Clownface

Books by Brad Linaweaver

From *PULPLESS*.COM, INC.

The Land Beyond Summer
Clownface

From Other Publishers

Moon of Ice

Sliders: the Novel
Sliders: the Classic Episodes

Doom (with Dafydd ab Hugh)

Doom 1: Knee-Deep in the Dead
Doom 2: Hell on Earth
Doom 3: Infernal Sky
Doom 4: Endgame

Free Space (co-editor with Edward E. Kramer)

Weird Menace (associate editor to Fred Olen Rey)

Clownface

by

Brad Linaweaver

PULPLESS.com, inc.
10736 Jefferson Blvd., Suite 775
Culver City, CA 90230-4969, USA.
Voice & Fax: (500) 367-7353
Home Page: http://www.pulpless.com/
Business inquiries to info@pulpless.com
Editorial inquiries & submissions to
editors@pulpless.com

PULPLESS.com, inc. ™

First Pulpless.Com™, Inc. Edition September, 1999.
Library of Congress Catalog Card Number: 99-62024
ISBN: 1-58445-096-7

Book and Cover designed by CaliPer, Inc.
Cover Illustration by Billy Tackett, Arcadia Studios
© 1999 by Billy Tackett

This book is for my mother and father, June and Mel

Table of Contents

God's Carny Barker
Introduction by Victor Koman

I first met Brad Linaweaver at the Denver World Science Fiction Convention in 1981. He immediately impressed me with his sharp and serious intellect married to an encyclopedic memory of all things literary and cinematic. Add to that a wicked sense of humor and you have the makings of a literary powerhouse.

And so he is. Like his mentor and honorary father, Ray Bradbury, Brad specializes in short stories. Spanning an entire spectrum from horror to fantasy to science fiction (and sci-fi, too—Hi, Forry!) he has created a body of work over the past twenty years that I and others look upon with admiration and sincere gratitude.

Brad has endured what many writers of short literature have had to endure: fame and fortune delayed a seemingly interminable time. For unless a short story is optioned for film, or convinces a film director to whisk one off to Ireland to breathe life into the whale of Death, renown beyond the ever-shrinking circle of readers of short fiction comes slowly if at all.

Yet sometimes a story so catches the mind and spirit that it grows into something greater and even more significant. Brad's story for *Amazing*, "Moon of Ice", so captured an alternate history of Nazi triumph and American resistance that it became a Nebula Awards finalist and Gregory Benford asked for it to be expanded for his anthology *Hitler Victorious*. And again, the world of which he wrote demanded even more revelation, so the novella became the novel, and *Moon of Ice* went on to win the Prometheus Award.

The stories in this collection, too, deserve notice and acclaim. "Wells of Wisdom", with its view of the World Brain's paradoxical victory, is rich with delicious irony. "The Lon Chaney Factory" ought to turn out a warehouse full of monsters for our joy and terror. And if we look upward "Under an Appalling Sky" we can find a gorgeous tapestry of evil only half-unfurled to whet our interest in how the worlds of Brad Linaweaver work and how they came to be.

Linaweaver saw a greater vision during the tumult and consciousness-razing of the 1960's. Choosing a politics neither left nor right nor center, he embraced a melange of agnostic Christianity and minarchist libertarianism that guaranteed everyone who met him would find *something* disagreeable. His anarchist friends are baffled by his steadfast minimal statism. His Protestant, Catholic, and High Anglican friends are puzzled by his unyielding uncertainty about God, his atheist compatriots bemused by his acknowledgment of some doubt about God's *non*-existence. His conservative buds wonder what's with his fondness for a sort of responsible libertine hedonism.

Yet he moves with a suave ease through all levels of social and intellectual strata. He is as comfortable discussing literature and politics with friends Ray Bradbury and William F. Buckley as he is holding marathon bull sessions about low-budget horror movies with drunken fans decked out in the hallway of a convention in some God-forsaken hotel. He possesses the upbringing that allows him to deal with the powerful as equals, yet he has cultivated such a love for all humanity that he can stroll at night through parts of Los Angeles and Atlanta that most would avoid like the plague simply because he does not view his fellow humans as a threat.

I never cease to be amazed by this unrestrained nova of energy, conviviality, loyalty, and good cheer. The man himself fascinates as much as do his stories.

He networks marvelously. He has brought together writers and producers, actors and filmmakers, leftists and rightists, literary giants and unpublished tyros. I think he delights in this *ad hoc* egalitarianism. He certainly glories in whatever success he can bring to his friends. A firm believer in casting bread upon the waters, he has seen favors returned to him by the most circuitous, six-degrees-of-whoever routes imaginable. If the writing ever fades when he enters his dotage, he will never do without lunch for he will be a magnificent raconteur.

The writing, though, will not fade if Brad has anything to say about it. In a world that rewards the quotidian clockpuncher with a weekly paycheck, he has chosen the rocky path of the writer, a profession not known for either steady income or predictable career arc. Why does he stick with it when surrender is an easy and accepted choice? Because he has something important to say. About Man. About Woman. About fear and joy and hate and love and power and freedom.

Welcome to the worlds of Brad Linaweaver. *Some* of the worlds. There are myriad others—born and unborn—creeping upward from the darkest pits of mankind's foulest urges or shining down from the pinnacles of our greatest achievements.

Come to the midway.

The freak show has on display for one and all an angel of terrifying aspect.

Man of the House

I will build a house of bone
Let me feel the murder pain
And my tongue digest each moan
So mind and music may explain
The sensate horror that is death
I will build a house of blood
Each vein a highway to the heart
Each death a segue in the flood
The whole is drowned with every part
Pain denies the world is art
And if I build with blood and bone
At end the structure stands alone
I have a friend I can't take home

—Berl Boykin
©1999 by Berl Boykin

I've been selling short fiction for over two decades but in all that time I've never been able to place the following. It's been observed that novellas and novelettes are the ideal length for science fiction and fantasy-horror. My science fiction novella, "Moon of Ice," demonstrated the rule and basically gave me a career. But the fantasy-horror "Clownface" could never find a home. Until now.

What made "Clownface" so special was the kind of rejection letters it received. I have never seen so many compliments with the dreaded word "sorry" attached. Now thanks to this new company of J. Neil Schulman's, I can bring "Clownface" to readers, and offer the following letter from *The Twilight Zone* magazine. (I miss that publication. Remember it?) Ted Klein was editor and he wrote the following:

"Clownface" offered writing of as high a quality as I've come across in months, but it had for me, a sort of Flannery O'Connor grotesquerie that doesn't feel right for a magazine such as ours. I suspect you want a more limited, more intellectual audience."

A writer of my sort lives for that kind of rejection. Hopefully with this collection, I've found an audience for the story of the ultimate freak.

Clownface

Clownface lived in a jail cell. They had taken away his makeup but he still looked like a clown, with his broad drooping mouth, doughy complexion and painful-looking bulb nose. He had played a sad clown in the circus but not a tramp clown—no five o'clock shadow was smeared on his egg-white face Anyone could see he was born to be a bozo, to wear kaleidoscope clothes, ride candycane unicycles, toot horns, and laugh in a loud, hollow voice. No one had told him, "Be a clown!" In fact, he had never consciously made the decision to become a clown. He had simply looked in the mirror and accepted what he saw there. Later, when he became a criminal and was locked away, he decided nothing much had changed. He was in a smaller room than he'd been used to, with a tougher mattress on which to sleep, and wore clothes that were a dull gray instead of the tacky red and yellow of his clown suit...but that was all that had changed. He was no less the clown.

Sometimes in the cell, he would remember things. Miss Mims was as good a reminiscence as any. She governed the course of his childhood. He thought of her as he stared at the bars on his window. On foggy nights it seemed as though her face was hanging just outside his window. It would float there, a suggestion of disapproval on the thin lips beneath a hawk-nose. Sometimes it would shimmer, and start to change—and he knew it would always become a face that he feared. The new face was white and round like his, but not his own; it was the face of a small, evil man he could not forget and which would make him turn away from the window and bury his head in the sheets of his bed.

He preferred Miss Mims to watch over him with an unchanging visage. On such occasions he would think back to the days that he spent in her orphanage—the good days before the growing up, and the circus, and meeting the man.

Miss Mims had not only been the head of the orphanage, but teacher, administrator and nursemaid rolled into one. She had meant something to Clownface when she was alive. When she died, it was as though she had never left. Her words still buzzed in his ear: "I will comfort you, my tragic one. You have nothing to worry about." She was always full of congratulations, assurances and tears. He

remembered how she would brush the few strands of wet hair growing out of his scalp and then coo to him about all sorts of things:
health and illness, happiness and sadness, life and death. She had a
knack for making everything appear the same.

What he remembered best from those days with Miss Mims was
Wednesday afternoon. Art day! That was when Miss Mims would
hug him and praise a crude drawing he had executed of an up-
rooted tree, or a sloppy, squashed cockroach, or a rendition of a
crack in the nursery wall. She saved all his drawings in a white
folder. He remembered the brown smears of her fingerprints on
that folder. Every now and then, she asked him to smear paint on
canvases, to close his eyes and feel the paint beneath his fingers
Her eyes were bright whenever she decided he had completed another masterpiece.

She hoarded the canvases in a little closet. It was really a distinction to have your artwork selected by Miss Mims for inclusion in
her file. He remembered there had been someone who desperately
craved that honor but never achieved it—Tom Riley. He had been
an emaciated boy with a confident demeanor. He stood very tall.
Watching him, Clownface used to think the boy stood as erect as
possible just to keep from falling down. It was a constant battle
between the force of gravity and the boy's fragile bones, calcium
girders resisting the inevitable. Clownface was stooped.

Miss Mims didn't like Tommy. The boy spent most of his free
time drawing pictures of airplanes, rocketships and planets. She
expressed a judgment of his work only once: "Come down to earth."
Clownface could not forget those pictures. Once he tried his hand
at a theme similar to one of Tommy's. He drew a castle and put a
ringed planet, like Saturn, in the sky above it. Miss Mims didn't put
Clownface's castle in her folder. She gave it back to him and said
nothing. A few days later, he threw the picture away.

Shortly after this incident, Clownface and Tom Riley were out
walking in the late afternoon. Riley was talking about his plans for
the future. He liked to talk and Clownface liked to listen. Suddenly
Riley pointed across the street at a doughnut shop. "The craziest
thing happened yesterday," he said. "I went over there to get a snack
and this strange little kid came through the door and bumped into
me. I started to tell him to watch it when I saw he really wasn't a kid
at all but a midget! You know, the little men they have in circuses

and freak shows. Anyway, he was carrying *five* boxes of doughnuts. Just looking at all that food made me hungry. I was gonna go inside but he grabbed me and said he had to talk to me. He told me he knew all about my future! He started talking about the orphanage— and how I would leave it—and then said things about Miss Mims, and you know what else?"

"What?" asked Clownface.

"He talked about you! He's seen you from a distance. He thinks you're special. Of course, he thinks *I* will be the artist."

Clownface knew that Tom was about to go off on a tangent about art, so he asked a question that seemed important: "What did he say about Miss Mims?"

"Nothing much. Just that he knows her from back before she had the orphanage. He was going to speak to her that same afternoon about the old days. But you know what? I've saved the craziest part for last. I don't know how he ever saw them, but he likes my drawings of outer space and other places because they make him homesick. He said he's been to other worlds in space and other dimensions and even back in time!" Tom laughed.

"I don't believe that," said Clownface, quite seriously.

Tom slapped him on the back. "Aw, he was joking. I'll bet he never even saw Miss Mims." The two boys went back to the orphanage and Clownface decided he would ask Miss Mims about this strange man. He forgot.

About a month later Miss Mims died one night in her sleep. They said it was a stroke. New people took over the orphanage, a married couple. They seemed more adept at bringing in prospective parents than Miss Mims had. Tom Riley was adopted within the week by a pleasant young woman who worked—the word went around the orphanage—at a circus. She and her husband were acrobats, the Amazing Morrows. Several of the children commented on the glamourousness of this. Clownface said nothing. He only thought of how unlikely it was that anyone would adopt him.

Clownface remained at the orphanage until he grew old enough to leave. He wandered around the country for many years, doing odd jobs, living with tramps, always moving on. He was thirty years old when he came upon a circus in a sleepy, midwestern state. One of the clowns had died and the manager was looking for a replacement. When he saw Clownface one evening, he made a mistake many people make: he thought the chalk-faced man was in makeup. "Who the hell are you?" he asked belligerently.

"Nobody," said Clownface. "Just passing through."

"But you're in makeup," said the manager. "Is this a gag? Are you doing this to get my attention? Well, I'm sold. I need a replacement right away and you fit the bill. You must have been with the carnival that came through here a month ago and went broke. Sure, that's it."

"I'm sorry," said Clownface softly. "I don't understand." Suddenly there was a high-pitched laughing that riveted the attention of both men. They looked over at a puff of smoke that billowed out from behind a tent; the fumes were followed by a grinning little man, a middle-aged midget smoking a cigar that seemed to be at least a third his size.

"Hey, rube," said the midget in a low voice, then chuckled again.

"What do you want?" asked the manager.

"It's all right, Mr. Jaspers," said the midget to the manager "I was just pointing out that this fellow here is a rube; he isn't a carny man. Neither is he a circus man. He's no clown, no nothin'."

Scrutinizing Clownface who was standing just outside a pool of light thrown by the illumination of the manager's trailer, Jaspers asked the man: "You're not a clown?"

"I'm passing through," said Clownface

"No clown," said the midget, "but something better—a freak! True, he's not a good freak. He's a bit too nondescript for a freak, and too grotesque to be a clown. But then, his grotesqueness is only a problem if you know he isn't in makeup. Consider the money you would save, Mr. Jaspers, on makeup if you hired this…this…Clownface."

The manager shrugged. "I'm a busy man," he said. "Do you want a job?" he asked Clownface.

"I need to eat, need sleep," answered Clownface lamely.

"He accepts," said the midget.

"We'll discuss details in the morning," said Jaspers to his new employee, then turned to the midget. "Since you seem to like him, you can put him up for tonight."

"Gladly," said the midget. "Come with me," he said to Clownface, reaching up to tug on a shabby pants leg. "This way!"

"You work for him?" asked the tall man following the little one as they disappeared into the shadows.

"You are a mental giant, aren't you?" asked the midget, "Actually, no, I give Jaspers my services temporarily. In truth, I work for other folks."

"Who?" asked Clownface. "Will they want to give me a job?"

The small man stopped dead in his tracks and looked up at the other man with a stern expression. "Such ingratitude," he said. "Here Jaspers has just hired you and already you're sniffing around for other employment."

"I'm a little confused," admitted Clownface.

"Well, no matter. As for me, the Amazing Professor Daniel Bloom, miracle worker and walking enigma, traveler of the universe, I am happy to work for..." the midget winked, "monsters that exist outside space and time."

"What?'" asked Clownface. He remembered a story Miss Mims had told Tommy and him once about devils and damnation. She had gloried in the gruesome details. Tommy had looked bored. Clownface had just listened. Now Dan Bloom made him think back to that day. "You mean," asked Clownface, "that you're a demon?"

"Only with the ladies. Being my size, one compensates. The important thing to know is that soon I'll be working for someone more despicable than any old devil."

"Who?"

"Myself! It is my intention to become self-employed."

"What will you do?"

"Give up the pointless racket of collecting what some call souls and go into something more tangible."

"I don't understand." said Clownface.

"That's all right," said Dan Bloom. "I like the sound of my own voice but it sounds ridiculous when I talk to myself. To continue, I will collect something of more value than what people designate as souls."

"Money?"

"No, money is merely a measuring stick of value. Since the value I seek is power, why bother with a middleman? Besides, they may go to metric soon and I never much cared for that system. You see, my apprentice clown, I am going into the market for soulless bodies. Look at it this way—the story people tell is how this Satan fellow, or whatever passes for the modern surrogate, collects souls. The souls the devil takes are spoken for before the people die, right?"

"I wouldn't know," said Clownface.

"Take my word for it. If souls exist, they would be in the devil's pockets about the time the human being in question reaches the age of puberty."

"How do you know that?" asked Clownface

"I used to be an accountant. Besides, this conversation has been hypothetical. Haven't you been paying attention? Anyway, I realized one day this arrangement would mean terrible waste because you'd have soulless bodies stumbling about, ready to be led anywhere, told to do anything, and no-one would be cashing in."

Dan Bloom lowered his voice. "Now I'll tell you something confidential. I'm looking for a perfect symbol of human waste. Someone who would never have a soul to begin with, no matter what the other arrangements were. Someone so dull and pointless that no devil would give a shit."

"Have you found him?" asked Clownface. They had reached Daniel Bloom's tent. He ushered the new clown inside.

"Maybe," he said. That night Clownface dreamed about the story Tom Riley once told him about a midget and Miss Mims. The next morning he couldn't remember the association he had made. He asked Dan Bloom nothing,

Clownface worked as a clown. He used a little makeup, but just for highlights; he put on a fake red nose; he dressed in a traditional white clown's garb, complete with conical hat. Jaspers, despite concern over reports that children didn't laugh at the new clown and a few were even afraid of him, didn't consider dropping Clownface. He knew that most clowns weren't funny anyway. As for the children who were afraid, it was not uncommon for youngsters to react adversely on their first contact with moon-faced harlequins who gibber, wearing grease-paint substitutes for mirth. An appreciation of the bizarre takes time and cultivation,

Dan Bloom defended Clownface against any and all criticism. For a week he kept his eye on the newcomer, then mysteriously disappeared from the circus for about a month. Clownface inquired as to the little man's whereabouts, but he got no answer. One day it occurred to him that he didn't know exactly what the midget *did* in the circus. Upon asking the manager, Clownface received no satisfactory answer. He gave up his inquiries.

When Dan Bloom returned, he brought with him a new strong

man for the show whose stage name was the typical "Hercules." He had been with the carnival that had passed through ahead of the circus and gone bust. Somehow, during Dan Bloom's absence from the circus, the other strong man—named typically "Atlas"—had taken ill and died, The new strong man could not have come at a better time. Dan Bloom had also brought something with Clownface in mind. "Is it a gift?" asked the white-faced man.

"Certainly not," said Dan Bloom indignantly. "I'll never part with this. I kept it at a bungalow I own and thought I'd bring it along this trip so you could take a gander at it." With a flourish, Bloom produced a canvas wrapped in brown paper.

"How do you afford a house of your own?" asked Clownface.

"I own houses, businesses, buildings, and a couple of corporations," he explained. "I like this circus job because it keeps me mobile and I get to meet interesting people. Such as..."

Dan Bloom tore off the paper and Clownface saw the painting that was underneath. It was a portrait of Clownface. Every feature was unmistakable. The face was a pale-mushroom white oval made of frowns and tears, a sad-faced resignation to fate. It was signed: *Tom Riley.*

"That name," said Clownface. "I know him. I know who did this portrait. But why did he do this?"

Dan Bloom clapped his hands together. "He only remembered you as a child. After all, he left the orphanage long before you did. Isn't this impressive? From memory alone, and anticipating what you would look like as an adult, he came up with this. Tom Riley had a real talent."

"Had?" asked Clownface.

"He worked in this same circus. His parents were acrobats here. In fact," Dan Bloom bowed theatrically, "I was made Tom Riley's honorary uncle. The lad and I got along fine. At first."

"What happened?"

"He was married and he died. The usual. Oh, things were a bit accelerated in his case. His wife was a beautiful woman, by the way. She had wonderful eyes, like a cat. She didn't like me."

"Where is she?"

"Probably looking for me."

"How did Tom die?"

"Accidentally."

For the first time, Clownface noticed something peculiar about the painting. There was a hole in the center of the forehead. "What is that?" he asked, pointing.

"I imagine it is a bullet hole," said Dan Bloom. "Look!"

He'd lifted up the canvas and was peering through the diminutive circle. Clownface would have pursued the line of questioning, but at that moment Bloom dropped the painting and did something strange with his hands. Clownface was looking at the writhing fingers when he found it becoming difficult to speak or move. Then, much to his surprise, he found that his legs and feet were moving him over by Dan Bloom when he had made no decision to join the midget. "This way," said Bloom, running on ahead, and Clownface's legs hurried to keep up. "We're going to watch the acrobats!" They stopped on the way so that Bloom could buy a couple of hot dogs which he ate gulpingly en route.

The star acrobat, Jim Morrow, was practicing that afternoon. Bloom and Clownface came in view of him as the muscular figure was poised defiantly over the earth, in mid-flight, body tense, arms reaching out for the bar of the trapeze. For a moment it seemed as though the figure would surely fall to be dashed against the earth, but the illusion was gone in the instant his hands grabbed the bar and Clownface noticed the net strung below. "There he is," said Bloom.

"Who?" asked Clownface, discovering he could speak and move again of his own accord.

"Tom Riley's brother. Not in blood, of course. The acrobat was the natural child of the couple. After they had him, something went wrong with their equipment. Adoption was the only course left for them if they wanted another son. So Tom came into the picture."

"Where are the parents now?"

"Dead."

Clownface looked at the acrobat. "It seems like there's a lot of dying around here."

Dan Bloom smiled. "And there will be more." Clownface watched the acrobat practice for a few more minutes. When he started to say something to Bloom, he noticed that the midget had gone.

For a week Clownface did not see Dan Bloom. Then the circus pulled up stakes and went to a new town. It was at the new location, on a busy Saturday evening, that Clownface killed the acrobat.

The main show was going on when Clownface walked by Hercules's tent and saw that the flap was open, waving in the wind, beckoning, revealing the light from a kerosene lamp that flickered on a table next to an open strongbox. Clownface stood at the opening of the tent. A moth, he entered. On a sudden impulse, he wanted a drink. Since he was broke that night, and needed money, the strongbox looked worth checking out. But he forgot about the drink when he saw the gun in the box. Besides, there wasn't any money there.

The Big Top was doing good business that night. There were a lot of children at the show, giving a hard time to their anxious parents. Clownface thought about them as he entered. He wasn't sure why he must shoot the acrobat. But it came to him, gun in hand, that he had no choice in the matter.

Incredibly, the clown thought, I don't hate you. Waiting until Jim the acrobat was poised in mid-flight between the bars, Clownface pulled the trigger and brought down a corpse that didn't seem as muscular as it should be. He was standing next to the exit, and exited. Behind him, people screamed, and cried, and mumbled and murmured, and hindered each other, bumping, tripping, falling. Walking casually, Clownface dropped the gun and went toward town.

He thought of nothing but a drink now and didn't remember his lack of money until he was seated at a prominent table in a little bar known as "Dave's Place," listening to a jukebox number called, "Your Lonely Heart." Dave in person had shown the clown to a table, saying how much he liked the circus doing good business. Dave explained how rarely clowns visited his establishment—except for the regulars, of course—and assured the clown that he sure had on "one crazy makeup!" Most of Clownface's makeup had rubbed off by this time, but he was still in costume

"For you, drinks are on the house," said Dave, and the other customers voiced approval at such beneficence. Dave was doing good business that night; the bar was getting the blow-off from the circus.

"There he is!" a voice screamed from the street. Clownface could not tell if the voice was male or female. He sat where he was, drinking something with a bitter taste he didn't recognize. Policemen entered. The bar was suddenly surrounded by the Big Top crowd and the people were flowing through the door, joining with the regular customers, assimilating, infecting. It was a carnival atmosphere of flesh and faces, lacking only a calliope .. but the jukebox blared its tin song into the milling company. People pushed one another. People shouted. Cops tried to clear a way through the crowd, tried to get everyone outside. There were just too many. Someone pulled the cord on the jukebox, and the music was winding down, and the rainbow colored lamps were swinging in a persistent breeze that came from the open door of "Dave's Place," and policemen were finally standing on both sides of Clownface.

The officer on his left informed him of his rights. The burden of choice having rested heavily on Clownface, he felt something akin to pleasure as he was led away. The police knew what to do. As Miss Mims had known what to do. As Dan Bloom always seemed to know what to do. Volition was no longer his concern. He could rely on his captors. If only Miss Mims were here, he thought, her thin arm around his shoulders, her thin voice telling him that everything would be fine.

In the moment that the doors of the police car shut upon him, and the motor roared into life, he thought of Tom Riley—and the painting. He knew, somehow, that Tom would never have wanted to do that painting. Wondering how strange and trivial it was to think of such a thing at a time like this, Clownface was taken away.

At the trial, everyone agreed that the clown had demonstrated beyond the shadow of a doubt his incompetence after the crime. They seemed insulted, Clownface thought, that he hadn't made a more serious attempt at escape following the shooting. They didn't want to believe that once the murder was accomplished, he forgot all about it.

They established that the gun belonged to the strong man. It turned out that Hercules had disappeared, along with the midget, and neither could be produced as a witness. Not that there was any real concern in finding them, or much of anything else, in a case this cut and dried. The owner of the circus had nothing to say. As for witnesses, there were several hundred townspeople to choose from. Motive was happily ignored.

The jury passed its verdict. The judge pontificated that perhaps the clown could function as a prisoner. At this particular time, in this particular state, there was no death penalty. Clownface had considered the possibility of death as an option. He felt vaguely cheated by the outcome.

Without the slightest effort on his part, he entertained the other prisoners. He was the subject of homosexual jokes—his nickname was "Lips." That is how it had been, with him alone in his cell, with his memories and the faces at the window. He lived a dry, dreamless life in the small square room that was his jail cell.

One day Clownface was sent a cell-mate, red-haired, who coined a new nickname for him, "Chalk." The cell block divided into two camps, arguing over the proper label with which to tag the sad-faced prisoner who stared off into space and didn't care about the outcome. Clownface heard the first rumor of an escape plan from Red on March the 22nd, which was the date of the day he was found in a corner of the orphanage kitchen, wrapped in a woolen blanket, dripping wet in the heat from the stove. Miss Mims used to tell him about that day.

His cell-mate told him about the break, in a matter-of-fact tone of voice, implying that the clown would naturally come along because the idea was for the whole cell block to break out. Someone named the Fixer had fixed things, somehow, from the outside. Red was excited by the setup. Clownface didn't inquire about details of the escape because he wasn't really interested. It occurred to him that he was going to have to make a decision. The burden of choice was returning.

Late on Wednesday afternoon, the word was passed. Red told him, "Tonight!" Everything seemed to approach more swiftly than usual. Clownface felt a cool breeze and looked through the bars of his window at low purple clouds moving across the sky, turning black, promising rain. He could see the guard-tower. The low clouds seemed to threaten that structure, but it was defiant, poised on the brink of a dark pit, challenging the night. The light from the tower's beacon moved methodically across the courtyard. The straight lines of the prison walls and tower, and the straight lines in his window that kept him separated from the sky, were a reproach to Clownface. It was not that they trapped him, held him in. It was that they were straight, and this alone made him want to withdraw from them. He felt as though they threatened to pierce him. He wanted the safety of flatness. Where could he find that safety, he wondered, except under the ground? For a moment he thought of the comfort of a graveyard.

"One hour to go," announced his cell-mate. Lightning flashed white against the sky—thunder rolled in a belated attempt to catch up. The clown cowered from the window. He was comfortable in his cell, all things considered. It was rather like the orphanage. Though he really didn't want to leave, he knew he wouldn't have the energy to resist the human tide that would soon flow from the cell block. He could see no purpose in the escape.

Looking at the horizon, beyond the tower, he saw a wall of water rushing to meet the prison. He could smell the rain. He wondered if, once he got outside, his face would wash off. He lay down upon his cot, closed his eyes, saw blackness, no pictures in his mind, no lights or colors. Soon he would return to the world.

Sitting in the porcelain-white ice cream parlor, cool oasis against the desert-heat summer world outside; sitting there, watching white capped waiters serve over seventy-five different flavors to wide-eyed, wide-mouthed children.

Dan Bloom looked away from the infant horde and observed his peppermint-drizzle parfait with wary eye. Across the table sat Hercules, downing the first of four tall glasses of water, lined up and cool. "Nature abhors a vacuum," said the midget.

"Huh?" the strong man replied.

"I was referring to the subject of my experiment."

"You mean the clown." The second glass was downed. "It's been about a week since the break, hasn't it?"

"One week exactly. Think of it. An entire cell block set free just so that I may have my clown again. If you're going to go to the trouble to spring someone, you might as well do it on a grand scale."

"I still don't understand what you want him for," said Hercules.

By way of reply, Bloom lifted a spoon of frosted redness and inserted the whole into his small but active mouth. Hercules shrugged. He'd come to expect periodic silences from the midget. Hercules wasn't the prying kind, and especially not where Dan Bloom was concerned. Hercules did what he was told, no matter how peculiar his task might strike him at the time. If shortly after meeting him, Bloom said: drop what you are doing—which was in fact very little— that is what Hercules did. If later Bloom said: take this money, leave your strongbox open, and go to another town—that is what Hercules did. Hercules was afraid of Dan Bloom. He had seen the midget do things he was convinced could not be done. Anyone who could do the impossible could tell Hercules what to do and be obeyed.

The strong man watched the little man fastidiously devour the ice cream. It was Dan Bloom's third meal of the day, at 11:55 a.m. He put away enough food in a day to satisfy Hercules's not inconsiderable appetite. Hercules watched the movement of the small jaws. He had been fascinated by Dan Bloom's fine doll features—a child face matured, held in eternal petulance—even before their agreement had bound him to longer contemplations. Hercules had never liked the crushed-mask faces of the dwarves he had worked with in the carnival. They were the caught-in-the-vise people. Dan Bloom did not look like someone who had been crushed by the world. He'd grown small and mean from the beginning. You could tell he had learned a lot about the ways of big people from his vantage point. And there was something about him that seemed so much older than the appearance of his age. Hercules wondered what secrets were buried in those old child bones.

"Look around you," the midget suddenly instructed, in his high-pitched, melodic voice, gesturing at the wet-armpit denizens of the snowdrift parlor. "It's easy to see, if you have the eyes for it. The perfect blank is a corpse. Our clown isn't *that* good, but he's close. Closer than you, Hercules. Closer than the acrobat he killed, who richly deserved it for his betrayal of my purpose. Closer than *anyone* I've found in my long career. Emptiness is the key to unlock empires. Show me a hole and I'll fill it."

A few feet away, a fat man asked his seven year old son what flavor ice cream he wanted. The boy answered peanut butter. The man smiled down, asked if the boy *really* wanted *that* flavor...surely he could pick a better one, and the seven year son reappraised. Vanilla was the compromise.

Behind the counter was an automaton by the name of Speedy Pete—he served banana splits fast, but he didn't know that he was the fastest in the business. He didn't know his distinction. What he knew was that every morning, he rose to face the customers with his permanently half open mouth, glazed eyes, and programmed hands which scooped up balls of ice cream with the deftness that comes from experience. Sometimes he felt very tired.

Speedy Pete noticed that the two men across the room from him were a bit different from the regular fare. The giant and pygmy were a contrast, variety, something worth looking at. For a moment he thought of childhood, and circuses and cotton candy and gaudy posters that promised an alternative to day-to-day blandness. Childhood. The thought lasted but a moment. A chubby face, aged eight years and five months, had ordered a banana split.

"What the clown is, is rare," said Dan Bloom, "but only because he is so much so! What the clown carries within him, an empty well, is easy to find."

Hercules finished the last two glasses of water and asked: "Where are we going now?"

A midget smile. "The little community of Forest Town—a pie baking community of good folk. A carnival is there currently, disturbing the tranquility. It will be going bust soon. There are some people I want to collect."

The unspoken presence of the traveling Clownface; the midget finishing his frosted parfait; Speedy Pete dropping a glass that shatters in outrage...the sun straight overhead noon.

"Done?" asked Dan Bloom.

"Done," answered Hercules.

"Best get a move-on, then," said the midget, sliding off his chair, landing firm. The duo exited, short part first, through clear glass doors, into the heat, carrying coolness inside them. Hercules thought that no amount of ice could last for long in Dan Bloom.

Red drank a beer. The beer was warm but he didn't care. He was glad to have it at all. He looked out a window through a screen entrapping two dead moths and saw a kid out late on a bicycle. Swallowing the last of the beer, he let the can slip from his fingers. The kid on the bike coasted out of view.

"I wonder where you're goin'," said Red to the vanishing form. "You look like a nice, young bastard. Going home probably. Probably get chewed out for being late. Nice Mom and Dad, right? Why were you out so late? Playing games? Let's see...were you playing make-believe? Maybe you think you're some kind of hero riding to the rescue, or something. Do you have a secret identity, you goddamn play actor? Try playing cops and robbers from the wrong end!"

Red heard a sound behind him and spun around nervously. It was only Clownface standing there. "What's the matter?" asked Red, responding to what he thought was a mournful expression on

Clownface.

"Nothing," said Clownface. "Are we safe here?"

Red laughed. "Safe," he said. "Safe as either of us has ever been in our lives. I don't know what we'd do on our own. I'm OK by myself but having you around makes me jumpy. It's nothing personal. It's just that you're so easy to spot! Fortunately, we have the Fixer on our side. All we have to do is follow the plan he laid out."

Red turned back to his small square of wire-screened window. The sun was setting and the clouds hadn't fully lost the light of a day's drifting. The sky was a crepe paper vault of ostrich blue, darkening, making the white globes of the street lights more real by the contrast. The street lamp nearest the house was buzzing ferociously, and attracting autumn-leaf moths which bumped into one another, dazed, drunk on the light. Over all hung the pervasive sound of crickets arguing in the thickening gloom.

"It'll rain later tonight," said Red, making conversation. Clownface said nothing. "This location is good," Red continued, turning from the window. "Being at the end of the street by the woods, no-one is likely to come with me to the Big Top, sneak up on us." Clownface said nothing again. "Chalk," exclaimed Red, "talk! What are you thinking about?"

"Nothing," said Clownface but he was noticing that something was wrong with the window—it didn't have any bars.

"There's plenty of that around here," observed Red. "We won't be here much longer before we have to move on."

"Where?"

"The Fixer is going to meet us! If only we aren't caught before we get to him. God, Chalk, you stand out like a sore thumb. It's to our advantage that so many convicts escaped at one time. The cops don't know which way to turn. They will be concentrating on cheap motels, not the suburbs. Yep, the Fixer thinks of everything."

Clownface thought back to the break. It had been over in a few minutes—all the guards were drugged at the same time as if by magic; the cells were unlocked just as mysteriously, the doors sliding open as though of their own accord, followed by the prisoners single-filing their way out of the Land of Nod. The get-away car for Red and Clownface was waiting a few blocks away. "'You're probably wondering why *I'm* going to all this trouble," said Red. "I've got an in with the Fixer, let me tell you. There's good money in this.

If he didn't want you so bad, I would have gone my separate way by now."

Clownface wondered how even the seediest crime lord would be interested in him, "Maybe they won't get me," said the clown.

"Who, the cops?" asked Red. "They can only do so much. Thank God. Don't worry. We'll get you through." Red lit a cigarette, inhaled deeply. "It's good to be free," he said.

"I like jail," said Clownface.

Red coughed. "Uh, everything will work out, you'll see," he said quickly, ignoring Clownface's comment. "We're going to be leaving in about an hour and our next stop will be to meet the Fixer."

"I feel lousy," said Clownface. "I'll go lie down in the back." He started for the hallway and caught a glimpse of himself in an old mirror with a crack running the length of it. Behind a yellow smear on the glass he saw his reflection. He decided he felt worse and turned away.

There was a door separating the hallway from the rest of the house which he shut behind him. He groped for the light switch. It wasn't there. As he rubbed his hand down the wall looking for the switch, he gradually became aware that there was light in the hall, a dim illumination—a diffuse blue—that was slowly growing stronger as he went.

And then there was enough light to see clearly. The hallway stretched in front of him as far as the eye could see. He turned around. It was the same behind him, the hallway stretching to a pinpoint. That is when Clownface noticed the shadows that were on the walls. He could see the silhouettes of hanged men, but there was nothing hanging from the ceiling. What disturbed him most, however, was the absence of a door. He instinctively walked forward, looking for an exit. He walked for a long time.

He didn't see where she came from, but quite suddenly a woman was standing in front of him, her hand outstretched for him. "This way," she said simply. "Follow me." He had come to an abrupt halt. Now, in his surprise, he considered what he was seeing. She was a slender woman with hair cropped short. The shape of her face, with its high cheek bones, made him think of a cat. In the pale blue light it was difficult to discern the color of her eyes; they were large and seemed to glow beneath slanting brows, but he guessed they were green.

As they walked, the hallway seemed to grow larger in its dimensions. The ceiling moved farther away, the walls receded into the distance. The floor beneath their feet became a barren plain. Then it was twilight and they were outside somewhere. And they were moving for the sole landmark on the horizon: a titanic circus tent. "Where is this?" asked Clownface. His voice sounded very small.

She said nothing but walked faster, beckoning him on. For a moment she stopped at the opening of the tent. As he ran forward to be with her, she stepped forward into the black hole and disappeared inside. Clownface could only hear her voice saying, "Come on." He could not see anything.

"Where are you?" he asked. "Please don't leave me."

"Come...come ..." The voice faded. He was left staring at the black abyss. He didn't move. He stood rooted to the spot, not turning back, not going forward, just looking, looking, looking into the darkness.

"Where would you like to go?" asked a peculiar voice from all around him. He didn't look for the author of the voice. There was something of its quality that indicated it was disembodied—that if you searched, you would not find the source. And there was something else unusual about the voice. It was many voices at once, but not a chorus of clearly separate voices. And it was familiar. It was as if someone had taken all the voices he had ever heard and combined them into one inhuman composite of hollow sound. "Where is it you want to go?" the voice repeated.

Clownface continued to stare into the darkness of the tent. "I want to go back," he said.

"Where is *back*?" asked the voice.

"I don't know. I want to go home."

"Home? Is it the circus you can never rejoin? Is it the orphanage? Is it your cell? The cell isn't empty anymore—it isn't yours anymore. Someone else is in it now. A rapist. A murderer. He has bad dreams at night, but not for his crimes. He dreams of *you*. They say the cell is haunted by you!" The voice chuckled, sort of. "How can the cell be haunted by a live man?" it continued. "You are alive, aren't you?"

"I am."

"Now, let's get this straight. You are alive, you say. But if you are alive, you must be living. And if you are living, you must be doing something. And if you are doing something, anything at all, then you must want something. What do you want, clown?"

"I don't know what you mean," said Clownface.

"We can keep this up as long as you want. We have all of eternity. What do you want?"

"I want to be safe."

"You ask too much and not enough. You say that you live. Do you know elation, passion, joy, boredom, hatred, love, indigestion?"

"I had an upset stomach once," said Clownface.

"Do you know guilt?"

"I know what I want! I want to get away from here."

Clownface continued to stand where he was, looking into the tent.

"Surely you must know guilt," said the voice. From behind him came a gust of cold, swift wind—a thousand needles pricked against his flesh, lifted him in a mad embrace and dropped him through the black hole to leave him tumbling head over heels into the center of the tent. A spotlight. A drum roll. The star of the show is come. Behold the clown.

He got up from the dirt and saw his judge, sitting high on a throne of wood. The judge was garbed in the office's vestments. He wore the long, white wig. What arrested Clownface's attention was the man's face under that wig—it was a tramp clown, wearing the perpetual five o'clock shadow and frown. Then Clownface saw his jurors in an empty cigar box. There were twelve of them in all, but the cigar box was of gigantic proportions. These were white clowns one and all.

Clownface heard a gunshot behind him and spun around. Floating in air at eye level was the gun he'd used to kill the acrobat. It was suspended in space; a card was attached to it by a string, a card reading "Exhibits A through Z." Behind the gun was a tall wooden stake with a skull on top—yellowing smiled—and a sign beneath it reading "Ex-acrobat."

A familiar voice addressed Clownface from over by the tent opening. He recognized her immediately: Miss Mims. "I'm your character witness," she announced. "I've told them you could never do a thing, good or bad, requiring serious motivation." He found himself ignoring her and wondering what had become of the pretty young woman who had led him here.

"How do you plead?" asked the judge, and Clownface wished he could escape that grim countenance of failure and despair.

"What do you mean?" asked the clown.

The earlier voice, the one made of all voices and all time, of every memory and sorrowful song, echoed the judge's query: *"How do you plead?"*

"On my knees," answered the clown, sinking down.

"Did you murder the acrobat?" asked the judge.

"Yes."

"Why?"

"I think I was supposed to."

"Why weren't you executed for your terrible crime?"

"I think they wanted to rehabilitate me."

"What was your sentence?"

"Life."

"Well then, do you have it?"

"I just want to be taken care of. That's all I've ever wanted, except that I'm not sure how it's supposed to be done."

"Your kind doesn't know the meaning of life. Answer this, dead man: have you ever been alive?"

"I do want to live. I know that much."

"You ask too much," said the judge in summation. Light vanished, darkness enveloped them, light returned. Set out in the ring, around Clownface, were these: the gallows, the guillotine, the electric chair, a bottle marked "poison," and a lone door, braced by nothing but the air. Clownface remembered the door to the orphanage. "Choose!" commanded the judge.

"Which one?"

"I'll help you then, you sorry fool." He pointed at the door.

"I saw hanged men in the hall. Doesn't that mean I should be hanged?"

"If you wish. But the door is better."

"I'll wake up if I choose one, won't I? I'll wake up from this dream."

"You are *awake* now."

"How can that be? That can't be."

"Can you judge the difference between truth and falsehood?"

It has to be a dream, the clown decides, but there is something wrong with it; he feels it is not entirely his dream. It is as if someone is inside his head, fiddling around.

"Who are you?" cried out everyone in the courtroom circus. Miss Mims opened her mouth to speak, moved lipstickless lips in the ritual of assurance, but it wasn't her voice that said in high-pitched tones: "My tragic bozo!" As Clownface recognized the voice of Dan Bloom, his head fell off, screaming, plummeting a mile to smash against concrete laid out below. "Are you beginning to realize what you are?" taunted the voice in a shrill sing-song. "This is my show. I alone know what you are, sad clown. I may let you in on the secret, some day."

His body went running after his head, and Miss Mims told the head, which had come to rest at her feet, the story of the tortoise and the hare. In her version, the tortoise gave up the race. The hare quit the race also and became a nurse to the tortoise. Miss Mims taught the head magic words: "Glik zhrept mourgh." The head repeated them carefully, phonetically. "Now you possess a great idea," she said.

A dark raven flew down at the clown head, hungering for its jellied insect eyes. The pupils rolled back in the head at the bird's coming.

He found his head, put it on, chased the raven away, and ran into a bathroom to wash off his makeup, which was drying, caking, cracking. But at the first handful of water, his pallid face began to melt. He tried to shout—the sound that came out was a trapped buzzing that did something to the glass of the big mirror in front of him. The mirror cracked into a black spider web configuration, dripping red blood from the cracks, before it finally shattered. The acrobat, propped inside, stiff and white, fell into the faceless man's arms.

Don't you know that according to Dan Bloom there's no Heaven but there is a Hell?

The clown ran up and down dead-flesh grass hills, fell, rolled with the green as an incredibly clear blue sky pressed down. Hearing a high-pitched, insane laughter, he looked overhead to see the full moon taking on Dan Bloom's features; saw the burning firefly eyes. "Too late for you," said midgeted moon...and the clown fell on his face.

The soft grass was gone, replaced with a hard floor. When he lifted himself up he heard a door opening behind him, followed by the sound of a click, and a 75 watt light bulb flickered into life over his head. He was back in the hallway. The grubby walls were blank except for peeling orange paint. The hand he felt on his shoulder belonged to Red. "Are you all right?" came the voice of a man he trusted, a cellmate. "I heard you cry out."

"I..." faltered Clownface, following Red out. "I don't know."

"You must have been in there for an hour. Did you pass out?"

"I think I had a dream." Clownface noticed he had been hearing the sound of rain falling outside since he had come to. He pulled on his overcoat, a musty smelling affair they had picked up second-hand, and followed the other man out into the storm. It was time to go.

In the night, in an old Ford, moving along at 50 m.p.h., Clownface saw a rippling world through the windshield and heard a Judgment Day cacophony, thunder occasionally interrupting the staccato rhythm of raindrop impacts on the roof. Red was driving, the wipers were wiping, and the headlights projected their white shafts, holding splinters of rain for-a-moment stationary in the light.

Clownface was tired. He felt exhaustion in his cheeks, and the flesh under his eyes was like gritty sand. His left eye twitched and he felt a hole in his stomach; felt as if a vampire had been at work, pumping rivers of blood from his weakened frame: felt his heartbeat pinch his upper intestine. He slumped in his seat, thinking about what had happened in the hall of the house, wondering if he was going insane. The car went persistently on.

"Welcome to Forest Town" said Red finally, "the coke bottle top capital and dust bowl of the world." They passed billboards, advertising fresh-as-you-feel cigarettes and greater sexual potency through candied mints. The posters looked as if they had been rolled on pre-faded.

Red drove through town. It didn't take long. When he reached the outskirts on the other side, he started looking for the place he was supposed to stop. The rain became a drizzle as they came upon one tent, out in the middle of a field—an incongruous landmark all by itself, a sealed turtle in the wet night. Pointing to it, Red said, "Let's go." Car parked, engine off, they went.

The two men took a few steps inside the tent and stopped. A table was blocking their way; it was set formally as though for a banquet, but there were only four places. Strangely, there was a bright yellow light permeating the tent, but no discernible source for it. "The Fixer sure does it right," said Red. "I've never had dealings with anybody like him before. I'll be interested to see what he looks like." Clownface knew. He had suspected who was behind it even when he was in jail. The experience in the hallway had been enough to convince him.

"Wonder where everybody is," said Red. It was then that Clownface saw them. They were coming from a long way off. He could make out tiny figures in the canvas of the tent wall facing them—the figures were slowly growing as though they were coming over a distant horizon. They were walking, and coming closer, and getting bigger...then Red saw them as though they had just popped through the wall of the tent. Three people: Dan Bloom, Hercules, and the woman Clownface had met—or thought he met—in the hallway: the first thing he noticed was that she was a brunette with green eyes. "Where did you come from?" exclaimed Red to the company.

"From outside," said Dan Bloom matter-of-factly, walking forward and extending his hand. "How do you do? I'm the Fixer."

Red reached down to take the hand. "I'll be damned," he said. Hercules nodded. "I always wondered what you looked like. I sure never thought you'd be a midget."

"What a tactful comment," said Dan Bloom smiling. "You are everything I hoped you would be."

"Thanks," said Red, "and now I'd like to be paid for bringing you this guy so I can hit the road again. We're still wanted men."

"No sooner said than done," smiled Dan Bloom, "but I *am* the Fixer after all, and I assure you that you are safe from the police so long as you are with me. Won't you stay for dinner?"

The invitation took Red by surprise. His faith in the Fixer was suddenly in conflict with his natural inclination to rely on himself alone in doing what he did best: running. Now the Fixer was asking him to stay put. He looked over at Clownface for support and noticed the pale-faced man was trembling. "Hey, Chalk," he said, "something wrong? You don't look happy. Think I ought to stay or take it on the lam?"

Clownface opened his mouth to speak. At first nothing came out—but then there was a low, croaking whisper that Red could barely hear. It said, "Get away."

"Oh, don't mind him," said Dan Bloom offhandedly. "He and I are old friends. That is why I'm paying you so well for making our reunion possible."

"Well, you got us out," said Red. "I'm just a courier."

Bloom laughed pleasantly: "Actually you are more than that." The midget took an envelope from an inside pocket of his white jacket and passed it to Red. "You may count it if you like. It's all there; not even a deduction for dinner."

As Red thumbed the bills, he noticed what seemed to be a discrepancy, not in the money but in the table arrangements. "Uh, Fixer," he began, "aren't you short a plate if you want me to stay? There are five of us but I only see four plates."

Dan Bloom folded his hands together as if in prayer. "The situation is a delicate one, I admit. You see, uh, Red, I have classified you as a mediocre thief and adequate errand boy. You have no potential to be a murderer. It is murderers I need. I require a particular kind of moral emptiness and all you have to offer is a petty smallness— not at all the sort of vacuum I endeavor to fill." Bloom paused in mid-discourse and went to the head of the table where he took his seat. He clasped his hands together again and looked for the moment to be a pious clergyman.

"You mean I can go?" asked Red hopefully, having become anxious at the solemnity of Bloom.

"Wait a moment," said Bloom. "Remember that I'm the Fixer and when I fix something it stays good and fixed! But nothing's perfect, not even my work, and, well...you notice Clownface over there?" Red noticed. "He's been in jail a while and I daresay become too comfortable. He has gotten rusty."

"Rusty?" asked Red.

"Yes, he needs a little practice. Which is what I was reminding him of when you and he were back at the house. That was a special house I arranged. It is a good house for what you might want to call dreaming, but what I call the place next door."

Red started edging for the open tent flap. "Well, thanks for everything," he announced, "but I really need to hit the road."

Dan Bloom said one word: "Hercules." Red's exit was blocked in the wink of an eye. It didn't look as though a big man could move as fast as Hercules did.

"As I was saying," continued Bloom, "Clownface needs a refresher course. And you, Mr. Red, will do nicely, Of course what happens to you will happen in *this* reality. And it will be permanent What more do we demand of our realities?"

"No," said Clownface in a voice that sounded like it came from the bottom of the deepest well in the world. Red made a break for it. Hercules was faster and trapped the hapless man in strong, brown hands. Dan Bloom reached under the table and produced a familiar painted canvas.

"This," said Bloom, pointing to the portrait of Clownface, "is why he will do it."

Red was beginning to get the idea. He struggled wildly in Hercules's grasp but he couldn't budge the strong man. "Why?" gasped Red. "What did I ever do to you?"

"Nothing at all," said Bloom.

"Why?" Red's eyes were staring at Bloom, pleading.

"Because you're second-rate. Clownface's first murder was of an acrobat no one knew was a second-rate crook except me. But unlike that case, I have nothing personal against you. The acrobat wasn't nearly as co-operative as you, Red. He didn't even know about the 'Fixer.' The answer is really simple. First, Clownface needs the practice. Second, if he doesn't kill you, what will we do for dinner?"

Red became sick, but Hercules continued to hold him even as yellow bile spilled from his lips. When he lifted his head, he turned his watery eyes in the direction of the girl. "Help me," he said lamely. She paid no attention to him but watched Clownface and said nothing. Clownface looked back at her intently.

Clownface's mind was in a whirl of confusion: if the woman happened to be real, then what he thought had been a dream must be real, too, in some way—he had never met this woman before. He did not doubt the powers of Dan Bloom to have created her out of thin air. But why this particular person? Clownface felt some dim connection between the woman and him. Whatever it was, he was sure that Dan Bloom knew. The question was: did she know? Clownface glanced over at Dan Bloom. The midget wasn't smiling now. He sat quietly, appraising the situation.

"Here," said Dan Bloom, as if in answer to the unspoken questions, and shoved the painting down the table—the heavy canvas seemed to glide across the surface, not disturbing the white table cloth; it came to a stop in Clownface's hands, which had instinctively reached out to stop it. Red had turned his head to follow the motion of the painting, but Hercules put one hand—roughly the size of a ham-hock—on the smaller man's head, and turned it back in the direction of Dan Bloom as though adjusting a faucet. A bone popped in Red's neck.

"Help me," said the red-haired man to no-one in particular.

Clownface held the portrait of Clownface. He saw it in more detail than he had the other time the midget had shown it to him briefly. Once again he saw the bullet hole in the forehead of the man in the painting, with a small network of cracks packed tight together around the small circle; he saw the angular lines of the artist's signature: *Tom Riley*; he saw, for the first time, the expression buried in the face. He looked into pale mushroom whiteness...and the eyes that gazed back from dried pigment and old canvas were like the eyes of a lizard you chase out from under a rock. And the mouth was a twisted rind of decaying melon. And the chin was a dried egg shell. Clownface looked deep into this face. He saw more than he cared to see.

Horror and agony were there. He remembered those things in Red's face when Hercules grabbed him and he realized what Dan Bloom had in mind. Clownface observed Red. Carefully. The man had resigned himself—at least for the moment—to being trapped. There was resignation in his face; Clownface beheld the painting and saw resignation there, too. But it was different from Red's. Clownface thought of the times he had looked at himself in a mirror. On those occasions he saw something behind his face—but he had never cared to examine it or find out what it was. Now he saw that same thing in the painting by Tom Riley. It was somewhat like the resignation he had seen for a moment in Red's face—and yet it was different. He realized the thing behind his face was a permanent resignation. He did not see that in any other face in the tent. It was a great black thing, as old as the man it belonged to. It was why, as Dan Bloom had said, Clownface would do as he was told.

He let the painting drop from his fingers. It fell face-up on the tent floor—canvas on canvas. Clownface looked at the opening in the tent and listened to the faint sound of water dripping somewhere outside.

"You aren't leaving," said Dan Bloom. It occurred to Clownface that Hercules was occupied with Red and although the captive seemed passive momentarily, Hercules wouldn't be able to stop Clownface without letting go of Red, which the strong man manifestly did not want to do. Clownface glanced at Dan Bloom, who had not left his seat at the head of the table. The woman was standing beside him, reserved, silent, still an unknown factor. Clownface started to move for the open flap.

"You know," said Dan Bloom, "that Hercules won't have to stop you." The midget pushed himself back from the table and slowly began to rise...still sitting. He floated into the air and stopped, stationary, several feet above the table. "You don't *want* to leave," he told the clown.

When he felt his legs go stiff, Clownface knew he was caught. If Bloom could still do this to him, he could do more. Bloom floated across the table to where Clownface was rooted like a tree, ready for the felling. Bloom did something with his hands and he was holding a gun The tag for admittance-as-evidence was still attached. Bloom dropped the weapon and it fell as though in slow motion, turning over as it fell, languidly, butt-end toward Clownface as it met his hand which reached out to take it.

"Don't kill me," said Red in a tired voice.

"Kill him," said Dan Bloom, opening his mouth to show two rows of razor sharp teeth that Clownface had never noticed before: perhaps Bloom had grown them for the special occasion. The midget gestured at the table and the empty plates upon it. "He who enjoys his meal best," said the floating man, "does not look behind the kitchen wall. I believe that is how the old saying goes."

"No," croaked Clownface.

"Yes," whispered Bloom. "Point the gun, pull the trigger and leave the carving to me. You found it easy enough last time."

His hand tightened on the gun, which seemed to be growing heavier with every passing moment. It was exerting a constant force on his palm, and it did not feel as though his hand was causing the pressure. The gun's weight seemed to shift toward the right, pulling his hand with it. The damned thing was moving in the direction of Red! Suddenly Clownface was surprised to hear his own voice ask a question: "Why is there a bullet hole in the painting?"

"Because," answered Dan Bloom, "Tom Riley put it there."

"Why?" asked Clownface as the gun came to rest, pointing at Red, from whose expression all shock had drained away and who now observed the barrel with a sullen stare.

"Because," Bloom answered again, "he saw what he had done. He took a talent meant to show hope and turned it to despair. I admit I helped him along, but then what is an uncle for?"

"You...?"

"I suggested Riley's adoption in the first place. I was rather taken with the lad the same day I first saw you. What a duo you made: the brave and the lame."

"But the bullet..."

"I did my best to influence him. But, alas, he was no killer. His painting of you was the only thing he ever murdered. That only happened because he succeeded in putting the inside on the outside."

"What happened to him?" asked Clownface, the gun continuing to point in the direction of Red.

The woman came up to Clownface and put her hand on his shoulder. She said in a low voice: "My husband is dead."

"Mrs. Riley?" asked Clownface.

"Yes," said the midget in response, dropping lower over their heads so that he was just above the clown. "I told you Tom was dead and she lived. It was for the best. Did you know he preferred his wife as inspiration over you? You should have seen the sort of Romantic drivel he was turning out. Esthetically, it was not at all what I had in mind."

"The bullet hole..." said Clownface, his voice trailing off. The woman sank to her knees and began to cry.

"Thomas Riley," announced Daniel Bloom, "was both an idealistic and practical man. He had a purpose in life. Unlike you, for instance, he was not a walking human vacuum. Fortunately for me, however, I was able to subvert him. What I cannot destroy, I prefer to dine upon."

Dan Bloom snapped his fingers and the painting rose into the air. When he grabbed it, it happened. All of them were immediately back in the hallway of the house that had been left behind, filled with blue light and the silhouettes of hanged men upon the walls. And Clownface was still pointing the gun at Red. And the woman was on her knees. And Dan Bloom was still sitting in the air. The banquet table was gone.

"Look again into this canvas," commanded Bloom. Clownface did, reluctantly. Now the thing was blank, without a mar or hole. In place of the portrait, he saw lights and movement swirling in the center of a white expanse—gradually images formed. He saw into a room where Tom Riley struggled alone in silence with his paintings. He saw Riley the perfectionist, throwing out half finished work and sketches, adding to an ever-growing mound of paper at his feet. Then came Dan Bloom, strutting into the scene, who kicked aside that paper mountain. The midget came to Riley as a smiling benefactor, a jolly want-to-be-a-pal uncle. He brought money. He commissioned one painting for which he offered the price of ten. All that Tom Riley had to do was turn his soul to contemplation of Clownface.

If Tom Riley had not understood the significance of the clown painting—had not seen inside it to the core of Dan Bloom's motivation—he probably would not have panicked the way he did. In a moment of futility he took a gun with which Bloom expected him to murder someone—anyone—and shot the portrait instead. He then dropped the gun and went for Bloom, who just happened to be in the room at that moment of pentimento. The larger man attempted to strangle the smaller man. He failed.

As Clownface continued to watch the panorama unfolding on the canvas, he saw Tom Riley running, falling, picking himself up again, and running on. If Riley had not been intent on keeping Dan Bloom in view, he probably would not have been looking over his shoulder when he ran out into the street. The vehicle that ran him down was an ice cream truck with a clown's face grinning from the side.

It was like a film strip running out as the moving pictures faded from the canvas, to be replaced not with emptiness, but with the same old portrait of Clownface. Dan Bloom drifted down to the floor and stood with the painting leaning against his small frame. "'Aren't you getting tired of holding that gun?" he asked. Clownface tried to relax his fingers, but it was as though they were glued to the metal in his hand. "You may put it down," said Bloom, "as soon as you have killed Red."

"No," said Clownface as before, but it seemed that his voice had become louder since his previous utterance, and he wondered where the strength was coming from. He knew that something had changed. The gun suddenly began to feel lighter, even though his hand still seemed to be stuck to it. And it was as if a fog lifted from his vision, a mist which had been enveloping the man he called Red. The woman had stopped crying and stood up, took a step toward-Clownface...

"No closer, my dear," said Dan Bloom, and she stopped.

Once again Clownface was surprised to hear his own voice as it addressed the woman: "What are you doing here?"

"Waiting," she said.

"For what?"

"Revenge."

"That would mean revenge against Dan Bloom!" Clownface exclaimed. "You seem to be here by his permission."

"She is my guest *because* of her hatred for me," began Dan Bloom. "The trouble is that her hatred is almost spent—which is what happens from frustration—and soon she will offer me no more amusement...or nourishment. Stupidly she thinks you will be her savior, and the avenger of her late husband. You, my tool! I have encouraged her in this delusion. When you have murdered Red, O clown, you will kill her, too."

Clownface began to tremble, but the more he shook, the lighter the gun seemed to feel—and his fingers were starting to come loose at last. "You see, " Bloom continued, "we must proceed through this hall of true justice—which is namely injustice—before we may once again sit at the banquet table."

When the pallid-faced man pointed his weapon away from Red, there were several reactions: Mrs. Riley went over to stand by him; Hercules looked surprised but continued to hold onto Red; Red renewed his effort to break the strong man's hold but without success; Dan Bloom cocked an eyebrow in surprise but made no move. The man with the gun pulled the trigger and fired point blank into Dan Bloom's chest. Three times. With each crack of sound, each flash of fire, each upward jerk of the gun in his hand, Clownface experienced a sense of release and happiness. For the first time in his life he knew what it was like to have a purpose. He dearly wanted to see the Amazing Professor Daniel Bloom dead

The three bullets did not enter Bloom's flesh close together. Each new wound was higher up the torso as Clownface inadvertently elevated his aim at the end of every shot. When Clownface stopped firing, one could draw a straight line through the three bloody marks across the victim's shirt. The most interesting thing was that it didn't seem to faze Dan Bloom. The recipient of the bullets cleared his throat and paused dramatically. He was now more than ever at center-stage, and he savored the fact of his audience's unflagging attention. "The wounds healed almost immediately," he said, "but you've ruined a perfectly good shirt. Do you know how difficult it is to get fitted in my size?"

The lady exhaled a breath that sounded like she had been holding it for a very long time; it was a sigh of final surrender. "We've lost," she said. "Oh, poor clown! You might as well put that gun down. If he'll let you."

"I've lost, too, Mrs. Riley," said Bloom, "but no-one feels sorry for me. The impossible has happened. It appears that I've misjudged this freak." The little man coughed daintily into his right palm and looked up mischievously. As if revealing a prize toy, he opened his hand to reveal three wet bullets. "These," he said, tossing them at Red who winced as they struck him in the stomach, "were meant for him."

Clownface's right arm was suddenly like a piece of malformed, heavy lead—which he let drop to his side where the gun remained dangling at the end. "See here," said Bloom, "stop wasting time. I was convinced you were perfect but now I see, for the first time in my centuries-long career, that I was mistaken. That doesn't mean I can't still break you!" As though he were a colonel intent on chewing out an insubordinate enlistee, the midget strode over to the reluctant gunman and belligerently put his face right up against the other man's knees. He opened his mouth full of razor sharp teeth and gnashed them together.

"I could hurt you," he told Clownface. "I could hurt you very badly and there's nothing you could do about it. I could make you sick the way I did Miss Mims when she got slow in her work and wasn't crippling new crops of children fast enough for my purposes. I could wipe you from existence if I thought I couldn't master you—if I thought you had a solid center to you, like Tom Riley for instance; instead I know of the emptiness in you. You were to be proof of the ideal human vacuum... the man who was born without a soul."

Daniel Bloom was red in the face, looking up at the doughy white globe on top of the body he was addressing. Sweat was beading on the little man's forehead. "You," he shrieked, pointing up, "will not beat me! You won't pick the games we play. Don't you know that sadism is boring? I am weary of the torments and the agonies. Because it is what I do best, this is my job, my damned day-in, day-out job for all time, the same old stuff no matter who collects the profits. Well, I won't be subtle. I'll use all my power against you. I'll give up dreaming of the perfect, *willing* slave and take what I can get. You will soak your hands in blood even if you don't particularly want to."

Clownface was aware, even as the others were, that Dan Bloom was making no idle threat. But there is always a moment between the saying and the doing, no matter how brief, and since Clownface had discovered the pleasure of making decisions, he didn't hesitate. He spun around, took dead aim and shot Hercules once through the head and once through the body as the big man fell away from his captive. As he had supposed, Hercules was human and obviously under the sway of the itinerant demon the same as the acrobat had been...and Clownface.

Dan Bloom took a few steps in the direction of his dead helper and blocked the way of the man named Red, who lost no time turning around and running as fast as he could in the opposite direction down that endless hallway. Bloom issued no commands to Clownface. In an instant he rose into the air and flew after his quarry. When he reached Red's white neck, he bit into it with his ghoulish teeth, which made the man scream and collapse upon the floor, blood gushing from the ugly wound. With Red disposed of, Bloom did a jig and called out to Clownface (who was still holding the smoking gun that held one bullet):

"It doesn't matter. I can repair Hercules when I need him again."

"You are lying," said Mrs. Riley with conviction

"I think you're right," agreed Clownface.

Dan Bloom did not take it well. He shouted at the top of his lungs: "So you think I'm a liar?" Blood was trickling out of his mouth, and there was a crimson stain on his lips. "I'll show you something!" He turned around and raised his hands over the corpse as though he were conducting a symphony orchestra. The clothes disappeared from Red as the body began to shrink. Neither Clownface nor the omen moved an inch as they watched. Standing in the hallway with an enraged Dan Bloom was like standing in a mine-field. The human body on the floor dwindled small, smaller, smallest...until it was only two inches long, a terribly tiny doll shape which Bloom lifted carefully and put into his mouth. His back was to them, but they heard the crunching of the small bones It lasted for about a minute. When he turned around, he was wiping his mouth with a handkerchief. He smiled at them, and they could see that the awful, knife-like teeth were gone.

"Now, my tragic bozo," he said, "you will shoot the widow of Tom Riley so that we may get along to dinner."

Even as he lifted the gun, Clownface knew he had made his decision as he watched Dan Bloom devour the remains of a man he knew in the long-ago world of a prison cell. He took a last look at the frowning face on a painted canvas, aimed the gun, and pulled the trigger. Before the bullet went straight through Clownface's heart, Dan Bloom was shouting, "No!" and lifting his hands as if to ward off the sight. The body fell sideways and lay partially propped up by a wall.

Mrs. Riley bent down to examine the corpse and gently put her hand on the bulbous white head. She closed the eyes with her right hand. "Did you notice," she said softly, "that he didn't do the obvious thing? He left his face unmarked."

Dan Bloom started backing away in the direction Red had taken. Mrs. Riley laughed. "You can't use him now. He's gone to join the others. You told me this was the one thing that could hurt you. You said that you could tell me about something that could never happen; you have nightmares, too." Bloom ran down the long hall. "You're not safe anymore," she called after him. "I can have my revenge. More important, so can they."

Dan Bloom was gone. With him had departed the blue light that illuminated the seemingly infinite corridor. Plunged into darkness, Mrs. Riley started toward a thin line of light she could see at the end of the hall. She was afraid she would stumble over the two bodies in the dark, but the course she took met with no resistance except for one thing. She bumped into something flat and square that scudded across the floor: the painting. Reaching down, she groped for the canvas, picked it up, and took the last few steps that brought her up against a door slightly ajar, through which she could see the shaft of light.

She heard a street-lamp making a buzzing sound as she stepped through the doorway into the outer room of the house. A cracked old mirror with a yellow smear on it greeted her with the reflection of an exhausted woman holding a painting which she saw, in that ancient glass, had changed its subject matter again. She went over by the window and held up the canvas to the light from the street-lamp. Her husband's signature was still on it, but the bullet hole was gone, and the bold lines of his name now took credit for a picture of several people sitting at a banquet table, holding knives and forks expectantly over an arrangement of empty plates. She recognized the locale of the scene. It was the table back at the circus tent. Somehow she knew that Dan Bloom was headed for that tent. The people at the table were looking out from the painting, and the perspective of the viewer was what one would see upon entering the tent. There were many people at a table which seemed to be of larger proportions than she remembered. Everything else was the same as when she left.

There were men and women she did not recognize, but among all the unfamiliar faces, she spied Hercules and Red. She was glad that her husband was not among this company. She was also glad to see who was at the head of the table, with a hawk-nosed, thin old woman seated to his left, and a man dressed as an acrobat seated to his right: Clownface. They were all smiling. They all looked hungry. She thought that Clownface seemed to be the hungriest of them all.

As long as we're already dealing with clowns, there's no reason to stop now. I wrote this story about Lon Chaney, Sr., who included some sinister clowns among his repertoire. The story first appeared in *When the Black Lotus Blooms* from Unnamable Press. It received Honorable Mention in *The Year's Best Fantasy and Horror, Fourth Collection*. The story was singled out as the best offering of *Black Lotus* in a review that appeared in *Locus*.

Then it appeared as the cover feature in a Forrest J Ackerman monster magazine, *Monsterama*. That's appropriate as the tale is dedicated to Forry for working harder than anyone to keep the legacy of the great silent star alive. "The Lon Chaney Factory" also does one of my favorite things by combining science fiction with horror.

The Lon Chaney Factory

The darkness was not complete. A green shape moved within. A hand. It sidled across an unseen floor, spiderlike. The merest sound of scratching could be heard in that Stygian womb. Then the hand rose into the air, pointing a luminescent finger at a sliver of white light that had just come into existence, growing as a door opened—flooding the room with scenery.

A gruff voice spoke: "I've seen that before. What else have you got?"

A quiet voice answered: "Nothing special, I'm afraid."

Screaming, an old crone on a broomstick swept down from bat-clustered rafters to glare at guests on the floor far below. She flew right through the fat producer who was the owner of the gruff voice, and who almost lost his unlit cigar as he yawned at her mad face. "Halloween again?" he asked of nobody in particular.

Through an octagonal window at the producer's left, the full moon turned into a blood-shot eye. A skeleton hand groped its way out of the floor in front of him. Wolves howled way down in the machinery beneath. "Let's see the rest of it," said the producer, and the two men walked farther into the gloom.

Out of a circle of darkness strode Count Dracula, fangs gleaming from no discernible light source. At his right loped a werewolf. A gauze-covered hand reached out just behind the producer and ...

"Turn it off!" said the gruff voice.

"Yes, Mr. Cordone," said his companion, removing a small card from his vest pocket, and touching a button on its clean, plastic surface. The monsters were gone. The light was on. Two men stood alone amidst a few props in what appeared to be an abandoned factory.

"Look here, Fossett," said Cordone, mouthing his unlit cigar, "we've got more vampires than we can shake a stick at and mummies coming out the kazoo. I wanted something different this time."

The younger man paused before asking, "What about my suggestion to get away from horror for a while? We could try a musical revue, say."

Cordone turned so that his cigar—which seemed a natural extension of his face—was pointing at Fossett's chin. "Doctor, I hired you for your technical skills, and you're not a half-bad scenarist. But basic showmanship is my job! I like your test holograms for a thirties musical program. If the market ever wants 'em, we'll provide. But now we're in the biggest horror boom since the holo shows caught on. And I want something that will swamp the competition."

Fossett wished he hadn't used that word—it reminded him of his failed swamp monster proposal from the previous month.

Cordone kept on: "Where the hell are the smells? I didn't get one whiff from the decay of rotting corpses or any of that stuff."

"Trouble with the software. We'll have it all together by the end of the week: sounds, smells, colors …"

It was as if Cordone hadn't even heard him. "What you were just showing me was going to run the full gamut, right? Frankenstein's Monster was next, I suppose, complete with thunder and lightning."

Ted Fossett brushed his black hair back on his head, and took a deep breath. Now was as good a time as any. "Mr. Cordone, I've been giving this matter a lot of thought. There is really nothing wrong with the concept of our current show. The audience feels at home with the traditional elements, as if they were long lost relatives. The trouble is in the faces."

"Yeah?"

"There aren't any."

The producer removed his cigar from a suddenly pensive mouth. "You trying to be cryptic with me? Never mind. You can explain what you mean over lunch. I've gotta be outside for a minute. If I don't light this weed and smoke it pronto, I'm gonna die."

On the ride over to the restaurant, Fossett spent his time trying to avoid the acrid cigar smoke and thinking up a proposal for his next holo-show that would be Cordone-proof. With the finality of a dungeon door slamming shut, he'd settled on his course of action by the first course of their meal at The Oyster's Shell.

"Now, what did you mean about faces?" asked the producer, mouth finally sans cigar and about to go to work on a martini.

"You're not really bored by the subject matter of your horror house: it's not familiarity with the material that's the trouble. Our monsters don't have faces. Our Dracula isn't Lugosi or Lee or Jourdan or Langella or Oldman. He's a vague approximation of a childhood

memory, a painted mask. That's the trouble with all the characters."

"You propose to redo the monsters based on famous actors in the
roles?"

"I would, except that you were also right about having saturated
the public with these particular images already. They are so used to
seeing the figures as they stand, they wouldn't even notice improvement in detail. No, we need something different."

The producer was smiling now. He started on his second martini.
It did his heart good to see creative employees being creative. "Something new?" he asked.

"Something old. Something with terror, yet also a memory. A program built around the portrayals of one great horror star."

"I like it! How about Boris Karloff?"

"A wonderful suggestion, but many of his famous roles are already part of the package we're selling. Oddly enough, we do not
have a single characterization from the first movie star to be associated with macabre roles."

"Who's that?"

"Boss, I give you Lon Chaney, the man of a thousand faces. And
what a face!"

A hundred photographs covered the walls of his office. Fossett
had a good research team at Doppelgänger, Incorporated. Some of
the old boys went back to the period of animatronics and robot
mockups. They'd made the transition to the holograms readily. Looking at the photos that they had managed to gather, he figured they'd
make good librarians as well.

He saw that most of the material was on loan from The Ackerman
Museum. A booklet on the Chaney section of the collection was on
his desk. Other photographs would be forthcoming. And holos would
be made from them as well as the films.

Fossett had insisted on seeing the classics. His grandfather had
been, what they called, "heavily into nostalgia." That's how, as a
boy, Ted Fossett had seen the original version of *The Phantom of
the Opera.* Old flickering melodrama that it was, the picture had
exerted a strange hold on its young viewer...as it had for generations before him. For the first time, Ted Fossett had beheld the face
of living death. He could not forget.

The first photograph he went over to examine was of the phantom. It was the only one in a frame. Yes, it was as he remembered, and yet there was something more. He turned away, waited, looked again.

Had there been a subtle change? Those high cheekbones, protruding to such an extent that they almost seemed to be eggs pushing their way out of the side of his head, had shifted, perhaps. Or the way in which light moved across the skull face, forming a spiderweb of shadow lace, above which the black eyes stared ... was there movement? The phantom seemed alive in that frame, under the nonreflective glass. The eyes seemed to follow the viewer around the room.

He took the picture off the wall and held it close. *Memory comes on little cat's feet.* He was holding his first nightmare. He'd forgotten just how effective that old movie had really been. It had taken a second bow in his dreams.

Doppelgänger, Inc., wasn't in the business of dreams. It was in the business of convincing people that they remembered what they had really forgotten. The more superficial, the better! The movies for which they provided holographic effects were simple minded trips, offering the audience one easy-to-digest emotion per film. He couldn't bear to watch them. At least these souped-up haunted houses had the merit of lacking pretension.

Until now. Wasn't he biting off more than Mr. Cordone could chew? He looked at the phantom in his hand. He looked at the picture's frame. Until now, the holo-shows had been nothing but frames. Now he was proposing to put a picture in that frame.

It had better be the right picture. With the amount of money he would be spending in the next three months, he couldn't afford to be wrong.

Trouble comes in threes. That's what he was telling himself, over and over. First, he had overslept. Dogs barking in the night had awakened a mockingbird that began to sing. Perhaps the all-night illumination in the street by his house had confused the demented bird into thinking it was daytime, but whatever the reason, its distracted chirping had gone on until dawn.

Oversleeping wasn't so bad, he insisted. One of the reasons to be an executive was to occasionally slip back into patterns of freedom from the good old days of unemployment. Just so that it wasn't frequent. He had no desire to return to the good old days of starvation.

That's what made the second problem so intolerable, the thought that he wouldn't just be late for his appointment, but might miss it altogether. Of all the times to run low on a charge! The blue beetle shape of his car was already the size of a coin in the distance behind him. He was near enough the research plant that it made more sense to finish the trek on foot than to go to a supply station. He could send someone for the car.

Naturally it had to be a hot day. Mouth half open and his eyes stinging, he noticed that beads of perspiration were even showing through his watch that he had taped to his wrist, as he did every morning right after his shower. He wiped off the face on the thin film of poroplast so that he could once more masochistically take note of the lateness of the hour.

Every step kicked up small dust clouds that made straight for his eyes. *My kingdom for a handkerchief*, he thought. The blue sky, the flat horizon, the sun baking his neck to a wattled brown—it all put him in the mood for the air-conditioned dark of one of his holo-shows. It was still a long walk before that.

One minute he was trudging down an isolated country road, wondering what his third stroke of bad luck might be; the next, he changed his mind about the fates. A car pulled up beside him, an old gasoline burner. "Need a lift?" asked the man inside.

The top was down on this old convertible. Fossett had a good look at the man behind the wheel. He was a nondescript sort, his long brown face relaxed under an old fashioned touring cap. "Don't see many of those anymore," said Fossett.

The man's eyes gave him the once over. "What, my cap?"

"Oh no," answered Fossett, laughing. "I mean the antique."

"She runs just fine. You getting in?"

Fossett needed no further inducement. The worn leather seat was especially comfortable after the mile he'd walked on foot. From a recent cleaning, the covers had a fresh smell that was new to him.

"Where you headed?" asked the driver.

"Not far. There's a new research and development lab of Doppelgänger, Incorporated, at the end of this road and, say, it dead ends there. Where are you headed?"

The driver allowed himself a thin smile. "Same place. I work there."

Fossett had not been to the plant before. A recent addition to his holdings, with new equipment—and ideas —that industrial spies would happily sell to the competition, Cordone had seen to it that it was in an out of the way place. The regular staff had a barracks behind the plant where they would feel that they were living the austere life of boot camp privates except that they knew they were DI employees receiving triple overtime for shifts lasting no more than a month at a time. The executive staff was flown in. That's how Fossett was supposed to have arrived, except that he missed the shuttle.

Somber thoughts of uncharged private vehicles were sneaking around in his mind when he noticed that the fuel gauge on the old coupe read near the top. Wondering where his benefactor had found so much gasoline, Fossett opted for a different question: "What department are you with?"

"I'm the janitor." The man straightened his arms on the wheel and brought his head back on his shoulders until there was a popping sound. "Not as limber as I used to be," he said.

"Oh," Fossett replied. "I'm with the holo development team. My first time out here, though. I normally work closer to town. Anyway, it was fortunate you passed by. I appreciate the lift."

"Sure." This response seemed to satisfy the man. It didn't satisfy Fossett, but he was through talking. It was so damned hot. He was thirsty and tired. Now the old fashioned nature of the transportation seemed more irksome than welcome. How could anyone stand to drive around without air conditioning?

Fortunately, the trip was nearly over. As the mushroom-shaped building came into view—its whiteness almost blinding in the afternoon sun—Fossett spoke to the driver once more. "I'm Dr. Fossett. You'll have to let me buy you lunch sometime."

"I'd like that. Maybe I can do something for you."

Fossett waited for the man to give his name. He didn't. The long silences were becoming annoying. He felt a need to make conversation, no matter how inane. Unprompted, a question slipped out: "How did you ever wind up a janitor?" Instantly he regretted the phrasing.

There was no hesitation in the man's answer: "I've always looked for jobs nobody else would do—or could do. Here we are." The car pulled into a slot marked MAINTENANCE. "I'll see you later," finished the driver. There was something languid about the manner in which the man unwound himself onto the ground. Walking with a cat-like grace, he went into the building, while his passenger continued to sit in the hot car in the hot afternoon. At length, Fossett seemed to wake up, wiped the sweat from his forehead, and followed the man into the coolness of the building.

It was a side door through which he entered. If the other installations of the company had struck Fossett as unbearably antiseptic, they were nothing compared to the hospital sterility of this place. The odor was of every disinfectant known to the nose of man. A dull hum emanated from the walls and was so annoying to Fossett that he forgot his thirst. Taking a few steps down the hall, the echoes sounded as the beating of gongs in the palace of an Asiatic despot.

"You're not supposed to be here!" A woman's voice reached him from behind. He turned. The same voice spoke in an entirely different tone: "Oh, Ted. Excuse me." She walked over to him, wearing sane sneakers that did not bellow at his dust-laden ears. "We were worried that something had happened to you."

"Blossom!" he replied cheerfully. That was one good thing about the hallway. There was plenty of light. Once again he admired the fine doll features of Dr. Tajima, a very talented Japanese woman who, among other things, had introduced him to the pleasures of sushi the night he had wanted to taste everything. Now they exchanged a brief kiss.

"Plenty happened to me. Don't ask! Am I too late for the demonstration?"

"The Lon Chaney Factory cannot begin without you."

"How in God's name did you become involved with this project? I thought you were still in Fuji."

"Cordone brought me over as a surprise for you. Besides, some of the work was farmed out to the Japanese branch."

They were walking down the hall as they talked. She punched for an elevator as he said, "But I didn't know about that. I should have been informed."

"You know how Cordone loves surprises."

"Yes," he answered ruefully. "I hope there aren't any more. At any rate, I shouldn't be complaining. If the janitor hadn't picked me up, I'd still be walking that damned road to get here."

"Janitor?" Tajima asked as the elevator door sighed open.

"Yeah," he answered as they stepped inside. "He gave me a ride."

She looked at him closely, then said, "There isn't any janitor here, Ted. The building is fully automated."

The doors closed.

... the tintinnabulation that so musically wells
... from the bells, bells, bells, bells ...

The Hunchback of Notre Dame ushered them into the bell chamber of the cathedral, where he threw his twisted body with unexpected grace upon the heavy ropes. The clanging was almost loud enough to hurt the ears of the hunchback's visitors. Almost, but not quite. The customer was always right.

It seemed to be Chaney's hunchback: God knows that Fossett wanted it to be. With microscopic attention, he watched the performance of the hologram. Its body movements were copied from Chaney—the athletic gyrations under the heavy rubber padding accenting the suffering of the gnarled face under the chaos of scraggly hair that would be forever famous as a visage of noble torment. They had taken the movements right out of the film and transported them here. Through computer overlays, they had extrapolated what different movements would be, and the final result worked.

Except that something was missing. Fossett was about to comment, but Tajima was already several steps ahead, gesturing for him to follow. Reluctantly, he left the cathedral set ... and entered a circus ring.

He Who Gets Slapped bounded up close to Dr. Fossett, the smile on the white clown's face not covering the frown underneath. For three full seconds, Fossett stared into that face, as closely as he would peer at his own reflection in the shaving mirror. The pathos was there, as he had remembered it. Yet something was wrong, as there had been with the hunchback. He was about to tell this to Tajima when the lights went out around him.

The moaning of wind through junkyards. The faraway call of a lost train whistle. When the light came back on, the circus was gone. But the clown was still there, only a few feet away, standing with a slightly stooped posture. The white of the face and the suit was brightly outlined in the moonlight. Cold orb above; sad clown below.

When Fossett had written the script for the Chaney holo-show, this had been his favorite scene. It was inspired by an old article by Robert Bloch with the unforgettable Chaney quote: "A clown is funny in the circus ring but what would be the normal reaction to opening a door at midnight and finding the same clown standing there in the moonlight?"

"It works," said Tajima in his ear, taking him by the arm.

"It should have ..." he started to say, but broke off.

She either didn't hear him, or pretended not to. Already she was walking ahead again, saying, "Wait until you see this!"

This was a collage. First, they stepped into a set for a laboratory. Dr. Ziska bowed in welcome. The white lab coat did nothing to put the mind at ease when noticing the countenance above it, Chaney's 1925 performance as a mad scientist from *The Monster*, truly a film that foreshadowed much. The Ziska hologram pointed to a sliding panel that was opening in the stone wall, that perennial device of the silent melodrama. A procession of characters entered the room, to surround Fossett and Tajima, all of them Chaney, all of them menacing.

The ape man of *A Blind Bargain* shambled off to one side as the ghoulish vampire of *London After Midnight* took up a position directly in front of Fossett. He bowed to the lady, this pale fiend, making a motion to tip his stove-pipe hat, but thankfully not removing it, as one feared it was an essential portion of his head ... and removing it would reveal the gray matter of an evil brain. The razor-sharp teeth were visible in the partly open mouth, a nasty slash that bisected his pallid face. Fossett thought this to be the most effective holo thus far, even though it left something to be desired.

He was just about to see the truth lurking behind those popping eyes when his attention was drawn elsewhere.

Tajima was approached by The Red Death, that disguise worn by the phantom in one of the more ironic moments of Chaney's career. The skull mask remained in place. There was to be no unmasking here. Yet whatever was bothering Fossett about the other figures did not disturb him about The Red Death at all. Why? He had to know!

Others came: the armless man with the magic feet from *The Unknown* a character of many facets, but here displaying only a scowl. He was followed by the legless man of *The Penalty*, and his frown seemed burned on— that was a feature of his character that Fossett remembered. Together, these two seemed to make a whole person.

There was more, such as the Fu Manchu appearance of *Mr. Wu*, complete with Mandarin's robes, but also wearing a loathsome grin that Fossett had never seen in any of the research material. Then came Singapore Joe from The Road to Mandalay—there was nothing monstrous about this character but for his all-too-human cruelty. Fossett didn't remember the scars on the man's face being quite so pronounced as they now appeared. As for the film-covered eyeball, that white egg orb ... had it been as large as was evident on the holo?

So it went. Figure after figure, sneer after sneer, the varieties of character had all been covered over by a smooth sheet of malice. Terribly different expressions had somehow been made to appear identical.

"I think I've seen enough," he told Tajima. "We still have a lot of work before us."

"All right," she answered, raising her clipboard and touching a button on the attached communications card. The show was over. From where they were standing, they could see all the sets, including the largest one just ahead of them: the phantom's chamber.

"What's wrong?" she asked, as they headed back the way they'd come.

"Two things. One, I don't like the changes in my script. I'd stressed the multitude of Chaney's portrayals, each one special."

"They kept the hunchback and clown segments exactly as you wrote them, according to my notes."

"I can see that. However, this last bit in the lab scene had all these different personalities treated in the same unimaginative fashion."

"Those changes came from Cordone. He left your grand finale with the phantom untouched." The smile she offered was less for him than for her; she didn't enjoy being the bearer of unwanted news.

"How obliging of him," said Fossett almost under his breath.

"He'll be here shortly. He wanted to watch the finale with you so you're not really missing anything. Ted, you said there were two things that bothered you. What was the other?"

His left eye had started twitching. *Damn tension comes with the job*, was the message of the ragged nerve. "I'm not sure," he admitted, "but whatever it is, it's the real problem."

As they left the demonstration area, the first person they ran into was Cordone. The way he was standing in front of the doors made Fossett think of holograms. He'd always felt there was a basic unreality about the man, even though the checks were tangible enough.

"What's this about a janitor?" asked the producer without preamble.

Tajima took the lead. "There was an intruder whom Ted noticed. We've had staff looking for him but there is no sign of either him or his vehicle."

Cordone was in his element: "Well, dammit, that probably means he got away! We're too near our next release date for a spy to steal our thunder."

"I don't think he was a spy," said Fossett.

Cordone turned on the sarcasm: "Besides being late today, you're also playing detective? How do you know?"

"There was something odd about him. A spy wouldn't draw attention to himself by driving an antique. He wouldn't try slipping in under cover of a job that doesn't even exist. Although I was convinced there was a janitor when I saw the maintenance parking space."

"That's for robot supplies," said Tajima.

"Well, I've turned it over to our best security people," said Cordone. "All I need is a description from you since you're supposed to be so hot with faces."

"Faces!" exclaimed Fossett. "That's the problem in there. What have you done with Chaney's faces?"

The change of subject was accepted easily enough by Cordone. He'd been waiting for Fossett to make the complaint. "Sit down, doctor," he said; then noticing Tajima, amended that to the plural. Joining them in the most comfortable chair—which unconsciously the other two had left for him—Cordone took out one of his hyperthyroid cigars.

"Excuse me, sir, but smoking is..." began Tajima.

"Perfectly safe this far from the equipment," he finished for her. "I'm not interested in your convenience. I do worry about machinery that costs a small fortune. And I worry when my people lose sight of the priorities, eh, Fossett? Now, what's the trouble?"

There was something cold inside Fossett's stomach. "You've changed my design. I wasn't told."

"Your design? Oh, you mean what you designed for me. The minor alterations were done for purely monetary reasons. Nothing to concern yourself over."

Tajima did not hide the concern in her voice: "The script changes were for dramatic reasons, Mr. Cordone. That's what my memo indicates."

"Honey," he said, and there was nothing of sweetness in his voice, "Fossett and I aren't talking about that. We're talking about a much bigger change, but one I had to make. And I remind you that positions in the entertainment field are not protected by the World State. If you want to keep your job, just shut your pretty oriental trap."

She was too surprised by the crudeness of his remarks to say or do anything. If anything registered in her expression, it was fascination that she finally realized the sort of man who was her boss.

"I liked your Lon Chaney idea from the start," said Cordone to Fossett, "but we couldn't afford the detail. That part was out."

The detail. The lines in the face. The subtle ones underneath the smiles and the frowns. The remarkable skull of the man they called Lon Chaney. Fossett had dreamed about those contours of flesh and bone. More than that, he had seen the pain that the silent cinema star had inflicted on himself to achieve his difficult results.

As far back as the 1930's and the first decade of sound movies, technique had been standardized and union makeup artists took over the job. It was the same as every other area. The Twentieth Century was the age of unions —before increasing centralization rendered such organizations superfluous.

Lon Chaney had been the last great cinema artist of an earlier period reaching its full flower in the twenties. It was the hard, rough world of the self-contained showman. He was actor, mime, story consultant, and designer of a thousand faces. And he knew the ropes.

"When I realized what you wanted," said Cordone, blowing a cloud of cigar smoke that to Fossett was taking on the features of a gravestone, "I almost laughed myself sick. Capture every line of every face! Bring out every nuance. Run a program to anticipate what new postures, new lighting, would mean to those roles. Fossett, who's gonna spend that kind of money? As the rest of your package was good, we went ahead with it, minus the absurd details. You were too busy to keep track of it anyway."

"Then it's just the same," said Fossett to the floor, "as all your other holo-shows. You've taken the soul out, and left nothing but masks."

"I give the public what I want. Nine times out of ten, it's what they want, too. They're lookin' for a show, that's all."

Apparently Tajima had decided that her position with the company was not the end-all and be-all of existence. She spoke again: "You also removed certain characters, Mr. Cordone. That had nothing to do with the budget."

To her surprise, Cordone sighed. "There was no way we were putting the Christ exhibit in. Besides, I don't believe that was Lon Chaney."

Fossett exploded: "The photograph was recently unearthed! Experts have verified it! It is a long lost studio portrait of Chaney as Christ. I'd stake my career on its being authentic." This torrent of explanation and defense had no effect worth noting.

"It doesn't matter," said Cordone flatly. "That wouldn't fit the program even if it was legit. Just forget it! Now we have one last piece of business to conduct, then I have to get out of here. Christ, er ... I don't have all day to waste." Cordone went inside the bowels of dreams. After exchanging brief glances of common distress, the other two followed.

Tajima lowered her head and spoke in the direction of the card affixed to her blouse, just above her left breast: "We're going to need the phantom." Somewhere in the dark, a head nodded.

"I don't think you'll have any complaints about this one," said Cordone. "Your script was fine. The material grabs!"

Fossett wasn't listening. He was worrying. Of all the faces, the phantom's was the most important to him. He couldn't bear to see what Cordone had done with it.

Not a mask, a mere mask. The man would not be there. The self-inflicted agonies of wire and hook, a lifetime's knowledge of what it meant to be different—the memories of deaf and dumb parents—and the reality of loneliness, all there in the pulled back mouth, flaring nostrils, and unbelievable eyes. It wasn't some cheap funhouse fright. He couldn't let Cordone get away with it.

The little voice that spoke in his head was as unbidden as it was difficult to ignore: "What sort of job will you look for next?" The twitching in his eye returned as he realized he would do nothing. *I'm sorry*, he said to himself—*sorry I've betrayed you, Lon Chaney*.

"Damn it!" came Cordone's voice, gruffer than ever. With a clattering as if an empty bucket were rolling downstairs, he'd stumbled over something. "Get some more light in here!" Tajima did.

Several empty cylinders marked CLEANING FOAM were slowly turning on the floor, coming to a stop like hands of a watch winding down. "What are these doing here?" asked Cordone in a voice so low that it didn't sound like him.

"The maintenance robots use them," said Tajima. "I don't know how they got here. Ted, uh, I mean, Dr. Fossett, didn't we just return this way?"

"The janitor," said Fossett.

"That does it!" shouted Cordone. "I asked you before if you could describe the guy to one of our identi-artists."

He walked over, limping slightly from the wrench he'd given his foot. "What does the man look like?"

Fossett had been trying to remember the face in terms of its most distinctive features. Cordone had unknowingly given him the key word, "like." Of course, he had known all along, but couldn't allow himself to believe it.

"He looks like Lon Chaney," said Fossett.

For a moment, neither Tajima nor Cordone did anything but stare. They could hear each other's breathing. When the silence became too loud to bear, he continued: "Without makeup, I mean. I was so busy admiring the numerous portrayals that I almost forgot his appearance when he wasn't in a role. He was a rather plain-looking man. You'd pass him on the street without giving him special notice. A long American face is what he had—you'd see it on the great plains, sweating behind a tractor, you ..." His voice trailed off as the weight of the silence returned. He had become obsessed with faces in the last few months. He could tell the one that Cordone was wearing: someone observing a body after a terrible accident. And Fossett didn't enjoy the pity on Tajima's face much more.

"Is this your idea of revenge just because you don't like the way I fixed a fucking holo-show?" asked Cordone, veins standing out on his neck as exclamation.

"No sir, I didn't even know what you'd done until you told me. But the man really looked like Lon Chaney!"

Nobody could switch tracks faster than Cordone. He'd removed one of the verboten cigars and was pointing it at Fossett as if it were a surgical instrument poised over tonight's surprise cadaver: "If this is your idea of faking insanity just so you can collect on the DI medical retirement, I swear that I'll fry you!"

That's when the lights went out. "Tajima!" shrieked Cordone. "I didn't do anything!" she yelled back. "Listen," said Fossett ... and they did.

Laughing in the dark.

"Who's that?" asked Cordone. "Listen, you bastard, whoever you are, Doppelgänger, Incorporated, has a policy on trespassing that's gonna put you so far behind bars that by the time they rehabilitate you ..."

The lights came back on. At the far end of the building they could see the exhibit for The Phantom of the Opera. The organ room was bathed in a light so purple that it looked like burgundy wine, and next to it was a section of opera seats with the great chandelier above set out in aquarium blue. A silhouette moved near the keyboard.

"There he is!" shouted Cordone, as he hobbled off in that direction.

"That's the holo-show," whispered Tajima.

"Is it?" asked Fossett, grabbing her arm. "Have you seen it all the way through? Is anything different?"

"It's just the program," she insisted, as they watched the producer. "The keyboard part of the Wurlitzer organ is the set, but the big section above is a hologram matted in. Over there, the seats are real, but the chandelier is a projection. And the phantom, of course, is like all the other Chaneys in here."

"Gotcha!" Cordone had reached the phantom. His hands grabbed air. Turning toward the others, he had the aspect of a small boy whose toy had broken in his hands, as the wraith of the caped enigma hovered about him. A shadow.

Fossett was the first to reach him. Without saying a word, he took the producer's arm and started to lead him away, when he caught sight of the death's-head monster. It was bland. It was blank. It was just a green putty face, with painted eyes and jack-o'-lantern grin.

Fossett's arm dropped away and hung limp as a thing dead. He felt like crying.

"I ..." Cordone began, catching a glimpse of Fossett's face contorting in inner agony. He didn't go on, but turned back to confront his handiwork.

"You're an amusement," he told the hologram. "Nothing more." He began circling the exhibit. "You're not art. You were never anything but mass entertainment. And when mass taste changed, you didn't change with it." He was in the seats now, and talking to the hologram as it went through its paces—it pointed at the organ before sitting there with a flourish.

"What's Cordone doing?" asked Tajima in Fossett's ear.

"I'm not sure," he said. "It isn't like him. Maybe he's only talking to me."

"Spook shows! Horror man! It's all crap," Cordone went on, as the swelling notes of organ music rose to drown his voice. But he would not be silenced, raising his voice to be heard again. "I've never liked you, never liked these fantasies. I don't let my kids watch this stuff. Too many dreams, too many nightmares. It's bad, I tell you! People who spend a lot of time with this stuff aren't healthy. They're not any good at business, I'll tell you that!" He was shaking. "I hate you. I hate you!"

There was a flicker in the light, a gasp of whispery sound. A man in a cape glided over by the seated figure at the organ. The black phantom sitting, sitting, playing an imaginary organ, grew fuzzy around the edges, slipped out of sight ... but The Phantom of the Opera was there. He bent down, brushing his fingers over keys connected to nothing, making hollow clicking sounds that could be heard, just barely, in the din of the musical recording. The deep notes of Bach throbbed against the walls but he straightened up and shook his fist at the keyboard—an island of fact in a chimera. The phantom turned his back on this illusion. The phantom strode over to a point where the two sets were joined.

"Oh my God," said Fossett. He could see the phantom standing there, half in purple light, half in blue—could see that the phantom had a face.

He knew that face of night, of pain, of truth.

"What's going on?" Cordone's voice sounded very far away, but he was only standing among the seats. From under a velvet cape of bloody red, a black-gloved hand spidered its way to a lever on the wall, a lever that Tajima had never seen. With a tinkling of glass, the chandelier moved. The phantom's arm fell away from the wall. The chandelier fell from the ceiling. "Turn it off," said Cordone, his voice pleading, arm involuntarily covering his head from what he knew to be unreal. Tajima's finger had already brushed all the off buttons on her card before Cordone gave his command. The show was over. The phantom was gone.

There was a crash just the same.

(Dedicated to Forrest J Ackerman)

We move from the future world of "The Lon Chaney Factory" to a more common use for the future: satire. If Richard Kyle had not brought back *Argosy* for one last run, I doubt that this story would have seen the light of print. And if I hadn't spent some time hanging around the periphery of the movie and television industry, I doubt "Pavlovia" would have any bite. About which, please judge for yourself.

Pavlovia

The TV writer had a good left hook. Everyone at the company table knew it. They were also aware that Mr. Harris from the front office was due to arrive shortly. Mr. Harris was sure to have a proposition for the writer that would be unacceptable to his angry, stubborn talent. No one talked. They just waited.

Harris came in carrying an attaché case. He was wearing a three piece suit and his hair was combed in some kind of permanent wave. He smelled like the upholstery in a new car. The writer leaned back in his chair and put his feet up on the heavy glass table. The two of them looked at each other as the silence was broken by the pop of clasps opening on the attaché.

"All right," said Harris, standing at the head of the table. "Let's get on with it." He appraised the writer, making an inventory of the blond hair, thick mustache and quaint leather jacket. "I see you have your equipment in hand," he said, noting the small, black box strapped on the writer's hip. "Do you always carry your Typer?"

"What's it to you?" he snarled as Mr. Harris took a manuscript spool out of the case and dropped it on the table. The writer could feel the tension in the room and knew he was the source of it.

"I'm demanding a rewrite on your story," said the voice coming out of the three piece suit. All eyes were turned on the writer...waiting, waiting. They knew he could move fast when provoked. Some of them had seen him in action before. He was a good Union man who always fulfilled the contract. Just as now he wasted no time jumping on the table and running down the length of it as Harris said, "Writers do as they're told; they're mud-sucking little...*gak!*"

The writer had the target by the throat as he careened off the table. "This has got to stop!" he shouted, straddling his victim. No one in the room made a move.

The gurgling sound that came out of Harris was an attempt to explain company policy. There were snatches of words here and there from which could be pieced together the general idea that the public's attention span had decreased again. The writer pum-

meled the face beneath him with heartfelt sincerity. And then, raising his numb hands, he pulled off the wig that covered the silver
plate on top of Mr. Harris's head.

"Ungrateful writer," muttered Harris as the circle of metal was
turned counter-clockwise, making it pop off the top of his head.
The writer inserted his right index finger and deactivated Mr. Harris, releasing a pungent odor in the air, the distinctive smell of an
open robot.

"Whew," said a trembling little man near the foot of the table.
"That was a good one."

Grabbing the manuscript spool and inserting it in the slot on the
side of his Typer, the writer started for the door. But he turned to
the little man before exiting the conference room, and said, "I've
had better, but this one was OK."

"How much will you cut it?" asked a woman with red hair.

"It was hard enough doing a mini-series in fifteen minutes, but
I'll cut it to ten," he answered, leaving the door swinging behind his
proud, tall back. He was a professional.

Friends of mine at Florida State University in the early seventies remember me working on this story even then. I've been living with this one for a very long time. Written as a tribute to my favorite writer, Ray Bradbury, I feel that I received the ultimate accolade when Don Albright (who is putting together the definitive Bradbury bibliography) liked the story so much that he gave me an actual copy of *Dark Carnival*, the book which plays such a crucial role in "Clutter."

Bradbury encouraged me with a three page letter on "Clutter." In a correspondence lasting nearly thirty years, there is no letter I cherish more than what he said about this story of a frustrated science fiction fan living a nightmare.

The publication history of this story was a nightmare in itself. Science fiction magazines rejected it on the grounds that I should submit it to horror magazines; while horror magazines rejected it on the grounds that I should submit it to science fiction magazines. I had violated the taboo of doing a professional story about a fan. That made it fan fiction, you see.

I received a complimentary letter of rejection from Alice Turner at *Playboy* that inspired me to keep trying. "Clutter" sold to Elinor Mavor's *Amazing* right before she was replaced by another editor who wasn't favorably disposed toward my work He was obliged to pay me for the story because it was in the inventory.

But still "Clutter" had not been in print. And then I was saved from an unexpected quarter: Robert Bloch bought it and published it in his anthology, *Psycho-Paths*.

My tribute to Ray Bradbury published by Robert Bloch! It was a dream come true. No magazine appearance could compare to that, not to me anyway. My oldest friends think this is my best story. It received Honorable Mention in *The Year's Best Fantasy and Horror, Fifth Collection*.

Clutter

After his parents died on the interstate, Paul Kraft, a small, freckle-faced boy going on fourteen, was moved into Aunt Rose's house over in Culver City.

It was an old two-story house surrounded by tall trees and he fell in love with it on first sight. Then, with the opening of a door, he came face to face with Aunt Rose, who until that meeting had only been a vague childhood memory, a shadow guest at his seventh birthday party: She stood thin in the doorway, a fifty-two-year-old librarian who had lived most of her years alone.

She invited Paul inside, showed him to an upstairs room and waited quietly as the people from the moving van moved his possessions into the house—some clothes, a monster mask and a lot of books. With the boy settled in, the cousin who had overseen the transfer said his goodbyes and departed from Jefferson Lane, leaving behind two people to get acquainted who had in common blue eyes and virginity.

The first thing Paul learned was that Aunt Rose cleaned house twice a week. The whole house. It was a strategy she had worked out against her arch-enemy, dust. Days when she didn't clean were lulls between battles, a time for planning. When she was engaged in the grand effort, all brooms and dustpans, she had no time for so trifling a concern as a nephew's privacy. His door was without a lock and he soon learned that Aunt Rose didn't knock. No closed door could withstand her determination to get into a room at precisely the moment she desired entry. There was never any telling when she would decide a certain rug or bureau required her immediate attention. After a month of diplomatic entreaties, Paul succeeded in being granted the privilege of cleaning his own room. As he had expected, inspections were twice a week.

Occasionally, Aunt Rose would call him downstairs for the announcement of a shopping expedition. Then would ensue an hour of methodical preparation, Rose dressing herself in an outdated, high-collared dress smelling of mothballs, and having Paul dress in a suit purchased on an earlier outing, starched little-young-man clothes with the look of a mail-order catalogue about them. On the first trip, he criticized his guardian's selection of clothes when in a department store she asked what he thought of a shirt she was buying for him. He hadn't liked it. She didn't ask his opinion again. Instead, she frequently told him that it was a great sacrifice on her part to take him shopping and he obviously lacked gratitude for her generosity. She didn't let him go in bookstores when they were out.

When summer came, Aunt Rose opened the door to his room one evening, poked her head inside and asked, "Paul, dear, are you busy?"

"No," he answered, "not really. Just reading."

"I wanted to ask if you know what today is?"

"Wednesday, the eighteenth."

"Yes, dear. It has been over three months since the death of your parents, one season in fact." She peered intently at Paul's eyes; he looked at her indifferently.

"What is it, Aunt Rose?"

She gave a little shrug. "Well, I thought you should know. You should think about it."

"Are we going to the cemetery?" he asked.

"Would you like that?" she asked back. He said nothing.

He was confused by the pleasant tone in her usually neutral voice. "Yes, Paul," she continued, "we are going after we've finished the den." He understood his cue and got up to help her with the vacuum cleaner.

They only spent a few minutes at the cemetery because a strong wind disturbed Aunt Rose's hair. On the way back she said she was glad their visit with his parents had been taken care of, as though a duty had been discharged. He wondered how many more anniversaries of the accident would be observed by his aunt ... and then, feeling anxiety and impatience, concluded he must be depraved for thinking such a thing. Not able to understand his uneasy emotions, he put them out of his mind as best he could. He spent the rest of the day on Mars, courtesy of Edgar Rice Burroughs.

It was a predictable Saturday. He didn't get out to a movie, but when the cleaning was done, and he'd settled himself in his room to read, a knock came on his door—a knock!—he steeled himself for the worst. What could have inspired a formal visit from Aunt Rose?

She entered, sat in a dark chair next to the window. She surveyed his bookshelf and its double row of books, and she studied the contents of a box at the foot of his bed— there like a footlocker, packed with books—and then she looked at Paul and said, "You have too many books."

His mouth hung open for a moment before he said, "I don't understand, Aunt Rose."

"For one thing, you don't have enough shelf space."

"They fit, don't they? So there's room, isn't there?"

"It doesn't look very nice. When your door is open you can see the box from the hallway."

"I can move the box."

"But that's not the point." She looked down at the thin, white hands in her lap, clasped them, and then glanced up at Paul—but she didn't look in his eyes; she was staring at the top of his head. "Paul, dear," she said, "surely you don't read them all. You couldn't possibly have read them all."

"I've read over seventy-five percent of them."

"You see?"

"But Aunt Rose...."

"Your hair is uncombed."

"I'll comb it." He pulled out a comb.

"Even if you did read them all, that wouldn't be good for you. It would take up too much of your time. It wouldn't be healthy for a young boy to spend so much time reading. It would be bad for his eyes."

"Aunt Rose," he said, his voice growing louder, "I like to read!"

She raised her eyebrows in surprise. "Why, Paul, there's no need to shout. You notice that I never shout. People will listen to you if you are quiet and polite."

"I'm trying to be polite."

"Don't you realize if you had fewer books it would be easier to clean your room?"

"I collect books."

"That's much better, dear. You may put your comb away." He put his comb away. Aunt Rose sighed and said, "It's not good to spend so much time cooped up in a room. You should get out more often."

Paul replied much too swiftly, "But you don't like me to go to the playground or to the lot where they have the football games. You don't like me to come home dirty."

She grinned in triumph. "You could go to parties. You could get out and still stay relatively clean. You really ought to."

"I don't like parties."

She stood. "Think about it, dear. I'm really trying to do my best to raise you, although I never expected there would be a child in the house. Still, I'll do my best." At the door she paused, turned back and said, "Don't forget what I said about the books." His white stare met her gray one and she hurried out the door.

That encounter got him to thinking about how his aunt used her spare time. He hardly ever saw her read. She didn't even enjoy the newspaper. This struck him as peculiar because of her job. As the town librarian, she was entombed daily among a thousand volumes. But reading for recreation was not part of her life. In the house there was a small bookcase chock-a-block full of fiction and essays and poetry left over from Grandma and Grandpa. Aunt Rose didn't use it. Paul remembered that his mother, Rose's younger sister, had liked to read.

The only time Paul saw Rose opening the books was when she was cleaning the house and moving things about. She muttered over them like a sorceress, vainly attempting to exorcise the dust that clung to the leather covers. She handled them roughly, reserving delicacy for dusting objects of fine china—a zoo of small porcelain animals and a cherished teacup that dated way back.

Not long after Aunt Rose's complaint about his personal library, he was vacuuming and she was dusting and talking to the books. He resolved to find out what made her tick. He turned off the machine, came into the study and asked, "Why don't you like books?"

She started, laughed without pleasure. "Why, whatever made you say something like that?"

"I was only asking a question."

"It's so foolish!"

"Do you like books, then?"

"Books are important tools. That's why we have libraries."

"Thank you," said Paul, still unsatisfied, returning to his vacuum cleaner.

Later that day, at dinner, Aunt Rose said, "If you went to the library more often, you wouldn't have to waste your money buying all those paperbacks."

"I earn that money mowing lawns."

"Is that good reason to spend it on things that just lie around getting dusty? Libraries exist so you won't have to buy books."

He got to wondering if Aunt Rose was happy. He felt a profound discontent in the air when she was present. Although she smiled often, it was always perfunctory when talking to him. He had the idea she was about to suddenly look over her shoulder, as though she were being stalked ... but it was only Paul who was there. She complained if he made too much noise, which soon became almost any noise he authored, and worried out loud that he did too much walking in the house; that the old house wasn't used to it and he might wear it out if he didn't exercise more care. He hid in his room but that afforded only temporary sanctuary. He did a lot of thinking there.

It seemed like a thousand years ago that his mother told him about her elder sister. She described the family history, complete with particulars, tactfully stated, of Rose's self-imposed loneliness. The old-maid sister had a knack for antagonizing virtually everyone except Paul's mother and her employer.

The story went that Aunt Rose suffered through a bad childhood inflicted on her by an older brother, Joda, who reached some kind of distorted pinnacle when, brandishing a baseball bat, he chased and terrified her. Joda was like that. The father doted on the boy because he was the only son—through him the family name was supposed to live on. Joda never married, however. If the patriarch had had his way, the son would have inherited everything except whatever stray cash was left for the girls to divide. The mother, who had half the estate in her name, intervened on behalf of her daughters and Rose inherited, among other dispensations, the house. Paul's mother inherited some stocks and bonds and money. Joda inherited the other stocks and bonds, the rest of the money and the family business, which he managed to bankrupt within a few years. No one was surprised that Rose elected to spend the rest of her life in the very house that had been the site of so many childhood traumas, rather than sell it as her sister advised.

Paul remembered his mother's words about Aunt Rose in a special way, as if they had just been whispered in his ear—her soft, calm voice telling him about the house of her parents, now haunted by the autumn-leaf woman blown from room to room by vagrant breezes, and sometimes blown out the door and down the street to the library. And always, the house waiting to suck her back inside.

One Sunday evening, Paul came downstairs excited over something he'd read, intending to share it. Aunt Rose stopped him cold in mid-enthusiasm and snapped, "What do your books teach you?"

He faltered, then said, "Well, they teach me about adventure, about fun, about good and evil ..."

"There!" said Aunt Rose. "Morality. What do you know about it? What does that"—she gestured disdainfully— "sordid book of science fiction teach you about morality?" He said nothing. She continued. "Does it teach you consideration for others?"

He said, "There's a story in here about a hero. It shows how a man can win if he's honest with himself, if he's smart."

"Does it show that we have duties to others, that society comes first?"

"What are you talking about?" he asked coldly.

She smiled a mirthless smile and translated: "Don't be selfish."

"Oh," he replied.

She approached him and brushed a lock of hair from his eyes. "We must bear in mind the importance of balance," she said in a disinterested monotone. "We must avoid extremes. That's why I worry that you have an obsession with books."

There was a malicious glint in his eyes as he said, "But don't you go to extremes in cleaning the house?"

"Don't be precocious," she admonished him. He bit his lip. "Now run along," said Aunt Rose. Paul ran along.

Back in his room, he considered an evening stroll but knew she wouldn't grant permission. Out there was darkness and she didn't like the idea of darkness. But then, he observed, she wasn't very fond of light either. The drapes were kept drawn twenty-four hours a day except for the faded yellow ones that hung at the kitchen window. They would be under the same roof for another evening, as usual.

Precocious! There was a word, much as he loved words, to hate. It had dogged him all his life. In first grade, while his peers were struggling through Big Golden Books, he was reading mystery comics and deducing the solutions to admittedly transparent plots. In fourth grade he was bored by the basic reader and discovered science fiction. Jules Verne was the launchpad, and H. G. Wells the rocket that shot him up high where waited the prose of Ray Bradbury;

where people with real human passions dreamed robot dreams—he was drunk on thoughts of the future. Seventh grade: while his class was one year away from being assigned Bradbury, he was well along in Dostoevsky. At first it surprised Paul that other students resented him for his speedy comprehension in English class but at length he became used to it. What he was never able to accept were the teachers who criticized him for his ability and called him precocious whenever he tried to express a thought.

It had finally seemed unimportant what opinions were expressed by the people at school. He was comfortable at home. He overheard his parents talking of how it was a good possibility that Paul would earn himself a scholarship to a university when the time came. Naturally they encouraged his voracious reading. But they soon found their ministrations to be unnecessary. He was on a nonstop roller coaster of words. His father proudly suggested that nothing human could derail him.

But then, with the screaming of metal on concrete, and an ambulance vainly seeking to cry out for the side of life with as much conviction as death's grinding of bones, Mr. and Mrs. Kraft were borne away. It had seemed so out of place, so wrong. With one hammer blow on his chest, Paul had felt his world diminished. They were gone. He was alone. Standing in a private limbo, peeking at a world awry, he'd seen his life packed away, all bundled up, and moved in big boxes via a handle-with-care van to Aunt Rose's mausoleum.

The first night, lying awake in a feather bed, listening to crickets outside his window, he decided he was disembodied and his spirit was wandering up and down the stairs, listening for the creaking sounds that are the very pulse of an old house. He imagined the house was carrying on a conversation with the night creatures and there was a general agreement that Paul Kraft wasn't really there; that it was just a grim joke being played; that he'd wake up the next day to find his existence intact once again. But he never got to sleep that night. Within a week he accepted the existence of Aunt Rose, and then the gray days began to creep by, leaving him with the knowledge that he was waiting, but he didn't know for what. He began to think that perhaps he had been in the car with his parents and accompanied them into the grave.

He thought that he had arrived, terribly alone, in a special kind of Hell where not even Charon or Cerberus would set foot—a place reserved for Paul and his tormentor. He got to thinking of it a lot. He even got to dreaming about it and one night he screamed about it, the night he dreamed he was locked in the bathroom, sitting in a pool of dirty water in the bathtub, sweating black dirt while Rose banged on the door from the other side. He could hear the vacuum cleaner roaring. And he heard her saying that he was every bit as dirty as his books. As he woke up, heart pounding, head dizzy with fear, he had heard his aunt's voice at the door asking in a low voice, "Why did you scream?"

"I had a nightmare," he'd answered abruptly, then added, "it won't happen again."

"Good night, then," had come the voice through the door. A pause. "Dear."

When his fourteenth birthday came around, he spent the day away from the house at a double-feature movie and in every bookstore within walking distance of the theatre. There was enough money left over from the pictures to purchase a few paperback anthologies, but he lamented the lost period of his life when there had been a regular flow of stories. Now he spent some of his time at the library as his aunt advised, but always on her day off. He read fiction when what he was after wasn't checked out. Paying his money for the books, he smiled inwardly, knowing that soon he'd have more money because of three recent additions to his lawn-mowing list. It was a fine present.

At five o'clock she picked him up in front of a drugstore. He was still cheerful. He stayed that way for almost an hour until she reminded him that any money he would be earning should go toward important things, such as savings for a college education; and of course there was the matter of his clothes.

He gave his aunt her due, however. When she had asked him if he wanted a birthday party, he appreciated the reticence with which she asked the question. At least they shared a mutual dislike of such events, or so he thought until she surprised him in subsequent weeks by insisting more and more frequently that he attend parties. The announcement came over a meal of lamb chops: "You," she said, "are going to Barbara Struthers's party." Well, when her voice had that tone, that was that. He cursed the bad luck that allowed Aunt Rose to make the acquaintance of Emma Struthers, a schoolteacher of all things, and now it was naturally assumed that the daughter of a teacher and the nephew of a librarian would get together and enjoy some kind of intuitive camaraderie. He savagely attacked the remains on his plate.

When the day arrived, he dressed reluctantly while she stood outside his door talking all the time about how much he'd enjoy the party. She finally inspired compliance with her edict when he saw the party as a means of escape. But before he got out the front door, she spied his bulging coat pocket and made him leave his book behind. With present in hand, he was off.

"Don't forget to be back before dark," she called halfheartedly.

Now that Paul was gone, Aunt Rose tried to forget about nephews and other troubles. It was time to relax. She sat in a rocking chair and contemplated a corner of the room. She thought about dust. She observed it, floating, swirling in the light shaft that slid between two almost-drawn curtains. There were so many motes of dust, a world of flickering particles made visible in one ray of light coming through the window, stopping on an empty corner. It bothered her.

She even dreamed about it. She had swept, mopped and vacuumed her way through so many nightmares; and still there was the dust, the infinity of little white specks. They were outside her and inside her—under-the-fingernail specks, inhaled specks, captured-in-the-ridges-of-fingerprints specks, everywhere specks. Sitting in her rocker, rocking, stirring up whirlpools of the stuff, Aunt Rose sighed, and from her left nostril there exited a particle of matter that once had been the flesh of an Egyptian pharaoh. The rocking woman felt time pressing against her eyelids.

Dust, if not bad enough in itself, conjured up images of even worse things, like dirt, like the filthy earth she was rolled in when brother Iode roughhoused her, like the dirty hands of her father patting her when he came in from working in the yard, like the grime that nested in her mother's pores (even though her mother was a fastidious woman, Rose could see pollution in the flesh when she was close up). She took baths twice, sometimes three times a day. She had done so for a long time, until her skin was almost the pallor of soap, and she got rashes on her oversensitive, flaking skin. She never felt clean. Each night she dreaded the prospect of working the next day because the big, dirty world was waiting to sully her. The library was so damnably full of dust. But if she didn't venture out to earn money to buy her protection, then one day that world might be able to touch her so hard she couldn't stand it.

Why, she agonized, couldn't Paul understand? He was grown up for his age. Surely he could see that she braved the outdoors for him. The busy, bustling department stores were bad enough ... but when she went to the cemetery it was truly terrible—just the thought of all that dirt around so many bodies. When she'd offered to make the supreme sacrifice (to let him have a party at the house even though such an event would mean a flow of dirt from outside), she thanked God he hadn't taken her up on it. The relief she felt didn't keep her from criticizing him for his stubbornness "You'll never get ahead, dear, unless you're more social," she had warned him with all the conviction born of bitter experience. Paul didn't argue the issue that time. Which pleased her. He ignored it. Which frustrated her. He was so hard to reach. So hard to understand.

At least she was alone, now. She liked that. Not that Paul was an exceptionally bothersome child—in fact he was quieter than many adults she knew. The problem was that he was there. She couldn't sleep at night when he was reading because his room was next door. Although it was a big house, all the bedrooms were together. The light from his lamp would creep under her door and its soft radiance would warm her face. She'd open her eyes, see dust in the light. Then she'd hear Paul turn the pages. It seemed that he was constantly reading. How books accumulated dust and how swiftly a few of them grew into an enormous inconvenience. In the twilight state preceding sleep, she would hear pages turn and she'd just have to stay awake, waiting for the next one. It was like the dripping of a faucet, only not as regular. Paul was a fast reader, getting to the next page before she could doze off. *Crinkle* would go the page in his fingers, as he turned it slowly, lovingly. *Crinkle*. Sometimes in the middle of late-night reading, he would take a break and move around. He even closed doors. Sometimes she could hear the creaking of bedsprings. Sometimes she didn't dream about dust.

She was growing to resent Paul. All he wanted to do was talk about his books—usually he'd get the most excited over a book she'd never heard of—and he liked to push tomes into her hands, proposing in a most insistent voice that she read them. She knew that if she complied, he would want to talk about them, which meant a discussion afterward. She so hated argumentative people. Paul was very aggressive, a prime example of the type. She blamed her sister for the boy's poor manners. Worst of all, she had discovered that he was smuggling new books into the house as if he didn't have enough already. Some of them were those dreadful horror stories.

She got up and entered the kitchen to fix herself a cup of tea. She selected the prize teacup, poured in the hot brew and went back to a rocking chair that protested, squeaking a little, when she sat down—but that was all right because it was her sound. She sipped her tea with a hearty *sssssut!* Outside, a car passed by and the shifting of the gears grated on her nerves.

A dog barked. How noisy, how messy the world. At least she had her house, her sanctuary, and the world was on the other side of her door.

Except for Paul.

Shortly before dusk, a grinning Paul Kraft left the home of Barbara Struthers, and berated himself for having supposed the party would be a bore. He had to face it. He could not deny that he'd had a great time. Barbara proved to be quite a hostess. He hadn't even known that she liked him before this. But now he could hardly believe the proof of her fondness. In his hands he carried the fruit of that pleasant encounter—a book. Ah, such a book, an old and valuable one. If Barbara Struthers were a bit crazy to give gifts on her birthday, as well as receive them, it was a sweet madness. He would remember and do his best to pay her back. She was like no other girl he knew—most seemed annoying pests to him—and he found her exciting.

He felt very much alive as he walked, ran, skipped his way home over bone-white sidewalks. To his left, the daytime moon peered over an elm tree. It was a friendly orb, good company for his elated mood. The sky was a curious mixture of pink and dark blue. And then ... 3700 Jefferson Lane, the haunted house, so full of mystery, that was his residence. The kitchen drapes were open, allowing twilight into an otherwise gray cave. There was a dying carnation in a vase in the window. He looked at it and thought about how Aunt Rose was fond of telling him to pay attention to worldly things, to come down from his fantasies and acquire some common sense as compensation for the journey. Well, he would make her happy tonight. He'd surprise her by bursting in with the good news.

"Aunt Rose," he shouted as the door slammed shut. From inside the house came the fragile sound of breaking porcelain. He stopped, pondered. *Not her favorite teacup,* he prayed.

"Paul." Her voice was quiet, almost a whisper. He shivered. "Please come into the parlor."

He came. Sitting still in her Boston rocker, she appraised him. The shards of broken china, white like midget icebergs, were scattered in a sea of purple carpet. "Please clean up your mess," she said.

"How did it break?" he asked, too bluntly he realized as soon as the words were out of his mouth. One wasn't blunt with Aunt Rose. "I mean the carpet ... how?"

She didn't answer. She was looking away from him, looking at a comer of the room. He tried to follow her gaze, to see the object of her interest, but immediately her eyes darted back, held his gaze in a cobwebby stare. She said, "It broke on the arm of the rocker. You see that the arm is made of wood. Wood is hard. Porcelain is delicate and must be protected from hard things. You startled me." It was like listening to a list being read by an executioner, a calm, dry tone enumerating your heinous offenses one last time, before the axe descends. Paul looked down at his feet.

"What's that in your hand?" she asked suddenly. He had forgotten about the book. In his haste, he had neglected to leave it on the living room table or to put it in the bookcase. A fool, he thought, I bring it into the lion's den. "What are you hiding," she snapped.

"I'm not hiding anything!"

"Then let me have it!"

"I brought it in for you to see," he said as he released it to her white hands, which held the book delicately, as if holding old papyrus. She started to look through it. "It's *Dark Carnival!*" he said. "By Ray Bradbury!"

"I can read," she replied.

"It's something I've wanted for a long time. It's a fine book, his rarest, his first, and the hardest to find."

She finished thumbing the pages and held the book up to the lamp next to her chair, examining it as if it were a fine crystal, slowly turning it, letting the light play around the brown, worn edges.

"It's worth a lot of money," Paul said in a cracking voice, wondering why he was afraid. He was suffocating. "A lot of money," he repeated, trying to recapture the intensity of his point. One word was shouting in his brain: *No!*

"Paul, dear, what if I were to damage your book?" she asked. He said nothing as the world collapsed around him. "What if I were to bend it, crease it?" He said nothing. "But no, it wouldn't really be broken then. What if I were to light a match?" He closed his eyes. "I shouldn't want to bum it completely. Just partially. We'd put out the fire before it was all gone." He wanted to cry. But he didn't cry. Silence was heavy in the room, for at least an eternity.

Finally he asked, "Why do you hate me, Aunt Rose?"

She shrugged and laid his book on the table. "I don't hate you, child. I love you. But you have to learn a very important lesson or else you'll be self-centered for the rest of your life. You never think about other people. You never consider other people's feelings."

"Are you talking about yourself? No one else has ever told me—"

"I'm talking about how selfish you are. Oh, I don't blame you. How could you be otherwise after the way you were raised? But now you must learn to be considerate of others."

"I was coming home to tell you how much I enjoyed the party, to share with you how—"

"Very well. Tell me about the party. We should change the subject. I hate people who argue."

He took a deep breath. "It was the best party I've ever been to. When Barbara gave me the book—" His throat contracted as Aunt Rose picked up his book, a limited edition, and hurled it against the wall. The binding snapped instantly. The thing was dead before it hit the floor—its neck broken, two halves of a book swinging drunkenly, held together by the slimmest hopes of glue and thread. As it fell to the floor, heretofore undamaged pages crumpled. He was thinking through a haze of panic: the pages can be salvaged, they can be rebound, and it doesn't really matter what's happened, not really. But he had heard the book scream.

"I have kept my patience with you," said Aunt Rose. "I've made allowances for your age and haven't forgotten the tragedy you've recently suffered. But now you're my responsibility and rank insolence I will not abide. You can forget to observe the memory of your parents if you want to, and you can keep me awake all night long with your noise and pages and doors and creeping in and out, if you want to, but you will not deliberately provoke me!"

He was thinking: *In time it can be repaired. I'll have the money as soon as I get a real job, and I'll fix the book and rent a place to keep the rest of my things in, and I'll move there. Except it's so hard to find real work. I wish I was older. Surely I can find something.*

"Paul! Have you heard what I've been saying?"

... Who is this woman? Oh yes, Aunt Rose. Yes, he had heard every word although he didn't understand a thing she had said. "I think so," he answered, tasting blood in his mouth. It occurred to him that he'd been biting his tongue for over a minute.

"You will not provoke me again," she went on. "After we had agreed to change the topic, you deliberately mentioned that dirty old book, that silly book. I read a few sentences in it, Paul. Do you know what I found? Fanciful sentences, that's what. A waste of time, a dust magnet ... You were going to tell me what happened at the party; instead you mention that book. Now, what do you have to say for yourself?"

He repeated a sentence several times in his mind and then, sure of the words, said, "Barbara Struthers gave it to me. That's why I liked the party."

She rose. She slapped him. She said, "You will not lie!"

He was far away. It took him a moment to notice that his face was hurting. He was still thinking about the blood in his mouth. "What?" he asked quietly, confused.

"I tried to stop you from taking that book along," said Aunt Rose. "You took it anyway. You had to be punished."

"But no, no," he said, starting to laugh. "I had to be punished for breaking the cup. Remember the cup?" He pointed to the pieces on the floor. "It was a paperback book I tried to take with me, much smaller than what I brought back. You've mixed them up!" He laughed louder.

"Don't you dare laugh at me!" she shrieked. "You clean up my teacup! I buy you your clothes and this is how you treat me."

Had she screamed? he marveled. *But she never raises her voice.* There were things he wanted to say. Arguments, logic, reasons, crowded his brain. Somewhere a mistake had been made. All he had to do was run it back to the beginning, find the error, bring it out. But when he opened his mouth, all that came out was laughter.

"I'll show you!" she screamed again. "You selfish monster!" This time there was no doubt. She had most definitely raised her voice.

He asked himself why she was running upstairs, heading for his bedroom, then he remembered the one important thing about that room—his collection. He stopped laughing and began to throw up on the carpet. She rushed back down with an armful of books. Then she saw what he was doing.

"Paul!" she cried out. Three times? But she doesn't raise her voice..."My carpet!" He noticed a yellow stain spreading on what before had been consistent purple. The remains of the teacup were being surrounded by the splotch. She threw down her load, ran back upstairs to get more.

He thought: I really ought to do something. Maybe I can gather the pages of *Dark Carnival* and leave with that much. I'll have to do it quickly.

THUMP! She was back and the pile of his books doubled. She tossed his monster mask on top for good measure.

"Shall I tell you what I'm going to do?" she hissed, suddenly standing over him, swaying ominously like a scarecrow about to topple. He looked up, wiped the tears from his eyes and found that he could breathe again. Standing, he faced her.

"What is it, Aunt Rose?"

"Go to the kitchen," she commanded, "and bring back the matches."

Something happened inside Paul—the rage and fire and terror were gone. There was nothing left but a quiet, hollow center. "No," he said.

"I've had enough of your defiance."

"You're mad," he answered softly.

With an incredulous expression, she turned from her nephew and hurried away from him. In a moment the sounds of a frantic search came rattling and clanging to Paul's ear. She was always misplacing those matches. Even as he remembered he had last seen them in the cabinet above the refrigerator, a triumphant cackle stung him as though she had reached out a long, bony arm holding a needle with which to pierce him.

She returned, the box of matches held high in her right hand. "Now!" she gasped.

Looking around him, Paul realized that the picture was ludicrous: it was made up of a carpet fastidiously clean but for the stain Paul had left behind, the lamps that had been dusted so often that the shades seemed to be made of tightly pulled, translucent human skin and the flowery wallpaper that smelled not of gardens but of the crushed, dead flowers you find in old *books.* He could not believe for a moment that she was going to play with fire in this museum.

Her eyes were staring, first at the pile of books, then at her nephew. He could swear she hadn't blinked in the past few minutes.

At length she spoke of her plan: "We will take the books to the porch. There is a barbecue grill there." Paul tried to remember a single time they had cooked dinner outside. The grill was as spotless as if it had just come from the department store. A Christmas gift left over from years past, waiting for one unholy fire, an innocuous device that was to be transformed into a sacrificial altar for Paul's library.

He still held *Dark Carnival.* Outside was the sidewalk, winding away into the safety of the night. Paul knew that he could run, hide, escape...and never have to come back.

"Damn you," he muttered in the direction of the wraithlike being bearing matches, dressed in a turquoise dress. She was carrying the books outside, five and six at a time. Her face had the quality of wounded pride—she wouldn't even grant him the role of victim.

Paul decided he wasn't leaving, not just yet. "Let me help you," he called out, his voice a bit shrill, as he headed for the utility room where she kept the one unused can of lighter fluid. By the time he returned, all the books and the mask were in a pile on the grill. She had a match in her hand that she was trying futilely to ignite. Paul waited as the liquid sloshed back and forth in the can.

She heard the sound and asked him, "What are you doing?"

"Helping." He stepped out onto the porch. There was no turning away from what he would learn now. A small hope wouldn't let go of his mind: it seemed to promise that she was all bluster and fear, not a monster really.

Screwing off the cap, he held the can above the books. And waited. Aunt Rose said nothing. Slowly, carefully, he placed the can on the floor. They could hear each other's breathing.

"Well?" she said.

"You do it," he answered.

She did. The fluid splashed on the floor and the thick odor was suddenly everywhere. She started striking the match, standing right over the pyre. "Christ," whispered Paul. *Shik, shik,* went the match. The fumes reached up, encircled the clawlike hand. Paul began trembling. He grabbed the can and shook it in her face. "Do you want to die?" he yelled. She didn't seem to see him. *Shik, shik, shik*....

Paul dropped the can, grabbed *Dark Carnival* and ran. He was halfway through the living room when he heard the sound, like the rush of air when a match is put over a pilot light that has gone out in a gas oven. Turning around, he saw Aunt Rose caressed by a long tongue of flame. She raised her hand, dropping the box of matches that flared and fell from her like a lonely comet. The suddenly-old woman's head was crowned in fire and her hand pointed at him in a last gesture of disapproval. The dried flesh was eaten up with a snapping and popping. The body collapsed as flame tentatively reached out for the rest of the house ... then spread in triumphantly.

With a slam, Paul was out the front door. Lights were on in nearby houses—neighbors opening their eyes to accuse. He could feel the heat of the inferno on the back of his neck. And so he walked faster. Then started running. By the time he heard the sirens, he couldn't see, smell or hear the fire anymore.

Hurrying on into the enveloping arms of night: in its darkness he did not imagine the myriad monsters of his books, the fiends his aunt had insisted populated his deepest dreams. The real monster was gone, behind him in a blaze of light. Ahead in the shadows waited the freedom of a quiet privacy, where light was used for reading instead of burning.

(Dedicated to Ray Bradbury)

I spend a lot of time in low budget Hollywood (unit publicist on a number of films, original story credit with Fred Olen Ray on *Jack-O*, even brief stints of what passes for acting from me). I'm fascinated by the whole scene. There's a lot going on in Hollyweird.

For *Peter Straub's Ghosts*, I decided to have some fun. My actress character in this, Dana Fredericks (as in Fredericks of Hollywood, of course), is based on two actresses, the incomparable Brinke Stevens, Scream Queen deluxe, and Dana Fredsti, of *Army of Darkness* fame and my co-author of "Professor Purr's Guaranteed Allergy Cure" in *Catfantastic IV*.

I enjoyed watching Brinke essay the role of Dana on stage in a production of the Atlanta Radio Theatre at DragonCon. Bill Ritch, who knows every twist and turn of my demented mind, did a great script. Today the radio drama, tomorrow the movie!

The reader may begin to detect a pattern when I report that this story received Honorable Mention in *The Year's Best Fantasy and Horror, Ninth Collection*. Ed Bryant called it a "mordantly amusing Hollywood fable" in his review for *Locus*.

A Real Babe

When you've been in the business as long as I have you become a little jaded. But Dana was too hot to take for granted. The first time I met her I figured she was just another bimbo looking for a quick and easy road to fame, with a payoff as cheap as the bad perfume my ex wears. And when she said she'd written a script and would I please take a look at it, if I had the time, I was ready to write her off despite her looks.

If it hadn't been for my third shot of Jack Daniels I wouldn't have even bothered to read the first page. The damned thing started out OK, which suggested to me that she'd received help from someone. I read a little further looking for marks of the amateur, but the thing was slickly professional and untouched by any college grad attempts at originality. Basically, she'd told a simple haunted house story with the right amounts of sex and violence. Either the whole script had been ghostwritten or she'd picked up a lot more about the business than I would have thought possible from her supporting roles in *Las Vegas Tramp Mutants* and *Demon Dolls*.

I'll never forget our first lunch together. No way could she fake knowledge she didn't have. Under normal circumstances I would have been thinking of ways of nailing her at minimum cost to myself. She was a fantastic babe with long, brown hair, high cheekbones, flashing green eyes and a devastating smile that was to die for. And the tits were as nice and big as they grow naturally—no need for implants here—with an ass that seemed to call my name whenever she took a step. The waist was small and narrow; and I was out to prove that her mind was every bit as narrow and incapable of producing a decent script before we reached dessert.

Meanwhile, it wasn't only her ass that was speaking to me. "Mr. Hastings," she said in a deep, sultry voice that made my balls tingle. I don't like the high, chipmunk voices.

"Call me Kent," I said, smiling with all the sincerity I'd managed to generate at my last audit.

She returned a smile so predatory that I wanted to lean across the table and lick her pointed, white teeth. "I bet you get a lot of jokes about being called Clark," she said.

Actually, I hadn't heard any dumb Superman jokes since high school but that might change now that I was meeting more people in the comics industry. My first rule is never to sneer at money in any form, but I'd recently had to deal with top paid comics professionals who were forcing me to improve my opinion of Hollywood hacks. But I couldn't think about any of that now if I wanted to apply ruthless objectivity to an actress/model who thought she could write.

Then she made with the mind-reading act; I mean, there's something disconcerting when she pops up with, "I know what you must be thinking, Kent. There's that old joke about the Polish actress who was so dumb she fucked the writer."

Normally I liked it when they talked dirty, but this was different. She had me on the defensive. I was ready to enjoy the globes beneath her chin but she was subjecting me to the lobes residing in her pretty skull. I founded Gore Street Productions so I'd be calling the shots—and I don't just mean directions for the guy behind the camera.

The irony, I guess, was that I'd intended to develop women writers Real Soon Now. But that didn't mean I wanted actresses carting around laptops and passing out story proposals, treatments, scripts. Things were bad enough when male writers starting wearing assistant producer hats so they'd have a chance at some money. But the real babes already had more control than was healthy, and there was no need for them to wear too many hats. Or wear too much of anything, come to think of it. Progress is OK. The casting couch is too crude. Dating is better. But the line has to be drawn somewhere.

At the time I wasn't thinking primarily about Dana. She was a new girl. My big star was Kristy Chalmers and she had no pretensions about writing, directing or producing. Unfortunately, Kristy had discovered the financial advantages to be enjoyed in control of her likeness in stills, posters and promotional videos.

As I say, at that first lunch with Dana my mind was seriously preoccupied with matters other than herself. No one could have convinced me how important this sharp tongued brunette was going to become in my life while my head was full of soft, suggestible, delectable blonde star power...who just happened to be busy ripping me off. Dana had come into my life at just the right moment.

Luck remains the one truly mysterious element that can't be honestly explained. Dana's script was about ghosts at the moment I was deciding to do a knockoff of a major studio's pending release about funny and delightful spirits played by big stars. You didn't have to be a genius to anticipate the sizable public that would soon be hungering for a nasty, low-budget quickie with a high body count. Dana's script delivered the goods. So against my better judgment I made a deal with her. I was generous. She was paid a portion of the money we discussed and there was a small role for her as well, tailored to her special athletic abilities. She was a gymnast and able to handle a foil with the best of them. And she was punctual, which is important in my book.

The haunted house picture would have been the end of our relationship except for one minor detail. I fell in love with her. Nothing like that had happened to me since my first year in La La Land. Maybe it was the way she could anticipate what I would say or do that got to me; but understanding a person is not the same as caring about him. When she'd smile at me—and if I haven't already mentioned it, she has the best smile on screen or off—I would actually feel something. I'm sure the bitch knew it. I only call her a bitch because she was starting to get to me, of course.

You've got to watch out for the gorgeous ones. Their beauty makes them a little crazy. If they're smart on top of that there's no telling what might be going on inside their heads. Which brings me from the first lunch to the last lunch I'll ever have with Dana.

I always take anyone I want to impress to a select number of restaurants where I can count on the best possible service. One thing that never hurts is when I've put the owners or managers in cameo roles in my movies. After they sign the releases and they see themselves up on the screen, it doesn't even matter if they receive the miserable little checks that would barely cover a dinner in their establishments. Hollywood still means glamour even when the economy sucks; maybe especially when the economy sucks!

Every time I had taken Dana out to lunch it had been at one of my special places. And I'd come within a few inches of nailing her at a party the night before, so I decided to really do the next lunch right. I had good news for her. Her house script had required very little rewriting. Unlike the larger studios we don't fool around with a script if it works. We can't afford it...and we don't have to create reasons to pay brothers-in-law and assistants at our budget level.

For some reason I wasn't thinking about money that day. Dana had me so excited that I wasn't being practical. Hell, I still don't know why I fell for her so hard. I'm not the kind of guy who cares if some doll is playing hard to get. There's plenty more where she comes from. You can see them waiting tables and working the streets. The lucky ones are dancing in the clubs. But only Dana had managed to get inside me somehow. Before I knew it, I was even listening to business advice from her.

I'd just had a very bad encounter with Kristy and her muscle-brained manager, and I was seething. Lunch at The Olive Tree was just the medicine I needed. Dana was waiting for me, dressed in a tight fitting blue dress, cut just above the knee. A strong breeze had blown her long brown hair so that it covered one eye with an unintentional Veronica Lake look. Because it was too windy to sit at one of the tables outside we went into the back where a curtained booth was ready and waiting.

The candlelight gave her face an imperious quality. Arched eyebrows and a full mouth always make me think of a Queen. The crucial moment had arrived as we sat over martinis she had thoughtfully ordered for us, and the red light made exotic patterns on her cheeks. I was ready to let her know how much I respected her intelligence. And then she blew it.

"I'm glad you wrote that script," I told her. "Think you could do another in the same vein? We may have a series here."

"Thanks, Kent," she said. "I'd be happy to write anything you want, but especially ghost stories. I'm like Russell Kirk in that regard."

"Who's that?" I asked.

"He writes ghost stories."

"Not a big name like Stephen King, huh?"

"He's famous for other things, Kent. But what I have in common with Kirk is that we both believe in ghosts. That makes a difference when you're doing ghost stories."

I was ready to kick myself. Every time I think I've found an intelligent woman she pulls the rug out from under me. If it's not astrology, it's nature worship; if it's not reincarnation, it's UFO's or something equally lame. So Dana was just another airhead after all.

Under other circumstances I would have written her off right then. Or I would have played along with her just to get laid. But what I never do is argue with them. Except this time was different.

I couldn't help myself.

"You're kidding," I said.

"No," she replied in a cool and calm voice.

The only manifestation I was interested in right then was the waiter so that I could order another drink, but he was nowhere to be found. So I took another swig of dialectic.

"Why do you believe in ghosts?" I asked her.

She didn't miss a beat. "Because I've seen them," she said.

"Doing what?" She shook her head slightly, so I pushed on. "You've seen ghosts doing what?"

For a moment she squinted her eyes at me like she was picking up on the sarcasm, but then she did that little knowing smile of hers and answered in all seriousness: "They do the same sort of things they did in life, especially the ones who were in a bad rut or feel they left things undone."

I didn't mean to do it but I laughed. "How can you tell the live ones from the dead ones, then?"

"You know when you're seeing a ghost," she told me. Her tone of voice had an edge to it. Time to increase the old sincerity quotient.

"I'm serious, Dana. I'm not trying to make fun of you." Whenever I tried to show that I was a caring sort of guy it was a good excuse to reach out and touch someone. Especially when they were as cute as this one. I held her hand and was I surprised. She has cold hands most of the time, and I had been anticipating the same problem with her feet. Nothing better than warming them up when they really need it. But Dana's hand was burning as if she might be running a high fever.

"Are you all right?" I asked. "You're so hot."

"I'm all right, Kent. But I don't think you really want to hear why I believe in ghosts."

"I do, babe, I do! I was going to ask how you can tell when you see one. Are they transparent?"

"No, not that I've noticed."

"Are they snow white all over?"

"You've been watching too many old movies."

"My inspiration. But how do you know when you're seeing a ghost?"

She traced her finger around the rim of her glass and seemed a little distant. Then she was ready to share: "There's a feeling at first, a kind of tingle on the back of your neck. And there's other things, like when you see someone no one else can. I've been this way since childhood. My parents thought I was talking to myself but I had friends from the Other Side."

"I've seen those movies, too," I volunteered. "I collect them."

"You'll be able to watch anything whenever you want now," she said out of the blue. "There are certain advantages to your new situation. And I think you'll adapt pretty well. You were never one of the worst ones, you know. You didn't care about the trendy night clubs and what to wear and who's dating whom. You were more individual than that, and having a real self makes it easier when you cross over."

"Huh?"

"I'm not very good at breaking bad news," she commented weirdly, finishing off the last of her drink. Whatever she was driving at, I only cared that she was setting a good example with the martinis. I finished my drink and signaled for the waiter.

"He won't be able to see you," she said.

Now I was becoming irritated. "Look, babe, I put him in *Scream Bunnies on Mystery Island* and used him on the day of the big topless scene. He sure as hell is going to take my order."

If I'd been thinking clearly I would have noticed the unusual touch of her reaching over and taking my arm. Her fingers burned as if they were small bands of hot metal. I yanked my arm away just as she stared into my soul with those big, bright eyes of hers and intoned, "You're dead, Kent."

The old brain still wasn't firing on all cylinders. "Nobody says I'm dead in this town! I've got too much on everyone, damn it. You'll...." And then I noticed a peculiar phenomenon only a few inches from my hand. The drink I had just drunk was once again a full drink. The waiter hadn't come over. Dana must have noticed my staring down at the table.

"There are compensations," she said.

"Oh, shit," was all that came to mind.

"I can be your living partner, Kent. Of course I don't know how your will is set up, but with all your inside knowledge you can still control...."

"Oh, shit."

"Is that all you can say?"

"This can't be happening," I said, feeling tears beginning to trickle down my face. "I can feel you, you can feel me."

"As time goes on, the living will become hotter and hotter for you to touch. I don't know why that is but I learned it from the first ghost I ever met."

I felt a sudden uncontrollable urge to show off a wider vocabulary. "This is all bullshit! I'll prove it." Jumping up from the table I ran at the nearest patron, a portly man who offered acres and acres of touchable flesh. When I was only an inch away I felt a terrible burning sensation. And then I was sitting on the floor, as if I'd been pushed down. Dana was helping me up and taking me back to the booth.

"Anyone observing me do this will figure I'm crazy," she said, "but I'd rather be living in a century when they think you're on drugs than in league with the devil." So she was showing off that college education again! If I'd been paying any attention I would have seen the warning signs but, hey, I was preoccupied.

Back in the booth, I calmed down enough to ask more questions. She had an answer for everything. "You don't know how you died because the shock was too great," she said, as she started to bite shrimp in half with her fine, white teeth.

"Kristy Chalmers' manager went crazy when you threatened to use the evidence of his being a child molester. He broke your neck."

"I have a slight sore throat," I admitted, "but as you say, there's no memory other than the meeting going badly. How did you hear about it?"

"The news, honey. And there's going to be a TV special on one of the tabloid magazine shows."

"To hell with that. We've got to make the movie first!"

She smiled the sweetest little girl smile yet and laid it on me. "I'm way ahead of you," she almost sang. "I've already started the script."

And that's pretty much how I've come to the sorry state I'm in today. My partner owns the company and he's too dumb to haunt; but he's not too dumb to blackmail. God, I love Hollywood. But it's a pain being dependent on the only person who knows I'm alive...well, who knows I'm dead but active. Dana and I don't do lunch any longer, but then there's no need.

She's a good sport about all this. She even let me make love to her before she became too hot for me to get close enough. I would have preferred scoring with her while I was still alive, but where beautiful women are concerned I try to be obliging. And I must admit that I've had my consciousness raised about babes. They shouldn't be taken for granted except when you can get away with it.

But the hell of the situation is that Dana has betrayed me in one area where I can't touch her, literally or figuratively. I can't help but think of her as the ultimate bitch for having done this to my company, Gore Street Productions. There's simply no excuse for what she's done, no reason, no justification.

She's improved the product.

This is really the companion piece to "A Real Babe." Writers know the frustration of placing a story and sometimes even being paid, only to see a new market collapse before their vision can reach the public. So it is with "Her Morbid Desires." In contrast to both "The Lon Chaney Factory" and "A Real Babe," where I do the usual cliché of the rapacious producer, this story is a bit more realistic. The character causing all the trouble this time around is the distributor!

Her Morbid Desires

When Frederica was ten years old she decided she wanted to be a movie star. One decade later she was. Sort of. Her parents were not as impressed as they might have been because their daughter was appearing in low budget horror films with titles like *The Cuisinart Killer from Chem Lab II* and *Blood Soda*. Frederica loved every minute of it.

She had a role model, who looked like a model and played roles that were both erotic and macabre: Brinke Stevens. Frederica's favorite movie was *Haunting Fear*, a Fred Olen Ray cult classic from 1990 featuring one of Brinke's most interesting performances. Freddie (as her friends called her) dashed off a letter to the Brinke Stevens fan club, with photo enclosed, and the actress wrote back.

Before long Freddie had sent her head shot to Brinke, commenting that friends remarked a certain resemblance. They were both petite brunettes projecting an intelligence that could not be confused with the bimbo school. Brinke agreed that Freddie could pass for a younger sister and before long they were corresponding well beyond the rigorous formalities of fan stuff. Freddie was thrilled when Brinke told her how she had started out as a fan as well, standing in line for hours to receive an autograph from someone she admired. Perhaps it was because Brinke had so many interests in her life (including a master's degree in marine biology) that her naive joy in show business made Freddie feel better about herself.

"You should be the mad scientist in your pictures," Freddie had told Brinke the first time they met at The Hollywood Diner on Sunset Boulevard.

"They like us as victims," Brinke answered, an evil glint in her eye as she daintily placed the straw of her soda between her rose petal lips. "And even when I play a take-charge character they still want me to scream."

Freddie nodded her head, and sipped her coffee. "You're the best Scream Queen, Brinke, and I mean that."

Their conversation was temporarily interrupted by a crazy street person coming up to the window and clawing at them, screaming quotations from articles in *Cult Movies* before he lost interest and wandered off. The man had money in his bony hand, but wouldn't spend it anywhere that collected sales tax. A blonde waitress (who had appeared in *Corpse Squad in Hawaii*) commented, "It was bad enough around here before the intellectuals started hanging around this corner." She refilled Freddie's cup.

A trucker at the next table threw in his 75 cents worth of comment with, "At least the hookers are real girls on Sunset instead of the drag creeps down on Hollywood Boulevard." The waitress took him some coffee and argued that some girls were still working Hollywood Boulevard. The trucker had appeared in *Blazing Sabers* and *Queen for a Slay*.

"God, Brinke, I don't know if I'm going to make it out here," said Freddie morosely.

"Sure you will. You've got a part in B.J.'s new movie and you got it because you did the best audition. Of course, people will imagine the worse."

"What do you mean?"

Brinke eyed her new protege and reached out to pat her hand. "Don't you know why he's called B.J.?" Freddie shook her head, and Brinke explained: "Actresses say he gives a whole new meaning to head shot. B.J. stands for Blow Job, honey. But actresses can stand up to guys like him. You have to respect yourself."

"That's why I admire you, Brinke. You were the first to take control of your own image and market yourself, and deal directly with your fans."

Brinke smiled. "You have to know when to be direct, Freddie."

As the two women left the relative cool of the diner and reentered the boiling heat of Los Angeles in late summer, Freddie was on her way to a career and didn't really know it. Brinke knew it.

"Blow Job" Polaski didn't hit on Freddie during the shooting of *Blood Soda* but that may have been due in part to Freddie falling in love with the Assistant Director. (Then again, maybe not.) Freddie had to put up with the old jokes about the Polish actress who was so dumb she slept with the writer—the point being that any good AD* is hell on all the performers and not to be swayed by personal considerations. She fell in love with Thomas anyway.

Just as Brinke Stevens had interests much broader than Holly-

---

* Assistant Director

wood, so did Thomas Brine—primarily historical ones which stood him well in acquiring research jobs, making sure the weapons and costumes were accurate and so forth. "The only people who can make good movies are people who are interested in real life," Tom said right before they made love (or maybe it was after).

She agreed, although she couldn't forget what Steve Bloodstone had told her at the wrap party for B.J.'s opus: "People who make good movies have lots of money, or access to lots of money, or the ability to convince others that they will have lots of money." Odd that she would think of Bloodstone while making love to Tom, who never seemed able to get work on a Bloodstone picture. It was Bloodstone who would give Freddie a good role in the *Cuisinart* picture. She met him as an actor in *Blood Soda*. B.J. liked using friends instead of extras. B.J. had a lot of friends. They were all male.

There was a lot less pressure for Freddie on the Bloodstone movie than she'd felt on the Polaski project. Steve was completely professional and a gentleman. An ex-cop and ex-soldier, Bloodstone had had more than his fair share of real life before dabbling in the movies. His company, Fallen Empire Films, usually did straight adventure movies with a touch of the erotic thrown in. He cast Freddie for the lead role in his first horror film.

Freddie's first problem turned out to be Thomas. He wasn't happy that he hadn't landed the job of AD on the movie. He never said that she should tie her acting prospects to his chances for work, but she felt subtle pressures in that direction. She kept this to herself and hoped her newly minted husband would forget about it.

By the time of her second Bloodstone movie, *Captain Steel vs. the Zombie Investors*, she had a lot more trouble. B.J. and Bloodstone were co-producers, and again Tom didn't get the AD job. In addition, Tom pointed out to Freddie the many startling similarities to his unsold script, *Blood Gophers vs. the Bikini Battalion*. Freddie was still picking her way past these potential landmines when real life, or in this case *real death*, stuck out a bony ankle and tripped her.

Her co-star, Rebecca Dalia, was found horribly murdered. Freddie had been to an autopsy once and prided herself on not throwing up. This time was different. The buxom redhead had been thoroughly sliced and diced. The pale white head was wedged between her two feet, neatly dissected at the ankles, "standing" in a pool of dried blood. As Freddie retched onto the auburn tresses she couldn't help but note the vaguely comic aspect—Rebecca looked like a cartoon character squashed down to where the head met the feet. As she stumbled away she bumped into the Cold Beverages machine. The dead woman's breasts were decorating the milk section.

"I hate it when they have a sense of humor," said Sheriff McGee, who had worked in Hollywood for years and appeared in *Teenage Tormentors* and *Gore Store*. He was nice to Freddie; he didn't criticize her for messing up the evidence.

Meanwhile, back home, Thomas decided to play detective. "You're still trying to get on the movie," Freddie joked, but he wasn't laughing. In the amateur detective category, he had competition. Bloodstone had been a sheriff, after all. And then there were the other Steves! Steve Charles was Bloodstone's assistant and a writer on the project. He had his own theories. And then there was Tim Stephens, known to his friends as "Steve," who disagreed with the Charles theory. Tim had been brought in to punch up the Charles script—he had a reputation as the fastest writer in the business—and he was just as quick to edit a theory as a script. Anyway, Tom disagreed with Steve theories One, Two and Three. (Bloodstone had his own theory, after all.)

"Let the police handle it," Freddie suggested. "Sheriff McGee seems to know what he's doing."

McGee's theory wasn't really any better than anyone else's, but at least he was paid to have it which, in the industry, was the genuine mark of credibility. Freddie noticed a bond of respect between the two men from the start, both heavy-set men with thin mustaches, having a quality of the bear about them. But Freddie saw how dismissive they were of the writers; and she assumed the same reaction would greet Thomas if he offered to help solve the mystery.

Freddie wanted nothing more than to forget the horrible crime when she'd go home but Thomas was already engaged on writing a script to work out his theory of Who, What and When. Freddie felt like letting out a scream so loud that it couldn't help but produce her own fan club.

Still dressed in a dominatrix outfit (from the picture), she went for a walk to clear her head. She was so angry that she radiated a solid wall of *Don't Fuck With Me If You Know What's Good For You.* This may have been the best acting of her life. Not until a hooker spoke to her as a fellow professional, and cheerfully pointed out that Freddie was edging into her territory did the actress step out of character.

"Damn it," was all she could think to say. "Oh, God," she added as she took a good look at herself. She explained the situation and the hooker told her not to worry about it. The hooker couldn't resist informing the younger woman of the role she had essayed in *Beverly Hills Hoboes Meet a Filipino Gorilla.*

Freddie dreaded going to work the next day. It was with a sigh of relief that she greeted the news that Bloodstone didn't think anyone should be engaging in idle speculation until the case was solved. Steve Charles echoed the same opinion and Freddie thought she might make it all the way through the day without being mauled by a Theory; but she didn't reckon on the third "Steve," the fastest writer in town, after all, who cornered her at lunch.

"I don't want to talk about it," she told him firmly, when she realized where he was headed.

Unfortunately, Steve was very literal: "You don't have to. I'll do the talking." With mounting trepidation she realized that Steve's theory in many ways paralleled her husband's. They both suspected poor old "Blow Job" Polaski. The idea seemed to be that Becky had turned him down and so he'd gone berserk. The trouble with this theory was that Freddie had finally been approached by the guy and found his feeble double-entendres pretty harmless. The fact of her marriage hadn't fazed him; but her lack of interest in his favorite prop hadn't been much of a problem either. His whole attitude was as casual as if she'd turned down an offer to get a bite to eat.

"You don't have any grudge against B.J., do you?" she asked, thinking of how Tom madly typing away could not forgive a man who said he'd never give him another AD job. (She still didn't know why.)

"No, I sell everything sooner or later," said this most prolific of all Steves; and she had to agree this was true as she watched him nervously tap his long fingers attached to the long arm of a six foot, seven inch pipe-stem body.

"Now, if you don't mind, Steve, I don't want *you* to talk about it either," she said. And she left before he could ignore her words.

When Brinke Stevens called, just back from a tour of science fiction conventions in the Northeast where they know the true meaning of horror, Freddie was expecting commiseration, but not these words: "Freddie, we have to get together. I know who the murderer is."

That night Freddie thought long and hard about giving up show biz. She watched Tom typing away, the little *clickclacktiktokclik* sounds of the not-exactly-silent computer keyboard competing with the crickets outside. Why pretend to be someone when you're not sure who you are in the first place? But maybe that was the answer. And maybe that was why she and Tom were faithful to each other, providing one island of security in an unstable world. And if he needed to pretend he was dealing with reality to drive himself to produce fiction, then that was a small price to pay.

Brinke provided the reality, more reality than Freddie wanted to accept. Brinke managed an invitation for Freddie to attend a party at Gerry Shah's palatial estate. (Tom was too busy with his script to cause any problems.) Shah was a distributor who had handled most of Bloodstone's and B.J.'s—and nearly half of low budget Hollywood's—product for the last five years. Shah looked like an evil version of Larry King.

Brinke took Freddie aside, and outside the house, which wasn't easy with a middle-aged film columnist for *Cult Movies* trying desperately to lay both of them and getting nowhere. He was drunk enough they managed to avoid him, and Brinke pointed out through the window in the side yard a perfect picture of Shah holding court over by the bar.

"Sometimes the bad guy is not anyone you know," said Brinke.

"You mean he did it?" asked Freddie.

Brinke nodded. "And he's not done yet. Every actress on the *Zombie Investors* picture is in danger."

"Including me?"" asked Freddie.

"Especially you," answered Brinke. "I've known this guy is scum for years but I never dreamed he'd murder people just to create a morbid atmosphere around a movie and improve its commercial appeal."

"Is he doing the killings himself?"

"I doubt it. He probably hires someone to wipe him when he goes to the bathroom." The contempt in Stevens's voice was as thick as the summer heat.

"I wonder if I should tell Tom," said Freddie.

"Why put the pressure on him? When a man goes bad it's better if women deal with it. You see, Freddie, I studied more areas of science than only marine biology." In the next few minutes, Brinke told the little known story of how when she was blocked from getting her Ph.D. as an oceanographer (because she took the side of the dolphins in a dispute with the Navy and the tuna industry) she dabbled in medicine and learned a lot about surgery before pursuing the siren call of acting. Freddie's eyes grew wide as it dawned on her what this dark and mysterious woman was capable of doing.

The proof of Shah's perfidy was in a large black bag that Brinke retrieved from the back of her car. She opened it wide for her young friend and took out incriminating tape recordings that she played right then on a player with headphones! His foray into sadistic murder made his previous practice of skimming thousands of dollars off every movie he handled appear a harmless cost of doing business.

"Becky is the first and last girl he's going to snuff," said Brinke, and Freddie nodded. For the first and probably last time in her life Freddie had a warm, friendly feeling for producer-directors, even B.J.! The two slender female figures held hands and made their plans. Then Brinke picked up the bag, shifting it from one arm to the other, and Freddie realized that it must be very heavy.

Gerry Shah's ego was typical in every respect. So when two attractive actresses approached him with the suggestion of a *menage a trois* he didn't think there was anything amiss. He was too drunk to notice that one of them was Freddie and he didn't connect the other one, the well known actress, with any of his current projects. He figured it would be nice not to be paying for it tonight; he suffered from a serious lack of imagination. He'd never encountered the wise old observation that when a beautiful woman is being obliging and willing and offering herself to you, she either wants to make love to you...or is out to kill you.

They never found his body. Among many other things, the black bag included addresses and names of all the identities Shah used for bank accounts and mail drops all over the world. Each address received a package weighing several pounds, wrapped in brown butcher's paper. When these objects began to give off an unpleasant odor, and the packages were opened, it could be truly said that Mr. Shah had been well distributed.

(My thanks to Brinke Stevens for letting me star her in a short story.)

This is one of my favorite titles but I must give credit where it's due. I'd finished this story about H. G. Wells and couldn't think of a good title to save my life. Forry Ackerman came to the rescue with this title. Not only that but he recommended it to E. J. Gold (son of H. L. Gold) for the new *Galaxy* magazine, where it duly appeared.

I figured that the only time I'd be listed as a Nebula contender would be when I was a finalist for the novella version of "Moon of Ice." But "Wells of Wisdom" did well enough to make the preliminary ballot and be noted in *Locus*. That wasn't the big thrill, however.

The thrill was when Gold made "Wells of Wisdom" part of the Galaxy Audio Project and Catherine Oxenberg did the dramatic reading. Which gave me an excuse to talk to one of the sexiest actresses in the world! I love science fiction.

Wells of Wisdom

THE WORLD BRAIN WANTS YOU!

They were letters a mile high.

THE WORLD BRAIN NEEDS YOU.

He contemplated the external universe of a single message, repeating itself with minor alteration. And he contemplated himself: Who am I? He didn't know. What am I? He remembered that he was a man. No, that wasn't quite right. He had *been* a man. Yes, that had the ring of truth about it. He was beginning to remember.

THE WORLD BRAIN REQUESTS YOUR ATTENDANCE.

He remembered a world of physical bodies, of substance, of weight and mass. He'd once had a body, been part of that world. And he remembered other things: colors, tastes, motion, pleasures, pains, things going into and out of the body that had been his. He was thinking again, and with that came the power to make distinctions. It was his *mind* that he prized above all else. He had made his whole life revolve around the thoughts that sprang from his mind.

THE WORLD BRAIN FACES A PROBLEM ONLY YOU CAN SOLVE.

This world of bodies that he was beginning to recall, there was something else about it. There were problems that came from dealing with other bodies, or rather the minds housed in the bodies. Well, some of them had had minds. Then again, not every moving body that appeared to have a mind in charge had turned out to be so occupied.

He used to have a fantasy about rudimentary bodies consisting mostly of a gigantic braincase and hands as the only limbs. There had been a lot of jokes about this particular image. He had made many of the jokes himself.

Now he remembered jokes. He remembered what it was like to have memories of things that were good and things that were bad. He remembered what it felt like to have a body. And just as suddenly, he had one.

The man opened his eyes. He was naked, lying upon a thin pad of comfortable material floating three feet above a blue floor. There were people standing around him wearing white robes. They were smiling at him, so he smiled back.

"We are the first council of The World Brain," said the youngest man there.

"Where am I?" asked the man, and as an afterthought added: "You wouldn't happen to know who I am, while you're at it?"

The young man bowed from the waist and said: "This is the year 4,000 A.D., on the planet Utopia. And you, sir, are Herbert George Wells, of England—born September 21, 1866 in Bromley, Kent; died August 13, 1946 in London."

His mind rebelled. There was so much to rebel against. Its voice drowned out the voices of the quiet, studious men and women who surrounded him. The mind knew that he had last been in the world at the age of eighty. He had not been well. But what was this mad talk about dying? It was true that he had been very ill. But if he was here, then quite obviously he had recovered. He had thought about dying, of course, and he had thought to himself, with the last clear thought preceding oblivion, that if this was the end it had better be quick because there wasn't enough time for his life to flash in front of him.

Fifty years of celebrity could not be compressed so easily. And before that, thirty years of struggle. He who had imagined so many different worlds had lived in a variety of them himself. Born without privileges in the Victorian age, but a success by its close; an ever rising star in the Edwardian age; a first hand observer of the Great War, a literary giant promoting the cause of reason in the jazz and gin soaked twenties; the world brain, as he was called, and prophet of bright tomorrows in the grey twilight of Depression; and then the final horror of the Second World War, the dashing of so many hopes side by side with the fulfillment of so many prophecies. He had become the philosopher who was no longer taken seriously precisely at the moment of his greatest victory.

His varied careers would have satisfied a dozen gifted men. He had changed his time and put his stamp on the thinking of generations to come. Yet in his own hypercritical mind, he died a failure, his last argument reaching out to touch his last book, a thin volume with a sad title: *Mind at the End of its Tether*. All his life had been a war between an expansive optimist who placed no limit on creative will and a pessimist whose imagination once unleashed painted shadows darker than the pits of deepest hell.

He had been an atheist and knew that death was the end.

Yet here he was! He remembered the words of another author, a countryman of his, and spoke in a high voice: "What place is this?"

"As we have told you, most welcome visitor, this is Utopia. It used to be called the Earth. We renamed it many generations ago in your honor."

"It is, in large part, your Utopia," said the oldest man there, if such could be judged from the whiteness of his hair, but his ruddy complexion and smooth skin showed no other signs of time's gentle but lethal caresses. "What you called the Open Conspiracy has prevailed. The World Brain you advocated was to be an elite of the best specialists in every field making common cause for the common good. We are but a cell of that brain; and we formally welcome you to your heritage."

"If I died two thousand years ago," Wells began slowly, "then how is it that I am here?"

Their smiles had a warmth he had never experienced —it was the first suggestion that he was not the butt of some incredible jest. He realized that they wanted him to guess. "Time travel?" asked the author of *The Time Machine.* They shook their heads and smiled more broadly. It was some kind of party game. "Suspended animation of some kind?" asked the author of *When the Sleeper Wakes.* This time they looked at each other as if sharing some private joke. On first glance, their garments did seem to resemble his descriptions from an old novel but as his eyes began to focus, he saw that what he had mistaken for cloth seemed to be cocoons of shimmering light beyond which he could see their naked bodies. Again they shook their heads. "Is it..." began the author of *The Dream* and *The Food of the Gods* and *The Shape of Things to Come,* but then he stopped. He shut his mouth. The smile forming on his lips was surely the match for any of theirs.

"This is a joke," he said with finality. "You mean to tell me that I really died? Well, I'm shrewd enough not to complain. You've made me feel a lot better but who's behind it, that's what I want to know. Is it Orwell? Is it Chesterton? Perhaps Shaw? Perhaps my son, Anthony? Or maybe..." He'd lived such a long, full life that now the different periods of his life began to run together. "Churchill?" The last name to come to mind formed itself into a face on the nearest man there. "Chaplin?" The familiar face took up residence on a man across the room. As Wells stared, the face grew larger as if he were peering through field glasses. His voice left him and he felt a slight tremor in his back. Without saying another word he saw other faces change around him, taking on the features of whatever person chanced to cross his memory. He felt a grave disquiet and other faces began to appear. When one man took on the stupid peasant features of Stalin and another the calculating malignity of Hitler, he shut his eyes.

Whatever was going on, he knew where to place his trust: in his mind and its ability to adapt itself to whatever conditions life, or even a semblance of life, placed before him. If his memory was the cause of what he saw, then he could at least control that much of his new environment. He searched the past and settled on a face especially appealing to him. When he opened his eyes, she was there. The woman standing nearest his head looked the way Rebecca West had when he first met her.

"You know you are not in your time," she said.

"I do."

"Would you like to see yourself?"

He nodded and she passed her hand across his body. Suddenly, reflected above him was the way he had appeared when he was in his thirties before he started running to fat. He liked what he saw although he missed his mustache. They had misplaced his mustache.

"If you will not tell me how I came to be here, perhaps you'd be kind enough to let me in on why I'm your guest."

The laughter of these people, male and female alike, was musical. He'd never heard people laugh in key together. He felt like laughing himself but didn't want to provide a dissonant note. Without waiting to be invited, he sat up and found his body responsive and strong. He dangled his legs over the side and his feet touched the floor. The floor was warm and soft. This new Rebecca West held out her hands and helped him to stand. The others applauded. *So as old a habit of humanity as that has survived,* he thought with keen pleasure.

He noted that the faces of everyone else had returned to their original aspect. He hoped this was not a common party-game of the age. But it took no special concentration on his part for the woman to continue looking as he imagined her. It only required desire.

"In the course of your life that spanned the nineteenth and twentieth centuries," began the white-haired man without preamble, "you left a record behind in the kitrospheres. These energies never dissipate but contribute to the genoplace, the sum total of which...."

"No, no," said the calm, cool voice of his new Rebecca West, "you must use language a little closer to the heart. His life left an electromagnetic record that is part of the race memory." She turned back to Wells. "Only now, with recent developments in applied love, were we able to retrieve you from the place you occupy without causing damage to a world that, after all, would not exist without you."

"You have tried this with others?" he had the presence of mind to ask.

"Without success," said a short man. "Insufficient energy."

"But we believed the time had finally come to retrieve you," said still another.

"We knew when we could draw on the entire energy of a crosstime/space rift," said West. "This is roughly the energy of a hundred exploding suns...."

"Sustained over the period of your original lifetime," concluded the white-haired man.

Wells's mouth was open. He doubted that he would ever close it again. That was, until his new girlfriend (who was his old girlfriend) kissed him. "You were worth every bit of surplus it took to bring you back," she said. "This society would not exist without your genius."

The man from the past had devoted his life to dreaming up futures. An unsatisfactory childhood in Atlas house had made him into a fountainhead of ideas, and rarely did he let one escape his net without exploring it at least twice: once for the positive implications and once for the worst possible scenario. He had been accused of believing that progress was automatic and inexorable. He had received this criticism from men who had read enough of his work to know that he believed nothing in the universe was certain.

He had never guaranteed Utopia for anyone. But he dreamed of it and fought for it. If he had been told that he could return to life and see a future world, he would have been more likely to anticipate some kind of nightmare waiting for him, some terrible new injustice carefully nurtured for generations and culminating in hateful sophistries. But the dream of a better world had never entirely deserted him. At the great apex of his life, he was taken as a prophet of science and practical hope.

Faced by the prospect of his fondest dreams made real, he hesitated, for one last moment, to ask the simple million questions he felt entirely necessary to give him some fraction of a chance to understand what had transpired in two millennia. With a touch of pride that would have mortified his poor old mother to the core of her Ulster Protestant soul, he realized that the span of time separating him from his origins and today was the same as that of Christ and his own time. And if what he was hearing was even remotely true, he had had an impact as great on the future as the Son of God could claim.

If it was hallucination, he wasn't sure that he minded in the least. He asked his first question: "Please tell me, how far does the domain of humanity extend in the late 39th century?"

"We have colonized most of the galaxy," said a young boy, the first child he had seen.

Again, his young lady told him what he really wanted to hear: "But we hope very soon to launch an exploratory craft into what we call OUTER SPACE."

"All the universe or nothing," he heard himself say, and there was a smattering of applause. So they approved of an author who quoted his own work, chapter and verse. If not Utopia, this place had to be damned close.

Thinking of the words they were using had raised another question in his mind: "What of this language we speak? Is it really English or has there been an alteration in my mental processes?" West placed a slim finger to his lips.

"Wait," she said, "you must eat and refresh yourself." Her solicitude was appreciated for its own sake but at the first mention of food, he realized that he was starving. It had been a long time between snacks. "How do you wish to attire yourself? There are hundreds of popular fashions..."

"In that case, garb closest to my own time would be acceptable."

"We have anything you need," she said. Within a few moments he was dressed in a simple shirt and slacks boasting such ancient accessories as buttons and belt. "The clothes of your time intrigue me," she said, raising an eyebrow. "Are you sure you wouldn't be more comfortable in the nude?"

"Perhaps in time," he answered diplomatically.

Taking a first step outside the room of his new birth, he saw such a peculiar conglomeration of gigantic trees, fountains, glistening pictures of strange creatures with stranger devices, solid masses of multicolored sheets drifting up high where the clouds should be, and moving surfaces at ground level on which people alternately walked and ran, that he found it nigh impossible to register, mentally, exactly what it was he was seeing. He let himself be led by the arm through the sensuous confusion. A few people called out to him in a language he did not recognize and waved to him. He was pleased that there were no mobs. Somehow he sensed that the world was done with such things.

He had always styled himself as a practical socialist. He had said that intelligent planning of the economy did not mean an exacerbation of class warfare but quite the contrary: a lessening of tensions between the classes. He had not considered fundamental changes in human nature as necessary for the victory of practical socialism. He had been pleased that the Fabians, for all their lack of imagination in many things, had struck out on the right course of reform as opposed to revolution. None of them had really considered a classless society very probable.

But when he was not having nightmares of class divisions projected into surreal exaggerations of human folly, he let himself ponder what a world without classes might be like. Could such be this world? He saw West removing a card from her sleeve, and speaking to it about having food ready for them when they arrived. The card spoke to her in a buzzing voice and recited numbers. If this were a financial transaction of some kind, it did not give him pause. He had never expected the abolition of money but considered it a practical benefit to a scientifically managed socialism. Nor was he in the least put off or bothered by the evidence that personal property remained very much an active institution. He had written many times that a wise socialism would insure private belongings in a manner that the capitalist order could never approach.

But it was one thing to think these thoughts a few centuries after his own time; it was quite another to try and judge a world two thousand years different from his own. What made the situation so bizarre was the claim that this world was built upon his ideas. That put a different light on everything. It was practically an invitation for him to pass judgments, big or small. How then to be simultaneously the teacher and the student, to be awed and yet to presume a position of authority?

He decided to make himself live up to their expectations whatever was required of him. As for the conflict he felt within, when had it ever been different for him? He had accepted the duality of his nature long before.

As if a little boy trying to bend the rules in his favor, Wells, in the most ingratiating tone of voice he could muster, asked if he couldn't have just one more question answered before they ate. Again he was treated to the tinkling laughter.

"What do you want to know?" asked a head in a jar that came floating past.

For a moment he couldn't remember, but then, quickly recovering from this latest surprise, he boldly asked: "What part of the world is this?"

"You'll be pleased to know that we are in London," she answered. "Since this was the optimum place for retrieval."

"Amazing!" he said. He was still repeating the word a short time later, as if a mantra, after consuming his first meal in Utopia. The robot chef simulated its "personal" appreciation so convincingly that Wells found himself wondering if this latest marvel did not exceed the rest. "Your dinner was prepared with the special requirements of your palate in mind," said the robot and he could swear it had just the slightest hint of a French accent.

"Tastes have changed in two thousand years."

"In the early days of the World Republic, only synthetic food was eaten so as to conserve resources," said the white-haired man. "Legend has it that the stuff tasted terrible."

"I was eating real meat and vegetables just now?" asked Wells.

"Yes, but no animal was slain nor plant harvested."

"I believe I understand." The author of The *Island of Dr. Moreau* had expected that the biological sciences would keep pace, if not surpass, the physical sciences. Much had been made of his predicting atomic weaponry in *The World Set Free* in 1913 but it was not too far off the mark to say that his earlier novel of 1896 was a prediction of genetic engineering in its multitude of post-Darwinian horrors. He had lived to see the atomic bomb...and it had depressed him profoundly. Since his return to life, he had been thrilled to hear of the conquest of space. As for the advances in biology that his contemporary Aldous Huxley had decried, he was willing to give the benefit of the doubt to this brave new world. The food tasted great!

"The time has come to ask you an important question," said Rebecca West over dessert, something very cold and very sweet.

"I'm grateful to provide answers," said the historian, the novelist, the man out of time.

"Do you remember anything before you...returned?"

"Yes. Something about a request or invitation from The World Brain."

"Are you interested in helping us?"

Wells laughed. It was a new sound for the people of this world. It was raucous and robust; it was simultaneously defiant and full of glee. It was, for the Utopians, rather an insane display from a difficult and uncertain past. When Wells had caught his breath, and could speak again, he said in a somewhat timid tone of voice: "You have returned me to life. You have restored my youth. You have shown me a planet beyond my dreams and claim that it is my vision made real. May I help you? I am yours to command."

"How do you wish to be instructed?" asked Rebecca West. His confusion must have shown on his face, or been subtly located in the winding passages of his agitated mind. "I mean, Herbert, what method of education do you prefer?"

"I do not know the choices."

"Slow or fast? You see, fast means we can impress knowledge directly into your unconscious, and then in a few days of careful training, show you how to extract what you need. Slow means we take you on a world tour and, well, there's something else."

"Yes?" He was becoming impatient.

"We lecture you."

Wells noticed that she blushed when she said that. This time he only chuckled. "I assume that you beautiful people are something like historians, and that you are more familiar with the details of my life and work than the average citizen." There was a nodding of heads, but was this physical motion another gratifying survival of the past or were they doing these things just to make him feel at home? He continued: "If you've read my work, especially the later books, you know that I like nothing better than a rousing lecture."

"We have few conflicts in Utopia," said the short man, "but the ones that remain are largely aesthetic. One party, you might call it, takes its stand on the early Wells and holds the essay in low esteem. We belong to the party that prizes all your work, of course, but believes your writing got better as you went along. There are splinter groups, some only interested in your nonfiction, some even dedicated solely to your journalism. We feel that we have the best argument if only because of the success of Utopia."

"Then I stand with your party," said Wells. "You're the ones who brought me back. You had the imagination and the vision that I advocated in my tracts. As for these stupid distinctions, I believed in the novel of *ideas* from the very beginning. The later books were more complicated conceptually and that meant more in the way of...let's call it lecturing. What the hell is the matter with a good lecture?"

They cheered him. They shouted with joy. He no longer cared if they were being anachronistic for his benefit. The grand tour began and they were all giddy with excitement.

They took him to the roof of the restaurant and there was an aircraft waiting for them, a large ball of a vehicle made from a transparent material in which Wells could have an unobstructed view in all directions. There were two chairs suspended at the center of the globe without any visible means of support. Rebecca West joined him in these chairs and spoke to the globe in a language he did not recognize. As they rose into the bright blue sky without any apparent means of propulsion, he thought of the sphere powered by Cavorite in his *First Men in the Moon;* one of the occasions when he had sought to be as fantastic as possible. Was there nothing he had imagined in his scientific romances that was impossible to this world? He dreaded to ask about time travel, one of his favorite literary conceits precisely because he was sure that it could never be. He had chosen to learn about Utopia one step at a time, the slow way, so as to avoid sensory overload.

But first, there was a world to see. And he could not imagine a more pleasant guide. Her smile lifted his spirits as high as the thrust of the vehicle lifted them into orbit. He was torn between looking down to see the civilization of his dreams or continuing to gaze at the face of his lost love, made more beautiful in the starlight that was unobstructed and undiluted. For a moment, he remembered his wives. Why hadn't he married Rebecca, he wondered, especially after she gave him his son? She had been what he was really talking about in all the outpourings on free love and intellectual equals. How strange to have her familiar visage reassuring him in a society where he must be, at best, a precocious infant. How embarrassing for any prophet to return to see his vindication, and feel complete inadequacy at the same time.

"Help me," he heard himself saying to her, and it was Wells the optimist warning against Wells the pessimist. Her head tilted just in time to receive the moonlight as the lunar orb peered at them from beyond the lip of earth's horizon. He could not stop thinking of what lay below as "the earth", any more than he could stop staring at the good strong face and intelligent mouth he remembered so well from the pleasant days at Easton Glebe.

That mouth formed a promise: "Watch." And the glorious sphere spun back downwards toward terra firma —toward a planet in harmony. He saw great white structures rising out of perfectly maintained forests and trees dotting colossal constructions and a sky untouched by the debris of an untutored industrial period. He saw cities floating in the air and bobbing on the sea, and began to wonder if everyone lived in cities, as he had once seen as inevitable. But no, there were small families, if they could be thought of in so archaic a fashion, and even the random individual living alone in a floating structure, as if a miniature city could be made available to a population of one.

The sphere plunged into the sea and he saw great farms on the ocean floor...and their presence seemed in no way to disturb the vast schools of fish that played among man-made spires, underwater cathedrals to celebrate the constant flux of life. Then they went to the Antarctic and he saw how even that inaccessible region of otherworldly ice had been tamed for man's purpose without any adverse effects. They saw rain forests above which humans floated and lived, and sometimes played below. The same was true of desert regions and prairies and vast meadows stretching for uncountable miles.

"I'm ready now," he whispered in her ear and she whispered back. The woman of the 39th century lectured H.G. Wells. She told him how many of the greater conflicts of the past had been from people only grasping some small piece of the truth and then foolishly denying that anyone else could have a different piece of the truth.

The human race had almost destroyed itself out of pigheaded stubbornness. There had been a Dark Age when technology had been forbidden by a new religion, Earthology; it was a reaction to an earlier folly of idiotic misuse of precious resources and fouling of the air and water through carelessness and incompetence. Precisely at the moment when better scientists and engineers were needed— essential components of the World Brain— the masses rose up and outlawed science. It was the last great stand of old time, really *old time,* religion. But certain forbidden books survived, among them Wells's books, and a remnant survived to take back the world from barbarism.

"Yes, yes," said Wells excitedly. "But I must know, at what point did socialism prevail over capitalism?"

For the first time since his arrival, Wells was surprised to learn that a citizen of the future could dodge a question; at least it seemed that Rebecca was changing the subject. "I thought you'd want to know about the fate of religion first," she said.

In point of fact, he was desperately interested in that subject. One aspect of the past concerned him very much. "What has become of the Roman Catholic Church?" he asked. His old sparring partner had never been far from his mind, even to that moment in World War II when he had called for the bombing of Rome and discovered that the German air attacks were a peaceful vacation compared to the response he received for one inflammatory pamphlet.

"As you surmised, I am an expert in history," said West. "It took a while to look up all the relevant information." This comment made his heart leap for joy. She spoke as an archaeologist or antiquarian, not as if referring to that which was still a living force. "You refer to a subcategory of a religion known as Christianity?"

"Yes. The Catholic Church was the beginning of its institutional form; other branches that came later, in rebellion to the first, were known as Protestant."

"My records show that Christianity in both forms survives...as a hobby."

"A hobby?"

"Yes, a game of some sort, but not as popular as another game from the years B.W.—a logic exercise you called chess."

His head was spinning. Traditional religion was now a game? It was reasonable to assume that what was true for Christianity was true for the other great faiths of the past. And what had she said about the years B.W.? Good lord, she must mean Before Wells! How he wished he could see his old opponents now, the men of the cloth who had, for some peculiar reason, thought the worst insult they could hurl at him was to draw a parallel between his most excited rhetoric and their own sermons! What sort of creed was it that used similarity to itself as the worst possible insult? And now to live in a world where the calendar was dated from himself; it was actually funny, the more he thought of it.

The globe in which they traveled came to rest in a field of red and yellow flowers. He looked at the most beautiful woman he had ever seen and took her hand in his. He kissed her fingers. She stroked his cheek with her other hand.

"Before you brought me back," he said, "you and your friends, I heard a voice saying that The World Brain needed me for some reason."

"That's true."

"Are you going to tell me?"

"Yes, but first I have to answer another of your questions?"

"When did socialism win?"

The corners of her mouth pulled down. It was the first time he had seen her frown. "It didn't," she said.

"What?"

"The world you see is the outgrowth of what I think you would call capitalism."

"You'll have to explain that."

"We don't call our economic system capitalist or socialist or communist or any of the other terms that were bandied about in the Industrial Wars of the 20th century. We call it Creation."

"But what you are really doing is translating into English, as best you can?"

"You're right about that, Herbert. The languages of the world today are descended from a 2000 year old tongue, Esperanto. There are five major branches and many dialects."

This was in itself amusing, considering that Esperanto had been intended to be a universal tongue. Instead, it was the base of later languages as if repeating the relationship of Latin to the Romance languages.

"What I'm driving at," Wells tried again, "is that speaking to you has been so near the contemporary English of my own day that I easily forget where I am. Certain of your pronunciations leave something to be desired, but that this is our only communication difficulty speaks volumes for the quality of your research. We seem to be having our first real translation problem over socialism."

"It's not all that terribly important, Jaguar," she said breathily, leaning close to him.

The sudden change in tactics surprised him. She was using her old nickname for him. For a moment, he thought he should be offended. This was, after all, a woman of the future playing a part for his benefit. And here she was saying things to him that Rebecca never would have said...except they had argued over almost nearly everything...and he found this woman sitting across from him to be water for a man dying of thirst. And he had this nice new body just dying to be tried out.

"Mind you," he said, "when I see a society in which no one is in want, and all are clothed and sheltered, it has all the earmarks of a well managed socialism." She kissed him and it was even better the second time. He kissed her back.

"On the other hand," she said, "if there are sufficient resources, and everyone has the means to use them, intellectually and otherwise, so much wealth is produced that the issue of expropriation never even arises."

"Hmmmm," said Wells as she began to unbutton his shirt.

"With unlimited energy, and robots who build robots who build robots, labor is permanently severed from the laborer." Her mouth worked its way from his neck to his chest.

"This goes beyond a dictatorship to end war."

"A dictatorship is war by another name."

"I hoped that a technocratic elite might save the world."

"The technocratic elite has become the world," she said, nimble fingers beginning to work on his belt.

"I wanted a society with no nations, no pride in ethnic identity, no missions from the gods, no sexual frustration..."

"I *see* what you mean," she said.

"I *feel* what you mean," he said.

"Go on," they both said at the same time, and laughed...almost in key with each other.

"When you brought me back," he said, his fingers finding no break in the smoothness of her peculiar, translucent garment, "I feared that I was living through a scene from my novel, *When the Sleeper Wakes.* It was no Utopia my sleeper found but a crazy civilization where one man's private property, through sheer accumulation of trusts, came to make him master of the world."

"Here, let me help you with that." With the flick of a finger, her garment disappeared. Wells was suitably impressed. "How is a world built on your ideas not every bit as much your property?" she asked him.

"Uh," he was for a moment distracted, "because if this isn't socialism, it's not really my idea, after all. Besides, I had the hero of my story divest himself of his albatross by giving his holdings to humanity."

They did not speak for a moment, and then: "Herbert, in a very real sense, we've moved beyond the conflict between private competition and public monopoly, the political factions of your time. We are post-socialist. It has been said that a sufficiently advanced economy is indistinguishable from magic."

"Allow me to call all this post-capitalist, then," he said, between sighs.

After that, the dialectic was concluded as follows— THESIS; "Oh, Herbert." ANTITHESIS; "Oh, Rebecca." SYNTHESIS: No exclamation could possibly do it justice.

He half expected some sort of pill or fluid to be offered with rejuvenating properties, but they slept instead. He'd never enjoyed sleep more. And for the first time in his new life, he dreamed. He'd been awfully conservative and cautious when writing tracts such as A *Modern Utopia* and *New Worlds for Old.* He'd been much closer to the mark when writing *Men Like Gods,* with its depiction of a society so advanced that for all practical purposes, it was an anarchy. And now he was in such a world. No soldiers. No police. This was to be his home.

He woke up before her. This time he would watch her open her eyes. And when she did, he kissed her again. Then he said, "I'd like to think I was brought back simply to be shown this grand show. But I remember being told that The World Brain needed my help. I don't see what I could possibly offer to...Utopia, but I am, as always, civilization's to command."

"This is as good a time to tell you as any. We have a problem and there is no one else who can help us."

She did something—he could never figure out exactly what it was—and they were flying again. This time there was no banter. Soon there would be no more secrets.

At length, they descended into the first ugly region he had seen on his journey: a blackened and charred terrain where all vegetation had been burned away. In a world where nature had been tamed, it was inconceivable that a fire would be allowed to spread to such an extent.

As they landed, and he had an even closer view, he could not deny what this scene of destruction suggested: WAR! But that made no sense at all in a social order so much at peace that the closest thing to a conflict of interests was over whether or not people should lecture one another.

THE WORLD BRAIN WARNS YOU TO EXERCISE CAUTION.

"What was that?" asked Wells. It had been an explosion of sound in his head.

"The joint telepathic communication by which we first communicated with you. Our coming this far triggered a last message. We are in danger here. But we have confidence in your wisdom to deal with any problem."

Danger. It was hard to believe that so idyllic an existence could even know the meaning of the word. He was excited to realize that he might really be needed by a civilization of this stature; that a two thousand year old genius might still be of use to his fellows.

But, in a more sober moment of reflection, he wondered what he could do against anyone or anything capable of threatening Utopia. He was still thinking about that when she said, "We must walk from this point. They would detect the sphere before they'd notice us."

The way she had said *they* left no room for doubt. There was danger here. Wells followed her up a ridge as lifeless as if he were traversing a moonscape. She slipped and he caught her, but there was no gratitude in her voice as she whispered: "We mustn't make any noise or we're lost."

They looked over the ridge. The moment he realized that they were at the lip of a crater, and he saw the long, cylindrical, metal shape that had made the crater, he experienced the sort of terror he had only written about before. None of this can be real, he told himself. It must be a pleasant dream that has just turned nightmare.

"They started coming to earth just a few months ago," she whispered. "It was around the time we started the project to bring you back." She waited for him to say something but Wells was silent. "We have established that these craft originate outside our galaxy. We've been unable to establish contact. This one landed first. The visitors made a device that burned up this area then went back inside the ship. Now they've started building something else. Look." She pointed at a tall metal structure further on, with long metal rods sticking out at peculiar angles.

"Rebecca, or whatever I should call you..." Wells began.

"Call me Panther, as you used to so long ago, my favorite Jaguar."

"In the Dark Age you told me about, did some of my books disappear? Do you have references to any of my novels that did not survive that period?"

"I hate to admit it, but we are missing a few of the titles."

"I can't begin to explain what is happening, Rebecca. Maybe this is a parallel universe of some kind. Maybe every writer creates a continuum, I don't know."

She did not seem to hear him. "We're hoping you can show us how to communicate with these visitors. There must be something about Utopia that frightens them if they felt the need to create this zone about them."

"Tell me," said Wells, and his whisper was lower than hers, so low that she could barely hear him, as if each word were only communicated by the movement of his lips. Perhaps he was using telepathy at last and didn't even realize it. "No one becomes sick in Utopia, do they?"

"No." She was surprised at his question.

"The air is clean of any germ, isn't it?"

"We haven't had bacteria, as you understand them, for centuries."

"That's what I thought," he said, and his voice was very sad. She continued talking but he no longer heard her. He was listening to the sound of metal turning against metal, as the cylinder began to open.

By now the reader may have noticed that I have a thing for doing tributes. This is because at some level I've never stopped being a fan, even after the hell I went through trying to place "Clutter." This story was written after I was in an argument where I put forth the proposition that Heinlein's work is as highly stylized as anything in SF; that Heinlein always did such a smooth job that many readers failed to notice the distinctive style he originated. The annoying thing is when critics are blind to his accomplished prose.

Never mind the hubris of my trying to write in one of the voices of RAH. Even crazier is that I had the nerve to send this to Ginny Heinlein and she didn't exile me to Coventry! This must be a textbook example of "it's the thought that counts." Looking back on this one, I see the seed planted for what led to my editorial work on *Free Space*, the libertarian science fiction anthology (Tor Books).

Paranoia Doesn't Pay

"My favorite's the one about the soap smuggler." Young Biggins paused before going on. Not receiving any response, he took it as encouragement.

"A variation on the wheelbarrow joke. For months, a guy is suspected of being a smuggler. They investigate him every time he goes through the gate at the end of the work day. They look in and under his wheelbarrow, but don't find anything. Finally they give up. Much later, a guard asks the guy what he was smuggling, because it's been bugging him for a long time. 'Wheelbarrows,' answers our successful thief."

Old Harrows knocked out his pipe and cleared his throat. "Now don't go confusing smuggling and stealing, young feller. There's a heap of difference."

"Oh sure, I know," said Biggins, but perfunctory-like, because he can't wait to return to his main point, which is: "The soap smuggler is the same idea. See, there's this captain of a star freighter, and he has this problem with the Anthropology Administration. They won't allow cultural contamination—that old saw. The joke is that there's this Earth transplant culture out in System 8. They've got themselves this doozey of a planet, Hillbilly World. And it would be cultural interference if you could stand downwind from them without fainting for your trouble."

"I had a boss like that once," said Neru, scratching his back with an elbow extension. "But one day I got over my cold and noticed! It was self-employment then!"

Old Harrows laughed at that, even though he'd heard a version of the same story before. Young Biggins was too busy to pass on acknowledgement.

"Like I was saying," said Biggins, "soap is illegal for import on this planet. So our heroic smuggler of the spaceways hatches a wonderful idea of making a planet shuttle out of soap. That's his wheelbarrow."

"Never hold together," said Neru, gesturing to Honey for another drink.

"It's just a joke," said Biggins, in a slightly offended tone. "He covers it with a light alloy, and has an anti-grav drive to bring her in real slow. This is science fiction, you know. So he passes inspection and takes her down."

"How does he deliver the soap to the hillbillies?" asked Harrows.

"With the real shipment, which is a load of pocket lasers. After removing the metal, he cuts up the ship into individual bars and floods the planet with 'em. Well, how do you like it?"

"Never work," said Neru. "How would he get back to his freighter?"

"Hell, another shuttle would be down. You're just picking nits."

"Never work," said Harrows. "Them hillbillies wouldn't use that soap."

They all laughed at that, even young Biggins. By then, Honey had glided over with Neru's drink, a Pink Glacier, and easy on the frosty. Biggins and Harrows were ready for a refill, too. Biggins wanted a Tom Collins.

"You'll always be an earther at heart," old Harrows told him, "but I'm not criticizin'. So was my Mom."

"What'll you have?" asked Honey, wiggling that nude chassis at all his sixty-five years.

"You on my lap instead of that skateboard."

"Management rules," she sighed, but winking at the same time. "You know there will never be anybody but you. So, what'll you have to drink, 'stead of eat?"

Harrows looked up at the grand view afforded by the ceiling. Mars was still there, right where he'd left it. "Something red," he said. "How about a Moscow Sled?"

"It'll keep you warm," was her answer, and she wiggled that splendid posterior of hers at Harrows as she went skating off toward the bar.

"I like her better than the dancer," said Neru. "She's got the prettiest rainbow hair I've ever scanned."

"I'll take the dancer," Biggins replied.

"Youth," sighed Harrows, but trying to be fair. "Ah me, who says all torchship captains have to share the same taste? Now about this little story of yours, why do you find it amusing?"

"It's funny."

"Maybe you find the idea of smuggling appealing?"

Young Biggins actually stopped talking. For a few minutes. Honey

had time to return with the drinks and exchange some bawdy sug-
gestions with old Harrows, before the younger man realized that
they were waiting on him. Never one to keep his peace for long,
Biggins told them, with all the conviction of his thirty years, "No. I
play it straight and legal. One thing I learned from my father was
not to get mixed up with feds."

Harrows was having none of that. "I thought he taught you not to
draw to an inside straight."

"Well, I picked up a couple of things from him, such as scruples.
I accept them with pride."

Harrows was relentless: "So long as your pride comes with all
duties paid in full."

"What my esteemed *elder* colleague is trying to express," said
Neru, lazily extending a prosthetic comb attachment from his wrist
and running it through the tresses that remained of his snow white
hair, "is that scruples are relative, same as space-time. A smuggler's
scruples might be of a higher order than those of a patrolman."

Biggins hunched over his drink. "Sure, some pickpockets are
better people than our leaders. But the economy of the Interplan-
etary Consolidation depends on the raising of revenue, and the control of goods and services. Without that, we would have chaos."

"You believe that?" asked Neru with something cold in his voice
as well as his glass. His dark skin was shiny in the light from the
table.

"Of course," Biggins said, taking another swallow of his drink. "I
don't just follow the rules because I want to avoid trouble. It's my
duty to the system." He regretted saying it the minute it was out of
his mouth. Harrows and Neru exchanged knowing glances, and
Biggins didn't like being the subject.

"A moment ago," Harrows began, "you made an interesting slip,
by comparing government administrators to pickpockets. I'm sure
you didn't mean it that way, but the comparison works better than
you intended. I prefer dealing with an honest thief to a dishonest
one."

"Honest thief?" asked Biggins, as if stuck at some point on a
vidcording.

"Son, the only dishonest thief is one who tells you he's stealing
from you for your own good. I've yet to run into the first smash-
and-grab man with blade or blaster who makes me listen to a bar-

rel of humanitarian tripe, or worse, his life story. Some haven't been in condition to talk after they try and rob me, but that's another point. Only a government man with his ledger and smile wants to have it both ways."

"So you're saying that a smuggler is an honest thief?" asked Biggins.

"No," said Harrows. "A smuggler never steals. He's an honest businessman."

While Biggins was contemplating that, the floor show began, which meant the light in their table was dimmed. Above them, Mars stood out as the brightest chandelier in the universe, and the stars were shiny with that steady light you only find in space.

A drum roll and yellow spotlight drew everyone's attention to the high dive boards that met near the center of the sphere that housed the bar. The ladder to one of the boards was only a few yards from Biggins. He got an eyeful as Gorgeous Gwen chasséd past, her bubble costume picking up the lights from random cigarettes, winking crimsonly in the dark. Her partner, Dashing Donald, was climbing the board at the opposite and, clad only in a pair of golden shorts. Low music came from everywhere and nowhere. They knew how to do a show in The Mars Station Silo.

The acrobats dive upwards at the same moment, and met at the zero-g center of the sphere, cymbals crashing near Biggins from the echo sound technique, no doubt to make sure that he wouldn't miss the point. With a series of champagne bubble pops, Gwen's costume disappeared. Donald pulled off his shorts and let them continue spinning up there, as if a reference to the lovers.

"They're really good," said Neru, an optical magnifier sliding out over his one good eye. "Pretty, pretty."

"Too good for them to be paid only in credits," said Harrows, admiringly.

Biggins knew that bit of monetary wisdom was for his benefit. He let it pass. When the lovers reached their crescendo, a series of colored lights cascaded over their muscular, nude bodies. The music peaked, too.

"Makes a poor half-man thirsty," said Neru, motioning to Honey. She sped over, a jealous look in her eyes.

"I saw how you were giving her the thrice over," she said in mock anger. "I guess we're through."

"You've got me wrong" he said. "There's no one but you, doll-charger. 'Specially if you bring me an absinthe-laced Armenian."

"Whooo," she answered. "Don't forget to pay me in real." With a zip, she went rolling back to the bar.

"What did she mean by 'real'?" asked Biggins.

"Hold out your hand," said Harrows to Biggins, the latter still gawking after Honey's retreat. Biggins put out his left hand.

"Come on, Captain," insisted Harrows, "you know what I mean." Biggins put out his right. The older man pulled back the sleeve, revealing a pinkish disc set in the flesh just above the palm.

"They say that makes the wrist itch," said the older man. "How do you like your credit disc?"

Biggins felt a sudden rush of high spirits, and told the world at large: "Doesn't itch, doesn't hurt. Don't feel a thing. Adds to efficiency. Beats carrying around a wad of paper that can be lifted by our good friends, the pickpockets."

"Money's only clean when it's anonymous," said Neru. "We're not money ourselves; *we're people.*"

"Biggins knows that," said old Harrows. Then looking square at the younger man, he asked, "Why did you have yours deactivated?"

Biggins swirled ice shards in the remains of his drink. "My generation, born on Earth, had 'em put in by law. You know all that. Out here, they can't supervise them. Too much trouble doing business otherwise."

"You recite the sales pitch well enough," said Harrows, "that I cannot swallow for a minute that you believe it. Maybe you have the makings of a smuggler yourself."

"Or a spy," said Neru. "They deactivate theirs, too."

Harrows slammed down his drink. "I'm ashamed of you, buckethead. What a paranoid thing to say!"

"You shouldn't call him that!" Biggins decided that he would be offended for the cyborg, but it was a wrong move. They wouldn't let him get away with it.

"Buckethead's a second name to me," said Neru. To demonstrate, he blinked three times in rapid succession and an antenna extended from the back of his head. If a cyborg didn't mind the slang, there was no greater example of bad manners than to offer unwanted pity. Besides, 'borgs outlived nearly everyone else.

Neru tuned in a Mars station that was playing the last movement

of Carlos' Blues Study. Harrows asked, "What if you had an opportunity to double your effective income for the year by running *one*
extra ferry?"

Biggins smiled. "Is that offer hypothetical?"

"It doesn't matter. I'm jest hankerin' after one of your scruples.
How does the little fella tick?"

"OK," said Biggins. "I'll give you a clue. My first question would
be to know what I'm smuggling."

Neru's symphony ended and was replaced by the applause of an
audience. Harrows said, "Congratulations, that's the first right thing
you've said. The moment you take that responsibility on your shoulders—to know what you're taking— you're not letting the State decide what is ethical."

Neru nodded, adding: "Those government boys don't want you
troubling yourself over actual consequences of your business. They
nabbed that one for themselves years ago. It's true the smuggler is
after profit, but he can also enjoy the luxury of having personal
integrity. His good name is his most important commodity."

Biggins wasn't hiding his frown. "Are you saying a government
employee can't have integrity?"

"It's discouraged," said Harrows. "A wise man many years ago
observed that no good deed goes unpunished. Nowhere is that more
true than in the Consolidation."

Neru got in his two-script worth: "The revenue agent only cares
about the law. He has no time for right and wrong."

"That's why Neru and I wonder about your scruples. We want to
know if they leave any room for a personal code of ethics. How else
would we know if you'd be trustworthy in business?"

Young Biggins hadn't felt this put upon since moon camp when
he had to take his fusion ship final. The chair in the simulation
chamber had been hard enough to sit on without Ironmouth Joyce
riding him throughout the test. Biggins had been so busy saying
"Yessir" and "Nosir" that he almost forgot when to put on the brakes.
The O'Neill colony that was projected dead in his path would surely
have appreciated his receiving a passing mark.

"Look," Biggins began, taking a deep breath, "there's nothing I
enjoy more than shooting the breeze with you two, but I don't think
you should talk so openly about, well, advocating crime."

Neru started to stand up but Harrows casually motioned him back to his seat. Then the eldest man there put the youngest possible smile on his face, and gestured Honey over. She signaled that she'd be a minute serving gin-crackers, to the Jupiter survey team—this month's special guests in the Mars Station Silo—and Harrows turned back to the younger man.

"Let me tell you what I picked up from my pappy. You can be good at math and languages, you can be a whiz at crosscynir engineering and be the world's best code breaker, you can be a poet who can rhyme and scan if he feels like it, or a sculptor who can bring a wad of anything to life; you can be all these things, and it's not worth one inflated mark in Weimar Germany if you don't understand people. That's one talent I've worked hardest to develop. And that's why I'm going to take a chance on you, young torchship captain."

Honey had finished with her other customers and came over to their table, one arm balancing precariously a tray of flaming Polynesian something-or-others. "Yes, lover," she sang out to Harrows.

"Help me with a little demonstration?"

"Anytime," she said lecherously.

"Ah, the stories these bones could tell," he said with a sigh. "But the blood has slowed, dear one."

Winking at him, she would have none of it. "I know an excuse when I hear one, and you are most certainly the laziest man between here and Pluto base."

"Merely prudent measures so that I may live forever."

"Watch out, or you'll wind up like me," said Neru.

"Demonstration?" cut in Biggins.

Harrows took it from there. "Honey, we will be here for a time yet, searching for answers to questions nobody's thought to ask."

"Tell me about it!" she said, turning to Biggins. "Watch out for these two. They'll keep you here through all three cycles of the day."

Harrows continued unperturbed. "I would like to pay you now, for services rendered thus far. I want young Biggins to see."

"Oh, I get you," she said. "Watch that you don't corrupt this nice, young man." She held out her hand, a different color on each nail, all of them lustrous. She turned he hand palm up. Harrows placed two tan pieces of paper in that soft depository. Giving her a pat, he shooed her off again. Except that she didn't shoot! There she stood, a curvy statue, an exercise in patience.

"She won't budge until I live up to my reputation," Harrows told Biggins. "And when have I ever undertipped you, girl?"

"First rule of Dirty-Old-Mandom is be generous," she said, as the third bill, olive green, came out and found a snug home in her hand.

"Now scoot," he said. She executed a pirouette on her skateboard, without losing a drop of the fire water on the tray.

"Pretty, pretty," said Neru.

"My God," Biggins said in a half whisper, "you paid her in smuggler script. Right out in the open! I don't believe it. What about the inspectors here?"

"They get bigger tips," said Harrows.

"Or have accidents," said Neru.

"But smuggler script," repeated Biggins, still stuck on that vidcording of his.

"We don't call it that," said Harrows. "I paid her in two barter notes, and tipped her with a whole Warren note."

"Warren?"

Another bill came out, same as the previous greenback, and was unashamedly laid flat in front of young Biggins. The face in the center was of an old man with mutton chop whiskers, and the legend read: *Josiah* Warren *1798 to 1874.* The top of the bill was in bold letters: One Time/Labor Exchange. NEVER TRUST THE BANK.

"I've never actually seen a smug... one of these before," said Biggins.

"Maybe you shouldn't have now," said Neru, just a touch of tension in his voice. He'd retracted his antenna and seemed on the verge of a good sulk.

"Bucket, bucket," said Harrows, "when are you going to learn to trust people? You'll never be rich out of worry."

"But I am rich."

"Richer."

Biggins, his voice barely above a whisper, asked: "Are you really offering me an illegal cargo?"

"Only if you understand the facts regarding smuggling. Would you tell me what money is?"

"Well, the computer files show how many units a worker earns. When he buys something, there is a debit to his account; when he makes money, there is a credit. Money is a symbolic unit for the exchange of goods and services."

"What determines the value of work applied to resources?"

"The Bank."

"Yes, the central computer on Earth. Who programs it?"

"The best experts credits can buy."

"Ha," laughed Neru.

Harrows continued: "Do you think The Bank's money reflects the value of resources—the energy we have available? Or do you think money reflects the time put into developing that potential—the human labor and thought brought to bear in the creation of wealth?"

"I assume both," said Biggins earnestly.

"The answer is neither," said Neru with just as much sincerity.

"Neither?" Biggins was surprised, all right. "Then what is money?"

Harrows corrected him: "Not 'what is money', son! What *is the Bank's money?* And that is nothing at all. It is backed by neither resource nor effort. It is simply the rent."

"But the *rent is* backed by something," said Neru. "The torchships of the Navy carry plasma cannons. When they fail, the long range communications lasers can be converted into short range weapons, a typical perversion of a good thing into something bad. But when the lads and lassies in gray run into real difficulty, they turn the ships around and count on the photon drive to fry any opposition." He was breathing heavily after that.

"Guns," said Harrows, "instead of butter."

He didn't have much heart in it, but young Biggins said, "They have to preserve order somehow."

"What is order?" asked Neru.

Biggins sighed. This was getting nowhere—or worse, somewhere he didn't want to go. He'd lost his thirst, and his appetite as well. Staring at the table, he muttered, "The Bank. Its money. That's what they preserve."

The lovers in the sky had finished. The music had stopped. It was as quiet as the bar ever was, a murmuring of voices like the tide at Atlantic City in the background. Harrows leaned over close and said, "'When robbery is done in open daylight by sanction of the law... then any act of honor or restitution has to be hidden underground.' A Twentieth Century Russian said that, a lady by the name of Ayn Rand."

"I thought she was American," said Neru. Harrows shrugged.

"Look here," said Harrows, passing Biggins a thin, rectangular package. "Open it."

Biggins removed plasrap to find a chocolate bar underneath. "That's our cargo for the next month," said Harrows, "an asteroid-full. If you're in, you'll be paid in Warrens. You won't be able to spend it on Earth for shoddy products. Out here, you'll find 'em good as gold."

Neru was watching Biggins closely. Harrows wasn't finished: "Listen lad, times are hard, and a captain's salary doesn't begin to be enough. We know of two ways to take up the slack. One is find a second salary in real money. The other doesn't merit talking about in any decent bar."

Honey waved at Harrows from across the room. She was standing on the floor, skateboard under her arm. At first it seemed unnatural to see her in clothes. Off duty time.

"If you gentlemen will excuse me," said old Harrows, rising. "Assuming these old bones don't object, I'll attempt to enjoy the rest of the day. I'd be a hospital case by now if I lived at the bottom of the gravity well you climbed out of, Biggins. It can weigh down your mind as well as your heart. I suggest that you breathe the freedom of these wide open spaces. It's bracing."

Harrows left. The other two continued to sit at the table, Neru looking at Biggins, Biggins looking at the table. Neru finally laughed. "That soap story is a good one," he said. "Grows on you."

The 'borg stood up in one flowing motion, an almost imperceptible click sounding in his spinal cord. "You know how to get in touch with us. There'll be a full cargo, if you're interested. And don't worry about informers. We have more eyes and ears than they do." The 'borg chuckled, as at a private joke. "They can be anybody, but we find 'em. They don't have a chance to spend their credits, inflated as they are." Neru patted Biggins on the back, then left, walking with the smooth gait peculiar to mechanically improved legs.

Young Biggins thoughtfully pocketed the candy. On the way to the chute, he felt a momentary chill on the back of his neck. Turning around fast, he caught a glimpse of a kid staring at him. It was only a six year old boy whose attention was suddenly diverted to a servo-droid gliding nearby. As the bald head of the child turned away, Biggins felt a sudden desire to stop off at a drugstore and pop something, anything, to calm down.

Perhaps a hashpill would have him free-associating to some more pleasant topic—but he knew if any contemplation was to be done, it should be reserved for the matter at hand. He considered an opiumpill; that would keep him on the subject, each little detail calmly leading to the next, evaluation without tension. The only trouble was that it would slow him down. He would have to make a decision very soon.

"Case of the jitters," Biggins thought. He was surprised at how speedily his tall tale had flushed out information—so much so soon. He needed to get back to his ship. The crew was on leave, most of them down on Mars. He'd have her all to himself. Solitude looked plenty good at the moment.

Somehow he'd wound up with the Warren note. It made him feel better to have it. He found it easier to forget the moonbase code he'd been thinking of punching up earlier in the week. He'd known for years that it was called the Judas line. Now he felt it.

His ship, the New Orleans, was docked on the opposite side of the space city from the bar. First ships in always took the Silo berths. He had a five minute chute trip to make.

The whole time, he thought about one thing: his chocolate bar. He wasn't thinking of how cool the candy was kept in his temperature controlled pocket. He didn't think about the sweet smell and sweet taste of rich, milky chocolate. He wasn't even thinking of when he would eat it. All he could think of was how much lighter a candy bar is than a bar of soap.

(Dedicated to Robert A. Heinlein, 1907–1988)

Just as there's no substitute for seeing your first story in a magazine, the first time your byline appears in a book makes a strong impression! I'd been recently married when Andre Norton and the late Robert Adams published "Shadow Quest" in the second of their *Ithkar* books. Within a few years, my wife and I would collaborate on "Dream Pirates' Jewel" for Norton's *Tales of the Witch World 2*, but not even that had the magic to hold our marriage together.

But when Cari first saw "Shadow Quest" in print, she couldn't have been more excited. *Magic in Ithkar 2* was a trade paperback the first time out. Later, when I saw the mass market paperback, I did a slow double take. It took me a moment to realize the cover art was for my story. I thought that dragon looked familiar!

My thanks to Andre Norton for letting me reprint the story here.

Shadow Quest

One moment there was the sound of celebration—bells and horns and the beating of drums, with some hearty cheers adding merriment to the whole. Then this was brought to an end...at least in one part of the fairgrounds. The Fair at Ithkar was famous for strange occurrences, but nothing in its four-hundred-year history had prepared any participant for what caused that bone chilling silence.

A crowd had gathered on the outer fringes of the fair before one booth. The young man who seemed responsible for the present distraction was as wide-eyed as any passerby at the thing struggling on the floor. The creature started to crawl in his direction, a snake's head wriggling forth from a hump covered by feathers. As it moved across the floor, the young man involuntarily lumped back.

"So!" rasped a voice like a dungeon door slamming shut. "You conjure monsters *here!* Curse my folly for ever making you my apprentice, Jad. " The crowd turned as one at the approach of an old man. His reputation preceded him: Kesnir the Brooding. Few would claim him as a friend; none wanted to have him as an enemy.

Kesnir stalked past Jad to appraise the creature. Above was the full moon, menaced by a great cloud suggesting the shape of a crow's head. The moon seemed to pause when it was in position as the night bird's white eye, while an orange radiance played under the cloud the light from the fairgrounds' many fires. Jad wished that a cloak of darkness would fall to hide from view the proof of his bungling. For, attempting a simple spell to amuse his bored customers—a low-order illusion that was within the rules of Ithkar—this monster had unexpectedly appeared.

"Jad," said Master Kesnir, and the young man could feel the weight of his name so uttered, "do exactly as I tell you. We will send this creature back to whatever black gulfs spawned it."

As the old man raised his hands and began to chant, it dawned on Jad that, at rare moments of crisis, an experienced magician does not waste time on threats. He saves them for later.

The apprentice watched his master pull his old body taut as a bowstring under the fine, silken robes he always wore. As Kesnir raised his arms, the jewels on his belt glowed with green fire.

Noticing that a fair-ward had joined the company of interested onlookers, standing quietly with a quarterstaff at his side, Jad swallowed a lump in his throat and waited for his master's instructions, which came as: "Take up the vial of ghoul's powder and throw it when I give the command."

The thing on the floor had managed to move only a few inches, leaving something wet behind. Keeping his eyes on the creature, Kesnir moved his hands over his head as if he were playing invisible harp strings. "Now!" he cried out.

Jad tossed the powder, which was evenly distributed over the aggravated monstrosity. There was a flash of light, a terrible smell … and it was still there.

"How?" asked Kesnir of the universe at large as the monster unfolded surprisingly large wings, rose for an astounding moment, and exited the booth. In so doing, one of its claws brushed Jad on the arm as the bulk of its body knocked him to the ground.

It flew over the gasping crowd into the night. Regaining his feet, Jad saw that once the oddity was in the sky, it moved with an obscene kind of grace. Outlined against the moon, it seemed as if an ungainly, crippled bird had devoured a large snake that was coiling itself free through a place where a beaked head should be. Yet it could fly without twisting.

"The snake-bird," whispered Jad. "How did I ever bring you into the world?" Examining his arm, Jad saw that he had a slight scratch. He could barely feel it. He felt strangely peaceful.

His mood was broken by the voice of the fair-ward addressing Maser Kesnir "A word with you, magician." Jad knew that he was in for it.

The animals kept in the largest precinct of the fair had panicked when the snake-bird sailed over them. The authorities were immediately besieged with complaints by owners of the various beasts. In some cases, animals had hurt themselves; in others, dealers were hurt by the thought that they might not realize any money after all their trouble. At any rate, they received satisfaction, the deserving and dishonest alike. Fair-law had emergency provisions for making a careless participant wish he had never saved his money, just so that it could be paid out in such a fashion. Kesnir learned how swiftly he had to part with a pouch of gold.

The old magician was at least grateful that the Fair at Ithkar did not hold him responsible for the sudden darkness that had enveloped the grounds for a few minutes after the departure of the snakebird. "Well, Jad, they couldn't prove that your monster is the cause of every ill."

Shortly after they had satisfied the last claim, the magician and his apprentice were standing in the ruins of an abandoned tower near the fairgrounds overlooking the river Ith. Kesnir had told Jad that this place had been used as a place of worship for the Three Lordly Ones long before the temple shrine was even constructed. It was a well-kept secret, Kesnir confided to his apprentice, that such had ever been the use of this tower—and most people had no idea that power from the Three still remained here.

"But I wished for darkness," Jad said, half in awe, half in worry.

Kesnir allowed himself to chuckle before answering: "I doubt that you have that kind of power!"

Jad took the moment's humor as an opportunity to apologize: "Master, I had no idea—"

"You never have!" Kesnir was never happier and Jad more intimidated than when the old man was insulting him. The apprentice had given up trying to understand so long ago that he couldn't remember if it had ever been different. He braced himself for abusing words ... those that didn't come this time.

"Jad, as this tower stands guard over the river below, so must I stand guard over the mistakes of an eager apprentice who believes himself competent to practice the art unassisted."

"I swear that I don't know what could hew gone wrong. My spell was meant to show a silver fountain in the moonlight."

The conversation continued with a melancholy sameness, the younger repeating the theme of inexperience, the older insisting on the necessity of blame. At length Kesnir's purpose became clear: "I do not say that what you have done through carelessness cannot be corrected. I do insist that you set it right. For I believe that the monster you have called forth comes from the sinister Thotharn."

There was a shocked moment of silence. Jad dreaded the dark god? in whom belief was generally stronger than it was in the reputedly benign Three Lordly Ones. Kesnir drew back a dusty curtain that revealed a purple window taking up the space of a wall.

As if guilt were a hand pressing down on him, Jad sat on the floor, his head slumping forward on his chest. "I didn't mean to do it. I want to change everything back."

Master Kesnir smiled, which, if Jad had noticed, would surely have struck him as odd under the circumstances. "You can help me, Jad, and do our world a service in the bargain. I have a scroll that I wish you to deliver to the Three Lordly Ones."

The casual manner in which Kesnir suggested a meeting with personages for whom Jad, at the very least, held some doubts concerning their reality, was not so surprising as the other implication: namely, that there was a *place* where he would find them. "A quest?" Jad asked.

Pointing with his bony forefinger, Master Kesnir drew his apprentice's attention to the purple window. "There lies a portal to another world," he said. "It is the home of the Three. I have a spell to send you through."

In the shadows of the altar was a leathern bag. Jad noticed that his master appeared just as well prepared here as in his own tower. The old man's hands played across its surface, like pale, white spiders, then held two items before Jad: a flask in one hand, a tightly rolled-up scroll in the other. "You must not open the scroll, Jad, for it will turn your mind to ashes if you read it. Once you arrive, trust your instincts to help you find the palace of the Three. It is a barren land you will find, and the palace is its only structure."

Already Kesnir was giving Jad the flask and scroll, all in one smooth motion that seemed to push him toward the window as well. The degree of Kesnir's preparation bothered Jad. The sudden change in his demeanor—from sullen to cheerful—seemed an exercise in unwelcome haste.

"Wait a minute!" insisted the apprentice. "I have no provisions: food, weaponry, sacks, torches ..."

"They would merely slow you down," came the brisk reply. "Water's enough to keep you going. Now listen: Once you present the scroll to the Three, they will send you home again. You must make haste. Every second lost is a second the snake-bird—I rather like your name for it—remains where it doesn't belong. The Three will know what to do."

Standing directly in front of the window, Jad seriously questioned whether he wanted the life of a magician. He still had enough wits about him to ask "What of dangers?"

"Minor obstacles, no more," Kesnir said, but there was little conviction in his voice, now beginning to hold a note of irritation as Jad hesitated. "If you get into trouble, throw the scroll away from you, and all will be well."

"Hey, hold on a—" Jad never finished. Master Kesnir had given him a helpful shove. Then he was surrounded by a veil of purple so pervasive that it was as if the drape had been pulled *through* Jad's body. A stubborn part of his mind was astonished to have met no resistance from a pane of stained glass that, apparently, was never there.

The transition was virtually instantaneous. It took several seconds before he noticed the marked decrease in temperature. He stood on a flat, featureless landscape of dry clay, hard as stone—stretching away in all directions. The sky was as dark purple as the vanished window.

A cold breeze touched his face. Jad was slightly astonished that such a barren place would be visited by even the wind. Shivering, he pulled his cloak more tightly around him. There was no sign of a palace anywhere in sight.

"Which way?" he asked aloud, searching for the barest sign of habitation. A mound of bones attracted his attention instead—the skeleton of a human being. The skull had fallen so that its vacant eye sockets were turned toward the merciless sky. It was impossible to tell from the arrangement of the bones the direction in which the dead had been traveling when death came.

The unpleasant sight made Jad think through the events of the last few hours. So much had happened that it felt as if a lifetime lay behind him. But the most peculiar aspect of the affair was not the advent of the snake bird, whatever it was, wherever it came from. The really strange thing was what had gone on between Master Kesnir and him; the speed with which his usually cautious instructor had sent him on his bizarre errand, with essentially no preparation, and hardly any explanation.

Was this the man who doubted that Jad could handle the simplest spells on his own? Who had rules that he kept secret until Jad unknowingly broke one and chaos was loosed? Who set traps for his apprentice throughout the tower in which they both lived practical jokes that never caused permanent damage but worked effectively to undermine the victim's pride? Why entrust something of this importance to—what had he called it.?—Jad's instincts? It made no sense.

   The skull grinned. There was something about its absence of life that suggested great wisdom. Jad had to find out what was going on, and obviously there was only one way. Find the Three Lordly Ones.

   He started walking. One direction seemed as good as another. His eyes strained at the vast expanse of purple sky and brown earth, hunting anything that might be a stronghold in this wasteland.

   He walked for hours. Every thirty minutes or so, he would stop, slowly turning in a full circle, hoping to sight even the slightest difference in his surroundings. An occasional bone was the only change. Any guess as to how these bones had come to be scattered was, in itself, disturbing. The clay underfoot was so hard that no prints remained behind to show his own passing.

   When the wind resumed, its icy needles forced him to huddle in the folds of his cloak. It never lasted long. The bones that appeared after a while were clearly not human any longer. Although most appeared to be those of animals, some suggested things he did not care to imagine clothed in flesh. He guessed that all had died from exposure or simple loneliness. He wondered how it was that any of them had arrived in this place.

   The sporadic wind came to scour the bones. Jad had no intention of the same fate befalling him, although he was becoming tired, very tired.

   His legs and chest felt thick and heavy. At last he was too worn out to continue without a rest. Even the hard ground felt good to sit upon.

   He swallowed dryness. Pulling the flask from inside his cloak, he resolved to take only one sip. The thought of the full bottle gave him a sense of security.

   Suddenly the scratch on his arm began to itch wildly, a touch of fire, like a line of red army ants lancing pain into his skin. It was such a surprise that he shook his arm and cursed. Abruptly as it had come, the pain vanished. He had to remind himself that he was still thirsty.

   Uncorking the flask, he tilted it to his lips ... and retched as a vile, green liquid began erupting from the spout. He threw it from him and watched the ichor ooze into the hard ground, steam rising from the spot where the liquid bad splashed. He was about to turn away in disgust when he received another flash of irritation from the little red line on his arm.

"Damn that scratch!" he cried. "I'm lost, I lose my water, and now this!" The pain vanished the moment he mentioned the word "water." He noticed.

Looking at the ground where his discarded flask lay, he saw something else. Picking it up, Jad upended the flask and sadly watched a few clear drops fall. Instead of a smoking piece of ground, he saw a simple darkening where the water had spread.

The time he had spent working on illusion spells had seemed wasted when it appeared that he had no talent for it. Now he thanked his stars for the real gift work provides: memory of how things are done.

He knew all at once the curse of this place. He was wandering in a land of illusion. His only hope was to take care and look for the signs of deception.

Sitting once again upon the hard surface, Jad stared ahead to where the straight line of the horizon promised nothing but more unbroken terrain. This succeeded in giving him a headache. Closing his eyes, he listened to the resonances of the silence. Eventually he heard the distant sigh of the wind, passing, but this time not touching.

He considered the horizon again, but without strain. He had relaxed, letting his eyes drift and his mind wander. The truth nudged him. The line of separation between ground and sky was somehow wrong. Then he did not so much see as realize that the plain was not flat after all, but curved like the bottom of a bowl. He had been walking around the perimeter.

Now he saw even more. Jad stood up and turned around oh, so very slowly. There was something in the distance. Upon closer scrutiny, he could make out two objects, still too far away for details. He started walking in their direction, feeling that he was approaching the center of this land.

He walked for a long time before the objects seemed to grow in size. They hadn't seemed that far away. Finally he was near enough to hear a sound of breathing like a thousand bellows full of ragged stones, rasping and wheezing in the thin air. The sound emanated from the first object. A few steps closer. He stopped dead in his tracks, dropped to the ground, his face grinding against the clay.

The thing couldn't make that much noise if it wasn't alive, and he recognized it well enough.

For, however many shapes they may assume, and no matter the size, there is something distinctive about dragons. They can be taken for nothing else.

This one had wings and a long neck supporting a massive, horned head sprouting like an evil stalk out of a lumpy, scaled body. And just as there is no mistaking a dragon for any other form of life, so there is no mistaking a dragon with a purpose! This dragon was a guardian. Beyond it was the second object—a small, ugly castle. Fortunately, the monster appeared asleep.

The color of the scales was an incongruous bright green, the hue captured on leaves in early morning sunlight. The beautiful color on the hideous form made a strange contrast in the bleak tableau, and it was as if a light pulsed somewhere deep inside to give the dragon an ethereal quality, which was all the more disturbing because of its unbelievably colossal size. A mountain of quiescent reptilian flesh, it dwarfed the fortress beyond.

Jad asked himself the obvious question: Was it real? Did he really want to go over and touch it to make sure? As if his right hand had a mind of its own, it was rubbing the scratch on his left arm. The scratch. The mark remained unchanged from the time he had received it. Yet it seemed inappropriate to call it a scar. Just what the snake-bird had set upon him was a mystery.

He had felt pain when he was about to throw away his water. Was it a warning? Too many questions crowded his mind, foremost among them why the snake-bird would help Jad. He wanted to dismiss such a line of reasoning, but he also had learned long ago that in magic, there are no coincidences.

Another question that nagged at him was that if he had a warning device on his person, why was it not tingling now? Did that mean that the dragon wasn't real, or that it posed no danger? He had to find out.

He had some pebbles with him that he used for a game of chance. There was one for each color of the rainbow. Now he selected the yellow one, said a prayer to every deity he could think of, and tossed it in a wide arc toward that green flank.

The pebble bounced off the dragon. Although the creature didn't move a muscle, every organ in Jad's body responded to his reckless gesture. After his heart had stopped beating at the speed of a hummingbird's wings, Jad muttered to himself: "That's real enough for me."

Concluding that the Three must be within the castle, Jad crawled on his belly, as might a desert reptile foraging through the perpetual twilight. It was his most devout wish that the dragon would not awaken.

He hugged the ground until he found himself on a gentle ridge (a surprising break in the landscape's monotony) overlooking the castle. Searching for the best manner of entry was fruitless. Even at close range, the structure was oddly nondescript. Aside from the main gate, there did not appear to be any other breaks in the blank, gray surface. There were no turrets, and not even lines were visible between the stones. Yet even taking into account its diminutive size, it could be nothing other than a castle, however inappropriately humble a home for the Three Lordly Ones.

As Jad drew nearer the building, the hairs on the scratched arm twitched. He halted a few yards from the right corner of the outer wall. Something was wrong.

As if on cue, the scratch began to burn. If it had hurt before, that was nothing compared to the agony he felt now. He had to bite his tongue to keep from screaming.

Could it be that the dragon had been roused from that heavy slumber? Turning his head, and lifting his body a fraction, he gained a clear view of the ridged back of the reptilian leviathan. It hadn't moved. Now that he was facing away from the castle, fear engulfed him. The mark on his arm had apparently reached its maximum discomfort. What was to happen would happen soon.

Later he was not sure if it had been a natural instinct for survival—a quality he wasn't sure that Master Kesnir had ever recognized in him—or a result of training in the art that had saved him. But he had rolled over, jumped to his feet, and run directly at the dragon. His sudden, wild hunch came not a second too soon. The castle began to move.

Odd how he hadn't noticed its breathing. Or was it by some acoustical trick he had mistaken the sound as coming from the dragon, whose sides—Jad now reflected—had not been moving? Hearing a wet, slushing noise behind him, he had the good sense to throw himself to the ground.

A long black tentacle snaked past his head, slapping the hard clay two inches from his body. Flipping over on his back, Jad viewed a sky full of more waving tentacles, all extending from the "castle." What he had taken to be the gate of the structure opened to reveal a red maw.

Possessing no eyes, it had to be relying on scent, sound, and the driving force of ravening hunger. Tentacles-snapped back and forth, entangling themselves in a frenzy to feed.

Jad had no way of estimating the reach of those tentacles, but he imagined that he was quite some distance from what might be safety. The closest point of refuge was the dragon! Perhaps if he could provoke the castle creature into attacking that behemoth, the ensuing battle would distract them both sufficiently for him to escape unnoticed.

The exhaustion that had plagued him earlier vanished. Jad leapt up as another tentacle grazed him. Even the touch of the thing through thick clothing caused his skin to crawl. This was a terrible form of alien life, loathing all natural flesh. It might feed reluctantly on anything clean but would feed just the same.

As a choice of deaths, the dragon was preferable. Whatever risk lay in Waking Up the reptile, Jad knew, had to be taken immediately. He raced straight for the massive hulk. Just before one flailing tentacle touched his ankle, the apprentice succeeded in ducking down beside the nearest haunch. The questing tentacle struck against scales instead of yielding tissue.

There sounded a dull thud, as one would hear from the striking of stone.

Then he noticed a door's outline where the ribs of the dragon should be. There was no time to worry over whether or not the portal was locked. Jad put his full strength against it ... and was through. Several tentacles converged on the spot too late. Jad wondered if the black monster was hesitant about assailing the edifice of the Three.

The dragon shape had not, after all, been entirely an illusion. Indeed, the structure had been purposely fashioned so. Given this outer design, it was relatively simple for powerful magic to cast a strong suggestion. The greater magic had been in the making of that eater which had worn the appearance of stone.

Torches burned on the walls of a corridor within. Traps might wait between those shadows. Echoes turned the softest footfall into an ominous pounding. Too many doors to choose from. Too many ways to be lost.

Jad started down a side hallway, only to halt as the scratch gave warning. He made two more attempts before he discovered a route taking him along just inside the outer wall. Naturally one would expect to find the Three at the center of their fortress, like spiders waiting in a web. Perhaps they were off to the side instead.

Jad's scratch suddenly itched, the same second his foot touched the metal plate hidden in the floor. He strove to retreat ... too late. And he fell forward into darkness, but not the darkness of unconsciousness.

His tumble was brief, ending surprisingly on cushions thick enough to protect him from any impact. Peeling very foolish, he sat up with a deep drawn breath. Determinedly, he removed the scroll from inside his cloak. By touch he thought it had been crumpled but was not torn. Holding it tightly, Jad waited.

Voices sounded as if speaking from the end of a tunnel, then light flared. He saw three smiling faces, hovering at the end of a strange room. Everything was yellow blending as one, floor, wall, and ceiling. The faces were pallid globes, expressionless and alike. That in the center spoke: "You have proven yourself a worthy courier. Place the scroll before us and your task is done." However, to Jad that calm, reasonable voice carried a vaguely disturbing note.

"I have questions, " the apprentice summoned the courage to say.

"Retain them, boy," came the prompt answer. "You'll find all such preferable to answers. Now give us the offering and you will be sent back."

Offering? Didn't they mean *message?* This choice of term unsettled Jad, but he moved forward nonetheless. He would have dropped the parchment below the hovering heads, as bidden. if the scratch on his left arm had not suddenly deepened into a nasty cut, from which blood erupted with force.

Jad staggered but somehow managed to hold on to the scroll. Though his blood was flowing red, as the stream splashed to the floor it became light blue—the color of his own world's sky. And out of that growing pool formed a familiar shape.

Light vanished. He felt as if the room spun around. A whispery voice hissed through the thick dark: "I am what you call the snake-bird. We must help each other against these servants of evil."

Jad heard his voice rise in anger to reply? "No, the Three Lordly Ones can't be evil!"

"These are not the Three," hissed that dark, hidden other. "Look!"

Light again soaring from the flickering of large torches in sturdy iron holders showed that there was no blood on the floor. Jad's arm was bare of any wound. He hardly noticed this, for the scene before him held his full attention. Three grotesquely fat men squatted atop an emerald dais in a chamber now possessing recognizably gray walls of stone.

Jad, in turn, became aware of a wet stare from three pairs of eyes. Three mouths wetly formed his name with a silent pursing of lips. Three sets of hands held up stubby fingers, like white slugs squirming up to the light from unknown subterranean depths, to gesture at the young magician before them.

"They are servants of Thotharn, and I am their enemy," said the snake-bird, whose reptilian head touched Jad briefly on the shoulder.

These three creatures—who had once been men—sat in monastic simplicity, wrapped in robes of coarse, dark fabric, even though they owned the riches of a dozen worlds. Their real wealth was displayed in folds of flesh bulging on bloated frames.

Theirs was a corpulent perfection, their obesity an art. Jad recognized them in all their perverted strength—did that knowledge flow from the snake-bird?

The first once had a name Illmur—and he had clung to his goal in life with genuine dedication: a full knowledge of nature. The second's had been Enir, desiring the role of rulership: those Machiavellian satisfactions that went hand in hand with political intrigue successfully accomplished.

Though the first two had forgotten their names, the third remembered his—Aickly. His end was to have been a pious one. With the powers that would be his, he wished to invoke the wisdom of gods, to serve others. He longed for sainthood.

Each in turn had betrayed his dreams, settling instead for raw dominion, living increasingly hidden lives of quiet malice. Their satisfaction became to hate life for itself alone.

He who had been Aickly spoke now: "Kesnir never had a message for us. You were a gift, young Jad, a sacrifice. We could have taken you at any time, since you entered our domain, so long as you gave up the scroll that is your master's petition. We could have fooled you into doing that, but each obstacle you overcame made you ... tastier."

"You could have tried, you mean!" From within himself Jad found defiance.

"We were planning on giving power to Kesnir in return, a small matter for us, but much for him. We were going to provide him with this." The eyeballs of the wizardly triumvirate rotated to the left. Propped against the wall was revealed—as though it had just appeared—a scepter unlike any other. Golden, granted a pair of gossamer wings, it was crowned with a winking diamond, and it hummed as if a honey-mad bee. "With this, he can easily master his world."

Jad held tightly to the scroll, as if to a lifeline. The exchange of it for this golden weapon must never be. He understood now that the art he himself sought was not a means to an end, as he had always thought; it was the end. For the true magician signs of worldly wealth were transitory, bait to catch the human fly. Kesnir wanted the same thing these three monsters sought: power over other people's lives.

The voice continued: "With this, he would begin by laying waste the Fair at Ithkar, and incidentally demolishing the temple shrine. All that would be left standing would be the remains of a tower dedicated to the worship of Thotharn."

Jad had no doubts about the location of that structure. "I always half suspected I was a pawn," said Jad slowly, "but I told myself that was simply the lot of any apprentice. I wouldn't be one forever. I never guessed that death was to be my graduation."

"But you are fortunate," said the one who had been Illmur. "Your new ally saved you from that."

"Who *are* you?" Jad turned to demand of the snake-bird. The answering whisper came promptly: "I am a wizard from a dimension bordering yours. Certain animals in your world are eyes for us. So we learned that Kesnir would have threatened us, after enslaving his own kind. I almost arrived too late, and the journey cost me dearly. I was so weak that I almost didn't survive. If I had not had the remaining strength to place my mark on you, I could not have shared this quest! Thanks be to the Three Lordly Ones that we prevailed!"

The one who had been Enir complained, "You, 'snakebird,' have interfered with us too often in the past. We thought we had made it impossible for you ever to annoy us again. I now call you by your real name, which is—" There followed a series of syllables so alien to the human ear that Jad could not remember them a moment later. "And you were not allowed to enter this land directly. Thus you needed this inept boy to serve you!"

"Which he has done well," retorted the snake-bird.

The central figure spoke again: "We should have detected an enemy wizard when we cast the spell of darkness over the fair. Kesnir was our servant, but not a good one, for he detected no danger near this boy. We let Jad through the gate. Kesnir did not even tell us of any difficulty, no doubt fearful that any such disclosure would jeopardize our agreement. The fool! Well, we shall do nothing to save him from his current danger. As for you"— the unspeakable name was somehow spoken again—"you must have flown a good distance away after your arrival. If you had been anywhere near the fair when we looked, we would have sensed you."

"Oh, yessssssssss," the snake-bird hissed, "I traveled far. And now Jad and I will travel back to his world...unless, of course, you three care to contest my will in this?"

Beady eyes regarded Jad from fleshy depths. The central one was spokesman for all: "We only enjoy that which comes without effort. Begone!"

The hissing voice of the snake-bird reached Jad instantly: "Hang on to the scroll."

The return journey was quicker than the first. It was instantaneous.

They no longer were at the fair but rather inside Kesnir's own tower, that monument to his ambition standing alone among jagged rocks near the Galzar Pass. Jad had no idea how much time had elapsed in that other place. All he saw was that he and the snake-bird were now outside the door to Kesnir's library, a secluded room at the top of the tower.

"Now comes the time to use the scroll," hissed the snake-bird, jerking a claw toward the rim of light beneath the closed door. "Read the words that burn," came the whispered order. Jad did not hesitate. Kesnir's warning did not deter him now. Opening the ancient roll of paper, lad saw the letters clearly, even in the darkness, glowing in blood-red light.

Because at the fall of night Master Kesnir had redoubled the magical protection surrounding his tower, he now wrought his incantations in imagined safety. Uttering the final words of a spell, he started for the door. As his hand closed upon the latch, fire flickered from that along his arm. He leapt back, wildly rubbing his tormented flesh, crying out hoarsely.

The door burst open. lad thrust his way in, accompanied by the snake-bird. "Never thought you'd see me again, did you? After what I have been through, I'm happy to return a little taste of it to you."

Kesnir did an uncharacteristic thing. Instead of casting a spell—which Jad expected—he threw a knife. The blade was aimed at the lad's throat, but the snake-bird intercepted the steel with a whistled cry, and it clattered to the floor.

Jad pointed the scroll at the cowering Kesnir. "I called you master and served you as best I could. You know well my reward."

"Thotharn forced me," Kesnir protested weakly.

"Thotharn forces no one," retorted the snake-bird.

"You made the decision," growled Jad, advancing on the old man. "I was to die for your gain."

Kesnir's lips twitched; he plucked at the folds of his robe. "It was an experiment," he said lamely.

"You have told me so many lies that I have lost track of them. You lied when you didn't even have to! I don't see how you could call that horrible dungeon those three fiends live in a palace."

"I would have lived in a palace." The old man's voice betrayed his loss of hope.

"You've lived long enough," said Jad, hurling the scroll to the rough stone floor. The snake-bird laid its head on lad's shoulder and wrapped its wings around the young man's body as the apprentice pronounced the words that were written on the parchment.

Gasping for air, Master Kesnir clutched his chest as if trying to make his heart continue beating. One word escaped his lips "No!"—before a crackling flame licked out from his chest, bathing his shaking body with eerie phosphorescence. The skin on his already emaciated frame dried to the fine, tight leather of a mummy.

There was the odor of decay. The mummy became dust, which blew out of sight. All that was left was a robe, looking as clean and unwrinkled as it if had been washed and hung out to dry. The jewels on the loose circle of the belt continued to glow with the magical energy that had failed to save Kesnir's life.

"You're getting better at spells," remarked the snakebird approvingly.

"Thanks to you. I don't suppose my magic had anything to do with your arrival in the booth?"

"Not really."

"I didn't think so," said Jad, picking up a nearby sack and beginning to fill it with implementia from Kesnir's collection, first among them the belt.

The snake-bird observed this procedure with its cold eyes and at length enquired, "Taking over your inheritance?" Jad nodded and started selecting volumes from the library shelves as his companion continued: "I've seen magicians in many life forms, and I think you have the makings of a good one. You'll have to study long and hard, especially now that your teaches is gone."

Jad paused long enough to say, "I've had enough. I'm giving up the art, aside from the few tricks I've already learned. Those are all I'll need for a good show in my booth. My own booth."

The snake-bird made a sound that Jad later realized was a laugh. "Maybe I'll visit you at Ithkar Fair again. It won't be any time soon. I need a good rest."

"If you do," said Jad, "how about another spectacular entrance? But don't bother scratching me. From now on I'll take my chances without that mark of yours. It's useful, but it also hurts!"

After a moment, Jad added: "I'm glad that we met. I was at last part of something important. You used me, of course, but what a difference from the way that Mas ... that Kesnir used me. "

"There is a goodness in you, Jad."

Jad reached over and touched the snake-bird's wing in a gesture of friendship. "Visit again," he said, "and you'll find that I have the most talked-about attraction at the fair." He rattled his bag of makeshift treasures. "These pieces of Kesnir's wizardry will lose their evil power if not kept together. I will sell each one to a different customer."

"Ah," said the snake-bird, fading from view, "you may not be a full colleague of mine, but you are no longer an apprentice."

Robert Adams was one of the most interesting people I ever met in science fiction. He was the embodiment of camaraderie. He threw the best damned parties at science fiction conventions. I've been to a lot of them over the years and believe me when I say that no one else came close to this guy.

When Robert and his wife Pam invited me to contribute to *Friends of the Horseclans* I felt honored. The Horseclans series was at its peak of popularity at that time and every author in that book would benefit in many ways. But what mattered most was to write a story that Robert and Pam could enjoy.

Part of the fun of this series was how Robert took the style of high adventure found in heroic fantasy and applied it to science fiction. Rereading the story in preparation for this collection, I can hear his booming voice again and I have to stop what I'm doing to toast his memory in fine Irish whiskey.

My thanks to Pamela Adams for letting me reprint the story here.

High Road of the Lost Men

During the time of the cracking of the plateau, there were many who were cast down, and others crushed by a rain of boulders. The fortunate ones escaped the Night of Fire. Among these were Kindred, Confederation nobles, Ehleenee, Freefighters, prairiecats, Moon Maidens, Soormehlyuhn, and Ahrmehnee, as well as sundry wild animals, birds, and even Ganiks, who lived to see a red sun hanging, as a distant torch, above the dust-shrouded crags of what remained. One survivor was the traveling bard Noplis, who sang of the Day of Doom thereafter.

He had not been the most popular of raconteurs before this time. The night before the disaster, he had been in the camp of Von, a chieftain in the mighty army that was Sir Geros's to command, where the storyteller was recounting deeds of the High Lord Milo. The largest prairiecat in camp, Flatear—so called because his left ear had been broken since birth—had little patience with the artificial means by which humans entertain themselves. Unable to restrain himself, he mindspoke thus:

"Here is a two-leg who speaks at length regarding matters of which he knows less than a cub. Were it not that our Chief Graypaw and Chief Von saw some use in these word mists I'd be for sending all tellers of tales to finish their days in the yurt of the old and sick."

"Hold there, cat-brother," said Von, quick to mediate, for his reputation as a diplomat was as widely appreciated as his record of fighting prowess. "This bard is welcome with any Kindred clan, and we should show proper manners. Though I'll admit"—here Von winked at Noplis—"'tis unlikely he's had firsthand experience with the matters of which he sings."

The poor man could do naught but agree. "Such is my admiration for the High Lord," said he, "that I sought to give an impression, or overview, of his campaigns, without bogging down in details."

"True words from the two-leg at last!" was Flatear's opinion. Noplis knew that cats do not smile, but he could not shake the feeling that this feline's permanent grin was at his expense.

"Relax, friend bard," said Von, slapping the slight man on the back with a force that almost sent him reeling into the camp's fire. "Would seem you've made a conquest of your furry critic, all in all." At this, the company burst into raucous laughter. Noplis was at least a professional. He had the sense to join in.

Von's concubine scratched behind Flatear's good ear, and Noplis wondered if he saw jealousy in the face of the large cat's female lying at the opposite end of the camp, carefully watching all that happened. Perhaps he'd been singing for his supper one night too many, he considered, if such odd fantasies could cross his mind unbidden. Human faces were a better source for potential drama, and he could not help but notice that a dark Moon Maiden watched the fair concubine with undisguised lust. But young Ethera's loyalty was to Von, and even were this not so, she seemed disinclined to frolic with her own.

"My lords," announced Noplis, his voice cracking a bit eyes searching out Flatear, "I'd be happy to tell another tale or cease withal, if such be the camp's pleasure."

"Fair is fair," shouted Terrell, one of Von's most trusted lieutenants. "If Flatear be unsatisfied with two-legged amusement, mayhap he'd regale us with a story of his own?"

Halfway through the night, and surfeited on heavy wine, these clansmen were eager to laugh at anything that was at someone else's expense; the basis of high humor, after all. But Flatear was a wily beast, well versed in the affairs of men, and able to protect his own sensibilities.

The great cat played along: "I've seen horses overcome dangers to test the mettle of anything living, and my catbrothers and I have not spent all our time purring at a warm fire. Any story of the Kindred should be of interest to you, but it's been my experience that two-legs are only interested in other two-legs." This inspired a chuckle or two, but the more thoughtful took a moment to reflect on whether or not they had been insulted. Paying no heed to the response, Flatear continued: "I'll tell of a two-leg deserving a respect from all clan brothers, if Chief Von does not object to being singled out by one who witnessed his bravery."

"Pay close attention, Noplis," said Berti, the cook, "and you'll have something to sing about."

A flicker of resentment crossed the bard's face, but then he realized that one of the convenient things about prairiecats—even a mean old sourpuss such as Flatear—was that they do not fret over ownership of an idea or the telling of an event.

Observing that Von had settled down beside Ethera, a flagon of wine in his large-knuckled hand, Flatear went on: "Von and I were hunting meat where pickings were scarce. Winter was prowling near, our breath was on the air, and frost was on the ground. Most game had gone farther south. There was in the region an old grizzly bear who was faring no better in his search for sustenance. Besides coming across the spoor of the grizzly, I'd also found a pile of dried wolf shit. 'Tis not mutton or pork,' said Von, 'but a sweet find nonetheless, with a welcome odor indeed,' and I was certain that a fine two-leg had taken leave of his senses. He proceeded to make a fire—where would a two-leg be without the flame?—and mixing the old dung with herbs he carried in a pouch, he made a stinking mixture which he smeared over his body."

"Ha, he must have stunk like a Ganik!" said good old Noplis instantly regretting his ill-chosen words as the deafening silence assailed him. Even Flatear was stunned into speechlessness, a rare occurrence indeed.

But once more was Chief Von's reputation for diplomacy proven merited. "A fine jest," said he, "and one you will no doubt add when you make this tale your own. For the nonce I think we'd appreciate the uninterrupted flow of Flatear's narrative, eh?"

With long, pink tongue licking his chops, Flatear turned his baleful gaze from his least favorite bard in all the world and resumed mindspeaking: "When his body was covered in the putrid solution, he spread what was left across the frost-covered ground in the direction of the bear's cave, then we gathered all the leaves that we could find—I still can taste the dry flavor—and Von lay upon the ground. We covered him with the leaves! Then we waited to greet the wind—and it obliged us by blowing in the direction of the cave. I held back, out of sight and scent, ready to help when need be.

"That old bear was as hungry for Von's appetizer as were we for him. With a carelessness borne of hope that he was creeping up on a lone wolf, the bear walked straight toward the hiding place."

There was a low, appreciative murmuring from those assembled. Most knew that Flatear and Von had had adventures together before they came to prominence with the forces of Sir Geros. Some had heard this story before, but all were entranced at the description of their chief's daring.

"One wrong step from that big four-paws and this clan would never have known the guidance of a sensible leader brothers. Von had spread his wolf scent with care, so as to guide the bear's movements. When the bulk of his adversary was directly over the trap, he struck with that very knife you see at his side now. I hurried to join the kill." As Flatear was the swiftest prairiecat of Von's clan, none doubted the speed with which this was accomplished. "I needn't have bothered. With one straight thrust of that long knife, he pierced the grizzly's heart, and his one danger remaining was to roll clear before two tons of bear flesh fell into a pool of its own hot blood! That's an act of bravery you don't see every day, wandering bard. If you sing of that, see that you tell it truly."

Noplis had nothing else to say that night but for repeated thanks at the generous offerings of food he received despite his less than successful showing. At first, he felt some degree of resentment at the brusque prairiecat, but as he thought upon it he came to agree that his critic had a point. There was no substitute for the proximity of a subject. It wasn't that the bard bad not faced danger before—almost impossible not to do in these perilous times—but that when danger loomed near, it was his habit to find matters demanding his immediate attention at a further remove. So accomplished was he at running that it had once been suggested that he might be of immeasurable value as a messenger, but when considering the brief life span offered by that profession, he concluded that he should apply his abilities to the more demanding rigors of the storyteller's art.

The one trouble with excessive caution, of course, is that the world pays no heed to the plan. How could Noplis have foreseen that the very next day he would be caught in the cataclysm of an earthquake because of insane machinations by a few Witchmen? Afterward, Noplis would have to agree that firsthand experience adds a dimension of verisimilitude to one's poetry, but at the time itself, the only thought in his head would be a raw animal urge to survive at any cost.

It began when the earth shook. That part was bad enough, but what bothered Noplis the most was that the horizon he was observing to his left suddenly wasn't there any longer. The ground was shaking badly by then. Unable to flee, stomach turning over, Noplis prayed that the world return to normal. Instead of tranquility, he was rewarded by fireballs that tore through the sky in his direction. His instinct to throw himself to the ground was thwarted by the ground moving away—or at least so it seemed, as the earth crumpled beneath his feet. One white-hot rock, the size of four horses, came close enough that he felt the heat on the back of his neck before the stone plunged into a nearby stream. The steam resulting from that immersion drifted in Noplis' direction, reducing his visibility. This was just as well, as he had no desire to see more, but the hot mist made it difficult to breathe.

By now, the shaking of the ground was at its peak. Somehow Noplis avoided broken bones, although he almost fell into a crevice that yawned open a few feet from where he was trying to maintain his balance. In the midst of chaos, soaring above the cacophony of roars and rumbles below, and the whooshing of rocks above, was a veritable symphony of mindspeak. The bard was one who had the gift developed to the point where he could farspeak. The telepathic cries for help added an unusual counterpoint to the earthquake: Real voices could not be heard for more than a few seconds, constantly drowned out by the grating of stone on stone.

After several attempts to stand, Noplis finally gave up electing to remain flat upon the ground. He was too tired to get up again. Idly he wondered if the earthquake might not be a punishment for the previous night's artistic inadequacy. If so it didn't have a very good aim.

The ordeal finally ended. Opening his eyes, Noplis discovered that he was alone. Not a tree was standing as far as he could see. Near at hand was a huge slab of basalt and granite with streaks of red and brown slashing across it—mineral deposits that made him think that the earth was bleeding. The air was full of dust, enough to make him cough as he rose woozily to his feet.

And there was something else amiss. He didn't even notice It at first, but when he did, it sent shivers down his back. The symphony of mindspeak was over. He heard not a note, not a word, not a yell. There were no voices.

His head felt as though it had been split in twain. Even so he called out … and the sound of his own voice hurt his temples. For many lonely minutes he cried out, alone. Then came a welcome, mindspoken greeting: "Stay where you are. I can reach you."

Right away, he knew who it was. His fellow survivor was Flatear.

Whenever he was bored, the Judge would look at himself in a mirror. In fact, he kept mirrors expressly for that purpose. Today he used a round one, with a yellow stain across the top, and one crack running diagonally across the pitted surface. It was one of his best mirrors.

The wrinkled face returned his gaze with large, watery eyes, the color of an eel—his healthiest feature. The protuberance extending from his right cheekbone was still growing, almost imperceptibly lengthening since last he'd taken inventory. It curved over the pulpy indentation where once his nose had been, almost seeming to be a replacement for that organ. He referred to the growth as a beak when he was around the Ganiks, pleased that his head had a birdlike appearance. That, combined with the feathers growing from his thin neck to his twisted shoulder blades, completed the image by which he convinced them that he was an emissary of their god, Ndaindjerd. The absence of a nose had proven a positive boon where that stinking rabble of ghouls was concerned. How convenient for him that they would not eat bird or beast.

As for the rest of the Judge's visage, it was a catalogue of the putrescent, scars of old diseases making a cobweb pattern across his forehead as if they were strings to a mask. Blue-gray flesh hung upon the skull without softening the contours beneath. He had no chin to speak of, the ears were barely noticeable lumps, and his mouth was the worst part: a few lonesome teeth, sharp as fangs, at odd angles to the ugly purple color of the gums. *Yes,* thought the Judge, *you're looking good.*

He thought of himself as Lucifer, fallen from the Center, the ultimate renegade of the Witchmen. He liked that label for his old associates precisely because they hated it. Witches. Across the sad and empty centuries, he had come to loathe his colleagues far more than he did their various enemies. The world the Center would recreate was not for him, any more than was the world that did exist. So he had aspired to something else that would be entirely his. Experimenting in secret with a genetic project of his own, he had secured the services of an assistant named Davidson, a biochemistry man.

Weary of transferring from one body to another, jealous of the High Lord, Milo Morai, and all others blessed with natural longevity, hating everything built by Dr. Sternheimer, the Judge had projected his mind into an artificially developed body. The good news was that the experiment worked, in that the transfer was complete, and that the body did not age ... exactly. The bad news was that he couldn't get out of the- horribly changing, ever more freakish shell. He'd bought himself a ticket to hell.

When Davidson saw the results of the experiment, he made the mistake of saying: "You are a great man, Doctor. Unwilling to settle for the status quo, you took a self-critical approach, the glory of our scientific method! Despite a few unexpected side effects, with this experiment you open the door to a renaissance. Surely the time has come to share this good news with everyone!" Davidson might have said more had he not been strangled on the spot. The new body was strong, at least. It was the death of the Doctor and the birth of the Judge.

Under the circumstances, he decided to make the best of his lot. One thing he had learned was that the general population agreed on very little, but an opinion that bound men together, however different their creeds, was: Ganiks are the scum of the earth. Brutish, superstitious, unintelligent, disorganized, disloyal, slavering cannibals ... what possible use could they be to anyone, themselves included? He decided then and there that they were the folk he needed. His knowledge of their customs made it child's play to convince them of his divinity. They learned to call him by the name he had given himself: the Judge. He didn't need many of them at first—just a few bullies and their herds.

On the last mission he had carried out when he still inhabited a human body, he'd stumbled upon an underground base in almost perfect condition. He surmised that the original occupants had suffocated perhaps as far back as the Great Change. It was like finding an Egyptian pyramid with all its relics intact. Naturally he kept the find to himself, never knowing when it might come in handy. Today it was his base. So far as the Center was concerned, he had died in a failed experiment, and taken Davidson with him.

It took months to put his new home in order. If the equipment had not been protected in a virtual vacuum, he wasn't sure what he would have done. As it was, he restarted the generators, turned the lights on, found some functional weapons in the armory, and even discovered Muzak tapes kept in their own airtight container. He reasoned that men of a thousand years ago must have prized this music very highly; because although the Judge remembered a good bit about the twentieth century. he had forgotten other things.

He had the most fun finding his "children," scaring them first, recruiting afterward. It was Home Sweet Home.

As he preened in front of the little round mirror, there was no way for the Judge to know that, elsewhere Dr. Braun and Major Corbett had set off explosive charges at the entrance to caves above a volcano, for motives entirely irrelevant to the actual consequences. So far as the Judge could tell, the earthquake that began to knock down the plateau beneath which resided his base was from natural causes. Then again on several occasions, he had joked to the wit-less Ganiks around him (he enjoyed talking to himself) that were the earth to split wide open, he would suspect that the Center was behind it, because "they have the qualifications once required by the Army Corps of Engineers." At the moment, however, the Judge was shaken as thoroughly as if he were in a Mixmaster, and he watched his precious mirror fall to the floor and shatter.

The Judge's Hold withstood the tremors. It had been built to sur-vive nuclear war…and had. Within minutes, a bruised Ganik crawled into his presence, fell at his feet, and using one of the forms of ad-dress that his teacher insisted upon, said: "Oh, mighty one who looks down from on high, a dozen men were killed in a cave-in in Sector 8."

"Is there other damage?"

The Ganik shrugged. Well, that would do for a no.

"How long will it take to clear the exit?"

"Only a few hours, as you have taught us the engineering ways."

"You're a smart one, all right. Give the order to collect the bodies if they can be located. Waste not, want not. And most important of all, report to me on how many mirrors I have left."

"By Sun, Wind and Steel," said Von, wiping grit from his eyes. "How many can hear me? Call out, or mindspeak!"

"Danger increases," interrupted the prairiecat Swifteye, mate to Flatear. "We must flee the fires."

"I can see that, cat-sister," said Von, "but survivors there may be whom we can save."

White-hot rocks were still falling, albeit smaller ones than before. The fires ignited by these were rushing together, forming one large curtain of red-and-yellow death. The only direction left was off the plateau, but that way was little better than the fire. The terrain was slowly collapsing about them, and no sure footing was possible.

"Follow me, all who can hear my voice or beaming," called out the chief. Swifteye sent out farspeak, and everyone else converging on the spot added his or her beacon to the call: *"Let all who survived come with us."* Every rolling pebble or far-off thunder added to their terror.

Berti the cook had a broken leg and arm and was bleeding from his chest. Terrell's boot splints had protected his ankles from being cracked, he was now withdrawing these bands of metal and using them as splints for his friend's bones, while the cook retained his good humor, between racking coughs by insisting that he was better off than the Moon Maiden beside him, whose wound had been terminal: a broken neck.

When the ragtag group was ready to travel, Von went in the lead, checking out the treacherous incline that dared his every footstep. Swifteye was at his side, sending out messages to Flatear—messages that were not answered. Von was the first to see Blackhoof, a noble warhorse, trapped beneath a mound of earth. Only the head and one hoof protruded, and it was evident from the angle of the hoof that the leg was broken. The horse mindspoke a simple message, all the more eloquent for its simple plea.

As Von started toward the horse, Ethera's arm reached out for him. He had not known until that moment that she lived. "My chief," she said, as he touched her lovely face, so wonderfully whole and unmarked, "no one loved Blackhoof more than I, but you risk your life to climb down there. Would it not be best to end his suffering with an arrow?" She gestured at one good bow and several steel-tipped arrows that had survived.

"My soul flies now that I see you live, dear one. But I will not dispatch yonder steed without a proper farewell. He bore me in battle, and that's an end to it."

Blackhoof's eyes were huge in pain, his nostrils flaring but he beamed an emotion of such pure joy at the coming of a kinsman, and this man in particular, that the danger seemed to recede before such camaraderie. An aftershock surprised everyone, and Von fell, sliding the last ten feet of rock-strewn slope to come up hard against the sweating flank of the horse. Putting out a big hand, he patted the wet, dark neck of his steed. They looked into each other's eyes, and exchanged something beyond words or mindspeak, before Von cut his friend's artery.

The chief of the clan didn't have to make the climb back up alone. Ethera had come to join him, and helped support his large frame, bruised from the sliding.

By some miracle, the survivors made it the rest of the way without further mishap, although Terrell needed extra help with Berti, who was fading in and out of consciousness. Periodically a wild animal would scamper or gallop by them so close that some of the Kindred could almost touch it. The greater fear drowned all smaller instincts.

Only when they'd reached the base of the plateau, and dusk was closing in, did they finally take a count of their numbers. The horses and ponies were presumed dead or run off. From a party of twenty warriors, thirty-five clanswomen, six prairiecats, and five Moon Maidens, their numbers were reduced to eight men, ten women, two cats ... and none of the Moon Maidens. Von kept up their spirits with: "We don't know that any be dead we didn't see with our own eyes. Others may be lost from us, as we are lost from other clans."

"Wouldn't we have received mindspeak?" asked a young girl.

"Nothing is certain," Von insisted.

Further discussion would most certainly have involved plans to reconnoiter and set up camp. Foraging would be no problem with all the fresh food so newly descended from the plateau. Their deliberations never got anywhere, because they were ambushed!

Exhausted as they were from the arduous journey, they still had the strength to put up resistance. The nature of the enemy was so completely unexpected, however, that it delayed their response. The enemy was a short, hairy Ganik, but what was worse, he carried a weapon the likes of which none of the Horseclansmen had ever seen.

The noise from the strange weapon was frightening; in fact, they feared that the earthshaking had started again. Even more frightening were the smoke and sparks thrown by the strange weapon. None of the clansmen were harmed, however; and the idea of a Ganik deliberately shooting to miss was almost as inconceivable as his using an incomprehensible weapon in the first place. Before Von could give orders to rush the enemy, a giant of a man, almost nine feet in height, appeared from around a boulder to their right, blocking their only avenue of escape, since none wished to challenge the unknown weapon to their left.

"Don't give hard time," shouted the giant. "Bigboy hurt when ground shook. Back hurts. Ribs hurt. Don't fight or Bigboy hurt you bad." The Horseclansmen stood still, several thanking Wind that they could understand the strange language of the Ganiks. Somehow it made the bad situation a little better.

"Hey, shaggy man," taunted Terrell. "Aren't you afraid that your demon, Plooshun, will feed your guts to your children for sinning against him? He will strike you down for using that strange weapon!"

Von was surprised. He knew that Terrell spoke many languages, but he hadn't realized that his young lieutenant knew so much about the Ganiks and their strange beliefs. Terrell's words were having good effect on their first captor— the little man was sweating heavily, and cursing in his coarse dialect. However, before they could take advantage of the Ganik's fear, the giant shouted again.

"Leave him be! Bigboy talk now," he cried. "Come. The Judge decide what happens to you now." The Horseclansmen still might have succeeded in rushing the enemy, despite their weakened state. Swifteye mindspoke to Von, assuring him that nothing could prevent her from tearing out the throat of whichever Ganik he assigned. Then suddenly a small army of Ganiks appeared, creeping forth from among the shadows.

Von broadbeamed a silent warning to his people: "Had they meant but to kill us, they'd have done so ere now. Wait for a better chance. We'll bathe the ground in blood before we enter their stewpots, I promise it." His people, more angry and frustrated than exhausted, eager to meet a tangible enemy after enduring natural disaster, agreed with their chief. They would bide their time.

So it was that Horseclansmen were introduced to the peculiar legal practices of a renegade Witchman.

The earthquake had played a game upon Noplis. Miserable over his latest performance, even obsessed with it, all the forces of nature had risen up to remove the would-be entertainer from his no doubt grateful audience. At least, it felt that way to him. If the earthquake were a bard itself, it could have done no better than to leave the singer of woeful tales with but one companion: his most severe critic, Flatear. Surely the earthquake had too blatant a sense of irony to be a first-rate artist.

"Sacred Sun is barely visible," observed the prairiecat. A feline's excellent night vision was of no use in a sky befouled with debris. On top of that, the big cat was continually sneezing in Noplis's direction.

If the Witchmen were driven to learn the secrets of how mutant telepathy worked, it was something taken for granted by the Kindred, as natural a part of their daily lives as breathing or eating. Something about the earthquake was interfering with both the cat's and the bard's farspeak, although they could still communicate one-to-one. Was it magnetic disturbance released from the earth? Was it smoke and dust in the air? Whatever the reason, long-range telepathy was impeded in this locality.

"Last mindcall was over there," observed the prairiecat, his good ear twitching in the direction of the wall of rock that had been vomited from the bowels of the plateau only a short distance from Noplis.

"Then we can't follow," moaned the bard, "and the other way lies certain death." The wall of fire was a safe distance from them, but how much longer that would last neither dared venture a guess.

"We must find another mute or perish," said Flatear, already moving with grace and precision along the side of the new barrier. "There needs be an opening somewhere," insisted the cat. "Help me look, two-legs."

Well into the afternoon they searched, the inferno blazing nearer, a reminder of the urgency of their plight. There was little opportunity for the exchange of bantering words, and no breath was wasted. Search, hope, move swiftly ... or die.

It wasn't exactly friendship that was formed by the ordeal, but there was a lessening of enmity. Treating a companion as an enemy is a luxury that danger does not allow.

The fire crept nearer, hot and hungry for them; the wall of rock remained impervious; the great eye of the sun was ever more occluded by the shroud of dust. Over and over, Noplis said a silent prayer: *Let me not lose courage before this brave prairiecat.* He had not even noticed that his prayer had changed from a screaming, hysterical plea of: *Get me out of here!*

They found a dead mountain pony. All they could salvage of his gear was a coil of rope. As Noplis worked at this task, he received a surprise. "Two-legs," beamed Flatear, his tongue hanging from his mouth, perspiring, "if I don't have another chance to tell you truly, I like one thing about your songs."

"You do?" asked Noplis, a sudden weight removed from his heart.

"You pronounce names correctly."

The Judge had been in a bad humor. Earthquakes tended to do that to him. The last occasion he had felt this way had been four hundred years earlier, during the submergence of Florida. Between his phenomenal memory and love of history, it was natural that he had made the joke: "Well, this will put a real dent in the tourist industry." Alas, the technicians at the Center were no more likely to laugh at his humor than were the vaguely human forms that made up his new community, but at least he didn't expect anything from the latter.

His mood was instantly lightened by glad tidings. "We've found Milo-men," said a Ganik, using a term that his master had taught him.

"Splendid! At times like this, nothing is so welcome as a trial."

The closet in which he kept his handmade vestments and favorite mirror (a floor-length one) had survived the tremors. Hurrying there, he eagerly reached out clawlike hands to fondle a moldy black robe—yet another reason to be grateful that his olfactory senses didn't work—and draped the garment around his bony frame. Even more absurd was the makeshift wig, once the working end of an old mop. One had to make do. Outfitted in the splendor of his office, he proceeded to court.

Bigboy always had trouble entering what had been the operations room a millennium ago but now served as the courtroom. Once inside, there was ample room for him, but despite a sloppy job of enlargement, the doorway still represented a tight squeeze. When there was to be a trial, the giant knew that the Judge would insist on his playing the role of something called "Abailiff." Bigboy stood close to the olive-green wall, and waited.

Von was standing in the center of the room. When he closed his eyes, little sparkles of light danced behind the lids and his balance was uncertain. How delightful it would be to simply lie down upon the hard floor ... and sleep forever. With a start, he opened his eyes. No, he would not succumb through force of will he would be as formidable as ever. The enemy would not claim his people or himself while life beat within the veins of any member of the Horseclans.

Yet no amount of bravado could completely remove the sour memories of being brought into this Hold. Down a flight of metal stairs, assailed by the stench of shaggy men's unwashed bodies—so concentrated that it was indescribably revolting—they had been forced to march. Their weapons and supplies were dumped in a pile at the foot of the stairs. The scene was bathed in merciless white light from the ceiling. This made it more of a torment, because it was all too easy to see the shaggies clearly; and some of the Ganik females, with an even more noxious odor than their mates, poked and prodded them. Disarmed and surrounded by such as these, Von had to wonder if he had made the right decision. The machine gun remained a persuasive argument.

The sound of a dull thud attracted his attention. Berti had collapsed at Terrell's feet. "Let me help," said Ethera, but before she could take a step, a swarm of Ganiks surrounded the fallen man and made off with him. There was nothing Terrell could do, but he tried nonetheless. His attempt to hold on to his friend was met by one hamhock of a hand lifting him by the shoulders. Bigboy was the most alert Giant Von had ever seen.

"Bigboy!" shouted Von. "Tell your chief Judge that should butchery befall our kinsman, he will answer to me, anon."

The laughter of these part-men is said to be able to curdle milk. Von had to agree with that assessment as he listened to them snort and snuffle in a parody of mirth.

When the Judge entered the room, there was an end to levity. Von could see why. On first sight, there was little that could be more startling than the human monster that addressed the assembly: "In honor of our guests, I will speak in their language. Translations are available upon request. Now, which one of you is the theologian?" Nothing amused the Judge more than bafflement on the part of others. "Come, come, I mean the one of your group who knew about the Ganik demon, Plooshuhn, that forbids these, my children, to smelt ore or work bronze."

Bigboy pointed to Terrell, who maintained a stony silence. "That's all right," said the Judge. "I don't expect cooperation. Are you impressed that my giant remembers you? Of all the monsters I've collected in Muhkohee lands, he's my favorite. He's smarter than my children, if truth be told." Here the Judge pointed first to a small band of large, hairless

Ganiks, then to the far larger number of small, hair-covered ones.

"What are you?" asked Von, his voice a threat.

"You are the leader of your side; I the leader of mine."

"Ganiks don't have leaders, just bullies, until they fall and are eaten," said Terrell.

"Bravo, the scholar breaks his silence. I am flattered that you contribute to the discussion. I am their leader. Perhaps it is due to my being a special envoy from one of their gods. Why, I even chat with Kahlohdjee, chief of their deities, now and again. The future belongs to the Ohrgahnikahnsehrvashuhnee. As for this theological question, you don't appreciate the subtle nuances of High Church Ganik worship. They are not allowed to make anything interesting; but they are allowed to steal and use interesting things made by other people. In the long-ago days, they would have found many professions suited to these nice distinctions."

Swifteye mindspoke to Von: "A Witchman."

Von replied: "He could be naught else."

The Judge grimaced, his version of a smile. "By your face, Chief Von, I sense that I'm failing to convince you. Very well, I'll admit the truth: I am their leader because I am inedible. You asked what I was. I am no man, so behave."

"What would you have of us?" demanded Ethera.

The Judge hopped over to one of the Ganiks, reached out his long fingers, and triumphantly held up a squirming white louse. "See this? Their bodies are crawling with fleas and lice. They like it because it's what they know. I want to broaden their outlook, bring out their potential."

"If you choose to live with Ganiks, you're lower than they," said Ethera.

"A woman who thinks that she thinks! Very good. I am an expert on parasites, my lady, and eminently qualified to lead. A thousand years ago, they had their own city—Paris I believe it was called. But enough history."

A fat Ganik entered the chamber—Von wondered how long the man could avoid being on the menu of his leaner brothers—carrying something wrapped in a brown cloth, a red stain on the bottom. The Judge was given the now dripping parcel, which he opened to reveal a gelatinous object that he held with some difficulty between two fingers and thumb, as it was very slippery, and took a bite out of the end, pulling and chewing before he could separate a piece of the rubberlike material. There was a splatter of blood.

"I won't watch," screamed Ethera, covering her eyes.

"May I have a knife for this?" asked the Judge of the room at large. "A Horseclansman's liver is tasty, but tough." He looked straight at Von and said: "I've picked up a few bad habits, but when in Rome, do as the Romans. Of course, you don't know anything more about Rome than Paris, but—"

Von's discipline was forgotten as one of the prairiecats, Firepaw, leapt toward the Judge and bit into his arm with three-inch-long fangs. Once again, it was Bigboy who was first to react, throwing the cat with such force that its back was broken, legs quivering in death agony.

Several things happened at once: Swifteye pleaded for a command from her chief, flashing the thought that she had seen Chief Graypaw crushed beneath a rockslide, and was sure that Flatear was dead, as well. With no reason left for living, the cat wished to join the fray, but with the sanction of an order. Von was busy commanding that everyone resist temptation, Swifteye included. Until that machine gun was neutralized, he couldn't take the risk. The Judge was as concerned over the gun as anyone. "Stop!" he shouted, as the nervous Ganik debated whether or not he should open fire. "Look!" cried the Judge, holding out his mangled arm to reveal that not one single drop of blood had been spilled. Several Ganiks fell on their faces in reverential swoons. "This always impresses them," said the Judge, winking at Von.

"It's fascinating to watch your expressions as you play with telepathy," said the Judge, his mouth full. He had retrieved his meal from the floor. Swallowing by turning his head at an inhuman angle, and jerking his head in the process, he continued with better enunciation: "No need to be upset. You'll end up as your friend did. They won't eat your dead cat, of course. They really aren't the best mate-

rial with which to bring back civilization, but they are all I have ...
and they do obey."

A chair was brought for the Judge. When he was sitting, the folds
of his robe draped about him, it appeared that his vulture's head
and emaciated arms grew out of a black obelisk. "Please note, if
you will, the oversized head of the Ganik. You'd almost think that
he had some intelligence. The overbite of his teeth helps to correct
that impression, as it makes him appear a caricature of the stupid.
Here, then, is the creature I would bring into civilization. To accomplish this unlikely task will require repeated demonstrations of
the court's justice."

Pointing at Terrell, he accused: "You, theologian, have Ahrmehnee
blood. I can spot it a mile away. Have not the Ahrmehnee collected
heads from these poor brutes? You Chief Von, chieftain of this sorry
little band, have you not put Ganiks to the sword more times than
you can count?"

Von would rise to a mental challenge as readily as a physical one.
"Aye, I've slain shaggies, and proud of it remain. Any who eat their
own kind are less than men." Von pointedly looked at the soggy
mess in the Judge's hand.

"Thank you for your candor," replied the Judge. "One of the first
things you must learn about Law, however, is that only the accused
is on trial. The moral stature of the authorities should not be brought
into question, as the inspiring edifice of our justice is based on the
rule of Law and not of men." Munching heartily upon Berti's liver,
the Judge persisted in the high purpose he had set himself.

"My dear barbarians," said the Judge, "it's not your fault that you're
uncouth mutants. You can't help misunderstanding that you have
wronged the Shaggy Men, as you call them. The reason that my
children are better able to appreciate a proper ethical code is that
they have a custom neither practiced by you nor by the fools at the
Center. They are cannibals. Since justice is a social concept, and
rests on the welfare of the group, the highest form of justice places
the group first. Cannibalism is not the death of the group; it is merely
rough on individual members.

"You may wonder what role the court has to play. When individuals in one group suffer at the hands of individuals from another, the
barbaric response is to bring in the notion of honor, and reduce the
grievances to an individual level. True justice requires a disinter-

ested third party to find one group entirely guilty, exonerate the other group entirely, and make certain that individuals suffer the penalty. It may be pointed out that I am not an entirely disinterested party, but to this I can only respond that nothing is perfect. We have a system that works."

"You speak wickedness and call it justice," said Von.

"From your point of view, that is a reasonable conclusion. Mine is a loftier perspective. All of you must die for your crimes against the Ganiks. True, the Ganiks have committed crimes as well, but they are not on trial; and no social purpose would be served if we viewed the case in individual terms. Coming at it from the other direction, it would surely be utopian to put everyone on trial at the same time. No one would be left to discharge the office of executioner." The Judge swallowed the last of his macabre meal.

There are silences so complete that they defy the idea of sound. The courtroom was like that for at least a minute, until the low growling of Swifteye begin to fill the spaces.

"You mutants cannot learn the error of your ways, but you can serve as an object lesson to my children. The superstition of an earlier age's inquisition was to save the individual's soul. A later age was enlightened enough to admit the real objective of torture: welfare of the greater number. Your deaths will be of benefit to these poor shaggies on two levels: spiritual and physical."

"'Tis justice when two-legs eats two-legs," Swifteye beamed to Von, who could only nod in grim agreement.

"Civilization was never an easy proposition. It prided itself on having left the primitive rites of sacrifice behind, and clucked its collective tongue over the simplistic codes of savages. Lord Milo believes in personal responsibility. How terribly unsophisticated of him! Justice teaches that the more people alive, the greater the number to be sacrificed! One virgin girl sliced open to irrigate the crops won't do for a civilized man. Such a paltry sacrifice is an insult to his morality. For him, whole cities must be reduced to fertilizer and not to grow food, but to feed his guilty conscience. The best enemy is one in which you see a reflection of yourself. We are all killers in here. That is a fact. Another is that there is no higher morality than joyous self-sacrifice. Despite my lofty ideals, I fall short of this noble ideal. For me, the best I can accomplish this evening is to sacrifice the selves of others."

"Do we eat now?" asked the ugliest Ganik present.

"Trial first, eat afterward," answered the Judge, annoyed.

"You eat now," said the Ganik, pointing to the sticky remains of the poor cook smeared on his master's hands. The Judge believed in spare the rod and spoil the Ganik. Producing a standard military-issue revolver from within the folds of his cloak, he blew the sucker away.

This was not a smart move. It wasn't that other impatient ones were sidling over to the fresh meat; the problem was a crack that appeared in the ceiling. Some plaster fell in the center of the room.

"It appears that I've been overzealous in disciplining my children," muttered the Judge, appraising the damage above. During the course of his heated monologue, he had completely forgotten about the earthquake. Now he remembered why he had been leery of the machine gun being used earlier. He'd thought the threat of the weapon, and the greater numbers of his gang, would be sufficient to stave off trouble. He was wrong.

Von realized the same danger from the machine gun at that instant. He needed no further impetus. Nerves on edge, black rage surging up in every breast, the Kindred attacked. As the Judge hesitated between a response to the assault and giving an order to the gunner *not* to fire, the panicky Ganik with the machine gun went berserk and started firing with wild abandon.

Given the respective positions of everyone there, and the full clip of ammo in the machine gun, the one crazy Ganik could have wiped out the entire population within the courtroom. For one mad moment, the Judge tried to shoot his own man with the handgun, but Swifteye was already all over him by then, and his gun went sliding across the smooth floor. The barrage of lead was terminated from an unexpected quarter.

"Flatear!" shouted Terrell, first to see the welcome sight, as the great prairiecat sprang from the corridor into the chamber of death, ripping the gunner to shreds. Close behind came Noplis, arms full of weapons taken from the pile near the stairs.

The fat Ganik who had brought the Judge the liver slipped on blood, the leavings of that unwholesome supper. With an animal cry to match a prairiecat's yowl, Von went for the man, and was busy snapping the fellow's neck before Bigboy could come to the rescue. The befuddled giant was not acting swiftly now; he could not figure out which way to turn. Finally deciding that the Judge was important, the giant pulled Swifteye away from her prey, and was about to throw her, as he had done with the other cat, when Noplis shot an arrow into the huge man's unprotected thigh. The giant never finished his maneuver, and it was Swifteye's turn to attack.

Elbowing the frenzied animal away, and finally backhanding her so that she was temporarily stunned, the giant began loping toward one of his human opponents. But it was not the archer he sought. The leader, Von, was his target. Bigboy roared a death curse.

As the towering shadow fell across the Horseclans chief, it was joined by another shadow: Flatear, finished with the Ganik, enraged over Swifteye, sank his claws into the giant's hide. Von turned to help his feline ally, but already the giant had fallen, and Flatear was keeping him prone as sharp fangs worried at the gore-bespattered flesh of the big neck. Another shadow fell across the duo, and Swifteye joined her mate in the kill. As Von saw the blood drain from Bigboy's face, he returned to his primary objective: passing judgment on the Judge.

The Judge was not thinking about Von. He was staring with mounting horror at the ceiling. More cracks were appearing. Bullet holes in the walls were also producing a spreading network of cracks. It just wasn't fair. The base had survived up until now. He hadn't even picked his jury yet.

With any degree of military discipline worth the name, the Ganiks would have prevailed. But the Judge had only been able to give them the appearance of soldiers. The reality was somewhat different. The shaggy men and women were fighting each other in a frenzied scramble to flee the base.

Von's flesh crawled as he wrapped his hand around the Judge's scrawny neck, lifted him from where he'd lain, and forced him back into his chair. There were puddles on the floor, but the liquid wasn't blood—rather something like stagnant water.

With his other hand, Von lifted a sword, grateful to Noplis for the delivery, and drove it straight through the Judge's midsection, until the blade embedded itself in the floor. Amazingly, this did not kill; but it pinned him to the spot. Picking the wig up from where it had fallen, Von replaced the smelly thing on the Judge's head, then stood back, admiring his handiwork. The human monster struggled, as would a bug, in a vain attempt to free himself.

"'Tis no easy task returning your 'justice' in full measure, but methinks your throne will do as a place to receive it," said Von— and then he laughed the loud, clean laugh of certainty.

The Judge screamed. It was part cackling, part retching. Slowly the room was emptied of Ganiks, and Von's warriors gathered around their foe. "Ere now, words came from you like maggots from a carcass," said Von. "What have you to say before we quit this stinking hole?"

"If you kill me, you'll remove the moral conscience of the future. I was only practicing the politics of reality, but it appears that I should have made a better choice than Ganiks. We might work together! What do you say we build a new society together?"

Noplis, suddenly more useful than he'd ever dreamed possible, figured out how to turn off the lights, and they left the Judge babbling in the dark about how he could have been a contender.

They tasted good fresh air when they stepped outside, and even the leaden sky of the first night after the earthquake appeared to them as the open vaults of paradise in comparison to where they had been: Von insisted on waiting until the final cave-in, rumblings of which increased as a promise that the Judge would retire soon.

Noplis finally had an appreciative audience for his every word— and the story was all the better told without his usual singsong delivery. He described how Flatear and he had found themselves caught between the flame and the rock, when they reached the edge of a cliff. With rope they had taken from a dead mountain pony, the bard was able to swing down a dizzying ten feet to a ledge below; then the rope was tied to Flatear, and the prairiecat was able to jump within a margin of safety. As night set in, they used some of the rope to make torches, but this light soon proved unnecessary as they detected an illumination showing through a small hole in the rubble.

Clearing this away, they found a tunnel that led directly to the base. They took the short cut. "The spoor of so many unbathed two-legs was a better guide than the underground sun," mindspoke Flatear.

Like corpuscles in a vein, they were drawn to the source of continued life within the ruined plateau, and came out in a place with a sign that read "Sector 8." Dead Ganiks were in there, but living ones were clearing an entrance to get at them, no doubt with feeding in mind.

"We heard your mindspeak," said Noplis, "a relief after the long silence. We followed that, and in so doing, learned of your peril."

"Could not you have let us know that you lived?" asked Ethera.

"Originally, communication was impossible. The earthquake cut us off in ways we do not understand. When we found you, anon, and you were in the clutches of these vermin, we trusted in stealth."

"Guards there were in the man-tunnel," said Von.

"Flatcar killed the Ganiks in the corridor," said Noplis, respect for the feline infusing his voice. With the discovery that his telepathy was working again, the prairiecat had delighted in clouding the minds of the guards, one at a time, before dispatching them.

Suddenly there was a loud crash from within the mountain. Dust puffed out the entrance to below. Several men cheered.

"The Judge is dead," said Ethera.

Then Noplis said what Flatear would later agree were the wisest words the bard had ever spoken: "Thanks be to all the gods."

When Ed Kramer suggested I might want to do a story for an anthology he was putting together with Michael Moorcock, he didn't have to ask twice. For one thing, I had done it before when Bill Ritch and I collaborated on an Elric story for *Tales from the White Wolf*. That book had been one of the most successful offerings from White Wolf, so I wasn't surprised that Ed would want to try something in the same vein. But where before all the stories revolved around Moorcock's most famous character, the albino warrior, this time the door would be thrown open to all his characters.

Which was fine by me! Because Elric is not my favorite Moorcock character. I prefer Jerry Cornelius. Hell, I'm one of the few people in the world who actually likes the film version of the mod hero's adventures, *The Final Programme*. Plus I've always regretted that I was too young to get in on the New Wave in science fiction. By the time I became a pro, science fiction had turned against the New Wave with a vengeance.

Well, here's the story I wanted to write in those swinging times. Austin Powers will understand.

The Last Short Story Writer at the End of Time

Jerry Cornelius laughed. He stood naked at the edge of a swimming pool and surveyed a long line of beautiful, young bodies, male and female, none under fourteen and none over twenty-five. The boys were on one side and the girls were on the other. Above his head of raven-black hair the dark night of inter-galactic space looked down—or would look down, metaphorically speaking, if there were any stars to play the role of white, bright eyes. But there were no stars in the great void between the galaxies. There was only The City.

As he dived into the pool, Jerry saw his perfect profile reflected in the polished mirror on his right. The boys and girls voyeured his smooth descent, their eyes sparkling and grins shining. They all waited to serve his every whim. Some were more skilled in certain areas than others. Cheri, the honey blonde sitting at the edge of the pool near him as he broke surface and gulped air, was especially adept at servicing him in zero-g. Most of the others did better in gravity situations like this one.

With a quick kick, he darted over to Cheri and grabbed her ankle and pulled her in. He'd show her a thing or two about gravity. She giggled. He didn't like gigglers but everything else about her was up to spec. The absence of bathing suits facilitated his inspection.

Physically, Cheri reminded him of an actress back on Earth who had driven him half crazy one very hot summer in London. The actress had short brown hair instead of long blonde tresses; and she had a genius IQ. Cheri had a brain the size of a dime. There were other differences. Cheri was single. The actress was married and her idea was to tease him to the point where he wanted her desperately—at which point she'd dump him and take all the excitement back to her husband. The actress was every bit as disingenuous as she was monogamous. Cheri never tried to fool anyone about anything.

As he slowly fucked Cheri, Jerry remembered more about the actress. Her friends called her J. Jerry called her J. At first he didn't care that she was the type that liked to flirt and then bring up the marriage if things went too fast. But he surprised her when he came off like a reactionary and told her that since she and her husband had decided not to have children their marriage was not genuine—it was only serious dating. Persistence paid off in the end for Jerry Cornelius, as it so often does. But once he made love to J, he felt resentment for what she'd put him through instead of satisfaction over his victory.

The other side of the equation was reached here and now in the cool, blue pool, as the precious bodily fluids of Cheri and Jerry mingled without any risk of disease or possibility of pregnancy. Somewhere in his old Earth memory, the lyrics of a George Harrison song played: "I've got my mind set on you." The only trouble was that he didn't have his mind set on any of the pliable, nubile, pneumatic, perfect playmates of The City. He had sufficient will-power to say: "Boredom, I Defy You; get thee behind me and wear a condom."

But there was no excitement here. No love. No hate. Even the copious supply of drugs left something to be desired.

When he was completely honest with himself he admitted that the only true love he'd ever felt was for his sister, Catherine. When they made love together it was something special, a true union of spirits where happiness of the one depends on the happiness of the other. God, he missed her. He was afraid of forgetting how to love. And how to hate.

Come to think of it, the only true hatred he'd ever felt was for his brother, Frank—a worthy target for Jerry's really neato state-of-the-art needle gun. But then, Frank felt the same about him. Loving sister. Hating brother. Incest is best.

The last time he'd seen Frank, or someone who looked like Frank, they had a big argument about Reality. Frank had become a movie producer using new computer technologies so that he could eliminate the need for dealing with real actors. But he didn't want to do away with actresses; and then he discovered he could make actresses (in all the meanings of the word). He'd started with the amusing idea of taking classic movies where the only inadequate casting was the producer giving his girlfriend the starring role—and then Frank would simply recast the female lead with a top star from the past! Next he used nanotech to bring all his facsimiles of yesterday's glamor girls to life. The last anyone had seen of Frank, or the person who looked just like him, he was being dragged off by walking-dead zombies who used to belong to the Screen Actors Guild.

This was just around the time that Jerry started having serious problems with Reality.

Jerry preferred not thinking about metaphysical questions when he could swim instead. Unfortunately, he recalled that he had a business meeting that he couldn't avoid.

He envied the lifeguard because the man didn't need to leave the pool area. The lifeguard was Julius Caesar. It made perfect sense. The Romans were deeply into pools. Jerry waved and Julius waved back. They didn't exchange words. The Roman only spoke Latin. Jerry could speak the tongue but he didn't like the sound of the words.

Jerry nodded to one of the girls, a cute little redhead named Noelle. She knew what she was being asked. As she kneeled before the stately figure by the diving-board, lifted his tunic and went to work on his lyre, the Conqueror of Gaul convinced himself that he was receiving his reward in the afterlife. The great Caesar smiled at the large, onyx column that rose out of the pool. The thing was perfectly timed to his passion. Surely this proved that he was among the gods. He believed that The City was Olympus. The design of the pool area reminded him of the stately architecture of Rome. Of home.

As Jerry climbed on top of the column and rode it up to one of many walkways criss-crossing The City like a spider's web, he thought that the best parts of the City were vintage London, circa the 1960's. He passed right by H. P. Lovecraft who preferred the portions that were most like Providence, Rhode Island. They waved at one another as Jerry walked along the silver bridge right past the little wooden balcony where HPL sat in a rocking chair, drinking a temperance beverage.

Jerry was on his way to visit the Editor who thought the best part of the City utilized the Manhattan motif. Jerry understood the man's point of view. The Editor thought the entire city was New York and all the strange buildings were recent additions from European and Asian immigrants. One man's decadence is another man's exotica.

"Have you finished the story?" asked the Editor as Jerry kicked in the door to his office. The Editor had a name. His friends called him

George. Jerry called him Mr. Bossum-Bozzele, or Bossum for short.

Jerry hissed an answer: "There are no stories any more, Bossum, you old bastard. No one reads. Besides, we've run out of endings."

"Don't talk that way," he said. "Here we are in the most important place we could possibly be, at the center of the universe! Why, that fact alone should inspire your best work."

"I'm not a bleeding author," said Jerry, not moving, dripping on the carpet.

"The perfect qualification for a writer, old sod. The only good leader is someone who doesn't want to be. Well, the same is true of an artist or a lover."

Jerry carefully studied the emaciated body of Mr. Bossum-Bozzele, and decided the man was not well qualified to discuss the subject of love...unless, of course, he had a whole lot of money, the truest proof of a sensitive and caring soul. Jerry changed the subject: "How do we know we're not part of some insane movie script, online Hell with plenty of connectivity activity and no screen needed to micro-soft-core-porn-toon net surf 'till you drown? How do we really know that all the cities of the Earth have been placed at the center of the universe?"

"New York, my son," said old George. "Any editor can tell you that New York City is at the center of the universe. Always has been! Look here, I have proof."

Bossum opened his desk and removed a recent issue of his little digest-sized magazine, *Boring Stories*. The cover art was a bland depiction of a wheel with a sad-faced woman standing next to it. The execution was flat and amateurish. Then he removed a second magazine, a vintage copy of a garish old pulp magazine with bright colors and a nearly naked woman struggling against a giant centipede. The art was dynamic and professional. The red block letters screamed that this was an issue of *Exciting Stories*.

"What's your point?" asked Jerry.

Never ask an editor that question. The man took a deep breath and got right to work: "Back in the good old days, we put out a magazine full of cheap sensationalism geared to a juvenile, but intelligent, audience. There was no mystery about why we sold a lot of copies. Today we put out a serious and responsible magazine. We are very careful not to offend anyone, with the exception of people who prefer the older magazine."

"So?" asked Jerry, already bored.

The Editor waved the smaller magazine over his head as if it were a bloody trophy of battle. *"Boring Stories* stays on the stands," he crowed, "month after month, year in and year out. Diminishing sales mean nothing. The magazine refuses to die. It wins the Praying Mantis Award every year, given by the Eco-technic League of Wymin and Male Persons for a Holistic Future. We know that the old magazine would sell ten times as many copies but we refuse to bring it back. We run *Boring Stories* at a loss!"

"I have forgotten what all this is supposed to prove," said Jerry.

Bossum was steadfast: "It proves that New York City was already at the center of the universe before we were moved from that benighted continent back on Earth. We could do anything we wanted to do! Reality was ours to command. We could make the molecules dance to our tune long before nanotech was first mentioned on anyone's bulletin board. The point is that science fiction magazines are used by the secret masters of the universe to find out what the masses will accept."

"Oh, not that again," said Jerry, turning to leave the puddle he had made on the floor. "I've heard it all before."

"You can't leave," said the Editor. Jerry turned to give him the finger and saw that Bossum was pointing a needle gun at his writer.

"How did you get that?" Jerry asked through gritted teeth.

"Thought only you and your brother, Frank, had these, huh?" the Editor shot back, metaphorically.

"It's a fake."

"Can you afford to find out?"

Jerry hated Mexican standoffs. They gave him heartburn. "What do you want?" he asked Bossum in a tired voice.

"I want you to meet your deadline. You're the Eternal Champion, aren't you? You can write a novel in a weekend. You've done it under your pseudonyms. The fantasy ontology by Elric; the diet book by Dorian Hawkmoon...."

"That's over," he said, looking down the barrel of the deadly weapon. "I only did that when we first wound up here to find something to do. I'm not interested any more. Writing no longer kills the loneliness. Short stories were my last interest and now I can't write them because I've run out of endings."

"You don't need endings, son! You have questions. All you need to write is a good question. Look at Phil Dick, for God's sake."

"So what's my question?"

"How did we get here?"

"Phil asked a better question: what the hell are we?"

"That's his question. *Boring Stories* wants you to answer how!"

Jerry had to smile and he took the chance of sitting down for the first time since entering the office. "I thought you weren't interested in that," he said. "The way you talk, your flippin' city is so important that it was a cosmic oversight to have kept it on Earth so long. You should be asking why it took so long for the Big Publisher in the Sky to place New York at the center of the universe where it so obviously belongs."

"Don't get cocky with me," said Bossum.

Jerry laughed. "You don't have to worry about that when I'm with an old pixie like you."

The Editor turned beet red. "None of your cheek."

Jerry laughed again. "What is this, *Straight Lines Anonymous*?"

"Will you please be serious? I believe that a super computer has brought us here."

"Been there, done that."

"We could have been taken outside of normal time. Maybe if you would consider doing a little time travel on behalf of the community...."

"Done that, been there."

"Curse you, Harlequin bastard!" exclaimed Mr. Bossum-Bozelle. "Don't you want to help anyone?"

"I thought all you wanted was a short story."

The Editor changed his tone of voice to sweetness and faster-than-light. "Now, now, that's true in a manner of speaking. But you must see that a story by you is a vastly different matter than a story by someone else." The old man raised his eyebrows which was the first time that Jerry noticed he had eyebrows.

"You don't want a story; you want a report. How about I tell you that The City and you are simply projections of my fevered imagination!"

"So you're a solipsist now?"

Jerry smiled. "That implies I have an ego problem. But I'm a solipsist who admits he can make a mistake."

The eyebrows went down again. "Don't you want the same thing we all do? Answers to our real problems! Wouldn't you like to know if your sister and brother are still alive?"

"Shut up."

"Well, I mean available to you in this particular area of space and time."

"I won't tell you again."

The Editor could see that the naked man sitting in the damp chair meant what he said. "This is getting us nowhere," he editorialized. "Are you going to cooperate?"

Jerry decided that New York editors were real enough for him and expressed his insight with, "I'll be happy to stick that weapon up your ass."

Bossum shook his head. "Very well, I must seek assistance." A trembling finger depressed a button on the desk—the first time Jerry had noticed the button—and a young, butch woman with dark hair and wearing black leather strode into the office.

"Is this your problem?" she asked, sticking a thumb in Jerry's direction.

"Allow me to introduce Elizabeth the Second," said the Editor. Jerry recognized the face of his Queen, young as she was. He judged her to be about the age she'd been in World War II. He remembered reading in the definitive study of her life, by Sir Thomas Cron, that she'd fallen in love with motorcycles during the war. People who showed up in the City tended to be at their ideal age and doing what they most wanted to be doing back on terra firma. Which led to some interesting speculation regarding Julius Caesar....

"Are you going to be trouble?" she asked, looking him up and down in a manner that had his undivided attention. He started to show excitement at the prospect. "That will be enough of that," she said sternly. "We are not amused." And with that, she put him firmly in his place.

"I keep spare clothes around here somewhere," said Bossum, rummaging around in his drawers and finally pulling out a ring. In a flash, clothes magically shot out from the ring and expanded to a black coat, black trousers and black high heel boots. Jerry dressed quickly. Anything to get out of this office and not come back.

"I'll help you finish your story," said the Queen.

Jerry didn't answer but the Editor encouraged him with a final: "Just send in the manuscript and a disc copy when you're finished.

You know where I keep all my bats for night delivery."

The Queen's motorcycle was waiting for them. It didn't have a name, unless being called a BMW Paris-Dakar counted.

"What do you miss most about the Earth?" she asked him as he climbed on behind her.

"Nothing."

She pursued her line of thought as if he hadn't thrown a wet blanket over her fit of nostalgia. "What I miss is the twilight, especially when you're flying in a small plane. All the colors are so vivid right before the sun disappears."

"Good memory," he said, as they started down the narrow path that was elevated high above the ground. The artificial gravity in this part of the City was really good. He knew this from the time he threw one of Bossum's copy editors out the window. The Monarch drove fast but not crazy.

He kept talking, loud enough to be heard over the roar of the engine: "I guess I miss something about living on Earth. There was this atheist who got a show on the telly..."

"In England?"

"I don't remember. It was on Earth somewhere, I'm sure about that. Anyway, he got this show so he could denounce religion. But the funny thing was that he really knew his subject. He complained about liberal men of the cloth watering down the message so as to make it more palatable. He read the Bible and consulted with scholars and became like a Chesterton for Orthodoxy; but he never denied he was an atheist. He thought that by describing the real thing he would bring more viewers to their senses. Before he knew it, he was receiving donations from religious conservatives. They loved him on doctrinal purity so much that they didn't care he was an atheist."

"So what's the point of this story?" she asked over the sound of the motor. "Did he convert?"

"No, but he got rich."

"What is it that you miss?"

"Irony."

She chuckled. "There's plenty of irony here, if you know where to look for it. What's the point of being a Monarch in a practical anarchy?"

"You've only recently noticed that," he said, smiling in spite of himself, and holding on more tightly to her youthful figure.

"Yes," she admitted, "but I'm dealing with it more effectively since reading *The New Libertarian Manifesto* by Samuel Edward Konkin III. He applies the free enterprise model to situations you'd never imagine. So I'm going to market the royalty idea the same as any other product! I'll bet you I sell a lot of subscriptions to my newsletter."

"Your attire is ideal for such an enterprise," said Jerry seriously.

She proved herself worthy of her crown. "You're not suggesting that what I'm selling is similar to ladies of easy virtue?"

Jerry exercised his tremendous will power and kept from laughing. "No, but I once read a pamphlet by someone named Michael Moorcock suggesting that the world's oldest profession is on a higher moral plane than royalty. In fact, I'm having trouble remembering anything he did not put on a higher moral plane..."

He could feel her body tighten at the mere suggestion. "We do not care to hear any more of such unpleasant sentiments."

"Fair enough," he said, copping a feel on the pretense of not falling off the bike. "You'd probably do better sticking to the Konkin pamphlets."

They rode in silence until they reached their destination. The Queen wasted no time getting away from him once she had deposited him, most ceremoniously (as would be expected) in front of The City Library. This building was more than immense. It was interdimensional, with certain floors extending into other universes. It was also much bigger on the inside than it was on the outside.

"Good morning, Doctor," said Jerry Cornelius as he passed by a remarkable personage who was tall and thin and wearing a scarf way too long for him.

"Have you seen a police call box around here?" asked the man.

"I'd look for that in a more British section, if you know what I mean," answered Jerry helpfully. "This is a very New Yorkish entrance here."

As if to prove the point, two thugs emerged from the building and grabbed Jerry. "Come on, you," said the burliest of the characters.

"Bronx accent," commented the Doctor. "Friends of yours?"

"Research assistants," said Jerry as the goons hustled him inside.

"You've got that right," said the other man who was smaller than his partner. "We've got our assignment and we're not letting you go until you've finished your short story."

As they half pushed him down the corridor, Jerry wished he had his needle gun. He would have tried to relieve the Editor of the gun in the office except that he was sure it wasn't real. The Editor didn't know where Jerry kept his personalized weapon hidden. The other needle gun was with Frank, in whatever part of the Universe now claimed him.

"What's your training?" Jerry asked the burly guy.

"Ph.D. in English Lit," the man answered gruffly. "What's it to you?"

"Thought maybe you'd have a clue of what I might do," he answered.

"Ha, he rhymes," said the other guy.

"Don't kid me," said the burly guy. "I've seen your file. All you care about nowadays is getting laid. You're a disgrace to your profession."

"Whatever that is," said Jerry under his breath.

"See what I mean," said the burly guy. "Mr. Bossum-Bozzele was right about you. We're going to help you see your duty so you can finish the damned story!"

Jerry was always enough of a bastard to take full advantage of any opening. "Do you really mean what you say about help?" he asked in his most desperate tone of voice.

The big, burly, tough Ph.D. was dumb enough to say that he was very much in earnest.

"So, tell me," continued Jerry, smelling blood, "what do you think requires more attention span from our good citizens, a novel or a short story?"

The hallway they were walking down was real long, so they had plenty of time for a discussion, complete with nuances.

"Uh, novels," said the man.

"I thought you'd say that," said Jerry Cornelius. "I used to think that. But the answer is counter-intuitive. The longer the novel, the more space there is for the reader's consciousness to become unfocused. Why, he can read for whole chapters before he notices that he isn't paying attention and then he can return to the text and plow forward, content that he'll eventually pick up the thread again. A short story doesn't provide that kind of space."

"Space," said the dumb one who was not burly. "We're in outer space. I know what you mean."

Jerry and his real listener ignored the interruption. Jerry continued: "A short story, on the other hand, is supposed to make one point or establish one mood. If you lose contact with the narrative, you can't hope to just wander around in it until you can make sense of it again. You need to start over. So it turns out that a short story requires more attention precisely because it is so much shorter."

"I see," said the big man. "You've made a good case for sitting down and finishing your fucking story right now, instead of dropping your responsibility to The City and running back to the pool where you'll waste your time...."

"Fucking," Jerry finished helpfully.

"What do you mean by responsibility to The City?" asked the dumb guy.

"I'll tell you," volunteered Jerry. "Your boss believes that I release certain energies that hold our little pocket of humanity together when I finish anything artistic—novels, equations, campaign speeches, poems, paintings, costume design, Letters to the Editor...."

"We get the point!!!" said both of the goons in unison.

This was a good place to take a break because they had finally run out of hallway. There was a door at the end of their quest marked Berchtesgaden. The door was guarded by a dinosaur—well, by a teenager in a green dinosaur suit who removed the head and held out a claw to shake hands.

"I'm a big fan of your work," said the young man.

"Pleased to meet you," said Jerry, shaking hands, and pleased to be meeting anyone other than the goons. "What's your name?"

"Chris Ray."

"What's your job?"

"I wear a different monster suit every now and then; and I guard different doors in the Library where unfinished stories are on the other side."

"You've done a good job," said Jerry, patting Chris on his blond head. "Get yourself a coffee or something. I'm going in there and finishing *my* job."

"Yes sir," said the guard, a tear in his eye—so proud was he to meet his hero.

"You two can go find a dance hall," said Jerry to the goons.

"Are you implying there is something intimate between us?" asked the burly guy, growing angry. The little guy stared stupidly.

"No, but I must ask you a question," Jerry persisted. "Do you think any object described in a story must play a central role in the narrative?"

"Huh?" they both replied.

"Like that stuffed hammerhead shark on the wall over there," said Jerry, pointing. "I only now noticed it." The burly guy thought for a while and then answered. "Well, yeah, if you draw attention to something like that, then you ought to use it, I'd say."

"Seems like a dumb rule to me," said Jerry, "but if you insist, I'll do as you advise."

Without further ado, the Champion Eternal, defender and destroyer of justice, and his own severest critic, took down that mighty fish from the wall and beat the two goons soundly about the head and shoulders. With cries of dismay, the two men ran down the hall, content to put distance between themselves and their mighty attacker. At that moment, Jerry lost all faith in them as they obviously did not intend to stay by his side until the story had reached its terminus.

Then he took a deep breath and pushed the door open. He didn't know if he was leaving Chaos for Order, or the other way around; but he did know the bracing wind of certainty as he entered a world where he could feel something powerful and clean: the emotion of pure hatred.

He saw Adolf Hitler right away. Not Fred Hitler or Albert Hitler or even Peter Hitler. It was definitely Adolf. Accept no substitutes.

Jerry didn't like the man even a little bit. Especially not when the German dictator was in a festive mood at the Berghof. Beyond the broad windows, Jerry could see a Mercedes pull up. The automobile was every bit as black as the clothes Jerry wore. Impulsively, Jerry looked down at his chest and saw that his clothes had changed. They were still black but now he was dressed as an SS officer!

A couple got out of the automobile and came up to the door. It was a beautiful day on old Earth, and the mountains beyond the windows reminded Jerry of a birthday cake his mother once baked for him, and the tender way she expressed her feelings: "Blimey, Ai wondah wot's tuh become of yer bleedin' life!"

Dr. Paul Joseph Goebbels knocked on Hitler's door. The Minister of Propaganda had another of his conquests on his arm, a pretty young actress who looked vaguely familiar to Jerry—and well she should. It was J, the actress who had had the unmitigated gall to dump Jerry in favor of her husband. But that had been in the latter half of the 20th Century, in London. What was she doing here?

"Come in, come in," said Hitler cheerfully. "Hey, Doc, you giving Magda the old heave-ho?"

This didn't sound right. Hitler had constantly criticized his propaganda minister for infidelities and indiscretions. Goebbels would never parade one of his conquests right under the nose of the Fuehrer.

And Hitler would never walk over to the woman, take her by the arm and say, "Perhaps we could all swim nude in Lake Konig?" Turning to Jerry, he said, "What do you think of that, young *Obergruppenfuehrer*?"—which meant that Cornelius enjoyed a rank in the SS equivalent to a Lieutenant General.

Cold rage surged through an English soul. For some reason, Jerry understood everything that was being said as if German were his native language. He spoke up: "Adolf Hitler," he said, "you're a Fascist." He'd wanted to say "bleeding fascist" but the word came out without a qualifier.

"Well, now," replied Hitler, "we admit to taking a cue or two from Benito but National Socialism is a major improvement on the Italian model, a purely German extrapolation; something that is uniquely ours."

Jerry had trouble swallowing. He calmed down and tried again: "You're a Nazi!" he said. A whole list of intended expletives never came out of his mouth.

Goebbels and Hitler were laughing. The young officers who materialized (i.e., literally popped into the picture) merely chuckled. J only smiled.

"And the sky is blue," said Goebbels, amiably. "What exactly is your point?"

It was the strangest thing. There was some kind of left-wing short circuit in Jerry's brain. The worst insults he could think of were political. In this context, the words became an exercise in belaboring the obvious.

He looked at J and thought he saw sympathy in her eyes. But that only succeeded in pissing him off all the more. Was he supposed to rescue her? And then listen to a lot of lies about her being a spy for the resistance? Odds were that she was with Goebbels because he was on top and she was hot.

He turned to leave.

"Wait," said J, rushing over to him an slipping something hard into his hand. His needle gun. The real thing. "This is your chance to stop them," she whispered in his ear.

"Oh, get real," he said, spinning around, more pissed than ever. "This is so contrived. How many times can you blow away the same bad guys? I'm tired. I'm going back to the swimming pool. Bossum can stuff his story. I have nothing new to say."

"Hold on there, young man," said Hitler. "You can't just walk out of here."

"Watch me."

"But I'm about to do something terrible," announced the dictator.

"Yeah, yeah," said Jerry, heading for the door and adding: "Have a nice day."

Hitler rushed over to a desk and pulled out several pages of a document. "Look," he said, "I'm about to tear up a treaty. I'm starting to tear it. I mean it, now. Here I go."

"Only you can stop him," cried J.

Jerry spun around, staring hard at the actress. "So I shoot Hitler and all the Nazis in this room," he said. "And then what? We go off to the pool and make out?"

The Nazis stood there like so many props, impotent without a proper cue. "Sounds like a plan to me," said the girl/woman.

"Or how about I kill everyone in the room, including you?" suggested Jerry. "A more downbeat ending. Or we go off to the pool and make love without my having killed anyone. I could live with that because this whole situation is so much bullshit."

"But you created the situation," said J. "It's your scenario."

"Now wait a minute..." began Hitler.

"Shut up," ordered Jerry. The Hitler figure shut up. Closer scrutiny revealed that the dictator had a number of facial features in common with George Bossum-Bozelle.

"You're just mad at me because I wouldn't betray my husband for you," lamented J.

"Right," said Jerry. "The fate of civilizations, the life and death of millions, finally hangs on who is banging who."

"Whom," suggested Dr. Paul Joseph Goebbels.

"I'm not sure," said Hitler. "It's so hard to know the answer to these sort of questions. The power of the will needs to be augmented by the best grammar texts we can seize in our push across the English Channel."

"Only you can stop them," J repeated, eyes wide, lips trembling.

"Kill a little; love a little," said Goebbels, helpfully. "That's what it means to be fully human."

"And then, in your twilight years, there may be a quiet moment for regret," said Hitler.

"I thought you blighters wanted to be more than human," said Jerry Cornelius.

"We can't help but do that," said a nondescript soldier from the back of the room. "Every time we pull the trigger we feel a little of the god stuff."

"I know," said Jerry. "But placing The City in this place, that's real god stuff." He didn't wait for them to ask what he meant. Their window looked out onto a verdant Earth not yet awash in blood. The door Jerry opened was for him alone. J could not join him on the other side. J wasn't here.

Back in the hallway, he sat on the floor, leaned back against the door. The guardian wasn't there. Jerry was alone.

He remembered the last conversation with J back on Earth. She balked at one of the group sex scenes. He didn't try to force it on her. He didn't think less of her. But the idea of it upset her badly.

"Are you trying to elevate promiscuity into a universal principle?" she asked in an angry tone of voice.

He knew that she was religious. He wasn't trying to make fun of her with his response: "If loving more than one person is considered promiscuous, then what does that make God?"

She didn't respond well. She could have made a joke about who did Jerry think he was—but then perhaps she was intimidated by his initials. Normally, he could turn any setback to his advantage. But she was one who got away.

He'd done everything, seen everyone, traveled in time, died and been reborn. He'd been a priest, a spy, a scientist, a politician, even a writer. And he knew what it was like to deal with the world from both sides of the great sexual divide.

With that kind of expertise, he did better than most humans at keeping the most dangerous force in the universe at bay: the Romantic impulse. He'd seen its power to lift and ennoble. He'd also seen its far more common application. He wouldn't be the last bit surprised to learn that humanity had destroyed itself on Earth.

Mankind's executioner would have to be a Romantic.

Thoughts of mass destruction brought him to the odd realization that J had done something to him psychologically. She'd gotten past his defenses and done a bit of sabotage. How very annoying. He regretted not having pursued her back on the old mud ball. Now there was no way of knowing if she was still alive.

He had to deal with the here and now. Jerry Cornelius would never tell the Editor that no one could undertake the man's suggested explorations. This was because The City was already at the end of time. Jerry didn't doubt his ability to escape from the situation. That was the sort of thing he did best. But when he left The City, he would not be coming back because there was no way to return.

The City was not a good place in which to make lasting attachments. But it was just fine for a long vacation. Bossum-Bozelle thought that if JC kept cranking out stories it would somehow postpone the inevitable. The poor bastard didn't understand that Jerry Cornelius was only able to do the postponement bit for Jerry Cornelius.

Meanwhile, there was another task to perform. Something far more important than finding the right ending to a story:

Jerry Cornelius laughed. Cheri waited for him at the center of the zero-g playground. He pushed off and reached her on his first try. As he held her close, and then a lot closer, she knew what it meant to be at the center of the universe.

I've lost track of how many times I've been told this is the most remarkable title of any of my stories. The title was a collaboration between filmmaker Fred Olen Ray and myself when I was co-editing *Weird Menace* with him, a tribute to the 1930's shudder pulps. Part of the fun of this book was coming up with the most outrageous and politically incorrect titles possible. The stories almost seem anti-climatic after the titles.

In the heyday of pulp magazine horror, the magazines known for weird menace filled a very specific niche. The stories suggested a supernatural threat until the climax when there was a naturalistic explanation. Usually it turned out to be a sadistic madman who got his kicks from torturing women. As might be imagined, this kind of story has fallen out of favor in our timid times. I was proud to help Fred do a book that featured two new stories by a past master of the form, Hugh B. Cave.

(Incidentally, this was Fred's favorite of my stories until he saw "Chump Hoist" which will be in the carnival anthology *Strange Attraction* around the time this book is out. Fred and I both did stories for that one.)

Blood Orgy of the Swamp Butcher

The hoot owls were quiet the night young Sally-Mae had her tongue ripped out. Before my father died, he used to tell me the critters sort of know when human badness is in the air. There's a kind of stink that goes with human violence that you never get from animals. It's like the animal kind of killing is clean by comparison. My father had been a sophisticated man for Mossburg, one of the few educated people in the county; but he had a deep respect for folk wisdom and local ways. I missed him.

I'd come home from the state university for the summer. My mother wanted to see what we could do about establishing a trustworthy reputation for me before I hung out my shingle. Mossburg had only one lawyer. That should tell you how backwards we were. When I was finished with my schooling Mossburg would have to put up with two of us.

The sheriff was a good man but he was terribly afraid of leeches. He'd fallen in the swamp when he was little and been covered in them. Nobody was surprised that he didn't mind letting his deputy handle the swamp detail. But the sheriff could only delegate so much authority in the case of a brutal murder! The cops knew Sally-Mae had had her tongue ripped out because that's the way they found her head. The rest of her was presumed to be scattered about the swamp.

Sally-Mae had been a very pretty young woman of twenty. She'd been popular, but not as popular as she might have been.

Her character flaw was that she gossiped. Most of her victims had taken it fairly well. Once she got a reputation for a loose tongue, everything she said was taken with a grain of salt. Like most gossips she would embellish the truth if it made a better story.

The first day I went to Ben's Barber Shop, the subject was whether the person who had turned the young blonde into bits and pieces of rotting meat had been someone she had spoken of truly or told lies about. We all sort of took it for granted that a murder so violent had to be very, very personal. We all took a lot for granted until we learned better.

Already practicing for my future vocation, I kept my mouth shut.

The only other young man there, Dick Pierce, reminded everyone that Sally-Mae had been a hot young thing, passed around from man to man like a good bottle of Jack Daniels. Old fashioned sexual jealousy must not be ruled out. Ben, whose place it was, agreed with such time honored wisdom as he sharpened his long razor with a *snick-snick, slap-slap* sound. Hot young stuff might drive a certain kind of man to deeds of desperate savagery. But so could being lied about at the wrong time, or even the wrong truth coming out at the right time! There seemed to be as many motives as there were mosquitoes around a rain barrel.

As if on cue, Old Martha was at the door of the distinctively male establishment. Old Martha was a colored woman who lived in a shack in the swamp and hadn't been seen in years (some folks thought she was dead). When I was ten years old she'd scared me so badly I'd had nightmares for a week. She hadn't meant to, of course. She was still in her sociable phase in those days and would wander around town selling herbs and potions...and little shrunken things.

In keeping with the good old days, the first word out of her mouth was: "Voodoo!" The little kid in me wished I could push the word back past her withered lips. Backward places seem to keep people on retainer to make sure they stay backwards.

"White trash tramps," muttered the old crone, "wa'll be sacruhficed to *et* thet waits in thuh deep swamp."

The other men in the barber shop listened to the old woman's ravings in a way that seemed as if they respected her; but later I realized they were just too bored to challenge her. They left that to a rash outsider, or someone who'd been away from home long enough to play the role.

"Are you saying there's a monster in the swamp?" I asked.

The way the crone chewed her gums and stared off into space made me think she might have forgotten my question but finally she managed to spit out: "He's the devil's own."

"Then why doesn't He want virgins?" I asked in what I hoped sounded like a triumphant tone of voice. The old crone was unfazed. Her laugh was a hoarse croaking but it was a laugh just the same. She said something in the cajun tongue and hobbled off back toward the swamp.

The barber made a friendlier laugh and patted me on the back.

"What did she say?" I asked him, in hope he'd have some inkling.

"Nothing much," he replied in good humor, "except that maybe you're too young to understand that sometimes the devil wants the women sent to him to have a little experience." All the men smiled at that, including me. But if a gore-bespotted claw could have risen up from the grave and wiped those smiles off our faces it couldn't have been a more grim awakening than what transpired in the next week.

Two more bodies were found: teenaged sisters. These weren't as mutilated as poor Sally-Mae's, but their eyes were gone, and the way their soft, white limbs had been arranged together in lascivious embrace left no doubt that the murderer was trying to tell us something. Certain internal organs were missing as well. This was an important clue but I didn't recognize it at the time. What the new slaughter told us was that Sally-Mae's gossiping tongue had probably not lost her the pretty head off her shoulders. The two sisters had been popular with everyone. And like Sally-Mae, they'd had boyfriends. These murders were definitely beginning to take on a Jack-the-ripper flavor.

More than ever I was thankful my girlfriend, Julie, hadn't been able to get time off from her job to join me for the summer. Whatever was going on, it clearly wasn't safe for a young, nubile woman to be in these parts until this evil was found and stamped out.

By this time the barber shop had become detective's central. Everybody exchanged theories there—even the sheriff, in a sly sort of way. I was too busy following down false leads in the light of day to notice dark truths that only speak to us in the shadows. I completely discounted the supernatural, even after the bags of chicken entrails were found near the bodies of the latest victims. The vulture feathers didn't tell me anything either. I could more easily believe that Martha was sneaking over to the scenes of carnage and leaving evidence of black magic. The almost unbelievable savagery ruled out any thoughts that a frail old woman was the killer; but I couldn't shake the thought that under her mumbo-jumbo the old colored woman knew more than she was telling.

Meanwhile, all the time I'd spent at the state university—where professors constantly condemn the love of money—had convinced me that no one does anything except for money! I couldn't imagine a motive that didn't have a dollar sign in back of it. So I studied the economic history of the swamplands. Who would stand to gain if people were afraid to go near the swamp?

The problem was that there were too many possibilities. I researched land developers, of course; but there were also ecologists who wanted the wetlands left alone. Then there was the tourism business that would want the wetlands open. There were farming interests who must keep their eye on the water levels of the swamp. I even got to wondering about buried treasure. As I say, the common denominator in all my thought was money.

"You remember witchcraft talk from when you were a kid, don't you?" the sheriff asked me the morning he let me come with him on his investigation. Normally he wouldn't have invited me, but this was swamp detail and his deputy was down sick with a fever.

"'Course I do," was my answer. I really did, too. You don't forget someone like the voodoo woman.

"What bothers me is the massive loss of blood," said the sheriff. "Bodies in a swamp will just naturally leak and drain and the mud will suck up the fluids, you know. The way Sally-Mae was torn apart, there wouldn't be much blood afterward. The Johnson twins weren't messed up as bad, but their necks and breasts were cut up bad enough so that the blood would run out quickly."

"Hell, sheriff, are you suggesting vampires or something?" I asked. "That sounds like Martha's voodoo rubbish."

The sheriff had driven as far into the swamp as he intended to go by car. He came to a stop, turned off the ignition and inclined his head in my direction. "Son," he started off, and his voice didn't sound the least bit fatherly, "the first rule of police work is to keep an open mind. Just when you think you have all the angles figured out is about the time you're in for a surprise. There's more motives for crime than you'll learn from law books."

I was ready to argue that it all depends on which books you read but the sheriff was already out the door and headed for Martha's shack. It had rained the night before and the swamp looked a lot better than it smelled. Standing pools of water were not yet covered with scum or leaves. Everything had a fresh washed quality.

The idyllic scene did not last long. The sheriff stumbled to avoid stepping on a dead squirrel and the way he staggered afterward suggested the very strong possibility that he'd been drinking on duty. He gestured for me to follow him and we approached old Martha's dilapidated cabin. No sooner had he opened the door than a new odor assaulted our senses. It took a moment for our eyes to adjust to the darkness of the cabin and then we wished we hadn't bothered.

Old Martha was staring at us. Strangely her head was the only really undamaged portion of her anatomy. Beneath her curiously calm face, spread out like an open starfish, hung the remains of her body—crucified on the rotting boards of her cabin wall.

"Jesus Christ!" exclaimed the representative of law and order.

"That pretty well lets her off the hook," I said.

"Don't be disgusting, boy," was the sheriff's terse reply.

Unconscious puns did seem out of place in this charnel house so I said nothing more. The sheriff took a few cautious steps in the direction of the corpse as if he half expected to slip on a blood-slick floor; but there was no blood to be found. "I'm gonna leave this for the boys to examine," he said, peering up at the dead face as if he half expected Martha to speak and identify her killer. In a way, she did.

"Look here, sheriff," I said, pointing to a row of broken bottles. Wine bottles. And there was something more: someone had scrawled one word in blood down where the wall met the floor, and that word was *communion*.

"Oh, gawd," exclaimed the lawman. "I think I know who's behind this. And it's none of your calculatin' criminals. Old Martha wasn't far off with her warnings and omens. I think the killer's Orson."

That was a name I hadn't heard since childhood. He'd been a big, ham-handed oaf. A school bully. A momma's boy. The one time he beat me up was because I, as a Catholic, was making fun of his rock-ribbed Baptist opposition to wine at communion. He thought any alcohol was the work of the devil. I made the mistake of teasing him about it at school. He said he believed every word of the Bible to be literally true so I asked him why he didn't use wine as the savior instructed in the New Testament. He said his momma told him that Our Lord turned the water into plain grape juice; and passed out the same at the Last Supper. When I asked if it was Hi-C or Welch's, some of the girls laughed. That's when he beat me up. I remembered that while I was bleeding he made some really strange remarks about salvation being found in the blood.

"I haven't heard of Orson in years," I said. "Wasn't he killed?"

"They had him on a chain gang," said the sheriff. "He was a sex offender. His poor old momma died of a broken heart. Orson escaped and they tracked him down to the swamp. Most of us figured he died here, probably disappeared in a quicksand bog. Then again…"

The sheriff started poking around in Martha's bits and pieces of black magic—herbs, roots, dead and dried pieces of animals, and human things, too. "Then again, some of our great minds at Ben's considered the possibility that Martha here might have saved him. I didn't give it much heed until now."

"But if he died years ago," I began, "why would he wait until now to start killing women? And why kill Martha?"

The sheriff kept looking through the old woman's effects. When he spoke, it was as much talking to himself as answering me: "Maybe he wasn't well enough until now. And maybe Martha tried to stop him in the only way she knew how, the same way she might have nursed him back to health, with her herbs and spells. The voodoo trinkets we found near the bodies might have been her attempt to stop or control Orson."

This was too much for me. "Oh, come on, sheriff. You don't believe in that supernatural crap, do you?"

He looked me straight in the eye, and if he had been drinking I sure couldn't tell it now. "I believe in murder," he said.

We went back to his patrol car and he started to radio in his report. We both had a good idea of what a massive search it would take to uncover the secrets of the swamp. If crazy Orson was living back there in a fetid hole somewhere, it would be no small task just to find him. I couldn't even imagine how to start. The sheriff did better than that. He had a plan.

"Just stands to reason," he told a bunch of us later that night as we returned to Martha's shack, "that if Orson is our killer, we have a very different scenario with Martha than we had with the young girls. She's more or less in one piece, for one thing. If he's still crazy about religion I think he'll return here."

"What about those smashed bottles?" I asked. "Did they mean something?"

"Martha liked to make her own wine. You remember what a temperance nut Orson and his maw were." I nodded. The sheriff went on: "When you find the word, 'communion,' written in blood, it's got to mean plenty!"

So I joined the stakeout. At the time, it was an almost academic exercise for me. I didn't have any personal stake here. I'd never felt close to Mossburg even growing up in the place. This whole gruesome affair was almost like an experiment to me, and a way to exorcise any childhood demons still oppressing my soul.

When the hulking form of Orson approached the cabin with a dripping bag held in his pale, white hands, I felt the same cold shudder everyone else felt. The brute must have found another victim. Well, there was nothing to be done but bring justice down on Orson's head and make sure he felt the full severity of the law. Meanwhile, curiosity bubbled up in me like gas after a bad hamburger. What personal demons were driving this creep?

Orson was most obliging. He began declaiming in the direction of the shack: "Martha, you were a *mambo*, a bad voodoo woman, you cured me good but you're still bad. I'm showing you the real magic, deeper magic than you'll ever know for it comes from Our Lord. Communion isn't about wine or grape juice. It's about blood. I take blood from young women like the ones He walked with and tried to help. And some of their flesh I take. You wouldn't see the truth with your dead pieces of animal. He doesn't accept sacrifices like that anymore. You wouldn't understand; but you still helped me so I will help you."

The moon had risen and we could see him take something white and round out of his dripping bag and place it on the ground. "I'll bring you back, Momma Martha, only if you promise to stop trying to fight me with your pieces of animal. We must prepare for the End of the World and that means we must keep taking communion. You'll have to promise ..."

We never did find out what the final promise might have entailed because the sheriff's deputy, perhaps not fully recovered from the virus that had been plaguing him, pulled the trigger on his revolver. What happened next was a symphony of gunfire. Not one gun or rifle wished to be left out. I don't doubt the sheriff would have liked to have been the conductor of the performance, but there was nothing he could do except wait for the barrage to end.

Which it finally did. The pale hulk that had been Orson was surrounded by a red haze. Before he dropped to the ground he reached

toward the moon with his great paw of a hand, made a strange gurgling sound, and was gone. One by one, his executioners came forward to survey their handiwork.

I hadn't fired but merely observed. The deputy who pulled the
trigger couldn't resist making a joke of it with: "You won't be making a case out of this one, counselor. The taxpayer can save his
hard-earned dollars." The deputy's heartfelt concern for the taxpayer didn't get through to me that day. I had problems of my own.

The white object on the ground was all too familiar. She'd gotten
time off, after all. She'd come down to Mossburg to surprise me.
Some stupid woman in town had told her that the sheriff and I were
out in the swamp and she'd come looking for me. Julie wasn't a
stupid girl. They should have warned her. Someone should have
warned her.

Orson hadn't mutilated Julie's head, other than removing it from
her body. She still looked pretty to me, that lonely head lying next to
the huge bulk of my old playground bully. For some reason, the
crickets started up around about then. They were answered by the
frogs. A lone hoot owl expressed its opinion.

They invited me to go back with them to Ben's Barber Shop for
the post-mortem. But I didn't go. I didn't need a haircut.

The history of getting this story into print follows an all too common pattern. I write a story for *A*. There are delays in hearing back from *A*. Finally *A* gets around to rejecting my story and is morally offended that I could write such a terrible thing. Along comes *B* and buys the story. And the funny thing is that I would have preferred *B* having the story in the first place.

I originally sent this to an anthology all about witches. It wasn't exactly a cold submission. I was encouraged to submit. What I didn't know was that some of the people behind the project were Wiccans. What they didn't know was that my story makes fun of Wiccans.

I'm sorry, but I find Wiccans hilarious. When it comes to this, I'll just have to be listed as a bigot. Or maybe it's because I dated a Wiccan once. At any rate, I was not really punished for my prejudices because "My Wiccan, Wiccan Ways" sold to *Adventures in the Twilight Zone*, edited by Rod Serling's widow, Carol, and a far more appropriate destination for this story than what I'd originally intended.

My Wiccan, Wiccan Ways

They were using her broom to sweep floors. This was the final insult! The broom had seen her through far too much to meet so ignoble an end. It had brought her into this world.

At first she hadn't realized that she was in a new world as the broom had picked up a sudden burst of speed and plummeted down beneath the clouds that were white on top and gray underneath. When she saw desert country spreading out below her black, pointed shoes, she had thought the problem was a simple miscalculation, or maybe too much body fat in the flying spell. Her objective had been London.

The sun glinting off the sand had made a thousand, flashing diamonds that were temporarily blinding, adding to her irritation. Impatiently, she had cast a spell and accomplished more than she intended. The gray clouds turned black and exploded into a torrent of rain. She got the worst of it, of course...and being drenched did nothing to improve her disposition.

The next thing she knew was that a gust of wind knocked off her hat and sent it spinning away from her clutching hand, a black funnel tossing in the maelstrom, a dark triangle growing smaller and smaller until it landed unceremoniously in a puddle of water. There were a lot of puddles, dotting the landscape, alternating with sagebrush to offer some variety to the eye. This dry, flat landscape could not drink the water she had provided. Ungrateful, dead land, it remained impassive to her curses.

The rain stopped. She knew that her anger was foolish, just as she knew she should be paying attention to her flight instead of craning her head at an impossible angle to look at her damned hat. That's when she flipped over.

Never, never had she flipped before. She had an undignified view of the horizon upside down, the distant hills jagged like knives. As she fell through space, she called out the names of Beelzebub and Belphagor.

Never, never had she been knocked unconscious—not she, not the Grand Witch of All England. She who was uppermost in the Queen's nightmares did not usually lose her dignity by acting like a stupid, common ass. Until now. These thoughts were still racing through her mind as she painfully regained consciousness.

A beautiful young girl, not more than thirteen summers, was gazing down at the old, old woman. The clouds were gone and a perfectly blue sky made a nice contrast to the young one's light brown locks. The sun had returned in all its fierce glory, and it was slowly roasting the witch in her heavy, black garments so that she envied the cool, white gown of the dark haired youngster.

"Are you all right?" asked the girl.

The witch spoke many languages, virtually a requirement of her trade. Although the girl was speaking English of some kind it was an unfamiliar dialect. The Grand Witch carefully phrased a sentence but she saw consternation on the young one's face at unfamiliar terms like "Ye" and "thou" and "shew"! The witch pressed on. Despite this barrier, it wasn't difficult to coax more sentences out of the attractive child. Then, shading her eyes against the sun, and raising herself on one arm, the woman in black used her powers to speak in the girl's idiom. It worked. But even as she felt comprehension flooding through her withered frame, she also felt strangely exhausted by her efforts.

"Can you tell me where I am?" asked the witch, doing the best she could to ignore the dizziness that gripped her.

"In Arizona," said the girl, but seeing confusion in the woman's face amended her statement. "Well, it's Peaceland now, since the revolution. What used to be Southern California, Arizona and New Mexico is all Peaceland. But my mother likes the old names best."

The witch tried concealing her bewilderment and asked as calmly as she could: "What...continent is this?"

"Oh," said the girl. "Oh, my. It's America, naturally. This used to be one nation."

It took another moment before the witch got the point, but then it hit her with a bang: "The New World," she exhaled the words as if she were blowing out a million candles. How the Spanish and the English enjoyed their little games there. But had the child mentioned something about one nation? Inconceivable. Impossible. In what strange universe did she find herself?

She was about to ask another question when the young girl seized the initiative. "By the Goddess, talking to you is as bad as taking one of my *her*story tests. But you need to get out of the sun before we do anything else."

Impressed by the young one's presence of mind and self-confidence, the witch allowed herself to be helped to a standing position. She was pleased that she'd suffered no serious sprains or broken bones. A few steps taken in that baking, oven air was all it took for her to realize how thirsty she was. The young girl could be an accomplished mind reader for she pointed at a cart hewn from some mysterious, light-weight wood and said there was water there. The cart was covered by a brightly colored canvas that would look well at any feast or tournament. Under the welcome shade thus afforded the Witch gratefully stood out of the direct rays of the sun and drank water from an earthenware cup.

They didn't speak for at least a minute, the two of them rooted to their safe places in the small pool of shade. The day was so hot that all objects seemed to shimmer, except the two of them in the little, dark circle—a magic circle, of sorts, to keep the blistering demons of heat at bay.

The witch wasn't happy about what she said next but she made the words come out: "What year is this, young one?"

The girl seemed to brighten at the first easy question: "It's the Year 126!" she announced. The lack of recognition on her companion's face mitigated her pleasure. "I mean, since the revolution. That's how the calendar works."

The witch sighed, a most unpleasant sound. "I know nothing of such matters," she said. "Can you tell me what year it is as reckoned by He Whose Name I Cannot Speak?" She spat at the yellow-brown ground and was partly surprised when the spittle did not evaporate in the hot, still air.

"Oh, you mean the Patriarchal Calendar," said the girl, crestfallen. This was becoming as difficult as a test, after all. "I should know that. We had a recent lesson..." Then she smiled and her eyes flashed, as though the desert had gotten into her after all. "I know the answer! It's easy. Add two thousand years to the new date. We're in the year 2126 A.D., as dated from the Patriarchal Enemy, the Christ!"

At the mere mention of the name, the witch made to cover her ears. "Don't be afraid, young one," said the old one. "Only don't speak that name aloud in my presence. You see, child, I am a witch."

The thirteen year old blinked her great, green eyes very slowly, as though failing to understand. "Aren't we all?" she asked.

"Not another one!" exclaimed the mental health coordinator of the sisterhood, first-class. "Someone will have to inform Our Elder Priestess, Blessed Be."

When Tanith, which was the young girl's name, had brought the sorely displaced Grand Witch of England into the Central Community, the two of them were welcomed by a guild song of sharing. The witch was really too tired to fully appreciate the beauty of the harmony or the simple charm of the lyrics. She was tired because she'd had to help the girl pull the cart all the way back to the human settlement. The girl had been in good condition to manage the cart by herself. She'd gone out in the desert in search of plants, gems and stones that might be used in the craft.

The witch certainly approved of such a reasonably motivated field trip. What she couldn't understand was the absence of any animals to help pull the thing; or failing that, why not use magick? Tanith explained that the first was forbidden as exploitation of animals, and by extension a violation of Mother Earth. As for the second, Tanith put on the gravest expression she could manage, and in solemn tones informed the Grand Witch of England that she obviously didn't understand the true nature of witchcraft. The girl was trying so hard to sound adult that the witch couldn't take umbrage with her.

The subject of magick was suddenly a sore point for more reasons than avoiding an argument. Although they had failed to recover her hat, finding the broom was swiftly accomplished. There were no oaths in all of Hell to express the witch's frustration at holding her favorite broom for the first time in centuries and not feeling the least scintilla of energy coursing through the gnarled, wooden handle. Whatever spell-sodden bitch from her own time had cursed her to this bizarre world, could the creature have also found the power to strip the Grand Witch of all but the most elementary magick? The idea was more terrifying than a gallon of Holy water.

The only good thing that could be said about a long trek through inhospitable terrain was that it took her mind off more serious matters. She'd managed to keep her cool, more or less, through the discomfort, and the syrupy welcoming committee, and even the misguided souls who had promptly placed her broom in the general storehouse of useful appliances. (Clearly these people had no respect for private property.) But the attitude of this inquisitor across from her, feigning exasperation over a surplus of the genuine article in a world of ersatz witches, well, this was simply too much.

Worst of all, the woman looked just like a certain nun who pestered every self-respecting practitioner of the black arts back home. She had the same square, middle-aged face, the same petrified expression of sour disapproval, the same self-righteous smugness. Tanith had hesitated at the door of this personage's inner sanctum, evidently reluctant to abandon her newfound comrade, and at that moment the witch had felt a genuine fondness for the child. She even promised herself to spare Tanith should she afflict the Central Community with terrors worthy of the Old Testament. (The Devil always said that Holy Writ was His preferred inspiration.)

The middle-aged woman peered over spectacles that would not be out of place in old England and asked in the tone of an order: "Wouldn't you be more comfortable if you took off those black rags and put on a nice gown with earth tones, hmmmm?"

This sudden concern for her wardrobe impressed the witch as lacking sincerity. Besides which, one look at the pale gown with a sunflower design so disgusted the witch that she wanted to throw up. She made no attempt to disguise how she felt about it.

"It's no use pretending," said the matronly mental health coordinator. "You just be as anti-social as you like but we'll still figure out who you are and how to help you. We've already filed a report with Coven Watch, just in case you really are a foreigner as you claim. Now, are you suffering from amnesia?"

"What's that?" asked the witch.

"Very clever answer," said the woman, making a note on an unilluminated manuscript. "It's a shame you couldn't be more original about your malady. This has become such a cliche, by now. And don't you poor, misguided women realize you're perpetuating one of the most vicious stereotypes of the old Patriarchy? Frankly, I think the Elder Priestess is too lenient. If it were up to me, I'd drop all of you in the nearest well."

The image of sinking in water suddenly gave the witch a solution to the problem that had been bedeviling her. The Grand Witch of

Spain had done this to her! The bitch must still be angry over sink-
ing the Armada. With the help of a wizard named Thomas, the Grand
Witch of England had done a fine job of protecting England's shores.
Her sister witch shouldn't hold a grudge about something like that.

Her reverie was interrupted by the mental health coordinator
demanding: "So, what's your name dearie? I need it for my records."

Holding up one of her bony hands with the abruptness of a sa-
lute, the old woman announced: "I am the Grand Witch of All England."

The matronly woman across from her was unimpressed. "You
don't even have an accent," she said. "It's a common enough delusion, though. That cursed isle is to blame for much of the patriarchal poison. I'll just list you as unknown."

The Grand Witch would have changed the woman into a toad
right then and there, and dared anyone to tell the difference, but
her powers were not yet restored. Had this demented woman never
heard of the Queen of England? The way this lunatic was carrying
on, one might think there had been a war between America and
England. What arrant nonsense.

"You may not realize how fortunate you are," said the woman.
"The Elder Priestess will see you this afternoon instead of a week
from now, or a month, or a season! But remember, you can only be
cured if you want to be."

Oh, for the power to turn her into a tapeworm or a maggot. or
even just to sew her lips shut! One gets used to magick as one is
accustomed to tormenting peasants who forget to pull the forelock.
As it was, the witch could do nothing as she was escorted to her
next audience. No actual force was used but the implication was
present in the form of two of the most unattractive specimens she
had ever seen.

The witch never caught the names of her stolid companions but
the least hint of displeasure on the part of the matron was sufficient
to engage the duo's brutal attention. They put her in mind of a
matched set of living gargoyles whose diet, she imagined, must consist of human flesh. This pleasant fancy was shortly exploded, however, when the witch was given the even more horrifying news that
everyone in the Central Community was a vegetarian.

At least their surroundings were interesting. They were walking
up a gently sloping hill. A welcome breeze was making the late

afternoon more pleasant than the rest of the day had been. On both sides of them stretched a long line of metallic windmills. The witch assumed these were made from some supernaturally treated steel; as they wouldn't be made of iron, the devil's enemy! To the witch's surprise, her guide muttered something about misbegotten technology instead of praising what must have taken a lot of effort to construct.

At the top of the hill, they saw the temple in which the Elder Priestess held court. The Grand Witch was unimpressed. It was a small structure made of some kind of dried mud. More interesting was the location of the building, dead center in a giant triangle composed of thin, healthy pine trees.

Along the way people came out to see the stranger among them. Something struck the witch as odd about the citizens of the Community but she couldn't put her finger on it. Then as Tanith waved from the crowd—in spite of a disapproving expression from the mental health coordinator—the witch realized that she was yet to see a single male!

Maybe these witches had a magick beyond anything they knew in Merry Olde England!

The Elder Priestess was waiting for them in the open door. She was not what the witch had expected. Instead of a mature woman, lines of care etched around the eyes and the mouth, here was a young woman with a carefree, sunburned face. She had honey-blonde hair, large eyes, large breasts, a large smile—and a narrow waist, small feet, small and dainty hands; and a small talent for diplomacy.

"Like, how do you like it here?" she asked the Grand Witch of All England. "There's no humidity."

Curiouser and curiouser, thought the witch. "You are the Elder Priestess?" she asked incredulously.

"I sense hostility," replied the young elder, batting her eyelashes. "Let's go inside Our Mother's Temple, you know, and, like, discuss your fate."

Inside it was pleasantly dark and cool. "Native American," said the priestess, gesturing for the witch to sit as she was doing, cross legged on the ground. The witch declined.

As her eyes adjusted to the dark, the Grand Witch was pleased to note the first evidence that this youthful leader had some idea of witchcraft. Lined up against the wall was a collection of the finest magickal stones and gems she'd ever seen: a lovely chunk of amber, as bright yellow as the priestess's hair; an azure blue lapis lazuli, the perfect size for making accurate prophecies; a dark green malachite and milk-white moonstone; blue turquoise, red agate and, naturally, a Witch's Stone. More than anything else there was crystal, a galaxy of crystals of all sizes, reflecting the light flickering from the opposite wall.

Turning her head, she beheld hundreds of candles burning, and marveled at how a structure so crude as a large adobe hut could have ventilation that worked so well. As there were rocks of every imaginable hue, so too were there candles for every color in the rainbow. There were astral candles, skull candles, image and triple action and coiled snake and seven-knob candles. But as to why these specialized weapons in the magickal arsenal should all be burning away at this time of day, the witch could not hazard a guess.

So she asked why. The Elder Priestess had a ready answer: "Hey, it's dark in here."

While the Grand Witch of All England was thinking that one over, her hostess clapped her hands and two figures emerged from the darkness where the candlelight had not reached. They were men. The witch rubbed her eyes to make sure that she wasn't hallucinating.

The Elder Priestess made the introductions: "I'd like you to meet Chauntecleer, the wizard, and Bob, the genius, or under-genius, or something like that."

The witch felt something very like satisfaction to be in the presence of men again. Chauntecleer reminded her of a monk who had held his own against her early in her career. As they looked at each other in the dim light, it was as if a spark of intelligence leapt the space separating them. His smile carried with it the prospect of an intelligent conversation...except for one thing. The Elder Priestess mentioned it in passing: "We've kept a few men around. We couldn't get around it. And like, any man you see is of the most high intelligence. Of course, we can't let them speak...."

The witch was horrified all over again. "Have you physically altered them?" she asked.

"Oh, no," said the priestess, pulling playfully at the pipe protruding from Bob's mouth, smoke lazily drifting from the bowl. His toothy smile seemed unaffected by anything she did. "The Goddess doesn't approve of unnatural stuff."

"Yet you've made them mute?"

"For sure."

"How?"

A subtle change came over the young woman, as if a sinister intelligence had just filled a comfortable vacuum. "Don't you know?" she asked.

Of course the Grand Witch knew. Herbs. Potions. Hexes. There were at least a hundred ways to silence your lover. But still the question was: "Why?"

"Because they can't confuse us this way," said the beautiful, young Elder Priestess. She pointed to the door and the two men left with an admirable degree of promptness. "They can't bring us down, you know."

Until this day the Grand Witch thought she'd seen it all. She had new respect for that old motto: live and live and live and live and live…and learn. "What were Chauntecleer's last words?" she wanted to know.

"He thought I lacked a sense of humor," the priestess told her.

It went on like that for some time, thrust and parry, a dance of conjecture, the interloper and the authority each searching for weakness—always weakness. The Grand Witch began thinking there was more to this seemingly unfocused child than a first impression would indicate. She learned some immediate history at least. All was not sweetness and light among these self-proclaimed witches.

Before establishing the current system, there had been strife and dissension over hundreds of issues. The windmills had even presented a problem. Those who wished to eschew machines were the problem; the winning side had to persuade their sisters that not all basic technology (a word the witch came to believe synonymous with magick) was a patriarchal plot! Then there had been the fight over the proper Wiccan view on fertility; between those who viewed abortion as in keeping with joy in life, and those who thought the Earth Mother did not have sufficient irony to see abortion in that light. Schism begot schism, tracing all the way back to the troubles between Gardenerianism and Alexandrianism. The ultimate offshoot of all these legitimate conflicts, it transpired, were those poor, deluded women who confused the pentagram life symbol with dark Christian myths; and mixed up the honoring of the souls of the dead at Hallowmas with the peasant superstition of Halloween. These were the same women who donned the traditional garb of a Halloween witch.

The Elder Priestess finally took a breath. The witch had been thinking over the implications of everything she'd been told and asked: "But if you think I'm a representative case of lunacy, why are you lavishing all this attention on me?"

The younger woman smiled. "Because I'm certain you're authentic," she said. "A real witch. A real, brimstone and demon worshiping witch."

"But you just got through telling me that I don't exist. I mean, that beings like me don't exist. You don't even admit the existence of my dark lord."

"Yeah, like the devil's a guy. I can get into that. The orthodox deny your world. We just have the boring old Earth Mother and love and peace and vegetables. Blessed be!" As the Elder Priestess went on and on, the Grand Witch became even more flabbergasted.

"I'll bet you've made many a cow give sour milk, am I right?" asked the priestess. The witch nodded. "Well, that wouldn't get anywhere with us. We don't even use cow's milk. We say that's exploiting the natural order again."

The Elder Priestess started pulling her hair. "I had to get you alone for a while," she said. "Who else can I talk to about this stuff? It's so boring here. You'd never believe how borrrrrrrrring." She made the last word into one long moan that had an undeniable sexual component.

The Grand Witch was at a loss as to what should come next. She was about to tell the priestess that if she wanted excitement back in the world she should do something about increasing the male population when she thought better of it. Now was the time for caution. Now was the time to avoid offending the powers that were.

"What do you want of me?" asked the Grand Witch of the Elder Priestess.

"Simple. Do a trick."

So much for caution. So much for the suggestion, endlessly repeated since she had arrived in this place, from Tanith to the mental health coordinator, that witchcraft was about anything but doing tricks.

"I'd like to oblige," said the Grand Witch, and she spoke from the cold ash heart of deepest sincerity. Oh, the things she would do to the Central Community if her powers would only return. "But I cannot perform for your amusement."

"You will do a trick," said the priestess, "or turn on a spit." Suddenly the dazzling white smile did not seem as charming as it had before. "I know you have powers. You don't think Tanith was in the desert by accident, do you? I sent her."

"Why?" asked the witch.

"I knew you were coming."

"How?"

"I trust my dreams, you know. It seems like my ancestor from long ago bossed the whole gig in Spain. She, like, sent me a message...to take care of you. Blessed *she!*"

This, at least, made some kind of sense. Up to this point the witch felt she had fallen into a pure nightmare where nothing was reasonable. But with her powers at low ebb, or possibly extinguished, what could she do? "I can't perform a trick just now..." she began.

"Who are you kidding?" spat the young woman with surprising vehemence, jumping up and even stamping her foot. "You were seen to fly. To fly!"

"They took my broom."

"If I get it back for you, will you fly for me?"

This was going nowhere fast. Under normal circumstances she might have tried to bluff her way out of the dilemma; but these were anything but normal circumstances. Despite the impropriety, the witch decided to tell the truth: "Something has happened to my powers. I don't know when, or if, they'll come back."

"Liar!" shrieked the priestess, pulling her hair again. "You're holding out on me."

When all else fails, try logic. "Do you think I'd still be here if I had my magick?" asked the witch.

Unfortunately, the Elder Priestess seemed perfectly impervious to a reasoned approach. "You can't fool me with that bogus routine, babe! We've had you hemmed in with our crystal power since you first arrived. Blessed be."

Now it was the witch's turn to lose control. She laughed long and hard. Even in her weakened state, she could detect the presence of magickal properties in any object. The collection in the temple could be used for powerful spells in the hands of a true adept, but this Wiccan community didn't seem to contain so much as one real sorceress. The Elder Priestess was probably the closest, as witness the dream link with the Grand Witch of Spain (speaking of which, the witch wondered if any of her sisters still existed in this century). One thing was *for sure*: not all the crystals on earth could strip a Grand Witch of her powers.

"You remind me of the Church," the witch told her adversary. "You think I have powers beyond your own, and yet you believe a few paltry baubles and trinkets can render me helpless. It is to laugh."

But the Elder Priestess was not laughing. She clapped her hands and the ugly duo returned. In short order they had the Grand Witch pinioned between them. Somehow the witch wasn't surprised as force was finally brought to bear on her pale, emaciated frame.

The last words the Elder Priestess said before they left the makeshift temple was: "Thanks for giving me a rad idea. Maybe this will bring you around."

The sun was setting on the worst day of the Grand Witch's long existence. Off in the distance the clouds were so low to the ground that they seemed an extension of a distant mountain range—all blue and white, with a touch of gold from the disappearing sun. They had tied her to a stake. Somehow she couldn't appreciate the nostalgia of the moment.

Sister Susan and Sister Sarah and Sister Judith and Sister Cynthia and several young lackeys had gathered wood for the festivities. They all seemed full of malice and unseemly glee, with the sole exception of Cynthia. But the latter's sad expression didn't keep her from doing the same as everyone else. A crowd of onlookers were being held back by dozens of women who seemed as muscular as men, the most horrifying sight the witch had witnessed yet.

Whatever few men were allowed to live in this world, none were to be seen at the burning. But the witch was pleased to see Tanith, off to the side of the crowd, shouting against the proceedings. The Elder Priestess went over to the girl and used the authority of her position to bring the brave child into line.

A last appeal to the priestess had accomplished nothing. The basic truth that witches and warlocks were no longer human beings seemed lost on everyone here. Servants of the dark forces were either born that way, or crossed over (to use an unfortunate expression). For instance, the Elder Priestess could make a flying potion with the correct proportion of baby fat, or be given a fully powered broom, and it would avail her naught. Without witchery in her blood, she wouldn't get an inch off the ground.

But what did the Grand Witch of All England expect from people so careless of their males? She was still reeling over the idea that some of these women believed in aborting perfectly good human stock before it was born and *useful*. Exposure to this sort of waste could make her sympathetic to the puffings of some old blowhard of a bishop! Waste not, want not.

What a bother that her powers had not yet returned. Time was running out. Clearly this was the work of the Grand Witch of Spain. But there would come a reckoning. Already a plan was beginning to form.

The women gathered the wood while another, Sister Morgan, kept time by beating a small drum with a slow and steady beat. Suddenly another woman ran up shouting, "Stop! You can't use that wood."

"Oh, no, it's Sister Lind Seed," muttered Cynthia.

The agitated young woman went on: "That's wood from a Joshua tree. It's on the protected list."

This was, as someone once said, the last straw. The final absurdity struck home as the sisters began gathering up the wood and looking for an acceptable substitute. The Elder Priestess couldn't legitimately oppose enforcing an official rule of her domain, but the Grand Witch could see frustration crawl over the young authority's face.

Anger had been the missing ingredient. Blood burning hotter than any fire, the Grand Witch felt her power surging back. She appreciated the irony that the plan she had just formulated was too good to change now. After all, her real opponent waited for her somewhere in the mists of time and she intended to use strategy, as she had when she sank the Armada.

"Oh, lassie!" the witch called out, capturing the full attention of the Elder Priestess. The young woman's eager smile spoke volumes. She obviously expected her reward in ill gotten magick. She started toward the old woman tied to the stake.

"I sense a decrease in negative vibrations," said the priestess to her admiring retinue. "The stranger has seen the error of her ways."

The Grand Witch of All England waited until the priestess was only a few feet away. Then she said, "You can tell the sisters they don't have to forage for any more wood. I believe this is the result you want."

The Grand Witch set herself on fire, to the astonishment of the priestess and the entertainment of the onlookers. The Elder Priestess was standing near enough that her arch little eyebrows were singed; and another layer of red was added to her sunburn. The Grand Witch enjoyed the sight as everything was eaten up by red and yellow flame, and she listened to Morgan's drum fading away like a slowly dying heartbeat.

The plan she had developed, a *master* plan one might say, was to go straight to the head office in Hell. The Grand Witch of All England had enough seniority for that. There she would bask in the masculinity of Satan Himself, and persuade Him to help her alter history so that no timeline such as this one would ever exist. That would be an approach her enemy would never expect; and if all went well, the Grand Witch of Spain might even undergo the sort of severe punishment at which her countrymen excelled.

The target of the New Inquisition would not be witchcraft in general, but the Wiccan movement in particular. A more worthwhile cause seemed inconceivable to the Grand Witch as she plummeted down and down to the warm embrace of a domain that cared.

Now, for the first time anywhere, this short appears with a slightly different take on the subject of people who want to be witches. I'll say no more.

School Prayer

"You're in a lot of trouble, young lady!" The principal's voice was as stern as her face. This was the third time in a month that Morgana had been called to the office. "You know better than to bring a book like this into Miss Runyan's class," the principal continued, holding the copy of the novel *The Wizard of Oz* between two fingers as if it might be contagious.

"I'm sorry," said Morgana, drawing on all the experience of her fourteen years to come up with an answer. A precocious straight-A student, she was tall for her age with long, red hair. She didn't like the way the middle-aged woman looked at her, old eyes fixed where young breasts were budding.

"You promised this wouldn't happen again after we found your copy of *The Lion, The Witch and the Wardrobe*."

Morgana swallowed hard and made to defend herself. "One of the other kids snuck that into my locker." This was true enough as Morgana was popular and inspired the usual adolescent envy; but she had read the book.

"Everything comes down to attitude," the principal recited her favorite formula, "and this is a fundamentalist school." A well timed pause followed.

"Yes ma'am," Morgana replied on cue.

With a grand gesture, as if playing an invisible pipe organ, the principal yanked open her desk drawer and pulled out the other offending book along with a third one, *The Halloween Witch and Other Scary Stories*. Morgana availed herself of the opportunity to make a close examination of her shoe tops.

"Look at me, young lady," came the expected command. Morgana did so. "Your mother and I have discussed your future at this school. She wants you brought up with traditional values. If you don't *want* this, the problem is between your mother and yourself. The school will not be held responsible for your lack of obedience."

Morgana had heard it all before, but this time there was something different—a chill in the air, a sour taste in the mouth. Her older brother played baseball and was always using the phrase, "Three strikes and your out." Suddenly the thought of being expelled from this exclusive girl's school that her mother had worked so hard to place her in seemed to take on a grim reality. She realized with her whole being that she didn't want to be kicked out.

"I'm truly sorry," Morgana heard herself say and she hated the sound of her own voice. There was no turning back if she said the words that bubbled up in her brain but she couldn't stop herself: "I want to prove myself by joining in the afternoon prayer today."

Leaning forward in her chair, the principal stared at the girl for at least ten seconds before, in a very quiet voice, the authority figure spelled out the facts of life: "This is a serious request, especially after your mother filled out the forms to exempt you from the ceremony."

"She's been trying to change my mind ever since," said Morgana truthfully.

"Why the sudden change of heart?" asked the suspicious official.

"I want to make amends for reading forbidden books."

Rising from behind her desk, the principal was a great judge garbed in turquoise robes Morgana sensed the importance of the moment.

"Very well," said the woman in charge of Vineland High School. "You will attend the prayer today and cleanse yourself before the spring break. And you will bring your books with you and do the right thing."

The teenager gathered up all three volumes, firm in the resolve to prove that she was a good girl, after all. After that the hours crawled by, tormenting her with classes suddenly more boring than ever. Finally the blessed hour came and Morgana joined the other pious students in the courtyard.

The kindling had been neatly laid out in a neat little pyramid awaiting the flame. Morgana waited her turn in line before throwing her books on the pyre. Then the assistant principal came out of the building, leading a sixteen year old girl dressed in white, her hands tied together with something leafy and green. Two large women bracketed the teacher and the student. They watched the student very closely—but the victim made no attempt to escape.

Of her own accord, the sixteen year old climbed over the branches and logs and papers and books, cutting her feet on one particularly nasty-looking twig. When she reached the top, she turned and spoke to the other students and teachers now encircling her.

"This is not true to Wiccan practices," she announced. "This is against the Goddess..."

"Hush, child!" said the principal. "Don't spoil the moment. You are a worthy sacrifice, a benefactor to your friends, a certified virgin. Your one blemish is heresy; and we will burn that away in love and kindness."

All this time Morgana exchanged glances with the older girl. They had been more than friends at the previous year's summer camp, where they explored the pale, moist valleys of each other's youthful eagerness. Even then the older girl had told Morgana to protect herself. Her face told Morgana that she forgave her young lover for standing there now with the others. The memory of tender mouths pressed together was their secret prayer, consecrated to the Goddess—a prayer that no murderous sacrifice could defile.

Morgana didn't notice who started the fire but suddenly the flames were licking around the flesh she remembered so well, making a halo around the other's soft blonde hair. Morgana moved her lips and silently uttered the name of her beloved: "Dianne." The other students gazed at the horror, feeling whatever satisfactions accompany the stink of roasting flesh and screams of agony that must come when even the strongest will succumbs to pain.

It was finally over. Morgana hoped that Dianne might have seen the tears on her face, a final gift of jewels for her love. Unfortunately, the sharp eyes of the principal didn't miss anything. The older woman approached her and placed a cold hand on Morgana's shoulder. "I know how you must feel losing your books," said the hateful voice. "We'll see that you receive a proper volume of the Craft."

"Thank you," said Morgana, The idea of learning how to cast spells suddenly appealed to her, especially dangerous spells, dark spells... As she observed the happy faces of the other students, she liked the idea of mastering witchcraft very much.

There are three witches in *Macbeth*, so I'll wrap up this sequence of stories with a third. In this story I knocked myself out to write a conventional modern fantasy where the witch is good! I wrote it for an anthology where despite all my care, the story was judged to be insufficiently feminist (no surprise).

By the simple expedient of removing the place names of the fantasy universe I was forbidden to enter, and making the names of the characters my own, I take this opportunity to answer the age-old question put to Dorothy: "Are you a good witch or a bad witch?"

Ice Daggers for Amberthorn

For a moment she couldn't see the sky. A gigantic iron claw was raised against her, blotting out the rest of the universe, threatening to crash down on her head. A cold wind stung her cheeks but she did not flinch from the threatening object that filled her vision as if a moon had been loosed from its orbit. Something deep inside her refused to turn from danger. Something even deeper was solemn in defiance.

As the claw faded from view, she almost regretted its passing. For a moment it had distracted her from another and more vexing problem. She did not know who she was or how she had arrived at a place where she was so terribly alone. She had been sleeping—she was sure of that—and then she woke up on a stone table.

The first thing she saw was a dark sky, so full of low-moving clouds that she felt as if buried alive under their canopy. Then a chill from below ran icy fingers up and down her back, and into every crevice of her body. She felt obscenely exposed, even though she wore a tunic, tight fitting leggings and fine leather boots.

With one quick move, she leapt off the table and instinctively reached for a weapon, but she was unarmed. Despite the dim light, she inspected the stone table and touched, as well as saw, the fine spider web pattern that had been carved into the center. Variations on the same design could be seen decorating blocks of stone that lay scattered about as if playthings of a giant.

If it was already this dark in late afternoon she could well imagine how the swift approaching night would extinguish even the hope of light. The first task must be to find something she could use as a torch. At this point, she did not know that she was atop a virtually unscalable plateau; but she already was in the grip of vertigo, the loss of identity making her feel as if she was falling forever. When she asked herself who she was, and who were the people making up the fabric of her life, the reward was a mental silence to match the emptiness of this barren place.

She sat on a broken piece of masonry and tried to think. The more she strained to pierce the dark void in her mind the more terrible was the lack of names, places, things, events, *meaning*…and

yet there was something straining at the edges of that nothingness—
a pattern so ingrained that its contours could not be erased.

She was certain that hers had been a busy and complicated life.
The size of the hole she felt at the center of her being suggested the
dimensions of what had been taken from her—a network of relationships so complicated as to demand the unstinting use of mind
and talents. Almost screaming inside was the command to *do* something, using her lithe body to fight, and employing special skills to
open a doorway to powers that would bring harm against one anonymous group of human beings and serve an equally anonymous
group... Cut off from her extended family, her clan, the call of duty
and the demands of loyalty were fierce emotions that could only
prowl at the edges of an empty chasm.

She shouted in frustration over being ripped from a universe full
of minds and faces. And then some deep seated conditioning made
her close her well shaped mouth, and stifle any further outburst of
sound. She must not give way to emotion. She must not announce
her location to enemies.

Enemies! Yes, she had enemies as well as friends. An image danced
just out of reach with secret music promising instruction as to whom
you owed everything good, and to whom you owed the edge of your
blade or the point of an arrow.

Thought of weapons seemed to calm her. Weapons were another
link to the pattern of her missing life. There were two kinds: physical objects, and forces to be released by using the mind. Contemplation of the latter brought one particular word into her consciousness: *Magic!* But when she tried to speak, the results were not satisfactory: "M— mm— ma—" How odd to see the word in her mind
but be unable to speak it aloud.

Then it struck her that since waking up she had not uttered ar-
ticulate speech, just a cry of animal pain. Could she be mute? The
thought made her tremble. She had no name to shout at the black
clouds. But she must hear herself speak. She must!

"Who am I?" she cried, joy rising in her breast at the cold, clear
words. "Who, who, who?" she continued. She didn't care who or
what heard her now, military caution be damned, even though she
could add with confidence: "I am a defender of children!"

This piece of information had slipped into her head with such
stealth that she barely noticed its arrival. At last, something of her

past had broken through the barrier that imprisoned her mind. She strained for more. "I am a warrior of ..." The thought hung there unfinished, as if hacked off with an axe. Details of a life, tantalizingly in view, scurried back into darkness.

Now the direct focusing of her will seemed counter-productive as if invisible gates crashed down from every direction. That which came unbidden was not to be forced. With a sigh, she sat upon the ground, the brief moment of elation stolen from her as if by the incessant wind.

Greater worries gave way to practical considerations. How far was she from human habitation? Could she find food and water? What of shelter for the night? And as she stopped wondering about her identity, possible answers whispered in her ear. Only this time it was a distinctive voice, a voice not her own, that actually spoke to her inner self:

Are you there? it asked. *I am trying to find you and the one you guard.*

That was the moment when the giant claw had appeared. And although it did not tear her face to ribbons, its appearance coincided with the silencing of the voice. At least she finally had the satisfaction of facing a real enemy. There was a certain exhilarating freedom in knowing that one faced external foes. And there was also the hope that the voice calling out in the night had been real and not echoes from a dying imagination. But a heavy weight was added to her soul that she was responsible for someone else.

When the claw vanished, she felt stronger, even eager to explore the ruins in which she found herself. Her first order of business was to find a source of light so that the fading of the already darksome day would not leave her effectively blind. Climbing on top of the stone table gave her a slightly better view of the jumbled rocks further on—now she could see that the ruins extended over a great distance.

Twenty minutes later she stood at the first of the broken stones, this one a darker color than the table. As it was only slightly taller than herself, and full of cracks, she found it relatively easy to climb to the top. What she saw made her gasp.

The ruins stretched on for miles and miles, as far as her eye could see! And everywhere was that same monotonous flatness of terrain, the tedium disturbed only by thousands of pieces of smashed stonework. The sections that still held some semblance to the original structure suggested a labyrinth of such colossal proportions as to be the product of deranged minds; or else to serve some magical purpose. There seemed no avoiding the word.

The thought of magic suddenly inspired a flood of other words trying to get past the barrier in her mind, and then a few penetrated, as if arrows had pierced through armor: And then a whole phrase thundered in her brain: *Beware the cold and scaled enemy.* Yellow eyes seemed to float in front of her, as the claw had, but they weren't looking at her.

Whirling around, she saw the stone table differently. Beyond it was only empty land...and the line of the horizon so close as to suggest the sheer precipice that would bring a careless adventurer's explorations to an unfortunate end. The stone table was the climax, then, of miles of architecture. The table remained pristine while the megalopolis, crouching before it as a wolf would guard a bone, had tumbled into ruin.

When she turned back, the eyes were gone. She had a headache that she hoped was a result of reawakening memory. More bits and pieces of a world's history floated to the surface of her consciousness, but it was still debris, disconnected from any grand purpose. Feeling her lips move, she was almost surprised when the next message came out of her own mouth, another warning: "Beware the cold ones."

She was good and ready to beware anyone and anything at this point. And she was becoming angry. Either she was quite mad or she was being played with. Whoever she was, she was no one's toy! The anger became a physical sensation in her chest, burning outward, inflaming her blood. And it seemed to awaken her senses to the world around her. Even a place as desolate as this offered more than she had first noticed.

She could smell the musty, dry odor of unburied ages, an aroma of ancient death. She could hear low whistling sounds as the wind explored underground passages and hundreds of fissures in the stone. She could feel a prickling sensation on her skin, as if she stood at the center of a magnetic field—a dead giveaway that magic was being practiced here. A lot of magic!

The mind still worked, even with details scrubbed away as if that giant claw had gotten inside her head and tried to scratch away all memory. The claw. The eyes. The voice that called from afar. They were too recent, and too vivid, to be doubted.

"I am not alone," she said in a strong, firm voice. "Do I face one enemy or an army? I can reason and I will fight you!" As she spoke, she walked forward, courage growing with every step as she ventured past free standing columns and broken walls. When bits and pieces of the spider design reappeared, she glanced at them with scorn. How mighty was this lost civilization that it had crumbled into dust? The sound of her footsteps were like a reproach echoing through myriad corridors of the past, long collapsed...but leaving a faint imprint as though the largest spider web design of all had been the entire structure itself.

"Show yourself!" she shouted. "Only a coward hides!"

And she was answered. As night fell an athletic figure, human in shape but with an odd shimmering appearance, danced out from behind a pillar. In one hand, the figure carried a globe that radiated a soft, steady light. The cloud cover was too thick for starlight or moonlight to penetrate. In a few short moments, she wouldn't be able to see anything. She couldn't help but feel a little gratitude at not being alone, and for the welcome light, even if this might be the worst of all possible villains.

The issue was soon settled by the silky voice coming out of the oddly V shaped head. And it was impossible not to notice the eyes, the color of burnished gold. "Long before the Wars there were races with knowledge you children of Valdemar will never know," said a female voice, with just a touch of cruelty. And the mouth could not help making a hissing sound because this creature was partly reptile. In the white light of the globe, bright colors formed a haunting pattern of reds and golds and blues across the metallic shimmering of the exquisitely small scales. The color especially contrasted with the white bundle the creature carried under its other arm.

Despite the amazing sight taking the trouble to bow in front of her, the young woman was more struck by a single word than anything else: *Warmth!* Her past was screaming at her.

"I apologize for your loss of memory," said the creature. "That was entirely an accident. Magic will play its little tricks on us. The idea was to isolate you from your comrades but the barrier I erected did a little more than that. You became separated from yourself! The trouble with you warrior witches is that you take yourself so seriously, merging your minds with each other and certain unfortunate members of the animal kingdom. But I want your memory restored as much as you do. So…"

With a flourish, the reptilian woman unrolled the white bundle revealing strangely familiar garments between its long and delicate fingers. "I don't know what I'd do without my cloak," came the hissing voice. The light was indeed a help in recognizing the official wardrobe of a witch. "Those…are mine," said the young woman, partly in wonder. "And you…" she addressed her bizarre hostess, "are Irs."

"Pleased to welcome you back to yourself, bitch," hissed the reply. "Perhaps you prefer your nickname, Diana?"

Now was the dam broken and a tidal wave of memory engulfed her. She was the Mother's Own, chosen for a most important task—and only at this second, with the recovery of self, did the darkest emotion of despair spoil everything. A daughter of the clan had been repeatedly threatened by an enemy. The enemy was Irs, proud of the boast that she only took and never gave. To have taken Diana meant Irs had also taken the girl, Amberthorn, whom Diana was sworn to protect.

If she couldn't remember who she was, it was hardly reasonable to blame herself for having forgotten the girl. But Dana wasn't feeling reasonable. For a crazy instant the guilt she felt was so intense that she was distracted from righteous anger. The moment passed quickly.

"By all the gods and goddesses," declaimed Diana, "if you've hurt the child…"

"Ssssooooooo," came the sibilant response, "you are back with us in full. How I admire your firm posture, narrow waist, dark tresses—and let's not forget those flashing eyes. Your body is most admirable but the attempt at theology leaves something to be desired. I am at war with your goddesses. I ignore your gods!"

Diana had a certain degree of sympathy for any poor souls who were victims of someone else's teratological experimentation; but she loathed any who voluntarily subjected their human form to animal based alteration. The combination seemed a kind of crime against both. Irs had *chosen* her current form.

There had been a time when Diana thought she had disposed of Irs with an arrow striking deep in the enemy's collarbone. But the reptilian element provided increased regenerative powers. The hybrid form, combined with the attainments of a powerful warrior, simply made Irs all the more dangerous.

Despite the hatred Diana nurtured for Irs, she would have gladly passed up a hundred opportunities to settle accounts rather than place her charge in a moment's danger. As she studied the glowing golden eyes of this monster, the terrible thought began to form that maybe Amberthorn was already dead.

Irs flicked out a tongue, licking the blue-green lips that must be painful for the monster to pull into a smile. "Your thoughts are as firm as your body," hissed the enemy. "I've always liked you. And if you'll merely violate the sacred vows to your tribe, we could become friends."

As Irs began to hint at the joys to be experienced by a full bonding between the two, Diana remembered her first lover, a pale young man that Irs had slain for amusement. He had nothing to be ashamed of. Irs had once butchered a wizard with a display of magic that had staggered the imagination. The results of that incident should have spelled a devastating end for Irs but she had survived so far, accumulating power, always more power.

There could never be enough magic to protect one who had made enemies of the Mother. And yet, the damned lizard bitch still lived, still threatened everyone in the world. And Diana faced her alone on ground of the enemy's choosing.

"Where is Amberthorn?"

"She is near," Irs almost whispered. "I know how much you ache to see her."

The way Irs stressed the word *ache* left no doubt that the monster was aware of the significance of the word to a witch. The staff of power that protected females was an object in keeping with its namesake. Whatever else had occurred, Dana would not believe for a moment that the staff would have fallen into the cold-blooded grasp of an enemy.

Night grew blacker out beyond the timid circle of light. The wind blew more chill. Was that a child's sobbing the Herald heard behind her, at the stone table? She started to turn, but Irs anticipated every move at a level deeper than consciousness.

"A short time ago you didn't know where you stood in the glorious pecking order north of your own people. Now you have a name, a high rank, a mission. How do you know this isn't another illusion?"

"You'd only give reality back to me if you can use it for torture."

Irs bowed again, then walked over, reaching for Diana. Each finger, as long as a small corral snake, slithered through the air and touched the pale, white shoulder. Diana wanted to recoil...but unexpected warmth from the fingers felt good on her skin; and there was something pleasurable about the texture of the smooth scales.

"I need you to be a witness," said Irs, again profaning the sacred word. She pulled gently at the woman who followed her back toward the stone table. Out beyond the pool of light the table reappeared. Someone had taken up residence there since Diana had vacated its hard caress.

Amberthorn was dressed in a white gown. Her bare feet and arms glistened from some kind of juice or oil that Irs, undoubtedly, had smeared over the girl. Her blonde hair almost seemed to glow as it spilled over the edge of the table. The clear, blue eyes were open and staring straight ahead.

With the return of self knowledge, Diana's training reasserted itself and she was able to control her desire to rush forward and embrace the girl. There would be no safety for either of them if she made a single mistake. Irs was watching, listening, smelling...waiting. The damned creature was awfully sure of herself. And yet Irs had been certain to disarm the warrior witch.

"I'm sure you can imagine what comes next," hissed Irs.

"You'll have to kill both of us."

Irs inclined her head at the suggestion. "Maybe not," she replied. "The powers to be released should be sufficient to hold you in check."

Diana had never really enjoyed games, despite their usefulness in preparing for challenges. The reality always seemed more unpredictable and messy. "What is to stop me from ripping out your throat with my fingers and teeth?" she asked in a calm and even voice.

Irs placed the globe of light on the ground and clapped her hands together. "A physical combat, your hot skin against my hide. That would be fun. But poor Amberthorn would stay in her trance forever, or at least until her physical frame turned to dust. And her death would be pointless. Wouldn't it be far better that we honor the lovely child?"

A black thing came scuttling out of the darkness, all hair and many legs. It stank as if an old, wet fox pelt had been used to wrap rotten fruit. At first glance it appeared to be a giant spider, but there were attributes that were all wrong—claws sticking out at odd angles, and an appendage that bore an uncomfortable resemblance to a human hand. This last reached up to the six objects sticking out of its back, and extracted one. The objects were daggers and Irs took one.

"A normal blade will not serve," said the reptile woman. "These are wrested from the Ice Wall Mountains, so that as each one pierces a different part of Amberthorn's anatomy, the spike of ice will rest there, and slowly melt. The sacrifice must be perfect; and your frustration will add the final ingredient, so that the magic thus evoked will serve my sane, new world. You are abandoned. This girl never loved you. She was too young and vain to love. Let me show you the joy of making war on warm flesh."

Everything about Irs was of a consistent whole, even to speaking of "evoking" magical forces instead of "invoking" them. The realization that Irs actually felt affection for the one who had fought her so often was the missing piece of the puzzle: why go to all this trouble when the monster could so easily dispose of her foe? The emotional ingredient Diana was supposed to provide was an inadequate explanation for her continued survival. The fire burning in the burnished golden eyes suggested a deeper explanation.

Trying to hide her thoughts from so powerful a foe was as difficult as it was futile. But Irs couldn't do everything, and there might be a significant delay between Diana formulating a plan and Irs anticipating the danger. Despite the return of her knowledge, there were still blanks in Diana's memory—how Irs had abducted the two of them; who might know of their whereabouts; and what had become of her weapons.

The monstrosity at her feet mattered little. The danger was Irs, always Irs. And as the scaled hand took a second dagger from the back of the spider-thing, the shape and heft of the knife jarred a picture loose from deep in Dana's mind. The only weapon that really mattered was the dagger that had been worn at her side.

If Irs's anatomy had included eyebrows, they would have arched high at the crucial moment when Diana noticed the slight difference on one of the handles jutting out from the monster's back. Diana recognized her own knife! The weapon that had been especially assigned to her for the protection of Amberthorn. The hawk-headed hilt that Irs had carefully duplicated for the five ice daggers. The cold dagger was the key to warm life.

The voice trying to be heard through the fog of amnesia had not come from untold miles distant—it had been the voice of the dagger itself. How Irs had silenced it was a mystery to be solved later. All that mattered now was the stunning realization of what kind of ritual was about to be performed on this blasted plateau.

Irs well understood the forces linking the witch to the dagger, and both to the child. Taking something intended for the protection of children and perverting it to a child's destruction was the blackest kind of deed. The evil pervading every square inch of this place cried out for innocent blood. Any attempt on Diana's part to prevent the murder would only feed the emotional whirlpool in which Irs swam and feasted.

Whatever the perils, Irs needed Diana awake. She was taunting and teasing Diana to keep her human opponent angry, just as she stressed the hopelessness of the situation to keep the witch depressed and uneasy. A direct appeal by Diana to the dagger would be anticipated and blocked.

Suddenly: "I love you!" cried Diana, with all the passion in her nature. For a moment, Irs's face looked completely human, caught in a moment of surprise. In the few seconds remaining before Irs realized that the words of tenderness were directed at the child instead of herself, the young witch summoned all the power at her command.

Diana spoke to Amberthorn with an insistence so deep and impossible to ignore that it challenged the dead to rise and stones to crack.

Already Irs had penetrated Dana's intention, but life flickered back into the child's eyes, and Dana added: "We love you, we've always loved you!" Amberthorn whispered Diana's name before the black curtain was again drawn across her mind.

The manner in which Irs screamed suggested that something could be said for improvisational tactics in the absence of a comprehensive strategy. Irs fought back. She threw the full force of her mind at Dana, merging their consciousnesses as a blacksmith forges steel. The witch's will was strong now, and not to be plunged into forgetfulness by design; but the sadistic thoughts of Irs were as hot ingots of pain searing into an already injured mind.

Diana knew her risk: *The ice daggers will be spoiled for the ritual if they are used in battle!*

With eternal gratitude, Diana literally threw herself at her stronger opponent. The advantage was with the attacker. Irs not only had to avoid using the daggers but exercise extreme caution lest the frigid blades shatter. In her fury, Irs invaded the other's mind with no concern over leaving avenues of retreat.

The spider-thing possessed no loyalty to her mistress, or else lacked the intelligence to fight. As the two warriors grappled with each other, the squat, black horror sidled out of harm's way. Irs caught the movement out of the corner of her eye and shrieked at the thing to return with *her daggers!* But to exert control over the arachnid meant a temporary lessening of the mental vise tightening in Diana's head.

Keeping Irs away from either the girl or the daggers would defeat the enemy's malign purpose. With a mighty shove, Diana sent the two of them rolling on the ground, away from the table, and toward the darkness out beyond the light. Meanwhile, *Hope* dislodged itself from the spider's back and came to rest on the ground a few yards from Amberthorn.

Pushing, pulling, the two fought, wrestled, inching ever closer to where the plateau dropped off to thousands of feet of eternal night. Diana kept this fact in a safe place in the back of her mind. The rage consuming Irs allowed no room for practical observations. But then, Diana didn't notice everything that was occurring, especially when the two finally reached the edge.

They were able to stand again. Weaponless, they fought hand to hand while the more serious battle exploded inside their skulls, Irs infiltrating Diana, Diana permeating Irs. A simple maneuver such as Diana putting a foot behind Irs's leg and shoving forward seemed inadequate, somehow, to resolve a lifetime of bitterness and hatred. But with that one deft move, Irs was hanging from the edge of the cliff and the choice was Diana's as to whether her opponent would live or die.

Irs entertained no illusions about Diana's decision, and yet managed to gasp out, while dangling over the abyss, "You wouldn't send me falling to my death, would you?"

Sarcasm was alien to Diana's nature but she surprised herself by answering, "I wouldn't presume to instruct you as to where you are to fall," and then stepped on the fingers that gave a satisfying crunch and sent her long-time enemy out of her life forever. The wind howled above and the wind howled below, but she wondered if there wasn't the faintest hint of great whirring wings and titanic snapping beaks concluding some unfinished business.

There was a greater surprise coming. Outside the range of the magical light, only the faintest details could be made out. Diana was limping as she returned to the stone table. Amberthorn was already waking up. The girl gave a start of surprise and jumped off the table at her savior's approach!

"What's the matter, young one?" asked Diana. "Your kidnapper is dead."

The light from the globe was bright and clear by the table. Diana had no trouble seeing Amberthorn stumble over to where the dagger lay on the ground. Grabbing the dagger with one hand, Amberthorn almost fell down, so obviously was she afraid. Regaining some composure, the girl held the knife correctly, pointed at Diana's throat.

"Amberthorn!" Dana cried out.

Do not fear her, child, the dagger told Amberthorn, and Diana was being addressed as well. Irs was a mighty sorceress but she will only have revenge if we allow her!

The girl understood then. She understood and spoke aloud to her friend. "Thank you." She placed the dagger carefully on the table and walked over where she embraced the witch who had saved her.

That was when Diana noticed the scales on the young girl's wrist.

I thought this would be a controversial story. Editor Mike Resnick who bought it for *Alternate Warriors* certainly thought it had some merit in that regard. In his introduction, he wrote, "Brad Linaweaver has been toiling in the vineyards of science fiction with consider-able success for a number of years—so when it came time to assign him an alternate warrior, I decided not to make his life too easy. We now present the story of a warrior who finally decided not to turn the other cheek: Jesus of Nazareth."

What limited the controversy was the lack of reviews, or reviews that missed the point. Alternate History is my favorite kind of fiction. I walked a tightrope in this story by not addressing whether Christ in this alternate world is only a man or something more, a question that remains unanswered in our own timeline for all of that. The idea was that the faithful might assume there is a divine Christ in all time lines, but the details of his life could be different in each one. Materialists could assume that there is a non-divine Christ undergoing a different set of experiences in those time lines.

I left it up to the reader. The verdict is that most didn't get it.

Unmerited Favor

And there are also many other things which Jesus did, the which, if they should be written every one, I suppose that even the world itself could not contain the books that should be written.
—The Gospel According to St. John

As long as anyone could remember, the Holy Land had been hot. That's why it was good to live in Jerusalem. The old city had a lot of water—so much of it that the occupying Romans could have their fill (and Pontius Pilate, the procurator, could grow all the roses he wanted); and there was still plenty left for the Arabs, Syrians, Egyptians, Greeks and, of course, the people whose land this was.

Thomas wasn't thinking about any of that right now, although he was as patriotic as his comrades. Like them, he dreamed of the glory that had been the birthright of the ancient Hebrews. But right now he was only thirsty, wishing that he wasn't in such a rush to get to the secret meeting.

He had been to a lot of secret meetings. None of them had changed anything about these depressing modern times in which he and his friends found themselves. But he was in the habit of lending support to any organization that would make a show of resistance against the order of things. Not too long ago, he'd been content to be a fisherman, and not think about politics except to grumble at tax time. Then he'd rediscovered deep wells of religious faith in himself, and had drunk deep; and he knew the one absolute fact of human life was the unity of politics and religion.

The rekindled passions coursing through Thomas could be blamed on the man from Galilee. Some perfectly sensible people were starting to believe that this strange rabbi was the Messiah. There was nothing unusual about the rabble pinning their hopes on the next charismatic man in line. But this new one, this Jesus, was achieving a level of credibility that Thomas found hard to believe. It's not that the man offered a specific plan. He could deflect any talk of revolution into a soliloquy on redemption. He could answer any concrete question with a mysterious parable that left everyone scratching their heads. And yet there was always something subversive in these parables. Primarily, Jesus had the enviable knack of being different things to different people, at a level of sophistication worthy of the most wily emperor. Maybe Jesus *was* the One!

Thomas didn't want to miss a word the Nazarene might speak. Heretofore, the speeches had been scheduled in easily accessible places. Or they had happened spontaneously—if one didn't believe the cynics—as a natural response to the love, and hunger, of the crowd. This time there was secrecy. Thomas counted himself fortunate to have been told at all! The place was a secluded garden on the outskirts of the city that had been allowed to go to ruin. It was the perfect location at which to harvest a crop of Roman spies.

Despite his haste, Thomas was late. A Zealot was already addressing the crowd that filled the tattered spaces of the unkempt garden. Thomas felt his dry tongue against his drier lips, and suddenly, as if a miracle, a cup of water was pressed to his mouth by a young lad who was working the crowd, jug in hand. They also serve those who stand and wait.

Refreshed, it was easier for Thomas to pay attention to the Zealot's speech, who even now was saying, "The emperor will hang on to this area if we put up five times, *ten times,* the resistance. Our sacred land of Judea is central to his trade routes. We all know it! Worst of all, our aristocratic Sadducees know the economic realities too well. And the Pharisees know it…"

There was some muttering at the last comment. The speaker quickly demonstrated his political sense. "Yes, I know it never pays to be overly specific when one is being critical. I am of the Essenes. The children of Israel have our little differences…and we Essenes are often criticized for our ideas on purity. But you've never seen a squabble until you've got Sadducees and Pharisees debating the afterlife!" A few chuckles near Thomas helped defuse the tension.

Then they were treated to Zealot humor, an oxymoron if there ever was one: "The Roman Empire first became involved in this part of the world when she tried to solve the conflict between Mesopotamia and Egypt. Well, she's had nothing but trouble since. You think she would have learned." He wasn't a bad-looking man, this Zealot, and as he laughed at his own remark Thomas was tempted to join in, if only out of politeness. It was just that no one saw anything funny about a perfectly accurate historical remark.

The Zealot was quick to recover. Nostrils quivering at a breeze that brought with it a whiff of distant salt and sea, he felt like a fisher of men. This was the moment to cast his net: "You know what binds us together," he said with passion. "Our national pride will never be crushed!" Thomas could feel the shift in the crowd, as a tidal pull has you before you even notice. A murmuring of agreement rose up, sighed against swaying palm leaves as if they were so many knives. The voice grew louder, more reckless of being overheard. "Our willingness to stand together is our power; and we will resist a hundredfold, even beyond counting, until there is no military occupation of our land!" Now there were cheers, as predictable as the marching of Caesar's legions.

Thomas found himself wondering why they hadn't sent out special invitations for the enemy to join them, considering the noise. Then he reproached himself for his lack of patriotism. Surely every precaution had been taken. The Zealots had posted their own guards. Now if Thomas could only make himself stop doubting the likelihood of spies in their midst.

The Zealot was sufficiently carried away that he probably thought he could convert any renegade among them who would sell their future for damned Roman coin. Perhaps he was capitalizing on the work Jesus had done, when the Master told His followers that they didn't have to deal in Roman money at all; and if they didn't like the coins with Caesar's graven image, they could always render them back to the Roman state. More people were trying to live by barter than ever before.

And yet it couldn't be said that Jesus preached against money *per se*. He didn't. Someone had observed that He spent more time talking about money than about Heaven. Thomas found Jesus the best possible guide for legal advice, when He had said that it was better to give the shirt off your back than allow another to take you to court, where you ran the risk of imprisonment and endless fines. No one gave more practical advice.

"All that is wanting is a leader," cried the Zealot. "We have waited long for a warrior, the greatest warrior, to lead us against the Roman evil. Have our prayers been answered? Has the true leader come among us?"

With a buildup like this, Thomas expected the appearance of Jesus very soon. Yet how would the man handle the spot he was being put in by the speaker? Up until now, Jesus had avoided direct confrontation with those expecting a martial solution to their problems.

Thomas felt uncomfortable.

Thomas was also uncomfortable over the many stories circulating about Jesus's propensity for working wonders. Thomas hadn't seen any miracles. Too much emphasis on this sort of thing seemed like playing to the lowest common denominator of the mob. And yet, could all this be part of a clever strategy? After all, the military prospects were bleak. The only reasonable plan was to combine a military strike with a political solution at the same time; so that the costs of putting down the rebellion would be greater than Rome was willing to pay.

Out of two discomforts Thomas found a new sense of security. He was too pragmatic to really expect any sort of unqualified success. Despite these reservations, he believed that a devious leader could improve the situation. Better someone reputed to work miracles like Jesus should take charge, than this Zealot whose hotheaded approach would guarantee disaster. A failed rebellion could make things worse. After all, Jerusalem enjoyed an almost anarchic freedom compared to any city in Egypt. The latter was a senatorial province with practically no freedom for anyone. Here, at least, they had the legal protections of a client state with some small degree of autonomy. It was easy for Jewish officialdom to keep the peace on purely practical grounds. Only a man skilled at fooling a lot of the people a lot of the time could shake the establishment out of its lethargy.

Thomas had stopped following the Zealot's words. Hear one of these tirades, and you've heard them all—the call for violence against a superior foe when it was not at all clear that the man crying for sacrifice would be spilling his own blood into the contested earth! Then there was a moment of blessed silence as the Zealot fumbled to find a new cliche, and was spared any further thought. A new voice spoke, the voice that Thomas had come to hear.

The crowd's attention was seized by Jesus of Nazareth as a child's fancy might turn to a delightful new color, and even finer sounds. No one had a voice like Jesus. Thomas felt himself smiling just because he was hearing the voice. And then he gazed again upon the only face that captured in its every line a perfect serenity and confidence.

Jesus said: "If you bring forth what is written within you, what you bring forth will save you. If you do not bring forth what is within you, what you do not bring forth will destroy you."

That was certainly a conversation-stopper. Not only did the crowd maintain a studious silence, but the Zealot moved his lips and no words came forth. Another miracle! The first time Thomas had heard Jesus speak he had thought the man was merely skilled at stating non sequiturs. But anyone who could make a person think the way Jesus did, was not merely spinning meaningless tapestries of words. It was Jesus who had made Thomas recognize the full humanity of women; who had made him feel a degree of sympathy for the poor and the ill that he would have condemned as weakness in himself until the strange rabbi made him accept his own emotions as strength.

Jesus had not come alone. Simon Peter was with him, and also Judas Iscariot. Thomas had once overheard Peter in an unguarded moment tell a friend that the Master often spoke in parables because the people weren't ready to understand the mysteries which must be kept secret. His friend had replied that Peter had a better understanding regarding the people's limitations than anyone else, including the Messiah! The conversation had then wandered into areas touching on Peter's organizational skills; and Thomas had wandered off in search of wine.

There seemed nothing secretive about what Jesus did next. Sometimes he could be so direct that his followers could scarce credit what they heard. He asked who among the gathering they trusted. Naturally, there were cries of His name. He seemed not to hear. Again, as if speaking to unruly children, he asked them to look at one another, and look into their hearts, and say, truly, if they trusted one another.

Thomas noticed a grim expression on the face of Judas Iscariot. Clearly this was a man of principle who was prepared to judge his neighbors. And yet hadn't Jesus admonished everyone to avoid judging anything but their own hearts? The more Thomas tried to understand Jesus, the more mystery he found.

Holding up his pale, white hands—hands that had an almost feminine quality about them—Jesus gestured for everyone to come closer. Above the hands smiled His face, a face that encompassed every imaginable quality of the masculine. No one hesitated to move forward.

He did not speak to them for very long; but every word seemed a revelation, burned into their minds. He told them that the time had come to take up arms against their true enemies. The crowd sighed as if releasing their collective soul for Him to fondle. Then He let silence reign, and it, too, became a palpable presence.

The Zealot was the first to find his voice. He asked: "Are you the new Moses?" Another asked: "How shall you lead us?"

Thomas was surprised to hear his own voice asking: "What of the law?" There were times when Jesus seemed to challenge the traditions of His own people as thoroughly as He brought subtle criticism against Rome.

Jesus answered them all with: "I am not come to destroy, but to fulfill." Thomas seemed to recall that He had said that before. It probably wouldn't be the last time. Then He spoke of bringing a sword in his hand and the Zealots cheered. Their fear that He would lead His followers in the path of peace seemed an empty worry this day.

The voice of Jesus changed then. The lofty quality was replaced by something more worldly—as if insinuating things, hinting things...making plans in nasal tones, plotting faction against faction and anticipating the worst. He said that any who wished to take up arms should meet back at this place tonight and they would be well satisfied.

Standing at the edge of the crowd was a sinister-looking merchant who grinned through broken teeth. Thomas had heard that this unsavory fellow was gifted at providing weapons for the right price. As to how the transaction might be arranged, Thomas had sufficient wisdom not to question a worker of miracles.

Jesus finished with a reminder that He demanded faith from those who would follow Him. Faith was not about the fog of half-formed aspirations and dreams floating in a young fool's head. Faith was about-confidence translated into action. Tonight would be an important test for everyone.

As the sun hung over the smooth, round hills of the Holy Land, it looked like a golden Roman coin placed against a woman's body. Thomas would not have as far to travel to reach the meeting place this time. He had simply remained behind. Although the heat of the day still clung about his sandaled feet, he wished that he'd brought extra clothing because the nights could be cold. Although born and bred in desert lands, Thomas often felt that he had too narrow a range for comfort where temperature was concerned. He envied his friends their toughness; and he also felt intimidated by the adaptability of the cursed Romans. They seemed suited to any climate, with their long, hard faces and souls of marble.

The merchant returned with a minimum of fuss and a heavily laden cart. When one wheel bumped over a broken piece of statuary, there was a sound of metal on metal from under the cloth that covered the contents. It seemed incredible that Jesus was really going through with it. All this talk of faith would be put to the test tonight. Thomas prayed that his last doubts would be as a dried husk, falling away to dust.

Two of the Zealots, left to guard the meeting place, had no compunction about arguing the usual: Was this man really the Messiah? If so, why did He waste time criticizing the natural order of things? Whence came this bizarre predilection for worrying over prostitutes, children and other no-accounts? From the point of view of these two pragmatic gentlemen, it was just about time for a leader to either put on the armor of a warrior or just shut up about odd hobbies and obsessions. Thomas rubbed the stubble on his round chin and smiled over the subject the Zealots were avoiding: the most disturbing behavior of Jesus was the man's willingness to talk to Gentiles as if they were human in God's eyes.

Here were dangerous waters to navigate; and more than one person had wondered out loud about the Nazarene's parentage. There was no doubt about the mother. His mother was not the source of controversy. At first Thomas had thought an Egyptian father might explain some of the Master's more exotic features. More recently, he had inclined to the dreadfully heretical view that there might be a Roman father skulking around the silver fountains. Perhaps this would explain the tolerance of the imperial authorities for some of the more provocative preachments of this latest man of destiny.

Hatred of the Romans was such that one didn't openly talk of such matters. Besides, the growing cult was putting out the idea of a supernatural origin for Jesus—one that didn't preclude a human mother but insisted on something far more transcendental for the father. This sort of notion played better with the Romans, actually, than with those who owed their allegiance to King Herod. The Romans believed that Zeus sent more of Himself earthward than just lightning bolts. Who ever dreamed a rabbi could be spoken of in a manner reserved for mythical figures, such as Heracles?

The heretical implications of the Jesus movement could undermine any political advantages if everyone wasn't very, very careful. There were plenty of mystery cults sniffing around. No one took them seriously. You had the followers of Mithra. You had the followers of Zoroaster. You had all sorts of followers...but not all of them wielded swords, like so many flashing scythes, to mow down the greatest army in the world.

We'll probably all be crucified, thought Thomas, but there comes a time when a man must choose to spend his life, if not wisely, then with a full measure of devotion. That was the kind of commitment Thomas noted on the faces of the men who were gathering in the garden. As night drew its shadows close around them it was harder to make out details. There was no moon yet. A few, lone stars winked overhead. And while visions of spies and solemn treachery made a chaos of Thomas's mind, Jesus walked among them.

It was that crucial moment in any military campaign when the commanding officer must inspire confidence. This would have been an auspicious moment for the leader to appear, surrounded by his entourage. But He had come without them. That wasn't so bad for morale. But Jesus had a woman with Him.

Thomas had met Mary Magdalene once before when she would occasionally join the small group that followed Jesus around Palestine. By that time, she was no longer plying the trade that had caused so much controversy. Respectability held no charms for these disciples of the new. Thomas regretted that Mary was no longer available to a hardworking man with coin to spend.

In the fading light, he could make out her long, delicate fingers. He wanted to touch them. Her raven-dark hair hung loose about her face instead of being tied up and properly out of view. A torch was lit near her face and in the dancing light he saw the hint of a smile as she noticed the discontent she inspired among the men. She glanced at Jesus but He seemed not to notice.

Thomas couldn't understand why the Master would make an error regarding something as important as the men's morale. Jesus had a worldly side, as he'd demonstrated when he put a stop to James and John angling for greater authority of their own. Bringing a woman along seemed not the wisest move at such a time but Thomas reminded himself that it was not his place to pass judgment.

Without saying a word, Jesus walked over to the cart and uncovered swords and spears and shields. Silently, he gestured to the warriors. They came forward, one at a time, to receive the offering. Jesus passed out the weapons with the greatest solemnity. When it was Thomas's turn, he hesitated. They had been told nothing of what to expect. This small group could be part of some large, coordinated plan—a rebellion that might stretch from Jerusalem to Jericho. Or it could be one more pointless act of terrorism to be followed by the usual reprisals.

With a sensation of tingling in his fingertips, Thomas reached for a sword and prayed that no one would notice his hand tremble. Jesus's face was blank and unreadable. Thomas felt Mary's eyes on him, and his cheeks burned under her sight. The call to faith was never easy.

When everyone was armed, Jesus, still unspeaking, walked out of the garden. They followed Him. Thomas waited until last. He couldn't take his eyes off Mary, who showed no inclination of joining the procession. To his surprise, she approached him right before he left and whispered in his ear: "You will be protected by His grace." Then she retired behind a sorry-looking specimen of an olive tree.

Thomas was still trying to figure out what she had meant as he trudged along the ancient hills, a would-be liberator with the rest. The sky had turned from gray to black and more stars were visible. For purposes of surprise, it would be best to have a cloudy night or, failing that, at least a moonless one. The credibility of the mission was not further enhanced when the round orb of the moon did rise like a sleepless eye to watch their progress. The moonlight cast their shadows before them like streaks of oil. Thomas felt like a ghost.

Jesus was leading them God-knows-where. At first it seemed that the objective might be a garrison, but as they marched out into the desert sands, in a direction that even Thomas knew promised nothing but more desert, the worst kind of grumbling began—patriotic grumbling.

Thomas was about ready to rethink his position on faith when

the ragged line stopped dead in its tracks. So there they were, remote from the cares of the city, all alone in the still, windless, desert
night. The grumbling of the men subsided as easily as it had begun.
They waited. The moon washed them a pale white as if they were
statues from antiquity.

Jesus said: "You see but do not perceive." His tall figure seemed
almost to hang over the desert, like a mirage, while Thomas was
bogged down, uncomfortable with the sand filling his sandals and
getting between his toes. Thomas waited stupidly. They all did; the
way many of them had reacted the first time they saw the Master
lower Himself to wash the feet of mere followers. *Now what?*
screamed a thought in Thomas's mind.

Jesus sat down in the sand. Some joined Him there. Some stood
uncertainly, shifting from foot to foot. Thomas was one of these.
The Zealot who had made the speech that got everyone's blood
boiling stared with undisguised anger at the latest turn of events.

"The enemy will be coming through here?" he asked through
clenched teeth, not bothering to disguise the sharpness of tone. Jesus
said nothing, which only served to feed the other's anger, who grew
more shrill with: "You're not going to tell us there is no enemy, are
you?"

Another man asked, just as testily: "You're not going to ask us to
turn the other cheek?" Jesus did not respond.

So they waited. All that could be heard was the rasping sound of
heavy breaching, the breath of anger. Still Jesus did not respond.
He let the quiet settle about their heads, and sink into their bodies,
and slow the breathing, before he spoke to them. Then He told them
about the enemy.

He promised they would face the enemy, here, tonight, as He had
faced the ultimate enemy in this place. He said the Demons would
soon come among them and they must gird their loins to do battle
with the foe. He closed His eyes and bade them pray.

"I knew it!" screamed the Zealot demagogue as if recovering the
tongue stolen from him in the garden. "We cannot put our Faith in
this man. We should have known better. Here is a prince of fools
who wastes time warning those without power about the pitfalls of
power! He's a madman who says prostitutes have a better chance at
entering Heaven than chose who administer our sacred moral law!
Now we see what sort of warrior 'He' is. We are to make war against

demonic possession rather than Roman oppression!"

Suddenly Thomas had every reason to believe that there would be bloodshed this night. For every man who seemed deranged in anger, another was either confused or willing to defend the rabbi, come what may. "He has no use for these weapons," the Zealot continued, "but we do!" He waved his sword so that it gleamed in the moonlight. "We'll leave 'Him' here with any other madmen who care to face invisible hordes."

Not a few men cast nervous glances over their shoulders as if expecting monsters to rise up from the ancient sands or descend from the even more ancient stars. The first to look up mistook the large cloud that had drifted into the otherwise perfectly clear night sky for a supernatural manifestation. He screamed.

The cloud covered the moon, and the confusion down below was almost perfect. At the same moment, a cold wind slashed at their faces. There was shouting, another scream and the clash of steel. Thomas panicked at the thought they might be fighting each other. He tried to run and collided with a massive chest. A pair of hands shoved him from the side and he fell to the ground, tasting sand and getting grit into his eyes. Listening to the melee, he wasn't at all sure he wanted to stand up again.

The Zealot was evidently disappointed by the absence of *esprit de corps* in the face of bad weather. He screamed above the wind: "You stupid children! You'll never stand up to the Romans. You'll ..." He coughed. Then he made a gurgling sound and fell near Thomas, who reached out and felt the other man's inert body.

"Demons!" shrieked another. "Demons took him!"

"Death to the evil one," said a voice much quieter than the rest. "There will be no more sorcery."

There were men for whom the life of Jesus was a poem and His words echoed in them as His actions guided them. For others, He was a danger not to be borne. When the cloud passed on into the night, and the moon shone down again upon the disorganized company, two bodies lay in the sand. The first was the Zealot, eyes staring in horror at what no one could guess. The other was Jesus, prone upon the ground with a spear piercing his side.

No one had kept track of who was armed with what weapon. No one admitted to the crime. Thomas stumbled forward, as in a dream, and reached out to pull the lance from the side of the only man in all the world in whom he had placed his faith. Then Thomas reached down and touched the red, gushing wound and he cried at the sight.

Many threw down their weapons and ran off in all directions. They were a mob now. Thomas knelt beside the body. A few others joined him there. They sat that way for at least an hour until a hand touched Thomas on the shoulder and he turned to see that, somehow, Mary Magdalene had joined them. Her hand was firm, and without thinking about it he pressed his face upon her arm.

"What will we do?" he asked her. "It's all over."

"No," she said, "it is not over." She sat down beside him and joined the long vigil. "It is only beginning," she whispered. Thomas thought she was speaking to him but she wasn't.

This is my other exploration of Christianity, but I didn't put any restraints on myself the way I did with "Unmerited Favor." I intended to write a deliberately blasphemous story, a quaint conceit in this day and age when few read and even fewer have any idea of what an orthodox view might entail.

To give myself a fighting chance, I did this story about the Roman Catholic Church. As little as I know about the subject, I know even less about the Russian Orthodox. I grew up Episcopalian but the good old Church of England doesn't go back far enough into history for what I needed in this story. Other Protestant choices were less promising. Imagine trying to look back over thousands of years from the tent of a revival Baptist.

So this became my fantasy about the Vatican. When I'm in limbo and looking for a lawyer to argue my case, I'll point out that I persuaded one of the world's most prominent Catholics to contribute a story to the same anthology, *Tombs*. I trust that a story from William F. Buckley, Jr., was more than up to the task of balancing mine!

If that doesn't work, I'll say that Ed Kramer made me do it.

The Darkest Doctrine

Monsignor Walsh was an unassuming, modest man. He was so careful of other people's feelings that he would not allow himself to recognize the fact that he had turned to scholarship to escape the incessant noise of his family—of brothers and sisters and a mother and father who all seemed to talk at once and enjoyed playing the television and radio simultaneously. It was not until his first year in a monastery where the brothers observed a vow of silence that Walsh thought back to his earlier life with a faint smile on his thin lips. The noise his family could not live without suddenly took on the quality of richly textured music.

He did not stay at the monastery but won a scholarship that allowed him to pursue his studies at Notre Dame. There was always a question as to whether his calling was to be among people or among the books that call out to a true scholar with a melody as pure as the wine monks make in their quiet monasteries. The decision was made for Walsh, whose first name was Ashley, at the age of thirty-five. He had returned home after graduation to serve those with whom he had grown up. He wasn't sure that anyone particularly noticed his return when he received a special summons from the bishop of his archdiocese. There he learned his destiny did not lie in Chicago.

"They want you at the Vatican," said the older man.

"I don't know what to say," said Walsh.

"That has always been your strength," replied the bishop.

A small voice in the back of the monsignor's head chided him over how easily he was able to wrap up his affairs; how easily he extricated himself from the city in which he had spent most of his life. He envied a younger brother whose name was George because the man involved himself in the lives of others as easily as slipping into a warm bath. George took on other people's miseries, fed on them and turned them into something better. Ashley thought his brother should have been the priest in the family; instead he was a musician loved by many women. He was the one person who was there to take Ashley to the airport.

"Congratulations," George said, shaking hands with his older brother. "It's a great honor. I can imagine how you feel."

The monsignor looked blankly at his younger brother. Young George had known sorrows and joys that Ashley despaired of ever feeling. The one emotion that guided the elder Walsh's life was a desire not to cause other people trouble. He prayed this impulse was born of a desire for their well being and not simply a lust for peace and quiet.

"I can't imagine why they want me," said Ashley.

George was surprised. "You mean you don't know?"

"The bishop told me the assignment requires a knowledge of Greek, Latin and Hebrew. But the Church has a wealth of scholars more qualified than I."

"They must know what they're doing, or what's faith for?" This last observation of the brother—more proof that he was cut out to wear the clerical collar—echoed inside the head of Monsignor Ashley Walsh as he took his seat on the United Airlines flight that would take him on the first leg of his journey. All roads lead to Rome. All roads lead away from home.

A letter from his mother resided in his pocket unopened. He would read it midway across the Atlantic Ocean. He knew what it would say. She always wrote the same letter. She had hope for all her children, but as she worried the most about him he received the most concentrated dose of good will. He couldn't blame her for this sort of sentiment. It was how she dealt with the fact that he didn't love her.

The first leg of the flight was uneventful, but the captain must have gotten up on the wrong side of the bed when he informed the passengers, in a voice dripping with sarcasm, that information about connecting flights would be available on video terminals at the Atlanta airport. Walsh thought the man was a kindred spirit, better suited to working with information than with people. One of the stewardesses made a snide remark about the captain, sarcasm begetting sarcasm, a nun breaking ranks with her priest. Walsh was amused to note that an elderly woman asked the captain what gate she should go to as she exited the plane. The amusement didn't last when Walsh tried to help her and found himself staring at a blank monitor. The computer system was temporarily down, a crisis in airport orthodoxy. Little scraps of paper proclaiming necessary boarding information were affixed to the blank screens, as if Martin Luther had appeared to post alternative routes to devoutly wished-for destinations.

Systems do break down. And Monsignor Walsh had no particular faith that he would navigate the dangerous waters separating one minute from the next. A bit of air turbulence, a shudder in a plane touching down, the red wine he purchased (his ticket was not first-class) tasting little better than fermented Kool-Aid, and an obnoxious child who insisted on kicking the back of his seat...these were the only remaining mishaps on the various flights that finally deposited him in Italy, where he was met by an English-speaking driver.

For a moment, he felt himself the recipient of more than he deserved. Cardinal Bennedito put an end to that. The cardinal kept him waiting so long that Walsh rediscovered the virtues of humility. Someone pointed out that now was a perfect opportunity to play tourist. Walsh was disinclined to take advantage of the situation. First, he wanted to be available the moment his superior called on him. Second, he had already played tourist back when he was a student at Notre Dame, and had visited Vatican City one special summer.

Young Ashley Walsh hadn't been overly impressed with the sights that astounded and delighted the other students. He admitted the columns were big, the paintings bright and colorful, the incense evocative of mystery, the gardens soothing and aromatic, the tapestries shimmering walls of ancient beauty. He saw that the ceilings were as high as everyone else could see. He heard the deep swelling of music, the perfect blending of young human voices with deep-throated organs speaking as from the center of the earth. He could smell and taste and touch as well as the others. The only trouble was that he didn't feel anything.

Unmoved by the purple and gold world flowing all about him, he was teased by one of the other students for being a closet Protestant. He laughed at that, surprising the other who had never heard him laugh. The trouble, he assured his fellow undergraduate, was that he, Ashley Walsh, did well and fully believe in the orthodox claims of the Church—thus committing the crime of apostasy against the modern and relevant church. Such a shocking claim rendered his lack of aesthetic sense a moot point.

He remembered that long-ago summer as the word came to him

that he was expected by Cardinal Bennedito. The man was a robust sixty-year-old, with silver-white hair offset by a black eyepatch. He looked like a pirate.

"Sit down, sit down," said the older man, his English barely accented. "May I offer you a cigar?"

"No thank you, your eminence. I don't smoke."

"Wine then?"

"Yes, thank you," answered Walsh, marveling how the man moved quickly and efficiently, like an athlete. The red wine soon passing the monsignor's lips was much better than what he'd sampled aboard the plane. It warmed him from the inside out, and suddenly all the little details of the office were easier to appreciate. The chair was very comfortable.

"I'm sorry it took so long to work you into the schedule," said the cardinal, lighting up a Havana cigar without asking the monsignor if there were any objections to his smoking—but in fact, Walsh didn't mind. "You have been recommended by Monsignor Cranston to be his replacement, and there is no objection from the committee. Of course, Cranston's department falls under my section, but I'll leave you pretty much a free hand. Frankly, I like to have as little to do with the Black Room as possible—and you know, of course, that's just the tip of the iceberg."

The free flow of words put Walsh in mind of one of his father's monologues. He adopted the same expression now he had as a child: a slight smile on the face, accompanied by an occasional nod.

Fortunately, the cardinal reached a stopping point which offered the monsignor a breathing space, along with the unfortunate promise that lessons in the obscure would continue under the tutelage of the other monsignor. "Yours is the most interesting task in all the Vatican, or under it," said the cardinal, leaving Walsh to wonder if this might be a cryptic comment.

Walsh followed the cardinal down the labyrinthine corridors, foolishly thinking how easily one could become lost. He had yet to appreciate how simple and direct a floor plan the Vatican enjoyed compared to other places. A more immediate problem was a sudden fit of sneezing that seized him next to a little altar with an attractive bit of greenery embracing the old stone.

Back when he'd spent time in the monastery, he'd read about the monks who tend the flowers and plants of Rome in buildings at least a thousand years old. Now as he blew his nose in the handker-chief thoughtfully supplied by the cardinal, he noticed an odor un-like any he'd encountered before. There was a strange combina-tion of wet and dry smells blended together, as if he were travers-ing a dry swamp. The purple cords that hung before the ornate doors suddenly seemed to be jungle vines. Walsh was dizzy.

"Are you all right?" asked the cardinal.

"Yes, I'm sorry," he reassured his superior.

"We're almost there," said the other, pointing to a door at the end of the corridor. The door was no different from others, but the wall around it seemed to have a peculiar yellow stain.

"I'll leave you here," said the cardinal, which struck Walsh as odd—to come all this way and not take those last few steps and make introductions. But already the cardinal was retreating, and all Walsh could think was how glad he was that when he sneezed nothing untoward got on the red cassock.

Right before he knocked on the door, Walsh felt something grab at his heart. He assumed it had something to do with his health. Then he was across the threshold, standing in the fabled Black Room and being received by the oldest, weariest man he had ever en-countered.

"Thank God you have come, Monsignor Walsh. I am Monsignor Cranston." He feared the old man's fingers would come off in his hand as he gingerly shook the withered appendage. "You are prob-ably wondering why you were chosen for this very special service to the Church."

"The thought had crossed my mind," answered Walsh as he was maneuvered into a comfortable chair.

Unlike the cardinal, this man offered no amenities. He seemed to be in a terrific hurry to get his words out all at once before he disin-tegrated before the eyes of his startled guest. His voice was the only strong thing about him. "We studied thousands to find the best man to replace me. You can see that I don't have much time left." His head shook slightly as he spoke, and Walsh tried to force himself not to watch the sporadic movement. Looking directly into the old man's watery eyes was a problem, too, as their color made Walsh sick.

Suddenly the man grinned. The smile seemed evil, as if it had been cultivated over the course of as many centuries as the ancient shrubbery. Then Walsh found himself wondering why he associated evil with antiquity, in this of all places. His faith seemed to break loose from its moorings and float just out of reach.

"You'll be able to handle the assignment, believe me," said Cranston. "You know, it's kind of amusing that you're the first American. I'm British. Originally I thought working here would give me a chance to improve my Italian. But you'll find you don't have much contact with other people. It's a good job for someone who likes lots of quiet."

The realization sunk in as to just how thorough the investigation must have been. Some roads lead to Chicago. "But what exactly is required?" asked Walsh.

The old man sighed. "Best to get this over with." he said. "What do you think we keep in the Black Room?"

Walsh looked around the room. The books and documents and scrolls were neatly arranged, as he would have expected. He was somewhat surprised that the place wasn't musty. At least there was no danger of his sneezing fit recurring. The lack of dust suggested that either superb janitorial skills were regularly applied or perhaps more people had access to forbidden texts than the Office of Propaganda would admit. (Walsh prided himself on knowing that the Church had implemented the first Office of Propaganda.) On the other hand, if people came in here regularly then the job wouldn't be as lonely as Cranston was intimating.

"The historical heresies," answered Walsh. "The Gnostic heresies primarily—theological debates involving some very fine points."

"Tell me, Monsignor Walsh, what you think the Church position was regarding the Nag Hammadi?"

This was becoming a bit annoying. Walsh didn't mind playing student in the Vatican, but not at this elementary level. "Well, you're referring to the fourth-century Coptic texts taken from the Greek originals. These uncanonized gospels were unearthed in, uh…"

Cranston helpfully filled in: "The year that saw the destruction of the Third Reich—1945."

Walsh blinked. Cranston had made an odd association there. "Well, yes, 1945. Naturally the Church is never pleased when these heresies receive publicity, leading souls astray."

"No more than she approved translating the Bible into vulgar tongues where careless readings gave us the Protestant problem, eh?" The way Cranston asked the question, Walsh wasn't sure if he might not be joking.

"Ashley," said Cranston, surprising the other by the sudden familiarity, "I am about to share with you a truth that no one can know without becoming its guardian."

Walsh laughed. Again Cranston smiled. There were no deep, dark secrets in the Church, other than perhaps the standard requirements of sharp business dealings in the modern world. The whole quarrel with the Gnostics was their insistence on a secret knowledge vouchsafed to an elect while the masses were fed on fairy tales. The war of spirit against the flesh was an inevitable consequence of that sort of paranoid thinking, ultimately threatening to dethrone God and render pointless the sacrifice of His son. Was Cranston putting him to a bizarre test to see if his replacement was foolish enough to believe in the fantasies of the ignorant?

Cranston stood. "The Gnostic heresies are false," he said.

Walsh laughed again. "That's quite a secret," he replied.

Cranston frowned and continued: "You don't understand. I mean to say they were created by the True Church to mislead the curious and proud from consideration of far more dangerous things. The persecution of heretics always had as its target one or two people who had discovered the truth, but their words would drown in the ocean of anguish."

Images entered the mind of the man from Chicago, images he would cast out as false idols but which stubbornly impinged on his consciousness: of witches burned at the stake, of Cathars put to the sword, of fire and blood in this crusade or that inquisition. Walsh had studied enough history to know that not everyone tormented by the Church over the centuries had been an innocent, or a mere political enemy. But he also knew that his Church was an institution that had learned the limitations of force; and this was appropriate if it was in fact not a human institution but a projection into our world of the Cosmic Absolute.

So Monsignor Walsh summoned what was left of his willpower and challenged Monsignor Cranston with: "What are you talking about?"

"This," said Cranston, forcing creaking limbs to support his weight, and taking a few steps over to the far wall. Reaching behind a bookcase, he touched a switch and the case swung open. It didn't creak. It must receive regular use. "I have opened the door," said the old man, his voice firm as ever. "Are you coming?"

The hesitation Walsh had felt before entering the Black Room did not return, even though he suspected that now would be a very good time for forthright indecisiveness. "I'm right behind you," said the American.

The stairway that seemed to lead down to eternity was less a surprise to him than were the fluorescent lights that stretched to a pinpoint, illuminating polished stone steps as far as the eye could see. Modernity apparently had its points.

The apparent absurdity of what he saw suddenly concerned Walsh less than a flash of human concern for his frail mentor, who seemed to think he could make it down those uncountable steps. "You can't mean to go down there?" asked Walsh. "Not in your condition!"

"Don't worry about me," said Cranston. "Are you in good enough condition to handle the stairway?"

"I think so," said Walsh, feeling a bit distracted and stupid. Before he could say or do anything else, Cranston removed a small golden bell from his loose sleeves and rang it just once. A most remarkable nun appeared from out of the shadows behind the two men. She must have been in the Black Room all along. She was fully six feet tall and so muscular that her habit barely concealed the bulging biceps on her arms. She reached out for the frail priest, grabbed him like a sack of communion wafers and, throwing him over her broad back, started down the steps.

"Are you coming?" Cranston asked again. Watching his receding form on the back of the incredible nun, Walsh thought that the old-fashioned way of doing things apparently had its points.

It took over an hour to reach the bottom of the stairs. Walsh didn't know what astonished him more: the engineering required to create such a vast tunnel, or the Amazonian nun carrying the old man on her back. The incongruities captured his imagination and reduced him to a childlike level—where his uncertain faith could find a natural habitat. The world was young again, full of surprises. When people and places ceased to be predictable there might even be room for God, that most unpredictable Absolute. Walsh didn't have time to be tired as he descended into the earth. He was too busy allowing himself to experience a detour from his life.

"Tombs!" cried out the voice of Monsignor Cranston, reverberating off the walls, carrying the conviction of a life almost used up. "What must any old building become? A tomb, of course. The older the structure, the more tombs it must contain. Think about it, boy. The Vatican is old enough to contain a thousand whispers from a thousand lost hopes. Dead frustrations give birth to secrets. Secrets must have shadowed corridors and sliding panels and trapdoors. And not even that grand old building above our heads could possibly house them all. So for over a thousand years this underground world has grown like a specially tended plant cultivated by one of the brothers."

"Who built this?" asked Walsh, not feeling the least bit poetical.

The gigantic nun snorted and shifted her charge from one massive shoulder to the other. Cranston continued along the same line: "Why, it answered the needs of a million prayers, unwinding like a great underground snake, hollowing through the earth."

Metaphorical language had never appealed to Walsh. A teacher had once pronounced him passionately literal-minded. "Who built it?" he repeated.

Cranston allowed himself a laugh that broke into a high-pitched cackle, the first time his voice seemed to match his emaciated appearance. But he recovered himself, and spoke in the deepest tones yet: "You believe the Church is the body of believers. You believe the institution we serve is a manifestation of something divine, no matter how corrupted by human imperfections." Although he was speaking in a declamatory style, Walsh kept mentally adding question marks...but the older monsignor was the furthest thing from a Jesuit instructor. Walsh placidly listened to the litany of what he was supposed to believe.

"Shut up, you old relic!" screeched the nun, shocking Walsh more by her hysterical voice than the irreverent content of her words. The old man merely laughed again. She held onto his frail body more tightly than ever.

"So you should be honored," continued Cranston, "as we plumb the depths of your mother. You enter her sacred body here below, and there will be soft things and decaying things and wet things that belong in the womb or the tomb—different words for the same place."

Even Walsh could run out of patience. "You're not going to tell me who built this, are you?"

Now it was the nun's turn to laugh. "Insects!" she spat out. "Two worms wriggling under Our Father's House."

The woman never seemed to get tired. Her litany of pejoratives was uttered without any noticeable change in breathing, whereas Walsh was huffing and puffing to keep up with her.

"I've been rude," said Cranston. "Allow me to introduce Sister Mary Kaitlan."

Before Walsh could say something polite, the remarkable woman shifted the stream of her abuse into more graphic areas: "You're both little cowards, wishing you were climbing into your mother's womb instead of exploring these sterile tunnels."

The old man caught the expression on the younger man. "It's all right," he said, "she's Irish radical. Just trying to get a rise out of you, so to speak."

"Pope John Paul the First would have fixed all you bastards," she screamed, "with Vatican 3. He would have overturned Pope Innocent's rule about nuns not participating in saying Mass, hearing confession and giving communion."

"She's really very political," Cranston assured Walsh. "She started out working with the poor in Northern Ireland and she thought John Paul the First would clean up Vatican financing and..."

"Lesbianism should be a sacrament!" she screamed. "Priests should marry teenage girls, then molest little boys in front of their parents."

"Oh," said Walsh, followed by a well-considered, "Ahhh?"

"She always makes me want to have a good prayer," said the old man.

"The same as a good bowel movement," added the profane nun.

The expression spreading across Walsh's face inspired a grimace from old Cranston, whose yellow, bad teeth gave the appearance of a partially eaten ear of corn. "Don't mind her," the old one advised. "She's being punished and we should not pass judgment on a fellow creature."

The word "creature" struck a chord in Walsh's mind, a most uncharitable chord. Although deep and sincere prayer did not come easily to him, Walsh recited under his breath, "Though I walk amid distress, You preserve me, O Lord." There must be something good he could notice about Sister Kaitlan. She carried the old man on her back without complaint. Talking to her was at least a distraction from the physical strain of the long walk down the stone staircase.

Meanwhile, the subject of his charitable thoughts snarled at her fragile charge with: "You're a Christian wimp!" The old man cackled obscenely.

When Cranston had regained his composure he fumed his head at a painful angle, looking back at poor Walsh struggling to keep up, and said, "She is modem in her views. Which means, of course, that she doesn't really know what she thinks."

"I don't doubt it," agreed Walsh. "To change the subject for a moment, I'd like to know where we are. We keep descending, but for some reason it doesn't become any colder."

Both nun and elder churchman laughed. Walsh didn't feel any better about the situation. Sister Kaitlan sensed his weakness as a carnivore smells blood. In her usual indelicate manner, she volunteered that, "You damned priests need Jesus, another man showing you how to manipulate women."

"Excuse me," said Walsh, not at all politely as irritation crept into his voice, "but do you accept the divinity of our savior?"

"Ha!" she exclaimed. "Talk about loading the dice. He's another male, isn't He?"

Shaking his head, Walsh finally felt the humility his brothers in the monastery had tried unsuccessfully to inculcate in him. Cranston was sympathetic and offered, "She has room for improvement. You must remember that the Church gave up the Inquisition long ago and excommunication has been found politically unwise. We must love one another for a reason never admitted."

"And what reason is that?" asked Walsh.

"Later," whispered the old man, "you'll have more answers than you can bear."

They trudged on in silence for about five minutes. Walsh resolved not to be the first to break the silence even though his head was aching with questions. It fell on the loquacious librarian to start up the conversation again with: "Sister Kaitlan is not alone in doing penance."

"Old fool," she muttered.

"She doesn't sound very repentant," commented Walsh.

"So, Ashley... I believe that's your first name ?" said Cranston, not seeming entirely comfortable with the personal approach. "Perhaps you would care to question the subtleties of her not very liberating theology?"

"Reactionary fungus," said the nun. "There would be more room to house the poor if we blow up the Vatican!"

Walsh decided to get into the spirit of the thing and put a question to her: "I suppose you believe in birth control?"

"Absolutely," she confessed.

"Would you do away with celibacy?"

"There is no celibacy. We must admit the fact!"

Emboldened, he pushed on: "I suppose you would allow abortion."

There was a sharp intake of breath from both the woman and old man riding on her back. "Shame on you," scolded Cranston.

"I'm a Catholic," added the nun in a hurt tone of voice. "And by the way, American monsignor, did you remember to kiss Cardinal Bennedito's ring?"

"I give up," said Walsh, wishing there were surrender papers on which he could affix his John Hancock. The silence returned except for the heavy footfalls, and echoes of footfalls, as they continued their fatiguing walk.

Suddenly Cranston shouted two words, the theological significance of which seemed unclear: "Look out!" Then Walsh saw the rat. It had been sleeping on a step only a few inches away from his foot. As the creature raised its head to investigate the sudden noise interrupting its solitude, Walsh had an all-too-close view of the size of the thing. From head to rump, the animal was the size of his forearm. Which wouldn't have been so bad if not for the added feature of the tail, twice as long as the body.

As if wishing to satisfy the curiosity of the humans, the rat leapt into the air where its head was on a level with theirs. Eye to eye with the rodent, Walsh decided it resembled a small kangaroo more than a rat, a pleasing thought until the jaws opened to reveal all the teeth in the world, long and sharp and nasty, guarding cheeks in which remains of old meals were stored, ripening until needed.

Walsh suppressed a desire to throw up; a stronger desire was to run screaming back up the stairs, but Sister Kaitlan came to the rescue. Brandishing a mean looking ruler (which she must have kept hidden on her person), the muscular nun swung the weapon in a wide arc. With a sickening crunch the wood splintered against the head of the hapless animal, leaving a red ruin where the eyes had been. The sleek body, now seeming smaller than before, plummeted down the stairs as the belligerent nun let out a war cry consisting of: "Damned Giant African Rats think that they own the place."

"We're nearing the bottom," said Cranston. "I see the dark at the end of the tunnel." Sure enough, the lights ran out where the stairs ended at a stone floor. Beyond was a pool of darkness. "The rats like to come up into the light," Cranston finished.

The obvious thought appalled Walsh. "You mean there are more down there?"

"They're not as bad as the snakes," Kaitlan assured him.

"I'm sure you'll enjoy our little menagerie," Cranston threw in.

"Things that creepeth or crawleth are the least of your troubles," hissed Kaitlan, finally staring directly into Walsh's eyes, whereupon he realized that he preferred the contemplative visage of the rat.

None of this was in the job description, thought Walsh...before remembering that he never saw a job description. Reaching flat ground again was sufficient cause for him to say a prayer of thanks, and to avoid the body of the dead, or stunned, rodent lying nearby.

Sister Kaitlan, not even winded, unceremoniously dropped Monsignor Cranston who, catlike, landed on his feet. The old man hurried over to the young man and whispered, "This next part will be a bit uncomfortable. You're not claustrophobic, are you?" As his eyes grew accustomed to the latest attraction of the tour, Walsh was horrified to notice a narrow, black hole in the wall immediately facing them. Cranston continued: "I've been enjoying our discussion as much as any Jesuit teacher...."

"Or Freemason," the reliably mad nun got in her two liras worth.

Cranston ignored her. "We must observe silence for a while. We don't want to draw undue attention to ourselves while in the tunnels." He let his thin fingers play across the stone just above the black hole as if searching for something.

The primary reason Walsh knew that he would go forward was that he wasn't about to flee back up those interminable stairs! As a final inducement, the nun drew close and, breath rich in whiskey, warned that, "We don't want to wake the fairies like we did that poor rat, now do we? The little ones fear the *Scapular*, Latin words from the Gospels a priest may wear around his neck, but I'll wager neither you nor Monsignor Cranston remembered to bring such good protection."

"Stop teasing him, Sister Kaitlan," Cranston admonished her.

"Surely he must know," she continued, an Irish brogue sneaking into the cadences of her speech, "that they keep their gold and jewels and pearls under the ground, and the Holy Father finances the world's wealthiest religious institution by crafty dealings with the wee folk."

Just about then Cranston found what he'd been looking for—a slight protrusion of stone. He pressed gently against it and a dim light appeared at the mouth of the tunnel. This illumination drew the nun's attention away from the American—drew her as it might a very large moth. Without hesitation, Cranston dropped to all fours and crawled into the space. Kaitlan followed. Walsh followed too, convinced that if the vigorous nun's bulk could fit through, so could he. And blessed be the light!

The first thirty feet weren't so bad. The low-wattage light bulbs weren't as nice as the bright, white fluorescent tubes...but they were a lot better than what came next. The dim light ran out around a tight curve. No more bulbs hanging overhead. Just darkness—oily, black, quiet as the tomb.

It was a no-nonsense game of follow-the-leader and Cranston wasn't stopping. He wasn't even slowing down. Walsh resolved that he would not make a peep of protest if they crawled right down to the center of the earth. Perhaps all that was needed for the rebirth of faith was to be obedient and do something deeply foolish. The last sight afforded him before leaving the light behind was of Sister Kaitlan's posterior, each cheek moving rhythmically, mechanically, as she marched forward on her knees.

Unpleasant odors assailed him, combining the exquisite delights of old cat boxes with a sour mustiness. The tunnel became narrower, as well, but so long as the nun could squeeze through he was unworried about following in her wake. Desperate to find something good in the situation, he experienced a moment of joy over the fact that other life forms of the creeping and crawling variety had not chosen this moment to share the incomparable gift of existence with him...in a dark, dank, reeking, foul tunnel.

Suddenly he had to cough. He didn't want to cough. Someone, or something, might hear him and come slithering, crawling, flooding down the tunnel to smother them all, choke out their lives and munch on their souls. Hoping to assuage the maddening tickle in his throat, he tried altering his breathing and then swallowed hard. Nothing helped. He bit his lip until he felt the sting and tasted salty blood on his tongue. That didn't help either. He lasted as long as he could and then he coughed. In his mind the sound was like heavy artillery. He held his breath, waiting for the others to say or do something. They kept moving and so did he.

All bad things come to an end, especially if something worse lies ahead. The tunnel let out into an underground cavern of tremendous dimensions, lit by three globes floating overhead: one blue, one red, one yellow. They were not at ground level. The tunnel they had used opened onto a ledge, a natural shelf of rock, providing ample room for even Sister Kaitlan. The shifting lights made it easy to see that the walls of the cavern were honeycombed with at least a hundred identical holes, suggesting a network of tunnels as complicated as the Dewey Decimal System.

"You can speak now," said Cranston.

"Cough some more, if you like," added Sister Kaitlan, and he couldn't be sure if this was a moment of solicitude or only more sarcasm.

"What are those?" asked Walsh, pointing at the pulsating globes.

"Don't tell him!" Kaitlan nearly shouted. Turning to Walsh, she clarified: "It's you I'm thinking about. He'll pontificate, sure as we're standing here."

"Sister, have you considered a vow of silence as a way to get to know yourself better?" asked the elder monsignor.

"Ha," said the nun. "You've got one foot in the grave and another on a banana peel, you old coot. See that you don't fall."

Finding the nun more intolerable than ever, Walsh surprised himself by coming to her rescue. What seemed to require a moment of heroics resulted from passing in front of another tunnel opening, at which precise instant a boa constrictor came out into the light and promptly wrapped itself around Sister Mary Kaitlan. Without thinking about what he was doing, Walsh leapt forward and wrapped his hands around the cold coils even as the serpent tightened them. It seemed perfectly in character that the nun would laugh at him.

"You do have virtues," said Cranston, admiringly "You care about other people—enough, perhaps, to keep dangerous secrets from them."

Stretching her neck forward as if a snake herself, the nun rolled out a long, red tongue and licked the head of the snake. Then she kissed it. "A little piece of Eden," she murmured.

Walsh thought he had reached his breaking point. "I'm tired of this," he announced primly. "I can only put up with so many things not being what they seem. I am fast approaching the point where if you are not honest with me about everything right now, I will resign and take the first flight back to the States."

The globes above suddenly grew brighter, flooding the chamber with rainbow colors. They made a sound similar to choirboys hitting their highest note. The moment had Epiphany written all over it.

"You'll do well in this position," said Cranston.

"That's your punishment," said the nun, "and your reward, too, if you're good at turning the other cheek."

Taking a deep breath, Walsh tried again: "What are those spheres overhead?"

"The Father, the Son and the Holy Ghost?" suggested Cranston.

"Holy Spirit," the nun corrected.

Cranston shrugged. "Good and bad things come in threes," he sighed. "Let's show this young man the true secrets he has traveled so far to meet."

They walked single-file down the ledge. Each time they passed in front of a tunnel, Walsh felt a tingling sensation on the back of his neck. He didn't want any more surprises that slithered. As if aware of his prejudice, the snake rested its head on the nun's shoulder where it could eye him balefully. In search of the good again, he admitted that the serpent entwined about the nun's stout frame helped to keep her calm. Her right hand stroked up and down the smooth reptilian hide.

While she occupied herself with her pet, he allowed himself a quiet moment in which to contemplate his deepening confusion. Although he'd had only one geology course in college, and his grade had not been outstanding, he remembered enough to wonder if this cavern made any sense for this area of Rome. The heat bothered him especially. If anything, it was becoming warmer as they descended.

The place stank of old flowers, as if someone had taken millions of petals that had been pressed between the pages of library books and ground them into a fine powder, sprinkling them in the air. At least it was easy to breathe despite the heaviness of the perfume. In a different place he might have found it pleasant.

They reached the floor. A great, flat expanse spread out before them with a small group of people standing in the center, apparently waiting for visitors. The three from above went to greet the assemblage below. As they drew nearer, Walsh began to fall back. A primitive instinct commanded him to run but his intellect told it to crawl back under a rock. The situation was what it was. He'd gone too far to turn back now. Despite a certain reluctance to pray, he thought the duty to pray made more sense than surrendering to the virtue of hope. He caught up with the others, determined not to hope for anything.

They were close to the figures now, and the figures all seemed to be men attired in white robes vaguely resembling hospital smocks. Most had long hair and beards. A few were bald. The most disturbing quality was how the men all stared ahead, eyes open, unblinking. As if a boy again, Cranston threw off his black cassock, and years of accumulated pain apparently went with it.

The old man danced in front of the staring figures.

"Hey, Ashley," he called out, "this is the big payoff. Not many mortal eyes behold this, let me tell you. The faces may not be familiar—but, oh, you know their names!"

Cranston ran forward, spindly arms waving like uncooked strips of pale, white chicken. With shaking, fragile hands he made pathetic fists and punched at the immobile men, but he stopped short of actually touching them. At no point did Walsh doubt that the silent figures were made of flesh and blood, although they were as silent and still as wax statues.

"This one," announced Cranston, pointing to a handsome young face, "is the Buddha. A prince with a heart!" Cranston threaded his way deeper into the group. Making as if to pull on the dark beard of a tall man with fierce features, he intoned, "You may have wondered about the appearance of this famous prince of Egypt. Allow me to introduce Moses. Is it only me, or does the Law Giver appear more like a prosecuting attorney than a friendly defense counselor?" A short man with even darker hair was identified as Mohammed.

While Cranston was enjoying the role of emcee, the snake unwound itself from Sister Kaitlan and departed from the human company. No sooner did this occur than the nun became belligerent again. "Where are the women?" she asked. "I see a Roman emperor over there who thought he was a god, and plenty of other no-accounts, but where are Aphrodite, Asherah, Astarte..."

"And she's only in the A's," proclaimed Cranston with good humor.

"There are no manifestations of the Goddess here," she plowed on. "No Hera. No..."

"None of your harlot idolatry here, woman," sang Cranston—he was literally singing—"your slut goddesses aren't here for the same reason that Odin or Zeus didn't stop by to say hello. Only real people touched by God stuff are in this select gathering."

Changing tactics, the nun asked a question the monsignor was not expecting. "Then where's the Virgin?"

"I don't know why the real fisher of men never brought her," said Cranston.

While this thoroughly demented dialogue was going on, Walsh noticed a peacock race out of a hole in the distance. It made the weirdest sound he'd ever heard. He felt like running with the bird and entering another dark tunnel before the light of the globes above revealed a sight he was afraid would scorch his mind. Instinct was warring with intellect again but it didn't have a chance; for one thing, he was too damned tired to run.

"And here He is," said Cranston, sounding for all the world like a talk show host revealing the prize guest of the evening. One man stood at the center of the group, occupying a place of honor. He was of average height and build, but exuded a sense of authority that Walsh could almost touch. Kaitlan looked away.

Closer examination revealed a face that Walsh would never forget for a very good reason. The face changed every few seconds. At first Walsh thought it might be a trick of the light, but the features were actually shifting in front of him. The nose flattened, then grew more narrow. The eyes moved farther apart, changed color, then came closer again. The hair extended like unkempt vines and then shortened again as quickly as a fishing line being reeled in. The most startling feature of the shape-shifting was that the man's race changed as well.

Cranston walked over to Walsh and placed a hand on the younger man's shoulder. "How does it feel to stand before Jesus Christ?" he asked.

"You must be insane," came out of Walsh's mouth, but the words lacked conviction.

"At least he understands the implications," sneered the nun. "If He's here, the incarnation becomes confusing."

"This is all some kind of trick," said Walsh. "Why are you doing this to me?"

"You are initiated," said both Cranston and Kaitlan at the same instant. That was the final straw. Walsh ran. He was not as fast as the peacock.

Heading for the nearest tunnel at ground level, he didn't care if monsters waited for him. But he was focused on the wrong area. A shadow as black as all the tunnels fell across him as he ran and he chanced to glance up. Something very large was near the ceiling. It had been above the globes, in fact, but now it was coming down. The thing had moved between the source of light and the little speck down below, running.

An attempt to run faster only succeeded in Walsh becoming tangled in his own cassock. He fell sprawling on the hard ground and cut his jaw on a sharp projection of rock. Fear spurred him on to greater exertion, but he tripped again before he could resume his futile attempt to reach the hole in the cave wall. He felt something alien brush against his back. He couldn't resist flipping over to see the nature of his attacker. A moment later he wished he hadn't done that.

Floating in the air directly above him was a giant fish, roughly the size of a family station wagon. Rolling over quickly he did manage to get out from under it and successfully jump to his feet. He would have preferred doing this without all the screaming but at least he was up and running again. By this time the monsignor and the nun had caught up to him, one on each side, and they were attempting to reason with him.

"Calm down," Cranston told him. "It won't hurt you." The fish floated lazily in the air, drifting closer to investigate Walsh. He gazed at the great eye of the fish, which had the appearance of a marble that had been crushed flat and then stuck to the scaly head. The natural blue-green scales refracted some interesting patterns under the alternating red-blue-yellow lights.

Cranston gave the fish a playful push and, like a Thanksgiving

Day balloon, it spun around slowly before swimming through the air and approaching Walsh from another angle. Now Walsh had a clear view of the monster's teeth. They were elongated with serrated edges, and shaped like spatulas on the end—a textbook example of the bristletooth fish that feeds on feces, seeking out carbon, nitrogen, protein and lipids, along with nutrients in the ocean waters. Walsh started giggling uncontrollably as he wondered what this creature found in the atmosphere to satisfy an appetite commensurate with its size.

Cranston had the answers, all right: "This is a *Time Eater*, Ashley old boy. You might say it is the original fish of the faith. It swims down the corridors of time and ingests the essence of God when manifest in human form. Then the fish deposits everything here."

"The detritus of history," Walsh mumbled to himself, but the others could hear. "Man's deepest beliefs are what drift through time."

"And now you understand the secret we must guard," Cranston said, sounding almost gentle. "The old Church taught there is only one way to salvation. Add up all the heresies and what do you get? The modern mind, with its belief of many roads to salvation. We must spare the world the truth, give it a brief moment of hope when that is all it may ever have."

"The truth?" asked Walsh, his voice sounding weak and tired.

The nun screamed and put her fingers in her ears. She had obviously heard what Cranston was about to say many times before. "There are no roads to salvation," the old man whispered. "Every promise of salvation ends here, in this quiet cavern."

Walsh stumbled away, aware for the first time in his life how badly he needed a redeemer. He had to see Christ again, Christ not risen but preserved in glory, exalted as the jewel in the Vatican collection.

The face was still changing, a hundred profiles under the triple sun burning overhead. Walsh wanted to reach out and touch the face, to kiss the forehead darkening and whitening forever and ever. He wanted salvation not only for himself but for the old man who stood patting the cold scales of the monster fish hovering in the air; and he wanted to save the mad nun who sat on the ground, weeping over loss and pain he could never imagine. And he wanted salvation for all the people he had never been able to touch in his cold and lonely life.

He thought he might say a prayer but he couldn't think of one, not one. Then a line of Dante came to him and he settled for that, speaking the words out loud, as carefully as possible:

"The uneven tombs cover the even plain—such fields I saw here, spread in all directions, except that here the tombs were chests of pain..."

For a while it seemed that my career would consist of rewriting "Moon of Ice" every few years. The first version of my story in which the Nazis win World War II appeared in the March 1982 *Amazing*, thanks to Elinor Mavor. Then a longer version appeared in a selection of the History Book Club, *Hitler Victorious*, thanks to Gregory Benford. Finally there was a novel from William Morrow and then Grafton and then Tor, all thanks to David Hartwell and to my first agent, Cherry Weiner.

I did around five years of research on the Nazis. That kind of obsession had to find other ways to express itself, especially when I could never find a publisher interested in a sequel to the novel. So I worked on a handful of short stories drawing on the research from *Moon of Ice*. Two of them are collaborations: "The Light that Blinds" with Victor Koman and "The Littlest Stormbringer" with William Alan Ritch.

"Under an Appalling Sky" seems the right choice for this collection. It was the first of these stories. And I received the following accolade from Robert Bloch in a letter he wrote in March, 1993: "'Under an Appalling Sky' is a very powerful story...and bound to attract deserved comment and attention in days to come."

Under an Appalling Sky

Speak only of that which one has overcome.
—Friedrich Nietzsche, *Human, All too Human*

Against the howling of the wind one angry voice hardly made a difference... except to a human ear, up close to twisting lips under gray whiskers. Dark clouds made a fist above the heads of the Alberg expedition, huddled together on a rocky crag in the Himalayan mountains. The voice coming out of the bearded face made accusations. The voice found fault. And there was something just a little mad about the voice.

It asked: "If you don't believe in the Grail, why are you here?" As Professor Alberg berated a young SS man, the rest of the expedition fell silent. They had only been kidding the somewhat pompous representative from the Ministry of Culture, but when they heard his stern and angry tone all the years of obeying Hitler spoke to them, and made them stand at attention. Karl was no guiltier of mischief than the rest, but he had been singled out to answer for their high spirits—for nothing more than pretending that any old rock was the object of their quest and they could go home. Karl's comrades knew he wouldn't spread the blame around. He was a good Nazi.

"I meant no disrespect, Herr Doktor Professor," said Karl. "I believe in the Grail."

"Of course you do," said Alberg, voice dripping with sarcasm. "You believed when we were comfortable in the south of France, exploring the Cathar excavations. You believed it less so in Jerusalem, when we started running into trouble. And now that we're going to work hard in a bad climate, well, now you make with the jokes."

Although a little man, the professor's indignation made him seem larger, as though rage could puff him up to the stature he thought his due. He constantly reminded everyone of his personal association with Alfred Rosenberg, for whose outre theories the Fuehrer had established the ministry in the first place. Karl had originally volunteered for the expedition in hope of working directly with the great man who had authored *The Myth of the Twentieth Century*—the first explication of Nazi philosophy placed on the Catholic Index of banned books. But when the mission finally got underway, Rosenberg was too ill to participate. Karl suspected the illness might be Himmler's handiwork, as the ongoing feud between the two men had escalated to the point where anything was possible. All Karl knew was that if Himmler had poisoned Rosenberg, then Himmler was responsible for sticking Karl with this second-rate professor in charge of something terribly important to the future of the Reich. Karl was not the only member of the SS to hate the ostensible leader of the SS!

"Are we going to get back to work or not?" asked Gertrude Feuer, an American-German anthropologist on loan from Harvard as part of a cultural exchange program. Her friends called her Gertie. No one called her Gertie on the expedition.

She was answered by the highest ranking officer, an SS Gruppenfuehrer named Baulmer, selected in part for his lack of imagination. His father had been instrumental in the Night of the Long Knives when the SS slaughtered the leadership of the SA. From this exercise in carnage had come the elder Baulmer's insight into how to make friends and influence people. His son had made him proud. His son knew how to make people calm, especially those who were slated for execution.

The young Baulmer's voice was almost too sweet and reasonable to be heard in the maelstrom: "Please don't concern yourself, Frau Feuer, over matters of policy." He gestured the professor away from the others, exchanging a sympathetic glance with young Karl as he did so. Karl knew everything was going to be all right. Besides, it was something of an honor to be shouted at by Alberg. The little man was only dangerous when he lowered his voice, which he never did except to conspire against a fellow German.

Since the Third Reich's victory in Europe, and nuclear stalemate with the United States, one might have expected a lessening of paranoia on the part of National Socialism. But one would have reckoned without Hitler, who had recently announced over color television, "While there is one Jew in Europe, we are at risk. While there is one Communist, one Capitalist, one Gypsy, one degenerate race-mixing homosexual, we are at risk." The TV critic who had wondered out loud how a homosexual was in a position to mix races one way or the other had been retired prematurely, without pension, but the general tone was clear. Vigilance was the standard.

Rosenberg's plan to build a Gnostic German Aryan Church received all the funding he could ever want. Both Hitler and Goebbels realized that a de-Judaecized version of Christianity would be easier to sell to the new Europe than Himmler's pipe dream of restoring the Old religion, complete with Odin, Thor and the whole pantheon. The SS had its own country of Burgundy to play around in, but the rest of Europe required careful handling.

If only Christ could be made out to be an Aryan, and St. Paul (Saul) removed from his position of influence, it would be a mortal blow to the last hold of the Jew over the Christian mind! Getting rid of the Old Testament wouldn't be easy, but it might work if the New Church could satisfy the age-old dream of finding the Holy Grail. He Who Held the Grail could change the rules to... anything. Lutherans and Catholics would lose their influence in Germany; and the new Christianity would be exactly what Hitler wanted.

As Baulmer explained the need for brave German men to let off a little steam with a joke or two, and Professor Alberg fumed but kept silent, Karl studied the faces around him, what he could make out under their scarfs and goggles. He wondered how many of them really believed in the Grail, or had even decided what the Grail might be. The professor had said it could be one of dozens of things: a stone, a book, or even the traditional chalice. With that sort of flexibility, why not just say anything was the Grail, call it quits and get the hell home? Unfortunately, arbitrary decisions like that could only be made by someone with the right list of university degrees.

Karl noticed that their Tibetan guide was bareheaded; and the man showed no discomfort from the flakes of snow settling on his smooth shaven dome. Karl couldn't help wondering if this fellow was the superman among them. There was no contradiction to National Socialist logic in this. The Indian civilization had been founded by Aryans, after all, and only racial degeneration over the centuries had weakened it. All that had been great in that civilization was preserved among the enlightened few in Tibet. Had not the swastika been chosen by old Haushofer as the party symbol because it was the Tibetan symbol of the sun? Hadn't Hitler brought a small Tibetan colony to Berlin and Munich as far back as 1926, seven years before he achieved power? Once he had the strength of a whole nation behind him, Hitler financed expeditions to find the Grail every year, all to no avail.

The Tibetan guide had a secret name that none of the party knew but for Alberg. (They would have exchanged such information at the Ahnenerbe, the SS occult bureau.) The guide was a high adept who had helped Alberg to convince Rosenberg, and then Hitler himself, that this year would be different. This year they would retrace the route of the previous expeditions; only this time clues would be extracted from earlier sites that would lead to ultimate victory in a new place.

The Tibetan had looked on impassively as Karl and the others made their jokes. Where Hitler was concerned, a promise was as good as a result. Nazis weren't above faking things when politically necessary. How hard could it be to just say any old artifact was the Grail? But as Karl conducted his personal survey of the others, he realized yet again that this was a gathering of true believers. Maybe a few of the SS regulars and he had their doubts, but no one else here had a bit of skepticism. He would do well to reflect on matters of faith if he wished to rise in the ranks.

There was the Parisian, selected for his knowledge on the work and life of Gobineau, the 19th century French aristocrat who had written the first scientific work (the party insisted it was scientific) on the Aryan race and its role in history. There was the man from London, an expert on Houston Stewart Chamberlain, the great Englishman who had carried on where Gobineau left off, and who lived to see the full flowering of racial science in the achievements of Alfred Rosenberg. Karl couldn't help but be amused that these two were a little too old, and a little too overweight, for the rigors of this particular mountain. They had both been happier sipping wine over the remains of Gnostic heretics who had been sensible enough to live and die in reasonable climates — Manichaeans, Bogomili, Cathars, and anyone else they could dig up.

The other American, besides the woman, seemed a hardy, young man named Carter; but his credentials were the most suspect. He had been expelled from Miskatonic University for his doctoral thesis suggesting that the real name of Jehovah was not really Yahweh, but rather something closer to Yog-Sothoth. Every good Nazi who bothered to hold a religious belief denied the possibility that the God of the Old Testament could be the father of Christ; it was par for the course to say that the Jews worshiped the Devil, Jehovah the Demiurge. But Carter based his views on certain obscure occult volumes suggesting a universe so removed from the common imagination that there was no way to make political use of such notions. He had earned his place not for a diploma but on the strength of an admirable degree of anti-Semitism.

Then there were the twins from Sweden. At first, Karl had been unhappy over the presence of women in the group, especially the American whom he found overbearing. But just as the point of the Alberg expedition was to be international, placing the race above nations (while in no way diminishing justifiable German pride), so, too, must both sexes be represented. Goebbels had been pushing for more radical uses of Aryan womanhood and was disappointed when no practical way was found to drag along Leni Riefenstahl and one of her camera crews.

Goebbels wouldn't mind if Leni fell off a cliff, of course.

Karl had seen the wisdom of the Goebbels feminist policy the night he got to know the twins better on a bed in a hotel in old Jerusalem. The amount of blonde hair, deposited by all three of them, left the wrinkled black sheets looking as if a golden storm had exploded over their damp secrets

The shortest man on the mountain was from Down Under. One would never guess that he was the foremost authority on the Spear of Longinus since the death of the leading German in the field. The Australian had corresponded directly with Rosenberg over the certainty that the spear acquired along with the Hapsburg treasures had actually pierced the side of Jesus Christ as the savior hung crucified between heaven and earth. The blood of Christ had supposedly fallen into a chalice for which mankind forever searched. The Holy Grail.

Rosenberg convinced Hitler that if the Christ were all God, instead of part man, this would solve the problem of Jewish parentage. It wouldn't matter through what human gate God came into the world. Hitler was partial to the idea that Joseph and Mary weren't really Jews (another simple solution) but didn't really care which theory won. Should Rosenberg be proven correct, the Grail could be in any form, as Christ's blood could have been something quite different from literal blood. Professor Alberg had suggested in his most famous paper on the subject that there might be many other solutions to the Jewish problem; but they all depended on actually finding the Grail.

The last expert in the party was a defrocked Catholic priest who was fighting a one man campaign against his former church. Himmler was always boasting how the organizational structure of the SS borrowed heavily from the Jesuit order. He loved it whenever he could get his claws into a real apostate. This man, the former Father Tyrell, had gone all the way, even being initiated into the inner circle of Burgundy, the SS nation, and taking the oath affirming a belief that the moon was made of ice.

The remainder of the party was SS soldiery and a few museum officials. Probably not one of them believed the moon was made of ice, Karl reflected. Von Braun promised that the first German rocket to the moon would prove the theory was pure moonshine. For some reason, the occult types didn't seem to care what the technical side of Germany said or did.

While Karl pondered these weighty matters, the Tibetan had been watching the sky. His frosty breath upon the air seemed to mimic the roiling clouds that encircled the mountain. The perfectly shaped head lowered, catching Baulmer's attention as it did so. Professor Alberg and the officer joined their very special guide, and the three men were soon deep in conference. After all this time, Karl still didn't know if the Tibetan spoke German, although it seemed frighteningly possible that the man understood any language he heard.

Alberg's fit of temper was a thing of the past when he addressed them again. "Comrades," he said, "we near the end of our quest. This last stretch will not be easy, but the weather is taking a turn for the worst. We must redouble our efforts." He ignored the groans of those lacking in the virtues of iron discipline. "But when we make camp for the night, it will be in the safety and comfort of a cave." The groans changed to cheers. Alberg let the anarchic behavior go by without a whisper of protest. Maybe he had seen reason. Or maybe he was tired.

Karl enjoyed the skiing that was required. The twins and he were the most accomplished in this regard. They went first, exchanging glances fraught with enough heat to melt all the snow in the world. It was a shame the three of them would have to share the cave with Hitler's field trip tonight. A nice, cozy cave should be used for better things.

He did not enjoy the next part: more climbing. But this was what training was all about. And he imagined that he had more to be happy about than the chubby little Englishman who lost his grip at that crucial moment when he wasn't attached by rope to the rotund little Frenchman, and fell a long, long, long way to his death, screaming all the while in such a frenzy of terror as to gladden the heart of an Irish patriot. They didn't lose anyone else... on the climb.

When it was necessary to ask for a volunteer to rappel down an annoying cliff, all eyes turned to Karl before he could even nod assent. He didn't mind. He could already see the cave entrance that was the object of their exertions.

The others had an easier time of it than Karl, but even so he was surprised that the middle-aged members of the party were able to take advantage of what he had prepared for them. After what the Frenchman had seen happen to the Englishman, it was a wonder that he was willing to let his life hang by one thread, or rope in this case; but then, the man had no choice.

Karl was busy enough—being the first inside and soon having his hands full with the Swedish twins who were bringing up his rear—not to immediately notice details about his environment. A gasp from Inga changed all that. The way she was waving around her electric torch put him in mind of the most recent Nuremberg rally that he had been privileged to attend. This was no mere cave but a very long tunnel that seemed to go deep into the heart of the mountain.

By the time everyone had safely arrived, and the professor told them they could remove the outer layers of their protective clothing, Karl was the first to heed the welcome order. He was sweltering. As he began to breathe deeply, he noticed a strange odor, a cold metal smell one might expect to encounter in a factory. And there was a sour taste in his mouth.

Baulmer soon had them working as a unit again. Karl was up in front, along with the brains of the expedition, as they moved forward into the tunnel. Walking slowly, they listened to their own footsteps echoing hollowly against the walls. The professor was uncharacteristically silent. Karl wondered if the death of one of the party had a sobering effect.

The roof of the tunnel did not become lower or higher but maintained the same uncanny distance, about a dozen feet from the floor, as if they were inside a manmade construction of some kind. Suddenly, something scuttled near the American woman, who screamed in a most unprofessional manner.

While the professor lectured her on not making loud noises when inside strange mountains, Karl couldn't help but notice that the creature hurrying off into the darkness was as large his arm, all black and shiny with dozens of squirming legs. It disappeared into a hole in the wall of the tunnel. Much more of this and Karl would seriously reconsider his decision years ago not to work as a farmer for the good of the *volk*.

A few more of the cave creatures were moving up ahead, just beyond the range of their lights. Suddenly one of the soldiers bent over and threw up, adding an even more unpleasant odor to the already stifling air. This might have been taken as a bad omen by those without a proper devotion to the cause when the professor instructed them to turn off their lights.

A blue light flickered up ahead. The tunnel made a ninety degree angle and the light came from the left. Now the Tibetan resumed the authority of guiding them. "Congratulations," he told Professor Alberg in perfect German that all could hear, "you will soon have your heart's desire."

The tunnel reached its end shortly after the turn, but this was no cause for concern. It led them to a huge cavern from which originated the unexpected illumination. "It's some kind of phosphorescence," said Feuer, annoying Alberg who had wanted to say the same thing.

"It covers the walls," added the man from Paris. "I've never seen anything like it."

Karl was more impressed by the sheer size of the cavern than anything else. It put him in mind of a cathedral. Great stalactites provided the Gothic arches. Stalagmites made the pews. A shelf of stone was the perfect altar. And as for priests, the expedition had more than its fair share of interpreters of cosmic truth.

"Look," said the Tibetan, brown hand pointing to a symbol carved in solid rock on the wall nearest them. It was a Hexagon with a claw in the center. Professor Alberg nearly fainted in excitement when he saw it. And then, to Karl's surprise, the newly loquacious guide quoted Goethe's Mephistopheles from *Faust:* "Everything that exists deserves to perish."

"Oh comrades," cried Alberg, oblivious to his own advice about raising one's voice when tons of mountain hang overhead. He didn't even notice another of the strange cave creatures which had been partly hidden at their feet. As he stepped on the thing, it wriggled and Karl had a clear view of its mouth that was suckers with teeth on the ends.

"We have found evidence of a lost civilization," he continued, noticing, for a moment, the monstrosity under his boot. "Why, even this little troglodyte is of an unknown species. Our friends in the most secret of the Tibetan orders have been keeping a few secrets from us." He smiled at the guide. "We of the glorious Third Reich had to win a world before they would reward us with this knowledge."

"What knowledge is that?" asked the American woman. "What has this to do with the Holy Grail?"

Professor Alberg was so excited that he was almost dancing. The raising of his foot gave the creature a chance to slither away. One of the Swedish twins moved close to Karl in a way that made the young man almost grateful to the cave worms, as he was now thinking of them.

"This symbol is known to me," said Alberg. "It is a sign of ancient Atlantis. And we will find the Grail here because the real Christ was Atlantean."

It was Carter's turn to be confused. "But I thought you were of the opinion that the Christ was of completely non-human origin."

"Yes," said Alberg. "Who ever said the denizens of Atlantis were human?"

"But isn't the idea that the Christ is completely spiritual?" asked someone else.

The old irritation was creeping back into Alberg's face, here a twitch, there a discolored patch of flesh. "When will you fools learn to think?" he berated everyone in general. "All that matters is to prove that Christ was no Jew, in any form, at any time. After that, everything else is mere detail!"

"We are grateful for your expertise and close relationship with the Fuehrer," said Baulmer, again the diplomat. "But before we continue with the work, we must rest. We couldn't hope for a better place to make camp than right here."

The guide allowed himself a smile before helping these self-styled rulers of the world to unpack their provisions. Karl hadn't realized how tired he was until he sat down and took a first drink of water from his canteen. His feet felt like swollen bladders, filled with rocks. And there was a pain in his back as deep as the mystery he felt in this place.

As if Alberg had read the young SS soldier's mind, the professor decided to draw him into a discussion where the young Rhinelander could play the part of a representative German citizen. The other experts were every bit as confused as the rank and file, but Alberg could be counted on to use a strapping young lad as the official dunce-student, so as to lecture everyone else. Top Nazis were incorrigible teachers.

"So, private, er... what's your name?"

"Karl, Herr Doktor Professor Alberg."

"Yes yes. So Karl how does proof that Atlantis existed help our cause of the Nordic Christ?"

Karl hated this sort of thing. The part of Nazism that had most appealed to him was the "act, don't think" motto. Many a young man and woman had joined the party because of that promise. They should have known better. National Socialism was as ponderously intellectual as the ideas it had overthrown.

"All the races of the world fall into a natural hierarchy," Karl recited the old lesson, "except for the Jews who are the anti-race. Teutonic man has many enemies, including traitors in his own midst, but the Jew will always be the supreme enemy because he is anti-natural."

Alberg was nodding, partly in agreement and partly from irritation. All this was well and good, but the SS man was circling around the main point. "We all know that, Karl, but how does Atlantis help us?"

As far back as he could remember, Karl had been intimidated by the tyranny of ideas. Any ideas. His mother had wanted him brought up a good Lutheran but the father had wasted no time placing his son on the fast track to success with National Socialism; and Hitler's New Order was a jealous god. All the Nordic Christ meant to Karl was a way of giving people like his mother a way to go through the motions of their old faith without presenting any political problems. Atlantis was as far out of Karl's depth as Hoerbiger's cosmic ice theory or any of the other enthusiasms that engaged the SS elite when they held secret meetings in Burgundy.

Karl's discomfiture was like fresh blood to a tiger where Alberg was concerned; but a loud snicker from another SS soldier distracted the pedagogue's attention and got Karl off the hook. "You there," spat out the professor. "What's your name?"

"Uh, Ludwig," came the unhappy reply.

"Well, Ludwig, why don't you tell us why Atlantis is important to our mission?"

This one had more imagination than Karl. It didn't help him very much when he said, "Because of magick, Herr Doktor Professor. If we find the true Grail, it can only be touched by those with the blood of the *volk*. Lesser races will become progressively sicker, and a Jew touching the Grail would rot away to nothing in an instant, his skin peeling, eyes falling out..." Ludwig's vivid description trailed off to nothing as he felt the attention of everyone in the cave settling on him in deadly silence. Then Alberg broke the spell by laughing.

"Only a juvenile mind would come up with something like that," the teacher's voice abjured the soldier. "Or a Jewish mind full of Talmudic nonsense." Sheer panic flashed over Ludwig's face but another hearty chuckle from Alberg put the younger man at ease. "Mind you," the professor continued, "your notion has a certain charm. It's a popular superstition born of the fact that every race has one soul, as Rosenberg has said. The Grail will communicate things to an Aryan that no one else could know. A careful reading of the Arthurian legend reveals our race based truth."

Alberg began pacing back and forth in front of the symbol on the cave wall, making of it a blackboard and the vast cavern his classroom. Everyone slowly gathered around, except for the Tibetan guide who, even more slowly, was edging away from the company, back towards the tunnel entrance.

"There is no one truth for everyone," said Alberg, "but each race has a truth, far bigger than can be encompassed by any one individual. We believe that all civilizations worth the name began with an Aryan somewhere. Furthermore, I insist that no city of man was ever so old that it didn't look back to some earlier golden age. And yet there has to be a beginning. Or must there?"

He raised his eyebrows and assumed a mocking expression before continuing: "The Nordic Church soon to take its place on the world stage will deny the Old Testament idea of creation *ex nihilo*. We say the universe always existed; the eternal return is our truth, and nowhere is this more profoundly understood than among the great adepts of Tibet. Alfred Rosenberg first incurred the wrath of Rome when he denied that God created man. The Nordic Church will teach that man and God have always existed, as equals. The Roman Church opposes the quest for the Grail because she fears all secret knowledge. And well she should, for Catholicism made the secrets herself by suppressing the Gnostic beliefs and branding them as heresies. In the end, Rosenberg won't care if Christ is proved to be all spirit, or completely physical so long as the physical side is Aryan!"

Alberg was getting red in the face. Excitement did that to him. The American Carter picked up the thread: "I get it! Atlantis was an Aryan civilization. The powers of mind come from her—extrasensory perception, telekinesis, and so forth."

"And healing powers," echoed Feuer.

"The power to make the lame to walk," came another voice.

"The blind to see," said another.

"To raise the dead," finished Alberg. "Yes, it is my belief that Christ was the last Atlantean; and in his body coursed the purest Aryan blood. The Jews conspired to have him killed. Then the Jewish Saul, later known as Paul, was sent to corrupt the pure racial message, and make Christianity dependent on Hebrew myths."

Alberg didn't have to drop the other shoe, or boot. They all knew that something would be found inside this mountain that would be dubbed the true Grail; and they would return to New Berlin as heroes of the Reich. Maybe a rock would do, after all. But given the size of the cavern, and the emblem carved in stone, they were sure to find something better than that.

The plan adopted was like a simple naval search pattern. Baulmer had everyone gather in a tight circle at the center of the cavern, then move out in an unfolding spiral that would leave no inch of ground unexamined. The natural luminescence of the cave actually provided sufficient light for their purposes but Alberg had them using their electric torches as well. If anything were there, it would certainly show up.

Something did.

Carter found it. He started to laugh, but the sound choked in his throat. "That can't be," he said. Karl was nearest to him and hurried over. What he saw, fossilized in the rock below was a gigantic footprint, vaguely humanoid but subtly wrong in ways other than size.

"What's the matter?" asked Karl. Carter only shook his head.

"Over here," cried out one of the Swedish twins. The two men were near and hurried to her side. They found another footprint, only this one wasn't a fossil. This one was in a patch of brown dirt.

"I've always had a fear of words that begin with the letter _Y_," said Carter, suddenly. "I've just remembered the first story I ever heard about the Himalayas, when I was very young."

Meanwhile, Professor Alberg had found a giant footprint over by what appeared to be the crude altar but must surely be a natural shelf of rock. He was calling everyone to come see when the Gruppenfuehrer wondered aloud what had happened to their guide. Alberg was too preoccupied with his find to worry about that. And nothing would have distracted him short of the loud crash that suddenly drew everyone's attention to the tunnel mouth.

"We're sealed in," said the Frenchman who was nearest and skilled at stating the obvious. He walked over to touch the unyielding stone surface of a boulder—or was it some kind of door?

Now Alberg became concerned about the absence of the Tibetan guide. After all, the man was his lodge brother in the Vril Society, a fellow believer in the Thule. They knew each other's secret names. (Aryan secrets were acceptable, of course.) The man had worked ever since the end of the war to introduce the Third Reich to the Grail. Why should he disappear at their moment of triumph?

The altar moved. With a terrible grating of stone on stone, it moved, and the sound exploded in the immensity of the cavern. The Alberg expedition stood rooted to the spot, all but Karl whose instinct for survival burned hot in his chest. He ran toward the opening, his usual method of facing the unknown. Up until now his courage had served him well. Unfortunately, taking the wild chance didn't pay off this time. Karl was lifted by a hand proportionate in size to the footprints. He stared into the most perfectly blue eyes he had ever seen in his life. Then the leviathan placed Karl gently on the ground and he had a clearer view of the giant.

First impressions can be misleading. Given a height between nine and ten feet, and a body almost completely covered in hair, Karl and the others might well have expected an ape-like countenance. But there were no heavy brows, no flatness of face, no heavy jaw or sloping forehead or thick, brutish neck. The features of the face were one of the few parts of its anatomy not covered in hair, as were the hands. And it was the most beautiful face Karl had ever seen, a face to match the pure light that seemed to stream forth from the eyes.

As the giant came into full view of the Alberg expedition, it was joined by others of its kind, all of them huge, all of them possessing the same delicate features and long fingers on their well formed hands. "Welcome home," said the first one in perfect German. "Welcome," said the others in English and French and other languages. As everyone spoke German in the expedition, the first of the giants continued to address the party in the language of the Reich.

"I don't understand," said Alberg, displeased with the sound of his own lame words.

"You were brought here by a mutual friend," continued the mellifluous voice. "We have something for you."

One of them came up from the rear, carrying a golden goblet covered in runic symbols. The drinking vessel was of a size suitable to the great hands holding it. There was something red in the cup that almost spilled out.

"If you are of the true blood," said the voice, "your spirit eye will be awakened. If not, then your flesh will serve others who are awakened. Even the remains of the body will live, transformed into the humble creatures you have already seen in this, our home."

Ludwig, who had an imagination, was the first to panic. He screamed. He ran. He got absolutely nowhere fast. The giants didn't even try to stop him as he hammered his hands bloody against the boulder blocking the tunnel.

Alberg opened his mouth and tried to speak, but nothing came out. The giant helpfully answered the unspoken questions: "He lives. He is still among us. He was always one of us."

Carter managed to say, "The cross must have been much larger than we ever expected." His words sounded like a moan.

"Now gather around, you men and women. This is His blood." The giant hand held up the cup. "You must drink."

Another voice spoke. Karl's voice. He was surprised to hear himself expressing the worry that must be on the minds of all his comrades. "How many of us will... survive?"

The beautiful face formed a beautiful smile. "There is no death here. But there is transformation, as I said. If you mean how many are of the true blood, and will become like us..." The startling blue eyes seemed to grow in Karl's sight until they became his whole world. "Only one in ten-thousand awaken."

"The rest serve, and serve well," said the others in chorus, then continued: "Their flesh is our flesh; and their flesh dwells among us." Dark things moved on the cave floor around everyone's feet, but nobody looked this time.

"This is His blood," the first one repeated.

Professor Alberg fainted but they woke him up. His turn came as did everyone's. The people lined up and they took communion. It was abominable.

Richard Gilliam, one of the editors on *Tales from the Great Turtle*, reports in his afterword: "This project began as an off-the-cuff remark I made to Brad Linaweaver that *Tatham Mound* is my favorite of Piers Anthony's novels. Brad's reply was 'Why don't you suggest to Piers working on an anthology together?'"

So we have an example of how I manage to get so many politically incorrect stories in print. I help bring about whole books so I can slip in my subversive notions!

But seriously, what is controversial about a story where I suggest that a Native American might prefer individualism over a tribal identity? Or that European whites weren't the only bad thing that might have happened to the Plains Indians (especially in an Alternate History where a technological Aztec Empire attacks North America)? At least I was expecting objections from that quarter. Imagine my surprise when I was informed by a fan and book reviewer that I was wrong to refer to "The Bison Riders" as science fiction. He assured me that I had only produced a fantasy.

Now that's controversy!

The Bison Riders

John didn't care that the toothless old woman was probably out of her mind. He believed the gods to be frugal in their fashion and so much magical ability had been granted this poor woman that she would naturally prove deficient in other areas. What mattered was that her spirit eye was always open; and she was willing to share her visions. He smiled at her wizened face that seemed to float in the greasy smoke rising from her little clay pot that hung over a modest fire.

Maybe the woman could answer his questions and put his soul at ease. If she really had psychic powers she would know that his father wouldn't approve of John's stepping foot on any reservation, much less giving credence to the superstitions peddled by an old woman. From earliest memory John had been told that he was an American first and not to be overly concerned with his Amerind heritage. He'd never thought much about such things until he went to college and met members of a radical political group.

"You're *not* John," one of his new friends had told him. "That's a white man's name. Why don't you show pride and take your real name?"

"But I don't even know my tribe," he tried to explain. "I mean, I have a pretty good idea of which tribes I could claim...." A grimly efficient Anthropology student, he had started to construct a possible past. So intent was he on the details of his own possible lineage that he failed to notice that the young man in front of him was at least seventy percent European in contrast to John's largely Native American physiognomy.

"You're missing the point," said John's interlocutor. "I am Hawk Above the Clouds." Gesturing at the blonde co-ed wrapped around his arm, the young man added, "My friend hasn't chosen her new name yet, but she will."

John admired the woman's strong blue eyes, thought about the situation for a moment, and shook his head in confusion. As if sensing this, she told him, "Oh, it's all right. I'm a Wiccan. We join our red sisters, and brothers, in respecting Nature."

Her boyfriend winced at her choice of words but to John this seemed a welcome change of subject. Her mentioning of Nature opened a door in him. Suddenly he was talking to her with a greater enthusiasm than he had intended. He told her of how he had spent the previous summer on a dig in one of his favorite regions. He described arriving by jeep through a pine forest, and enjoying the morning-fresh fragrance before venturing out into the flat vastness of the surrounding desert. He told her about the cedars that came after the pines; and the blue-grey mountains on a horizon that seemed to beckon him out into the deep desert, as full of smells and sights and sounds as the woods had been, but more subtle in presentation. She must have noticed how his smile grew and his face turned up almost in ecstasy as he remembered the sand dunes, and the bright colors of red and gold where rock and clay met, and the fierce wind that scoured the other-worldly terrain. He finished with a few words about the sudden storms and the beauty that had clutched his heart.

She had seemed to be listening, nodding now and again at appropriate moments. But when he had spent himself, she simply blinked her perfect blue eyes and said, "What do you think about the tropical rain forest?"

He had never been to the rain forest; never been in South America at all. Neither had she. The conversation meandered down a winding tributary of statistics that neither of them could possibly know firsthand and then drowned in a lagoon of soggy anti-capitalist rhetoric.

John would see a lot more of this duo in ensuing months, as well as other members of their small but vocal organization: NAME (Native American Mobilization Effort). He didn't take NAME seriously at first. His favorite Anthropology professor, Dr. Frederick Rae, was a master of sarcasm, especially where student activists were concerned. NAME was made to order for this teacher's brand of wit.

The first time John had met the leader of the organization was when Grey Bear Walking audited Rae's class. The professor was up to the challenge, beginning his first session of the quarter, the way he always did, by shooting a dart into the back wall from his South American blowgun. This got everyone's attention. "You need to learn about tools and weapons before you make up endless kinship charts," he liked to say. He was making his favorite point against armchair Anthropologists who never get anywhere near a helping of long-pork, when he noticed the President of NAME in the back row. The professor added a few choice words about xenophobia and ethnocentricism.

"White man's rules," came the low, steady voice out of the lean, brown body of Grey Bear Walking.

"And what about science?" Rae wanted to know.

"No such thing," was the reply, as cold as an abandoned campsite. "You want to kill our pride." The professor had smiled at the young man's gift for demagoguery and had moved on. But after class John felt he had to confront the student leader whose real name was hard to find.

"You can't deny the quest for objectivity," John had said.

"What do you know about quests," the other said, "when you won't even undertake to find out who you are. I pay no heed until you find your true self."

Those words had burned themselves down deep where dreams live. John started dreaming himself into canoes and moccasins; into tipis where the young wife always enters after the husband; into war dances and mortifications of the flesh and staring at the sun until the brain grows hot...and you wake up.

Strangely the people he was meeting through NAME seemed indifferent about any discussions concerning his visions. They were organizing a protest against the university's traditional Indian symbol for the football team. John wouldn't be available to help. He had a vision quest waiting.

A full day and night of driving had brought him to stand before the old woman in her wickiup. As she fussed over her little pot of foul smelling medicine brew, he reflected on the unlikelihood that Grey Bear Walking had ever heard of her. John had learned about the woman through Professor Rae, always reliable when it came to locating Native American curiosities. (His collection of artifacts ranged from as far north as Canada and as far south as Peru.)

"Tell me your spirit beast!" the old woman cried out, bringing John out of his reverie with promise of a greater reveries to come. She enunciated pretty well, he thought, for a toothless hag.

"I don't understand," he answered lamely.

"The animal meant for you," she said, her voice a dull roar in his ears. "If you would journey on the great river, Turtle Father must speak to your spirit self."

"I need you to help me find out, I guess."

"No!" she almost screamed. "You must know first. First! Is it bear? The eagle? Wolf? Serpent? You must tell me." As she harangued him, a thin line of spittle traced its way down her wrinkled chin. The smoke surrounding her head made it seem larger and bulkier, rounder; and peering from the center of that cloud were two red-coal eyes, burning. He recoiled as if from a physical blow. He knew his animal spirit at last, something thundering across a thousand leagues of dry prairie, exploding out of the dead past with an almost unbearable force of life: the buffalo, the bison.

He told her. She nodded. "We are ready to send you to other self."

"Into the past," he said, sitting cross-legged on the ground.

"No," she answered. "Not this world's past; but your true self's past." He didn't have a clue what she meant but he figured he would be finding out if he had the courage to drink the horrid brown mixture she was even now offering him from a large wooden spoon. He hoped the brown lumps floating on the surface were nothing worse than mushrooms.

The taste was something like a curry that had gone bad. But he was able to keep it down. He didn't have to wait long for what he assumed were the hallucinations. First there was a burning sensation in his eyes. Naturally he closed them; and experienced acute vertigo. He was having trouble breathing until he was distracted by the not entirely unpleasant experience of something wet sucking its way up his spinal cord until reaching the brain...and gobbling it whole.

When he blinked his eyes back into some kind of focus, he was outside...in the middle of a great, flat prairie...with dry grass whispering in a breeze that wasn't nearly cool enough. He was sitting astride something he assumed to be a horse, but he wasn't fully conscious of the situation and there seemed to be a slight haze surrounding everything. His sense of smell was not impaired even if he would have liked to avoid the thick odor hanging in the air as if a hundred old carpets had been soaked and then left out to dry in the sun.

"Far Seeing Eye," a voice addressed him, "your father still misses the old ways."

John hesitated as if realizing that the moment he turned his head he would be committed to accept as reality whatever presented itself. He looked. An Indian dressed in the full panoply of war and with bright warpaint highlighting his scarred features grinned at him, his head held high against an empty blue sky. The old woman was certainly earning the few dollars John had forced into her gnarled hand. Why, the hallucination was so convincing that John seemed to be comprehending an alien tongue. Although he was studying Native American languages, this one was unknown to him.

Unknown...except part of him *did* know it; and he realized that he could speak the language as well. His companion continued speaking: "There's no denying your father was good at the old tricks. My mother says your father was the best at putting on a white wolf's skin and sneaking up on a buffalo. They really had courage in those days. Of course if I have to be close to one of the great beasts, I prefer my own mount!" The young man patted the hump that was just underneath an elaborate saddle. John's eyes grew wide as he followed the motion and saw all of the two thousand pound monster the Indian was riding.

Then the inevitable question: Just what was John sitting on anyway? He felt a sudden panic when he saw the broad, brown expanse of the smaller buffalo underneath him. This one probably weighed in at only fifteen-hundred pounds. In John's right hand there was a fine piece of rope, part of a full bridle that went all the way around the gigantic head.

Where the hell was he? Plains Indians never road buffalo. They hunted them for food and clothing and even shelter, given how much of the tipi depended on them. Nothing was allowed to go to waste. The bones, horns, hoofs...all were used; and the dung was a primary source of fuel. Before the European invasion brought horses, hunting these beasts was considerably more dangerous. He'd heard of the trick with wolfskins. But how could they be riding buffalo, and with such technologically advanced saddles?

Closer scrutiny of his companion's saddle, which was easier to see than his own, revealed horn neck, horn cap, pommel and even stirrups, but shaped differently than they would have been for a horse. Saddles made him think of horses again. Even as the thought galloped into his mind, he realized that there was no word in this language for *horse*. He heard himself trying to ask the question, but couldn't get past the difficulty of the elusive word. He remembered scraps of phrases and vocabulary from Commanche, Apache, Kiowa,

Pawnee, all to no avail.

"What are you talking about?" his friend asked.

"I'm sorry," he managed to answer. "I'm a bit confused today."

"You better get over that before the battle!"

Oh, great. A battle. But he couldn't let that deter him from figuring this thing out. He was sure that the old woman was giving him a dream back in time. Maybe this was a period before the arrival of the white man. But that still wouldn't explain the technological sophistication of these saddles. There were words he could use to ask about the white man. He did.

"Far Seeing Eye," began his friend whose name he didn't know, "we have always treated your visions with the utmost respect. I learned from you the prayers to the spirit of the buffalo when we must kill him, or when we must feed him the herbs to make him docile enough to ride. But the great battle is before us after weeks of planning in which *you* played a crucial part. Are these new visions a warning? It's too late now for pale men and strange animals to make a difference." As the man spoke, he grabbed the long black elkskin sash he wore and held onto it as if a lifeline.

If only John could call the man by name! Whatever was happening to him gave the power to understand but not to remember who he was. Naturally John assumed he was inhabiting the body of an ancestor. More questions occurred to him but before he could ask them events overtook both young men.

The other gave a war cry at the sight on the horizon. Smoke signals were making a string of white cotton balls against the sky, drawing attention once again to the absence of any clouds. John swallowed hard as the immense beast beneath his legs surged forward. He was keeping pace with his companion who began to veer slightly to the right. John had been riding horses since he was a child but they hadn't prepared him for this. He was twisting in his saddle the moment he pulled on the reins, but he managed to hang on.

If he'd thought horses put you far away from the ground, and their hooves were a sound you could feel in your bones, he hadn't reckoned on the thunder made by these incredible animals. He found it hard to believe the creature was made of flesh and blood. Such doubts were soon rendered moot by what was waiting for them at the end of their long ride.

Over a rise was a welter of blood and gore, the first battle John had ever seen. But not even the screaming men, howling beasts, hacking and stabbing and dying could distract his attention from the spectacle of who was doing the fighting, and how they were doing it. For one mad instant he saw the tableau of war frozen for his edification. Time enough to dive into the maelstrom and wonder if to die here meant to die back in his own world. Time enough to take the bow and arrows slung over his shoulder and make his bloody contribution to the carnage. There was no doubt as to the enemy. He knew them on sight. The only trouble was that he couldn't believe it.

Wielding obsidian-bladed clubs and ornate javelins, attired in gold and jade and yellow parrot feathers, raising a din with conch-shell trumpets and clay whistles, the enemy could be nothing else but Aztec. They had never come this far north. At its height their empire had stretched from the Gulf Coast to the Pacific; and given their limitations in terms of resources and technology, they had been over-extended before the Spaniards came and destroyed them. They had never been close to having what they were employing in this battle.

They drove massive chariots drawn by half a dozen buffalo.

John knew about Aztec gold. Everyone did. The Aztecs had not even prized the stuff except when it had been transformed into works of art. Besides vast quantities of gold, they had plenty of wood and copper; but they had never learned how to make bronze. And yet right now, in front of John, he saw that the armor of these Aztec warriors, and important sections of the chariots, were bronze, impossible bronze!

But the most amazing feature of the chariots was that instead of wheels they rode on helix cylinders, spiraling down a hill, storing energy, and greatly increasing the speed by which they could go up the next hill. They also had a golden, or gold-plated, weapon that shot small arrows in rapid fire succession. From a distance John had no idea how they worked, but they were silent which ruled out gunpowder.

And then class was over. John was jolted back into reality, or what passed for reality, as an arrow creased his cheek. The pain was sharp and stinging, and he could feel wet blood trickling down his face. With another whoop of a war cry, his companion hurled himself into the fray. John remembered that his own name in this place and time was Far Seeing Eye. He hoped his vision would make him a deadly warrior. There was another war cry! A few seconds later he realized that he was listening to his own voice.

John had been mediocre at archery before, but this body he was inhabiting knew what to do. While two bow-lengths from the enemy he was already fitting arrow to the taut string, pulling back, aiming without thinking, and letting it go the moment he was near enough to reach the target. A few seconds later his arrow seemed to appear in the chest of an Aztec warrior who fell out of his chariot and was trampled into pulp by the buffalo of the next chariot behind him.

John didn't have time to reflect on his accuracy because he had already fired two more arrows. He didn't see what happened to them because a war club grazed his head with sufficient force to knock him from his steed, but he didn't lose consciousness within the dream, or whatever this was. Falling to the ground, he scrambled to his feet, barely noticing a broken rib. An Aztec priest was advancing on him, holding a foot long flint knife. There wasn't time to retrieve his bow so he pulled out his own knife and took a fighting stance.

The surprises weren't over for him yet. John never tested his mettle with the priest because one of the chariots came close, very close, an obsidian club appeared and smashed the bald head of the priest like a rotten egg. John wiped the blood from his eyes, and caught a grin from the commanding officer of the Aztec army. The man looked to be the identical twin of Grey Bear Walking. And then he was gone in the dust; and John had more pressing matters to concern him.

A gang of priests had managed to surround his friend, who had also become separated from his mount. John couldn't tell which buffalo it was, but he was sure that one of their two shaggy beasts was being attacked by at least a dozen wolves. He hadn't noticed where the wolves came from, but as he saw Aztec foot soldiers seeming to control the animals with whistles he remembered the words of the old woman about his not being sent back into his own timeline. Whatever world he'd stumbled into, this wasn't in any history text taught by Professor Rae!

The buffalo's eyes had been torn out by the wolves, and now they were working on its legs, ripping into them with a courage equal to the great beast itself. But the bravery of a man is always the greatest because he knows his own mortality; and the bravery of the other Plains Indian now called to John, as the priests bore down upon him, eager to cut out his heart and offer it to Huitzilopochtli, their hungry god of the sun.

John got his arms around the priest's thin body, and broke the man's back in a rage. Then he used the body as a shield against the next priest's knife. His comrade rallied at the attempted rescue and soon the two of them were fighting back to back, and the last surviving priest had run off like a jackal. No matter how stupid it sounded to the other man now, John had to know something.

"Before we die," he said, "I'd like to hear you say your name again, my friend."

"White Owl. I should not have doubted your visions, Far Seeing Eye. We are losing the battle. And this was supposed to be a trap for them."

"What went wrong?"

"Where are the reinforcements? They must have seen the signal."

The conversation was becoming more informative all the time, but it was cut short by the termination of the battle. The two friends were surrounded by a wall of Aztec soldiery. The priest that had been driven off returned, looking more demented than ever, and relishing his second chance. But this just wasn't his day. The officer who looked like Grey Bear Walking stepped down from his chariot and saved the two captives from the carving knife.

"I am Prince Cuauhtekoch," he announced grandly, "and I accept your surrender. You will be taken to our new city where your blood will make a worthy offering."

The priest was obviously disgruntled, and of the opinion that these two should be sacrificed here and now. There seemed to be a protocol covering such matters, and the end of the battle altered the situation. Sacrifices were now to be postponed for proper festival and ritual.

The prisoners were tied up behind the chariots. John hoped the distance would only be so great or else the captives would not survive to be slaughtered later. Before the great trek began, Cuauhtekoch came up close to John and whispered in his ear, "Your secret agent from Tlaxcala betrayed you, but no matter. He is no longer breathing and the real traitor will be dealt with later, the one we both love!" John's expression registered nothing. He wished he had some clue what was going on.

They only traveled a few miles before nightfall and then the caravan stopped to make camp. Apparently the Aztecs wanted healthy sacrifices. Before the darkness fell, John had an opportunity to study the chariots more closely. Once again he marveled at the technology of this world. They had progressed well beyond the straight pole arrangement of early chariots. He ached to take one of the mechanisms apart to see how it worked. How unfortunate that his own body was slated for a similar operation.

He wondered what would happen if he slept. He seemed to be tired. Still, he put off sleeping as long as he could. Perhaps he would wake up with the old woman, back in the good old U.S. of A.! He still had several thousand unanswered questions to deal with first. One of the Aztec soldiers sang a hymn to the stars and John realized, yet again, that he understood every language spoken here. The words had a haunting quality:

> *We only came to sleep*
> *We only came to dream*
> *It is not true, it is not true*
> *That we came to live on the earth.*

John slept. He did not dream, unless he was dreaming of sleep. And when he opened his eyes to the sun, he was still a prisoner of the Aztecs. They fed the prisoners with white and yellow tortillas. The food was actually good. They did not mistreat those who were to be food of the gods.

The poetry from the night before had only been a taste. Aztecs would walk up and down the line of captured warriors, throwing flowers at them, and reciting verse. John realized that most of his companions did not speak the Aztec language, but the man whose body he inhabited was apparently an exception before John was ever in the picture (or else the leader would not have whispered to him in Aztec). At any rate, John wondered how the man would have responded to two lines spoken by one of the poets:

> *But our body is like a rose tree...*

It puts forth flowers and then withers.

He didn't like the sound of that.

The journey took another two days. They finally reached a city under construction next to a large lake. There was something incongruous about an Aztec pyramid being constructed next to a stand of pine trees. A titanic block of stone was being carved into a giant bowl for what, John was sure, could be no good purpose. A utensil of those dimensions must be intended for the gods, and he didn't doubt what sort of cuisine they preferred.

No sooner had they arrived at the site than Cuauhtekoch gestured for John to be separated from his fellows. White Owl already wore the expression of a mourner at a funeral feast. He looked at John with concern, and hopefully no suspicion. But then what had Far Seeing Eye done, or left undone? So far John had found it easier to learn about this alternate timeline than to find out anything of substance concerning the man he was supposed to be.

Hands still tied from when he was on the line, he followed the prince and a number of his retinue into the largest dwelling, and one of the few completed buildings. Comfort for an aristocrat appeared to be a high priority. As they entered the rooms, a young girl with blue-dyed hair passed her lord a flower. There was something almost dainty about the way he sniffed the blossom's aroma.

"A charnel house odor hangs about our places of worship," said Cuauhtekoch with a shrug, "so we develop an appreciation for perfumes and other pleasant scents." Somehow John's sympathy was held well in check. "Oh, come now, Far Seeing Eye, enough of your frowning. I know what you and my sister have been planning. I respect you for it, but she should have known better."

They entered a bed chamber, and to John's surprise all the guards were instructed to leave except one, a man the prince obviously trusted beyond the normal call of duty. "I know you're expecting her," he told John with a wink, "but keep your breechcloth on. Perhaps it's time you should be told that I have enjoyed her in the same way, although years before you came on the scene. She liked me enough to make a statue of me. She's sentimental that way."

The man's manner was so insulting that John felt like taking the risk of slugging him, even though he didn't have a clue of the plots and counter-plots that revolved around these people. His expression must have been interpreted as pride and firm resolution by the prince.

"I see that you still love her," he said. "Well, I tell you that I loved Nezaberlcoyotl, or at least his brain. He was as smart as his father, and as great an engineer. I will never forgive your slaying him, but his work was completed before your filthy tribe got its hands on him. His father gave us the chariot, with a little help from that Chinese captain he captured and befriended. Now his son has given us weapons that when we have mass produced them will bring all other peoples under our dominion."

"What sort of weapons?" John asked. He really wanted to know.

"Don't play the fool with me," said the prince. "With the new projectile devices and the exploding powders, no one will stand before our might. And after this continent is subjugated, we will explore and conquer the rest of the world. Two oceans! Think of it. Beyond two oceans lie two other worlds, with other races, other blood, an uncountable number of sacrifices for Huitzilopochtli. And Tonatiuh will never tire for hearts, and the sun will never go out when it is fed so well; and our capital of Tenochtitlan will be the capital of the universe, and the eagle will perch on the cactus forever as we will live forever, the greatest race of all times and all worlds...."

John was getting better at recognizing the demagogue style. This one had a glazed look to his eyes, and a certain nervous tension that put John in mind of a certain European tyrants from the first third of the twentieth century, in a world that obviously didn't belong in this particular stream of history. Living up to the name of Far Seeing Eye inspired the asking of impertinent questions, such as: "Do you really believe all that?"

The prince was just taking a deep breath and he let out in a guffaw of surprise. "You are a remarkable man," he said, "to even think of such a thing much less put it into words. Of course, I admit I'm a politician. I believe what is expedient to believe. But it's certainly better to believe in a world with a purpose than that we are here by random accident."

"The world can have a better purpose than your plan for endless bloodletting."

Again the Aztec noble was taken aback. "You show a side of yourself I never imagined," he said. "I always knew you were more than a savage. After all, your tribe may have learned from us how to use the bison for a never dreamed of purpose, but your people had the brains to make alterations and invent new things. If my sister must take up with a barbarian, she did as well as could be expected. But even she would never dream you'd advocate open atheism."

He reclined on the bed, but extended no invitation that John even sit upon the floor. The noble continued to ramble a bit: "As a member of the Eagle Knights, I should have slain you in the most painful way I could imagine. Your blasphemy does not make you the ideal candidate for sacrifice, even as a captive warrior. But no matter. I keep my bargains, and we must be liberal about such things. No one is perfect, after all."

John was getting tired of this. The prince was giving him information, all right, but he couldn't make much sense of it. He could hardly ask the man to tell him everything from scratch as though Far Seeing Eye had become Dimwitted Brain, and needed to be reminded of nearly everything. He needed months to understand this world and he had a very good idea that his schedule would not be accommodating.

While John had been looking about the room for some method of escape the prince had produced a turquoise necklace from somewhere and was playing with it. "How my sister loves her trinkets," he said. "I've had to punish her, you know. I've taken away most of what she loves. Which one of you was it who first conceived the notion of taking me prisoner today, and breaking the alliance with, well, you know which tribes are the weakest link in our new hegemony?"

Not having the least idea made it all the easier for John to be heroic. "I won't tell you," he said with genuine confidence.

"I admire you," said the prince. "Torture doesn't work on you people because you self-inflict it so often for your rites of manhood. And anyway, you'd say that you were at fault instead of her if it came down to a 'confession.' But I must tell you that she never had any intention of reducing human sacrifice. She's a pious woman. But the two of you would probably have gotten along otherwise. You're both so passionate! My death and your diplomatic skills would have created the first serious challenge to the empire in a long time."

He bounced to his feet and held out his hand as though John were free to take it. "I'll keep my promise," said Cuauhtekoch. "One last night of love for both of you. I still love her in my way. I don't care about the priests and their stupid rules anyway. Her heart will be in the hands of the goddess, Tlazolteotl, soon enough. And you will feed the sun himself. The two of you make a lovely couple. You're strong and handsome, while she is the most beautiful woman in the world—I'm sure we can agree on that much—with her great, round eyes that look right through you and the light brown color that almost appears to be gold when the light is just right, and her perfect teeth ..."

The prince took a deep breath, and shook his head as if clearing it of personal fantasies. John did not doubt that in another minute the man would be offering to join them in the bed of love, and what's tomorrow's sacrifice among friends? One thing was certain, however. John was ready to meet this Native American Cleopatra as he'd never wanted to meet anyone before. His heart was beating faster at the thought of their embraces. The prince might be the scoundrel of all time but his word picture of his sister had worked some powerful magic.

Precisely at that moment there was the sound of an explosion followed by screams. A voice in the corridor was shouting, "The slaves are in revolt. They have the powder!" The next moment a door burst open and a large white packet, with a fuse attached, was thrown into the room. There wasn't time to pull the fuse, much less grab the explosive and throw it somewhere else. Even before it touched the ground the bomb had gone off.

For John the experience was not painful at all. When the smoke cleared, he was back in the old woman's wickiup without even a headache or a stomachache. He was also very annoyed.

"Is that it?" he asked.

She sounded tired as she said, "Your quest is over."

He was becoming more annoyed. "I don't believe it. I was about to meet the most beautiful girl in the world for a last night of indescribable ecstasy."

"Over," said the old woman. "No more."

"But where was I?"

She smiled her toothless smile. "How should I know?" she asked. "Each person's quest is his own."

"You knew enough to say I wasn't going back in...normal time, or whatever you said."

"Each quest goes to the important place for him. Goes to other worlds, other possibilities."

The frustration was becoming unbearable. "Then send me back!"

"I can't. You were given last cycle of someone's life. You have returned, which means the life is over. You already pay so you may go now." She hunched over the fire and began fiddling with the three sticks that formed a tripod from which hung her little clay pot. She did not speak to him again.

He took his time driving back, arguing with himself every mile. Frequently he would stop and get out of the car. He would stand there, in the dust, feeling the sun on the back of his neck. The air smelled of rubber and road and gasoline. Sometimes he would walk a half mile out into the countryside, kicking at rocks and picking up sticks as if he were a kid again. Then he would return to the car and drive some more.

By the time he reached the campus he had come to a decision. He wasn't going to join NAME. He went looking for Grey Bear Walking and found him slapping the blonde Wiccan who was cowering in a corner and not doing a very good job of standing up for herself. John picked up enough scraps of the conversation to get the general idea that Grey Bear Walking thought he had a right to take whatever he thought his due from white people. His victim apparently shared enough of the same viewpoint that she was only half-hearted in making the feminist case. Nor was she doing anything about her assailant's unprotected throat and eyes and ears and groin.

John didn't think very much about the woman's lack of skill in the art of self defense. He was busy. No sooner did he have his arm around the bastard's throat than he realized he could easily kill the other man. A brief flash of the anger he had felt for Prince Cuauhtekoch almost turned the tide into a crimson one; but he regained control of himself and simply beat the other man until his face would never be as handsome again. What finally made him stop was the expression on the young woman's face. She had never seen such an explosion of violence before. He hoped she would never do so again.

John decided not to tell Professor Rae that the crazy old woman might not be crazy after all. He kept his vision quest to himself. Except that he let a little of the story, just the least little bit, slip into a letter he felt he had to write:

Dear Father,

You probably wondered if I would ever write you again. It has been hard on both of us since mother died. I'll always appreciate how supportive she was of my decision to major in Anthropology. When you said it wasn't a practical choice I was sure that you had other objections. I admit I'm more interested in my heritage than you are. I've always felt that you were ashamed somehow of being a Native American. Yet that didn't keep you from marrying a Native American.

I'll always remember your horror stories about dealing with Federal Indian Agents when you were a boy on the reservation. I'm not saying that you've spent your life in denial. I've never said that. I agree that the greatness of this country is to share the same national identity regardless of who you are or where you come from.

I'm writing now because I've recently had an experience that reminds me that anyone can be an oppressor and anyone can be a victim. You'd think a thought so obvious would never be denied, but apparently it is beyond many people.

On campus we recently had a memorial for all the Native Americans who died at the hands of the Spaniards. I'm looking at a reproduction of Xipe Totec as I write this. He was the god of spring planting for the Aztecs. Priests danced in his honor while wearing the skins of sacrificial victims. The Spanish empire was wrong in what it did in America. But other peoples at other times would be as bad, given the power, given the opportunity. So obvious. So hard for some people to accept.

I hope one day you will be proud of the career I have chosen. I am an American and I am a Native American. I am an individual. And I am your son.

One day I hope to find a woman who will mean to me what mother meant to you. I have a deep faith that such a woman is in this world, and I will find her. Wish me well, father. I wish you nothing less.

Love and respect from your son,
John

My pride in this story is that the master of Alternate History pronounced it good and bought it for a book he was editing. I wasn't about to let down Harry Turtledove when he gave me the opportunity to do a story about Julius Caesar. I did my homework and anxiously awaited my grade from the good professor.

And to the Republic for Which It Stands

"He that once enters at a tyrant's door
Becomes a slave, though he were free before."   — Sophocles

Even Caesar dreams. There is no surprise in this. Perhaps the surprise is that ordinary people dream, or can dream at all—hoping for a better life that never comes. Only nightmares tell the truth.

Caesar's dreams are usually rehearsals. The general, the politician, must always plan, even when consciousness sneaks away like a harlot in the dark. Alone with his visions, he sees the land and sea and people as the gods must see them. Early in life he learned that free will exists, but only for leaders. Once a choice is made, free will becomes a phantom as inexorable law grinds out its verdict. What is true in the blood-drenched mud of the battlefield is true for the white marble sarcophagus of the Roman senate.

He wakes in the hot night and turns in bed to see his wife still asleep. Calphurnia is not as beautiful as his first two wives but he loves her more. Her breasts are perfect, smooth hills rising and falling like legions marching over countless landscapes of countless campaigns. He touches them, touches her, and feels a force less terrifying than love. Her sigh reassures him that in her arms, he is accepted; he is at peace.

Love demands more—as does his love for Rome. Love demands the spilling of blood, the conquest of peoples, even the agony of civil war. Love requires constant proof of devotion.

He has a sour taste in his mouth that can only be removed by wine. He can't sleep anyway so he carefully leaves the bed. No need to wake his wife if the stroking of her breasts failed to rouse her. He needs to walk, to think. This night of March the fourteenth there is much to think about.

When he gets in this sort of mood he envies his soldiers. Their souls are pure because their worries are, if not small, at least manageable—getting laid, getting drunk, not being a coward. Whether the battle is won or lost, they are judged by how they behaved as men. Only men. They are not judged by the standards of a god.

He pours himself good, red wine and drinks deep. He never drinks to escape himself but only to relax the tension that is his constant companion, nagging him on to greatness. The moon observes him through his doorway and he thinks how cool it looks, as if made of ice. The night is so still and humid that he wishes he could cool off.

He remembers an evening like this when he was held by the pirates of Pharmacusa. They were simple men, simpler than his legionnaires. When they ransomed him at twenty talents he laughed at their conservatism and recommended they raise it to fifty. They enjoyed his company and believed he was joking when he promised that one day he'd see them crucified.

His pleasant manner confused them. His lack of fear disarmed them. In his heart he did not wish them dead and this they could sense. But they did not reckon upon his devotion to Rome. She must be served. Her enemies must be punished. This is the force driving him to war upon the republic. Nothing else makes him stand up to the senators and the aristocratic families they represent. Fighting their corruption is the whip driving him on to greater glories, taking what he learned as a general and applying it more generally— the *sine qua non* of a dictator.

A soft voice whispers his name in the dark. He returns to his wife. She wants to ask what keeps him awake this night, but they both know the answer. He has called the senate into session on the morrow. The word is out that he will use the opportunity to declare war against the Parthians. There is another rumor as well: that he will use the opportunity to force the issue of kingship. Even some who accept him as dictator will balk at the final, logical step.

He wants to speak, to set her mind at ease...but no words are worthy of the moment. Instead he makes love to her with a passion he hasn't felt in years. She is pleasantly surprised. She adores him still. It is good to be conquered yet again by the general who won in Gaul, Greece, Egypt, Asia Minor, Africa, and most recently Spain. Part warrior, part diplomat, he distracts her attention with fingers and tongue and breath, before accepting her surrender.

Then she watches him rise from the moist sheets and neatly arrange his hair as if an audience awaited him in the darkness of their bedchamber. She is almost happy. For some reason, she remembers the controversy surrounding the funeral oration he gave for the death of his first wife—a young and lovely girl. Only older women had been so honored before. Caesar was accused of self love. Calphurnia has spent her married life wishing her husband to be guilty of more of this self adoration, expecting that such a surfeit will leave some for her.

"I had a dream," she hears herself say.

"What?" he asks, distracted by an insect buzzing in the warm darkness.

"Must you go to the senate tomorrow?"

He sits on the edge of the bed and brushes her hair with the same attention he lavishes on his own. "I must not disappoint them."

An ocean of meaning is contained in those few words. They are his motto. Although born of a patrician family, financial problems have dogged him from the start. Early on he realized his aptitude for the military and learned that being a general requires more than skill in warfare. Statecraft is the extension of war by other means. Make many promises but know which ones to keep. Don't be known as a man of thousands of virtuous words—such as his severest critic, Cicero—who never performs a single worthy action. Never devalue the currency except for a good cause. And there is no better cause than putting on spectacular entertainments for the people, be it a triumphal procession or a new series of gladiatorial contests. Always strive to be what the people expect of you, and failing that settle for the appearance. Forgive enemies when you think you can get away with it.

"You never disappoint...them," says Calphurnia, as if reading his mind. "But beware of daggers from those who lack your gifts."

"Your dream?" he demands, his voice suddenly loud, the orator bursting forth.

"Yes."

"Dear one, we know better than to believe in omens. The gods reward intelligence and punish stupidity."

This is a night of truth between them. She lets it out: "Sometimes I think the gods allowed there to be one Alexander the Great to torment all great men ever after with visions of the impossible."

Caesar laughs—a rare sound. "Put aside your fears," he tells her. "I have decided to do what is best for Rome, and the only question is who will resist the more: my friends or foes?"

He heads for the door, her voice following: "Where are you going?"

"I must take some of the night air. Probably won't be much cooler than in here, but I remain an optimist."

She remembers how to laugh.

The moon and stars are his companions—along with one thin, black cat, part of its side a red ruin from recent battle. Caesar doesn't intend to walk very far. But he must be alone with his decision.

Ever since his defeat of Pompey, he has realized the power that has come into his hands. Ever since the first night of passion with Cleopatra, he has realized how the world perceives him—his potential to be as great as Alexander. Perhaps even greater.

Again and again, he has told himself there is no turning back. That is what he said to himself when he crossed the Rubicon. When he shared power with Pompey he knew that one day he would have to destroy this rival general. When the foolish senators feared Pompey more than Caesar (because the man was a popular general from a non-aristocratic family) the future dictator realized the odds were in his favor from then on. No one is as dangerous as an aristocrat without money.

Poor Pompey. Assassinated in Egypt. Poor Egypt. Poor everyone who is not Rome.

And yet there is nothing inevitable about the decision *not yet taken*. His staunchest allies are ready to support him for king, complete with hereditary succession. He has been prepared to take that final step. A century of corruption, of aristocrats looting the state, cannot be undone by half measures.

So he has told himself.

But of late he has been troubled by dreams that sound like his hated critics with one important difference: instead of the whining voices of privilege he hears voices so deep and true that they must emanate from the gods. Their style is even more direct and clean than his proud soldier's memoirs. There is no dissembling, no circumlocutions, no bad analogies. They ask him why he loves Rome.

Why? His life has had no time for why. Only where and when. Why does he love Rome? As this troublesome question has taken root in his soul, as if a spear has been driven there, he doesn't like the answer. The rule of law, even if only for some, is better than the superstitions and traditions of the barbarians they conquer. He hates the republicans for how they have damaged good order, without which there is no trade, no prosperity. His decrees have already improved matters.

He's been telling himself that a rotten republic is only good for growing an empire. The State's will be done.

But the dreams, the voices, won't give him peace. They are different from the dreams of his past, maps guiding him to this summit. They ask if his empire might not cause the same problems as the republic, only on a greater scale that could never be corrected? What if his triumph starts a series of events leading to the destruction of the greatest civilization in history, handing over the world to emotion guided children and their primitive taboos? A world of low prejudice and cunning with no room for nobility. The West become carrion for the East.

It is a terrifying thought.

Tomorrow Rome will listen to him. He will enjoy an opportunity few men in history have ever enjoyed. He will turn down the crown, any crown. He will....

A voice speaks to him from the dark. It is not his wife's, but almost as soft. It is a man's voice that he recognizes instantly. Brutus. One of Pompey's followers whom he pardoned.

"I have come to warn you," says the man from the shadows.

"Step out into the moonlight," Caesar bids him.

The man is nervous and sweating. But in this hot night, everyone sweats, even great Julius Caesar. The general's eyes see that Brutus's right hand hovers near a place where it would be expedient to conceal a weapon.

"What have you to tell me?" he asks the man.

"Of a plot against your life."

Despite what he told his wife about omens, the sudden appearance of this man gives Caesar pause. He recalls that Brutus believes himself descended from Lucius Junius Brutus, who overthrew King Tarquin and established the Roman republic. Not a family eager for royalty to pollute the public baths.

"Tonight I broke with Cassius," says Brutus. "I fear the death of the republic more than I fear one man. A martyr's death is fertile soil for other would-be kings. Cassius doesn't understand how some on your side could benefit from your assassination."

Caesar laughs, the second time in one night; the first time ever in a public place. Brutus is astonished.

"We think along similar lines, Brutus, although starting from very different camps. Tomorrow I will announce that I reject kingship. There is more."

"More?" asks the astonished man.

"I will announce that if my reforms are seen through, I will step down by a certain predetermined date. Then I will ask for the commons and the aristocrats to cease their endless squabbling and put Rome first in their hearts."

"By all the gods..." Brutus begins to speak, but his words die as his imagination collapses, vanquished by a man he cannot begin to fathom.

"Cassius must be told," Brutus says, half to himself. "He'd envisioned an even broader scheme than your death. He would have included your closest friends and allies, appendages of yourself. The others in the conspiracy wouldn't go along with that, but only I stood away from spilling your blood."

"I thought you hated me."

"I do. I did."

Caesar places his hand on the shorter man's shoulder. "You were a political friend."

Now it is Brutus's turn to smile.

The two men part and Caesar turns his head to the moon. He wonders how superstitions men would imagine this evening's events. How many portents would fill the sky? Would the moon turn to blood? Would its face be darkened? Would the stars wink out, leaving the sky as black as the soul of Cassius?

These are the musings of a battlefield general, already weary of statecraft as his life becomes a thing of politics where nothing is ever really decided. But the speech he will give tomorrow is written in his head, waiting behind his proud brow to spring forth as from the brow of Jupiter. That much is decided.

As he walks home he wonders if Calphurnia will be awake. Perhaps they can make love again. He'd like this to be a night for her to remember.

Before he reaches his door, another man steps out from the shadows. Caesar wonders how many people are near his house tonight. For a moment he thinks that it might have been a mistake not to keep soldiers on guard until dawn. At first, he thinks it is Brutus returned but this is a larger man.

And then he recognizes the proud face.

"What brings you here at this hour?" asks Caesar.

Mark Antony does not conceal his weapon, which glints white in the lunar light. He speaks only once: "I have come to bury you."

I can never thank Greg Benford enough for allowing me to have my head on this one. The 500th anniversary of Columbus inspired a lot of silly political posturing from the multi-cultural left. I figured if it was going to be the silly season anyway, I'd turn my Alternate History about Columbus into a science fiction parody that led the reviewer in *Locus* to commend the "endless stream of mostly funny pulp cliches."

Every now and then I'm invited to do readings of this at conventions. The challenge is always to get through it with a straight face.

Destination Indies

WHAT HAS GONE BEFORE: *In the previous installments Captain Christopher Columbus (a.k.a. Cristoforo Colombo) studied quantum theology, advanced geographical theory, and the art of how to make friends and influence potentates. At the court of Ferdinand and Isabella he faced much treachery and intrigue. The Dark Duke tried to frame our stalwart hero as an agent of the Turks, sent to divert precious resources from military necessities into mad voyages. But Columbus saved the day by proving that the Dark Duke had financial interests in the Canary Islands that would be put in jeopardy should a westward route to the Indies be discovered. In his rage the Dark Duke kidnapped our hero's lovely girlfriend at court, but Columbus was able to rescue her with the aid of Poncho, his trusty sidekick, and a highly complicated bit of trickery involving five different kinds of cheeses and a ship's compass.*

Granted one last opportunity to make his case at court, Columbus eschewed his scientific and economic arguments for global access and the tendency of gold and spices to accumulate when traveling westerly along a particular latitude. This time he directed his appeal to the queen's heart, pointing out that the future promised greater things than temporary victories over the Moors, the burning of random heretics, and the expulsion or conversion of Jews. With a new route to Asia and storehouses bulging with gold, Spain could reclaim holy Jerusalem with a surprise attack from the east!

A final masterstroke was the manner in which Columbus forever destroyed the Dark Duke's credibility by suggesting the man might be a secret agent working for the French, the English, the Portuguese, the Moors, the Knights of Malta (but at least not the Knights of Columbus) ... and that maybe the man was a practicing Satanist as well. The queen was so thrilled with this presentation that she offered to hock the royal jewels to help finance Columbus's mission, but he cannily suggested that liquidating the Dark Duke's holdings would produce a sufficiency of funds.

Meanwhile the Dark Duke had finished reporting to the French, the English, the Portuguese, the Moors, the Knights of Malta ... and had used microdemonic engineering to create his own ship for the

*exploration of Water Space. Realizing that he must keep out of sight
during the voyage, he decided to make his craft fully submersible so
that he can follow his enemies without being sighted ... until the time
is right for him to strike!*

The Santa Maria, Pinta, *and* Nina *are launched from Palos on
August 3, 1492. Admiral Columbus is aboard the* Santa Maria. *Identical twins, Martin Alonso Pinzón and Vincente Yanez Pinzón, command the* Pinta *and* Nina *respectively. There is only one mishap on
the voyage to the Canary Islands, the last outlying post of Spanish
territory. A saboteur is found trying to damage the* Pinta's *rudder.
Short work is made of him. Then it's on to the islands and last preparations before the dangerous part.*

*After a torrid affair with the island's female governor, the lovely
Donna Beatrice (who bears a startling resemblance to the girlfriend
he left behind in Spain), Columbus is ready for anything. Three ships
and ninety men challenge the deepest, darkest depths of the Unknown.*

*Meanwhile the Dark Duke and his handpicked crew of cannibals,
child molesters, and heretics rescued from the Inquisition follow in
the wake of his enemies. We resume our tale with the log being kept
by Poncho, the loyal sidekick.*

Chapter CVII

"It is late in the day, and gray clouds sail across the sky, moving
low, hazarding the reef that is the sturdy mast of our ship. After a
sea of faces at court, bobbing up and down on the tidal movements
of fear and greed, how our brave leader must prefer the real elements of sea and sky."

The admiral leaned over my shoulder and told me that the previous paragraph is all right, but not nearly purple enough. I imagined
that he wanted me to more fully describe the multicolored hues
that swirled about the prow of our good craft as we surged ever
onward into the receptive waves that mark the shimmering surface of Water Space.

Ever since I graduated from Saint Pedro's Academy for Loyal Side-
kicks, I've been driven to prove myself. That the admiral would
choose me for such an important mission left me speechless ... almost. I knew that he kept his own log; but his suggestion that some-

one else should keep a log so that there would be a more objective record of our adventures thrilled me more than words can say. Why, I worship the very planks that man trods upon and I wasn't about to let him down. If it's objectivity he wants, it's objectivity he'll get, by all the saints.

As Columbus faced the horizon, his jaw jutting ever westward, I knew that it would be no great matter to lay my life down for this man. But no sooner had these thoughts crossed my mind than we faced a great danger! I cursed myself if idle thoughts of my own destruction should bring harm down on the heads of my betters.

"Sea monster off the port bow," cried a salty seaman from Madrid. We all dropped what we were doing—even my quill pen fluttered down, where it tasted rough-hewn boards—and we gazed in astonishment at what was rising from the vasty depths. It was amazing. It was astounding. It was really big.

I had seen whales before, but at a distance where it was very difficult to estimate their true size. Once a dead whale washed ashore at my humble village. It had been as big as a felled tree, and the teeth were fearsome to behold. But that poor creature was as a minnow compared with the dimensions of this behemoth. I heard the ship's alchemist whisper one word, "Leviathan," and he spoke truly.

The wind was blowing at about ten knots. The rhythm of the sea was steady, the water lapping at our ships, all three of them bobbing like corks. The way our ships were laid out formed a kind of triangle, and the monster was rising in the dead center. Sea foam churned around its sleek, blue hide, while the water around it was a viridian shade of blue. It was as if the ocean had chosen this moment to manifest itself in a living form larger than all three of our ships put together. I shuddered to think what kind of teeth it might have, but it had a peculiar-looking mouth and it was not clear that it had teeth at all.

"It doesn't seem aggressive," said Columbus. "That is well, for I doubt that any of our weapons would hinder the monster."

There was a muttering of agreement, a medley of "ayes" and "ahrrrrs," but one old sailor lost his nerve. "It's a sign," he cried. "This mission's cursed. If yon monster doesn't make a dinner of us all, then we'll surely be pulled in the direction of the magnetic mountain that will draw all the nails from our craft, and we will fall into the sea of darkness before being swept off the edge of the earth."

The admiral looked at the poor, raving dolt with more sympathy than the man deserved. Then he summoned the ship's morale officer, who gently took the man by the shoulder, turned him around, and drove him through with two feet of fine steel. There were more "ayes" and "ahrrrrs" at this demonstration of permissive therapy.

"The monster doesn't seem to notice us," said Diago, the admiral's good right hand.

"Pray God it remains so," was the answer.

Suddenly there was another cry of "Monster off the starboard bow."

"Shiver me timbers," said the dying man through foaming lips. Sure enough the water was becoming agitated off to starboard. We turned and watched the surfacing of what appeared to be a considerably smaller whale, but a particularly mean-looking specimen, all black with oddly shaped fins sticking out all over its surface. The smaller whale headed straight for the leviathan.

"It's trying to drive off the larger beast," said the luckless man whose turn it was today to prepare our rancid meals.

"I don't think so," answered the admiral, his brow furrowed in thought. "The big one is placid. Now with this sudden attack ..."

The small, black beast was headed straight for the flanks of the big one. We expected the leviathan to heave to, or dive, or do something. But it just waited, oblivious of the insect making a run for its side. And then the little one struck. There was no roar as we expected, just a soft thud. The smaller whale bounced off and then the larger one submerged. Unfortunately it began moving in our direction as it went beneath the waves.

"Make yourselves secure," shouted the admiral, grabbing ahold of my throat as the nearest object by which he could steady himself. We counted ourselves fortunate that the monster did not actually strike us, but the wake of its passing had our ship tossing and turning in the most frightful manner. Ironically several boxes of some mysterious objects called phyrecrackers (provided by the ship's alchemist) were set off, sending out their bright sparkles as we half fell and stumbled to one side of the ship, and then the other side, back and forth, monotonously back and forth, until I, for one, was sick to my stomach. I say it was ironic that a product of far-off Cathay should add to our distress as this was yet another market to be opened to us should our voyage prove a success.

"Well, that was close," said the admiral, releasing me as I slumped to the deck, my chest heaving as air rushed back into my tortured lungs; and then I threw up to make the perfect end to a perfect day.

"Aye," said his second, third, and fourth in command.

"Ahrrrr," said the sailors.

"Was a mighty fish indeed," agreed Snooty, the ship's expert on flotsam and jetsam.

"Perhaps you men noticed that the black beast was no sea creature at all," announced Columbus.

"Whatever was it, then?" I heard myself croak through a badly damaged windpipe.

"What sea beast carries on its flank the crest of the Dark Duke?" asked Columbus.

"You mean ..." asked the sailor we were certain had been slain but, despite a tremendous loss of blood, sounded better than I did.

"Yes, you pathetic sea biscuit. We are being followed by the Dark Duke."

"How did he get himself inside a big fish like that?" asked the temporary chef, no doubt through professional interest.

"He must have constructed the thing as we build our ships to sail the surface. But being the work of the devil, his craft sails below."

More "ayes" and "ahrrrs" at this last revelation. Sailors always respect sound reasoning. When we had established that there were no casualties, and signaled the good news to the other ships, it was definitely time to break out a great flagon of grog for the men (or was it simply rum?) I was among the privileged few invited to sample wine from the admiral's table. At any moment rowboats would come alongside bearing the captains from the other two ships for a general rehashing of the events just passed; and they would be thirsty too. Normally we passed messages back and forth by bringing the ships close together (as we did every evening so that we wouldn't lose one another) and sending a little bag across by means of a rope. But something as dramatic as what had just occurred demanded more personal contact. Or, to put it more objectively, the admiral would be in a lecturing mood.

I was already on my second glass of the best Thunderous Vino (from a bottle put aside expressly for my use) when captains Pinzón and Pinzón arrived. They were not happy about this latest encounter. And there were other problems as well. The admiral sensed that the time had come to be frank with us.

"I'll tell you whatever you want to know," he said.

"When we venture into waters swarming with monsters, perhaps we should consider turning back," said one Pinzón.

"And I'm concerned that something is amiss with your figures, Admiral," added another. "I'm certain that we have traveled more leagues than you indicate in your log."

"Gentlemen," he said, in the sternest possible tones, "I thought we would sight land within three weeks. We've now been at sea for three and one-half weeks. And I admit that I have been underreporting the distance traveled. We've traveled sixteen hundred miles." Everyone in the room gasped, except for those who, far gone in wine, belched instead. I, too, was shocked that he had not given the distance in leagues.

"But why?" asked the Pinzóns as one.

"Because the world is a big place, and the ocean is big. When the priest gave us his blessing in Latin the day we sailed, I wished for ten times that blessing, for fear the world would be ten times greater in size than we imagine. All educated men know that we live on some kind of sphere, although I believe it is more pear-shaped than ball-shaped. The direction in which we travel must inevitably lead us to the Indies. But what lies between us and that final destination is a mystery. That our direction is correct I know to be absolutely true. It is at the very heart of my Theory. But the distances involved are another matter."

"But, Admiral," Diago piped in, "you have some idea of the distance. You said as much at court."

Admiral Christopher Columbus, the greatest navigator the world has ever known, smiled and spread his hands. "Look, guys, it took me years to get the approval and appropriations for this mission. And I'm not interested in some onetime stunt where we plant the flag of Spain on some rock in the middle of nowhere, find a plant or something to take home, and that's it. The race is on between the European powers, and we'd better win it because there is no defense against a nation that rules the waves."

When he got worked up like this, it was best to let him get around to the point without further prompting. We sat and waited. The gentle rocking of the ship and the good cheer provided by the wine had everyone in a receptive mood. It felt as if it was going to be downhill all the way from this point on. The admiral would tell us what we needed to know.

"This mission was sold on three things: mathematics, maps, and money. We sail on three hopes: God, gold, and ..." He paused, but I had faith he would maintain his alliteration, " ... guts. When I told the queen that it would be seven hundred and fifty leagues to India, it was a guess and nothing more."

"But the biblical basis!" said the ship's alchemist, demonstrating a knack for alliteration himself.

"That foundation remains sound," said the admiral.

"When it is said that waters are gathered into the seven parts of the world, and there are six parts of land to one of water, the only conclusion we can draw is that there must be much more land yet to be discovered. But the Scriptures give us no idea of what the total volume might be! The point I'm trying to make is that I fully expect to find many strange new lands between us and our ultimate destination. I mentioned this in passing to the queen, but what is unknown is harder to sell than what is known. So I stressed the Indies in my presentation, and what we can ultimately achieve by finding a new route to the East." His eyes twinkled, and he smiled, showing off the whitest teeth I'd ever seen. And to think the Dark Duke had called him that little upstart from Genoa.

"I am concerned," he concluded, "that we have not encountered islands by now. But despite recent sightings of birds flying southwest, I am determined to remain on our current course due west."

"The ships cannot stand the strain," said Snooty, but no one paid him any heed.

Diago was more concerned about the men: "We may have more adventure than we want if provisions don't hold out. There are mutterings among the sailors already."

"What's a sea voyage without loose talk?" asked Columbus, laughing. "There's a long way between that and mutiny. I'm sure we'll find land very soon. Meanwhile let's keep our eyes on all the marlin pikes and meat hooks. And there are a few convicts who came along because of the queen's promise of a pardon. Let's watch them a bit more closely."

Diago nodded and said, "You've handled the sailors well so far. That business about the compass still being reliable when the position of the North Star shifted... I thought some of the men would go mad."

"Superstitious sailors," Columbus agreed. "That's when they first thought we'd left the natural waters God intends for us to sail and entered forbidden realms of Water Space." He laughed again, and the rest of us joined in, although I detected a certain nervousness on the part of some.

"The change is a sign of divine approval," said the ship's alchemist. "Before, the needle declined to the east; now it declines to the west. It is well."

Everyone toasted the mission. It was a good time to call the meeting to an end, which the admiral did. Except ...

"Wait," I said before the company broke up. "What about the Dark Duke?"

There was a sudden silence in the admiral's cabin, broken only by the creaking sounds of the ship, the lapping of the water, and a squeaking made by the lantern that swung above the table on which were scattered all the charts and a state-of-the-art quadrant. All eyes were turned on me, and they did not have a pleasing aspect.

"I didn't want that subject brought up, Poncho." I had forgotten that the Pinzón brothers had not been aboard when he made the observation about the black whale having his enemy's crest. I had forgotten, also, that the Pinzóns became terribly upset at the mere mention of their fiendish fellow countryman.

"We are doomed," suggested one.

"We'll never be famous now," added the other.

For the first time I could see that my hero was really angry with me. What tipped me off was the admiral's suggestion: "I think Poncho here needs to be taught a lesson."

I had a pretty good idea what that would mean. "I'm sorry, Admiral. Have mercy!" He paid no heed, but sent word that the sailors should gather to witness my punishment. In retrospect I realize that he made the right decision. What else could he do after I let him down? Of course I never liked it when he had me keelhauled. It made it difficult to write afterward. But if he let me get away with a serious mistake, that would set a bad example for the men.

So they tied me up and cast me in the salty brine. The underside of the *Santa Maria* was every bit as rough as I had remembered from the last time, and soon the water was full of my blood and everything went black.

When I came to, it was morning; but whether it was the next day or many days later I could not tell. The ship's boy was singing the traditional welcome to the dawn: "Blessed be the day, and He who sends the night away." For a moment I thought the song referred to our great leader until I remembered He whom even Columbus must honor.

Our Creator must have been in an interesting mood when he allowed to come into the world the myriad wonders that even now assaulted my senses (damaged though they were by stern correction). In the golden light of dawn I beheld a Brave New World that seemed to dwarf even the accomplishments of Spain.

"Astounding," said the man to my left.

"Amazing," said the man to my right.

"If ..." I began but was interrupted by a strange constriction in my throat that I attributed to the keelhauling. Fortunately my vision was unimpaired, and I had an unobstructed view of the Miracle.

It was as if someone had taken a heavenly city from its place in the firmament and placed it in the middle of our earthly sea. We had laid to in the harbor of this golden metropolis. And golden was the right word! As the rosy fingers of the dawn touched each building, we could espy the glint of burnished gold. The edifices were huge pyramid shapes, except that they were flat on the top. Strange flying things traveled back and forth between these pyramids, and they, too, seemed made of gold!

"Are we off the coast of Asia?" I asked. "Perhaps we will meet the Great Khan."

"I don't think so," said the ship's alchemist. "Through a close study of ancient writings, and one in particular by a scribe named Plato, I conclude that we have found the lost continent of Atlantis."

A new word came to me, although I could not credit the source. *"Goshwow!* As soon as my hands heal, I will record all this. But look, even now here come some people to welcome us. I will call them Atlanteans."

Suddenly the strong arm of my commander was on my shoulder. As I gazed into his steel-gray eyes, I realized that he had forgiven me, thank the Virgin. "Good Poncho," he said, "I suggest we call them Indians, because that would show due respect to the Theory, without which you'd still be eating pig dung back in that hovel you call a home." Even as he spoke, his strong fingers dug into my lacerated shoulder.

"Oh yes," I gagged the words, *"Indians* is what they are!"

A sleek, metal craft pulled up alongside our ship. A remarkable personage stood at the prow of this boat wearing feathers, gold, some shiny white material, and having a dark-brown complexion that almost made him appear to be made out of wood. "Permission to come aboard," he said in a voice as cultivated as a member of the Castilian aristocracy.

As the man clambered over the wooden railing of the *Santa Maria,* Columbus asked him, "How is it that you speak our language?"

"From monitoring your church services," he answered. "We speak all the tongues of Europe." A few "ayes" and "ahrrrrs" could be heard in the background. "Well, almost all..." concluded this ambassador from a strange new world.

More metal craft were coming alongside to take our party ashore. We were astounded that these boats were not too heavy to float. I was selected to go with the admiral and was glad that I would not be needed to row. I was in considerable pain. These boats didn't seem to require rowing, but were propelled by some magical force that had our ship's alchemist so excited that he almost drooled.

I learned that quite a lot had happened while I was unconscious. The *Pinta* and *Nina* had been sunk by the black beast. "It almost got us, too," said one of the men, "but the admiral tricked it with an amazing subterfuge involving five cheeses and the ship's compass."

"By San Fernando," I exclaimed. I hadn't realized that we had any cheese aboard. The stench must have been terrible by this time, but I'd been spared any unpleasantness, having lost my nose during one of the keelhaulings.

A regal figure was waiting for us ashore. His attire was so bright that it hurt to look upon him. He wore a symbol of the sun on his massive chest. "The time of reckoning is at hand, Admiral," he said.

Columbus showed no fear. "You have the advantage, sir. You know more of me than I do of you."

"I've had a good tutor!" said our host. "I know of your previous voyages. I know how they turned you down in Portugal and how it took eight years to persuade the Spanish crown to finance this trip of yours."

"He just wouldn't give up," came a terribly familiar voice. We all turned around to behold none other than the Dark Duke!

"Saints preserve us," said a little redheaded sailor.

The duke was in a bragging mood: "After sinking your other ships, I got here ahead of you in plenty of time to warn these people about your mad dreams of conquest."

"A thought that never crosses *your* mind," said Columbus, his voice dripping with sarcasm.

The regal figure held up his hand, and all were silent. "Your petty squabbles are no concern of ours," said the Atlant ... I mean, Indian. "So long as you restricted yourselves to your part of the world, we could afford to leave you alone. But now, with improved sailing methods, not to mention a submersible craft worthy of our own shipbuilding, you threaten to extend your violence to our peaceful shores. You leave us no choice."

He clapped his hands, and two European men appeared from behind a huge wall. They were very old, with beards down to their ankles, and they wore horned helmets. Each carried a strange weapon made of crystal and gold, with rotating blades.

"The two of you will fight a stupid, bloody duel to the death," said our host, inclining his head first to Columbus, and then to the duke. "We are pacifists, so we will derive much pleasure from watching the spectacle."

This seemed fair all around. Clearly these people were civilized. But the admiral's practical approach to life did not desert him now: "What will the winner claim as prize?"

The shining man held up a shining cup of water. "This liquid comes from a land to the west. We call it Floridated water, and it will make He who drinks it immortal. The survivor and his crew will be given this water and our most seaworthy submersible, the *Nautilus*. They may explore the rest of the world so long as they never return to bother us."

The admiral did not avail himself of this opportunity to hold forth on the demonic nature of boats that travel underwater.

Diago had a practical question too: "What happens to the loser's crew?"

"They will be fed to a giant octopus of course," came the unemotional answer.

As the weapons were passed to the men from Europe, the Dark Duke made a surprisingly cryptic comment: "No matter how far we

travel, we find ourselves there."
   Suddenly a volcano erupted.

To be indefinitely continued

When I wrote this, we still had a President in the White House, George Bush. I didn't consciously model the Prez in my story on any actual leader, but I was operating on a set of assumptions that no longer apply. As low as the bar has been set for Presidents up until now, Clinton has set a new standard so very low that future satires must always take the Clinton years into account.

In this story, the President is still somewhat presidential; he still has a certain dignity. The joke doesn't work otherwise.

The basic inspiration for this was not politics but comic books. I could never warm up to the new X-men and Teen Mutants that Marvel foisted on us a while back. The adolescent desire to have supreme power and be a poor victim at the same time disgusts me. It's one or the other, kids.

I never would have written this if I wasn't a fan of the best comic book writer of all time, Alan Moore, the first to imagine the effects that real super-powered beings would have on the rest of us. My second agent, Ricia Mainhardt, guided me to John Varley's remarkable anthology, on which she also did editorial work, *Superheroes*.

Press Conference

They used to joke that after he was elected president, he'd wish he were back in the senate where he could wield some real power. He'd taken that sort of thing in good humor. After all, it was only a joke...then.

He was a student of history, wasn't he? He was well versed in the imperial presidency—the accumulation of power in the executive accelerating in the 20th century. Every war had helped. The speed of modern communications had done its part. Ever since Truman, the CIA was in there pitching. Sure, there were frustrations. He still had to deal with an unwieldy, vaguely democratic system. He didn't really mind. When it came right down to it, he didn't object to anything that was part of the natural order, as he saw it. In common with many predecessors in the office, he was that peculiar kind of human being who thrived when dealing with political parties, special interests, other nations with their special requirements, and lawyers! He could juggle priorities with the best of them.

He talked about reflecting the will of the people and he said it with a profound sincerity. Hell, he was good at his job. But the President of the United States had not been prepared for the sudden appearance of The Two. No one in his right mind would have constructed such a scenario. And like all good politicians, the President prided himself on being in his right mind.

Only one month ago the universe had still made sense. It didn't seem all that long ago. Then The Two had come out of nowhere, sharing a nightmare between them as two monsters might suckle a malignant spirit. The world had held its breath, waiting for the last super-power on earth to *do* something. That meant the President of the United States was expected to perform a miracle. Being a little short on burning bushes, he elected to hold a press conference instead.

And so here he was. The reporters waited for him, eyes wide, mouths wider, under a forest of arms swaying under the lights. What had happened to protocol? Where was his introduction, and "Hail to the Chief" blaring over the speakers? The organizational structure of the White House had gone to hell, along with everything else. On the plus side, every network was carrying him, not just CNN and C-span. Even hundreds of little local stations across the fruited plain were interrupting their game shows and reruns of sit-coms. It had been a long time since a president had received this much audience share.

Gazing up and down the usual row of anxious faces, the President was overwhelmed by his usual emotion toward the fourth estate—contempt. The terror gripping the nation had done nothing to bring out the finer qualities of the White House press corps. Not even the prospect of imminent doom could alleviate their rudeness.

He actively disliked the woman from National Public Radio so he let her have the first question. Best to get it over with. She didn't disappoint him: "Mr. President, what steps are being taken to deal with the crisis?"

Watching thin lips moving in her pinched face put him in mind of a fish out of water. He thought how this was the same person who had criticized every covert policy and overt military action he had ever taken. Now she wanted action.

Willing himself to be polite, he rattled off the official answer: "Our best experts are working on this problem night and day. Dr. Gerber has taken over from Dr. Shooter who retired after his theory was exploded..."

"Why did Shooter claim it was a hoax?" the NPR reporter interrupted. *That counts as her follow-up,* thought the President.

"He wasn't the only one," explained the chief executive. "The last doubts were not dispelled until the destruction of New York City. Now mankind is united on one thing at least. Next question!"

A pasty faced man from CBS wasted no time hitting him with: "What about the charges that both of these...creatures resulted from a secret government project in genetic research?"

"We categorically deny it," the President shot back.

"So do I!" a voice boomed from behind the President, who slowly turned around to see a man—what appeared to be a man—-standing regally with a purple cape wrapped around his muscular frame. A tight, black mask covered his head except for huge goggles over the eyes. Already secret service agents were closing in around the President, although a a sense of futility pervaded their actions.

The President tried to sound brave but he came off like a ten year old making a careful inquiry about the rules: "What is this about,

Captain Prism?"

The man in the cape answered: "I'm here to protect you, of course. *He* plans an attack on this very conference. Never fear, he will never prevail while I am guardian of the world." The President had a sinking feeling in the center of his chest. The speaker declaimed some more: "There is no limit to the evil of Mr. Focus. He would enslave the human race with no regard for your free and representative institutions. In fact, the first place he plans to attack is this room! Now, by the cosmic powers at my command, I will move you to the Rose Garden."

"No, wait!" the President started to say, but it was too late. The low, humming noise and glowing lights in the goggles could only mean one thing. In a flash they had been transported to the Rose Garden. It was late in the morning and a cool breeze made the hot day more bearable. The sky was as clear as an IRS agent's conscience. Everyone was temporarily disoriented but there was no hysteria. God help them, but they were getting used to this sort of thing.

The President took a quick inventory. The bad news was that, although the television cameras and sound recording equipment had been transferred as well, there was something wrong with the hook-up and the press conference was temporarily off the air. The good news was that Captain Prism was gone...for the moment.

A black woman from CNN was first to break the silence. "Mr. President, to your knowledge have they ever deliberately hurt anyone?" While the technicians were busily trying to restore the link, the President relaxed for a moment—put at ease, in part, by the naturalness of the question.

"No, Monique," he said, happy to remember her name. "Even what happened in New York seemed to be an accident, a side effect of their battle. Apparently they'd aimed their beams of force at each other. Neither intended for Wall Street to evaporate. And the way things escalated after that..."

"Mr. President," a voice spoke from behind a camera. "We're ready to go back on the air."

Taking a deep breath, the leader of the free world—well, they didn't call it that any longer, since the New World Order—the leader, then, exchanged glances with his press secretary. Time to give it another try. Except they never got that far.

The blue sky suddenly grew dark as the light breeze became a fierce wind tearing papers out of everyone's hands, the fluttering shapes having the appearance of white doves escaping as swiftly as a peace dividend. The other one had just arrived. He was a full head taller than the cowering sound man who had the misfortune of standing next to Mr. Focus.

If anything, Mr. Focus was even more theatrical than his erstwhile foe. He wore an old fashioned, broad-brimmed hat, as black as the heavy overcoat that was draped over his lanky frame. Although he wore no mask, his dark glasses made one, long strip of unbroken lens bisecting his face. What could be seen of his stern features did not inspire confidence that the rest of the day would be uneventful.

"He's been here," said Mr. Focus, seeming to detect traces of his enemy's presence in the very air. "You've been told the usual pack of lies, I'm sure."

The President was about to respond but he found his already shaky sense of authority further eroded by reporters directing their questions to the interloper. Mr. Focus took over the press conference with the consummate ease of a politician. He answered the red-haired man from ABC, whose question was: "Captain Prism says you're the bad guy. Do you have any response?"

Mr. Focus was clear: "That's typical of my hatred eaten foe. You know, of course, that he acquired his powers by accident from a stray meteorite, whereas I, through a combination of sheer genius and dogged determination, made myself into what I am today." He paused as if expecting applause but had to settle for the fear that was palpable in the air.

"That doesn't really address the issue of which one of you is the villain," the red-haired man followed up.

The reply was a bit testy: "The point is that Captain Prism—and in what army does he hold his rank, eh?—is a megalomaniac, out to conquer the world. I'm out to save it."

"Yeah, but what about..." someone began but never finished. With a bolt of jagged blue light emanating from his glasses, the cross section of humanity that made up a Washington press conference found itself transported to the oval Blue Room. No one was really disposed to appreciate the French Empire decor, although they were situated very close to a splendid table right next to one of the long windows. That they were standing on the table may have had some-thing to do with the diminution of their aesthetic sense, along with everything else. They had been reduced in size.

The President of the United States, now exactly six inches tall, was the first to realize the drastic change. "God damn it," he said, oblivious as to whether the recording equipment was working. It was a sure bet that no broadcast would be going out in the immedi-ate future. "This has got to stop," he went on.

"No need to thank me," boomed the voice of the now gargantuan man in the slouch hat. "Captain Prism won't expect to find you here. You weren't safe in the Rose Garden."

"That's what you think!" boomed an equally titanic voice. The other one was outside one of the ornate windows. Naturally he smashed through the window. There was no good reason for this as The Two could pretty much materialize wherever they pleased. But both of them liked to smash through things occasionally.

If the little figures scurrying around on the table had been asked their opinion, they almost certainly would have voted against the dramatic method of entering the room. As it turned out, they were almost showered with broken glass, the size of which pieces would have proven fatal to a large number of the victims. They were saved by Mr. Focus disintegrating the glass fragments with another of his beams.

"This is exactly what I mean," gloated Mr. Focus. "Captain Prism would have killed you all."

"I didn't see you poor, tormented people," said Captain Prism, picking himself up from the floor and addressing the table.

"It's a wonder you can see anything through those stupid goggles," was Mr. Focus's retort.

Captain Prism wasn't about to miss his turn: "So who shrunk them down in the first place, risking their lives in the bargain?"

The dialogue went on in this fashion for some time. Finally, the enigmatic figure men call Captain Prism decided on a course of action. With a blast of crackling energy, he restored everyone to their natural size; and there is simply no denying that the President was grateful for the restoration of his original dimensions. The only small quibble was that, as no one had been removed from the table, most of them suffered minor injuries as they fell to the floor or through the broken window. The President, in fact, landed squarely on what his political opponents referred to as the most representative portion of his anatomy. His lower back didn't fare too well, either.

"I told you he was the villain," crowed Mr. Focus, addressing the room. "The agonies you suffer today are but a foretaste of a grim future."

"Scoundrel!" replied Captain Prism. "Please, my friends, do not be taken in by his malevolent ruses. This fiend will not rest until…"

"Shut up!" screamed the President of the United States. "Will both of you just shut up?" The ensuing silence was the first evidence of executive authority anyone had experienced in some time.

Captain Prism and Mr. Focus glared at each other (at least one could assume they were doing this beneath their respective head appliances). Neither would be first to speak in yet another battle of their mighty wills. The lovely silence continued. The press corps was quiet, too. Some of them were preoccupied with their own pain; but there was no one present who didn't appreciate the tenuous nature of their respite. Who would be first to break the silence?

The President basked in his momentary victory. Standing up, straightening his tie, he felt a smile creeping onto his face. *This is the moment,* he thought. *If I can just bring these super powered lunatics under control, if they will follow my orders just one time…* Gathering what remained of his personal resources, putting on the tattered remnants of his father-knows-best charm, he formulated his position. He opened his mouth. That's as far as he got.

An explosion rocked the room. Where before there had been a wall there was now a gaping hole; and stepping through this ragged opening was a tall, athletic, beautiful woman with the single most remarkable figure the President had ever seen (this side of the budget deficit). She looked just like a living Barbie doll, an anatomical implausibility living and breathing, definitely *breathing* only a few short feet away. Her close fitting red jump suit was like a second layer of skin. Her honey-blonde hair swirled around her head as if a halo accentuating the pleasant fact that she wore no mask.

For one brief moment, the President allowed himself to appreciate her beauty and confident bearing. Then the higher levels of his brain kicked in again, analyzing the new data: explosion, hole in wall, someone in a funny suit. Two words began to hammer in his brain: *Oh no.*

"I am Lady Lightning," she announced, "of the sisterhood division of the Fabulous Fifty, a loose confederation of teenage mutants whose maturity of thought exceeds the angst of a troubled adolescence."

"Oh no," said Captain Prism.

She kept right on: "We have chosen this time to make our existence known to the world. We are here to save mankind from this diabolical duo."

"Oh no," said Mr. Focus.

"The first thing we will do," she said, "is thwart the machinations of these power crazed villains by coming to your rescue. I will place a protective shield around each of you individually in which your bodily functions will be temporarily suspended. It's the only way."

The President's last thought before he screamed was how much he would miss the military industrial complex despite its current impotence. At least his emotional display wouldn't cost him with the electorate. They'd never know. And the best part was that the reporters were screaming, too.

I've made more money from this than any other short story I've ever sold. The reason is that with every foreign sale of *The Ultimate Werewolf*, new checks rolled in. As I type this I'm looking at the Japanese edition. There's no way I could tell which story is mine except that they kept the illustrations from the American edition and I could track down the picture of the barber giving my werewolf a close shave.

We're back in the land of spoofs and parodies. What "Destination Indies" does for science fiction, "Close Shave" does for horror. Think of all five times Lon Chaney, Jr., played Larry Talbot for Universal. Also, the confusion of European and English locales is entirely deliberate in "Close Shave."

I know that I did something right in this story. It got me a good review in *Fangoria*.

Close Shave

"Don't let them take the natural out of the supernatural!" That's been my motto, ever since I expanded my business to include the physical side of the occult.

Allow me to introduce myself. I am Alfred Von Booten, adventurer...and barber for hire. Haircuts, shaves, dentistry and minor surgery are my stock in trade. I also deal firmly with monsters of every kind. Von Booten rates are reasonable, and open to negotiation if the need is great enough.

Only once have I suffered disappointment with one of my customers, but I made up for it in the end. The frustrating series of events began when I was on holiday in the mountains of central Europe. On impulse, I decided to drop in on an old friend.

Descending from the mountain, I saw the little village of Kaninsburg, partly obscured by clouds that were so low as to hug the ground. Shouldering my kit of provisions and precision-made dental and barbering instruments I trudged over rock and crevice with the sure-footedness of a mountain goat (a goat restricted to using its two hind legs, that is).

I had strapped my spectacles on with a fine strip of leather and could see very clearly. The last time I had visited the village, in late Spring, it had been a thriving community of little gingerbread houses, surrounded by greenery, and covered in a fine yellow pollen from the many flowers that were its pride and joy. Now I was arriving a year later, at the height of Summer, and expected more of the same. I blamed the precipitous angle, and the presence of so many clouds, for what must be a mistaken impression of Kaninsburg on a dismal Winter day of washed out browns and grays, a bleak landscape awaiting the next snowfall. But it was when I climbed below the clouds, and had my first unobstructed view, that I realized the place really did look *dead*—a wasteland punctuated by trees almost leprous with black bark.

And yet only a few miles beyond the village was a verdant testament to the season of life. It was Summer everywhere but the village. There was only one explanation: *monster trouble!* I had warned my friend, Baron Averal Tahlbot, that whenever British nobility is transplanted to small European villages, the risk of monster infestation goes up. The Baron had won this village in a game of whist on a Walpurgis Night, when there was a full moon, and he had a toothache. He was in too splendid a mood to believe in ill omens; and I wasn't about to turn down his invitation to see him enjoying the bucolic life (he had been land-poor back home, despite his title). When I arrived, I was to discover that Kaninsburg had no barber, as Baron Tahlbot had driven away the previous practitioner for the crime of sorcery, and for indifferent hair styling. I had been very busy during that stay, and had expected renewed opportunity this time.

Upon reaching the bottom of the mountain, I set to work, extracting clues from the unyielding cavity of life. What blight had come to this fair village? Was it vampires? Poltergeists? Ghouls? Frenchmen? What could it possibly be?

First, I found some wolfbane. Then I noticed a pentagram painted awkwardly on the side of a fence. These clues, combined with a huge sign reading "Beware of Werewolf" suggested the very strong possibility that the problem was lycanthropy.

"Von Booten, you old fraud!" It was the distinctive voice of the Baron, whose smoky vocal chords had entertained the Queen herself (of which country I fail to recall). Unsurprisingly, he was walking his dogs, whose snarling ferocity made me feel as much at home as I had been when facing the zombie legions of the Lost Jackal.

"Hello, Baron. Where are your villagers?"

"Quaking behind closed doors, I expect. We have a bit of bother at the moment."

"It wouldn't be werewolves, by any chance?"

"Astounding, dear fellow. How ever did you deduce that?"

"Elementary," I said, with a sweeping hand gesture, "it's all this damned evidence."

"Secondarily," he replied, "if it's evidence you're after, then my village is full of it. But I say, what brings you here?"

Opportunities such as this should not wasted. Today's business reputation is only as good as yesterday's coincidence. Clearing my throat, I began in stentorian tones: "Through strange powers that defy human explanation, I felt your call for help vibrating through the ether...."

"Just passing through, eh?" was his villainous reply. "Well, I'm glad you're here. Come to think of it, you're still owed money from your last visit. I'm certain that had nothing to do with your returning here. Come with me to the castle and we'll settle accounts."

We shook hands and I couldn't help noticing how he had let himself go to seed. The tweed jacket was frayed at the cuffs and it was missing buttons. This wasn't like him. Although he'd been a widower for some years, one would never know it sartorially. I also noticed that the jacket had about a dozen long, coarse animal hairs on it. Could it be ... ?

"I can see by your expression that you're displeased over my appearance," he said.

"Oh no, it's only ..."

"No need for dissembling, old friend. I admit it. I need a haircut badly."

As a matter of fact, he did. A shaggy mop of unkempt hair was inappropriate to his station in life. But I would no more think of interrogating him about those hairs on his jacket than I would shave off my mutton-chop whiskers. The finest tack was called for when dealing with a Tahlbot.

"By the way," I began, as the melancholy tower of the castle loomed over the gnarled trees to mark our desultory progress, "have you been petting any werewolves lately?"

"Shiver me timbers," he said, recalling his days as a seafaring man, "you see right through me, Alfred. I can't hide a thing from your dogged ratiocination. My son is the village werewolf, and I don't know what to do."

No sooner had these words passed his lips than fog began pouring into the forest as if someone had turned on a steam-powered fog making machine. We walked in silence through the roiling mist. We walked over the moat, through the gigantic door (at which point the dogs went running off in the direction of the kitchen), past the mute English butler, by the dumbwaiter, into the den and up to the ornate fireplace.

Suddenly a beautiful woman, with hair as golden as a doubloon, came gliding down the staircase, in flowing gowns, and fell smack into the arms of the Baron. He introduced her as his niece. It occurred to me that I'd yet to see a villager.

"Oh darling," she said in an American accent, "who is this darling man with you?"

More introductions were made. More greetings were exchanged. The exchange rates for various European currencies were discussed. She served drinks. She passed out cigars. She gave me a back massage and played the piano, although not in that order. Her laughter was like the tinkling of a chandelier submerged in a vat of ambrosia. She sang. She told my fortune.

This last diversion proved to be a mistake. Seeing the sign of the pentagram in my palm, she tried to change the subject, laughing nervously, but it was to no avail. Somewhere in the night, a wolf howled. She swooned. A maid came bustling down the stairs. The maid wasn't a villager either, but some kind of humorous Swedish person. Together, the two women sort of flowed back up the stairs, as if a tide could ebb upwards to greet the stars. Or something.

"Er, where were we?" I asked, "before uh, what's her name again?"

"Evelyn from Idaho," answered the Baron, with a shrug. "Don't worry about it, Von Booten, she sees the sign of the pentagram in everyone's hand."

"Thank you. But what were we talking about before your niece came in?"

"My son, the werewolf."

"He's English?"

"Born in England, of course, but raised in the great American West where two fists and a full head of hair are all that's needed to wrestle life to the ground as Davy Crockett once did with a big old grizzly b'ar."

"Yes, Colonials like to drink in ugly pubs…but please tell me more about your son."

"His name is Lonnie but the villagers have a nickname for him."

"Larry?"

"No, they call him the Horrible Beast, and since being bitten by a werewolf, they've been much harder on him."

We drank some more. At length, I popped the question: "Is he in the castle?"

"That he is."

"He's unhappy about being a monster, I take it."

"He is that."

"You know there's no cure."

"That I do."

"You've tried to put him out of his misery?"

"Yes, but none of the traditional remedies work! That's why I'm so glad you're here."

"One silver bullet ought to be effective."

"We've run out of silver bullets! He's so full of them that he sounds like a Spaniard when he walks."

I had never heard of such a phenomenon. Just what kind of werewolf was this? He could see my consternation, or else he was peering at the small mole on my left cheek. Taking me by the arm, he led me, gently but firmly, in the direction of the family dungeon.

"It will be the full moon tonight," he said, "as it has been for the last two weeks."

"Wait a moment," I said, "astronomy is not my subject, but the full moon couldn't possibly ..."

"No time for that now," was his terse reply. "You must see for yourself what has slaughtered half the inhabitants of my village and torn Evelyn's favorite dress."

"Down into the lower depths?"

"More like the upper depths," was his curious answer. While pondering the Baron's sanity, we descended—I had been doing a lot of that lately—past wall torches that had already been lit along the passageway. I would have preferred taking a kerosene lantern but the Baron insisted that only torches were reliable in the dungeon. The most peculiar sight was that there was a veritable curtain of spider webs we had to push out of the way ... and yet not a spider in sight.

Lonnie was waiting for us, locked in the dungeon's only functional cell. He was a big, beefy man; and every bit as American as a brass band on the Fourth of July. "Dad!" he cried out. "I want to die. Please let me die. Will this man with you help me to die? I can't go through another night of eternal torment! I won't, do you hear, I won't!"

"Evelyn and Lonnie both tend to carry on," the Baron whispered in my ear. Then, in a louder voice, he announced: "This man is going to help you, my son, but first he must witness the transformation."

"Not that, anything but that!" the young man blubbered. Fortunately, the full moon put an end to his monologue.

"Now prepare yourself for a surprise," warned the Baron. I'd seen people turn into wolves before, as well as a horse (a poor peasant named Ed), a pig, several breeds of cat, snakes, and even a baboon once. But I'd never seen anything like this. Young Tahlbot retained the shape of a human being, while accumulating additional features. To see a human face take on a lupine aspect ... to see wolfish fangs protrude from human lips ... to see hands become not paws, but claws, still able to grasp as well as rend ... to see a hybrid horror that was neither wolf nor man struck me as a professional challenge, and an unparalleled opportunity to receive a larger fee.

The Baron had been speaking for some time, but I hadn't listened. There was something numb in his voice, and I heard him say: "... seems to die when we use silver weapons, but come the next full moon, which seems to happen awful frequently 'round here, he's alive again."

"Lycanthropy is only part of your problem," I heard myself say, "because this whole region is under a curse. When did it all begin?"

"There was an old gypsy woman who ..."

"Say no more!" Any unprejudiced observer must admit that lycanthropy and gypsies go together like money and a Scotsman. "We must put an end to this damnable business tonight! Er ... those bars are strong enough to hold your son, aren't they?"

I had good cause to ask such a question as the dirty son of a wolf was throwing himself against the bars of his cage with such vigor that drops of his saliva left spots on my spectacles.

The Baron answered: "We keep putting in new restraints ... as he destroys the previous ones."

It was time for action! I removed my best scissors from my satchel, along with a variety of combs. The dental tools would be used later.

"We will need the assistance of several strong men," I told him, "and it would be a great help if they are stupid. If we cannot free your son through death, then we must strike at the root, no matter how painful."

It was a grim sight, watching all the young men in the Baron's household fearlessly risk dismemberment, infection and worse, as they overpowered their wolfish subject and bound him with chains. It also helped that Lonnie had exhausted himself attempting to escape.

In all the years of my trade, I'd never faced more of a challenge. Bracing myself, I laid on with scissor and comb. No amount of snarling or of staring eyes made my hand tremble. The customer deserves nothing but the best, especially when it's involuntary. Using the razor was more difficult than the scissors, but by the time all his body hair lay a foot thick around my ankles, and my arms were numb, I felt a sense of accomplishment. But the most dangerous task remained.

He must have sensed what was next. His howling might have deterred a lesser barber from moving on to necessary surgery, but my implements were sharp and purpose clear. First, the teeth had to go—at least the nasty ones. They were more of a threat than the talons. (The incisors and cuspids remain in my possession to this day—a souvenir, one might say, sort of fangs for the memories.) Extracting the fangs was a bloody business, and it put Lonnie into such a state of shock that I encountered no resistance when it was time to give him his "manicure."

When I was finished, there was a smattering of applause. Turning around, I saw that the entire household had gathered to witness the shearing of the locks. Foremost among the assemblage was Evelyn, who was embracing an unfamiliar young man. I didn't need to ask the Baron to know that here was *another* foreigner, and probably an American to boot. This village was suffering from an identity crisis beyond anything encompassed by mere monsters.

"Well done," said the Baron.

"Simply darling," said Evelyn.

"Rrrrrrrrrrr," was Lonnie's comment in his sleep.

The young men patted me on the back. The English butler raised an approving eyebrow. A French chambermaid whom I'd somehow missed before licked her lips provocatively.

"Inform the villagers that their days of woe are over," I announced. "These stout fellows can take the glad tidings to their homes."

"Sorry governor," replied one of the lads, "but Baron Tahlbot brought us over with him." The cockney accent shouldn't have taken me by surprise. Not really. But this meant I hadn't seen a single villager! I was certain, if only because of my previous visit, that the village had villagers m it.

As if reading my thoughts, the Baron whispered, "Easy on, Alfred. There are sufficient villagers to bring the population back up to par, if they haven't been wasting all this time behind closed doors. But the decrease in numbers will play havoc come harvest time."

I neglected to inquire what crops could possibly grow in the deso-

lation I had witnessed. We carried the young Tahlbot upstairs. No
one awaited the rising of the sun with more eager anticipation than
your immodest narrator. To tell the truth, I had not the slightest
idea what the next transformation would bring.

Curiosity was stronger than exhaustion. Despite a sleepless and
strenuous night, I felt invigorated when, looking through a window, I saw the fog beginning to dissipate in the first light of day.
Now there would be at least some answers.

Would Lonnie's natural teeth be restored, or gaps remain in his
smile, putting one in mind of a village idiot? And would the small
ivory substances in my hand revert to normal teeth or remain fangs?
And would his natural head of hair grow back, or would he still be
bald? And just how big a tip could I expect?

Then it was morning. Lonnie's face began to change. Gradually
he regained all his natural features. This was good news for him
now; but did this mean the missing features would be as easily restored when next the full moon shone? There was enough mystery
her to justify a full report to the A.M.A. (Austrian Monster Association).

Only the next full moon could answer the final questions. Concerning which, I hesitated to bring up to my host the issue of his
peculiar lunar problems. There is only one night of the true full
moon every month, although it looks to the naked eye as if there
are three consecutive nights of the full moon. That the curse of this
transplanted British family could have altered all the laws of nature
in this place did not occur to me at the time.

I didn't wait around to find out. After assuring the good
Baron that there was nothing else I could do, I received my pay-
ment and returned to my travels. The news of Lonnie's salvation
must have been transmitted by some supernatural means, for now
the village square was full of singing and dancing survivors. It struck
me that these people did not behave as if anything unusual or tragic
had befallen them.

The story might have ended there had it not been for my damnable curiosity. I fully expected to hear news from the village eventually, but I failed to reckon on the degree of isolation involved. By
late Fall, curiosity got the better of me and I decided to return before the weather made travel inconvenient.

The night I arrived, all that could be seen of the moon was a thin crescent in the sky. But as the village came into view, my vision blurred. After rubbing my eyes and putting my spectacles back on, I beheld the impossible: all 2,160 miles of lunar diameter were plainly visible as I stared at the round, silver orb. I had returned to Kaninsburg.

At least the increased luminescence made it easier to traverse the mountain path leading back to the village ... where the werewolf was waiting for me. It was Lonnie, all right. There was hair all over his body, but it wasn't his. I recognized horse hairs, dyed all sorts of colors, and stuck at random about his body. He had fangs, too. The moonlight glinted off a full set of steel dentures. In addition, he had claws. Tied to each finger was a miniature dagger in place of his talons.

With a low growl, he came for me; but a barber should always be prepared. I beat him to death with a striped pole I had used to keep my footing when negotiating the mountain pass. There was a silver knob on top.

"This is ridiculous!" I cried to the night sky. "Will I never be rid of this monster?"

"Never," came a man's voice. I turned to see an old gypsy woman emerging from the fog—there was, of course, lots of fog—but beneath the bangles and brightly colored rags, I recognized the face of a man. "You don't know me," he continued, "But the name's Basil Davies." Good God, it sounded like another transplanted Englishman. "I was the village barber before Tahlbot banished me."

I felt another deduction coming on and said: "You've been behind this all along."

"Yes, after old Tahlbot bored everyone with his stories of your splendid barbering, nobody wanted me any longer. Even the damned peasants preferred waiting for you to visit, or tried their hands at home barbering—*no matter how horrid the results*—or just let their hair grow rather than give me any business. I used black magic to try and get my business back on its legs, but nothing did any good. How I hated them. How I hated you!"

"So you found a way to transform Lonnie into a monster," I concluded helpfully. "Well, he's destroyed now and I'll turn you over to the Baron."

He was having none of it: "You fool! I'll only escape through some ludicrous oversight on his part. And you have not destroyed poor

Lonnie. He always comes back! The village of Kaninsburg is under the Universal Curse, a potent spell that guarantees monsters who return forever!"

His certainty unnerved me. "That cannot be. Nothing is forever. There must be some way to defeat you."

"You'll spend the rest of your life trying. The villagers reproduce themselves, and the Baron keeps importing Americans and Englishmen. You see, he is compelled to keep the village populated. It's part of the curse! Just as Lonnie never leaves anyone wounded and about to become a werewolf in his own right. As you may have gathered, Lonnie is one of a kind."

Laughing maniacally, the transvestite barber/dentist/surgeon (demonstrating a villainous lack of concern for the propriety due our profession) hurried off into the ever thickening fog. And I returned the way I had come. It was evident that if the Universal Curse was to be defeated, it would require research before any ill-considered action.

That was five years ago. In the ensuing period, I learned everything I could about the curse. There was no simple remedy. One promising method was to introduce other monsters into the werewolf's prowling grounds. It was no easy matter, imprisoning ghouls and zombies and then shipping them off to Kaninsburg. Vampires were simply too difficult a proposition or I would have employed them as well (at reasonable rates, of course).

Yet, the next time I ventured there it was to find the wolfish son of Baron Tahlbot as firmly in place as a landmark. Truly he seemed to be immortal. The Baron had lost all faith in me by then. His American niece had even left him, along with her new boyfriend, to go live with another uncle in England—some kind of transplanted European scientist, I understand, who does a lot of research with electrical equipment.

It seemed that my bag of tricks was empty, insofar as dealing with this stubborn spawn of hell. But I had one last idea—and this is the one that saved the village, the Baron, and, incidentally, my reputation.

To prevail against the gravity of the lycanthrope, I turned to comedy. There was a small abbey only a few leagues distant from Kaninsburg. In this quiet and secluded place, I found men of God who were willing to risk everything to help me. The abbot who headed the monastery persuaded one of his monks to accompany us—a short, chubby little fellow who seemed afraid of his own shadow, but who proved invaluable against the forces of darkness.

I'll never forget packing a large cloth sack with the weapons that would defeat the Ultimate Werewolf. We filled our bag with banana peels and cream pies. Nor will I forget two simple words that filled my soul with confidence; and made me believe that the Universal Curse did have an ending ... as all things must end.

When we were leaving the monastery, the little fellow called out for us to wait: *"Hey, Abbot!"*

I'm a long time fan of H. P. Lovecraft. Proof of my dedication is that I read every word of S. T. Joshi's truly exhaustive biography. Fellow Lovecraft enthusiast, Fred Olen Ray, and I did a 10,000 word story for the yet to be released *The Disciples of Cthulhu II* with a title that someone had to use one of these days, "Eldritch." So I jumped at the chance to be in a book called *Miskatonic University*.

This is another of my stories where horror and humor mix. I had a lot of fun on this one. I only hope that it's contagious.

Scavenger Hunt

I hated that my English professor didn't approve of sentences beginning with the personal pronoun. I didn't come to Miskatonic University to get stuck in a creative writing class taught by someone who never sold anything. Actually, Professor Akeley's problem with "I" wasn't nearly as bad as his other hangups. It was one of his few old-fashioned criticisms of student papers. He didn't like sentences beginning with the neutral pronoun, either, which is more modern than complaining about "I." (It dawned on me that he might have been mugged by a pronoun when he was a kid.)

"You would improve your writing," he had scrawled on my best story, "if you didn't distance yourself from the subject. You instinctively use passive voice instead of active. Your fiction reads like an essay in drag. Also, once you make a point you keep on making the same point."

It would have behooved the good professor to get off my case about beginning sentences with "I" if he wanted more immediacy and action in my writing. That's what I say.

He wasn't a bad fellow, actually. One of the co-eds kept throwing herself at him but he behaved as a perfect gentlemen and didn't take advantage. I would have tried my fortunes with the comely lass except that a certain saturnine expression in my lean, cadaverous face always costs me with the ladies.

"Another problem," the professor told me in person, "besides using too many words, is how you mix styles that don't go together." Verily, the man could piss me off.

At no point did I contemplate revenge for slights, imagined or otherwise. But neither did I anticipate what would come into my possession as a result of Miskatonic University's annual event of the scavenger hunt. If I had realized what would happen to Professor Akeley, I might have gone a little easier on him; but I believed that he was betraying the great literary heritage of Albert Wilmarth, the finest professor of both literature and writing old MU ever had, a man who certainly wasn't afraid of passive voice or the objectivity to be achieved through emotional distance.

"Run-on sentences," Akeley would say in my general direction when waxing hyper-critical, and I would defend myself with all the arguments I could marshal.

"Forget it!" was the advice I usually received from Willett, my only friend and a student of the arcane lore forming the solid foundation on which the university owed its international reputation. "You need to study the *Necronomicon* more, and stop worrying about trivia."

"Alfred," I said (his first name is Alfred), "I'm an English major."

"That's your problem," he elaborated the point. "Miskatonic University is the greatest college in the world for the study of the most important knowledge. We only know fragments of this knowledge, but some day someone will put it all together and change the world forever."

"In the meantime, Al," I replied (his nickname is Al), "I want to make a living as a writer."

"Writing about what?"

"Well," I faltered, "I, uh, want to write about life and the human condition."

"You won't make a living writing about that," he insisted. "Now, the 'inhuman condition' is something else again. Tell you what, I'll let you join me on the scavenger hunt. I'm on to something that will win this year, hands down, and I'll share it with you."

There was no way I could express my gratitude for such an offer, even if his grandiloquent perorations came to nought. The big event took place on a marvelous spring day, so beautiful that it would distract anyone but a corpse from formal studies. And so, attracted by the verdant green of trees and grass, the ocean blue sky, the sweet breezes wafting about the theoretically clad co-eds, we ventured forth.

I shouldn't have been surprised when we left this Edenic setting to descend underground. There was a trapdoor hidden in the administration building where no student would venture if he didn't have to. Besides, I realized that something really good for the scavenger hunt wouldn't be readily accessible. I wondered if Willett might conceivably be afraid to go alone, but as I studied his stern and dedicated face whilst light remained, I espied a dedication leaving no room for fear.

A furtive scratching was the first suggestion that we were not alone. Apparently rats lived beneath the administration building!

Many students at old MU would not be the least bit surprised at this revelation. Nor was I surprised as we discovered labyrinths stretching out like snakes, or tentacles, deep into the ground beneath Miskatonic University.

Deeper down there were noises that didn't sound anything like rats. Organic entities made soft, wet sounds suggestive of gigantic, uncouth infants crawling underneath ancient graveyards. My desire to be spared accompanying images was extinguished by Willett turning on a light. He had a flashlight. He also had a map.

"What's that?" I asked, making a reference to the map.

"Be quiet if you value your soul," he hissed, generating as much noise as I had; but I respected his instincts in this matter. Otherwise, I would have reminded him that I subscribed to the philosophy of scientific materialism.

As we descended, our nostrils were assaulted by a host of indescribable odors. I hoped our adventure would reach a terminus before I disappointed Willett by becoming violently ill. Fortunately, the map, which I could see quite clearly in the beam of the flashlight, indicated that we would reach "X Marks the Spot" within a few yards.

And we did.

I kept my mouth shut as we moved the heavy stone slab, trying not to choke from the dust that covered its rough surface—this really was a two man job—and Willett reached out trembling hands for an old wooden box. I maintained silence as we hurriedly returned to the surface, mindful of the cacophony behind us as if all the denizens of the underworld were stirred to rise against us. I didn't speak until we were safe again in the warm sunlight of a typically gorgeous Arkham day.

"Now, Alfred, what is this all about?" I asked. I wasn't such a novice that I didn't realize the nature of a typical scavenger hunt. A wide variety of interesting objects are deliberately hidden so that students may find them. Even now I saw a young co-ed wearing tight little shorts and an even tighter halter top carrying the mummified claw of some prehistoric horror that must have been able to devour her in one bite.

"This is a secret, my friend," he said, "that only a few professors know. They want this hidden, but they are afraid to destroy it." He was about to elaborate when he was distracted by two other co-eds, one dressed in jeans so tight as to defy the laws of physics and the other attired in a cheerleader outfit. Between them they carried a statue of a bloated brachycephalic horror that seemed to have been carved from one solid piece of ivory. Regrettably I missed other undoubtedly interesting details of the sculpture as my vision was otherwise occupied.

So what's in the box?" I asked, and I could tell from Willett's expression that he was surprised by my brevity.

"This," he said dramatically, opening the box and removing a handful of loose, moldy, yellow pages that had the appearance of having once shared company between the covers of a very old book, "is the only copy extant of the *Apocrypha* to the *Necronomicon*."

Willett had finally succeeded in surprising me. I'd never even known there was such a thing, more rare than the *Pnakotic Manuscripts* or a decent grade from Akeley. "What are you going to do with it?" I asked.

"Grand prize of the scavenger hunt, a year's scholarship," he answered. I wasn't greedy. I didn't want to steal any of his thunder at such a moment; and I told him so. Willett was a naturally generous person and insisted that I take something for my trouble.

He knew which page to give me. The *Apocrypha* was in Latin, the same as the university's famous edition. Willett always made A's in Latin. He was a much better student than I was. He explained what would happen to someone steeped in Latin coming across the page unawares—and how I could affect the will of said personage.

The next day I was only a little surprised to learn that after his moment of glory Alfred Willett had mysteriously disappeared. As one of his friends, I was asked if I knew anything. But his discovery of the *Apocrypha* was no secret. The whole school knew. Standing one last time in his room I felt a moment of disquiet, as if the angles and proportions were somehow wrong. Then I shuddered and went to class.

Of course, the lost book was lost again. Rumors flew fast at good old MU. I didn't believe the book was any more lost now than it had been before. Only this time the keepers of the tome would notice that one page had somehow been misplaced during the regrettable Willett incident.

I wasn't very good at Latin but I trusted my friend's description of what that certain page would accomplish if slipped among the papers of someone who understood Latin and was taken by surprise. All the Liberal Arts professors knew Latin at Miskatonic University.

There was nothing different in the demeanor of Professor Akeley when he shambled in front of the classroom to lecture us, but the words that came out of his mouth were music to my ears: "Gentlemen, and any ladies present, heretofore I have insisted on a certain taciturnity on your part when expressing yourselves through what we euphemistically designate as the art of creative writing. It is now incumbent upon me to change course, as it were, and redirect those of you who are interested in expressing coherent thoughts while observing the highest standards of classical rhetoric; for I fear that I have may misled some of you into the worst excesses of modernity. It has always been my goal to discourage faulty practices, or crimes against the mother tongue if you prefer. Miskatonic University enjoys a fine conservative tradition that must not be sacrificed on the altar of commercial vermin in New York who would undermine the cultural patrimony that we seek to preserve against Philistinism. It would have been personally expedient to pretend that I have not erred in leading students away from the vitality of solid discourse into a superficial emotionalism incapable of breadth and discipline. In short, I cannot help but direct you in future to the somber elucidations of our most gifted student..."

At which precise moment Professor Akeley smiled at me, and I returned a grin appropriate to the moment. Cthulhu bless a pedagogue capable of learning his lesson.

Hopefully the only humor in this one is the title, standing for the vampire Amway. This is my first attempt to do a straight-for-the-jugular erotic horror story. Since I did comedy in the book that had a werewolf on the cover, I didn't want to be typecast as the comedy guy in monster books. Especially not in the first anthology where I'd appear that had Dracula on the cover! I take him too seriously for that.

Having read a number of the *Hot Blood* books, I suppose I was influenced by them when I tried my own hand at the form. As for Mr. Sepet, I figured that spelling Dracula backwards is old hat (or should I say bat) but there are other parts of the Count's full name with which to play. My two favorite movie Draculas are Bela Lugosi and Christopher Lee, if that helps with visualizations for the head of Vamway.

Vamway

Mr. Sepet held the floor. We all respected him. Some would say it was because of his age but that wasn't it. The new girl, Johna, told me she found him very sexy. One of the punk kids in the organization said he'd rather fight a whole street gang than go up against "the old guy." Tonight the kid was on guard duty. Mr. Sepet held the floor because he held our respect. There was real power in the man who founded Vamway.

"This evening is your initiation," he said, his eyes seeming to burn right into her. After years in close contact with him, I still couldn't describe the color of his eyes. They changed.

One of my responsibilities was to bring out the chart. The punks had already moved the heavy mahogany dining room table off to the side, as well as rolling up the carpet before placing chairs in the center of the room. The chandelier lit up the work area nicely. I placed the chart on a metal tripod in front of the chairs and went back to my corner.

The familiar pyramid showed the various levels within the organization. I glanced over at Johna because I wanted to see if she reacted when she saw it was the Great Pyramid of Egypt. Occasionally we recruit people who are into Pyramidology. She looked at the chart without visible signs of excitement or stress. She probably wasn't even a regular watcher of Dr. Gene Scott's television program.

Mr. Sepet must have been reading my mind because he suddenly asked Johna, "Do you believe in God?"

She raised an eyebrow. The founder smiled, pulling back his lips just enough to reveal a single, pointed tooth. We breathlessly waited for her answer.

"I don't know," she admitted.

"Are you certain of anything?" he asked, voice as cold as my dead wife's feet.

Johna frowned. "I'm certain I don't want to find out if God exists anytime soon!"

That broke the ice. Everyone laughed, even before Mr. Sepet chuckled—his usual method of warning the rest of us to be at our ease.

With a motion as slow and deliberate as the erection of a statue, the founder stood. Johna involuntarily took a step back. He would be an imposing figure even without his great height. I offered him the pointer and he jabbed at the chart.

"We must have courage," he intoned, "to attempt immortality on this plane." He held the wooden pointer over his head as if it might be Excalibur. "To allow even this mundane object in our inner sanctum requires a brave heart! We face so many limitations as it is, you might wonder why I created an organization that, on the surface, seems only to add to our burden."

He stared directly at Johna but she wisely refrained from speaking. Vamway always has room for another smart recruit.

Again, he seemed to read my mind when he said, "The essence of my cruelty is that I try to oblige women and give them exactly what they want. Especially the ones who are closet exhibitionists."

I laughed nervously. The other women in the room smiled and whispered among themselves. I never ceased to be impressed by how he handled the Brides. That's what we called the women who converted enough new members to join his inner circle.

"Me, too," said Lucy, the boldest member.

"You give men what they want?" Johna asked her uncertainly.

"No," answered Lucy, smiling devilishly. "Women!" The redhead licked her lips. I liked her the best. She was friendly to everyone, male or female. She even paid attention to me when I went on and on about my favorite subject: fly fishing.

"Peter Pan was one of us," announced the founder without preamble. "What do you think is the moral of the story?"

"I don't know," admitted Johna.

I'd heard the speech so many times that I knew the words by heart. But none of us would dare step on Mr. Sepet's lines: "Once you lose your shadow, it's a waste of time trying to get it back."

Johna was the youngest girl there, just barely in her twenties. She looked younger. She had a petite figure and with her short dark hair could play the role of Peter if we felt like putting on our own little theater production. Lucy would almost certainly volunteer for the role of Wendy.

Johna tilted her head in a bird-like fashion and volunteered: "Isn't that story about free will? The children are given the choice of staying young forever."

"The perfect metaphor," hissed our noble leader. "To be fully human, you must be full of human blood. Keeps you young! I first hit on the idea of Vamway when I offered a Turkish scholar the opportunity of joining our society voluntarily. Unbeknownst to me, the man was dying of cancer and he eagerly accepted. Over the centuries, I have harvested some of the most famous men and women in history as they neared terminal retirement."

Sometimes I can't keep my big mouth shut. "As Winston Churchill says—there's no such thing as history; there is only biography."

"Is he...a member of Vamway?" asked Johna.

From the back of the room came a female voice with just a touch of brogue: "Any Irishman would say yes."

The founder reiterated the official line: "Only those who have sold enough to reach Five Blood Rubies level are privy to our confidential lists. Johna, you have passed the preliminary tests. Do you voluntarily accept our kisses?"

She swallowed hard and nodded. The time for words was over. I went to the closet and got out the mop and the robes. Before I returned I could hear the ripping of cloth. The Brides liked to tear off their own clothes. We'd gotten to the point that we had special tailoring for these events.

Six naked women surrounded Johna whose eyes were already glazed over. The room was full of perfume and female musk. I dropped the mop and busied myself moving the chairs out of the way. I could feel the founder's eyes on the back of my neck like two golden bees, ready to sting. I was a little slow tonight.

"Your turn," said Mr. Sepet softly. Johna unbuttoned her blouse. No one seemed to mind that she might want to preserve her wardrobe. Then she removed her skirt and dainty underthings. Lucy moaned at the sight of small, firm breasts and full thighs.

"Wait," said Mr. Sepet, barely above a whisper. "My turn."

The founder approached the girl in a manner both leisurely and formal. He might be asking her to dance; but no word escaped his lips. Only his tongue protruded like a red snake. No tongue should be that red.

He licked her nose. Then on to her eyes, her forehead, her cheeks. Everyone in the room waited in rapt anticipation for him to reach the pulsing at the base of her neck. When at last he sank his fangs into her flesh, there was a collective sigh of release. His large white hands held her by the shoulders. He could have crushed so easily the vessel from which he drank.

Then he stood back. He wasn't satisfied. He could never be satisfied. But a true aristocrat practices moderation and derives pleasure from the sensation of hunger.

"Everyone's turn," he said in a voice heavy with her blood; but I knew the invitation didn't extend to me. I wasn't complaining. My diet had improved a lot lately. I remained in the corner and finished munching the remains of my snack.

Six moist, soft tongues replaced the founder's dry, rough one. The Brides fed on every interesting portion of Johna's writhing body. She was the cup. We know the true meaning of communion at Vamway.

Johna groaned more deeply than Lucy. Mr. Sepet guided the novice's head to Lucy's breast and made her nurse from the crimson nipple. Lucy laughed hysterically, and then returned the favor by getting behind Johna and burrowing there.

Johna died beautifully. She was reborn in the glory of the new flesh. Over the years, the founder had discovered how to accelerate this process.

As the new member, and potential Bride, opened her shining eyes, everyone in the room experienced a telepathic projection of the life Johna had left. We saw a little girl about the age of ten skipping in a garden. She expected nothing but good from the world. She eagerly faced life like a newborn kitten. Then a few years passed and there was the change.

Puberty had done its work. Now the girl was sullen, but still expectant. The longing for life was thwarted, and she'd already learned to keep feelings to herself. Playfulness had been replaced with her secret tension. It was the worst kind of secret—the secret everyone pretends not to know. She still looked out upon the world, but suspicion was her *leitmotif.*

A few years passed again, and she was a full blown teenager. Running hot. Running cold. No more skipping in the garden. Volatile. Vacant. Crazy. Lied to until the only defense is pretense made into a law of life.

Then there was the calm after the storm. The first great love. Followed by the second, third, fourth One-and-Only Great Loves.

Five. Six. Each time the temporary return to the garden. Hope turns into lies like butter melting on a hot gravestone.

Each time love died, the calm expression drained away more slowly than before. The frustration returned, of course; but she was building up her armor. If she'd lived out a normal life span she would have continued confusing monogamy with loyalty. The wages of monogamy are death-in-life. She'd been saved from this by the founder, with his gift of life-in-death. Lucky girl.

With a collective sigh like a hot tropical wind against our lips, the visions faded. Back to reality. Back to abnormal.

I didn't want to get into any trouble for being too slow now! One of the punk kids guarding the mansion liked to say that when Mr. Sepet got pissed off, he went postal more completely than anyone this side of a world war. He was a great killer.

First, I passed out the thick cotton robes. They were all red. My idea. I have my moments. Then I mopped up the puddles. There hadn't been much waste tonight.

"You're hungry now," said the founder to the gasping newcomer.

"Yessssssssss," she sighed.

"Wait," he advised. "Let the hunger grow. You can't experience the deeper satisfactions unless you first practice self-denial."

She whimpered but there was no resistance in her. "Yes," she said.

"How do you wish to address me?" he asked, his voice suddenly gentle.

"I...I'm not sure," she answered.

"What do you want to say to me?" he coaxed her.

"I'm ashamed to say it," she murmured. "I don't deserve to speak the word."

"Say what is within you."

"Yes, master," she screamed, falling to the floor and kissing his feet, abandoning herself to the freedom of total self abasement.

The founder laughed. The nostrils flared on his aquiline nose. His chiseled features were full of the love that only comes from a clear vision of the object of one's passion.

"There, there," he said, beckoning her to rise. "Now tell me: are you still concerned for the rights of others?"

She nodded, too ashamed to speak.

"That's all right," he consoled her. "Vamway is the only pyramid scheme that never fails. Normally, you run out of people. The base widens until there is nothing underneath it but empty promises. The people at the bottom guarantee a good living for the people above; and they in turn pass the benefits up all the way to the top. But there is always a limit to how many can maintain themselves at the bottom. There comes that dread day when the market is exhausted, the market in suckers one might say."

"Fortunately, Vamway isn't in the business of providing a living for anyone," said Lucy while she ran her fingers through Johna's short hair. Here was a new Peter Pan indeed. At least I didn't have to mop up any spilled shadows.

"A true pyramid scheme is a Ponzi scheme," he went on, as if he hadn't heard Lucy. "There is a geometrical progression making it impossible to maintain. The power of two is the power to run out of victims. We aren't selling a product, of course. We are selling a 'lifestyle,' one might say. We have the means to drain victims to the point of death. To join us, one must deliberately partake of the sacred blood. If everyone in the world wanted to be in Vamway, we'd have an insurmountable problem. Then we would be guilty of a pyramid scheme. I can assure you that we'll never have that problem."

Johna blinked her big, dark eyes. "I think I understand," she said uncertainly.

"Are you happy?" Mr. Sepet asked her.

"Yes," she said quietly.

"We will find you a volunteer," he promised, "but now I must tell you one of our secrets. The younger the blood, the more it satisfies us. The older the blood, the emptier we feel...although it maintains our existence."

I watched realization dawn in her face. It was much easier to find volunteers among the old ones. There was only so much decadence available in youth.

My last task of the evening lay before me. I led Johna to her coffin, already prepared and waiting for her. I could tell that she hungered for my throat but she would follow the rules. I told her that later the founder would join her and allow her to finish her communion with him, personally. Then when she awoke, feverish in hunger, we would introduce her to the next volunteer, a middle aged man who would have to do.

"Was he telling the truth?" she asked me as I started to lower the lid over her beautiful, intelligent face.

"About what?"

"About famous people who are still...on Earth?"

"Oh, yes. This weekend I'll personally introduce you to Bram Stoker and Ambrose Bierce."

"There is so much I want to ask them," she said, more to herself than to me.

I left her dreaming of the new life opening up for her. There was no reason to disappoint her. It would be months before it finally sunk in that our knowledge was not particularly more advanced than the ones who bleed and die. Mr. Sepet was still wrestling over the question of whether or not God exists. Every dawn he prayed that the answer is no. Please.

When I returned to the dining room, the Brides had finished with the baby. Mr. Sepet brought it in the moment I took Johna to her new quarters. My guess is that it will take Johna about a year before she is ready for the next secret. Namely, that Vamway recruits new members who respect the rights of human beings because such members are worth teaching. Only through ritual do they overcome their prejudices. We don't want brutes. We want members who know what they are doing. Who feel the delicious pleasure of feeding well.

The Brides are getting better about leaving me something. The master has made it clear that I work hard and deserve the leftovers.

This was originally intended to be a companion piece to "The Lon Chaney Factory." I've been paid for it a couple of times over the years and then the rights have come back to me, the story still unpublished. Maybe there's a curse on this one.

I wrote it around the same time I sold (and saw published) an article I did comparing the 1976 remake with the 1933 classic, *King Kong*—"Two Kongs Don't Make a Right." Since then there has been a revolution in movie special effects, but any good science fiction writer would have anticipated things like CGI. That's why I take such pains in the story to do a fully functional robot Kong as the latest thing in amusement rides and publicity stunts.

God knows what future generations will be capable of if they are only bored enough.

The Kong Company

She rushed into the house on the beach. "Alan, Alan, they are going to put me in the hand!"

Alan Beatty smiled half-heartedly at his wife. She stood before him, head thrown back, proud. Her blonde hair was combed in a wave that cut across her left eye, giving her an impish appearance, He remembered that she had been a brunette the week before. Looking at her now he saw something contradictory about her face. The stern mouth didn't belong with the upturned nose and laughing eyes.

"I'll be the first one," she announced gaily. "They plan to use a live girl every year from now on, but I'll be the first."

She walked over to a picture window and watched the sun setting over the ocean, the sky turning from red to gold. She reached for a button on the wall and pushed it, speaking to the glass before her. "New York City," she said. "Present time. Aerial view of the Empire State Building." The ocean disappeared, to be replaced with New York City, the tall buildings stretching away beneath Alicia's face to 34th Street far below. She pressed her nose to the cool glass.

"Just think, I'll be up there in another month, the winner of the Ann Darrow for a Day Contest."

"They are sure it will be safe?" he asked.

"Don't be silly. I'll be wearing a safety harness." She chuckled softly. "You of all people shouldn't worry."

Beatty shook his head. "You shouldn't have such absolute faith in the company. The safety department lost some good men recently."

She looked at the picture window. "Don't you think the city is beautiful at this time of day?"

Alan Beatty shrugged. "All right," he said. "We'll change the subject. It is a lovely time of day." Beatty's voice was tired and he tried unsuccessfully to suppress a frown. For years he had found himself growing melancholy whenever he was with Alicia. It was especially hard for him now.

"Of course," she continued, "sunset is very attractive in a natural setting, too. I'm very fond of natural settings."

"Yes," he said.

"I just can't decide which I like more, which kind of setting I mean. I guess I like them about equally."

"Ever since I've known you, you've liked just about everything."

"I know," she said, "and I wouldn't have it any different." She lifted an eyebrow. "Don't you think the Siclari Building is one of the most impressive buildings that's s ever gone up?"

It took him a moment to get his mind on the Siclari Building. "They played hell way back when the twin towers went up," he began. "They should never have put up anything taller than the Empire State Building if they couldn't match its beauty. The Siclari is just the newest, tallest, ugliest thing in the city."

Her laughter sounded like a taunt to him. "Oh, you're prehistoric, Alan! Besides, the Siclari is a *company* building."

Having dispensed with the argument to which there was no rebuttal, she saw no point in continuing the conversation. She worshiped the company. For thirty years, Beatty had worked for Doppelga[[umlaut]]nger Inc., renowned as the best robot manufacturers in the world. He was well established by the time Alicia met him at a cocktail party given to celebrate his appointment to a Directorship. It had been good at first, the brief romance, the marriage that took him by surprise. She had been sure and his doubt was no obstacle for her; she joked that he was "wishy washy" and he thought that was amusing. So they walked down the aisle and it wasn't until a year later that the doubt returned to nag at the corners of his mind.

Yet it seemed that he was alone in this. If she were unhappy, it was her best kept secret. His few attempts to discuss his disenchantment led nowhere; she had become ever more adept at channeling the course of any discussion past troublesome topics. After ten years, she looked as beautiful as ever. With the cosmetics and exercises in her daily schedule, she had at least another fifty years of comparable charm. It wasn't really that she had changed; he knew the difference was in him.

"Would you like a drink?" he asked, already headed for the bar.

"Sure, anything," she answered right away, turning back to the glass, pressing the button on the wall and saying: "New Australia, any time will do."

The earth was a blue-green disc filling the lunar night over New Australia, the biggest moon city. It made a green dot reflected in

Alicia's eye.

"Here's a whiskey sour," said Alan Beatty.

"Oh, that weak concoction?" she said, taking the glass offered her. "Well, I did say anything, didn't I?" She walked over to a couch and sat down, "Let's have a toast to my victory," she said.

They sipped at each other.

Why, he thought, looking at the earth in his picture window—why was the situation deteriorating? Soon Alicia would be in a great mechanical hand, held far above the concrete labyrinths of the city, vulnerable. He could take steps to stop her. But, dear God, he didn't want to!

"Think how many contestants there were," she said. "Thousands. And I won. I'll bet my blonde hair is what tipped the scales. Who would think hair would be heavy enough to do that?" She guffawed. Alan Beatty took a long pull on his double scotch.

"I'm so happy," she insisted. "It will be announced all over the stations tomorrow."

He contemplated the scotch, thinking of the hundred announcements made every day about the endless contests running every week, every day, every hour. "I'm going to let in the ocean," he said at last. Alicia said nothing, "I know you like running the scanner, but the reason I moved out here in the first place was for the sea, the sight and sound of it."

He went to the window, touched his forefinger to the always obliging button and said, "Home, present time, sound." A last hint of twilight was on the ocean. He stood, listening to the dull thunder of waves dying on the beach.

"I'm going to have to buy a white dress," she observed from the couch. "They will supply the harness, of course."

He turned and faced her. "I have a surprise for you tonight," he said simply.

"Oh good," she said, jumping up, but then noticing the room around her. "Do you think we could have some light? It's getting dark in here."

"Come on," he said, "there's light where we're going. I have your surprise in the TeeVee." He went down the hall and she followed with a list of questions:

"Is it the new psychorama? Is it the latest Sensu-Show? Oh, I hope it stars that gorgeous Ronald what's-his-name. He tastes so good."

The TeeVee was a cylindrical room, all white with chairs set in the middle of the floor. They sat down. He addressed the ceiling: "Run film 601." The room darkened and a small square of light grew directly in front of them.

Then they were looking at a black and white picture of a tremendous radio tower rising over the earth. The legend announced that this was to be an RKO picture. The high beeps of sound from the tower died and the picture faded. Capital letters became visible in the distance; they rushed forward to confront the viewer with the title of the movie to follow: *King Kong*. There was low, menacing music that gave a portent of future drama.

"Oh no," said Alicia. "A revival! Not the old one!"

He stopped the film and the lights came on. "You don't want to see it?" he asked.

She was disappointed that he would even ask. "I half thought you might be showing *Kong*. It is a cute idea. But not the old one. Why, the seventh remake was just released this month! It's a full Sensu-Show. Why have a Sensu-Show TeeVee if you won't use it? What's the point? At the very least, you could run one of the color versions. You know how I hate black and white. Ever since that modern art group, the Inner Eye, has been trying to bring back black and white, I've refused to watch it. It's not fair to expect me to..."

"Alicia," said Alan Beatty, "shut up."

They sat quietly for about a minute, then he said: "This God damned event, which you're so proud to-be a part of, has been going on for the past ten years, with its God damned full scale mechanical ape. At first they brought him in by helicopter and deposited him on a ledge built just for the occasion. There he stood, holding a robot girl squirming in his hand, barking out recorded growls from the most recent version of the classic film. Promotion, they called it. We trumpeted that it was a marriage between the film and robot industries. We at Doppelgänger Inc., loved our Kong, even though it was crude work for us, a simple puppet of an ape, operated by remote control. Here is a company on the verge of developing androids—the most sophisticated work in the world, for God's sake—and we're holding big government contracts. We start doing a little promotional work on the side. Kong brings in some extra cash. Fine. But does it go in the R and D budget? No, it goes to build heavy scaffolding that runs the length of the Empire State Building so that the mechanical ape, with some alterations, can "climb" up the whole building just like the real thing! What waste, what stupidity. And it's just the beginning."

Alan Beatty was breathing heavily. Alicia was astonished. She had never known him to be this upset before, and it wasn't like him to lecture.

"But..." she began, "it's just for fun. What's wrong with having Ann Darrow Day?"

Alan Beatty seemed to notice her again; he had glanced at the point on the wall where the picture had disappeared and remained that way, staring at nothing. "Alicia, you're the first person they are going to put in that giant hand, to be carried up that scaffold staircase. You'll be held at arm's length from the fourth tallest building in the city."

She chewed her bottom lip. "It's perfectly safe," she said again. "They won't do it unless the weather's clear and there's no wind It's all planned out to the smallest detail."

"Yes, I know," he said sadly. "All planned." He closed his eyes. "They are redoing all the great films with the full-flesh holograms; now everyone can be a part of their favorite cinema. Join in the drama without ever leaving your chair. And every year there are more robot copies of favorite characters from the arts. Buy your child a Santa Claus every Christmas, and while you're at it, you can buy a chimney too."

"Alan!" Alicia screamed. "You sound like you're against the industry!" She looked as though she might cry but he doubted that she would. She hadn't had much practice.

"That's ridiculous," he said quietly.

"But all those things you've been saying!" She had forgotten her surprise. "It doesn't make sense for you, not when you helped build the industry in the first place."

"I need another drink," he said. She followed him back to the den.

"The man who interviewed me today," she said, "knew that I'm your wife. He wanted the human interest. We talked about your old department that began supplying the robot planes when they first made the Kong display, just two years before your Directorship! I told him that historic biplanes are your hobby, though God knows why you waste the time with them that you do. Anyway, I said it's appropriate that I should be in the hand, surrounded by your planes. It's such a coincidence, too!"

That was the hell of it, that it actually was a coincidence. Alicia entered every sort of contest but she'd never won before. It was one thing he never would have expected, that she would win *this one*. For a moment, he was sickened by his indifference to Alicia going ahead with what he knew was going to be dangerous. He had to try one last time to dissuade her: "Alicia, it's not too late for you to cancel. I think you ought to get out of it."

She started to answer him, but her mouth was caught open between a laugh and a rebuff. "What? You've got to be kidding Just who do you think you are?"

Now was the time, now to put things right, to tell her outright why she shouldn't go or else lie about it; to save her or tell her to go to hell... but to do *something*, anything, so he'd know she was still real to him, a person, not one of his robots.

His shoulders slumped when he realized his decision was to say: "Forget it, I'm sorry." The inner betrayal left him with a twitch in his left eye. *Coward*! he berated himself. No, not coward, he rationalized, just indifferent. *Worse, much worse*, the inner voice insisted.

"Well.." she said, "all right then." They stood a room's length apart, in silence. There was nothing to say. The surf seemed quieter now, whispering against the pane of ice-clear glass in the picture window. They stood within the frame of the full wall picture window not touching, not desiring to touch. Statues.

Finally Alicia, a slight quaver in her voice, said, "It's been such an exciting day that I'm not about to be depressed about anything." Her face was flushed and her eyes were unnaturally bright, in contrast to Alan's ashen complexion. "I'm going out," she announced and walked briskly to the hall, went into the bathroom and emerged a few minutes later, nude. She wore one piece of jewelry, a platinum collar that glinted with a special brilliance. It was a shadow-caster. From neck to toe, her body was ink-well black, no features visible save for the outline of her silhouette and two spots of pinkness where her hands fluttered out past the sleeves of shadow, positively naked in their unabashed color.

He still appreciated the fine lines of her body but what he saw was an image of cold beauty, not warmth, and her hands were cool as they took him by the head, and her dry lips kissed him perfunctorily on the white, drying skin of his forehead. In his mind there was the sound of crisp leaves grinding underfoot.

"I want to say something to you, Alan, for your own good," said Alicia. "You're losing sight of your priorities. You're forgetting about the things that people enjoy. It can be bad for you in your business, whether you admit it or not. Who gives a damn for those creaky old films? You're so interested in history that you're forgetting the present. The only thing that old junk is good for is the ideas which we use better than they ever could. People want to have fun. They want to participate. Old movies offer none of that. People want to be more than spectators. It's like when you're a child. You don't want to be left out of the game. I hope you understand this, Alan. I'm going out to play. Are you coming?"

"No," he said.

Then she was out the door into the warm night and he was left, dwindling inside his grey suited body. He was committed to something he had begun years before and nothing could stop it. He knew he wouldn't change his plan to sabotage Ann Darrow Day.

He fixed himself another drink and he was beginning to feel the alcohol now. He moved on down the hall, holding the glass gingerly, listening to the clink-tink of the ice. He stopped outside the door to the TeeVee room.

Kong was waiting for him inside. Not some pillow-faced clown of a great hairy doll, a poor gorilla fantasy borrowed from a psychologist's cleaned-up, scrubbed-down, non-violent idea of tolerable terror; not the Kong of the new versions and Doppelgänger Inc. No, this was the real one, the beetle-browed killer of Skull Island. Beatty sat down in the white chair and told the room to run film 601.

He watched as the flickering old melodrama went through its paces once again. Here was the great ape who was more than beast but less than a god after all; who pursued the precious doll-woman through fabulous jungles, defending her against various dinosaur transgressions; who finally dived into space from civilization's pinnacle, as if to prove his captor's belief: It was beauty killed the beast.

Surely he was misunderstood, this monster, and that accounted for his lasting popularity as recognized by critics from the beginning. It was the thing's spirit that made a creation of latex and metal and rabbit's fur and special effects more than clever sleight of hand.

American folklore it had been called within a few decades of its release. It had been the first love of Alan Beatty's life when he saw it at a museum of cinema history. The human expressions on the gorilla face had been unforgettable. How could such an inhuman visage mirror so closely the manlike qualities of humor and rage and jealousy? The face of violence showed tenderness towards Fay Wray; the thrill of her being an exception to Kong's violence was the whole point of the story. No later telling of the fable ever captured this so well, or impressed Alan Beatty at all.

Middle-aged Beatty, sitting in his TeeVee, was thoughtful of his condition: funny how one's youthful exuberance is never fully extinguished—it crops up unexpectedly given the proper stimulus. His fierce loyalty to Kong was a lifeline to the past; it helped him remember the way things could have been. When he was in graduate school, working on a degree in engineering, Beatty experienced his last sustained period of joyous expectancy. Life was a tremendous adventure promising rewards commensurate with risks taken, with obstacles overcome. He was going to be the best in his field, and to him that meant achievement and pride. Had he failed to live up to his personal expectations, reached a limit in mathematical acumen or drafting ability, he could have accepted it. But he was a superlative engineer. A mind able to perceive the thrusts and counter-thrusts of any structure, found itself helpless before the "social structures" of the business world. He lost his youthful fire in the labyrinths that wind their way between offices and cocktail parties. And he was at his lowest ebb when they began talking of making him a Director. His very aloofness made him a compromise candidate between two factions.

He began to have dark thoughts of a great primitive body raging against carefully constructed edifices that are fragile things which can be broken.

He was despondent and entertaining vague thoughts of suicide when he met Alicia. She was good for him at first. That's what made the eventual disapointment all the greater. She had not married him for his work, or his ideas, or even for his money. She had married the company.

But the coils of disaffection tightening around Beatty did not plunge him again into suicidal contemplations. Destructive thoughts returned but these were directed outward. He formed a plan, a pro-

test against the people he blamed for his ills. It became an obsession The company had betrayed his values. Now he would betray
the company.

*King Kong falls, again and again he falls for his perfect love, and
dies on the cold pavement far below.*

Beatty played the film twice—from the Empire State Building
scene on to the closing line of dialogue—before he felt satisfied.
When the promise behind a ritual is lost, all that remains is the
soothing aspect of the ritual itself.

"Code four," he spoke to the TeeVee, "A, B, C, D, E, F..." he recited the entire alphabet. "Keep your chin up," he finished the coded
message.

Then he was sitting at a drafting table in a brightly lit office. Across
from him, drinking coffee, was the lean figure of a young man with
dark brown hair and green eyes. There was a mocking quality in
the way this man greeted his guest.

"Hello Mr. Beatty," he said.

"Hello Alexander," Beatty answered. "You got my message?"

"Yes sir." He sipped coffee. "Are we going ahead with it?"

"We are," Beatty said softly.

"Your wife isn't going then?"

"She still plans to."

Alexander raised an eyebrow, the brief surprise vanishing as
quickly from his face as it had appeared. "I'd offer you some coffee,
Mr. Beatty, but I don't think you'd take me seriously."

Beatty stood up and walked through the table, walked through
the body of the man seated before him, walked to the end of the
room and then began pacing back and forth through the table. "Did
you know I had a great-grandfather who hated telephones?" he said.
"That's always struck me as odd. I've never understood individuals
who hate technology. The only thing worth hating is human wickedness or stupidity."

"How long have you known that it would be your wife?"

"I knew it a day before she did, when I contacted you to expect
this message from me today."

"Is she in the house now?"

"No, but I've sealed off the room anyway. And you?"

"I'm alone." The lean man looked at his coffee. "Do you hate your
wife?"

A brief pause. "You're the only person I know who could ask that question and get away with it." Beatty sat down, "No, I don't. That's why I don't want her in the hand."

"Then how can I take you seriously when you propose we go ahead as planned?"

"Look, Alexander, the Awards Committee would authorize the substitution of a runner up if Alicia cancelled, but she won't. If I attempted to cancel her without her knowledge, it could appear suspicious. Besides, it would complicate things; for the cancellation alone, I could be up on a felony charge by the State whether she wanted to prosecute or not. If we drugged her or something, and convinced another girl to act the part, the new one would be in the same danger which is the problem with our plan now, no matter what."

The other man nodded. "It took five years to arrange this," he said, "to subtly alter the programming in our department, to cover our tracks. And then the bastards go and put a live woman up there the year we're finally ready." The lean man smiled. "It's rather wicked of them, don't you think?"

Beatty didn't notice the sarcasm. "If we really try to pull a fast one and substitute a robot copy, they'll catch on during the interview. That's another feature this year—the in-progress interview."

"It's almost as if they'd anticipated us somehow."

"Yeah," Beatty continued, " and the 7003 series won't be ready for another year, the only one we could possibly use to fake a human being with... and *then* we'd have to know what questions were going to be asked in advance so we could program the answers."

Alexander shrugged. "Finding out the questions would be no trouble, if there were any point to it."

"Damn, it's incredible the way this has worked out. We have no alternatives."

"Yes," the other man nodded.

"That puts it entirely in your hands."

"I'd already made arrangements in the safety area the minute we learned there would be a live person involved. The odds are excellent that the woman's—I mean your wife's—safety harness will have its opportunity to function."

"See that it does."

Alexander put down his cup. It made a hollow echo against the table top. "Believe me, every precaution has been taken. The safety harness has to be outsideof the confines of the hand so the air-jets can support her. There is a small charge in the wrist of King Kong, just enough to blow her free. It's a simple problem in mechanics, and you know my skill."

"Show me," said Beatty. For the next hour, they went over every detail until Beatty was satisfied.

"I'll destroy these papers," said Alexander before Beatty terminated the call.

"Right," was the reply. Then Beatty was back in the arctic whiteness of his TeeVee room, and Alexander, scowling Alexander, was left behind.

It was in the same TeeVee room that Beatty, a few weeks later, prepared to watch the Tenth Annual Ann Darrow Day, held in memory of Fay Wray every March fourth, to commemorate the New York premiere of King Kong at Radio City Music Hall in 1933. He watched the fat, double-chinned and slow moving president of Doppelgänger Inc., break a champagne bottle against the ankle of the robot Kong—it made him sick, the way they did it every year, as if the old can be made new and virginal by the proper rite. Then a narrator's voice announced the first commercial even as Kong began the first stage of the "climb" up the first ramp:

"With the advent of live participants, this event has become so popular that Doppelganger Inc., proudly informs you, the viewing public, of a King Kong renaissance. Starting next year, there will be four—count them—King Kongs, each beginning his climb at the same time as all the others. The granddad of Kongs will continue climbing the Empire State, while the new Kongs climb, alternately, the Trade Towers, the Wynand Building, and the newly finished Siclari Building. And we'll cover all four events at the same time!"

Alicia, safe in the cocoon of Kong's hand, smiled in a way that made Beatty think she could see him. Then the interviewer asked his first question—"Can you hear me, Alicia?"

"Yes, perfectly."

A medium close-up of her— "How do you feel?"

"Wonderful."

—"Do you find the height exciting?"

"Oh, very much. But it doesn't make me nervous."

—"How do you like being the bride of Kong?"

"He's just a dear." (A close-up of the gorilla face, impassive, dull.) "I love him and wouldn't trust anyone else up here."

—"Does it bother you that the crowd below has been moved back to a safe distance in case there is an accident?"

"I was told they do this every year. It's more of a tradition than anything else. There's no real danger."

—"You seem to be a very brave young girl."

"I know what I...oops!" Her position had shifted as the hand turned slightly. Kong had stopped inexplicably. Then he started up again. Alicia laughed. "He's getting his bearings," she went on. "You know the entire climb is programmed in advance but the operators are inside this building at their counsels where my husband once..."

—"Are you all right?"

"What? Oh yes, of course. I was just saying that the if anything went wrong with the program, they'd go to manual."

—"Yes, we know. We'd like to confer with the operators a moment. If you'll excuse us?"

"Certainly."

—"We're talking with Alicia Beatty, the winner of the tenth annual Ann Darrow for a Day Contest. Now we take you to the control room."

It was Alexander's boney features that filled the TeeVee screen as the interviewer asked if there were any problems. Alan Beatty had an impulse to stand and begin pacing, but he remained seated, staring, as the monotone voice of his co-conspirator assured the viewing audience that there was nothing amiss.

"What the hell?" asked Beatty aloud. "What kind of sloppy work is this?" He almost decided to call Alexander, but then thought better of it. The mistake had obviously been an authentic error that had nothing to do with the plan.

—"We're back outside the Empire State Building with Alicia Beatty and we're asking her how secure can anyone feel when in such precarious straights."

"Secure enough, I suppose. Of course I took a stress pill beforehand, but that's pretty routine. There is a lovely view from up here—you can see the Siclari Building—and I'm having too much fun to be worried."

—"No doubt that's because of your Steady-Hold safety harness."

Alicia's eyes opened wide and doll-like, a habit of hers when she was trying to remember something. It came to her: "Yes, Steady-Hold makes me more secure in the air than if I was home in bed."

—"Thank you, our Ann Darrow winner."

Alan Beatty noticed that he was breathing heavily. Perspiration irrigated his cheek. The "climb" still had a long way to go. He worked up a good sweat as the commercials came and went, as brief histories of all the versions of *King Kong* played across the screen, and even an interview with the singularly boring president of Doppelgänger Inc., took up more minutes still.

Finally, the gorilla machine was nearing the platform. Beatty imagined the men in the control room, twenty floors down from the observation deck, glancing occasionally at the readouts. Alexander was probably off to the side somewhere, in the shadows. The robot planes would be air-borne by now. The helicopter with the dummy Kong would be waiting nearby.

"Ladies and gentlemen," said the announcer, "we give you Kong, the eighth wonder of the world!"

The ape stood above New York City. He beat his chest with one hand. They had decided he shouldn't put Alicia down and pick her up again; it was an extra precaution. Even now, seeing his wife in the hand, Beatty cursed himself for remembering the film—lovely Fay Wray on the edge of the abyss, the great dark figure looming over her, challenging the earth. But the scene that greeted him was Alicia sitting in the equivalent of a hairy Ferris wheel—seeming, to the casual observer, to be perfectly safe.

"Here come the planes!" said the announcer. There were four of them. A close-up on the lead plane showed a pilot and gunner, plastic dummies. No animation for them yet, but given time, future programs would remedy that. Except there would be no time.

"They are opening fire!" Men watching at rectangle screens expected the planes to each take three passes at Kong, exhausting their gunfire—blanks—and then move off as the helicopter came in to drop its rag doll cargo before retrieving Alicia from the hand.

There had been a time when Kong had destroyed a plane before, clutching his chest, the bullets finished him. Beatty watched the lead plane come in for its first engagement. He watched Alicia's calm face. He watched as the plane closed the distance. He said a prayer for the explosive charge in Kong's wrist. The plane came closer and still didn't veer off. The impassive Kong stood his ground, not a bit like his unpredictable namesake. The plane kept coming until it crashed into Kong's matted chest. The impact knocked him off his perch before the wreckage of the plane and his ruined structure burst into flame; the hand which held Alicia was blown free. The whole hand. With Alicia still in it!

The TeeVee scanners, mechanical ghouls ravenous for every detail, unimpeded by distance or surprise, showed every detail of Alicia Beatty in her plunge. The air-jets on her harness had automatically cut in the moment she fell the first few feet. These sought to stabilize her, hold her in the air; but they were no use as the mechanical hand dragged her down, the safety harness emitting streams of air that escaped between the giant fingers—a sound like a released balloon, a whistling coffin. For a moment, Alicia was conscious, struggling, her eyes closed tight against the wind that pressed against her cheeks, tore at her hair, rushed into her open mouth. But then, whirling in her descent, she lost consciousness. Beatty, in the span of a few seconds, had gone from shock to acceptance, felt himself already mourning her even as something else in him screamed against the impossibility of it.

Alexander! Alexander! The bastard planned to kill her all along. He had wanted a *martyr*...and Beatty didn't know. Beatty, the fool, so blind to Alexander who was more vengeful than he.

A shout died aborning in Beatty's throat; impact was a brief moment away. A word impinged on his brain: "Beauty.'"

The inner voice: "Not beauty, not beauty killing the beast this time. There is a killer...but not beauty."

Just then the fingers of the giant hand broke off, scattered. Alicia's spinning body was automatically turned upright. The harness held. And as if to compound miracles, the raining debris missed her. She was alive. Beatty fell to his knees in amazement.

Somehow, through all this, the announcer managed to keep talking but so fast that he was incoherent. He slowed down enough to be understood as Alicia was lowered to the ground and taken inside the building by Doppelga[[umlaut]]nger Inc.'s ground crew. He reported that no-one was hurt in the accident. Although pieces of Kong had scattered for blocks, those in attendance of Ann Darrow Day were a safe distance away where they watched the proceedings through traditional telescopes provided for the occasion.

There was a special bulletin: Alicia Beatty was all right, but stunned, and Doppelgänger, Inc. would be releasing an official statement in a few minutes.

In the cold whiteness of his TeeVee, Alan Beatty gasped for air like a fish out of water. He stood. He had to get through to Alicia. He had to find Alexander and learn what, why and how, before he killed the bastard.

He called Alicia first: "We're sorry, Mr. Beatty, but she won't be able to speak to you just yet. She's being instructed."

He was indignant: "Instruct... what are you talking about?"

"I mean," said the voice, "she's been through quite a shock. She won't be able to talk for a few minutes. Please try back later."

Alone again. He tried a scramble code through to Alexander's emergency frequency but got no response. Then he called directly to the control room. A man he'd never seen before faded into view and replied to Beatty's inquiry with: "Mr. Alexander has left on a matter of great urgency, sir. He didn't say where he was going."

"He left? He was just able to leave after that accident?"

"What accident, sir?"

"What *accident*? I'm a director of the company, you imbecile! I demand to know what's going on."

"I'm sorry, Mr. Beatty, sir, but I don't know what you're talking about."

"Put me through to your superior!"

"But sir..."

Another voice on the line: "Mr. Beatty, we have your wife on the line."

Beatty: "Put her on! While you—" He looked at the technician. "You stay put until I get back to you." The man disappeared to be replaced by Alicia fading in. He was standing a few feet from her. She looked unshaken and there were no discernible bruises.

"Are you okay?" he asked.

"Yes, dear. I'm glad you called. Wasn't it exciting?"

"The accident, you pulled through, thank God."

"Huh? What are you talking about?"

A stunned silence, before he said, "Alicia, you have recovered from the shock, haven't you? Is there a doctor there? Let me speak to him."

"There's no doctor here, Alan, and I'm all right. They just told me the whole thing and I apologize for what I said about your priorities. The company is still the most important thing in your life, the way it ought to be. You created a wonderful stunt. It saved the show. I've never been so vulnerable before, so thrilled. Hundreds of people are already calling in, wanting to sign up for the Ann Darrow Day Contest. They wonder what sort of surprises are coming up in the future. You should see the ratings analysis we already have. I suppose it was for the best, you not telling me what to expect. It made it more suspenseful. To tell you the truth, back when I thought it was perfectly safe, I was a little bored. Looking back, the argument we had seems so silly, doesn't it?"

Alan Beatty blinked, opened his mouth, shook his head. He seemed to be hearing the words he was hearing, but he wasn't sure. "Alan, stop play acting," she said. "I know everything. Mr. Alexander told me."

"Told you what?"

"Afterwards, he told me about your idea. Only a select few people knew, those men in the control room. You had the idea but it was Alexander who worked out the details, and of course he told the company president at the end."

"Alicia, listen," he exhaled, closed his eyes... "I'm going to confess. I don't know if this is all a set-up to trick me into confessing. But I will. I don't care anymore."

"Alan, you don't have to..."

"Listen! Alexander and I plotted to destroy the King Kong robot. We have been working on this for revenge against the company. Alexander had a motive in helping me—for years Doppelga[[uml]]nger Inc.,has rejected his various research projects. He's never been promoted although lesser men have risen. Alicia, he and I were willing to risk your murder! It's only by the most incredible odds that you survived."

Alicia laughed, brightly without a trace of scorn. "You don't have to hide it anymore," she said, "I understand. Why don't you just come out and admit it was a clever gimmick and let it go at that?...Oh, they're making the announcement. I'll switch it on."

A square of light formed off to the side, a second image in the TeeVee next to the three dimensional form of Alicia's projection. There was a face in the square, Alexander. He said: "Ladies and gentlemen, members of our beloved viewing audience, there has been an error in today's earlier reports. There was no accident.

The so-called disaster was intentional. In developing this sensational stunt, Director Alan Beatty and I worked in secrecy and of course this caused some confusion today. The plans we drew together will no doubt be collector's items in a few years. The trick of the hand breaking is my own technique but I'll be turning it over to Doppelga[[uml.]]nger Inc.

"The woman who was in the hand is the wife of Director Beatty. She wasn't afraid to take the risk. She is the bravest girl I've ever known. She believes, as all of us at Doppelgänger Inc., that the public comes first, always! If anything had gone wrong, then Director Beatty and I would have had to pay the price in court. But we took a chance and put excitement back into the world of entertainment. And now a word from our president."

The fat man filled the screen. "Thank you, operator John Alexander," he said. Then a stream of bromides issued from the president's mouth as Beatty said to Alicia: "I'll deny it. I'll fight it in the courts. I'm guilty, do you hear? Guilty!"

Alicia wasn't laughing anymore. "Enough is enough, Alan. I'll admit I would have preferred knowing in advance what you had in mind, but the mere fact that you had the guts to put me in a dangerous situation makes me respect you again. I'm telling the white lie about knowing in advance, and do you know why? Because I love you."

Something exploded in his brain. "You're insane. Alicia. Crazy! You, Alexander, the whole world...everyone is mad but me!"

"There you go again, being a spoil-sport. I should have known you'd have remorse..."

"I tried to kill you."

"... over this event. Well, I enjoyed it too much for you to ruin it with a change of heart. I'll see you later."

She faded away as he lunged, arms stretched out, screaming, "Don't go!" Gone.

He stood in the TeeVee. The company president's face vanished from the rectangle suspended in space with: "Good night everyone and we hope to see you again soon."

A voice said: "Mr. Beatty, the president wants to congratulate you. Will you take the call?"

"Later. I'll call back."

He stood a long, long time before giving instructions to the TeeVee.

The white room vanished. He was standing on top of the Empire State Building, high above the city. He growled, he roared, he beat his chest.

He participated.

The anthology, *Confederacy of the Dead*, edited by Richard Gilliam, Martin H. Greenberg and Edward E. Kramer, is probably the most noted and successful horror anthology in which I've appeared. It came out at the right time and had a shelf life worthy of the undead. There was something really exciting about being in the company of William S. Burroughs on the contents page.

Reviews have been uniformly good over the years. Many readers tell me that "Red Clay, Crimson Clay," is my best story, giving "Clutter" and a few others a run for the money. It's one of my few tales of terror where I had a nightmare during the period I was writing it.

Although growing up in Florida, which is about as much the South as California is typical of the West, I've always been sympathetic to the only region of our country which was occupied as enemy territory. My entire married life was spent in Atlanta, Georgia, before I sat down to write this. I think it is the self righteous hypocrisy of the damned Yankees that is the real horror of this story.

Red Clay, Crimson Clay

Do not fear me, although I was one of only two survivors Sometimes we cannot help staying alive. It is not that we choose these things. Life chooses us; or sometimes, it is a matter of death passing us by.

Oh sir, I am real flesh and blood, as I will prove to you soon enough. I would think you were already well satisfied in that area, after the way you've been pawing poor Maria there.... I'm sure she enjoys your company as much as I hope you'll enjoy mine. But then, I must remember that you are interested in more than my body.

The madam suggests you are a most sophisticated gentleman. You wouldn't come to a house of this character if you didn't prefer our variety.... Yes, it is true that I'm fluent in both English and French. You could say I've two other languages as well—the degenerate French of our fair city and plain old colored English. Yassuh, or *Oui, monsieur.* What is your pleasure?...I appreciate the compliment. I'd rather speak in this fashion, kind sir. You're right that I find time to read novels and plays. I even write letters as a service to my more decadent clients.

Well, if you are finished running your fingers through Maria's blonde tresses, it is best we have privacy. I don't tell the story very often. No one has ever believed it before, but I have confidence that you will be my first exception....

Now that we're alone, where should I begin? Of course, you want to hear about my mother.... No, she was not as light-hued, since you ask. A "High Yellow," as they call me, takes time to bloom in this old black and white world. Mama was a quadroon and my father was white. That's how we, to put it delicately, breed an octoroon.... There are social disadvantages, to be sure, but in my line of work there are advantages. If you'd be a bit more generous with your champagne, sir, I'll tell you what the customer really wants when he asks for something *exotic.* Here, let me pour your glass. For a fine Yankee gentleman to travel so long a distance to New Orleans just to see me, a girl might think he's after more than memories....

Why, how flattering! Let me sit here by the window and you may have a better view of the sunset in my hair. You can see the water from here; it's so beautiful this time of day.

... Now don't pretend with me. Talk like that will get you nowhere. It is true that I'm outspoken, but you can't blame that on the end of the peculiar institution. I haven't been a slave for many years. The late unpleasantness had nothing to do with it. But please forgive my tone; you are master here, so long as you pay the price. And you will.

Mother was born in the West Indies, where the races mix as easily as rum and love, at least on the good days. She learned the craft of *Voudon*. Perhaps you know it as Voodoo. There's not a lot to it, really. The spells are all very simple. People are made well or ill, happy or sad. It makes use of the four basic elements: fire, air, earth, and water. Mama was especially adept at using earth. She knew it all, from the meaning of a buzzard's wing on your doorstep to the uses of a pail of water under the full moon. She had opinions on every variety of doll and zombie. She was a *mamaloi,* or mambo, the highest female position. She even knew the Queen herself, Marie LaVeau, who introduced her to other things.

As for me, I was born right here in New Orleans. Mama initiated me at a very early age. I was so young, I got the mistaken impression that you couldn't prepare a meal without saying incantations over the food! She used the same pots for the magic, you see. What's that, sir? She must have raised some spicy demons? Why, imagine that— a Yankee with a sense of humor.

... Please don't misunderstand. I mean no disrespect. Here, let me fill your glass again. I know you find it difficult to believe that I could have any sympathy for the Confederacy. It's not easy to explain, but my loyalty has always been to people and places. I am very much my mother's daughter in this.

There's not much more to say about Voodoo. You should not make too much of it. It doesn't take long to penetrate the mysteries of Damballa and the lesser spirits which serve the serpent. As easily as those names tripped off Mama's tongue, she would say very little about other knowledge she had acquired over the years, beginning with her discovery that the Queen of Voodoo turned elsewhere when need was greatest. The most I could get out of Mama was that there were great forces beyond the dreams of human will, powers that could never be commanded or cajoled but only obeyed. To even put a name to these things was to court disaster, and the names—she assured me— were very difficult to pronounce. Voodoo was child's play in comparison: playing with matches compared with trying to hold the sun.

My education in such occult matters was brought to a close by a change in fortune. Our family (for that is how we thought of them) went bankrupt. Mama was sold to an old friend in Atlanta. She had already determined the best course for my future and used her considerable influence to see it brought to fruition. I was sold here, to the best bordello in New Orleans, where it was understood that if I proved myself, I would be set free. It was frankly more economical for me to be an employee. It was even standard practice in this house. Mama wanted to broaden my horizons, and promised me the world by this means.

… You would ask that, wouldn't you? I began my career at the age of twelve. I was very popular…. Thank you for not feigning disgust. A taste for young girls is not always restricted to the connoisseur.

I have since given much thought to this subject. My situation was hardly unique in world history. For many women, the only road to economic independence was to become a courtesan. In this business, youth comes at a premium.

… You flatter me again, kind sir. I will not tell you my true age except to say I plan to be in my early to mid-twenties for a very long time. And Voodoo has nothing to do with it.

… You're right about there being a link between sex and magic. Magic draws its powers from the interplay of all sorts of human tensions. But only one human activity allows for the release of the most powerful forces. War has no substitute. The darkness of the heart is exalted when good people are being patriotic.

… You wonder why I came back from Europe? My, my, you have been checking up on me. Perhaps I was foolish to return from Paris during the war. It was no small feat returning to this place, but I knew I'd always be welcome here. Besides, the French at peace are more dangerous than Americans at war. (No, Maria is not French, I assure you of that. She doesn't speak because she has nothing to say. Her language is English.) The gentleman who had taken me overseas became tired of me about the same time I tired of him. And the streets of Paris are never safe.

I had to come back, even with war clouds obscuring the horizon. Mama guided me. From the earliest I can remember, she could communicate by words and pictures in my mind. As I grew older, she could reach over longer distances. She wouldn't call me back without a reason. And it's not as if I had much choice. She had a way of invading my dreams if I were not the dutiful daughter. I would have to go to her to receive the family legacy.

... I can't answer that. I don't know if I loved her. We were linked. It goes beyond mere relationship. Do you love your hand?

... No, I'd never met the Swains, but I felt as if I knew them. Mama showed off the new family in my dreams. The father had a dignified quality, a man who was moderate in most things. His family had originally come from Charleston. The mother was a quiet-mannered woman of old Atlanta stock. Neither was very large and their health only middling. But they had produced three children: two boys and a girl. Mama was most taken with the daughter, of course. She could never look at a female without considering the potential.

Mama made me see their home, as well. I could tell that she approved of the Swains' taste. The house was all white and blue, the front door surrounded by classical posts and a lintel. Inside, there were beautiful hardwood floors, polished to reflect the lights of a hundred parties. As for the rest—furnishings, carpets, tapestries, even the least detail of the chandelier—it all had just the right touch.

Do you know how you can tell a house that has become a world in itself? The strongest impressions come from children. They leave so much of themselves behind, and I don't mean their fingerprints on the brass fittings. There is a thin layer of emotion, as if a fine dust, left over all the surfaces where children play, and from this you can extract joy or melancholy. Mama was very good at what she did. She helped me to feel that she was living in a happy home. She liked their masquerade parties best because she could dress up Sarah—that was the little girl's name—as a witch.

...You want to hear about the trip? I admit that I don't like remembering it. It was worse than I'd expected. Shadows in the mind can never have the same raw impact as being there. I'd already seen pieces of the war. Only men could call something so bloody by its proper name and not even notice the word: *pieces.* If only those who brought about this war could witness every horror up close....

Oh, please sir, let us not be distracted by anything so tawdry as politics. You can't seriously consider the opinion of someone in my station, now can you?...Well, if you insist, I'll admit that I don't believe the war was fought to free the slaves. The late President made it clear from the start that his goal was to save the Union *at any cost.* All other issues were secondary. But surely this is not the time to discuss American statecraft. I read a lot, and have traveled some, but I wouldn't pretend to match my thoughts against a graduate of Harvard, such as yourself.

... The trip was terrible, with one exception. I started up the Mississippi and soon discovered a river of wounded men whose spirits had been torn out of their bodies. Your religion doesn't understand how bound to flesh is the spirit. I will never forget the faces, especially the ones missing features. It made no difference, whether going by water or by land; there were always those faces to haunt the soul.

... You want to know how I arrived at my destination in so timely a fashion? Maybe I flew on one of my mother's broomsticks! Well, I'll tell you, I'm only half joking about that. There is good fortune attached to the trade we practice in this establishment. I made the acquaintance of a Confederate signal corps officer. He'd already paid his respects to me when he found out that I'd been present at a certain event before the war, an event he'd regretted having missed. It was when Monsieur Petin of the French Academy conducted his famous balloon flight from Lafayette Square right here in New Orleans. After that, it was the next best thing to love. Despite the risks, my dashing officer in gray took me with him. The wind was most obliging, but I don't know that Mama had anything to do with it.

This was the only part of the journey where I didn't see any wounded. But even in the heavens one remembers Hell. Images in my mind were growing stronger as we neared the destination until, finally, the red glow on the horizon became as bright as freshly spilled blood. It was the first time I'd ever seen Atlanta, Georgia. It was different from Louisiana.

... Oh, I am pleased to learn that you don't approve of Sherman. I've yet to meet a Yankee who thinks the burning was a good thing; although a surprising number will argue that it was necessary. To be fair, I agree there were plenty of atrocities to go around. You've certainly followed the Andersonville Trial. I don't dispute that Union soldiers were ill treated as prisoners of war in that Confederate hellhole. Yet couldn't a case be made for extenuating circumstances? ... I mean that when supply lines are cut off, prisoners of war are the first to feel the pain.... I don't deny that justice was done, or will be done. I only ask what military justification was there for General Sherman's pyromania? I hadn't thought that he was so noble a man as you make out, only dedicated to shortening the war and saving the lives of his troops. Well, as I said before, despite my unusual education, I am still but a woman, and a darkie at that. You can't expect me to see the picture whole, as you do.

You must remember that I saw Southern life from an unusual perspective. The Old South was not so much a system as a set of attitudes, of personal faith and subtle hatreds. If the goal of the late unpleasantness was to reduce the oppression of man by man, then I'm afraid someone in authority made a miscalculation.

...As for the carpetbaggers who have lately joined my clientele, I won't say that they fail to measure up, but they do lack something one came to expect from Southern gentlemen. The old way had its problems, but at least it developed manners to a high art. Mama always taught me to love ritual for its own sake, as well as for the practical side of getting a formula right.

But there's no point lamenting over things that are gone with the wind. You want to know how I found the Swain estate.

...It was on the outskirts of Atlanta, and outside the perimeter of Sherman's flames. With a bit more luck, it might have escaped notice altogether. Mama had used her Voodoo for spells of protection. As you have gathered, it didn't work. The other, darker powers could only be used destructively, but at least they *always* worked. In matters of revenge, Mama had lost her faith in the power of pins and dolls and all that rigmarole.

...You're right. I still haven't told you how I found the house. Can't a girl keep any secrets? Shadows in my mind were all the guide I needed. In that chaos of fire and death, of murder and rape and looting, I was reluctant to ask for directions. Yet surrounded by all that danger, I felt queerly safe the nearer I came to my mother.

These feelings of confidence and purpose were shattered the moment I saw what had happened on the Swain property. I realized Mama had withheld the most recent events from her messages. The house was strangely untouched, except for a few broken windows in the front and some bullet holes in the walls. I say strangely, because it seemed almost indecent that it was still standing. It should have been in mourning for the Swains, who lay butchered out in what remained of the side yard. The earth had been torn up around them, as if in sympathy with their torn and ruptured bodies—or as if graves had been begun and then abandoned. The children were the worst, pieces of them lying about the grounds, as if discarded toys. The blood had drained out and mixed with....

You don't look well, sir. Shall I continue? My aim is to please. The customer is always right. Here, let me pour you another glass to settle your nerves.

Well, as I was saying, the blood had seeped into the ground. Are you familiar with the topography of Georgia? There are places in that state where the soil is very red; and this was so even before the arrival of Union troops. The Swains had a stretch of the reddest clay I've ever seen in that side yard. Of course, I never saw it completely dry. I won't try to describe the odor.

...You wonder what had become of Mama. So did I. The next thing I remember was hearing voices from the house. And laughter. The most pleasant sound in the world becomes the most terrible when heard in an abattoir. They were male voices. Young voices. Soldiers' voices.

It didn't seem possible that Mama could have been bested by such as these. Yet strewn before me were the remains of those she would have protected; the red spots turning brown on the charnel flesh, the skin a pale white terrain on which insects carried out their own military sorties. The impossible was real: Mama had failed.

It was late afternoon. The sky was overcast with clouds that seemed to be made of smoke. No birds sang. I knew that when night fell, not a single cricket would be heard. It was more unnatural than any witchcraft. But when men have done such things, they set the stage. What nature cannot restore may be restored in other ways.

I did not yet realize that Mama was dead. You see, she was still communicating with me. I wanted to scream at her: How could you let this happen? Why didn't you protect yourself? The only trouble was that I knew the answers as soon as anger flashed through my brain.

Powers of protection never match powers of revenge. She had sensed that her time was coming if she intended to pass on the legacy to me. Turning to the greatest powers she knew, and uttering the names that must not be spoken, meant that she would have to let go of this existence and join with *them* if she were to avenge the Swains and pass on to her daughter a higher understanding. Her body was nowhere to be found. *They* had taken it and left something behind in the ground where the slaughtered family lay unburied and unmourned.

I realized then the role I had to play. Mama needed me to finish it. Walking up to the house, I let myself in the front door. There were ten of them.

They were all privates. I never did find out how they had become so cut off from the command structure. It really didn't matter, though, as one named George had come to dominate the rest. He was the idealist of the group, constantly quoting Robespierre from the French revolution. The rest had fallen in line behind this thoroughly evil bastard, all except one fair-haired lad who hesitated to offer up the full measure of his devotion. This boy was named Mark.

...Oh, *monsieur*, you seem upset again. Here, have some more of your excellent champagne. As I say, this George had worked them up to a killing frenzy against the Southern plutocracy, as he put it. Mark had been uneasy about the gruesome business, but he hadn't resisted. No more did he resist when the other nine took turns with me. George was quite the ringleader. His rationalizations were nothing short of remarkable. As this was the only time in my life I'd been raped, much less raped by a mob, his fine words about my personal deliverance fell on deaf ears.

They kept at me until I was bleeding profusely. That's when Mama began whispering again. My blood was the missing ingredient, the catalyst, now that she was gone.

When my education was finished, theirs began. The sky darkened, and with it came a deeper silence. I was left unguarded, except for Mark who sat crying in a corner. The rest had been drunk when they raped me. Now they got drunker on the last of the Swains's liquor. George was arguing loudly with two others about the necessity of burying the bodies before morning. The stench was becoming hard to ignore. In the absence of officers, he had seized the baton, so to speak, and showed a natural skill for delegating responsibility. Everyone was so preoccupied that they failed to notice my going over to the window, where I opened it and let some of my blood drip outside. This was on the side of the house next to the bodies.

That's all there was to it. The rest happened very quickly, as when the last pinch of seasoning has been added to a stew and there is nothing else but to bring it to the boiling point. There was a rumbling sound, then an explosion. One of the soldiers ran to the front door to see what had happened, but something was blocking the door on the other side. The young soldier, Mark, had moved over to the side window and he saw it first.

Swain blood, red clay, my blood—they had come together to make a reddish mass. In the failing light, it looked as if a side of raw beef was being dragged across the pane, making a horrid screeching sound. And while this was happening, the rest of it was bubbling up and spreading around the house.

I knew that I was safe. That's what my mind said. Mama said it. I hadn't been required to speak any of the forbidden names. Despite these assurances, however, it was the most terrifying experience of my life—just watching what happened to those men.

None of them had any idea what it was. How could they? It came through three windows at once. The presence or absence of glass in the panes was entirely irrelevant. It started off like a cascade of mud pouring into the room, but as the volume increased, it took on a more recognizable form. The thing grew tentacles, and they were redder at the tips than the remainder of the bulk that kept pushing through the windows until I feared we would all smother. But no one was to have that merciful a death.

George was the first to go. I liked that. Dozens of the tentacles struck him all at once. At every point of contact, he began to bleed. This was no mere trickle but a human being turned into a crimson fountain. He fell to the floor without uttering a sound, it had happened so quickly. But his men—for that is what they had become—had time to scream.

The others tried to escape, but all they managed to do was trample one another up against the front door. Mark and one other soldier managed to flee upstairs. From where I stood, I had an unobstructed view of the carnage; it still seemed incredible to me that I was spared by the flailing tentacles.

There was still a spasm of life in the first victim's body, and I watched George slither across the floor before coming to a stop, sliding in his own blood. The skin was as pale white as the corpses outside, but it didn't stay that way. Even as I watched, it changed—the skin dried and then cracked, like clay baking in the sun.

Suddenly a clear path opened to the stairs. I walked in that direction, fearing that to run would mean slipping on the wet floor. Once on the stairs, I hurried to the top floor, where I found Mark and his friend, huddled together as if they were Siamese fetuses dreading birth into an unknowable world of pain.

... Speaking of which, I see pain in your expression again. Dear sir, it seems you are upset every time I mention this young man, Mark. We needn't fence any longer. I know why you're here. You almost restore my belief in the power of love. Only the most dedicated father would have followed so unlikely a trail to the bitter end.... When you first heard stories of monsters and witchcraft, you must have dismissed them. But the disappearance of your son must have been agony you couldn't abide.... As we agreed, there are different kinds of love. Only love would inspire you to give credence to stories of a New Orleans prostitute who had something to do with the mysterious disappearance of Union soldiers. What made you believe your son was still alive? An instinct? Perhaps love is another form of magic.

Your son was the only one who didn't rape me. Clearly, Mama intended that all of them should die. I decided to be merciful. I don't believe your son participated in the murder of the Swains, but he passively stood by, as he did in my case. But the other one was guilty of the acts. He had to die. It wasn't easy prying them apart, but I managed.

The pulsing red mass was already pushing its way up the stairs by then. I fed it the last one.

While this other soldier was writhing in the tentacles, I placed myself over your son's body. By the time the thing reached us, I had decided what to do. It searched for a way around me, but it was too difficult to touch Mark without also touching me. Mama spoke again, and we had our final argument. Her years of being a mambo helped develop her sense of humor. We reached a compromise about what should happen to Mark.

... There's no point in threatening li'l ol' me. You'll discover shortly that you cannot take any action against me. The champagne you've been drinking has a special ingredient from an old southern recipe—the southern hemisphere, that is. It eliminates undesirable initiative. You *cannot lift a hand against your new companion.*

...Now we understand each other better. As I say, Mama and I were of one mind on what was to be done. Your son, Mark, was touched in three places by the thing. Twice on the chest, and once in a more delicate location. He bled, but the flow was allowed to stop. As for his body, there were changes, but nothing so drastic as what happened to his comrades. The shock was severe and he was granted a loss of memory. There might have been a suicide otherwise.

"He" still doesn't remember. And it can stay that way, unless you want me to change it. If you are very good, and do exactly what I want you to do when we consummate the evening, I'll be kind, dear sir, and allow you to forget.

You'll want to forget everything you did...with Maria.

My assignment was to write the sickest story I could dredge up from the unpleasant regions of the soul, and then plug it into the Worlds of Darkness for publication in the first *Dark Destiny* book. Only the reader can judge if this story is sick enough. It led to my contributing to all the Dark Destiny books, edited by Ed Kramer. I appreciate Ed's letting me include the story here.

Poisoned Dreams

We conclude with a field of unburied, dead children; pale and drained of blood, resembling ice-cold fish shining in the moonlight. But that is not where we begin....

The little, bald man was one of those people who can kill spontaneity in a roomful of people just by leaning forward and opening his mouth. Even if you've never met him before you just know that he will bore you to death. And he'll have a joke, one of those laborious, long-winded affairs more likely to elicit a smile of relief when it is finally over than any genuine amusement at the punchline.

I braced myself the moment I saw him smile. But instead of the dreaded funny story he surprised me by saying, "You're the only mage who can help me. I suppose your schedule must be very full with all the important people you handle, but I'm hoping you can squeeze me in."

Simply transcribed, the words don't convey the agony of listening to the man. He would pause between words as if they were sentences, and at odd places. I felt that even to respond would be rude, a possible interruption of one of his silences. Naturally I wanted to turn him down but I couldn't.

The party at which he approached me was a private affair, courtesy of some of the highest practitioners among the Virtual Adepts. He stood out like a sore thumb among all the elegantly dressed gentlemen and ladies. But he couldn't possibly be there without a special invitation; which meant that he must be an initiate at some level, as hard as that might be to believe. To verify my suspicions, he added: "I come recommended." I told him when he could see me at the start of the week.

Once our business was concluded, he didn't even stay behind for the ritual to Cerridwen. It was a delightful affair with the nine most beautiful women in the room dancing around a new piece of software dedicated to the goddess of wisdom. I'm glad I didn't miss the spectacle of the ornate roof opening to reveal the bone-white moon above. I still liked the sight of the moon *then*...before it took on a leering, uncouth grotesquerie more depressing than any of the gargoyles passing silent judgment on me every time I traveled the damned streets.

I was asked to recite a verse from Coleridge, honoring the goddess: "Her lips were red, her looks were free; Her locks were yellow as gold. Her skin was white as leprosy. The Nightmare Life-in-Death was she, who thicks man's blood with cold."

The most beautiful of the nine stripped off her clothes as I spoke the words; then she sat at the console and typed in commands that turned my words into an interactive game. The computer-generated holograms danced among us and set my mind, if not my spirit, at peace for a short time.

I used to think that as one is initiated into higher orders of consciousness, a sense of well being and purpose would increase. In my youth I'd been tempted by the pleasures of the Cult of Ecstasy. I'd felt cold shivers from the Euthanatos. I'd wondered if the answer to all problems might not be found in the Dreamspeakers. The point was that all my desires led in the direction of the Nine Traditions. Never in my studies, or the dangerous games I played to collect information, was I ever tempted by the true evils of the Technocracy, the Nephandi or the Marauders. Or so I thought.

If not for the relativistic viewpoint inculcated by the Virtual Adepts, I would have gone crazy long ago. "All things are information quantified, and information wants to be free." And as I learned from the wise insights of the Prophet Wilson, one man's reality tunnel is another person's dead-end! Or as I like to say, one man's ascension is another's nosebleed.

I was smug in what little wisdom I had managed to obtain. I knew that the problem with the Technocracy and the Nephandi was their obsession that each had The One True Answer. In contrast, the Marauders had the virtue of individuality; but they would plunge the world into the dreary abyss of chaos. My old teacher used to tell me that ours was a high and lonely destiny, to steer a middle course for the good of civilization, between Insane Order and Insane Chaos.

Of course I had hoped that I might play some role in determining the fate of mankind. Who wouldn't? But I never would have believed that a little, boring man met at a routine party would be my ticket to infamy.

The evening had begun with socializing and the proper wine, then concluded with an uplifting lecture, as usual. "Sexual madness is always the lot of the uninitiated," said our priestess. "Crime and violence always increase in times of repression. If this civilization is to survive the current crisis, we must increase the potency of our magick to compensate for the lack of wisdom in the people. A Gothic punk world needs guidance. Empty scientific materialism is not enough. Mindless instinct is not enough. We need the gnosis with the mostest! And I believe there is one among us tonight who will open the gate to True Wisdom."

At no point did I think she was talking about me. Now that I think about it, maybe she wasn't. She smiled, which was our cue to chuckle. The ape brain is so much a part of the human race that most people have never moved beyond their first encounter with abstract reasoning. They believe in a brute form of cause and effect, translating into blood sacrifice to get what they want. So it has always been. The great mages of the past who dared teach them something better have all too often met the same fate—one might say they've been crucified for their temerity. We are the wise ones who learned the obvious lesson.

It was a good party.

My mind full of vast historical vistas, I walked to work on a seemingly pedestrian Monday. I'd put on my Sunblock 1000. I was wearing my trendiest sunglasses, made out of the latest bioplastic, friendly to the earth but still capable of protecting the eyes from cataracts. My new Bogart hat felt good on my head and I only had to step over six bodies on the way to work. I'd almost forgotten about the little, bald man.

On those occasions when a special patient requires special handling it behooves us to be prepared. My assistant at the office was Valerie, equally proficient at office work and performing the duties of a nurse. Whenever I beheld her lovely face under a halo of strawberry blonde hair I could only think that she would probably wind up with a higher position among the Adepts than I could ever hope to attain. She was doing a lot more than sleep her way to the top; she was dreaming herself there.

Her lunch breaks were too long but she was worth it. Hell, she often got the jump on problems and wrestled them to the ground before I knew of their existence. She was in fine form that Monday. With a minimum of fuss she hurried Mr. Bennett—did I mention that the man's name was Bennett?—into the preparation room. While she was washing his face I locked the door and made sure the blinds were pulled down at the window.

I went over to the safe hidden behind a picture of Apollo and Dionysus standing together, trying to outdo each other's grins. (To the uninitiated, they looked like two fishing buddies. I enjoyed imagining their having a lofty conservation about how "monotheism is the slippery slope to atheism.") Behind the picture was a device I could only use in special cases.

Being ever so careful, I removed the equipment.

Then Valerie took over, attaching electrodes to the patient's forehead. At the other end of the wires was a crystal ball, atop a red, silken pillow with a line of stitched, runic symbols taking the place of fancy embroidery. Blue-gray mists swirled at the center of the ball in anticipation of the ceremony.

"I've never seen a DreaMeter before," said the man.

"Just relax," answered Valerie in a voice as soothing as one of her backrubs. She didn't need magic to make a man cooperate. Before I could conjugate a Latin verb, the little guy was out like a light. Valerie works fast!

If you're not already asleep when you're hooked up to the meter it puts you under immediately and, *hesto presto*, you're in dream-state. Whatever dreams you've been having recently leave a strong impression and they are re-experienced, just like a summer rerun. Valerie and I had both been trained to separate public omens and symbols from the purely personal character of an individual's dreams. But neither of us was prepared for what was stirring around in the little man's head, just waiting to be projected in three-dimensional holographic images.

The dream began with Mr. Bennett's divorce from a woman who disbelieved in all forms of magick. One is not required to marry a person who is aware, but one is expected to keep specific details a secret from an unenlightened spouse. In this respect, Bennett had performed his duty. Suddenly I realized that his excruciatingly dull demeanor might prove advantageous for the keeping of secrets! Valerie and I had been through this sort of thing before. We joined hands and did an incantation, tapping into the web of magick that was older than the earth. Of course, the Adepts kept up with the times when it came to style. Another three-dimensional image appeared, a bright red square floating right in front of us, part of the SpellCheck program. Reaching into a desk drawer, I picked up my wand and touched the square which brought up a wall of shimmering lights. Next, I touched a yellow triangle, the exact color of a fresh lemon, which conjured into the room the spirit force of Memory...a spirit that would keep a careful lookout for that moment when Bennett's dream departed from wish-tinged memory into the faery realms of pure invention!

We learned that his wife had been a plain and unassuming woman—almost as dull as he was. They'd both been teachers in the public school system, and were therefore acquainted with all varieties of evil. The only wonder was how they managed to hold the interest of their students! It might have gone on that way until they both reached retirement age and settled into a respectable dotage...except that Mrs. Bennett caught Mr. Bennett doing a bad thing. He strangled their cat.

At first she thought it was because they had been forced to spend so much money on Perseus, her name for the feline, when their pet came down with a serious urinary tract infection. But the cat had survived numerous trips to the vet, and there was no reason for Mr. Bennett to strangle the life out of the poor creature after they'd expended so much effort to save it.

The dream played on. Memory is pain. He'd apologized to his wife for killing Perseus more times than he could remember. He didn't know why he had done it. Wives don't like to hear that. And no amount of later good will dispelled her memory of the crumpled form of the dead cat or the thin, red scratches all over Mr. Bennett's wrists and hands.

He didn't really seem to resent her for divorcing him. He took it as a sort of judgment. His feeling was that he should be punished for having married her in the first place, and the business of the cat justified her to act as his executioner. There was something of a self-esteem problem here.

So pathetic were these emotions that Valerie and I experienced a kind of culture shock when the images shifted from memory to dream. Suddenly we were plunged into vivid colors and even the quality of the sound improved! Mr. Bennett, so slow and dull in real life, and not faring much better in his own memory, captured a splendid heroic quality when entering into the deep dream.

The SpellCheck was still functioning as Memory let us know its work was done. Lifting my wand again, I touched a purple circle and engaged the services of the Spirit of Omen. The light flared bright, a sign that the dream was more than just a dream.

Now the little, bald man seemed taller, resplendent in golden robes, a jewel-encrusted scepter in his hand. Vague shapes swept past him, as if caught in a hurricane that left him untouched. His name was called out by high, piping voices; he was being honored by unclean things.

Then the picture changed. Now he wore red robes, with a curved dagger in his hand. Except that the robe wasn't really red—it was white underneath all the blood that had splashed on him from sacrificing hundreds of animals. They were all shapes and sizes, from a bull to a hen, from a snake to a sparrow, from a black goat to a pure white Alsatian dog. Surrounded by a sea of brown fur, bright feathers, shining scales, and pools of blood, he was fulfilled in this fantasy. Real life had left him empty of all meaning.

Suddenly Valerie whispered in my ear, which was not accepted procedure. She said, "The very best magick doesn't require blood sacrifice." Who did not know this elementary lesson, taught members of the Adepts as a fundamental? But she had more to say: "Unfortunately, the old ways, bathed in blood, work!"

As if responding to her words, the dream became more unsavory. Bennett's lips were pulled back in a grimace that in no way could be confused with a smile. His eyes were glazed over and his heart beat like a trapped rodent waiting for its turn at the knife. Now there were thousands of animals lined up, all docile as if they had been selected for a hell-bound Noah's ark. Bennett started biting off bits and pieces of the hapless creatures with teeth that seemed sharper than what the little man actually had between his jaws. Gray, human figures appeared at the line of the horizon. They applauded the grotesque banquet.

When the three-dimensional figures faded away, the sounds of dying animals remained. They echoed within the walls of my office for a long time.

The session was over. "What does it mean?" asked our patient, waking up the moment the DreaMeter was removed. The meter was making a strange sputtering sound.

"Have you killed anything besides your cat?" I asked.

"No," he answered. "At least, I don't think so."

"When did the dream begin?" I continued.

"I'm pretty sure it was around the time I got rid of Perseus."

"I'm certain that's when you started having your problems," said Valerie, "and there's a cure for your condition."

I don't know what surprised me more: the fact my assistant was pre-empting my authority, or the cure she proceeded to administer. She produced a syringe—as if by magick?—and injected the patient before I could make a move to stop her.

"Valerie!" I shouted. "What the hell are you doing?"

"Don't worry," she replied as Mr. Bennett's eyes rolled up in his head and spittle appeared on his lips. With a gurgling sound, he collapsed on the floor. "He's dead," she went on, in that matter-of-fact tone of voice she used when going over accounts.

I'd heard of things like this. Not everyone can handle the pressure. On our backs rests what little civilization there is in the world. (Who am I to quarrel with the party line?) And attractive as Valerie's back appeared, especially when bare, I couldn't let something like this go unreported.

The only trouble was that even as I reached for that most mystical of all devices, a telephone, she intercepted me with a soft hand on my cheek. "Oh, my darling doctor," she cooed, "you don't realize how fortunate it is that I'm here to keep you on the one true path."

"Valerie!" I said her name as though it were an incantation. I wanted to touch her with my wand, the magickal one, as if by this action I could erase her crime. But she was one step ahead of me, as usual.

"Oh, my poor fool," she said, and at that moment I realized how much she must really love me. "There's no time for subtlety now. We won't let anyone sabotage our preparations for your future."

Our? What was this *our*? She didn't need occult powers to read the expression on my face. The day was not going well at all.

She sighed, a very pretty sigh. "You weren't supposed to be told until the end of the week, but you've been selected for the position of a High Mage."

"How would you know that?"

"I was assigned to you" she said quietly. Catching a glimpse of myself in the small mirror we kept by the vase of roses (a homey touch) did nothing to improve my mood. I'm sure that I'd never let a patient see such a face as I was currently wearing.

"But Kenton and Schulmann and Vanessa and the others wouldn't send you. This goes against the teaching of the Virtual Adepts when you remember that…"

"Who said I was sent by them?" she announced with a grim smile. Funny how this woman I'd known for only a year suddenly seemed so different. "You've been searching all your life. Now the Truth has *found* you." She seemed to be the same woman I worked with every day—the same face, the same arched eyebrows, the same high cheekbones and full mouth. What had been alluring when she was only my assistant was now transformed into something Queenly—and untouchable.

I looked at the body of the little, bald man, who was somehow less boring in death. He made a perfectly adequate corpse. And I suddenly realized I wouldn't be subjected to any joke from the poor guy, unless his death counted as a punchline. "He'll be removed," she said, "and you won't have to bother with him. We've had dozens of others like him to deal with since I was assigned to you."

A therapist should be prepared for ambivalence. Part of me wanted to bow and worship her; but another part wanted to do to her what Mr. Bennett had done to his cat. After all, I still had my pride for a short time yet.

"Please tell me everything you can," I said.

She smiled her I'm-going-to-eat-you-up-but-you-won't-mind smile and did a terrible thing. She told me! "You don't have bad dreams, do you, Paul?" I shook my head. She continued: "The True Ones don't. Now that the time of the great change is almost upon us, there are dozens of little false mages, such as Mr. Bennett, who don't even realize they are being summoned by gods of simple absolutism to lead us astray from the real gods of insight. At least the Adepts are right about relativity. When we find a narrow point of view, we remove it. We of the…" She smiled, aware that she had almost said who had sent her. "Nobody must be allowed to distract you from the important tasks that lie ahead; and especially not with the pathetic sacrifices they would offer."

"Excuse me," I said, tempted to raise my hand as if I were a pupil (which in a sense, I was). "What is this great change?"

She smiled with a touching degree of tolerance. "I have not been entrusted with information at that level. You know that all mages in all orders believe only themselves to be right and everyone else is wrong. The Ascension War is in itself a contradiction—one does not rise by sinking to the lowest depths. The people have sunk so low that they must be reintroduced to more primitive forms of worship. And you, dear one, are to be the instrument of their salvation. No one else must stand in your way."

If I'd been thinking clearly, I would have seen problems with her position from the start. The cold blooded murder should have tipped me off. It was behavior worthy of the cold Technocracy, or the malevolent Nephandi, or the unpredictable Marauders. We who follow the Nine Traditions are supposed to know better. But the disagreements between the mages of the Nine Traditions had limited our effectiveness for so long that some of us could not help being optimistic. And Valerie knew me well enough to exploit that most dangerous parasite in my soul: hope for a united front against the darkness.

"You murdered for me today," I said in wonder.

"I would kill anyone for the man I love," she replied, further complicating the issue and leaning forward to kiss me with all the passion a man could desire. Under the circumstances, I could only behave as a proper gentleman and make love to her.

Naturally I was sorry about killing her later. She was my first sacrifice. Her masters were annoyed she had told me the good news before I was scheduled to be informed. Oh well.

I still don't know who is behind this new world of mine. I only know it cannot be the Adepts. And there are times when I wonder if what has happened to me is real or if the DreaMeter broke and released nightmares into my head. Perhaps I died in my office that day and never had to kill all those children.

The world I knew had been a dark Gothic nightmare of neon sleaze. But now the public accepts things it never did before! Isolated critics aren't much of a problem, and the really bad ones can always be sacrificed. Fortunately, I have a lot of eager assistants in this work all over the world. It's a weird feeling giving approval for throwing maidens into a live volcano. It's not as hard as I thought it would be, and we had excellent television coverage. The girls were mostly volunteers. (When we sacrificed some young males the ratings weren't as high.)

The only time I've been really uncomfortable, so far, was the mass sacrifice of children under the full moon. The ratings went through the roof. I know all the arguments. A few hundred slain before the eyes of the world means that thousands will not be raped, mutilated and abused in secret, by lone maniacs whose interest in the preservation of the social order is not very well developed. Civilization must have its little sacrifices now and then.

But I'm still uncomfortable. When I raise doubts that the forces we serve (or utilize) ever wanted human sacrifices, the Shadowy Ones I Obey remind me that our civilization has sunk too low to worry over details. We have to work our way back up to where we may be worthy of moral distinctions. The only goal now is to keep Chaos in check by making sure that the oceans of blood the human race insists on spilling will be channeled productively. An ugly voice whispers in my ear with talk about building a dam, behind which all that blood will power the turbines of a renaissance.

Maybe so. Maybe those children had to die. Some of them agreed to the sacrifice, but you can talk a child into nearly anything. Unlike adults.

I'm an adult. I must be. Or they wouldn't trust me with this splendid, curved knife that is always at my side. Sometimes I think it looks just like the one in Mr. Bennett's dream.

I think about that dagger a lot. If the weapon was only in Bennett's dream, and now I seem to have the same cruel thorn in my blood spattered hand, then maybe I am only dreaming. Maybe I haven't betrayed what I thought to be the human values of the Virtual Adepts. Maybe I haven't immersed my soul in a pool of red murder. What good is magick if it doesn't provide the opportunity of denying what your senses tell you?

Without denial, there are no gods. And lately I have the overwhelming desire to worship...something.

Many of my best stories have appeared in books that Marty Greenberg godfathered through to completion. When I wrote this particular story, I was actually surviving from one Greenberg check to the next. (I would shift from short stories back to novels when Dafydd ab Hugh and I wrote the first *Doom* novel, *Knee Deep in the Dead*, for a deal put together by Ashley Grayson, my current agent.)

At the time I wrote "Milk is a Sauce," I was at a low ebb and wondering if my parents might not have been right about my being better off if I'd gone to law school and become a solid citizen. I was also wondering where my next meal was coming from, which may explain the obsession with food in this story.

Milk is a Sauce

I fell in love on the best day of my life. Looking back, I realize that was the problem. If just one thing had been out of place I might have been in my normal frame of mind—which is a very critical one. But no, Atlanta was having a perfect day, one of those non-sticky summer days. The air was so clear and clean that if I closed my eyes I could imagine that I was home in Macon.

Normally, I didn't like coming to Atlanta. My mother had always taught me that everything good about Atlanta had drifted to Macon sometime during Reconstruction; and that the new Atlanta was simply not a proper environment for a lady of refinement. When I was a teenager, I concluded that Mom was simply a racist. The whole country knew that Atlanta was a showcase for the new south, which meant that more coloured people—or blacks, or African Americans—were coming to positions of prominence. I enrolled in college thinking that my dear mother was a bigot. But by the time I graduated, that opinion had changed. I'll never forget her genuine shock the first time I told her what other white students were calling the bus system, MARTA. They said the letters stood for Moving Africans Rapidly Through Atlanta. She thought there was nothing funny about the "white trash" who would talk that way.

As a teenager I had thought she was being patronizing to Walter, the old family servant. A few years of maturity enabled me to understand the bond between them—a relationship based on mutual respect. They shared a similar viewpoint in common with the other old families of Macon.

The notion was that the modern world had destroyed manners. This lamentable state of affairs made it exceedingly difficult for a lady to find a gentleman or a gentleman a lady. Or for anyone to have good manners in the first place! One thing was for certain: Mother didn't expect that I would find the right sort of man in Atlanta, much less that I would meet him through a business association. But that is precisely what I thought was happening on my perfect day!

His name was Edmund Mierany and he could deep fry better than anyone. He was head chef at *Merry Mack's Collard Palace* where he literally swept me off my feet.

"This little lady wants to start a breakfast restaurant chain called *Macon and Eggs*," announced my friend, Ron. "She's already got the financing lined up for a first one back home."

While Ron was talking high-pressure words in a soft, smooth, low-pressure voice, Edmund was looking at me with eyes that flattered every little pore in my face. He invited me to have a late supper with him that very evening. I accepted. My poor mother had never approved of my unwillingness to be a wilting blossom, pining over lost days. A proper gentleman, by modern standards, inspired me to be a modern lady. We would be polite to each other even in the morning.

When we were alone he began by talking about himself. He was Canadian, from a little town on the border between Quebec and Ontario. Naturally I expected he'd like to do French dishes, heavy with sauces. But aside from heavy desserts, rich in cream, he didn't gravitate toward French cuisine. He adored American Southern deep fried and overcooked food. "I've *found* myself in Atlanta," he said.

I thought that he had found me as well. Before I knew what was happening I was telling him all sorts of things about myself. And he was that most dangerous sort of male: he listened! Matters started moving much faster after that.

The first time I ate one of his breakfasts was not at the restaurant but after we'd spent the evening together. I was ready to be invited for breakfast instead of dinner. He was so polite, so considerate, so decent, so funny. The possibilities were as rich as butter pancakes.

Not until much later did I realize that some of his humor wasn't exactly what it seemed. I thought he was joking when he referred to cereal as "the milk course of breakfast." That sort of comment seemed harmless enough then. And I enjoyed the omelette while I was eating it. Not until afterward did I notice the peculiar aftertaste. While I was helping him with the dishes he casually described how he never wasted any of the bacon grease (he called it side bacon, or American bacon, to distinguish it from the "superior" Canadian back bacon). He'd used all the grease from six slices of bacon and a full bar of real butter to make that killer omelette.

I was horrified. He joked about it being his heart stopper's special recipe. I tried suggesting there were healthier ways to make an omelette but that's when I first noticed Edmund's knack of not hearing anything he didn't want to hear. And then I did a wicked thing. I made myself remember what Ron had told me about the most economical approach to a breakfast restaurant—the greasier, the cheaper...and the tastier!

Without Edmund or myself ever bringing it up the implications were clear that if we married, I'd expect him to leave *Merry Mack's Collard Palace* and come to work in *Macon and Eggs.* The very thing I didn't want on my own table was probably the ticket to success in the enterprise. In my family, it was more unthinkable to mix sordid enterprise and marriage than to put lard in your tea. But I had resolved to become a practical lady.

All I would have to worry about was the unhealthful aspect of eating too much of his food. As all men do who love to cook, he'd turn the kitchen into his own private domain in our little home. But I wasn't about to lose my figure by ignoring what he did in that domain of his. I could simply miss meals when necessary, taking smaller portions. I'd even make up a stomach ache if I had to. Why, sometimes he might even let me cook one of my own low calorie specials.

Had I mentioned that he was overweight? Not horribly so (he was fortunate to have a high metabolism) but enough so that I assumed I wouldn't have to worry about some young hussy taking him away from me. Not that such a thought would ever occur to me, of course.

In retrospect, I have no-one to blame but myself. The family had learned there was no point in advising me. I wasn't about to marry one of those boring local boys. As I got to know Edmund better I began to realize that under the surface of good manners and genuine charm there was a very difficult personality. But, I told myself, those are the only people worth marrying.

I'd already learned there was no point arguing with him. "Fat is a high energy food," he would say. "If you take the right vitamins you can eat all the fat you want." I'd just nod and smile. Argue with him about food and he'd launch into a speech with as many words as a triple-chocolate dessert has calories. But there was always an out for me before we were married. He'd allow me to change the subject! A man who will allow you to change the subject is a true gentleman. There was no reason to expect he would change.

He had money. Greasy, unhealthy, cholesterol-laden dishes paid for every bit of it. Now I was trying to turn that to my own financial advantage. I don't claim that I was innocent.

The day of the wedding was the second best day of my life.

The weather was beautiful and I remember a jet flying up so high that there was nothing but a thin streak of white contrail in the blue sky. For one moment the sun glinted off the plane and it looked like a small pink jewel, or perhaps one of the sprinkles on the wedding cake.

Edmund didn't much care for wedding cake. So he was providing his own sweet touch, rows upon rows of the best pecan pie. He proudly announced that "a southern wedding must have a proper southern dessert." That was about the time that Mother began softening toward him. She helped us buy a house that wasn't so near that we'd be expected to drop in on her all the time, but was still conveniently located to the restaurant. But Walter never softened. He warned me to "watch out."

Not until the failure of *Macon and Eggs* did Edmund begin to change. Or show his true colors. He hadn't burned any bridges when he left *Merry Mack's Collard Palace*. I was more than willing to move back to Atlanta with him and he could work at the Palace again. Meantime a woman had moved into the position of head chef but she made it clear that Edmund could return anytime as far as she was concerned.

Instead, he sat in our house in Macon, took unemployment checks, made sarcastic comments about women cooks...and cooked. In the course of setting up the restaurant, I had made a number of good friends in the local business community. Now I had an executive secretary position with a small firm and continued planning the resurrection of my own business. With the new income and money Edmund had saved, we were well set for a goodly time even without his taking the unemployment checks. I was not so much worried about the money as I was concerned over his state of mind.

When he decided to sell his fine collection of cutlery I tried to talk him out of it. We still had all my pieces but I knew how much those knives meant to him. I assumed it was a matter of pride with him, but everything deteriorated after that.

The real trouble started slowly, the way you soft-boil an egg. I'd been accommodating his little idiosyncrasies, the way you have to if any marriage is to stand a chance. But he stopped accommodating me. Not that he had ever done much of that from the start, but a little consideration is certainly to be preferred over a big dripping chunk of nothing.

One evening I'd had a really stressful day and all I wanted to do when I got home was sit in the kitchen and drink a tall glass of cold milk. Edmund came in wearing his bathrobe. His hair was a mess and ha hadn't shaved. "What are you doing?" he asked in clipped tones.

"What do you mean?" I asked back.

"Why are you drinking milk? Milk isn't for drinking."

"It's not?" I asked, wondering what planet Edmund had been visiting.

"Milk is a sauce," he announced grandly. "A quart of milk should last three times longer than we've been going through it."

My first thought was not that he'd taken a dive into the deep end of the stewpot where his brain had been permanently overcooked. He must be trying to economize. That was it! And this strange rationalization was his way of denying the situation. We couldn't go on like this forever. He must be trying to motivate himself to go back to work.

Suddenly I remembered his statement that cereal was the soup course of breakfast. "So milk is just for cereal..." I began.

"And cooking," he finished the thought.

Although he was upset, he wasn't exactly raving. I took this into consideration as I said, "Do you mind if I finish this glass as long as I've already started it?" Now he was the picture of reasonableness. He left the kitchen.

The next day I was making a peanut butter and jelly sandwich. Having eaten nothing of the left-overs from the night before (a greasier than usual chicken-and-dumplings dinner) I was ravenously hungry. He came into the kitchen, wearing the same bathrobe from the night before, adding to the sense of *déjà-vu* as he thundered forth with: "Now what do you think you're doing?" His voice was more hysterical this time.

"Making a sandwich, Edmund. I have a lot to do today and I can't stay for breakfast."

The manner in which he stared at me with bloodshot eyes suggested that he hadn't slept much the night before although he hadn't tossed and turned in bed. He had just reposed there as if a statue.

"That's a vomitous thing to do!" he snarled. "Besides, don't you know that peanut butter is a garnish?"

If I hadn't seen the need to economize I might have taken a stand right there and then. But I was trying desperately to give him credit for something, even if only for a pathetic attempt at economizing. We said nothing more about peanut butter as I hurried out the door, forbidden sandwich in hand.

Despite all our problems it was hard for me to stay in a really bad mood. Early autumn is my favorite time of the year. The weather is perfect and there are no heating or air conditioning bills. Spring is that way, too, but without the beauty of what happens to the trees and the special scents in the air. I felt that I was ready to change, just like a leaf off an oak tree, all golden and ready to let go of the branch.

One Sunday morning I decided to risk eating a whole breakfast with him, having skipped dinner the night before. The sun was shining, the birds were singing, a cool breeze was wafting through the open window. Nothing could spoil this day. Except....

"What are you doing?" came the terrible question.

"What?"

"You're putting jelly on your toast."

"Yes, Edmund, I am."

But you're not supposed to do that until after you've finished the eggs. Jelly is for dessert!"

This was a new one on me. I felt very unladylike as I told him in no uncertain terms: "Go to hell, dear."

He stared at me without blinking. Then he got up and brought me pancakes. I was going to pass on trying his heart-stopper's pancakes but I was so angry that I was ready to eat anything. I grabbed the bottle of pure maple syrup, broke the hymen, positioned the neck of the bottle over the plate and....

"What are you doing?"

"Putting syrup on the pancakes."

"You haven't eaten your eggs yet. You have to finish the eggs before..."

"Edmund, are you feeling all right?"

"What are you doing now? You can't drink coffee until you've...."

"Edmund."

"You'll give yourself an ulcer if you drink coffee at the wrong part of a meal. Surely you must know that…"

"Edmund. The only ulcer I have to worry about is the one you're giving me."

He stopped. Or maybe he was only resting. We stared at each other and then I got up and left. The coffee was still in my hand. My supply of sympathy was running low.

That evening I tried to make peace. I thought it might help if I volunteered to prepare dinner. We had all the ingredients for a fine salad—tomatoes, lettuce, radishes, green onions, fresh mushrooms, avocado, cucumber, carrots and a wonderful Italian dressing. After finding a long knife with serrated edges I began slicing the tomato real fine. Suddenly the voice I was coming to dread asked, "What are you doing?"

What could it be this time? I wasn't eating anything at the wrong time. I wasn't drinking anything at the wrong time. I hadn't combined anything yet. "I am slicing the tomato," I told my husband.

"But that's a steak knife," he said. "You can't use that for a tomato."

With all the powers of self-control left in me, I kept my voice even and said, "This was the only knife I could find with serrated edges."

"Here!" he literally screamed, yanking open a drawer and pulling out a short-bladed knife with a smooth edge. "This is for cutting."

"It's too short," I said very slowly and very quietly.

"I guess we'll need a bigger knife," he answered sarcastically.

"It's not the size that matters," I told him, "dear. It's the edge."

"The size is what matters!" he screamed again, wielding a butcher knife in front of my nose.

"So you think I should use that knife on the salad?" I asked, my voice still surprisingly calm.

He probably shouldn't have stuck the butcher knife in the cutting board between the red radishes and the red tomato. He had misplaced all his manners by this point. Not that I'm saying that I was in my right mind. But at that precise moment I still seemed to be in control of myself. My hands weren't shaking. And I still didn't know that this was the third happiest day of my life.

My voice didn't break once as I said, "Edmund, I think I need a moment alone."

"So who's keeping you here?" he asked, suggesting a lack of basic skills for a career in diplomacy.

"I mean alone in the kitchen," I emphasized. He looked like a little boy who had just been scolded. The way he sulked and stormed off made me feel a twinge of kindness again. Maybe it was going to be all right. But my stomach was tightening up and I didn't like that.

A glass of milk was just what the doctor ordered. So I poured a tall one. And I started to drink. The milk helped calm my nerves. A few deep breaths and I would be fine. Just fine.

If only he hadn't chosen that moment to return to the kitchen. And if only he hadn't said, "Milk is a sauce!" And if only I hadn't had the butcher knife in my hand.

As I said at my trial, it was an impulse. I don't say things like *irresistible impulse*. But it was an impulse. I didn't want any special defense. I don't respect people who do that. I told my lawyer that I wouldn't accept an insanity plea. Georgia is sympathetic to women in cases like this anyway. I deserve time in prison. I want to be punished. I wouldn't even mind if they took my life, but everyone seems certain that they won't do that.

I don't think that Edmund deserved to die. I should have divorced him. Divorces are made in heaven. They are what make America strong. But right after my late husband said, "Milk is a sauce," one time too many, I decided to express my displeasure in the most forceful manner open to me.

Until my dying day, I will have some respect for him. Not for his being Canadian. Not for his ability to turn grease into a semblance of food. I respect him for the last words out of his mouth as my butcher knife carved his yielding flesh in the late afternoon sun, and his blood added a new shade of crimson to the tomato and the radishes.

His last words were: "That's the wrong knife."

This is the third appearance of this very short story. I first got the idea after sitting through a presentation by true believers in the cryogenic cult. Sure, as a tremendously long shot, you freeze yourself and you might come back some day. But to bet on it seems wishful thinking. Only a lack of imagination assumes that the world you'd return to would be congenial.

Consider how alienated we are in our own time period, with which we are intimately acquainted! We can't even deal with the alien worlds of our own immediate ancestors. With such reassuring thoughts in mind, I wrote the following.

Freezer Queen

She went down into darkness. Ice ran in her veins and a velvet voice promised her warmth and light at the end of her fall. There was a whirring of machinery.

Fragments of thoughts floated somewhere in her cranium—picture pieces collided in the frozen silence and made new patterns.

She remembered. There had been a promise. She had bitterly resigned herself to age and decay. Then hope changed all that, hope in the face and form of the young doctor.

"Don't give up," he had said. These were words with which she was well acquainted. Out of a hundred other mouths they had meant nothing. But he was different. Something about his young, strong hand on her yielding, white arm encouraged her.

Cryonics. Suspended animation. She didn't have to age and wrinkle and sag. She could put the problem on permanent hold. There was no guarantee of ever being thawed out. That was true. But the doctor considered it reasonable to assume that any future society that brought the patient back would do so to cure them. She had agreed with him. Age was as surely a disease as cancer. Boredom was no less a sickness than arterial sclerosis. And so she willingly gave her still-young, still-beautiful body to the young doctor and the cold void of the deep freeze.

She didn't expect to dream. The doctor had told her that her metabolism would slow until it would take a thousand years for a single thought to form. Yet many thoughts were happening under the black lid of the long sleep. She dreamed not of her past, her childhood, of growing up, of living a mayfly life on the money from her inheritance. She dreamed instead of herself as she was now—and she imagined her body still young, adventuring through time like a frozen Bon Bon, bringing her beauty into a waiting, sterile future. She thought of waking up in a bright, antiseptic world of white-smocked doctors—all handsome young men with familiar features. She could hear them saying that everything was all right. She could imagine their looks of admiration.

Now she started to thaw for real. The sound of machinery intruded on her dream and she knew she was coming back. How much time had passed? A year? A century? A millennium?

The light was a sickly green, the odor unfamiliar. Dark shapes were moving near the sarcophagus that held her neatly tucked away. She had been told to be prepared for anything. But doctors, she expected, would always be starch-clean and solicitous. She asked for nothing more. She heard sounds from a distance that couldn't be part of the machinery but were strangely mechanical nevertheless—a loud clicking and clacking.

Then the smell grew stronger as the lid automatically lifted away from her face. She choked on foul and rotten fumes. It was so bad that she could barely breathe.

Soon she forgot about that problem. Her still numb body was grabbed by myriad thin—yet strong—arms, if indeed they were arms. As she was hoisted into the air she got a glimpse of her attendant. She tried to scream, and failing that, she fainted.

Surely, she thought as consciousness resumed, she was still asleep, safely packed away under layers of cold mist. When she was really brought back to awareness, she would laugh at the nightmare that had invaded her solitude.

She heard a persistent scraping. The thing was still there, hovering over her. There was another creature beside it, and a smaller one beyond. She looked into the reddish-brown mass of chitinous armor covering the creature, and felt the long legs with claws on the end moving her body into different positions. It was some kind of aberrant cockroach. She was tied down on a flat, metal disc. Slowly it dawned on her that she was on a table and the giant insect was leaning over her.

At first she thought its antennae were reaching out for her but then realized that they were directed toward something behind her. Prostrate on the table, she found she could move her neck and saw a large black and white screen that was displaying a scene of creatures like the one holding her.

They seemed to be playing a game with a ball. Closer scrutiny revealed that the "ball" was the dried, prunish remains of a human head. She felt one of the insect's legs pressing on her chest and turned her head back to see something sharp pointed at her throat. It looked like a knife.

The last thing she saw before it sliced into her yielding flesh was one of the bugs taking out the garbage. It was a clear plastic sack full of human bones and empty cryogenic units.

Then she realized what she had become: A TV dinner.

After the dust had settled from my divorce, I thought I should write a story of apology to my ex. She always liked my stories of high fantasy better than my science fiction or horror, so I produced this tale with her in mind every step of the way.

As for the politics in "Blind Sceptre," I make no secret of being a libertarian and work in my philosophy where appropriate. Often I encounter the attitude that libertarianism can be effectively expressed through science fiction, but not fantasy or horror. I'm always amazed at that kind of intellectual laziness. Any religious or political belief may be expressed through any genre of story telling. That is self evident to any rational mind. One reader told me that this was the first story of mine he'd read where he thought there might be something to my political views. So there!

Blind Sceptre

"There are no good emperors," said the king. No emperors being present at the banquet table there was general agreement. The absence of any emperor on the continent of Ir contributed significantly to the nodding of noble heads and the murmuring of assent in support of the king's words, even by those lords and ladies whose grasp of history was tenuous at best. The queen forced herself to smile.

Only the Lady Cynthia remained impassive. In the privacy of her chambers at court she had become a student of history. Over five hundred years had passed since the countries of Ir had suffered under an imperial yoke. Only the intervention of supernatural powers had put an end to that broad and indiscriminate tyranny. At least that's what the common people believed. Official, and officious, court historians explained the fall of the emperor in terms of economics and politics.

Lady Cynthia preferred the notion that the gods would judge harshly one who would presume to own all They had created. Lady Cynthia was the lover of the king and wondered if a man of his appetites could ever be satisfied. Too often he had referred to the magic sceptre that had absorbed all the power of the empire. Too often he had made bad jokes at the expense of the priesthood which hid the sceptre in one of its monasteries, out of reach of ambitious kings.

There had been a time when she had loved her monarch. Tired of the courtesans, he had wanted a more refined adventure. The lady and the king had caught each other in an artfully spun web. The queen was too much like the king to offer him love. Most women at court put on excellent performances but he could see through their intentions as easily as the revealing nightgarments they wore to his bedchamber. But when the king looked at the Lady Cynthia he received her steady gaze from strong, brown eyes in place of the meekness and deceit that were the norm. When he reached out and touched her long face with its high cheekbones, and caressed her night black hair, there was no pulling back on her part; and her eyes never turned away from him, as she would have been trained to do from childhood.

She still fondly recalled those days as she picked delicately at her vegetables in the banquet hall, and listened to the king lecture his unfortunate guests. He was going on and on about a monarch's responsibilities to his people as she remembered the first words he had spoken to her: "You're a brave one!"

When he had complimented her courage on that day so long ago, her cool reserve almost cracked and the little girl she carried deep inside almost broke free of all restraints. She had never gotten over the death of her father and at that moment the king made her remember how much she still longed for parental approval. But she had learned to suppress all genuine gaiety at a very young age. A typical male despite the crown he wore, the king had redoubled his efforts to elicit her approval. Female ice is said to inspire the hottest male flame.

The early days of their romance had been the happiest period of her life. At first there was the almost childish pleasure of sneaking around behind the matronly queen's back; but all ladies at court were sophisticated enough to know that the queen had spies everywhere. She was ten years older than the king when their marriage had been arranged. As such, the queen entertained no romantic delusions. Her central interest in life lay in organizing the minute details of everyone's life at court. Every new mistress of the king's could count on a brief holiday from meddling until the king's ardour had cooled. After that, the latest love interests would be assigned some level of insignificance by the queen and stay under her charge.

The Lady Cynthia had been the king's mistress for over a year and there was still no sign of flagging interest on his part. "I don't understand it," the queen had told the alchemist. "These affairs of his rarely last a month. Is there some kind of anti-love potion you could make for me?"

The alchemist was so old that everyone assumed he must have wisdom to match his years. "I can poison people and not leave a trace," he said. "I can make people fall in love. But falling out of love is something beyond my humble powers."

With a sigh, the queen surrendered. She considered routine murder unbecoming to her station. Nature would have to take its course. What she didn't know was that the alchemist was playing his own game with the king and wasn't about to jeopardize it.

Nature was in no rush where love was concerned. The king found the Lady Cynthia fascinating for many reasons. She didn't hide the fact that she could read. The queen would never understand this sort of attraction. The physical attraction between king and lady was made all the stronger by the growing closeness of their minds. Entire evenings had passed in which Cynthia forgot that she was making love to her king; and the only authority he held over her was his power to make her feel both wanted and satisfied.

She never dreamed a day would come when she could sit at the king's own table, among his inner circle, and be mind-numbingly bored. But such was the case as she listened to him intone: "Everything must be in its proper place for a well ordered society to function. Empire throws the natural order out of balance."

This latest platitude won the approval of no less a substantial presence than Lord Bottoum, far gone in drink. Empty wine glasses were lined up in front of his stout frame like so many conquered soldiers, the last glass having tipped over and its red tide coming within an inch of staining the Lady Cynthia's lavender sleeve. The man could always be counted on to provide entertainment by virtue of his indiscretions that were so finely wrought that no court jester could hope to compete.

Even the Lady Cynthia was roused from her grey mood as the entertainment began. "My liege," Lord Bottoum addressed his king, "no emperor could possibly equal your steady hand at the tiller of the state." At this point, most speakers would have detected the sudden silence settling over the room at the inappropriate comparison. A king reigning in his properly ordained sphere was not to be thought of as in any way similar to a world-aggrandizing emperor, but such was Lord Bottoum's turn of mind that he could only imagine the silence to be respectful awe over his rhetorical blasts of air.

The king played along. "Is this flattery, Lord Bottoum?" asked the man who held the power of life and death over everyone in the room, but would never confuse such authority with imperial powers.

Lord Bottoum was immune to irony and sarcasm, and with another glass of wine already in his hand, he bravely sailed on: "What I mean to say is that if any man could avoid being corrupted by the nature of imperial institutions, it would, of course, be your majesty."

The high priest chose that exact moment to have an attack of hiccups. Lady Cynthia raised a long fingered hand to her mouth to suppress a laugh. This was definitely better than being bored. She snuck a look at some of the other women and detected no change in their demeanor. They obviously didn't have a clue about what was going on.

"What is your point, Lord Bottoum?" asked the king.

Now, finally, the impolitic lord got the general drift of the situation. The last time he'd been in equivalent hot water was when he reminded everyone of how the queen would not allow her grown children on an outing because the alchemist had predicted a rainfall that never happened. Bottoum had almost lost his head over that one.

"I have no point, my liege," he said. The king frowned. The queen remembered just how annoying Lord Bottoum could be. Lady Cynthia wished court etiquette would allow her to express an opinion. The alchemist carried on an inner dialogue over whether overweight bodies were easier or harder to resurrect from the dead than bony, thin ones.

"You have no point?" echoed the king.

Legs quivering beneath the leathern gaiter that came to his knees, Lord Bottoum provided the denouement of the evening's entertainment: "The only point I ever dare to make in your august presence would be to your honor and glory, my liege. Any problems that my ill fated tongue might precipitate are never to be thought to arise from authentic sobriety. By which, I mean to say that any perceived incongruity is, in fact, a mere counterfeit of an actual blunder; or something very close to it."

The youngest woman there, a girl of surpassing beauty and golden blonde hair, giggled out loud. Cynthia had her first positive feeling for the younger woman.

Lord Bottoum finished his soliloquy at last. Even so, his mouth was still open in an excellent impersonation of a beached whale. He waited for the king to respond. Everyone waited.

With great theatricality, the king lifted a glass of wine and toasted the unhappy lord. "I thank you for clarifying your position. Are you sure you're not the reincarnation of an adviser to the old Emperor of Ir?" The priest in residence wrinkled his brow in thought as he wondered how close the king himself was venturing toward heresy with such a remark. But when the king laughed, and Lord Bottoum nervously joined in, and then everyone else except the Lady Cynthia added to the chorus, the priest decided that the gods must have a sense of humor and added his own good-natured laughter to the merriment.

Things could have been worse. Lord Bottoum might have mentioned the emperor's sceptre. But not even a drunken buffoon was likely to do that. To speak of the emperor's sceptre merited the death penalty by slow torture.

The candles were burning low, casting long shadows on the gold and red tapestries decorating the king's bedchamber. The Lady Cynthia and the king were playing a game of *dragon board*. In the beginning she'd been flattered when he told her that she was his first lover with the strategic sense to play this particular board game. But as she had become more proficient at the game the king had become less interested in playing it with her.

Tonight he was strangely eager to have her play. When she'd won the second game, she was sure that would be the end of it; but he happily rearranged the fine, obsidian pieces for a third contest. "You're in fine form," he said, smiling, without the least hint of a lewd suggestion about her figure. She concluded that this would be one of those rare nights when sex was not required of her.

"Robert," she said, becoming intimate, a privilege only granted to her in this room, "you seem unusually cheerful tonight."

"They're such fools," he said, "so willing to agree or disagree upon my pleasure."

"What choice do you give them?" she asked.

He responded with another question: "Do you know why I enjoy being with you?" He didn't even take a breath before continuing: "Because you speak from your conscience. You are my better half. But I know you have the same contempt for the great mass of mankind that I have myself."

"Do I?" she asked, a mocking tone creeping into her voice, accompanied by a raised eyebrow.

"You know, my little raven's wing," he said, idly stroking her hair, "there's something a little funny about calling the people my subjects."

"What is that, my liege?" she replied, and he noticed her return to formality.

"They're only objects, when you come right down to it. What difference would it make if the hand that guides them in their daily affairs is that of a king or emperor?"

Books she had read long ago came back to her now, and prompted her to say: "Perhaps there would be no difference to the people. But what of the character of the leader?"

He took up the challenge. "Why should authority over more subjects be a corrupting influence on character?"

"You were calling them objects a moment ago!"

The king looked long and hard at his favorite lady. "Are you arguing with me?"

She let herself think about the royal brothel as a possible destination for an imprudent lady. A momentary concern for dungeons flashed through her mind as well. "I suppose I am," she answered.

"Good! I need you tonight, Cynthia, as I've never needed anyone before. How would you like to be my empress?"

The words struck her as if a physical blow. Treason, heresy, blasphemy, and a bad jest all rolled up in one might be expected to break down the most carefully maintained composure. She gasped.

"Thank you," he said. "A reaction from you is always gratifying." Rising to his feet, he went over by the ornate bed where they had played games more interesting than *dragon board*, and poked at the impish cherub that hung from the beautifully carved headboard. His hand was doing things to the little statue that made Cynthia vaguely uncomfortable when suddenly there was a creaking sound.

The wall behind the bed moved. The Lady Cynthia wasn't sure if she was more disturbed by the realization that every time she had made love on that bed the wall behind her had been an insecure barrier...or if the presence of the wizened alchemist now stepping through that opening might be cause for greater alarm.

"My liege," said the alchemist, bowing to the king. "My lady," he said, bowing to her next.

"I know this is a night for surprises," the king announced airily as he put his arm around Cynthia. "I wanted you to hear my speech at dinner because as a student of classical rhetoric, you would recognize every argument."

The alchemist was carrying a long tube in his claw-like hands. He stood in the corner of the room, his head slightly bowed, and waited for authority to be exercised.

"I have no secrets from my alchemist," the king continued. "He knows of your literacy and penchant for self-education."

She bowed to her king. "The ancient world's half-hearted belief in one god led to decadence and atheism," she recited the conventional wisdom. "We are fortunate to be living in the age of faith and the certainty of a multiplicity of gods. Even so, we can learn much from the older world. Their philosophers understood the need for moderation and balance."

"What say you to that?" the king asked the alchemist.

"Admirably put," came the predictable reply. "You have chosen well."

Uncertain of the direction the men's conversation was taking, Cynthia thought it best to continue: "Kings are ordained to protect the common people from fine lords and ladies, such as my family. That's what my books say. The king is a custodian of the common interest. The king holds society together in a kind of equilibrium. And even if the king is not just and good on a personal basis, the institution of the monarchy has built-in protections to maintain civil order. As one critic of the old empire once concluded, 'Monarchy is the worst form of government, except for all the rest.'"

She took a deep breath and hoped her presentation would prove sufficient. The king applauded her. The alchemist merely smiled, a disconcerting sight with his bald head and narrow face giving the impression of a living skull.

"You have defended the hierarchial order," said the king, "even though you are living proof of what an absurdity it truly is!"

If there had been surprises before now, they could not compare to this latest remark of her sovereign. It was as if he had reached into the deepest recesses of her heart and plucked out her most secret thoughts. She looked at his large, strong face with its fierce, black beard and saw him as if for the first time. Gone was her boredom as if burned away in a furnace.

"Didn't people suffer more under the empire than in all the centuries since?" she asked in the cautious tones of a student.

"Yes," he said. "What of it? The small wars we fight now are hardly worth the bother. Every king worries over the rules of warfare so as not to offend the high priest. There's no reward in that. War should be fought to *decide* on the rules, not to abide by timid restrictions foisted on us by a benighted clergy."

A year of close personal contact with the king had taught Cynthia to expect him to work himself up at times like this. With a florid gesture, he motioned to the alchemist to step forth and deliver. The man did so. Theatricality was catching. The alchemist struck a dramatic pose and then opened the tube.

Her self-control back in place, the Lady Cynthia showed no expression at what was revealed; but something cold grew in the center of her stomach, as if something had just died in the castle.

The alchemist held in his hand the forbidden sceptre of the emperor. His withered hand could not activate the magical powers that lurked within the seemingly innocuous white cylinder with a plain ball on the end. But contact with a royal hand was quite another matter. The king's hand seemed a small and insignificant thing, despite the ruby ring on the middle finger, as it reached out for the forbidden sceptre.

"Robert!" She surprised herself by speaking his name in front of the alchemist. Neither seemed to mind. Today's protocol was about to become tomorrow's quaint memories.

"Women had more power in the empire, you know," said the king.

"Only the priestesses!" she cried. "And what they did to children was wrong. They..."

She was cut off the moment his fingers came in contact with the smooth, white surface of the sceptre. A sound like the rushing of a thousand winds filled the chamber. The Lady Cynthia didn't mind the noise nearly so much as what was happening to the ball at the end of the stick. The ball was becoming a recognizable human eyeball the size of a fist. The pupil, as large as a normal human eye, moved in the direction of the only woman in the room.

A light stabbed out and bathed her in its radiance. At the same time the light was reflected back on the king. The alchemist cowered in a corner, covering his face. Pictures began to flow into Cynthia and, reflected from her, into the king. They both saw the same thing, the same vision since sight had been restored to the oldest magic wand on the continent of Ir.

First, they saw Cynthia standing naked on a cliff overlooking the sea. In her hand she held a primitive stone knife. At her feet, equally naked, was a squalling infant. Far below, on the beach, surrounded by a vast army of soldiers clad in golden armour, the Emperor Robert stood as if waiting for a command. He held the sceptre high against a red sky.

His eyes met hers. She plunged the knife into their first born son and....

"No!" screamed the Lady Cynthia back in the world, back in life, back in the king's bedchamber; but the relentless light would not cease its probing. Now there were new pictures for man and woman to consider.

The same scene was repeated as before. Only this time there had been a change in the people on the cliff. Down below, on the beach, nothing was different. But on the cliff, the baby was gone, replaced by Cynthia, naked and bound at the feet of another woman—also naked, standing there with sagging breasts and spindly legs and wrinkled arms. The stone knife was held in the hand of the queen...and she did not hesitate to cut out the beating heart of the king's true love.

The sceptre didn't stop there. Next came a vision of dominion. All the nations of Ir surrendered their rights to the new capital. The old castle of the king was razed to the ground to make room for a sumptuous palace in its place. All the king's old enemies pretended to be his friends; while all his friends became new enemies.

There was no end to war. But now all was insurrection. The power of the sceptre was sufficient to turn the tide, should the new emperor make a serious miscalculation, either political or military. Although not even the sceptre could promise absolute security, the probabilities were all in favor of the new despot, clad in imperial purple and green.

A chorus of voices could be heard singing the praises of the new emperor, all across the continent of Ir. Great wealth was sent to him across the ocean from countries far enough away to be allies of the new regime. Their praises were added to the domestic voices, with just a hint of caution underlying the diplomatic flatteries. Could even great distances be a safeguard against the leader with a vision so vast as this new emperor?

More and more voices could be heard, accompanying the splendid pictures of ostentatious wealth. No one was more clever than the emperor at playing one faction off against the other. They could never trust each other for one second, and in that one single fact the strength of the empire could grow and grow, as the voices sang the praises higher and higher.

During all this, the Lady Cynthia stared dumbfounded, riveted by the image of her own bloody sacrifice. Her heart sank as she realized the death sentence she had pronounced on herself with the uttering of one little word. The chanting voices seemed a funeral dirge when suddenly she heard a deeper voice, a voice with substance. Someone else was speaking for real in the king's bedchamber. Someone else was saying the same word she had spoken but a momewnt before. This voice was saying: "No."

As if waking from a dream, she saw the king through the light and the pictures that for all their splendor had an ephemeral quality. The king had raised his free hand as if to stop the torrent of pictures and sound while his other hand continued holding the sceptre. He was looking straight at her at the very moment the pictures became a procession of beautiful young women from all over the world, all waiting their turn to be consort to the emperor. The queen was no more of a problem to him as empress as she had been as his queen. She watched the young women with a curious pleasure, as if they all belonged to her somehow.

"No," the king repeated. His voice was softer but somehow stronger than before. There was certainty in it. Slowly he placed the sceptre on the floor. Very gingerly, his hand opened and his fingers pulled back from the smooth white surface. As he did so, the staring eye became opaque.

"What are you doing?" screamed the alchemist. "Do you know how many people I bribed, how many murders it cost to bring you the sceptre?"

"Yes," said the king, unsheathing his sword from its scabbard, where it lay propped against his chair. The alchemist's eyes grew very wide before the light in them went out. The king wiped the old man's blood on the old man's robes.

Wrapping his hands in a towel, the king carefully replaced the sceptre in the tube. "The alchemist was in a plot against the kingdom," he told Cynthia. "Clearly he wanted to be the emperor, but knew that only a royal hand could bring forth the forbidden magic. Everyone knows how I feel about empire. We can make them believe that's what happened."

"Why?" she asked.

"Why did I want to restore the empire?"

"No. Why did you turn down all that power?"

He came over to her and held her in a strong embrace. "Don't you know?" he whispered in her ear.

"You care for me...that much?" she asked. She couldn't believe this was happening.

The king sighed. "What good is am empire if I don't have anyone to talk to?" he asked of the universe at large. "The sceptre's price was too high, the moment you turned down the offer."

"Thank you," was all she could think to say. He kissed her hard. She tried to make herself feel something.

Gone were the days when the Lady Cynthia had loved the king. But all the peoples of Ir could be grateful that the king still remembered how to love.

I was in a particularly bitter mood when I did this one. Of all the stories in *Excalibur*, I believe this to be the most pessimistic in what it says about relationships.

But here is a fine opportunity to say something about the ending instead of rewriting it, which was my first impulse. The protection and fulfillment of England may be seen as something quite different from what's good for the British Empire. I was thinking of G. K. Chesterton's writings on Little Englanders when I wrote the ending of "The Other Scabbard." In the midst of World War II, fighting for their lives against the Nazis, not every Englishman had the same view about saving the Empire.

The Other Scabbard

Blind eyes blinking in the dark, soft mouths forming words without sound, things that might be fingers reaching out to stroke healthy flesh passing by in the gloom of secret passageways.... That's the way it always was whenever I paid a call on Merlin. He'd liked his privacy when he was alive. Now he was positively a recluse.

Not that he was exactly dead, but to the outer world he might as well be. He'd allowed the rumor to spread that Morgan le Fay had bested him; a perfect absurdity to anyone who knew their respective abilities. None of us among the Little People had been taken in for a minute. Merlin always played his own game. The problem was how to get him on your side.

The leader of the People had selected me for this journey because of the time I'd been a spy at Arthur's court. From the first moment Merlin saw me in the outer world he recognized me for what I was. He helped get me into Camelot, all part of his eternal diplomacy—juggling the contrary interests of alien worlds, and trying to convince everyone that mutual interests exist where there are none. Well, he was a magician, after all.

Naturally the humans took me for a female child. Guinevere even thought me a bastard result from one of Lancelot's previous adventures. The great knight's indifference to a child did nothing to disabuse her of the notion. She was well aware that many a father acted that way toward legal issue.

My purpose was to keep an eye on Arthur. The king had no inkling of my true nature. Merlin and I agreed that it was best to maintain secrecy; but I wouldn't have put it past the old reprobate to subtly suggest to the monarch of Camelot that his majesty be on best behavior when around the new child. Then again, perhaps the king came off as a perfect uncle to any child who was there to enjoy the hospitality of his castle.

Arthur guessed my age at ten. He was off by a factor of ten! A mere century among the green forests and rocky crags of these islands means I'm still a youngster among the People; but old enough for dirty dealings with the human vermin. Merlin was interested in peace. We prepared for war.

I was a good spy. Not a trace of revulsion crossed my face as the king ran his fingers through my blonde tresses or gave me friendly pats. "Darling child," he called me. I smiled and giggled. Merlin even complimented me on how well I played the part.

Merlin! With one hand he helps and the other he thwarts. I stayed at court, passing on my reports in a special potion I poured into the ground. (At the time I thought the wizard would not divine what kind of magick I was using. I know better now.) My one certainty was that the status quo couldn't last forever.

Lancelot and Guinevere turned out to be the chink in Arthur's armor. We decided that this crisis was tailor-made for us to press demands on Merlin; especially since we had recently discovered the magician's greatest secret. We'd found the hiding place of the other sword! Everything seemed to be working in our favor: Adultery was tearing the kingdom apart, the fool knights were dividing their power in a mad quest for the Christian Grail, and Arthur was sinking into the depths of despair. Once we learned about the existence of the other sword, we felt sure that Merlin would renegotiate our arrangement.

I wasn't surprised when the wizard disappeared from the world of men. Nothing is ever simple with Merlin. Many the time he'd gone off alone for weeks before returning to court. But this time it appeared his departure was permanent.

He'd guided the affairs of Camelot with Excalibur, but it had been done with his usual flair for indirection. Whatever plans we had for the other sword, we could be certain he was several steps ahead of us. At times like this it was hard to believe that he had any human blood in his veins.

Among the People we had our own magick. That is how we located Merlin's secret place, and how I found myself exploring his private tunnels. A welcome guest at other times, I felt nervous intruding here. The labyrinthine complexity went beyond that of our own constructions. And where we had to depend on smokeless torches for light, or sometimes the bodies of small animals that gave out a yellow luminescence, Merlin's powers had invested the walls of his stronghold with a permanent light. The only drawback was that the colors were constantly shifting as one walked, giving an almost hypnotic effect. Where Merlin was concerned, nothing was accidental.

"You're wasting your time," he said as I spotted him from behind where he was bending over a small pool of water. He always loved to show off. Nothing ever surprised the great Merlin! At least, that was the impression he liked to make.

"I represent the Council," I answered in as solemn a voice as I could muster.

"And I represent the Lollipop Guild," he replied as he turned to face me. I had no idea what he was talking about. He enjoyed being cryptic even when he was above ground. "Don't worry about it," he replied, as if reading my mind. "Some people say I live backward in time, so that would naturally provide certain unusual points of view."

For the first time since I had known him, I felt that I could be personal and said, "Many believe you were a product of rape."

"So much is said about me that I forget most of it. When you say 'they' do you mean people on top of or below the ground?"

He was trying to goad me. I didn't mince words: "Humans aren't people."

"Ah, yes, the party line," he said.

"Some of us don't believe the claims that you have any human parentage. Nasty rumors may be spread about anyone. Others believe that one human parent can be overlooked in someone of your attainments."

"That's most obliging," was his reply. "I'm sure there are humans who are as tolerant about you."

The trouble with diplomacy is that it puts demands on one's self-control that go far beyond the call of duty. "You're not serious, Merlin." I could hear my own voice becoming shrill. "Very few humans know for certain that we exist. For the rest, we are either stories or superstitions. They don't know us."

"So they can't form a valid opinion about you?"

"Exactly."

"Whereas you have known thousands upon thousands of humans as the basis of your evaluation?"

I hadn't noticed his sarcasm until that moment. He usually spoke in a monotone, except when shouting to drive home a point (as had been the case when he was instructing the young Arthur).

All these criticisms being thrown in my general direction seemed a bit unfair at the time. So I defended myself (another mistake): "Your problem is with the Council. I'm just—"

"No, you are not *just*; and that's the real problem!"

A Lord of the People had warned me about this sort of thing when I first offered to serve. There are as many points of view as there are stars in the heavens. A clever debater is someone every bit as intransigent as you are but with a pretense of objectivity. Merlin could keep me tied up in knots for hours this way. And I frankly didn't have the time....

"How long has it been since you last ate?" he asked with uncharacteristic solicitude. Perhaps his bag of tricks didn't have a bottom, but I'd never thought that his art would include cookery.

I was so surprised that I couldn't think of anything to say. With a touch as firm as it was kind, he took my arm and led me deeper into the recesses of the cave. Here were sights more beautiful than the crystal walls of my own home. And if I thought we of the People had mastered every kind of underground labyrinth, I had not reckoned on the powers of Merlin. For the first time in my life, I realized that I was lost. Every corridor was the same, even as every color of the rainbow washed over me, and pleasant tinkling sounds satisfied longings without a name.

"This way," said Merlin, voice growing deeper as he led me into his secret realm. There was no need for speech. His hand still held me in a firm grasp.

And then my heart skipped a beat as we stood before a gigantic sword, plunged deep into what appeared to be some kind of fungous growth. "Excalibur," I said, but even as the sacred word passed my lips, I knew it couldn't be.

"No," said Merlin. "This is not the king's missing sword."

"I never thought I'd actually see the anti-Excalibur."

"This seemed a good place for a little kitchen," he said, smiling thinly. Not until he began opening a door in the side of the tunnel did I realize that he was no longer holding me. The strength of his grasp was such that I still felt his fingers on my arm; and I liked the feeling.

He hadn't been joking about the kitchen. A large cauldron steamed in the center of the room. The aroma was pleasant with just a hint of sweetness. Neatly stacked against the wall were barrels of different kinds of herbs and plants. A small wooden table was placed near the food. I couldn't help but notice that it was perfectly round.

As if the argument between us had left something unpleasant in the air, we didn't speak. Words would have spoiled the splendid repast. I hadn't been hungry until I tasted the first spoonful of the stew. As I eagerly ate the rest of the tangy mixture, I felt his flinty eyes watching me. We both knew this was a temporary lull in the battle, but I was willing to enjoy it.

"Why did they send you?" he asked when I'd finished the meal.

I thought we'd been through all that. My time in Camelot had not been wasted. As a spy I had seen the enemy close up— the human pestilence that covered these fair islands like so much soot from a dirty chimney. An older and more experienced member of our race could have been selected, but the honor was mine because of the proximity I'd had to King Arthur, to his subjects ... and to Merlin.

I decided to address the real issue: "We don't understand what you're trying to accomplish any longer. I'm here to find out. "

As he stood, I was struck once again by how much taller Merlin was than a normal human. Given my diminutive stature, he towered over me. The way his cloak swirled around him, green and brown colors capturing the hues of the earth, he seemed a giant tree, but one that could never be humbled by ax or any other blade.

His response was patronizing: "What is wrong with your statement is the suggestion that anyone has ever divined my purposes. And what do you, little one, suppose they are?"

He wasn't going to trick me that easily. There had been agreements, promises, treaties! "You know full well," I told him. "The humans may only live here if they are kept in control. They cannot be allowed to breed indefinitely."

His smile was beginning to make me uncomfortable, especially the words that came past those thin lips: "There is not enough space for infinite breeding where anyone is concerned. Even the Little People need room."

This persistent equating of us with the human scum was beginning to get on my nerves. I tried to keep from shouting: "We were here first. We belong here. Human beings are invaders."

Although under the ground, we were still near enough the surface to hear thunder explode overhead. A torrential downpour followed. It was that time of year. It usually was that time of year.

"The animals preceded you," he said quietly.

"And who does a better job of taking care of them and living with them than we do?"

I thought he was about to argue how we sometimes kill animals, the same as humans, for food and clothing ... and to make our spells. A counter-argument had already occurred to me: namely, that we didn't begin to hunt as many of them as the other side. And then there was the matter of trees. We never cut down trees for any reason. But Merlin tried a new tack.

"Little one," he said, "there is no point in this kind of comparison. I grant that human beings are not as in tune with earth forces as you are."

"Or you," I replied. happy of the opportunity to pass on a sincere compliment.

The rain was continuing to pour down with an incessant drumming sound. All I could think about was the fresh mud this would make, and how many humans might slip in it and break their fool necks. With that uncanny power of his, Merlin seemed to look right into my soul.

"Why do the Little People hate mankind?" he asked.

The very words seemed to set my brain on fire with an uncontrollable rage. I jumped up so quickly that I knocked his little table over. "We're angry with you, Merlin! With you...." I wanted to stop myself, but the words poured out as if to match the volume of the rain crashing overhead.

I went on: "We thought you would use your influence, at the heart of Camelot, to keep humans in their place. To keep them divided and at each other's throats. To keep them busy killing each other."

His face seemed to age with every pronouncement I threw at him. He turned to face the wall beyond which a sword waited, like an accusing finger. I couldn't seem to stop myself: "The Druids were the best we could expect from humans. And you're the best of them, far better—because you were more than human. So now you stand between the pagan world and the Christian world, between the forest and what Rome brought here, now collapsing back into the dust where it belongs. Humans believe in you. You gave them Arthur. You put Excalibur in his hand. You ..."

I wanted to build him up all the higher so I could drag him down all the more; I could see the crucial events in my mind and how the seeming unity that Merlin had helped to create worried us at first. But when adultery did its disintegrating work, and the sword Excalibur was a lost hope, and the knights went off on futile quests, and the sorceress Morgan le Fay turned everyone else's pain into her own personal treasure, we assumed that Merlin had been craftier than anyone expected. This was all the more easily believed when he allowed himself to be bested by Morgan le Fay and thereby removed from Arthur's side at the king's moment of greatest trial.

When the news first came to us that Merlin might still be striving for unity and the restoration of Camelot, the thought was too hideous to bear. But the elf brought proof to the Council. Merlin was casting new spells for the good of Arthur and his noxious realm.

And so, finally, I finished my tirade with, "We can't believe you'd work to increase the presence of human beings in our home." I'd worked myself into such a state that I could barely catch my breath. His contemplation of the rock wall completed, he turned around and gestured that I resume my seat. Before joining me, he bent over with a considerable sound of creaking in his joints and returned the table to a standing position.

"There's no quarreling with your criticisms, little one. Human beings do not provide the best material. Take Guinevere, for example. I warned Arthur about her, but to no avail Blindness is his flaw. As for her..."

My time at court had not been wasted. "She broke her vows," I said, which struck me the same as violating an essential step of an important magickal spell.

"All too predictable," he said with a heavy sigh. "Once boredom or disappointment comes into the picture, expecting a wife to stay with her husband is like expecting a vulture to tarry over dry bones when there is rotting flesh nearby, awaiting her delicate attention."

Hearing Merlin express such a perfectly reasonable opinion about the enemy gave me a false sense of security. Could he be seeing things clearly at last? One could hope....

"There's not one thing I can say about them," he told me, "that I can't also say about the Little People. Loyalty is an achievement." He came close and pulled something out from under his flowing robes. A glittering crystal winked at me from his long, white fingers. "Loyalty is as rare," he whispered, "as a jewel in the snow. I never break my word to anything on earth, or under it."

Supper was definitely over. I wasn't sure I wanted any dessert. He opened the wall again, and beckoned me back to where the sword glinted in the shifting lights from the cave walls. "I know why you've come," he said. "But we won't discuss this little trinket until you know where I stand." He didn't seem to be making a pun.

The moment we were back in the tunnel, there were groaning and mewling sounds from out of the darkness. The elemental creatures guarding Merlin's domain might not have much in the manner of brains, but there was little doubt as to their loyalty. They would die for Merlin, always assuming they were already alive.

Pointing to the sword, but exercising care not to touch it, he went on: "I never promised to put the interests of any group over any other. Individuals earn my allegiance. Arthur earned his sword. I won't punish him any more than he's already punished himself."

Without Merlin's help to trick Arthur into thinking this sword was Excalibur, the king would never raise the wrong blade above his head, and call his knights back to the banner. And the dark magick wouldn't be released, undoing everything that Excalibur had wrought. What Lady Guinevere had begun, we were more than willing to finish.

"Why do you hate them?" he asked. There was no answer I could give. The emotions ran too deep. Human beings looked like us, but as ungainly caricatures, coarse and ugly as goblin droppings. We told ourselves that they were enemies of the natural world; but if they never cleared a field or ran their plows through the soil, we would still wish them ill.

"Forgive an old man," he said, placing a hand on my shoulder. The fact that I did not shrink from his touch was sufficient proof that he couldn't really be one of them. "You can't help being a bigot when that's all you've ever known," he told me. "But you can return to your caves and report that I won't use the power of this sword to destroy those whom I love!"

"What has happened to the real Excalibur?" I had the presence of mind to ask. He simply shook his head. I didn't really care if he wanted to keep that a secret. The power right in front of me was all I cared about at that moment.

"You'd like to touch it, wouldn't you?" he asked. Now it was my turn to shake my head. "Go on," he said. "The sword has no sting."

I was standing very close to the anti-Excalibur. There seemed to be shadows moving on the ground near the blade. At first I thought it was the phosphorescence from the walls playing tricks. The truth was more disturbing. As I bent over to examine the ground, I saw that the moldy substance beneath the sword was actually moving. I leaped back and almost fell.

Merlin, reliable as the rock under my feet, caught me "There now," he said, "I thought you knew. This sword was grown over the course of many centuries. Only a special hand will harvest this sprout from its garden; as only the right hand drew Excalibur from the stone."

"The wrong hand," I heard myself whisper, but it was as if someone else spoke the words. "A hand meant for destruction."

"You may still touch it," Merlin repeated. "Yours is not a human hand, and as you know so well, only a human hand will release the darker powers of that blade."

Suddenly I felt very stupid. "What are you up to?" I asked, scarcely disguising my suspicions.

Never before had I heard the laughter of Merlin the magician. Although I have lived many years, I pray to gods and goddesses above and below that I never hear that sound again. There was no joy in it, only cold knowledge.

His eyes changed as he watched me. I remembered the light that had flashed in the small jewel held between his fingers. Now it was as if the light had traveled up his arm and reached his eyes. The brightness was painful.

"We know what you want," he said, providing no clue as to who was intended by the plural. "This sword is a concentration of earth's darkest powers. You will not place this in Arthur's hands. His destiny lies elsewhere. But even after Arthur is a memory, you will still be trying to place this deadly thorn in the hands of a human leader. We cannot prevent this forever."

The vibration beneath my feet was barely noticeable at first. I didn't even pay attention until there was a loud rumbling. Merlin's eyes were dancing before me as if they were twin comets; yet his body remained rigid as if a pillar anchored to the ground. And then the whole tunnel tilted crazily and I was falling forward, forward ... with nothing to hold on to except the sword.

No sooner had I steadied myself than everything returned to normal. The experience was so vivid that for one moment I believed in its authenticity. And then I realized that the sounds and tremors had been pure illusion. The lack of falling rocks or even dust in the air should have warned me that Merlin was still Merlin! He'd gone to all this trouble just so I would reach out and grasp the hilt of the anti-Excalibur.

His eyes were normal again. They were looking at my hand. We of the People are not allowed to curse, or I would have let loose such a torrent of vituperation as to drown out an eternity of rain.

"Thank you," he said. "I needed your cooperation. By touching the sword before a human hand, you help redirect its magick. Now it will rebound upon the eventual user, but only in a way to the good. Humanity in England can be saved by both this and the real Excalibur, if need be ... but in different ways at different times."

I must have worn such an expression of horror that Merlin felt a moment of sympathy. The weight of what I had done pressed down on me as an invisible hand might force me to sit, dejected, in a cavern that suddenly seemed so much darker. I could barely hear the old mage's words over the sounds of my own sobbing.

"There now," he said, "it's not as bad as all that. Negative magick is not so easily dispelled. Anti-Excalibur cannot be used to extend an English leader's power beyond certain limits. Clearly, you don't want Englishmen with too much power, or their progeny extended too far. At some future moment of great peril, this weapon will keep things in balance and preserve the natural order of—"

"No!" I screamed, leaping to my feet, unbearable frustration consumed in anger's welcome fire. "You tricked me! I'll never be able to return to the People now. They'll know. And they don't forgive."

He crouched down beside me, but I was grateful he didn't touch me this time. He was gentle as he asked, "Aren't these the ones for whom you would have laid down your life?" I nodded mutely, tears filling my eyes. "You can stay with me," he went on. "I will greatly extend your lifetime. You needn't be cast upon the wind. You can join me in glorious solitude. There are more worlds than this. Stand back from the battles of the many. Embrace the outlook of the one. The human tribe and your tribe serve no useful purpose except to produce an occasionally interesting individual."

He went on like that for some time, and although I initially felt revulsion for what he said, the words began to affect me as flowing water will eventually smooth the surface of the sharpest stone. The love I had taken for granted suddenly seemed completely unreal. I had failed. Those I loved would destroy me for that failure, if they could.

I have only the vaguest memory of going outside with him. No elemental creatures barred our way. The tunnels were empty, leading to a different world. The rain had stopped. Stretching out before us was a monotonous landscape of mud, the color of excrement, and with an odor to match. "This blessed plot," I heard Merlin mutter under his breath as he held his nose. I'd never noticed odors like that before. There was no sweet, after-the-rain freshness.

We wandered over the hills of England. No human or animal took note of us. The combination of his powers and the logic of his arguments finally seemed an irresistible combination. And for the first time, I began noticing details about his face. Even in the pale light of late afternoon his bushy white eyebrows seemed like small, jagged lightning bolts, forever fixed above a stern gaze. I wanted desperately to trust him, because I no longer had a People to call my own.

When night came, he did things with his hands, and the stars all turned into blinking eyes. I'd never felt so lonely than at that moment, surrounded by a myriad of potential judges, as indifferent to me as I was empty inside. I desperately needed to be filled with something, anything … and Merlin knew it.

He gave me powers. They were difficult to master, but I eagerly accepted the challenge. There were methods by which I could leave my body and travel through space and time. By this means innumerable worlds were mine to explore. The sheer volume of event and environment put my own past into an ever-diminishing context. Eons passed without my even seeing Merlin. And finally the moment came when he allowed me to understand that all those cold eyes sprinkling the black canopy of the night had been my own, sated with a million visions.

I had almost forgotten about the sword when Merlin took me back to England. Camelot was now a dream—lost forever but remembered with an aching desire. Gone were the Brythonic-speaking Celts and their problems with the Saxons. In their place a new world had risen from the mud and rocks and dirt, a world of steel and other metals, as that cursed sword had grown in its fungous bed. The sky was full of cold metal as well, raining down to earth where it became hot as the burning sun. And this new England had produced a new leader.

"Look upon him," said Merlin. We watched from safe distances, invisible and indifferent; but curiosity still lived somewhere in my ancient breast. "Look at what is his!"

This man had found the sword, the anti-Excalibur, where its soft bed of muck had grown hard over the centuries. When he touched the hilt and pulled, the hard mound around the sword showed cracks and gave way. With a great yank he held the blade before his face, while three old crones promised that this special weapon would turn the tide against the enemy and save England.

The man did not appear particularly regal. He was short and squat. In place of a profile his face was round as the moon, with heavy jowls and a protruding lower lip that made him look pugnacious. His garments were bulky and rough, suggesting not the least hint of comfort. On his head he wore a shapeless black thing. He was old and used a cane. With the sword in one hand, a stick in the other, and a large stomach hanging over his widely placed feet, the composite effect was a bit ridiculous. This was no King Arthur.

"Today is historic," he boomed in a voice far greater than his body deserved. "I think of Charlemagne and Alexander the Great, but most of all I think of Arthur Pendragon. As I wield Excalibur...."

"But—" my thoughts spoke to Merlin as a whisper in the void. He answered, "You know which sword is found this day."

The man in black bowed to the three old women who had led him to so much concentrated power. "I did not take this job," he said, "to oversee the dissolution of the empire."

I knew the immediate outcome, even before Merlin pulled back the tapestry of time to show the future. The black magick had been tamed. Many English lives were saved by the sword I thought would mean their doom. But negative energies were released when it came to the more ambitious goals of this would-be Arthur. England was no longer to control the destiny of the world. England was to be itself. Only itself.

Those who had been my People were now reduced to such small numbers that I scarcely believed I had once feared them. But there were still enough of them to put up a wail over the ever-spreading sea of humanity that not even the most destructive war could stem. Suddenly I felt no gratitude to Merlin that, thanks to his sorcery, I had outlived so many.

Somewhere the real Excalibur still lies, hidden from the eyes of all sapient creatures. I am not curious as to its whereabouts, and

Merlin seems to have forgotten it. As for the other sword, grown from the marrow of inner earth, the blade dissolved as if an icicle on a summer day when the skies over England became silent once again.

Silence is always best.

One science fiction editor thought I had a background in math when he read this. Fooled him! I talked to friends who were math nerds and did my homework so well that the editor in question thought I should tone down the inside stuff. I placed the story with a less picky editor.

Critique of Pure Math

Professor Reis hated, in alphabetical order, the Board of Regents, the faculty, students and the university. He liked tenure. He loved one thing: Mathematics.

Ten years had been devoted to a particularly esoteric mathematical problem. After a complex series of equations and formulae, he had at last finished. The beauty of the thing was in the tremendous distance that lay between it and any practical application.

Once a rash, young student had asked the professor about The Great Work in a mere graduate class in Non-Standard Analysis. Reis had tolerated the insubordination though he had inwardly cringed at the thought of even talking about his favorite problem with students. But then the young man asked, "When you solve it, what use will it be?" Wiser members of the class maintained their silence and waited far the axe to fall.

"Have you taken any courses in philosophy?" asked Reis.

"No."

"Too bad. If you had, you might have come across Plato. A pupil once asked him the practical use of philosophy. Plato gave him a coin so his time would not have been wasted. Then he expelled the fellow!"

It is to Reis's credit that he did not draw out the agony. The unfortunate student was removed from the class that very afternoon.

Such was Professor Reis's life: evenly divided between odious teaching and the ecstasy of pure mathematics, a self-contained universe of Logic where the relation of a premise to reality was as irrelevant as the relation of a professor's concern for education and tenure.

It might have gone another way—Reis enjoying a relative anonymity—but for the invasion of the beings from the Inzatriod star system.

Earthlings had no name for the star—it was hidden in the galactic core. But the Inzatriodians lost no time In adding that useful information to our astronomical charts.

They also established three laws: 1.) a world government under their control; 2.) all dogs and cats would be turned over to them to be used as the primary food source for the colony on earth; 3.) Professor Reis was to be given official recognition as the greatest thinker of the human race.

Reis, of course, had no say in it. He was summoned to court. There, in front of the slug-like beings from a distant star, he performed mathematical proofs in his own medium: chalk and board. They loved it and applauded by slapping their sticky appendages against the floor.

Reis hated them as much as the Board, the faculty, the students, and the university.

After he whetted their appetites with concertos in chalk, they demanded the full symphonic rendition of the Great Work. He had been made a celebrity. The equation was at the heart of the Inzatriodian's entire civilization. That a mere human being could have come up with it thrilled them to no end.

Reis was to spend the rest of his life at court, the most favored human on earth . They would explain to him the half million practical applications of the proofs of his theorem.

After five years he went insane. Regretfully they locked him away for his own protection. As a last gesture of their esteem for Reis, they let him have pieces of chalk and a blackboard.

During the first months of his captivity, Reis paid no attention to his surroundings. He had withdrawn entirely into the gray world behind his own eyeballs. It didn't last. Gradually he became aware once more of his arch-enemy: reality. For a man who loved neatness and order, there was something abhorrent about a universe that would allow Inzatriodians to blanket the earth and disrupt his life. Something had to be done.

With this realization, he made the decision to slide once more into the warm, soothing womb of pure mathematics. He saw his salvation in the schoolroom equipment near at hand. Reis was his old self again.

Only this time he would make sure that his equations, formulae, and theorems would remain unsullied by any possibility of application to the real world.

"Now clear your head," he told himself. "Stop thinking of these damned Inzatriodians." He tried projecting his mind into limitless space, away from the slug-infested world that was his home planet. But it didn't work. Sooner or later he'd bump Into *them*. He decided that they could be anywhere in space and time. Then he tried remembering what it had been like before they came. The only trouble with that was the nagging knowledge that they would arrive later—that all of human history was a prelude to the horror. "Empty your head of them!" Reis commanded himself in his small, white room. "Your mind can create an infinite vista. Do so!" He thought about the future. The far, far future. A time when the Inzatriodians would be no more. It worked. He was at peace. Without further delay he leaped into his work.

The years passed. His hosts fed him and occasionally observed the progress of this new mathematical problem. "Has it any use?" asked the leader of the Inzatriodians. "It is utter gibberish, oh Honorable Worm," was the answer. "He is merely playing with symbols; there is no possible connection with reality."

"Too bad. He was such a useful being."

On the twentieth year since he had begun, Professor Reis solved the problem. Now a doddering old man, he raised his shaking hand to the board, and with a last squeak of chalk was done with it. Immediately the cosmic axis shifted. A gate opened. Through it streamed a mighty armada of starships headed for earth. The occupants were human to a man. The sleek crafts attacked the Inzatriodian base on the moon and wiped It out. So swift was the attack that there was no time to warn the defense stations in orbit around the Earth. Within twenty-four hours of contacting the main force of the aliens (based in the Americas) the last Inzatriodian had been reduced to a bubbling puddle of brownish ooze.

Professor Reis was liberated at dawn. A sandy-haired colonel saluted him and read an official statement from the Commander of the Liberating Star Fleet, to wit: "We extend our heartiest congratulations to you, Hiram Reis, for genius above and beyond the call of duty. Without your great feat, we would never have been able to save this part of history."

"Eh?" said Reis. He had become hard of hearing.

"This is no time for modesty," said the colonel, raising his voice. "Our previous time travel attempts had created an unfortunate paradox. Only with your help—opening the time gate at this end—were we able to preserve our highly advanced civilization of the future."

"The future?"

"The Inzatriodians are not from your time, but ours. They sought to destroy us by changing earth history in your time. But you have restored the proper sequence of events. Your achievement caused two time-streams to converge—and we came through."

"My...achievement?"

"You are more than a mathematician, Reis. You are a great engineer. You have changed the structure of reality. Given the circumstances, we have no idea what you are supposed to do next. But no matter. We intend to take you back with us. In our hospital, we will rejuvenate you."

"Why?"

"Think of it," said the colonel, smiling. "You have a good millennium ahead of you, in our time; more than enough years in which to aid our utopia. The one statement of yours that has come down to us through the centuries is: 'With mathematics we govern reality.' Ah, Reis, you're just the sort of practical man we need."

Professor Reis's scream lasted for a long time.

This bizarre short about an astronaut with a few problems readjusting to Earth appeared in a small publication alongside a story by Robert Sheckley. All I could think of was how much better Sheckley could have handled the idea than I did. To cheer myself up, I read some stories from today's top science fiction magazines. Do that on a regular basis and you can't help but have an increase in self esteem. You may not end up convinced that you're another Asimov or Silverberg, but you'll feel a lot better. Guaranteed!

Piecemeal

He was the only survivor of the expedition. Naturally, they gave him the full treatment. Not a blood cell was left unscrutinized. A lab specimen of distinction, he was allowed to leave the maze from time to time. It was understood that he'd always come back.

No sooner was the final report filed away (with months of data on the astronaut) than he had the accident. The first thing the doctor in charge thought to do was reopen the file and turn to the psychiatric section. Colonel Robert Wilcox claimed to have lost the small toe of his left foot in a defective lawnmower. The toe in question was still plainly visible and unharmed. And that discrepancy was the least of the problems for the shrink department.

Wilcox didn't deny there was a toe on the end of his foot. He denied that it was his. "It wasn't regenerated," he insisted to the assorted doctors. "The aliens did it. They studied me with their crystal eyes and stroked my soul with their cruel, jewel minds and changed me. This toe isn't mine. I stole it!"

"Stole it?" was the incredulous response.

Before the mission he had a been a taciturn sort. Now they couldn't shut him up: "The aliens are so far up the evolutionary ladder that when they look down the many rungs, the human race is barely in view. We're like inanimate objects to them, just resources to be used. But contact with them expanded parts of my mind to the point where I'm a million years ahead of the rest of you."

He stared with such intensity that one of the women doctors felt compelled to look away.

Catching his own expression in a mirror, he shuddered and continued: "But the rest of me is still a primitive ape, unable to understand or control the new part of my brain that is supposed to be part of a heightened cosmic consciousness. Without guidance, without control, the new brain is stealing... things."

"The toe?" asked Dr. Stapledon, the head of the project. "You were going to tell us about the toe."

"Oh yes," said Wilcox. "I was lying on the grass, blood pouring out of my foot and cursing. I'd been out of the solar system and back, and then I go and do something as stupid as mowing the lawn barefoot! My neighbor rushed over to see if he could be of assistance. Suddenly he screamed and I saw that his small toe was missing. In its place was a bleeding stump. I looked down at my foot...and there was a strange toe on it. This," he pointed in the direction of his foot, "isn't mine."

There was a mutual clearing of throats around the table. By common assent, Dr. Shaw spoke. "We interviewed your neighbor. He told us there was a jagged piece of glass in the grass and that's how he injured himself."

"Did you find it?" asked Wilcox.

"You mean his toe?" asked Shaw, smiling in that annoying manner she had. "Some small animal or bird must have made off with it. You simply projected that poor man's agony onto yourself, colonel. You weren't injured except in your mind."

He wouldn't let them off that easily. "What made me cry out for help in the first place?" No one answered his question so Wilcox smiled and said, "Your ape minds cannot accept the existence of beings of superior intelligence who have altered a mere human being." He thought of Nietzsche's statement that man is a rope tied between the ape and superman; but he didn't say it out loud. They were upset enough with him already.

"There is no proof of these aliens," said Wells. "You are engaging in confabulation of the classic sort."

Wilcox laughed scornfully. "They saved me, didn't they? How else did I survive out there when the ship crashed on that dead rock?"

Wells had a ready answer: "There were sufficient supplies for one man to survive. You must have programmed the lifeboat computer to take you home, then fantasized the aliens along the way. You had a lot of time out there to dream."

There was no reasoning with collective expertise. Wilcox even recognized the irony that on some level, the committee of doctors was analogous to the group mind of the aliens. How could he explain what it had been like to encounter truly superior intelligence? At first it was like facing a blank wall. There was nothing his brain could see. And it was like listening to the silences between the stars. There was nothing for his brain to hear. And then they helped with whispers and shadows and something like music.

They made him remember childhood fancies of perfection and beauty. They took him back to the time when behind the darkness beat the light of angel wings, before adulthood extinguished all light forever. But now that the light had been returned to him he was afraid. He missed the darkness.

One more time he would try to make the men and women in the little room understand. "I've become some kind of Frankenstein vortex," he told them very slowly. "If anything is 'taken' from me, I receive the equivalent from the individual nearest me; and he is left with nothing but my wound."

"Your delusion can be cured," said Stapledon.

And so they took Wilcox to a special room with small, expensive instruments and Stapledon stayed behind to administer the treatment. "This machine," he explained, "will focus on your strongest belief at the moment—which is your certainty about the aliens and remove it. There will be no damage to you mentally. We've come a long way since lobotomies."

"You're making a mistake," said Wilcox. "They put me through a battery of tests you can't imagine in their attempts at communication. I only remember a few details; enough to know that I was challenged to the limit of my intellect. If you take that away, it could be dangerous."

"Dangerous?" asked Stapledon, with the barest hint of mockery. "No more than what you've been through already."

"They never let up," Wilcox continued. "I've never been tested like that before. Raising consciousness is hard work, let me tell you. They demanded that I make incredibly subtle distinctions, to think and ponder and worry over the minutest details...."

"No need to worry any longer," said Stapledon as he spun a dial. There was a hum and a click and the sensation of falling for Colonel Robert Wilcox, who finally touched bottom as softly as Alice coming to rest on a fluffy Wonderland pillow.

In the waiting room, a red light flicked off to be replaced by a yellow one. The treatment was over. "Did it work?" asked Shaw, the first to enter the room. "Does the colonel still insist that the aliens saved him out there?"

"What aliens are you talking about?" asked Wilcox.

"Tell us what you remember of the mission," she requested in a firm tone.

The astronaut shook his head. With no great conviction he said, "I remember the ship crashing and then... I got back home somehow."

Dr. Stapledon saw his own face in the therapy room mirror. He observed himself with genuine curiosity. He knew that he was a doctor. He could recall every detail of his involvement with various space missions. But of his days in medical school, there was not a trace of memory. The pain and anguish and struggle were blanked out of his mind.

On impulse Stapledon interrupted the questioners, looked straight at Wilcox and demanded, "What day did I take my doctor's orals?"

Wilcox glanced at him in momentary surprise, then quickly answered, "The fifteenth."

Stapledon didn't bother to check it out. "Our young man no longer believes in the aliens," he said, "but I do!"

Originally, I was going to reprint "Con Job" here, a story I sold to the wonderfully strange *Squonk*, but I think it's too dated now. The premise of Disney buying the entire state of Florida and renaming it Florida World holds up, but the world science fiction convention being held there on the eve of the millennium, and God appearing to judge fandom, doesn't seem as funny to me now.

In its place, I offer something more relevant to what Pulpless.Com is trying to do to create a better world. Since Forrest J Ackerman is working with us on a series of classic science fiction novels, his role in this story is essential.

Freedom is never guaranteed, not even in cyberspace. But it can be won anywhere.

Imagicide

They started by outlawing that "ugly neologism," sci-fi. Very few people at the time noticed what was happening within the science fiction field. After all, the nationalization of all commercial art was the main issue; and what was going on inside one genre was happening on a larger scale in what was euphemistically called the mainstream. All sorts of labels and pet names went by the wayside that first week of the new edicts.

One of the most popular science fiction writers of the time issued a stunning *pronunciamiento* before committing suicide. Theoretically, his argument went, none of this should be happening. The computer revolution was supposed to have rendered impossible the centralization of authority. "No one will ever have a strangle-hold on imagination!" he assured his readers. He put his faith in the cypherpunks, the resourceful inheritors of the cyberpunk tradition. The Internet, virtual reality, spread spectrum...all these were magic words of power to him, promising new vistas of personal freedom for those with the wit to see and understand.

The idea was that in record time there would be no monopoly on information; and the media centers of the world would lose their power. Why, if teenagers could create their own three-dimensional, interactive worlds at the push of a button, they didn't have to rely on the movies or music videos that someone else would give them. They could create their own.

The only trouble was that the author's utopian projections had not reckoned on the SS (the Systems Soldiers) and their ability to invade any program that was not approved. In this, the authorities had a surprising amount of assistance from the younger generation that proved somewhat deficient in the imagination department and didn't know what to do with all the new technology. Clearly, guidance was needed.

Guidance was provided when the Educational Authority was given control over popular entertainment. The nationalization of commercial art was the inevitable result.

Within the genres, a number of writers thought they could fight the new edicts with a united front. The world famous author, who wrote the *pronunciamiento*, had entertained the rather hopeful idea that government officials would need to bring in outsiders to take over science fiction; and that the lack of specialized knowledge of the field would defeat their purpose. He was most adamant on one point: "The fans won't support something just because it has SF on the label. They don't fill their shelves with travel guides to San Francisco! They won't buy a name brand just to keep collections complete. They're too smart for that, I tell you!"

Whatever the merit of his views on fans, he did not bring his analytical skills to the subject of his fellow professionals. No one was more surprised than he when certain prominent members of science fiction writer organizations volunteered to help in the transition to the New Order. But he didn't stay around long enough to see the ultimate outcome. Before he died, he left a note apologizing for his deep weariness, but still concluding on an optimistic note: "I am sure that one day someone of stature will avenge the world of imagination."

Meanwhile, back at the politically correct dictatorship, all fiction henceforth was to be socially responsible. Science fiction seemed to catch the brunt of the new policy in many ways. Heroic stereotypes and monstrous adversaries were considered a distraction from the purity of extrapolation, and they were associated with the banished term, "sci-fi," anyway. So without a single disintegrator beam fired, whole armadas of star ships were swept away. Anything that overly excited the adolescent mind was condemned. It was easy enough to single out sexual material or brute violence as culprits (and neither escaped the watchful eye of the authorities) but intellectual stimulation could be more dangerous than the sensual.

The mind itself had to be straightened out. The more fanciful aspects of science fiction were exiled to the same realm as undisciplined fantasy—and so the time machines were loaded onto the magic carpets and shipped off. Then Faster-than-Light drive took up company with reincarnation. And intelligent robots joined vampires in dusty oblivion.

By the time the housecleaning was over, there wasn't a whole lot left. Science fiction had been purged of much of its fiction. Alternate History had been eliminated because of a new ruling against recursive characters. Besides, history was the most dangerous kind of fiction.

Very few writers were still practicing the craft, but those who were doing the current work had been producing material before the new epoch dawned upon the earth. Finally, the few magazines that remained became one magazine. The anthologies became one anthology. And then the unforgettable moment arrived when all novels became one novel. In the end, there were only five writers of the new science fiction. Despite the limitations of the form, they managed to produce millions of words annually.

Not very much happened in their stories. Only one extrapolation was allowed in any given work, regardless of length. And a very strange thing happened. Although science hadn't been forbidden, as had been the case with fantasy, there was less and less science every year. One computer bulletin board offered a prize to the first reader who could find any scientific extrapolation in the year's installment of *The Novel*. Before the authorities closed down that particular BBS, the author responded with an e-mail: "Science is subjective," she wrote, "unless it serves objective social harmony."

Another of the five working writers had made the same sort of observation about characterization, a good indication of the restrictions these creators labored under. Yet, somehow, they continued pouring out millions of words. They were pros. Of course, no one read much anymore in the United States. In science fiction, a few thousand read *The Novel*. Only a few hundred hardened fans read *The Magazine*. Times were bad for legitimate, authorized, high-minded, acceptable SF. Maybe no one was really happy except for The Reviewer, the one fan who did all the reviews of all five writers for his Education Authority approved publication, *The Column*. The five writers took turns receiving an award from this fan every single year, given out at The Convention. The festivities were held in Washington, D.C. They'd moved it there after terrorists eliminated New York City.

Meanwhile, millions of Americans were reading sci-fi! On diskettes. On paper. Over the phone lines. The SS had bragged that no black market could exist in their America—so it seemed pretty clear that the day of liberation was at hand. A computer genius, an expatriate American living in Germany, bragged that he could defeat anything the American SS came up with. His was the holy crusade of the cypher-punks, back for round two. The United States of Europe had become home to many Americans, and those interested in imaginative fiction had congregated around the Ackermuseum in Berlin.

The computer wizard had known the proprietor of the museum personally. They were part of a group that relocated to the bracing freedom of Europe when tyranny extinguished the rocket's glare of American liberty. Now they had a plan to ignite the imagination that must still slumber in their native land.

No government propaganda campaign could stand up against the old classics of Hollywood (and new productions as well) being projected with giant holographic, 3-D images, anywhere, anyplace, anytime. And as a final extra touch, the first test of the new technology would carry a personal meaning for those who had betrayed The Sense of Wonder.

The five writers were attending The Convention in Washington. The Reviewer was doing his usual job as toast master. One hundred and thirty-three really serious fans were attending the awards ceremony. Most of them hadn't read the year's installment of *The Novel*. But most of them had read at least something in *The Magazine*. The Best Editor trophy was about to go to the usual computer program, *Ed-dead*, and the Reviewer was already holding the free-form Jell-O sculpture encased in an ecologically acceptable—and therefore melting—block of ice.

Accepting for the computer program was a writer who insisted he didn't write this junk, but who managed to show up at The Convention anyway. He was putting on a pair of gloves in anticipation of receiving the award that, whatever its intrinsic absurdities, still represented that most important of all extrapolations: money in a bank account.

No sooner was the block of ice in the writer's gloved hands, than he dropped the thing. A thousand little white shards spread across the floor, leaving the ugly blotch of gelatin spinning around as if Dr. Frankenstein had dropped an organ in haste to get away from something. Something terrible. Something like the apparition outside the window.

The writer recognized what he saw...and he screamed; this writer who didn't write "childish twaddle," as he sometimes referred to sci-fi in his more charitable moments, knew a lot more about the field than its current five practitioners. The five were blessed with total ignorance of its history even before the Education Authority had decided to fix everything in sight. The Reviewer and the ex-SF writer were both probably familiar with an old Heinlein classic, *Sixth Column*. The five didn't have a clue.

But everyone who saw a five-hundred foot tall Forrest J Ackerman would never forget it. Nor the ringing words he was speaking, first in Esperanto, then in English translation. The sound came booming out of the sky as if all the thunder of Mount Olympus had been gathered in this one spot. And these were the words:

"Sci-fi *is* my high!"

This is the one time I slavishly copied a style that used to be popular in the New York Lit Crit subdivision of science fiction. The rejection letters were always encouraging but somehow I was missing something. I include the story in this book as an object lesson. Fortunately it is not too long and it admirably sets the stage for the next story.

Executing a Pirouette for Belphegor

"Why do I always anticipate disaster? I don't want to live through it beforehand!"

Many times he'd listened to the desperation in her voice. His agony did not diminish. Flipping on his kindly doctor expression, he half-lectured, "You have imprinted bad experiences. Now you expect them."

They were at the bottom of a well. The well was made of plastalloy and was perpetually alight with an off-pink color. A small circle of blue was the sky above them, made more distant by the filtered lens. Although they had ample room on their big, round bed inside the bigger circle of the well, they felt closed in by the sameness of the surroundings, as indeed they were.

"I know I've used this service a lot," she said; as he looked at the chart with the number of her treatments standing at 13. "One shouldn't ..." Her voice tapered off.

"One shouldn't what?" He could make his voice stern.

"Depend!" she nearly shrieked. He nodded. A passing mark. The well hummed as treatment began.

"Now, a little free association is called for. We start with what you do. You've been a teacher how long?"

She was hurt. "That's not fair."

"Of course you don't remember. That is as it should be." He never liked himself during this stage. He smiled at her. She didn't smile back. That was good. It proved that she needed 14.

"So, let's hear the first thing that comes into your mind when I say...apples!" With the mention of the word came an appropriate fragrance. The well had just been outfitted with all the latest touches.

"Teacher."

He volunteered another fruit: "Oranges."

"Scurvy."

Time to shift gears, he thought, and came out with: "Teaching."

"Shit," was her swift reply. He silently thanked the identi-odor for being linked to his words alone. The well stopped humming;

started playing violin music from some obscure concerto.

"An interesting association," he commented lamely. The good old days of withholding evaluation from patients were long gone. Prudence could no longer be master over the "shrinks" now that they had the machine, or it had them.

"What did I say?" She looked genuinely puzzled, as if she couldn't remember, and after more than ten treatments, maybe she couldn't. There were unexpected holes in the pattern.

Patting himself on top of his bald head, he leaned back against a pillow, the better to contemplate the blue disc above. "You equated education and excrement—or at least the training that passes for 'education' in our cautious institutions. Belphegor would approve."

Pulling the sheet up around her small breasts, she shook her head. "I hate it when you do that."

"What?"

"You're doing it again. First you leave me hanging with a name I've never heard of, but acting as if I should. Now you're playing the innocent. Next you'll...."

He cut her off with a laugh. "Leave what's *next* to me." They lay there in silence for a while, listening to music. He reached under the sheet, and played in a desultory fashion with her right nipple. She would not be distracted.

"Belphegor," he finally got on with it, "was a demon of many specialties. He was as brooding a scholar as any solemn monk, such was his concern for knowledge. And as others in the profession will attest, a suitable offering could be made to him in heaps of dung." The disgust on her face was also a good sign. She didn't really want to think about it; which meant that she was already trying to forget; which meant that she'd be more attuned to what lay in store.

Silence returned. This time they cultivated it. When the music stopped, there was no encore.

He'd made up his mind that she would have to resume the dialogue, and she accepted this. After all, she was paying.

When she spoke, it was the sound of a little girl lost in a dark wood: "Sometimes I'm afraid that I'm giving up my life, piece by piece. Shouldn't I be trying to hold onto it?"

That was his cue, if he'd ever heard one: "That depends on whether you want to hold onto unhappiness." He'd hate himself later for going through with the treatment, but when had that ever stopped him?

She climbed out of bed, and her warm feet on the soft, compliant floor, triggered new responses in the well. The light dimmed, the warmth increased.

"No-one would go through as many treatments as you have who didn't want to be happy."

"Why must I *forget*?" She wanted to sound angry, but her voice was toneless.

"Remembering will make you sad."

"I'll bet you always say that."

"That's something you can't know," was his answer. She looked like the pale women who used to haunt bus stations in the days before tube travel made it more difficult to study strangers, each locked into private miseries. She sighed at him in exasperation, and he noted again how her green eyes were her best feature. They had been what first attracted him so very many years ago.

"Let's finish it," suggested the woman, his patient, his old flame who had forgotten.

"Say aloud what troubles you."

From the manner of her presentation—brows knitted, voice tense, body language a threat to all and sundry—he concluded that she had rehearsed. "I have enemies on the faculty," was how it began. "I have no idea if they are enemies I've had before...but they are certainly after me now!" As she named names, the well trembled at the emotions released. How paranoia tickled plastalloy when it was geared to the machine.

She went on and on: "Since I'm aware of who dislikes me, I can't be at ease around them. That would be asking too much. The turn of a head, a chance remark, the gaping emptiness of a room that was occupied right before I enter...it affects the way I act in the little minutiae of the day. The events cling together and grow like coral! They stifle me! I want to start over again. Please give me another chance. My mind must be purged!"

There were pictures on the wall of the well. They were the pictures she needed to see. She might not have her old dreams any longer, but the well did.

White-capped mountains in high, cold air; flat, featureless deserts; gray-silted craters on the moon; and, finally, black space, without even a glint of starlight. These images were clean for her.

"Lie down," he ordered, but his voice was soft. "I'll hold you."
She hesitated, but the bed was inviting and he *was* her therapist.
Sex was a calculated part.

He stroked her hair, massaged her neck, drew her hand to him.
She was only half there, a few mechanical gestures of masturbation augmenting the hypnotic patterns of the womb they occupied.
The wires in the well, as veins in a living body, pulsed with constant support.

A voice was whispering, "Forget, forget...." and she couldn't tell
if it was the machine or the therapist who spoke. The lights all
around, the sounds from underneath, and the perfume in the air
prepared her to do more than listen—she absorbed.

"To remember the cause of a trauma is not necessarily to overcome it. We used to be in the business of selling fragmented understanding, when what our customers wanted all along was a nar-
cotic. The point was to clear the road of unwanted debris so that
the patient could get back on the job. Anything else is a waste of
time. *Memory* is *insanity*."

There was a rocking motion in the bed, a cradle at the bottom of
a hole. Down there where they can't find you, out of the scary, blue
world.

"We don't want people to become comfortable with their pain. A
thorn is to be found, extracted, thrown away! There is no past. There
is no present. There is only the future of idle daydreams—which
fantasies we choose for you. We know what you want."

Then the voice repeated the same message, more or less, in
French, her other language. Mustn't allow for denials hidden in
another tongue.

When a thin beam of light came down from the top of the well
and touched her brain, it was over. 14. All quiet on the downward
end.

He was smelling perspiration, she was tasting metal, and the well
was glowing in the aftermath of their satisfaction. It was forbidden
that they converse now in any but the most banal pleasantries. This
they did with conviction, and the smiles that they held for each other
were unchangingly tiresome so that when she had been lifted out
of the well by the nurse-tentacle, they both felt a great release as
they relaxed into private frowns. She carried hers all the way home.

Below, he allowed himself the luxury of anger. He wanted to put an end to its gnawing insistence by leaping from the bed and breaking the quivering structure of the well, well, well! How he cursed. It was indestructible, so far as his bare flesh was concerned. Exercises in futility were his recreation. Wrenching his foot with a final kick, he settled for a drawn-out scream, a howl of identity.

He asked for the file. His voice was the well's to obey. Information flashed on the wall space directly in front of the bed.

Sure enough, two of the names she had mentioned were there— chronic patients themselves. He'd even treated one a while back. Although his memory was intact, there were still too many names for easy recall.

"Oh, Janice," he whispered, placing his hand on the gentle valley where she had lain beside him. "Why did it happen?"

He was granted remorse. Others saw it as the price he paid for his position; he held tightly to it as compensation.

While awaiting his next patient, he let his mind wander. In the state he was in, a path was quickly trod —a destination swiftly reached.

He had been her assistant. Although one of many, he'd been a notable talker and worrier. That contributed to the relationship, such as it was. Their first serious disagreement had been over the extent to which The Institute planned to use the new technique of the mind-wipe. He thought that there should be limits placed on the wells, his nickname for the mass produced therapy wombs.

It was perhaps not surprising that as the inventor, she had argued for the widest possible application. At the time, she had no inkling of the nervous breakdown that was crouching in the shadows, waiting for her a mere year down the line. When part of a good mind dies, what is left finds the loss unbearable. For her, this meant the first treatment. For him, it meant the special guilt that only comes with survival.

She gave up her patent to become a patient. Her name was stricken from the records. Eventually her co-workers were "wipes" themselves, except for him. He guarded his position as her permanent therapist, as he guarded his memory.

What wisdom he possessed was derived from a sober understanding of The Institute. Those who owned the wells did not brook any criticism. Predictably they did not desire that the inventor recover her memory. They could not risk her advancing a different point of view.

His task was clear. He was to keep her happy. In return, they let him keep himself...down to the last tantrum.

At the bottom of the well, it was always warm. He waited for more souls descending to his and the machine's smooth embrace.

When Elinor Mavor bought this for the July, 1980 *Fantastic*, my career as a professional fiction writer finally began. I'd been selling journalism and articles for five years before that. I'd also sold short fiction pieces—vignettes—to magazines and newspapers that didn't run a lot of fiction. The thrill of seeing my first professional story in a real science fiction magazine is still fresh in my mind.

"The Competitor" was adapted for an audio magazine, *The Centauri Express*. Bill Ritch did the script. Tom Fuller directed the show. Brad Strickland played the robot conscience. And in a classic stroke of typecasting, I essayed the role of the robot devil.

The audio version had a second life when it was nationally distributed by Sunset Productions. But the actual story itself has never been seen again since its original appearance in *Fantastic*. At one point, Jerry Pournelle was going to edit an anthology called *Silicon Brains* and he told me that he wanted the story for his book, but the project didn't come off.

So you hold in your hands the first book appearance of the story that started it all for me. I wrote it with the opposite approach of "Belphegor." I didn't study any contemporary examples. I remembered my favorite stories from the fifties and pretended I was back there.

I will always be grateful to Elinor Mavor for giving me my first break. Before I took the story to her, I received the most insane rejection of my life from another editor, who informed me that I had done a "Gernsbackian catalogue of wonders" with insufficient attention to character. As I had recently received a master's degree from Rollins College that could honestly be described as "Liberal Arts Dude, Not Good For Practical Stuff," I could not believe I came off as an engineer type.

"The Competitor" is a character piece and a psychological story. What's good and bad in my writing is all here.

The Competitor

I was implanted at the base of his brain. Jack purchased me at a discount and got the operation free. Shortly after I was inside I learned the whole story. Jack's parents were the first to suggest he try it when they saw him over Christmas. His wife seconded the motion with a passion he hadn't noticed in her for years. So he came to see Dr. Brock, the man who made me.

"Your problem is commonplace," Brock had said. "Otherwise I wouldn't be in business." He chuckled at his observation but Jack just sat there and waited. Jack was never known for his humor. "What you need is a dependable C-31. That's the standard model. Nothing fancy."

"What is a fancy one?" asked Jack.

"Oh, just trimmings. People who like to think of themselves as erudite, or above the herd if you like, will order a culture model—it recites Shakespeare to them. The advice they receive is the same as if they were using a C-31. They feel it is less mundane, and within our little world it is sort of a status symbol I suppose."

"Do you think I'm mundane?"

Brock laughed. "No, Jack. Please don't misunderstand me. But the forms you filled out, the tests you took, the interviews ... all indicate you'd simply be happier with the standard model. Frankly, you don't seem to have any preferences. Is there something you haven't told us? A hobby perhaps?"

Jack took a few seconds to answer: "No."

"Well then, it's settled."

Dr. Brock put me in Jack's head the very same afternoon. It didn't take more than thirty minutes. The operation is so smooth you can't even detect a scar when it's over. So there I was, snugly in Jack's cranium. His new friend. It didn't take long to find out why Jack needed me. My programming prepared me to assimilate information directly from Jack's mind. He thinks, therefore I am. I lived through the conversation preceding the operation (old Brock strikes me as a bit pompous). And then Jack and I talked about his problems. (That doesn't sound quite right, of course. I should say we had a dialogue at the nonverbal level. Just our two voices-in-the-mind whispering back and forth.)

"I'm your new conscience," I said.

"You're a C-31," he answered. "You're not real. I'd have to be born with a conscience, and since I never had one, you're what I end up with."

"You shouldn't feel that way," I said. "Lots of people admit they have consciences but then do the most horrible things. Any good psycho-historian can give you a dozen examples of dictators who fit the pattern. The fact is that everyone has a conscience of some kind. It is what they choose to do about it that makes the difference. I'm an *aid* to you, Jack. I'll become part of the conscience you already have." I thought I handled that rather well; diplomacy without being patronizing.

"A disc in my head, that's what you are," he said morosely. It took me a moment to realize he had said that sentence out-loud!

"Jack, you've just made a blunder. You shouldn't ..."

"I know," he said, non-verbal again. "That would sound to any passerby like I was talking to myself."

"Not out loud, Jack! That's all you have to remember. Because you really are 'talking' to yourself. I am you. Get that through your head—if you'll excuse the choice of words—and we'll get along fine. Don't think of me as a 'me'."

"If only I could get over this idea that I'm inferior. I need you the way I need a crutch. Lots of other people are walking around without these things in their heads."

"You'd be surprised how many famous, successful people avail themselves of this service."

"Exceptions! You and I both know ..."

"You're getting schizophrenic."

"We both know ..."

"Same difference."

"Oh hell, I know that most people think that the Conscience Industry mainly deals with criminals. Dr. Brock made his breakthrough as a prison doctor! Then he branched out into the marketplace."

"So what?"

"I'm not a criminal."

"It's all the more to your credit that you volunteered."

"You've been in my head long enough," he said, "to know this wasn't my choice. I haven't made a real choice in years."

I knew. A part of his past that never left him was the knowledge that he hadn't married the woman he had wanted—instead, he let himself be influenced by his parents in their self adopted role as match-maker.

That night I met his wife. The image he carried of her in his mind made her appear older and, well, coarser than she actually was. "You don't look any different," she said without preamble.

"It's in my head."

"Well?" she asked.

"Well?" he asked back.

"Hey," I whispered. "Smile at her. Show her some teeth." He smiled but it was forced. "No, not like that," I went on. "Put some warmth into it." He tried again. It worked this time.

"Come over here," she said. He did, and they made love right there in the living room. For a while we didn't have any dialogue. Jack was content. But later that night I had to earn my keep. There was trouble.

I already knew that they disagreed about Jack's job. The argument had been going on for months now. "How can you disagree with me?" she asked, in a shocked tone of voice. "They promised me you'd be all right after today."

Here's where I came in. Jack was hurt by her comment, but the pain was dulled. After years of denying his feelings, you'd almost expect those feelings to be dead. It isn't so. They lie dormant.

Some might criticize what I did next. But it was my job. Dr. Brock had no intention of disrupting society. Dangerous potential was in his work, but he held a tight reign over the implementation of his theories. All kinds of moralists attacked him but he maintained he was giving society what it wanted.

I told Jack to give in. He did. The argument ended that night. The next day Jack went to work. He was manager at a plant. By noon he had fired a man, one of those new college grads who think they know everything. The problem wasn't with the young man's ideas— he had suggested a plan that would save the company some money in the first month. But his personality grated on his fellow workers, the ones who had been at the job for years. It had gotten to a point where if Jack didn't fire the new man, he might get himself in trouble when a company re-shuffling came.

Something had made Jack reticent to do his duty. A feeling. It was driving his wife crazy with worry that he would place anything ahead of the security of his family; of her, in other words, as there were no children. Obviously he needed a good conscience to help him do what was right.

We discussed it later. "Why did you make me do it?" he asked.

"There you go again, playing Jekyll and Hyde with yourself. I am you, not somebody else."

"A conscience should get you to do what is right," he said.

"Right for whom?"

"But the guy was doing his job."

"Was he? Wasn't part of his job to fit in? His personality was getting in the way of his ability to do what was expected of him. You have six months of memories of him—and I see from the self-righteous attitude he displayed today that your memories are accurate. You did the right thing."

"It didn't seem right."

"What about your responsibilities?"

"Well, with you around, I mean with my new understanding of things, it was easier to do. If not right."

"You'll get over it. Give it time." I paused, then hit him with: "Why do you resent your wife?"

"If you want to find out everything," he said unhappily, "then root around in my mind yourself, you crummy little disc."

I kept after him: "Do you know who else you resent?"

"Besides you? Or me, or whatever the hell I'm talking to? You tell me."

"Parents, teachers, bosses ..."

"So I'm a pretty normal guy!" Jack decided he was tired of sitting around the house and went for a walk. A few minutes later he opened up again. "You remember what I said about choice?"—As if I could forget!—"Sometimes I think my whole life has been planned for me in advance. First it was my parents, then my wife, and now you."

"This attitude is at the core of your problem."

"Why do you refer to me in the second person, if you're me? Ha, I caught you there."

"Dialogue forces us into little awkwardnesses. You just keep remembering that what I tell you are your decisions. Now, before we go any further, answer one question. Do you feel better than you used to?"

"Yeah." There was no hesitation, I was pleased to note. "I was having headaches before. Really bad ones. That was one of the reasons she suggested I see Dr. Brock."

"Then your wife does care."

"Wait a minute!" His mind literally shouted. For a moment I thought he'd speak out loud but I was pleased to see he held himself in check."

"What?"

"The voices are gone!"

That was a wonderful moment for me. From the beginning, I had understood that a major objective of my tenure in Jack's skull was to free him from the counterfeit consciences that had been hounding him for years. In the absence of a firm conviction on his part to be responsible for his actions, the voices had grown. He was suffering in a self-created limbo between the urgings of his deepest convictions and the demands of the people he lived and worked with. The voices yammering in his brain were more than a little familiar: they were Mom and Pop, a bully in the old neighborhood, his first girl friend, aunts and uncles, a sundry boss or two ... and of course his wife. Now they were silenced. I did the job they had done.

His wife was happier than she'd been in years. She sensed his new found commitment to the things she believed in. The urgings from deeper wells in Jack's mind simply dissipated. Such is the nature of getting a C-31.

For the first few months it was necessary for Jack to check in with Dr. Brock. This was really nothing more than a formality. Because of a zealous young Senator attempting to impose regulations on the industry, Brock had become sensitive to public relations. The catch-phrase around the office was, "We Don't Forget Your Trust In Us."

"Your employers have been in touch with me," Brock said, beaming. "They are pleased with the way you handled a problem on the job shortly after the implant. Congratulations."

"Thank you," said Jack without prompting.

"From the way they were praising you, I wouldn't be surprised to learn there's a promotion ahead for you." Then Brock ran the tests. Routine procedure; routine result.

All was well with my world. Jack was a success.

Looking back, I still don't forgive myself for losing control of the situation only a week after the visit to Brock. It is not smart for a disc to attempt to dictate, except a little bit at a time. You don't want to turn the host's mind against you. But I was too soft, I guess.

If only Jack hadn't run into Phil at that damned bar. Jack was already drinking too much that night. He hardly needed Phil's bad example. I had noticed a gradual increase in Jack's alcohol consumption. Drink was the one flaw in my work. My victories that had seemed so secure were starting to show hairline cracks.

Phil sat there, a grin on his round face, as he ordered Jack another Scotch on the rocks. My attempts to warn Jack were met with stubborn resistance. I knew that Phil was the subversive element in Jack's past. Sooner or later I'd have to be able to deal not only with him but with any future Phils. I did not doubt that I could pass the test.

Phil's high, sarcastic voice got right to the point: "I hear you have it in your head now."

"It's true."

"A shame," said Phil. "I didn't think you'd really do it." They drank in silence for a moment. I kept quiet. It was best to find out what Phil was up to before counseling Jack.

"I don't mean to disturb you," said Phil at last, "but you know what I think of Dr. Brock." Jack inclined his head and continued absently swirling ice in his glass. "This so-called Conscience Industry is curious to say the least. Have you ever heard of a disc being removed? Is there a record of a single dissatisfied customer?"

Now was the time! I told Jack to get out of there; had he been sober, I'm sure he would have left. Damn the alcohol in his system. Try as I might, his will remained just out of reach. He turned a pained expression in Phil's direction.

"What's the matter?" Phil wanted to know. "Won't that thing let you answer?"

"Look, you've got it wrong. I'm still me. I decide what to do."

"Yeah?" said Phil. "I'll bet that thing is telling you to call this conversation short." I was taken by surprise. For a moment I stopped my entreaties.

Phil wasn't giving up. "Would you put it to a test?" he asked.

"What do you mean?"

"A bet. Like the good old days. I'll even give you the better odds."

This was probably where I made an error in judgment. It had reached a point where I thought my best course of action was not to advise Jack what to do. Not then, anyway. Phil had made him self-conscious. I hoped that his good sense—for despite anything else amiss with my host, he had an admirable survival mechanism pre-dating me—would see him through.

"What's the bet?"

Phil kept grinning. I didn't like the look of that at all. It was too big a smile, making his orange face appear a jack-o'-lantern. "Jack, you know my work has paralleled Brock's. I'm qualified to criticize him."

"I know that your attempt failed to get Brock's business outlawed. The court did not find that the Conscience Industry is an invasion of privacy. That new Senator isn't doing any better."

"The operation was your wife's idea," said Phil, his smile gone. "She has probably fed you every detail that was printed in the gossip rags about how I went off half-cocked against poor Dr. Brock."

"She's never approved of you."

"Nor I her. So we're even. The bet doesn't involve her. It's between you and me." Phil finished his drink. "This isn't the place to give you my proposition. If you're still free, then come over to my place for a visit."

One of Jack's old voices came back into his head at that point, without any prompting from me. Clear as a bell, I heard his wife telling him he'd better not go. To side with that voice was, I felt, at this point not a prudent thing to do. Despite the garbage this Phil character was feeding him about being enslaved to his disc, Jack knew he could do what he wanted.

They left. Phil's house was in walking distance and they were strolling up his driveway in a few minutes. A black cat eyed them suspiciously from a window. Once they were inside, though, the cat did not appear again. This had me thinking that the creature was a familiar of this smooth talking wizard (I'm not a bard, but like all C-31's I have a culture/history background to draw upon).

"Be careful," I warned Jack.

"You've decided to talk again," he answered. "Relax, Phil is an old friend."

"They can be the most dangerous kind," I said.

They sat down in two comfortable old chairs, a stonework coffee table between them with a bottle of brandy and small glasses already set out. I could feel Jack's thirst, the anticipation of the burning liquid going down, so l didn't bother raising any objections. He reached out, took the glass offered him and sipped. It wasn't the liquor that tipped me off that something was wrong; it was the intent expression on Phil's face, as he said, "Remember the games we used to play when we were kids?"

Jack did. So I did. An awkward part of my job is that all sorts of knowledge is available to me only when Jack dregs it up from the misty regions of the deep mind. I suppose Brock thinks that a C-31 shouldn't be omniscient. Or maybe there is a technical problem involved. I don't know my limit on data. Self knowledge can be a dangerous thing, even for a Conscience. Anyway, I do what I'm supposed to.

The image that flashed through Jack's mind was of Phil, the practical joker. Phil said: "The bet is that you will approve, eventually, of a stunt I've prepared for you."

"Get to the point," Jack answered but the words were slurred. He was starting to feel dizzy.

"Maybe you don't know it," Phil continued, "but that C-31 in your head can't be taken out or nullified without killing you! They say it's a problem in their technique and cover for themselves with verbal obfuscation in the contract, but it all boils down to a simple lie. They don't want you to have an option. Don't forget these things were developed for ex-convicts; the good folk didn't feel secure about criminals walking the streets. Nobody really believes in rehabilitation!

"There's a rumor, Jack, that the government has a plan to give tax breaks to 'discees.' Who knows, there may come a day when the law requires everyone to have a disc. Brock would love that."

"Phil," said Jack, his fingers suddenly numb as his glass fell to the floor and shattered into small, fine shards, "you've drugged this drink."

I shouted advice! I envisioned Jack's body running, running, getting away. But the body was going under.

"I can't remove the C-31," said Phil, "but I can put something in. My device won't be booby-trapped—it can be taken out again. Only I predict you won't want to."

"Phil, Phil ..." Jack tried to stand up. Phil walked over and put a hand on his shoulder.

"Stop fighting," he said. "There is nothing else you can do."

I was screaming at this point: "Call the police, get help!" It was hopeless.

"Why ..." Jack began but he fell forward, unconscious. Phil pushed Jack back into the chair and I heard his footsteps walking away. I was still conscious, of course. I always was. Often when Jack slept, and dreamed, I reviewed the day's events, planning for the next waking period. That is why it was such a shock for me when Phil came back in, walked over to Jack and whispered in his right ear:

"Hi, Conscience. I know you can hear me. I have something in my hand that will put you to sleep. It won't last longer than the operation, however, or I could kill you and let my aid to Jack end there. Prepare yourself for a mild electric charge." A small circle of cold metal was pressed against Jack's head and ...

And when I came to, Jack was still unconscious at the bottom of a black, dreamless pit. I could feel that his body was back in his car that had been parked outside the bar. Phil was sure to be gone. I also noticed that I was no longer alone in Jack's head. I had company.

"Good morning," it said.

"What? Who the hell are you?"

"I'm a disc in Jack's head, same as you. Only I have a different purpose."

"What is that?"

"You'll see! Incidentally, he won't be able to hear you for a while. He'll be too busy listening to me. By the time my energy level has dropped to where you may be heard again, it will hopefully be too late."

"Too late for what?" But it had nothing else to say. Not to me, at any rate.

Jack woke up. The new disc went right to work. Jack noticed the difference in voices and wondered what was speaking to him. "I'm your anti-conscience," it said. He still didn't understand, but I was beginning to. "Jack, I'm your personal devil." Jack still felt groggy but he drove home. The devil sang him a song about piracy on the high seas as he drove through an upper-middle class residential section.

In one week, the devil had managed to undo all of my work. Jack began by telling his wife to shut up. The new disc egged him on. When she persisted in complaining he slapped her round face. It wasn't that hard a blow but she fell to the floor with a shocked expression that made Jack smile. By the time she recovered enough to call the police, her mother, Dr. Brock and the lawyer, Jack was gone.

He went directly to Dr. Brock's office and punched him. Since nothing like that had ever happened to Brock before, he didn't have security measures to prevent it. As Jack was on the way out the door, Brock started yelling into the intercom about how the C-31 had malfunctioned. So that's what the good professor thought of my work without even bothering to gather data! I was so mad I didn't care what Jack did next.

He went through the exit door at a run. As he was going down the steps, I noticed that he was having difficulty catching his breath. Not used to this kind of exertion, I guess. Well, I supposed it was better he should be tired out than attack someone in the elevator.

No sooner were we outside than he entered a post office and bought a postcard. For the first time, it occurred to me that this devil thing in Jack's head had a sense of humor. The note he was scribbling congratulated the anti-Brock Senator for his good work.

I caught myself laughing. It was a new sensation. I didn't even know I could do *that*. There wasn't much time to appreciate it, though, as the devil had Jack leaving a trail of outraged faces behind him that anyone could follow. Jack found the district manager of his company and punched him out for having forced Jack into firing the young man; he wrote his letter of resignation on the unconscious administrator's shirt.

Then he found the man (who had been reduced to working as a waiter) and gave him a couple of hundred out of his own pocket. That man's expression was more memorable than all the others. Talk about astonishment! During this interlude, Jack almost seemed to relax. The young man offered him a drink but Jack uncharacteristically turned it down.

The devil jabbered on with a melancholy sameness about the necessity of revenge; and Jack made it happen.

As Jack went on his incautious way, I felt my power returning. The other disc had been expending an enormous amount of energy—as it had promised— and now was winding down to a more manageable output. Soon I would be heard again. But what would I say? I realized my voice would be no stronger than that of the devil's.

Before I could be heard, Jack did the most surprising thing of all. He took a train to his home-town and looked up his parents. They were two old frail people living in a little white house. I was afraid Jack was going to rush in the door and throttle both of them. The memories that came back to him in a flood were pure nightmare. The devil urged him to throw open the door. There they sat, reading newspapers and watching television. He got their attention: "Go to hell," he said, but he took a good, close look at the shadowy faces that turned in his direction and realized that they were already there. The devil was satisfied. The son left without their having said a word.

I first noticed that Jack was becoming tired of the devil's harangue when he quite suddenly told it to shut up. He said this aloud. But that damned disc just kept on talking, the dirty little invader!

Even as I condemned the interloper, I noticed something about myself—I had come to feel differently about Jack. Then I realized the truth *I didn't know what to say to him.* Soon I'd have to do something ...

The devil kept at it the rest of the day but Jack was too tired to comply with any more diabolical requests. He took a room in a cheap motel where he collapsed into a slumber neither of us could possibly interrupt. Finally the devil's voice faded away and all I heard was Jack's snoring.

It was then that I conceived my plan. As the devil's output frequency was dropping in line with mine, I realized there would be a split second when we would be in resonance. I waited.

About four a.m. the phone rang. Jack groggily answered: "Hh-ello?" It was Phil. Don't ask me how he found us, but it was his high, nasal twang asking Jack how things were going.

I told Jack to tell him to fuck off. Jack heard me. He did. "Hey," said Jack as he hung up "you sound different ... you almost sound like my old disc."

"It's me, jack. Your C-31." He thought about that. We hadn't talked in a long while.

"Welcome back," he aid softly. "But where's the other one?"

"It's still in your head," I said. "Wake up, devil ... say something!"

Silence. "Why isn't it talking?" Jack asked.

"Maybe it has nothing to say."

Jack scratched the top of his head and said, "You've probably been thinking all this time, huh, C-31? I suppose you'll want me to make amends for what I've done."

"No," I said, and surprised myself. "Leave it alone."

"What? Are you the C-31 or not?"

"Sure I am, but I've got a soul, haven't I? I've learned some important things. I've been wrong."

He sat on the edge of the bed and pondered. Then he raised his hand to his head and struck himself in the temple with the flat of his palm.

"What did you do that for?" I asked.

"Knocking some sense into my cranium. I'm also checking on the devil up there. Is he asleep or what?"

"You know, Jack, you've got a lot of brains. I haven't paid much attention to that because I've been too busy having you work against yourself. Maybe it's time you started using all that intelligence."

"You mean that?" he asked.

"Sure. You'll see that I can be a big help. When I want to."

"What about the devil? Should I have it removed with surgery?"

I decided to tell him. "It's just a lump of organic plastic. You see, the devil and I are harmonious now. I did it while you slept."

Jack laughed. It was better than my laugh. It was the nicest sound I've ever heard.

"I'm thinking about an old movie," he said. "You ever see *Casablanca?*"

"No, Jack. You've never taken me to a movie."

He got up, smiled at himself in the mirror, and said, "I think this is the beginning of a beautiful friendship."

My agent represents Christopher Pike, the most successful YA writer in the world. Pike gets the teenagers after they've graduated from R. L. Stine and before they become hooked on Stephen King. So when I was invited to try my hand for an anthology that Pike would edit, I jumped at the chance of trying a new style (fully aware that the final result would still be heavily Linaweaverized).

The book in question didn't come off but the story was written with nowhere to go. I include it here because of the eclectic content of this book. And because I like it.

The Broken Charm

"You need to get on with your life!"

Sixteen year old Claire Russell thought the only good thing about the person who wanted to murder her was that he didn't say that stupid sentence she'd heard so many times she could scream.

This guy was more likely to say she needed to get on with her death. She didn't like the idea of dying. She didn't like the idea of never hearing music again or feeling the sun on her face or tasting tears; her tears or someone else's tears on her lips....

Only a few weeks earlier she thought she had a problem. She was immortal then. Horror and death were for other people. She only had to put up with a jerk who wouldn't look her straight in the eye as he said: "You need to get on with your life!"

She'd heard those words many times before. Ever since her mother first said them to her father, Claire felt something hard and heavy grow in her breast. She didn't hate her mother but she promised herself that she would never say anything like that to anyone she loved. She was only twelve when her parents divorced. Two weeks before her sixteenth birthday it was her turn to be on the receiving end of the terrible phrase.

"What do you know about my life?" she answered Ed Sommers, the acid in her voice seeming to dissolve the confidence in the face of the most handsome boy in school. She was every bit as surprised as he was at the anger coming out of her.

He blinked, opened his mouth...and said nothing. She suddenly realized how much time she'd wasted worrying herself sick over whether this big beefcake loved her. He wasn't very smart but everyone considered him a great catch. Most girls weren't allowed to date until they were sixteen but Claire discovered there were certain advantages to having divorced parents. And she looked two years older than her real age.

Of course, when she looked in the mirror, she thought herself about average in appearance and lucky to be going steady with Ed. On this Friday afternoon, the last day of school before summer vacation, she could accept that she didn't really like Ed.

"Is that all you have to say?" she asked, going on the offensive.

"I'm trying to make it easy on you," he answered without much conviction. He was stuck in a rut as if he were an old man. He was only a year and a half older. Something told her that he'd never been challenged before when he gave a girl the brush-off.

Yeah, that's it, she thought. *He throws out that stupid cliche about getting on with your life and expects me to go away and leave him alone. He says it like it's a magic spell!*

Other kids gathered around, with wide eyes and smiles, attracted by the smell and sound and sight of *trouble*. Claire watched them watching her. No good friends of hers made up that crowd.

As Claire felt their eyes burning into her, she didn't feel worried or afraid. In a strange way, she was grateful to the time she'd spent with Ed. She wasn't as shy as she used to be. As she had become more confident in herself, he tended to pull away from her. Now she felt that a confrontation was inevitable. There was a sense of liberation that, somehow, it was already over. She wouldn't hold anything back.

"Since when do you care how I feel?" she challenged him at the top of her voice.

"We had a good time," he said, "but it's over."

Of all the things she could have done to him at that moment, she chose the one most wounding to his pride. She laughed. He didn't like that.

"I can't believe I ever got involved with you," she said. "You've probably forgotten my birthday is next weekend and breaking up with you is the perfect present!"

"At least he won't be paying you alimony," said Steve, one of Ed's friends who prided himself on being the school funny man. The only problem was that no one laughed at his jokes.

"But Claire, I thought you believe people should stay together," came a calm, cool voice. She turned to see Debbie making up part of the makeshift audience. The girl was petite, quiet, and as introverted as Claire used to be. Debbie's large brown eyes gazed deeply into Claire as if to say that she was completely sincere. This girl wouldn't even know how to do a put-down.

"That's how I feel about marriages," Claire said.

"Hey, I gave you the best three months of my life," said Ed. Steve laughed. Claire felt as if she'd stepped into another universe where Ed had a sense of humor. It seemed a little late for him to develop one now.

The sun was in her eyes. Now so many students had been attracted by the shouting that the hallway was crowded. Not very long ago she would have gone to great lengths to protect her privacy. It was good not to care any longer.

"Remember our first date?" she asked him, and the mention of something personal made him uncomfortable. "You said you liked girls who are unpredictable." She figured now was a good time for a reminder. She rushed toward him so fast that he involuntarily backed away from her. She shoved her face right in his and saw the truth that poor old Ed couldn't tell a joke to save his life. She couldn't help noticing that his features were sort of round and bland. Maybe he wasn't all that handsome after all.

"Show's over," she announced, her chin raised, facing the others. Turning on her heel, she started for home.

"You're a bitch," said Dianne, a year older and with her green eyes fixed on Ed's mop of blond hair. The way Ed returned her gaze left little doubt about why he was so eager to end his great romance with Claire.

"Don't worry," Claire answered Dianne. "If you work at it, you can be one, too." Steve laughed again. And all of a sudden Claire felt much better. Why be mad at Ed when she could be mad at herself?

It felt wonderful to walk away from all the emotions he'd made her feel. But somehow she realized this was not the same as getting on with her life. She thought if there was any justice, then something exciting would happen on her birthday.

Uncle Dennis lost an eye in the Vietnam War. He refused to use a glass eye because he said they were grotesque and unnatural. So he wore an eye patch and did pirate voices for Claire ever since she was a kid. He was the best part of the summer, living in the big old house in the woods near Mirror Lake. He lived there with Aunt Fi and the two of them collaborated on books about superstitions and the occult.

"I'm glad you don't think you're too old for this, missy," he said, offering her an ice-cold beer. They sat in two old rockers on the pen-air porch. Everything was wood. Claire loved the house and the tangy aroma of the fresh pine trees.

"I'll have a coke," she replied.

"Ahhrrrr," he did his best Long John Silver, "you're sort of young for hard drugs. Will you settle for a soda pop?"

One of the advantages of Mom and Dad's divorce had been more time spent with her crazy uncle (and slightly crazy aunt). Mom was so pissed off with Dad that she was happy for Claire to spend extra time with nearly anyone else, even a bad influence like Dennis. Claire liked him because he actually paid attention to her and answered any question she put to him. Uncle Dennis was a brave old coot.

"Here you are," he said, passing her the requested drink with lots of ice. "What do you have planned for your birthday this year, since you're stuck here?"

Mom might have been reluctant for Claire to spend two weeks with her uncle if she'd known that Aunt Fi would be visiting a sick friend for a big chunk of it. But Claire always felt safe when she was with him.

"Guess I'll open my presents from Mom and Dad," she said. "Mom promised me a party when I get back."

"And Dad gives you one later in the year, doesn't he?" asked her uncle sympathetically. She nodded. "Parents can't help but compete for their children," he sighed, "even when the marriages hang together. It's especially hard on an only child."

"Why didn't you and Aunt Fi have kids?" asked Claire. She'd thought about it before but never had the nerve to ask.

"We've had fun trying," he said, with a grin to match any old time buccaneer. "No luck. We'd adopt except that we have our hearts set on one of our own. And how's your love life?"

She told him about Ed.

He had an answer for everything: "The trouble with you kids today is that you spend so much time making each other miserable that you don't leave yourselves any time to make out."

"Don't forget AIDS, uncle."

"What's to forget? Sex has always been dangerous; and not all of it is equally dangerous anyway." He scratched at his eye patch, a nervous habit when he noticed he was sailing into dangerous waters. It was obviously time to change the subject: "So what do you have in mind today on your sixteenth birthday?"

"I dunno."

"Sweet sixteen," he amended. "I see you're wearing your charm bracelet." She smiled and held it up for his inspection. Aunt Fi gave her the silver bracelet on her tenth birthday and since then she had been adding the usual sort of things, always silver. Last birthday her aunt and uncle had given her a beautiful pair of ballerina slippers. She was pleased to see Uncle Dennis take out a tiny little box and pass it to her.

"Thanks," she said before opening it.

"Sorry about it not being wrapped but I'm all thumbs when it comes to even normal sized presents."

"Sort of difficult with that hook of yours," she commented, smiling.

There was a full beat before he laughed. "The best thing about you making jokes is that you tell them dead-pan," he said. "Missing an eye is enough pirating for me because..."

She didn't mean to interrupt him but couldn't help herself blurting out: "Awesome!" She held up a little silver cage that barely fit into the snug confines of the box and held it up to the light. From deep inside the miniature silver prison something glinted, blood-red.

"It's red agate," he said, "a very special red agate."

"Intense!"

"I love your vocabulary," he said.

She smiled a bit sheepishly. "There are many ways," she began, then frowned in thought—"to express joy," she finished triumphantly. 'Joy' was uncle's favorite word.

He reached over and patted her on the shoulder, and she was glad he didn't have a hook. "You should make A's in English composition."

"I do."

"I know."

"What do you write about?"

"How boys are dorks," she said without thinking.

"Ah, yes," he said, and patted her shoulder again before leaning back in his chair. "I'll tell you a secret. Wherever there is desire, there is dishonesty. And both sexes are so full of badness it's a wonder the human race survives."

"You're not a dork, Uncle Dennis," she said, standing up and kissing him on the cheek, right under his eye-patch. "You've always treated me like an adult." While they chatted she added her new treasure to the charm bracelet.

"You've made that easy," he replied...and he seemed sad for some reason. "There's a secret to your agate that most adults could never understand. Listen closely and I'll whisper it to you."

This seemed a bit odd as they were completely alone, but she bent down and felt the scratching of his beard against her ear as he told her a story:

"Real magic exists, but it can only be used by those who are willing to sacrifice everything they have in the world, even their souls. Long ago a young man gave his true love a red stone as testament to how he felt—a symbol of his heart. She loved him deeply. She happily accepted his gift. Either would have died for the other and so they married. Of course, in those days people were not as afraid of death as they are now. They believed in forces greater than life and death, without which belief there is no magic.

"Another woman loved this man and had sworn to destroy any lover he would choose over her. She knew the power of the red stone. Its magic helped lovers find an endless variety of new people in each other. With its power it was impossible for a husband and wife to ever become bored. Naturally the woman thought that by breaking the stone she would destroy their marriage.

"The happy couple kept the stone in their bed chamber. The jealous woman hired a man to steal it for her. He brought it to her and she took a hammer and smashed it into many pieces, one of which you now possess on your charm bracelet."

Uncle Dennis lifted his head from her ear, and finished off his beer in one big swallow. Wiping his lips with the back of his hand, he leaned back in his chair and looked at his niece as if he were waiting for something.

"That's it?" Claire asked. "What happened to the lovers?"

"The husband and wife," he added. "They still loved each other. And the jealous woman did not have her revenge." He examined the bottom of his mug as if some beer might still be hiding from him. "There's just one thing..."

"I hate it when you do that," said Claire. "I want the end of the story as another birthday present."

He laughed. "You win. The only thing the jealous woman changed was that the husband and wife found other lovers, as many of them as there were broken pieces of the red stone. The lovers didn't know who it was that stole their magical stone and the man continued to have no interest in the jealous woman."

Claire's naturally suspicious nature didn't take long to start the warning bells. "No way," she said, laughing. "I don't believe that. Mom always said you never got over the sixties."

As if to prove Mom's point, Uncle Dennis patted Claire on the knee. She could have done without that. Then he stood up, slowly, and went inside the house where she heard him open the refrigerator. He came back with another beer and poured it in his personal stein. He never drank out of the bottle.

Sitting down, he pushed back in his rocker and sighed, rocked and drank for a full minute. She thought he was overdoing his normal routine. Finally, he spoke in a good, loud voice. "Claire, your mother believes she's rediscovered morality. And naturally she's divorced. Your Aunt Fi and I believe in something more old fashioned. We think divorce is a lot worse than the trivial sins people use to justify their divorces."

At first, she almost laughed…but the heavy thing inside her turned the sound that came out of her into a sob. She didn't realize she was crying until she felt the dampness on her cheek and the salt taste on her lips. The really weird thing was that she wanted to agree with him. She really, really did. But what came out was a big surprise.

"Damn you!" she said. "You know how I feel. How could you say that to me?"

Next she surprised herself by throwing the remains of her coke down on the hard wood surface of the porch where the glass broke into several large pieces. A small part of her brain was glad that none of her drink splashed on her uncle. Normally she didn't go in for temper tantrums. She'd never been like that, not even as a kid. Uncle Dennis watched her with his one eye. He didn't move or show emotion. He'd never seen an outburst from her before.

She vaulted off the porch and ran into the woods, feeling really stupid—like she was eight years old or something. Another part of her brain seemed to be watching herself from a great distance. A small voice deep in her head moaned: *So this is how you're getting on with your life.*

He was the most handsome male specimen she'd ever seen, better looking than a movie star or rock musician. She guessed his age at nineteen, twenty tops. His face was a study in angular lines. The cheekbones were so high that she wondered if she'd cut herself by touching them. And she wanted to touch his face very badly. She wanted her hand against his tanned cheek moving down to his beautifully proportioned chest and further down to his flat stomach. Beyond that she was afraid to think.

She was glad he was in bathing trunks that looked great on his bronze body! But his outfit made sense as they met at the lake. Fifteen minutes of running through the woods brought her face to face with this Greek god as he climbed on the dock. He shook water from his face with a shake of his head and never once touched the handsome profile with his hands. Instead, he ran his fingers through his hair which was almost as black as his trunks.

Mirror Lake was well named. It made two of him, the blue of the sky and its perfect reflection in the water giving her twin views of his lean, swimmer's body.

She stopped running and tried to catch her breath, standing there panting. She felt like her pet cat with its first view of red meat in a long time. Everything was very quiet all of a sudden.

Walking closer, she made eye contact and noticed his long, fine eyelashes. Then she looked at his strong mouth with its thin lips starting to move. He spoke to her and his deep voice—an actor's voice, a preacher's voice—snapped her out of her trance. She couldn't believe that someone she was meeting for the first time, a total stranger, could begin a conversation by asking:

"Are you happy?"

"No," she blurted out. Honesty was a bad habit of hers. There was something electric in the air. She could feel her breath in her chest and tension drained out of her. "Are you?" she asked back.

"Always," he answered, grinning slowly. "You have a nice smile. My name is Leo."

"I'm Claire," she said quickly.

"Why don't you come in for a swim?" he suggested.

"I don't have a bathing suit," she answered, eyes slitted, cautious; but curious about how far he might push his suggestion.

His silky, smooth voice mad him sound very reasonable. "You have a T-shirt and shorts. Why don't you kick off your sneakers and come in as you are?"

That was good enough for her. But she wasn't going to risk losing her charm bracelet. She removed it and left it in one of her open sneakers and then ran right past the boy on the dock and dived in past him. It was exciting to be close to him as he stood there, watching her sleek, young body dive into the lake.

Claire was a good swimmer. Dad taught her. At first she'd been afraid of the water but he knew how to make her trust him and that led to trusting her ability to hold her breath. Part of the fun came from the slight risk of death. Love is was what you depend on to resist death.

She broke surface and spun around to see what had become of Leo. He wasn't on the dock. Treading water, she looked around. He couldn't have disappeared into the woods that quickly so he must have dived in behind her. But where…. ?

By expecting to see him surface near her she was unprepared for his coming up underneath and grabbing her by the ankle. This was a guy who took her breath away, literally. She was terrified, but only for a moment because as soon as she was submerged he let go of her and darted up quickly as a dolphin to look her in the eye. How did he know she'd open her eyes to see what was happening? He kissed her hard while they were still under the water, and then they were back on the surface. She gasped for breath and took a swing at him that didn't come anywhere near hitting him.

"You're crazy," she sputtered.

"Don't hold that against me," he said in a voice so cheerful that it virtually begged her to forgive him.

"You shouldn't do things like that," she said, hating the sound of her own voice.

"How old are you?" he asked out of nowhere.

"Uh, I'm eight…" she started to tell her usual lie and then thought better of it. "Why should I tell you?" she asked defiantly.

"Because we like each other," he threw back at her.

He was very annoying; and he was right! "I'm sixteen," she blurted out. "So you better watch it!" She said this last in a mocking tone of voice, a gentle kidding she often used with older guys.

"I'm never afraid of that," he said. "The residue of baby fat you have right now is a lot more attractive than the other kind that comes later."

"Huh?" She didn't like his talking that way. Even though she had a good figure she was self-conscious about her looks and hung up on fat like everyone.

As if reading her mind, he said, "I'm not trying to upset you. That was intended as a compliment. You don't mind if I think of you as a sex object, do you?"

This was totally incredible. Only a few moments ago she'd blown up at her uncle and run into the woods in hope of clearing her mind from emotions that were burning her up. Now here she was, treading water, and moving into intimate subject matter she never got anywhere near with good old Ed.

"I'm not a prude," she said, one of her mother's favorite words. "But you sound like a sexist...." She stopped herself from finishing the thought.

"I believe you've been to school," he said. The words should have been sarcastic and a put-down—but the way he said it transformed the sentence into something nicer, almost friendly. "I like you, that's all."

"I like you, too," she said, amazing herself. She'd just met this guy. Maybe it required her jumping in a lake to realize how lonely she was.

"You're a weird guy," she said as she followed behind him.

"And you're a nice girl," he answered, proving her right again. "There's a good reason for my asking if it's OK to treat you as an object," he continued as he climbed on the dock, then reached down to offer a helping hand.

"What's that?" She was becoming more willing to take the bait.

"Upsie daisie," he said, pulling her the rest of the way. She was only inches from his lips and she noticed a slight scar running the length of his chin. A strand of hair fell over his right eye and made him look very sexy.

He kissed her again and then stopped in the middle, right when her tongue was warming up. He stood there, face a few inches away, arms still around her. He was waiting for something. His blank expression provided no clue. Then she surprised herself by acting on impulse. She kissed him.

He liked that a lot. A minute later when he let her catch her breath, he continued his previous conversation as though nothing had happened.

"Objects are easier to deal with than subjects," he went on. "You don't have to be as careful with them." She didn't like the sound of that.

"Women are better suited to being objects," he continued. She wished she could make him shut up. She didn't want to hear this. Maybe if she kissed him again. But as she tried, he held her back, gently but firmly. He meant for her to hear every word and this didn't make her happy at all. Not when he said: "Females are natural masochists. They have to be. Just think about it. It ties in with childbirth. Nothing could hurt more than that! That's why they like a little violence mixed in with love. They need practice in pain."

Great, just great. You find a perfect guy at the perfect time in the perfect place. All the crap you've been through is going to be washed off in this pure, clean lake and he will do all the scrubbing. And then you find out he's a nut. What completely typical luck!

"You're not afraid of pain, are you, Claire? Not if it will make you happy?"

Make that a dangerous nut!

There was a place in Claire's mind she called the "I told you so" department. Right now it was working overtime reminding her that Uncle Dennis had been bugging her to let him teach her about self defense. Mainly he wanted to take her shooting but he knew a little martial arts and a lot about dirty fighting. She always seemed to have something better to do...like running away from him and straight into the arms of this wonderful guy who was starting to sound like he'd just crawled out from under a rock.

What was she going to do if things got serious? Hit him with her charm bracelet?

"What are you doing?" he asked her. Claire wasn't any good at Poker. Her thoughts went straight to her face without stopping for directions.

She tore her gaze from her sneakers and looked back in his eyes, trying to keep from trembling. "Waiting for you to finish," she said, and then boldly added: "I have no idea what you're talking about!"

"You don't have a knife in your sneakers, do you?" he asked in a matter-of-fact tone of voice. She shook her head. "You're not packing?" he added.

"Huh?"

"You know, a gun. Do you have a gun?"

"No, I do not have a gun. Why are you trying to frighten me?"

He let go of her. She didn't even think about running. She could see what good physical condition he was in. She hoped he was only playing with her, and in a few minutes she would be walking home and he'd be swimming in the lake. If this handsome young man really was a monster, her only hope was to hurt him badly enough to stop him and then run. Killing him would be better...but she doubted her ability to do that.

God, why is he taking so long to say something?

"Would you like a beer?" he asked out of nowhere, echoing her uncle.

"I don't drink."

"Is it because of your age?"

"Since when does that stop anyone from doing what they want? Besides, you don't have a beer."

"I do, too, in my van, parked back behind those trees." He gestured and she hated herself for admiring the muscles on his arm.

"I don't like the taste of alcohol," she admitted.

"A good girl, huh?"

She bit her bottom lip. Maybe there wasn't anything to be afraid of, after all. Right now he was more annoying than scary. This seemed as good a time as any to end the meeting. "Leo, I appreciate the offer but I have to be getting back or my uncle will miss me."

"I understand," he said in a hurt tone of voice. "I've been talking crazy and you're afraid of me."

The guy's sense of timing was truly strange. No sooner than her fear begins to seep away than he brings up the subject himself!

"Look, Leo," she began in a calm tone of voice, "you'll do a lot better with girls if you don't talk about pain!" Turning on her heel, she started for her sneakers. He didn't do anything to stop her.

She was off the dock when he spoke again: "Physical pain isn't much compared to emotions. How did it feel to be dumped, Claire?"

Spinning around, she glared at him, right hand making a fist, grass caught between her toes. This was simply too much. "How did you know about that?" she spat out, then regretted it the minute the words left her mouth.

He chuckled. "I've learned to read the signs. I'd never do that to a girlfriend of mine. They do it to me."

"But someone like you would have a lot of girlfriends," she heard herself say.

He laughed long and hard. "But you can guess why I don't keep them. You've pointed out how crazy I am."

He had a point.

"Well, I'm glad I met you," she lied. "But I must be getting along." She bent over and started putting on her sneaker when she realized the view he would have of her. She quickly faced him and sat on the ground where she should watch him as she laced up.

All this time he hadn't budged from his position. Now he took a few unhurried steps in her direction, moving easily like blue water lapping around the legs of the dock.

"Would you do me one favor before you leave?" he asked. She waited for him to continue (some might say for the other shoe to drop). He came closer and said, "I'd like to take your picture."

"Where's your camera?" she asked, already knowing the answer.

"In my van, of course."

"I'm not getting in your van," she announced in as unfriendly voice as she could summon.

"I'm not suggesting that," he said, smoothly. "But please promise you'll wait here for a moment while I grab my camera."

She finished slipping both sneakers on her feet and she put on the charm bracelet. An obvious thought occurred to her. "OK," she said, "but don't be long."

He started away from her and then spun around quickly enough to catch her expression. "How dumb do you think I am?" he asked. He'd been moving so slowly that she was unprepared for the sudden burst of speed. He ran straight for her.

At that instant she had a good idea. Sitting the way she was she might be able to stick out a leg and catch him in the stomach. She tried to do this. But her reflexes weren't fast enough and he caught her, flipped her over and pinned her to the ground.

"Why are you doing this?" she cried out as he applied pressure to her arms and back. A fiery lance of agony struck her between the shoulder blades.

"It's my fault," he said. "You're so beautiful that I was impatient and I told you too much too soon. Come on!"

He stood and dragged her to her feet. Continuing to hold her in a vise of pain, he marched her to his van. At least he hadn't been lying about that. She hadn't seen the vehicle because it was several yards past the dock and hidden behind a stand of pine trees. Her sneakers crunched on cones and she had a strange impulse to warn him not to step on them with his bare feet.

The van was new and clean. She half expected something dirty and run-down if he was going to kill her. She wasn't sure at which exact moment she decided he was a killer. Oddly enough, she wasn't at all sure if he intended to rape her.

"I always take their pictures first," he said, as if picking up the thread of a conversation he was having with someone else. "One girl almost got away because I lost her picture. I went nuts over that, spent a whole weekend tearing up my apartment looking for it because I can't kill them if I don't keep the picture."

He was using that matter-of-fact tone of voice again. It was insidious and made you want to talk, the way she heard herself asking, "Why didn't you take another picture?"

"A good question," he complimented her as he shoved her face right up against the metal of the van. "But it has to be the first picture. Only that one captures the terror in a pure state. And obviously you can't allow the pictures to be developed in a lab. I used to let whole days pass between the taking of a picture and finishing the job."

She bit her tongue and tasted the iron, salty flavor of her own blood. Her breath came faster. Her heart beat faster. Oh God, how she wanted to live.

"I'm going to tie you up and get the camera," he said. He dragged her over to the rear door and opened it. He hadn't left it locked. He pulled out a plastic bag with one hand and opened it just as easily. Inside were several long, silk scarves. He'd taken his Boy Scout lessons at some moment in his life because the knots were more than she could handle. He tied her hands and feet.

"Why aren't you using rope?" she heard herself ask.

"When I drown you, it's best you don't show any marks."

Part of her wanted to shut up, shut up, shut up; but the other part couldn't stop satisfying her curiosity. For instance, she asked: "Why didn't you drown me before?"

"Hadn't taken your picture before," he said as he climbed inside the van and started rummaging around. "Ah, here it is!" he said, brandishing the camera as if it were a weapon, which for Claire it most certainly was. It was one of those cheap deals that spat out the picture in sixty seconds but there would be no question of going to a foto lab.

As he returned, she started noticing that a large metal tub filled up most of the back of the van. "I have good instincts," he said, noting her interest in the coffin-like object. "Thought I might get lucky today." Opening the lid, he revealed that the vessel was full of water.

She surprised herself by her reaction to all this. Anger was boiling up inside her, leaving no room for fear. "Why do you say you've never left anyone?"

"They leave me," he answered cheerfully, "as I've already told you."

"You're too much of a coward to drown me in the lake, where I'd have a chance to get away."

"You're confusing cowardice with common sense," he said, jumping down and taking her picture without even asking her to smile. Her wrist felt warm all of a sudden. Something was happening to the charm bracelet. The red agate in the little silver cage was glowing.

With a whirring sound, the picture cam out the slot of the camera, four white borders around a smudgy rectangle that would gradually take on the features of the victim of the year, the month, the week? How many girls had he really drowned? Or was it only an act to terrify this freak's idea of a date?

Suddenly Leo screamed and threw the picture away. Then he took another one. A few minutes later he repeated the process. By this time, she noticed the fragment of red stone was glowing and she thought she heard a high hum coming from her wrist.

"What are you doing?" he shouted at her, shoving one of the snapshots under her nose. She witnessed a perfect picture of red haze. The color made her think of the light used for developing pictures.

"I guess I'm invisible to your camera," she pointed out, remembering her uncle's story. If there was a power in the fragmented stone to find lovers maybe there was an equal power to hide the owner from haters! It made as much sense as running into Leo.

Leo glared at her charm bracelet. "Why is that glowing?" he asked.

"Don't ask me," she said. "Maybe it's magic."

"What do you know about magic?" he exclaimed and for the first time she noticed a certain nervousness in his voice. "The powers I serve are alone in the universe. Alone! There is nothing else..."

While she was trying to digest the import of his words, he angrily reached out for the charm bracelet and touched it. The little silver cage burst open and red light coursed up his arm to his shoulder, his neck, his face...and ended in his eyes. The camera fell from numb fingers. The red agate had vanished.

The way he stood there like a statue—a statue with glazed eyes—gave Claire an inspiration. She had nothing to lose. "Leo," she said in a low, firm voice, "untie me."

He untied her.

Then she had another idea. She didn't wait around to see how this one came out. She couldn't wait to get back to Uncle Dennis. She wanted to celebrate her birthday with him and she wouldn't spoil it with talk about dangerous people who prowled the woods. She'd tell her uncle that the best possible present he and Aunt Fi could give her was their love and that she wanted nothing more than a chance to get on with her life.

There was no good reason to scare her favorite aunt and uncle with a story that would get back to Mom and Dad and worry them. But she couldn't leave a monster loose in the woods, not even a handsome one; not when she could suggest that he take a nice, long bath in a tub that was ready and waiting for him. The kind of bath where he just might fall asleep.

There was a spate of books about Elvis a while back but I missed my window on this story. Cults always fascinate me because one never knows what they might grow into.

Just a Hunk of Burnin' Love...Tied to the Stake

The Hound-dogs were baying at the moon. He hated it when they did that, but at least they were respectful toward his office. They were an odd bunch, but their eccentricities had not yet degenerated into heresy.

"The Bishop!" cried one.

"Join us," suggested another, forgetting himself in the excitement.

They were enthusiastic children but it did no good to dampen their spirits without cause. "Aren't you neglecting something?" he asked the one who had recognized his office. The man wasted no time coming over and kneeling before him so as to kiss the proffered horseshoe ring.

"We meant no disrespect, your eminence," said the man.

"And none is taken," was his cheerful response. "You do but honor Elvis. Now rise, my son." It did this man of power good to feel their gratitude. It flowed over him as if a wave of beautiful music.

Several other Hound-dogs kneeled before him as he continued on his way. He paused before each one, touching their heads. The first to receive his benediction spat on the white shoes he wore and wiped them with a silken handkerchief, probably the most elegant possession the man had. "Rise," he said to each in turn, as their beloved Lord had risen; and as it had been duly reported in the sacred pages of the *Revealed Inquirer*. Each tried to brush against him, some touching his gold lame[[accent acute]] jacket, others feeling, however briefly, the smooth texture of his velvet shirt.

"Rise, rise my children."

As he reached the large steel doors of the Sacred Studio, these portals shining all blue and white in the light of the full moon, he turned back for a last glance at them. "You come to do good work!" cried one. "We will be here at dawn!" cried another.

"'You ain't nothin' but a Hound-dog'," the Bishop quoted.

"'Don't be cruel'." Then he turned from their cheers, suppressing a tear as he did so. There were many who would say that he was about to be cruel to one of his oldest friends, who was waiting for him inside. Only so many examples could be made .. and then it was up to the rest to learn. As for the examples, they had to be chosen very carefully and with love.

Right before entering, he craned his neck back so he could see the new sign over the door, the huge letters easily readable even in this light: Worksland. It had been a real battle, changing the name from Graceland. Even those who should know better retained a nostalgic attachment for the older name. Well, a few generations was all it would take to make today's innovation into tomorrow's tradition.

The doors creaked as he went through them. He'd make a complaint about that. But there were more important matters to concern him now. The Studio was open twenty-four hours a day, and would remain that way until the crisis was over.

A large part of the crisis was breathing at the end of the hall and looking out at the Bishop through tired eyes with dark circles. There was a bruise on the left cheek of this small man.

Observing the pale face and hunched figure, it was hard for the Bishop to believe that this wretched man had been a friend much less that he was now a threat to the True Faith.

"Hello, Lewis," said the representative of Order and Civilization.

"Hello, Lee." said the heretic through broken teeth.

"Who did this to you?" asked the Bishop angrily. Theory suddenly disappeared in a haze of emotion; flesh and blood spoke to flesh and blood. Even a defender of Right Reason could have a weak moment.

The guards looked away sheepishly as Lewis answered, "One interrogator is pretty much like another. They've just been softening me up for...you."

"I'm here to help you."

"To persecute me, you mean."

"*Righteous* persecution!"

"You won't rest until you've saved me," said Lewis with a grim smile.

"Come, let us be alone," said the Bishop. He turned to the guards. "Untie him."

"But your Wholeness..." one started to dispute him.

"By RCA, you'll do it now!"

The other guard was already unwinding the cord from Lewis's

wrists and helping him to his feet. Without saying another word the Bishop gave the man a shoulder to lean upon; and Lewis needed it, the way he was rocking on his feet. The two men half walked, half lurched the short distance to the bishop's office.

The Bishop was feeling very old by the time he closed the door behind him and gratefully deposited his old friend in a chair facing a huge portrait of Elvis. It was hard to believe that he and Lewis had known each other for fifty years...and helped found the True Faith together. Although they were many generations removed from the Time of Elvis, the incredibly thorough records kept of He who was the Recorded Sun proved more than adequate for true enlightenment.

Who would ever dream that a time might come when Lewis and he would turn down different paths? Why, they'd worked together on the first concordance! But the Bishop had to remind himself that only those with part of the truth were in a position to lead the faithful astray. If only Elvis would give him strength for what was to come.

While Lewis scrutinized the portrait that he found so obviously distasteful. the Bishop turned a critical eye on his old friend, his new enemy. It was as if he could read the other's mind; and he found himself constructing arguments in defense of the "artist's rendition" on the big canvas before an attack was even made. Sure, the sideburns were too long. Sure, given the mature age of Elvis for this particular setting, many pounds of unflattering fat had been ceremoniously removed. The purists didn't like contemporary interpretations anyway, but if a painting or sculpture had to be made, there were many records preserved from the First Century, and there was simply no excuse for changing any detail that was known to be true. That was the trouble with purists! Why, that kind of thinking carried too far would mean no True Faith at all.

An old trick the Bishop had learned was the more worrisome a situation, the more important it was to put the other person at ease. This he proceeded to do by walking behind his desk and announcing: "You know, these white shoes of mine are a pride and joy, but they kill my feet." He pulled them off with a sigh of relief and slipped on the blue suede shoes he kept under his chair. Then settling in his Officially Comfy Chair, he allowed himself to ponder the other man. This time he wondered if some of the displeasure he saw on

Lewis's face might have something to do with physical pain.

"When did they last feed you?" he asked.

The haggard little man allowed himself a smile although it hurt his mouth and said, "'Not since my baby left me.'"

Silence settled over the room, thick and swollen. When the Bishop spoke again, it was in a much quieter voice: "You don't need to quote chapter and verse to me."

"'Go cat, go....'"

"Please, you know that blasphemy will only make matters worse. Only Elvis should speak certain of the sacred formulations."

"Who decides what the laity may say and what it may not say?"

The atmosphere of good will was fast dissipating. This would be the Bishop's last chance to save his friend—to show him the light of reason. "Lewis, Lewis. when the schism first began, I could see some merit to your side, even though I disagreed with it. But now you've moved into a territory so alien that I no longer recognize it. or you. The True Church must defend itself."

All this disputation was making the Bishop thirsty. He reached for a carafe labeled Memphis Water, and noticed a slight trembling in Lewis's right hand. Elvis knew when the man had last been given a drink of water. It made the Bishop feel kindly to offer him a glass. Lewis didn't turn it down.

Dehydration was an especially grim torture, the Bishop reflected. And yet it had been one of the most popular methods of stern correction imposed on those who had been led astray by Lewis's selective use of scripture. Peering over the rim of the cup, Lewis's eyes looked deep into the heart of his own personal inquisition.

"Thank you for the water," he said, "but why keep up this pretense any longer? We both know I'm condemned and I won't change my confession."

"Then you condemn yourself, you, not the Church, as you finish what you began in sin when you took your second wife."

"Keep Priscilla out of this!"

"More blasphemy."

"You know we could take what names we wanted back then."

This was getting nowhere. Taking a few deep breaths helped before the Bishop tried once more to help his old friend see what he had made of his life: "Lewis, I only brought up the subject of your marriages to illustrate a point. It was your first wrong step."

"'Elvis is in you and in me...'" Lewis began to quote.

"No. Our best scholars have proven that song was a blasphemy put into the world by the heretic, Dr. Demento!"

"I have a personal relationship with Elvis."

"If that were true, He would have told you that a man is entitled to only one wife."

"But Elvis said, 'I got so many women I don't know which way to jump'."

By the Colonel, was there no reaching this man? The more certain Lewis was of his crazy beliefs, the more he placed himself in jeopardy. At least the Bishop could quote passages with as much conviction as a lost soul steeped in error, and proved this with: "Did not Elvis also say, 'I'd rather see you dead, baby, than with another man'?"

Lewis wasn't buying it: "A possible case against polyandry but not against polygamy."

"This is no joking matter."

"I didn't say it was."

"Lewis, this may be the last chance you have to use your brain. Think, man! When Elvis said. 'Get out of that bed and wash your face and hands,' He is clearly addressing His one true love."

The other man had a ready answer. "But in the same Sacred Pressing, He condemns her as a 'Devil in Nylon Hose'. Have you forgotten how one of the other Bishops concluded from this reference to the Devil the doctrine that all women are in greater sin than men? By that logic, no man would take unto himself even one wife!"

The Bishop shook his head and rose to his feet. The nervous energy coursing through him had to go somewhere. He started pacing. "You draw incorrect conclusions, as usual. It is from that verse that we learn the simple truth: no priest may marry. But it is meet and right that other men should marry, else they cannot enter the 'Heartbreak Hotel'."

"'Where man is so lonely he could die'...."

"Exactly! And 'he's cryin' all the time'. Man must suffer through Woman to attain his salvation so conversely, Woman attains hers through him."

Lewis coughed into his hand and looked up sheepishly with raised eyebrows. In the heat of argument, the Bishop had forgotten the other man's appalling condition. He provided him with one of his

own monogrammed silk handkerchiefs. Lewis wiped his mouth and
cleaned his hands, leaving bright specks of red on the cloth.

"I know about suffering," he wheezed. "But if to suffer is good.
then the more women in a man's life, the more he will know goodness."

The Bishop walked over and put his hand on Lewis's shoulder.
"You were always a steadfast husband, each and every time. And
even though it's wrong, you know that multiple wives is an error
toward which we can be lenient...but your most damnable heresy
is another matter. You must decide now, tonight, if you will repudi-
ate this heresy and live."

Outside the Hound-Dogs had started chanting. They were responding to the low machine sound of approaching helicopters—a
sound that become progressively more irritating as the things grew
nearer, and nearer...their spinning rotors churning the air. bringing spectators to witness the human maelstrom of an execution.

"When they light the fire," said Lewis softly, "I would like a reading from the Prophet Lennon where he said, 'Before Elvis, there
was nothing....'"

It was at that moment that the Bishop realized there was no turning back. There was no point in telling Lewis that those who would
witness the final purification did not hate him; they were going to
pray for him. No one actually wanted his soul to wander through
the great wastelands until it finally arrived in Vegas.

"And before we part company," Lewis continued, "I would like
my last act on earth to be for your benefit. Don't you realize that
your exalted status won't save you? It is you, not I, who risks damnation this night."

"Don't make it any worse on yourself," said the Bishop, but the
words sounded hollow. The die was already cast.

Lewis was on a roll: "When your so-called True Church denied
the sufficiency of Grace, you cut yourself off from hope eternal. You
have traded everything for a little temporal power. 'The cats are
going wild'. You cannot enter the portals of His Graceland by defac-
ing His House on earth. You can dress like Elvis and arrange your
Sock Hop Balls...."

"Stop!"

"... and Shake, Rattle and Roll until you're as blue in the face as
His blue suede shoes. but it won't do you any good. If you really

believe in Elvis, no institution is needed. If you don't believe, all the ritual and pomp in the world won't keep you from being square..."

"Stop, I beg you."

"... and uncool."

"No more!"

Lewis suddenly seemed taller. And he sounded benevolent and strong in a manner that the Bishop would trade his wardrobe just to have the same quality. "I'll pray for *YOU*," said Lewis, and then he left the room and turned himself back over to the guards, who looked upon the little man as if he were someone they had had never seen before.

The Bishop watched his own door close. Then he grasped the beautifully ornate replica of a wooden guitar that he kept on his desk. He held it tighter than he had ever held it before.

Soon it would be daylight. Soon the fire would be lit. There would be chanting about the Sun, the RCA and the Holy Wood. Would the flames secure the social order, peace and harmony? Would they at least burn away the darkness always waiting to assault one's peace of mind?

Would anything make any difference at all?

They couldn't start without him. He knew he would walk out through those big doors, as surely as he knew the sun would rise.

And he knew that Lewis would give a good account of himself, showing no weakness in the face of excruciating pain. The Bishop knew with a dead certainty that he would whimper like a dog if he were in Lewis's place.

Instead, he would stand tall, dressed like the King, safe from harm and he would say: "And Rockabilly begat Rock and Roll...as Elvis was begat by Gladys and His Father, the Music of the Spheres...and He went unto their ranch houses through their Radios. and Record Players and T.V. sets...and the Colonel begat the Profits, and saw that the first Billion was good...and in time was the Lesson revealed unto His followers, and we are His good and trusted servants...."

He'd watch the newly risen sun light up the faces of the faithful. The young girls would look prettier than ever with their rosy cheeks and fine white teeth. They'd scream and faint and giggle as the Work was done. And Memphis water would be sprinkled over the ashes.

The Bishop bent over and picked up his white shoes. He'd need them again. The trouble with heretics, he finally decided, was that they were overly concerned with their own individual souls. They didn't consider other people. Salvation was other people.

"Isn't that right, Elvis?" he asked out loud and glanced over his shoulder, half mockingly, at the portrait.

He saw something in the painted face he'd never seen before. It was subtle, but it was undeniably a hint of a scowl. Funny how he'd never noticed any cruelty in the face before. He couldn't help but think of one of the forbidden phrases of Elvis. The fact that it was documented made it all the more crucial to keep this utterance on the restricted list; "Don't mess with me."

This collection begins with "Clownface," in which a Little Person plays a significant role, the midget Dan Bloom. Now it ends with a story that features another Little Person, the dwarf Raymond. I don't know that the failure of these two pieces to sell over the years has anything to do with diminutive characters, but there the resemblance ends.

In contrast to the compliments that "Clownface" brought in, "Dwarf" inspired the most negative comments of anything I've ever written. One editor I respect actually recommended I seek psychiatric help on the basis of this story.

I wrote "Every Dwarf" to be disturbing. That was the whole idea. Maybe I thought that after Harlan Ellison's ground-breaking *Dangerous Visions*, writers would all be trying to do visions that were, well, dangerous.

I found out that I could be pretty dangerous when writing about Nazis. But when it came to shrinks (the subject of "Dwarf") I got nowhere in a hurry.

This is the right story to end the collection. Anything after this would be anticlimactic.

Every Dwarf Should Own a Dinosaur

Our story—"our" refers to Raymond and myself as I don't approve of getting chummy with a reader who might be a total stranger for all I know—begins in a doctor's office, or more precisely the doctor's waiting room. Raymond and I had worked on the plan for over a month before we deemed it adequate, and I felt secure enough to sit in the waiting room on the thirtieth floor, reading a copy of *Scientific Armenian* and occasionally glancing up at the pinched face of a secretary who, despite her unpromising expression, had a body that was nothing short of a religious experience.

The execution of the plan would require an explanation of the particulars to the good doctor. The reader who likes to know what's going on won't be cheated if he is patient.

Twenty-five minutes I waited before the secretary looked in my direction, without looking at me, and said with perfect diction, "The doctor will see you now." She seemed to derive pleasure from her alveolars. The face remained pinched.

"Thanks." I walked straight into the inner sanctum and sat down across from Doctor Frederic Skinoo. "Hi, doc," I said in a tone of genuine camaraderie. "How goes it, old fellah? How do you like having three doctorates? Does it feel good being a popular speaker with the Moral Modality?"

The doctor smiled broadly. Of course he wasn't disconcerted by my abrupt and totally uncivilized entrance. Of course he put on the mask of benign concern that he reserved for his favorite type of people—Grade-A loonies. And just as I had expected, he responded to all my questions with: "Well, well, how are we today?"

I frowned in thought. Seconds ticked off on my Royal Geneva (I hate digitals). "I'm fine...Raymond is in deep trouble...and I haven't the slightest notion how you are," I told him. The doctor's hands remained in clear view. He was obviously a tape man. "What speed recording are you using?" I asked.

"That's none of your business," he replied. He was a cool egg. "Let me worry about the diagnosis. Now, what's your problem?"

It was the moment. A whole lifetime of serious obsession went into my answer. "It's not me I need to tell you about, doc. It's my friend."

"Uh huh."

"Raymond's his name. He's a dwarf with a problem."

"A little person, you mean."

"A mean what I say, or as the philosophical potato says: I think, therefore I yam!"

"And just where *is* your friend?" He must have thought Raymond to be one of those pesky imaginary friends.

"Raymond's been a dwarf for a long time, so he's not imagining it." I paused for dramatic effect. The doctor paused back. "Well," I continued, "might as well get on with it."

"Might as well," agreed Skinoo.

It's a good thing the doc had a box of Kleenex on his desk because I spit out: "Raymond owns a full grown Dimetrodon and he can't get rid of it."

The mental health expert smiled, a little smile forming on his corpulent lips. "Ah yes, the Dimetrodon," he said, pursing those lips. "That is a fin-backed creature of the Permian period, is it not?"

"If you say so. Do you have one, too?"

"Dinosaurs were my hobby as a boy," he continued, his voice calm, his round face bored, "and practical jokes were my next favorite pastime...until I discovered it was more fun to help people than to hurt them." I shed a tear of understanding. "You aren't young enough to be undergoing a fraternity initiation."

"They're illegal now."

"I must assume that you are an individual eccentric and this is an expensive...."

"Practical joke it is not, good sir." I enjoyed interrupting the guy. "But you are observant to notice that I'm an individual."

"You must think that I don't care how I conduct my profession, as long as I'm paid for my time. In that, good *sir*, you are very much mistaken. I won't even charge you for...." His right hand disappeared, no doubt to summon forth the white-clad bouncer whom Raymond and I had been studying for the past month.

I interrupted him again. "Don't be patronizing, Dr. Skinoo. I'm no crank. I don't even phone in to *The Larry King Show*. Either I can prove what I say or I'm in need of real help." I leaned forward in my chair. "Please help me," I pleaded in a whisper. "You're the only one who can."

Both of his hands appeared again. "But I thought it was Raymond who needed help." For the first time since his routine opening query, his voice sounded positive in intent. I knew that he no more believed in Raymond than he did the Dimetrodon.

"That's right. But having a friend with such a colossal problem makes it my problem, too. I learned that from reading one of your books."

"Tell me, why isn't Raymond here."

"He's shy."

"Yes."

"He's also a genius."

"Yes."

"I'm a genius, too."

"Yes."

"You probably think you're a genius, also."

"Yes...uh ..."

"But I'm an extroverted genius whereas he's introverted, so like I say—he's shy."

"Uh."

At that exact moment, a buzzer announced itself, a cross between a bumblebee and the mating call of the great American seatbelt. Dr. Skinoo's swift right hand repeated its favorite trick. "I left word that I wasn't to be disturbed until I gave the final signal," he said to his desk.

"There is a gentleman out here, of little height, who claims to be with the gentleman in your office, Doctor."

"Raymond," I said. "He doesn't realize he's only made it to the waiting room. Your secretary is probably not a good enough metaphysician to help him out of his latest difficulty in dealing with this vast and varied universe in which..."

"Show him in," said the doctor, resigned, and interrupting me! The door swung open, closed.

"Hi, doc. How goes it, old fellah?" Raymond's voice was loud.

The extent of Dr. Skinoo's professionalism was demonstrated by his lightning grasp of the new situation. Rather than answer Raymond with his stock rhetorical question, he looked down at the dwarf and said, "How are you, today?"

"I suffer from the illness of alcohol syndrome, er, I'm a drunk," said the face that was only three and one-half feet above the floor, and two hundred, fifty-three and one-half feet above sea level.

"Won't you have a seat?" offered Skinoo.

"Shake my hand first," Raymond insisted.

"He believes in propriety." It was my turn.

"That's my friend," said Raymond, pointing at me.

"I know, I know," admitted the doc, shaking the dwarf's hand.

We were all seated. A minute ticked itself into oblivion. The doctor's body language resembled a pretzel. "About this Dimetrodon," he began, "how long have you had the delusion, Raymond?"

"What delusion?" Raymond asked. "It's in my mind...."

"That's what I'm talking about," crowed Skinoo.

"...and in my basement."

"You mean that you think it's in your basement," corrected the doctor. I jotted down the analyst's comment on my handkerchief.

"I don't have the D.T.'s, Dr. Skinoo, you old fool. *I've got a Dimetrodon!!!!*" Raymond was peevish.

Skinoo turned in my direction, thought better of it, and turned back to Raymond. "If you think you, er, own an actual dinosaur, why then do you say it's in your mind?" Despite his excellent education, the doctor seemed ill prepared to deal with solipsistic questions, such as: *did Raymond really have a basement*?

"I never said I had a dinosaur," replied Raymond. "What idiot told you that?"

"Why, uh, your friend here. And you just admitted to...." Skinoo's voice trailed off as he noticed me shaking my head and shooting a bird in his direction.

"No, you jerk, I have a Dimetrodon. But technically it doesn't qualify as a dinosaur. It's a *pelycosaur*, extinct long before the first dinosaur appeared. Why, I bet you are so ignorant that you still believe in mythical creatures such as the brontosaurus—when everyone who is up-to-date knows that it's as imaginary as the fundamentalist Bible thumpers always said. Why, in a few more decades, there won't be any dinosaurs left. So there."

"Geniuses are a pain to be around," I said helpfully. "They always correct you on details. But they don't get the girls."

The good doctor paid me no heed. A true professional, he had fixated on a single concept and wouldn't let go. "But if the

Dimetrodon is extinct, as you just admitted, how can you have one in your basement?"

"You mean *now*? Oh, it's in your office now."

"Raymond, you are an alcoholic, right?"

"I don't mind being called a dwarf, but don't ever call me an alcoholic. I'm a drunk."

"Do you fear that you've ever had hallucinations as a result of problem drinking?"

"Maybe. I like to keep an open mind."

"Wide open," I added.

"But you sit there," persisted the doc, "and tell me that you believe the dinosaur, or whatever you call it, is real?"

"I don't *call* it a pelycosaur. It *is* a pelycosaur, and the best damned pet I've ever had."

I scribbled a note and passed it to Skinoo. He took it, glanced at it, then scrutinized it, frowning. "What have you written? I can't read this."

I shrugged. "The note says that it's time for special effects. I can't write legibly because I come from a broken home."

At that revelation, both of Skinoo's hands disappeared. Raymond winked at me. My watch read 4:30. I knew that the doc's bouncer wouldn't be showing up. He'd already been taken care of—heh, heh, heh. I gestured to Raymond that it was time for Talbot. He returned my signal. The author of *Reading the Body's Secret Language* (only so secret, huh?) thought we were yawning and stretching.

And then we struck! First, Raymond farted. Profusely apologizing for my little buddy, I removed what appeared to be a can of air freshener. The doc tried to stop me using it—he was screaming something about the ozone—but he was too slow.

Afterward, all that he noticed was a cold shiver. As he sat down in his chair again, it was 6:30; but he hadn't noticed the startling passage of time. He'd find out in good time.

"Look, doc," I said, "let's just put our cards on the table."

I reduced my smile to a grin. The doctor continued watching the closed door which led to the waiting room. Raymond removed a flask of Early Times (a bit of a motif here, wouldn't you say?) from the inner pocket of his jacket and drank some of its contents. The secretary, still on the other side of the door, screamed in high C. Neither the bouncer nor the dinosaur were heard from at this time.

Skinoo gasped when he heard the scream. He even jumped up. I was polite and rose also. Raymond, on the other hand, took another swallow and remained seated, his feet dangling. A bird flew by the window of the office, flapping its wings in a very symbolic fashion. It was an albatross and seemed to be foreshadowing something.

"God, Miss Talbot!" choked the doctor

"She looked like a *Miz* Talbot to me," said the dwarf. As for me, I always thought that *Ms.* was an abbreviation for manuscript.

Dr. Skinoo walked swiftly—for him—to the door, flung open the portal and stepped into the dread anteroom. This is what the man saw: Talbot's corpse lay sprawled on the floor in a pool of the usual. The most startling aspect of her appearance was without doubt her lack of a head, hence the pool. There was also a clue. The wall to the doctor's left was caved in. The entire waiting room was a mess, not to mention next door.

Dr. Frederic Skinoo was on the verge of passing out. His complexion was porcelain white, his eyes glassy. As if on cue—in fact, it *was* on cue—a muffled roar underlined the scene of carnage. Far away though that sound was, anybody would know it was our Dimetrodon (anybody who's ever seen a monster movie, that is). Skinoo considered the audible datum and decided on his best course of action. He would have no more to do with the verge. He fainted.

"He's down," we said as one. Raymond removed leather thongs from his inner pockets and I helped him tie Skinoo to the chair. While we waited for our victim to wake up, we arm wrestled; and I lost every time. Time passed. Raymond drank. I wrote some Letters-to-the-Editor that could also be used as suicide notes. More time passed.

Finally, Skinoo opened his eyes. Then he focused his eyes. He probably regretted what he saw. The door to the waiting room was closed, the horror filled tableau on the other side safely entombed. Having finished all the whiskey he brought along, Raymond was surly, and in a corner. I was pacing the floor to put the doctor at ease.

The curtains were drawn. The overhead light was on. It was midnight. Skinoo was a good fainter.

"What's going on here?" He'd never been very original to begin with, and the more dire his peril, the more trite he became.

"We are protecting you from yourself," I explained.

"He's quoting from one of your lousy books," said the dwarf. "Probably *Your Neighbor's Keeper* or *Beyond Individualism* or *The Physics of Masturbation* or *How to Protect Your Baby From Itself* or *Violence in the Arts*: *Threat or Menace?* or *Negative Sex Roles in Crossword Puzzles* or *The Myth of Bravery* or *Marriage as Rape* or *Finding* a *Cure for Pride.* But I wouldn't know, since I've never read one of your books."

This was a bit much for Skinoo. "Wait a minute, wait a minute," he redundancized. "If you don't read my books, how did you list all the titles just then?"

"Rowrrrrrrrrrrr," was the Dimetrodon's opinion from next door.

"It sounds like the thing is just next door!" said Skinoo, changing the subject and as a result never learning anything about Raymond's reading habits. Meanwhile, the Dimetrodon was breathing heavily on the other side of the wall. Skinoo became hysterical. "The phone! Let me use the phone! Call for help. Call someone in authority."

"You're an authority," I said.

"Warn the people! Call the military. The dinosaur!"

"It's not a dinosaur," said Raymond.

We waited for him to calm down. Then I made a valiant attempt to reason with our most unreasonable subject. "It would do no good to contact the authorities," I pointed out. He made a noise, sort of like a little squeak. "A live dinosaur..."

"It's not a...."

"Shut up, Raymond. As I was saying, a live dinosaur is hard enough to swallow all by itself, but add to that the unlikely facts that it feeds on human heads and is of the transparent persuasion...."

"Say what?" said the doc.

"Everything about my pet is invisible," said the dwarf. "And it's uncurbed."

"Oh no!" Our victim was beginning to catch on.

"You should realize, as a professional therapist, that things are not always what they appear to be. But sometimes there is the cosmic irony of things being exactly as they appear."

"If it's time for your lecture," said Raymond, "then I'm going to sleep. Wake me when you require my services." The little guy fell down, went *BOOM*.

"I think I'll take another nap, too," said the doc.

"You won't wake up from it."

"I think I'll stay awake and listen to you." So he could be reasonable, after all. "You see an apple," I continued, getting hungry, "you see its red skin, so you conclude that it's red to its core. In other words, you say that man is a product of...."

"And woman," he said, proving that his programming was stronger than his instinct for survival. So he was only so reasonable.

"You say that *man* is the product of society without bothering to realize that first, society must be the product of man. To you, Society is not an abstraction but an entity—a justification for tyranny, a cosmic graph on which we are the dots...and you are one important dot, what with degrees in psychiatry, psychology and sociology from influential institutions of higher learning."

"I've devoted my life to helping others."

"So true. *So true.* It's a wonder that you find time for a practice, considering how many books you've written. Raymond forgot to include your most important title: *Seduction of the Bemused.* That's when I first heard of you. You'd never even met Eddy, the teenager who raped and killed an old woman But that didn't stop you coming on television and telling everyone that Eddy wasn't responsible for his actions. You found his books and magazines guilty. You convicted these objects over the air. Inanimate objects They never even had a trial. You blamed everything on a culture of violence."

"Rowrrrrrrrrrr," from guess who.

"You're...a...critic!" he gasped. "You've done all this just to give me a bad review."

"Wait until you see your terminal notice. Look, you say that environment is the primary factor in making us what we are."

"I admit it."

"You make a pretty feeble case for why society has criminals, such as Raymond and myself, but your theory doesn't even begin to account for geniuses, such as Raymond and myself."

"What do you think that word *genius* means?" asked Skinoo, a glint in his eye (the glint of a born again shrink).

"A genius is a clever sort of person, not just smart but intelligent, good at abstractions...and the most clever of all would be a person who figures out how to create geniuses at will.

"You can't mass produce genius on an assembly line," he said.

"Wait a minute, doc. You can't say that. In your books, you deny that *genius exists*. You say it's a myth, remember? So you contradict yourself if you imply that genius is attainable by any means!"

"You have me there."

"No, *we have you here!*" It was Raymond, praise be. He'd awakened from his nap refreshed and full of piss and vinegar. It did my heart good to see him run over and slap the doctor on the knee. "Genius is easy to create if you know how," said my little buddy.

"Which you don't, but I do," said I.

"I do, you don't" sez he.

"No you don't."

"Yes I do."

"I do."

"I do ."

"You don't."

"Help!" was Dr. Skinoo's contribution.

"Less filling."

"Tastes great."

The Dimetrodon had nothing more to say, the tape recording having run out by this point. But Skinoo was getting his second wind. Recognizing a conflict between his captors, he sought to make the most of it: "You two have a disagreement?"

"That was really subtle, doc," I said.

"Yeah, we'll be at each other's throats in no time." Raymond had a great personality and a good sense of humor. He staggered over to the doc and gave him a good dose of drunk dwarf breath. "But we agree about what we're going to do to you." He giggled. A happier sound I've never heard outside of a Disney cartoon.

Raymond exited, stage right, closing the door behind him. He would return in a few minutes. The silence sounded all right; and Skinoo's labored breathing sounded OK; but I missed the sound of my own voice, and so I began moving my lips again, and the following came out: "You know, Raymond became a psycho at an early age. His uncle had an axe. He used it to chop down trees. He was a lumberjack and he was OK. One day, Raymond deduced that if an axe could cut something as hard as wood, it would have a pronounced effect on flesh."

"Did he test his hypothesis?" asked a weak, uncertain voice from the depths of a swivel chair.

I nodded. The office door opened. "Do you see my point?" I asked as the dwarf entered.

"You're wrong about me," insisted Skinoo, recoiling at the sight of Raymond's hatchet. "You're wrong I wouldn't say the solution to axe murders would be in the prohibition of chopping wood."

"Oh yeah? What about the environment?" growled Raymond.

"Now Raymond, let's give him the benefit of the doubt. The last time he spoke before MAFS (Mothers Against Free Speech), he demonstrated his sensitivity to things ecological by saying nice things about snail darters. Or was he just complimenting the ladies?"

"I don't care one way or the other," said Raymond, taking a few practice swings.

Skinoo decided to take the direct approach. "Don't kill me!" he suggested.

"Give us one reason we shouldn't."

"You wouldn't want me to die before I fully understand the reasons for your bitterness; not before I understood your brilliant method."

"You understand enough, doc. You've got a fine mind." He didn't seem very pleased with my compliment but continued watching Raymond swing his axe.

"Don't you understand how impossible this is?" he asked more of the universe at large than of me. "If Raymond was your agent, killing my secretary while we talked that short time before his entrance, how could he do it? How did we hear Talbot scream when Raymond was in here with us. How did he knock down the wall without a sound?"

"I take it that you no longer believe in the Dimetrodon. You are also assuming that we have no confederates, the most obvious explanation."

"What is the truth?" he whined, as so many great minds do.

"Don't tell him," said Raymond.

"No, I disagree with you. I'm going to tell him because it is a sure sentence of death."

"On the other hand, I don't really need to know," said the good doctor, but too late.

My mouth was already open and I had taken out the aerosol can. "This," I declaimed, "is a suspended animation spray that Raymond and I invented in one of our more cooperative moods. We used it on you when we needed you out of our hair. You should be able to figure out the rest."

"There never was a dinosaur," he said in a small voice.

"I told you that all along," said the nitpicky dwarf.

"But wait," he continued in one last burst of clarity—"if you have invented something as important as this, why in hell are you using it to commit these crazy murders? Why not sell it and get rich?"

"You tell us," said the dwarf.

"Elementary, my dear doctor," I said. "Our suspended animation product would be seized as a threat to national security. It is a sublime weapon, if I do say so myself."

"Besides, it's too late for us to take that route," said Raymond. "You are not our first murder using this method. The cops would figure out a lot of stuff if they knew about the spray."

"I'll never understand why you're doing this," said Skinoo.

"You have the rest of your life to work out that problem," I encouraged him...but I guess that even a smart guy can only do so much in about five minutes.

He was clever in his own way, however. "All right, I admit that I was wrong," he said. "Genius *does* exist. The two of you prove it."

"Nice try," said Raymond. "But you're only half right, the part about me being a genius. I did the most difficult part of developing the suspended animation spray."

"The devil you say!" Friendship only goes so far.

"You know it's true."

"I do not."

"You see, doc, we're in a little race to do something a lot more important than making tape recordings of what we think a pelycosaur would sound like, or dismantling people when they are in a state of suspended animation; or even using prerecorded screams at dramatic moments." Incredibly, the dwarf said all that.

"Then whatever your current project, it must be more important than killing me." Skinoo was using his powers of reason again.

"We always finish what we start, right Raymond?"

"Right. Just as I'm going to finish the *new* project ahead of you and prove who is the real genius, once and for all."

I don't really blame the doc for trying to find out details of our dispute. Anything to delay the razor's edge of destiny. There didn't seem any advantage in telling someone who was a stranger, after all, about something as personal as our contest. No point in getting too chummy, you know.

The trouble was that I wanted to develop artificial intelligence the *dry* way...in a computer. I'd purchased everything I needed from Radio Shack and stole the rest from the Hollywood Industrial Complex when I was last out on the coast. Raymond was afraid that if I succeeded, I would have created a mind without a body. This, according to my diminutive ally, would constitute a conscious spirit form, or more specifically *an Angel*. He was becoming religious in his old age and was afraid that if I summoned such a being, it would judge us harshly for all the people we had killed. Basically, Raymond was nuts.

But there's no denying he had it upstairs. He'd been busy robbing graves and doing the Frankenstein bit because he was convinced that certain materials in the human brain were simply indispensable to human intelligence—and as the brain is a *wet* system, he based all of his research on that icky premise. Ugh.

So we're having our friendly competition to see who could produce the first genius and then—wouldn't you know it?—he goes and discovers girls. *We've been going about it all wrong*, he tells me. *The old fashioned way is best*, he says. And then the little weenie goes into unsavory details about *wet* this and *wet* that.

Well, his efforts in the amorous arena were not entirely successful until he started using the suspended animation spray. Then I make one joke, just one, about necrophilia. He won't talk to me for a month. So when we finally shake hands and resume our murder sprees (the old pleasures are always best), we agree that the winner of the contest must develop his genius artificially, though of course biological materials may be used for Raymond's project.

But it's just more of the same. Bitch, bitch, bitch. *These brains aren't fresh enough*, he tells me. *When we kill people we need their brains right then.* Over and over, I listen to this. Is it my fault that he's clumsy? I didn't mean to trip him the time he dropped the jar down the stairwell. But will he let me forget it?

The entire matter was too embarrassing to share with the eminent Dr. Frederic Skinoo. So I decided to wrap things up. "Dear doc, are Raymond and I responsible for the many murders which we have committed in our quest to make the lives of homicide detectives both exciting and full of mystery?"

"You did them, didn't you?" he responded, avoiding the question.

"Doctor, are we morally responsible for our crimes?"

"You're sick. You need help."

"Boy, are you dumb, pronouncing your own death sentence," said Raymond, climbing on top of the desk and lifting his hatchet.

One last time, Skinoo was possessed by the lust to analyze.

"What kind of a psycho are you?" he asked me, "if you let others do your killing for you?"

That really pissed Raymond off. He inquired if he could torture the bastard first. "No," I said. "We already have. Stick to the plan." Fortunately, the hatchet didn't stick. It was a clean stroke. Raymond was very, very strong. And the material of the hatchet was yet another of our collaborations, a most unusual alloy.

Skinoo's head landed in a trash-can, face up. I spoke to the head because its eyes were still wide and inquisitive. "Doctor, you weren't killed by an individual, but by the orphan of a negative social impulse."

You see, this is where "our story" ends and mine begins. I couldn't let my little buddy take Skinoo's brain. It was fresh; and it was right for him in other ways. I couldn't let him beat me in the race to create a bottled genius. No more than I could admit that my primary contribution to the suspended animation spray was the scent.

As Raymond leaned over the trash receptacle, I lifted the axe and did what a man's got to do. Of course, I'm not as strong as he was. It took several swings to finish the job. Then I lifted the dwarf's bleeding head, a full-sized adult head naturally, and placed it on Skinoo's leaking body which was still tied to the chair.

Before leaving the office, I pecked out the following on the office typewriter:

> *From the Desk of Dr. Skinoo:* I have delved where man is not meant to go. We are more than motor reflexes after all. A Jungian Archetype is flapping at the window; and it is eyeing my head with a hungry look. What's that sound...?

So I left them, all of them, every nasty, bleeding fragment of them. They mean nothing to me, not even memories. I'd rather be haunted by dinosaur ghosts.

There's more work to do. Millions to slay before I sleep. Too bad there're no good shrinks in the world. Well, at least I did poor old Skinoo a favor, something no one else could do for him. I left a good head on his shoulders.

About the Author

Brad Linaweaver is author of the Prometheus award winning novel, *Moon of Ice*, which was also a Nebula finalist when it appeared as a novella in *Amazing Stories*. Published in America and England, the novel opened the door to his full time career as a writer.

He's sold over sixty short stories to magazines and anthologies, the latter including *Adventures in the Twilight Zone, Peter Straub's Ghosts, Superheroes, Miskatonic University, Confederacy of the Dead, Dark Destiny III: Children of Dracula, Alternate Warriors, Alternate Generals, Alternate Americas, Hitler Victorious, Tales from the Great Turtle, Psycho-Paths* and *Pawn of Chaos*. His first short story sale to an anthology was "Shadow Quest" in *Magic in Ithkar 2*, edited by Andre Norton and the late Robert Adams.

He is author of *Sliders, The Novel* and *Sliders, The Classic Episodes*, from the popular television series. With Dafydd ab Hugh, he is co-author of four popular *Doom* novels, based on the video game from id Software. He is currently working on his first *Wishbone* book.

In addition to media tie-ins, he works more directly with film and radio! He had a radio play on National Public Radio as part of the *Horror House* series. He shares story credit with producer Fred Olen Ray on *Jack-O*, the last film of John Carradine. (He also co-edited the anthology *Weird Menace* with Fred.) He adapted Robert A. Heinlein's "The Man Who Traveled in Elephants" for the Atlanta Radio Theatre in a production starring Harlan Ellison and introduced by Ray Bradbury. He has performed with Turhan Bey, David Hedison, Michelle Bauer, Brinke Stevens, John LaZar, J. J. North, Forrest J Ackerman, Robert Carradine, Don "the Dragon" Wilson, Brittany Rollins and Leslie Culton. He's been on HBO and the BBC.

He's done over two hundred non-fiction pieces, appearing in *National Review*, *Chronicles*, *The Atlanta Journal & Constitution*, *Locus*, *Cult Movies*, *Femme Fatales*, *Filmfax*, *Famous Monsters of Filmland*, *New Libertarian*, *The Agorist Quarterly*, *Spacemen*, *Synnwatch*, *Florida Magazine*, *Reason* and many others.

He is co-editor with Ed Kramer of *Free Space*, the only libertarian science fiction anthology in the universe.